D1494262

ALSO FROM JOE BOOKS

Disney Frozen Cinestory Comic
Disney Cinderella Cinestory Comic
Disney 101 Dalmatians Cinestory Comic
Disney Princess Comics Treasury
Disney • Pixar Comics Treasury
Disney's Darkwing Duck: The Definitively Dangerous Edition
Disney's Frozen: The Story of the Movie in Comics
Disney Big Hero 6 Cinestory Comic
Disney • Pixar Inside Out Cinestory Comic
Disney • Pixar Inside Out Fun Book
Disney Gravity Falls Cinestory Comic Volume One
Disney • Pixar The Good Dinosaur Cinestory Comic
Disney • Pixar The Good Dinosaur Fun Book
Disney Zootopia Cinestory Comic
Disney Winnie the Pooh Cinestory Comic
Disney Descendants Wicked World Cinestory Comic Volume One
Disney Alice in Wonderland Cinestory Comic
Disney • Pixar Finding Nemo Cinestory Comic
Disney Star vs the Forces of Evil Cinestory Comic
Disney • Pixar Cars Cinestory Comic
Thor: Dueling with Giants
DreamWorks Kung Fu Panda 3 Cinestory Comic

Don't miss our monthly comics…

Disney Princess
Disney Darkwing Duck
Disney • Pixar Finding Dory
DreamWorks Madagascar
DreamWorks Shrek

And Disney Frozen, launching in July!

Disney · PIXAR

FINDING NEMO

CINESTORY COMIC

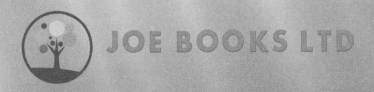

JOE BOOKS LTD

Published in the United States and Canada by Joe Books, Ltd.
567 Queen St W, Toronto, ON M5V 2B6
www.joebooks.com

Library and Archives Canada Cataloguing in Publication information is available upon request.
ISBN 978-1-98795-584-2 (Softcover edition)
ISBN 978-1-77275-297-7 (Ebook edition)

First Joe Books, Ltd. edition: June 2016

Disney · PIXAR

FINDING NEMO

CINESTORY COMIC

ADAPTATION, DESIGN, LETTERING, LAYOUT AND EDITING:
For Readhead Books:
Alberto Garrido, Ernesto Lovera, Puste, Ester Salguero,
Rocío Salguero, Eduardo Alpuente, Heidi Roux, Aaron Sparrow,
Heather Penner and Carolynn Prior.

Disney

PIXAR

ANIMATION STUDIOS

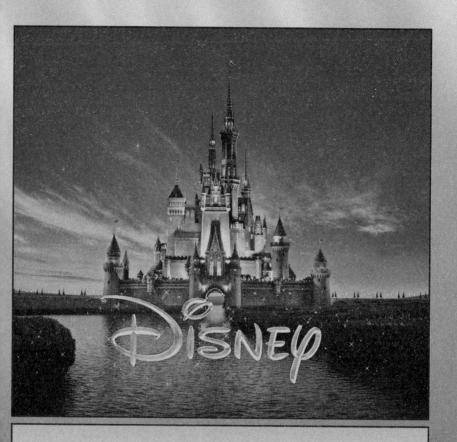

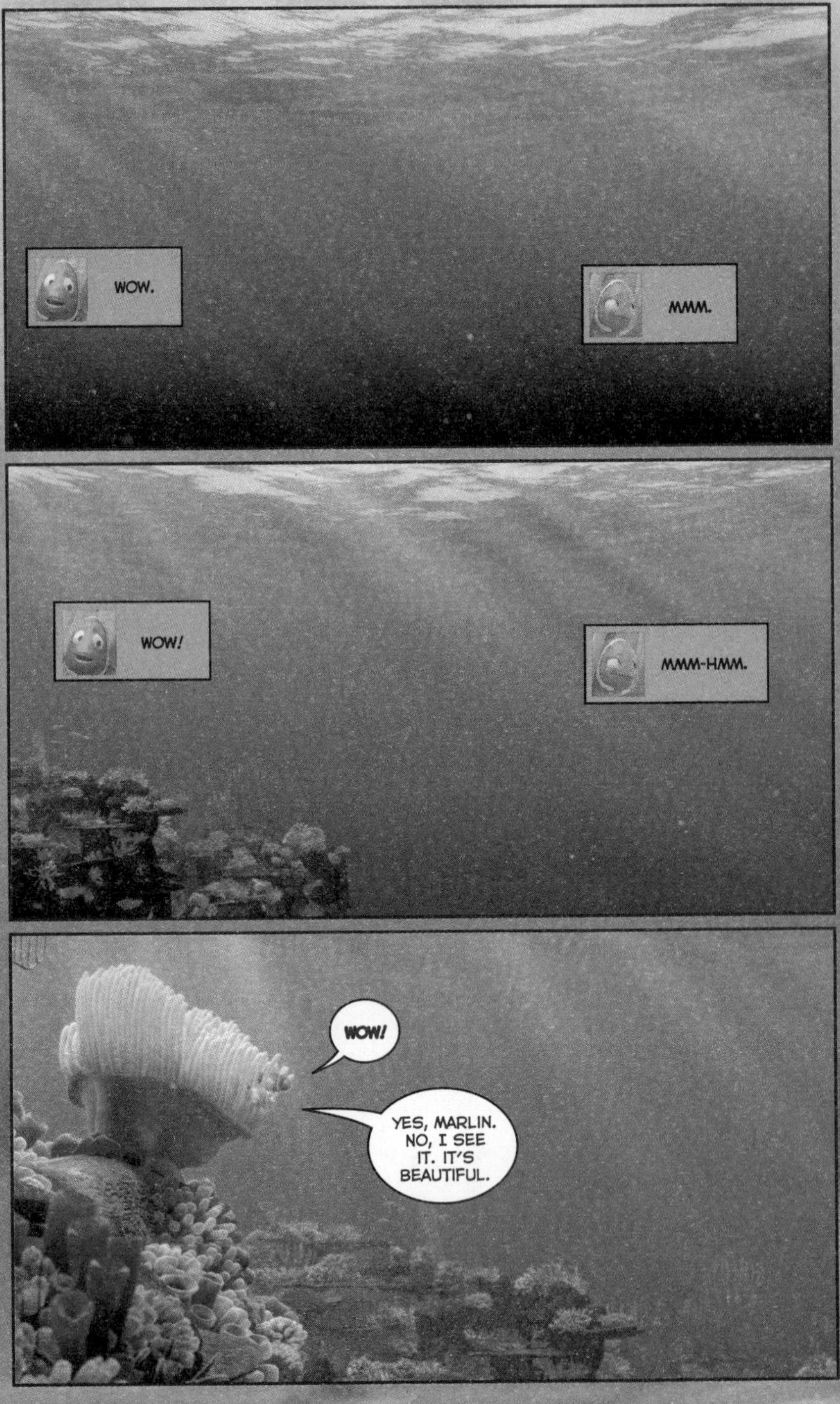
WOW.
MMM.
WOW!
MMM-HMM.
WOW!
YES, MARLIN. NO, I SEE IT. IT'S BEAUTIFUL.

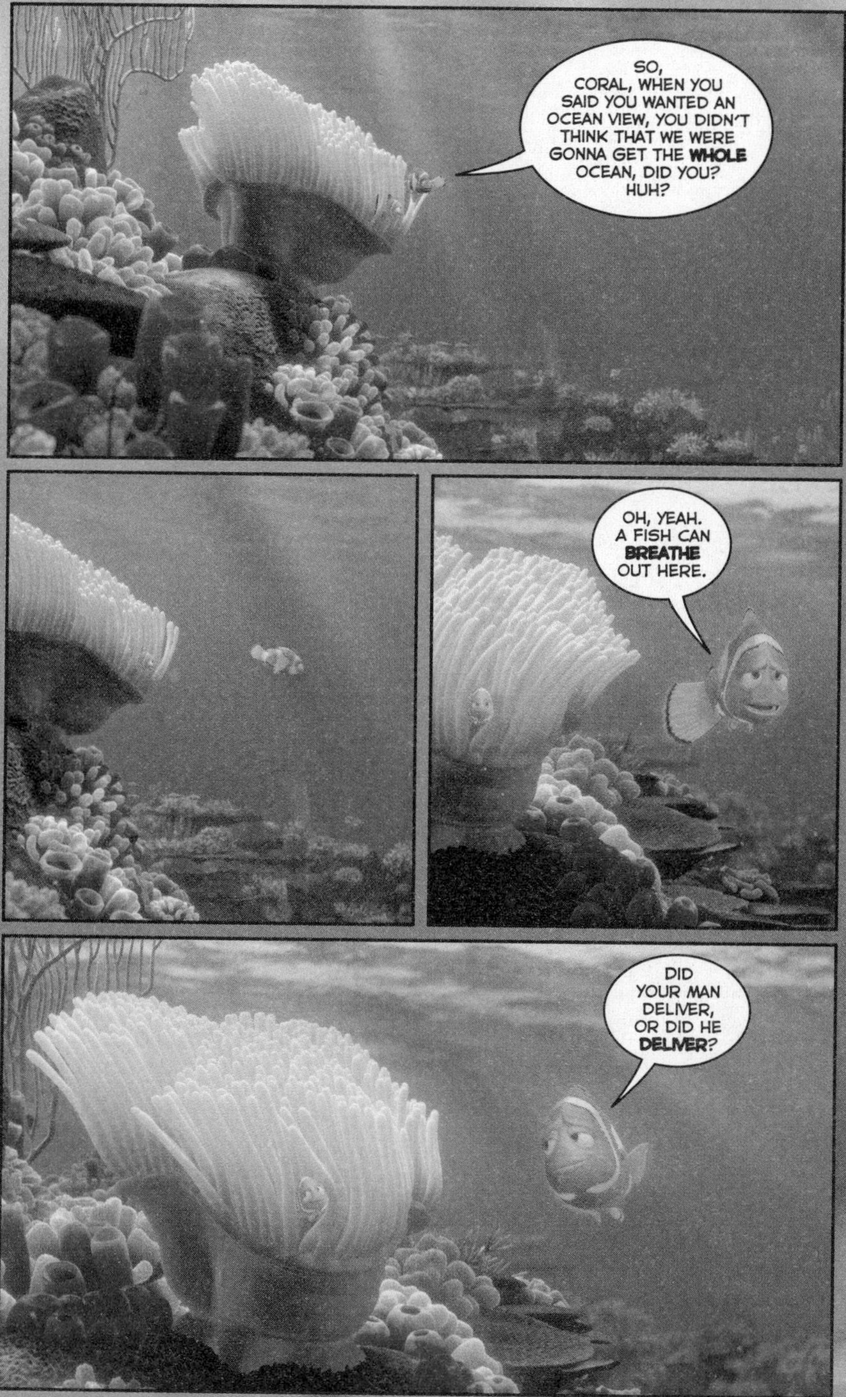
SO, CORAL, WHEN YOU SAID YOU WANTED AN OCEAN VIEW, YOU DIDN'T THINK THAT WE WERE GONNA GET THE **WHOLE** OCEAN, DID YOU? HUH?
OH, YEAH. A FISH CAN **BREATHE** OUT HERE.
DID YOUR MAN DELIVER, OR DID HE **DELIVER**?

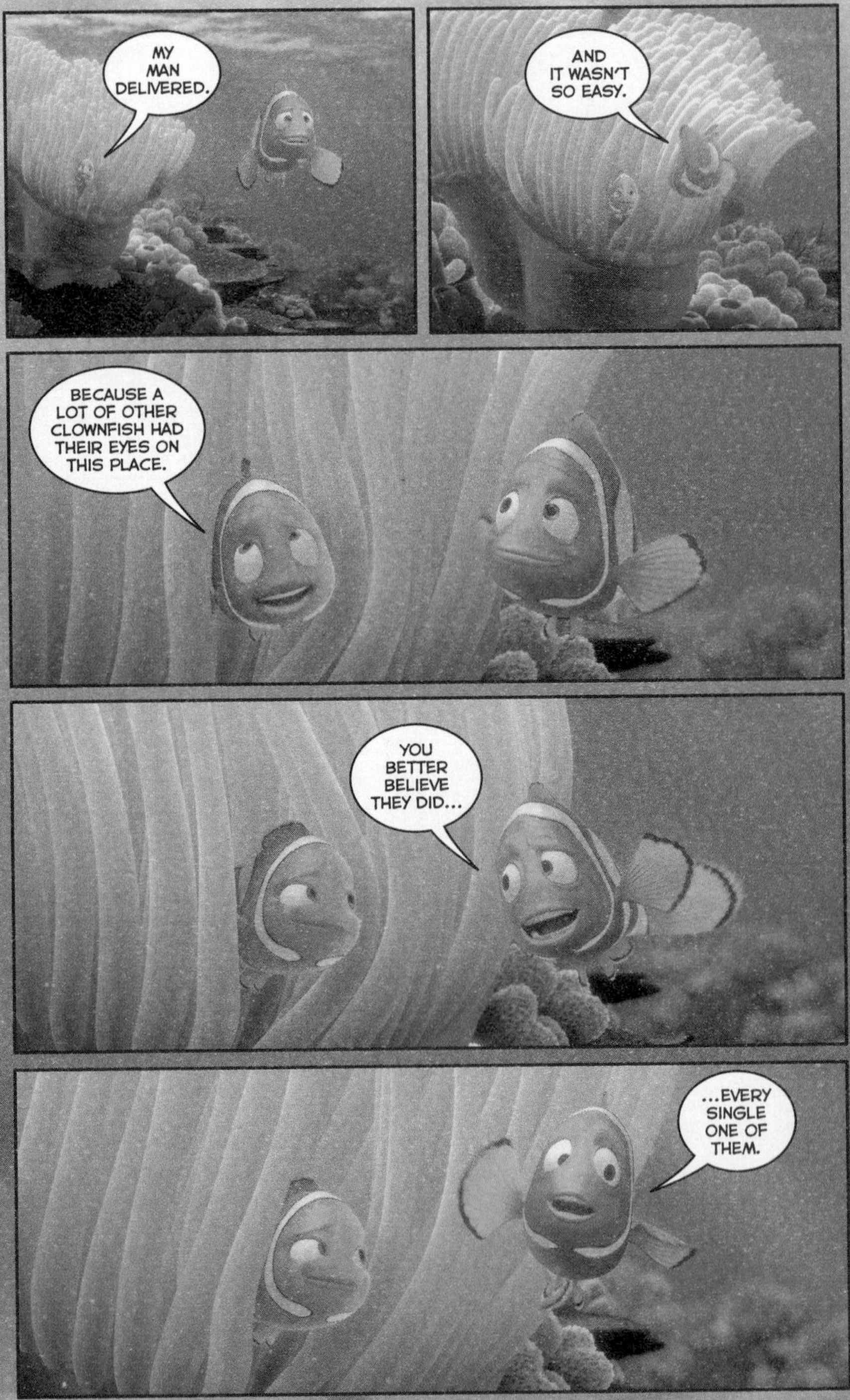
MY MAN DELIVERED.
AND IT WASN'T SO EASY.
BECAUSE A LOT OF OTHER CLOWNFISH HAD THEIR EYES ON THIS PLACE.
YOU BETTER BELIEVE THEY DID...
...EVERY SINGLE ONE OF THEM.

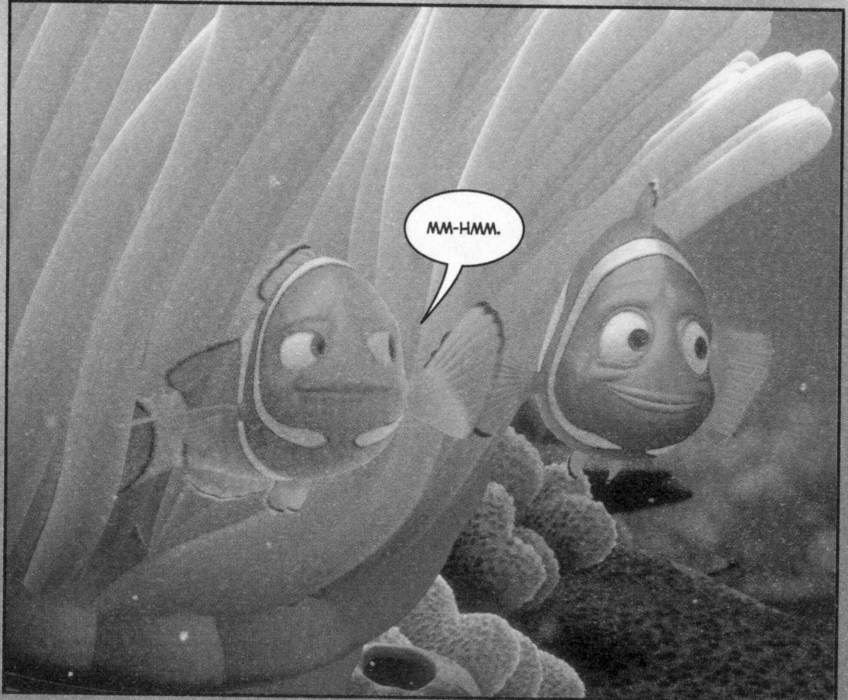
MM-HMM.

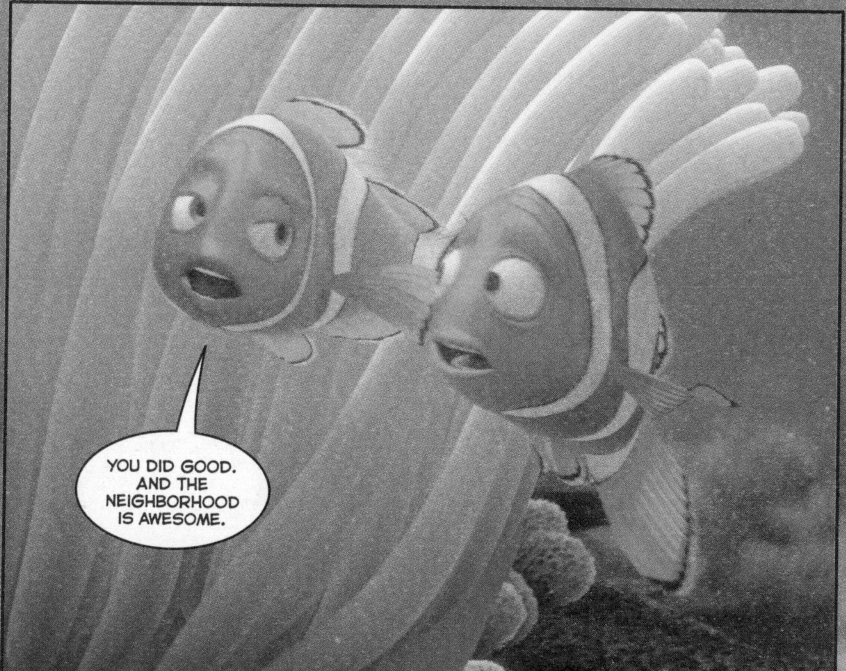
YOU DID GOOD. AND THE NEIGHBORHOOD IS AWESOME.

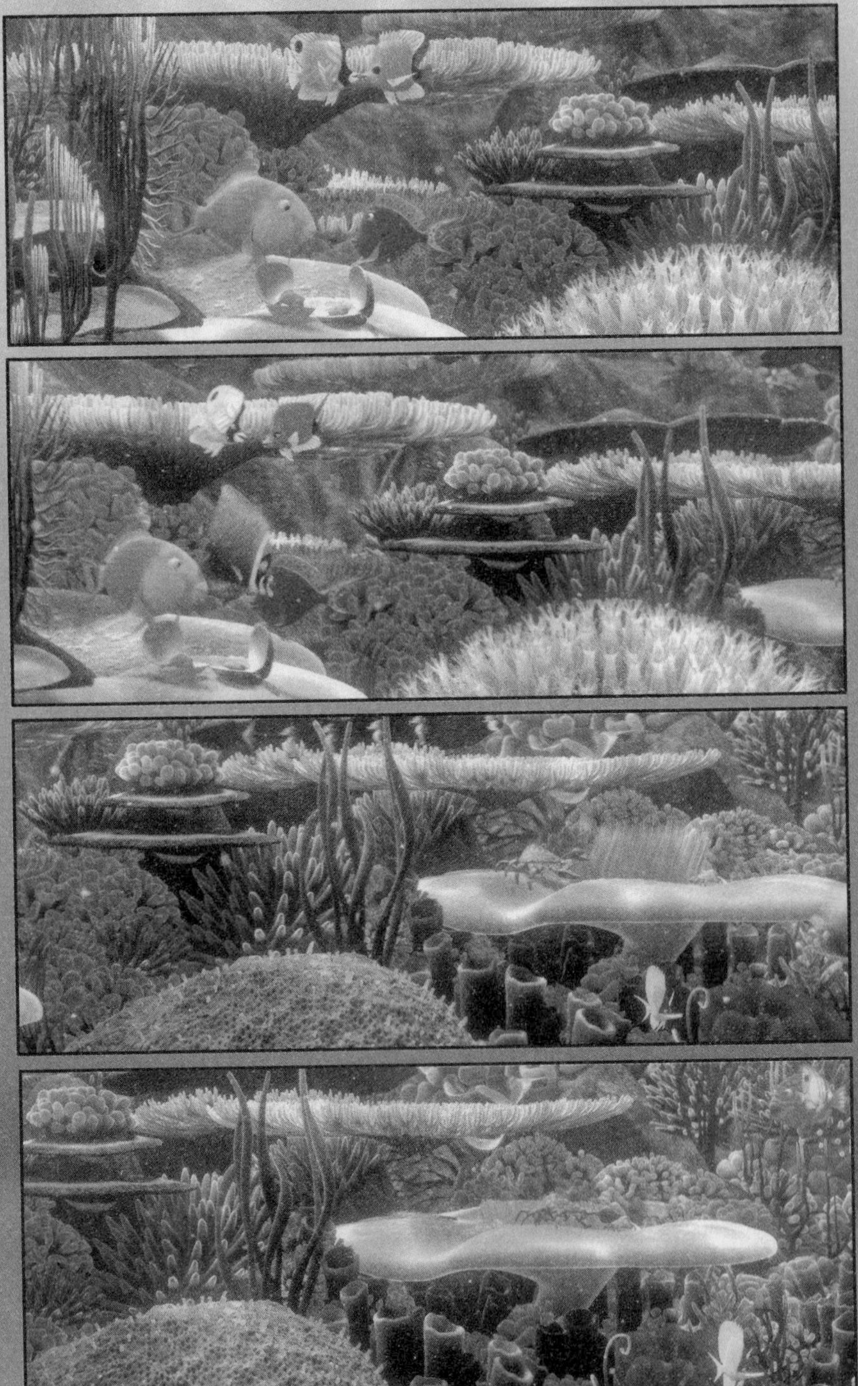

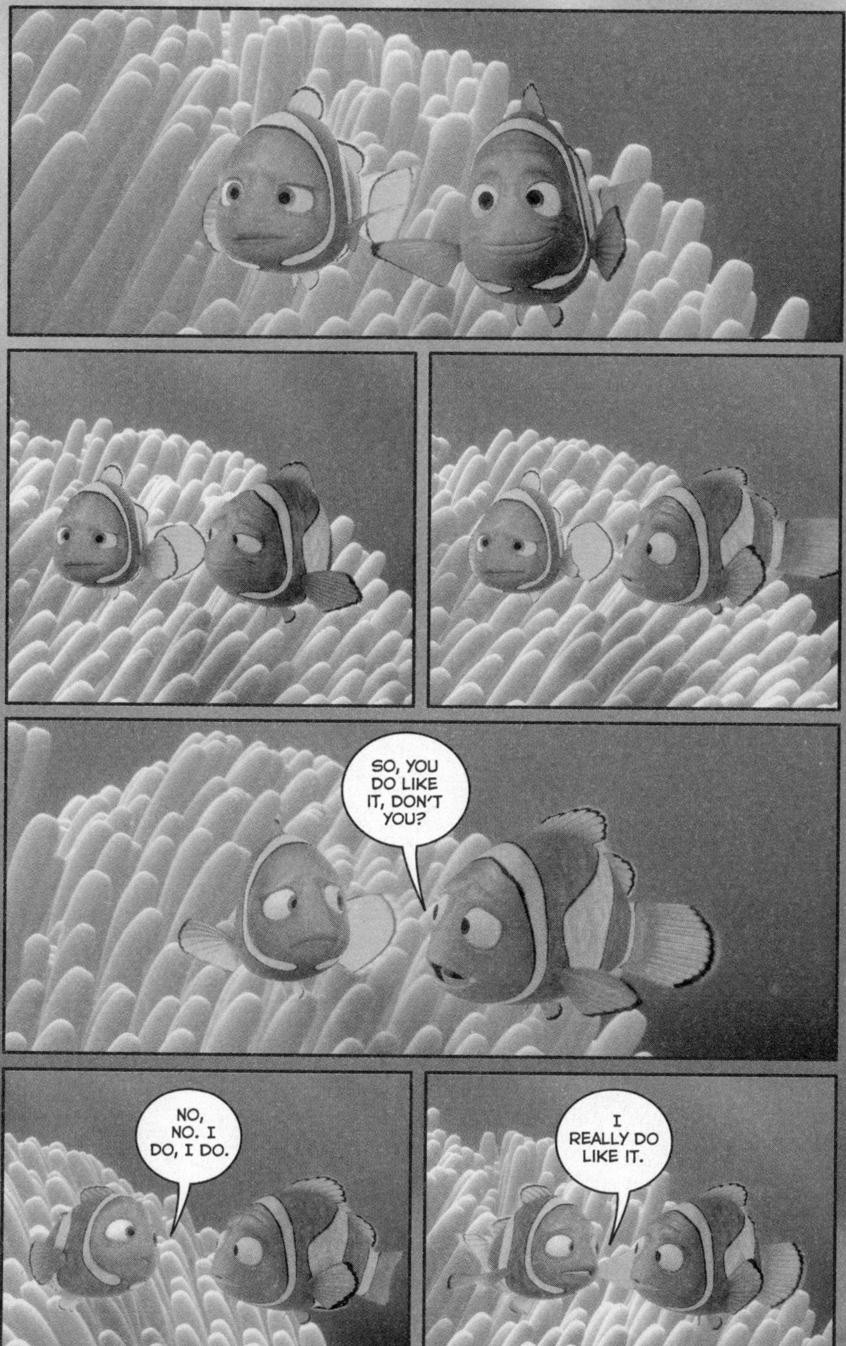
SO, YOU DO LIKE IT, DON'T YOU?
NO, NO. I DO, I DO.
I REALLY DO LIKE IT.

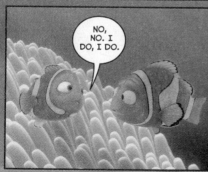

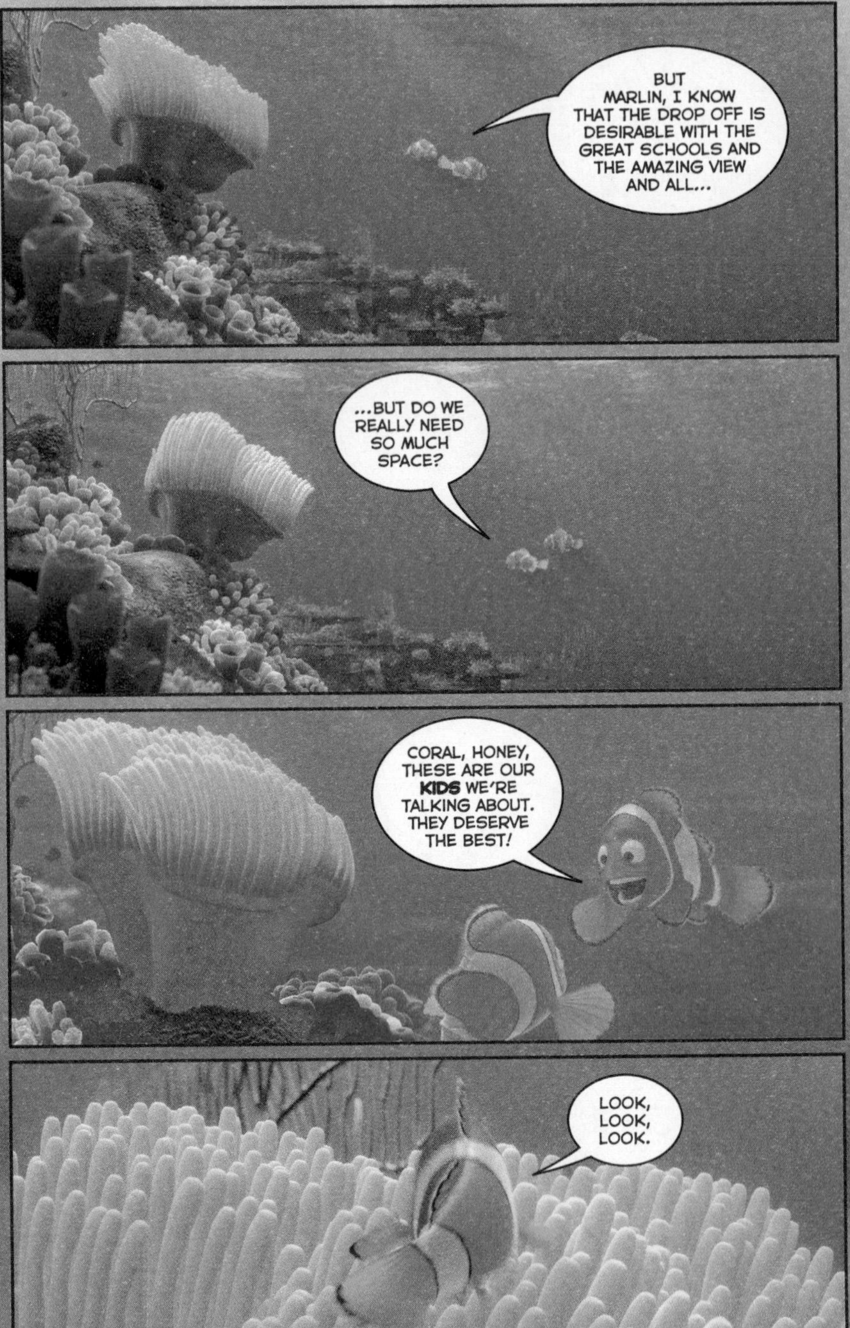
BUT MARLIN, I KNOW THAT THE DROP OFF IS DESIRABLE WITH THE GREAT SCHOOLS AND THE AMAZING VIEW AND ALL...
...BUT DO WE REALLY NEED SO MUCH SPACE?
CORAL, HONEY, THESE ARE OUR **KIDS** WE'RE TALKING ABOUT. THEY DESERVE THE BEST!
LOOK, LOOK, LOOK.

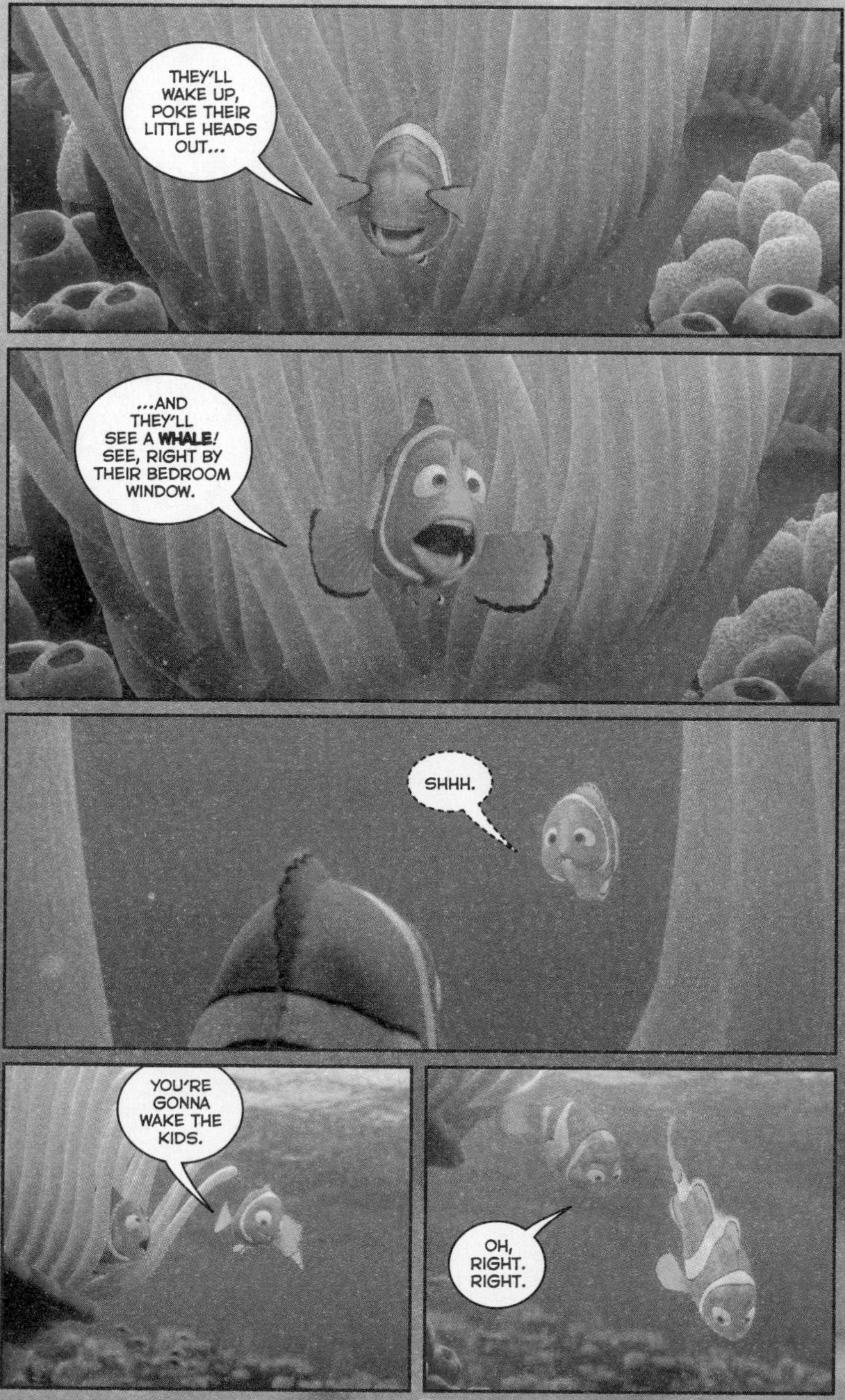
THEY'LL WAKE UP, POKE THEIR LITTLE HEADS OUT...
...AND THEY'LL SEE A WHALE! SEE, RIGHT BY THEIR BEDROOM WINDOW.
SHHH.
YOU'RE GONNA WAKE THE KIDS.
OH, RIGHT. RIGHT.

AWW, LOOK.

THEY'RE DREAMING.

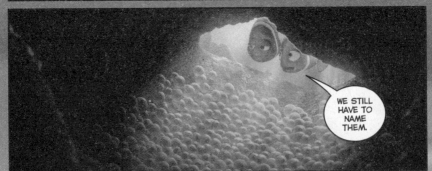

WE STILL HAVE TO NAME THEM.

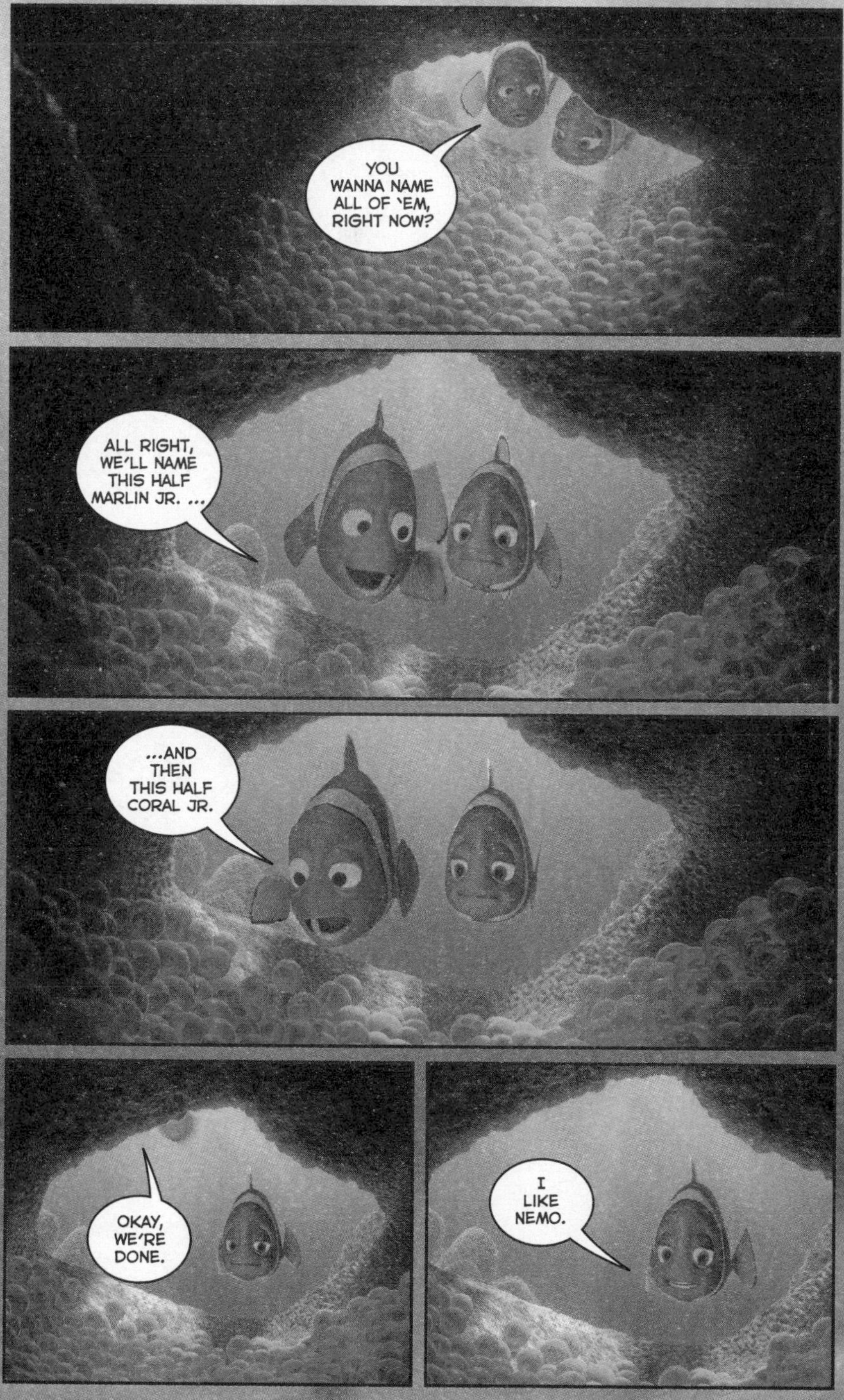
YOU WANNA NAME ALL OF 'EM, RIGHT NOW?
ALL RIGHT, WE'LL NAME THIS HALF MARLIN JR. ...
...AND THEN THIS HALF CORAL JR.
OKAY, WE'RE DONE.
I LIKE NEMO.

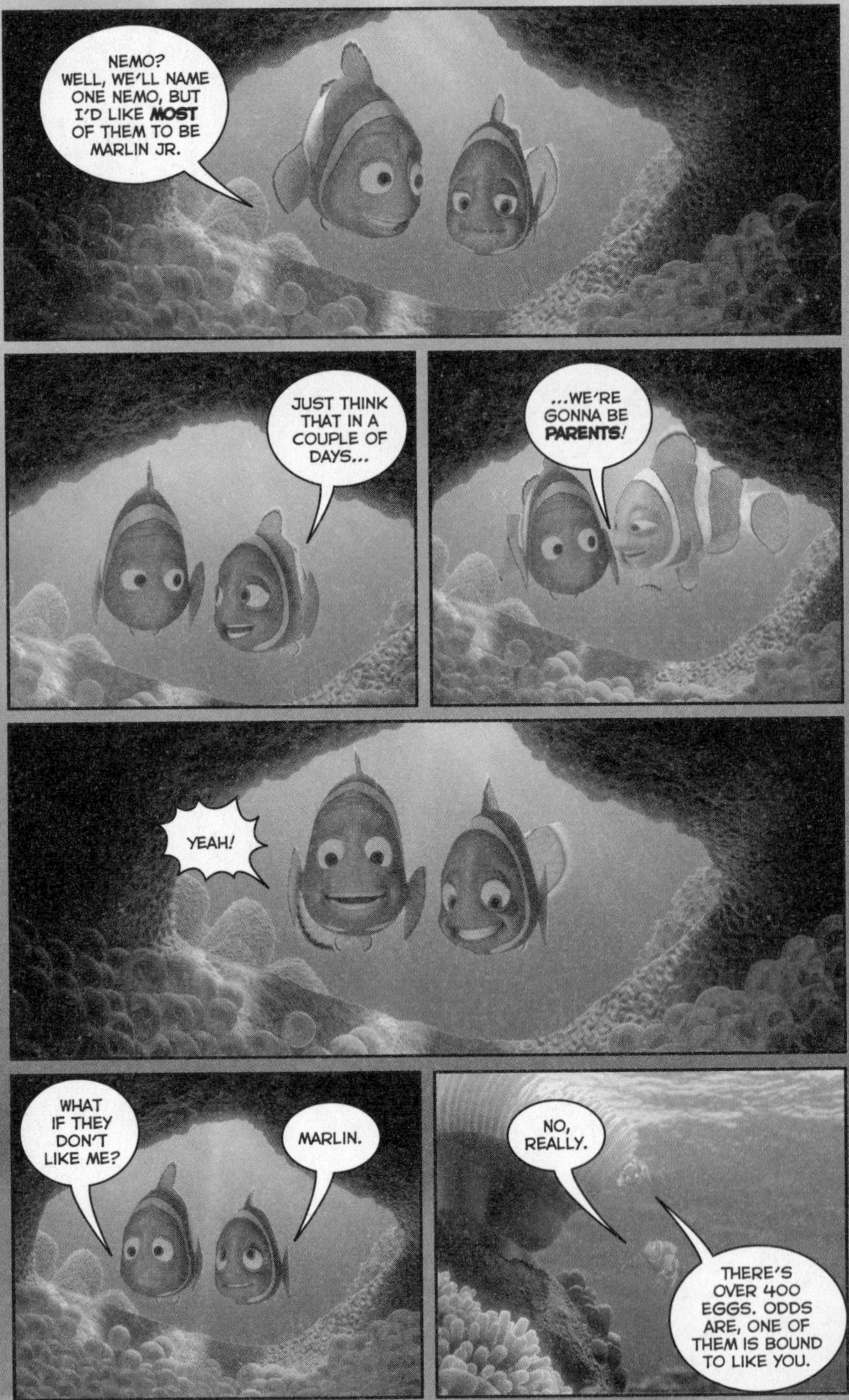
NEMO? WELL, WE'LL NAME ONE NEMO, BUT I'D LIKE **MOST** OF THEM TO BE MARLIN JR.
JUST THINK THAT IN A COUPLE OF DAYS...
...WE'RE GONNA BE **PARENTS**!
YEAH!
WHAT IF THEY DON'T LIKE ME?
MARLIN.
NO, REALLY.
THERE'S OVER 400 EGGS. ODDS ARE, ONE OF THEM IS BOUND TO LIKE YOU.

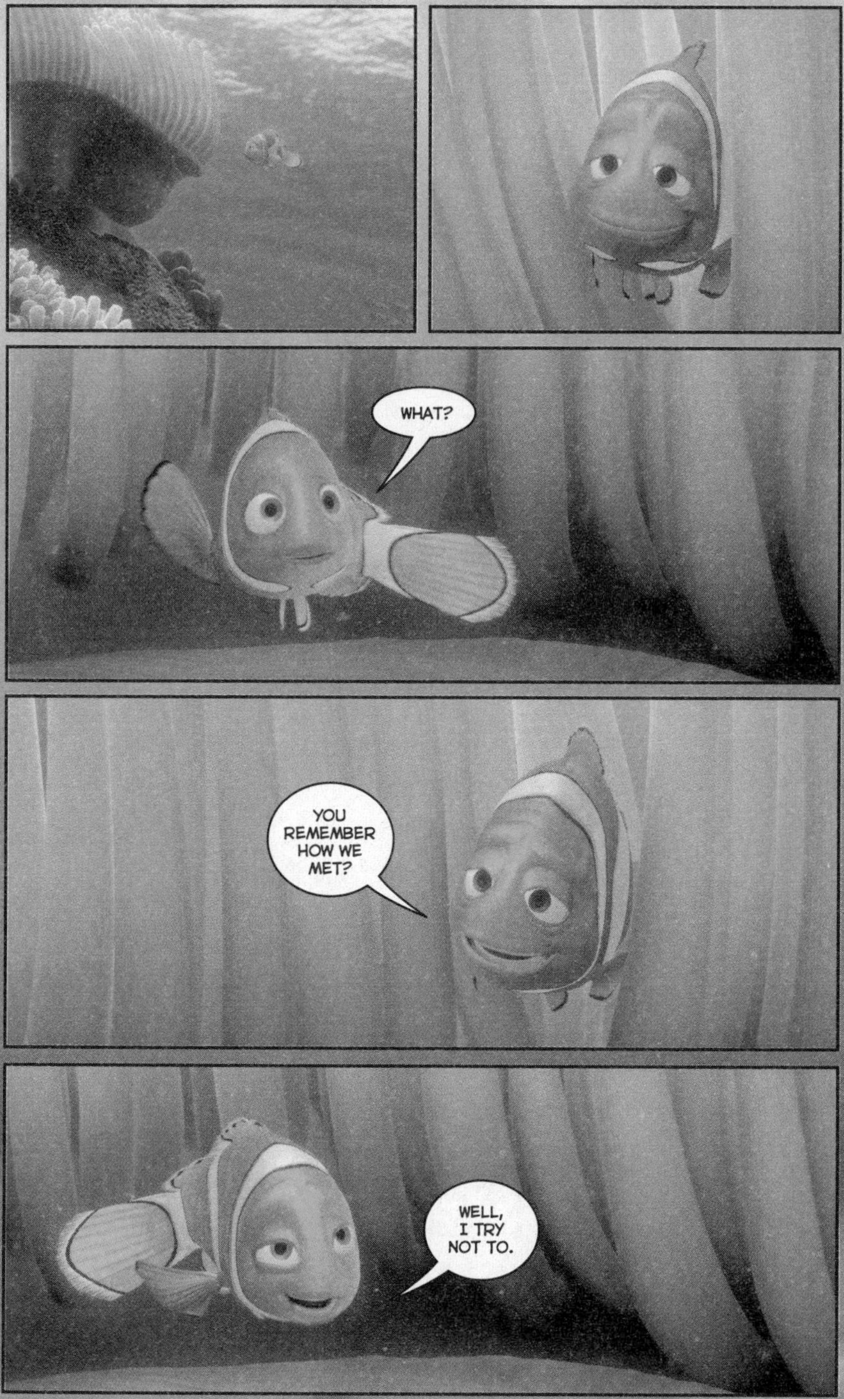
WHAT?
YOU REMEMBER HOW WE MET?
WELL, I TRY NOT TO.

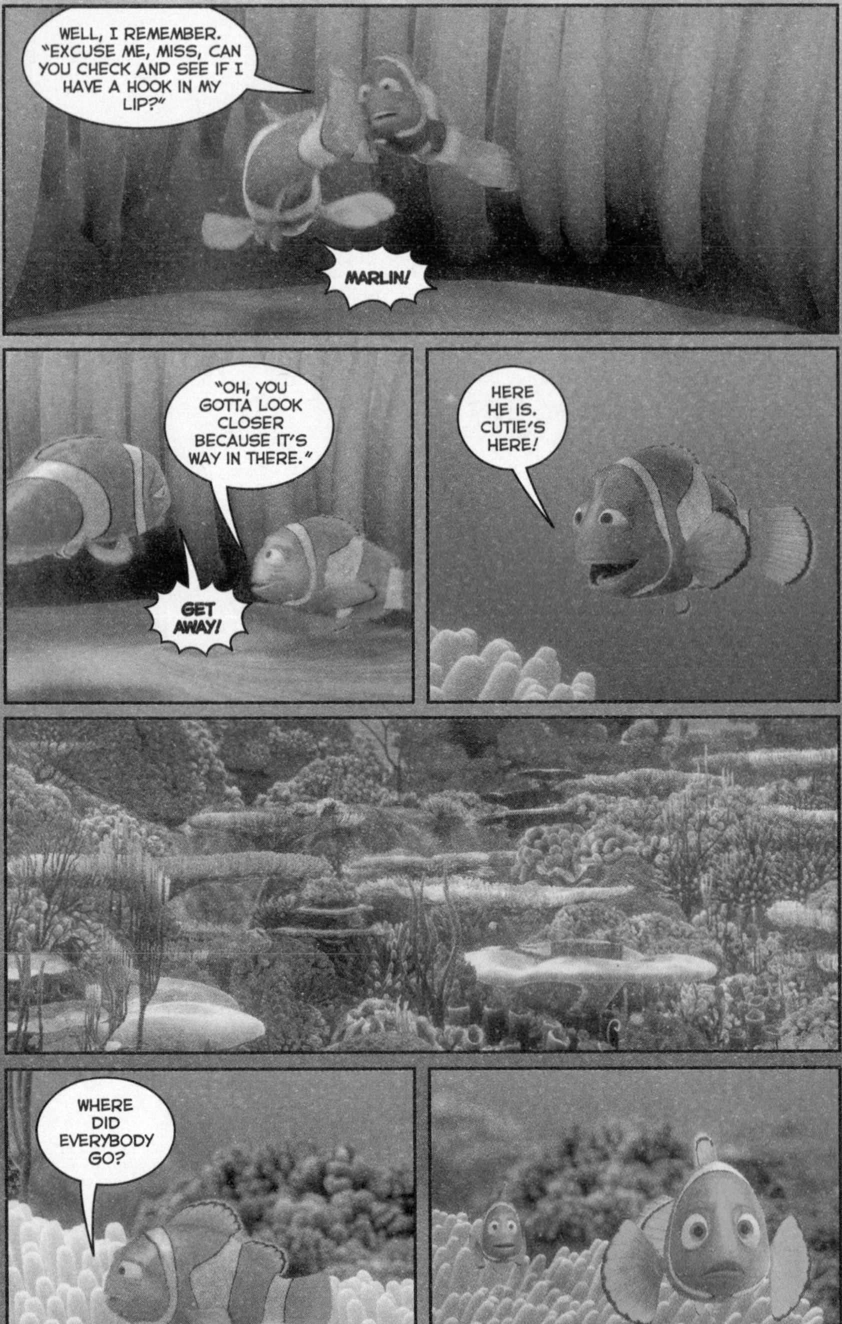

WELL, I REMEMBER. "EXCUSE ME, MISS, CAN YOU CHECK AND SEE IF I HAVE A HOOK IN MY LIP?"
MARLIN!
"OH, YOU GOTTA LOOK CLOSER BECAUSE IT'S WAY IN THERE."
GET AWAY!
HERE HE IS. CUTIE'S HERE!
WHERE DID EVERYBODY GO?

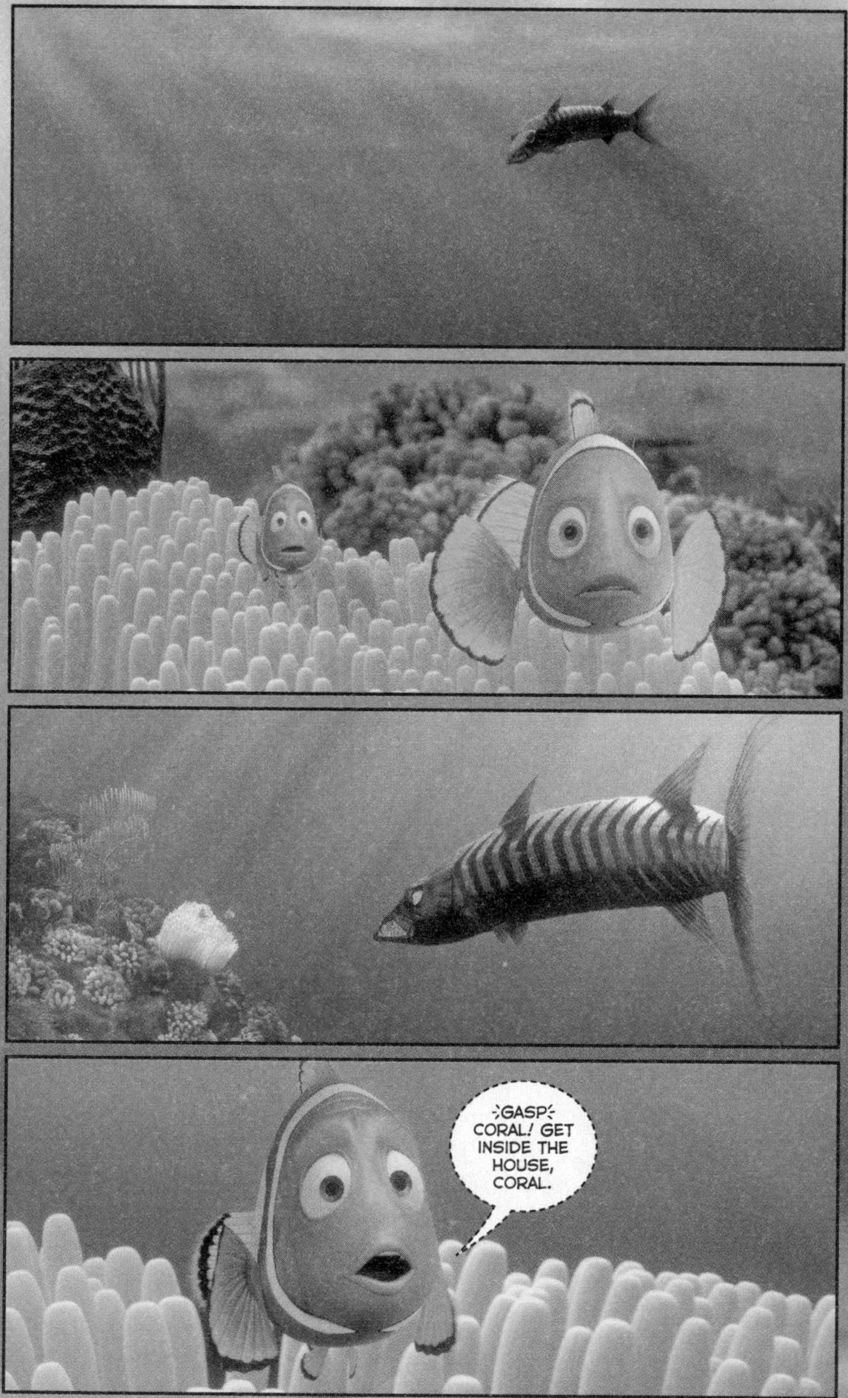
GASP
CORAL! GET INSIDE THE HOUSE, CORAL.

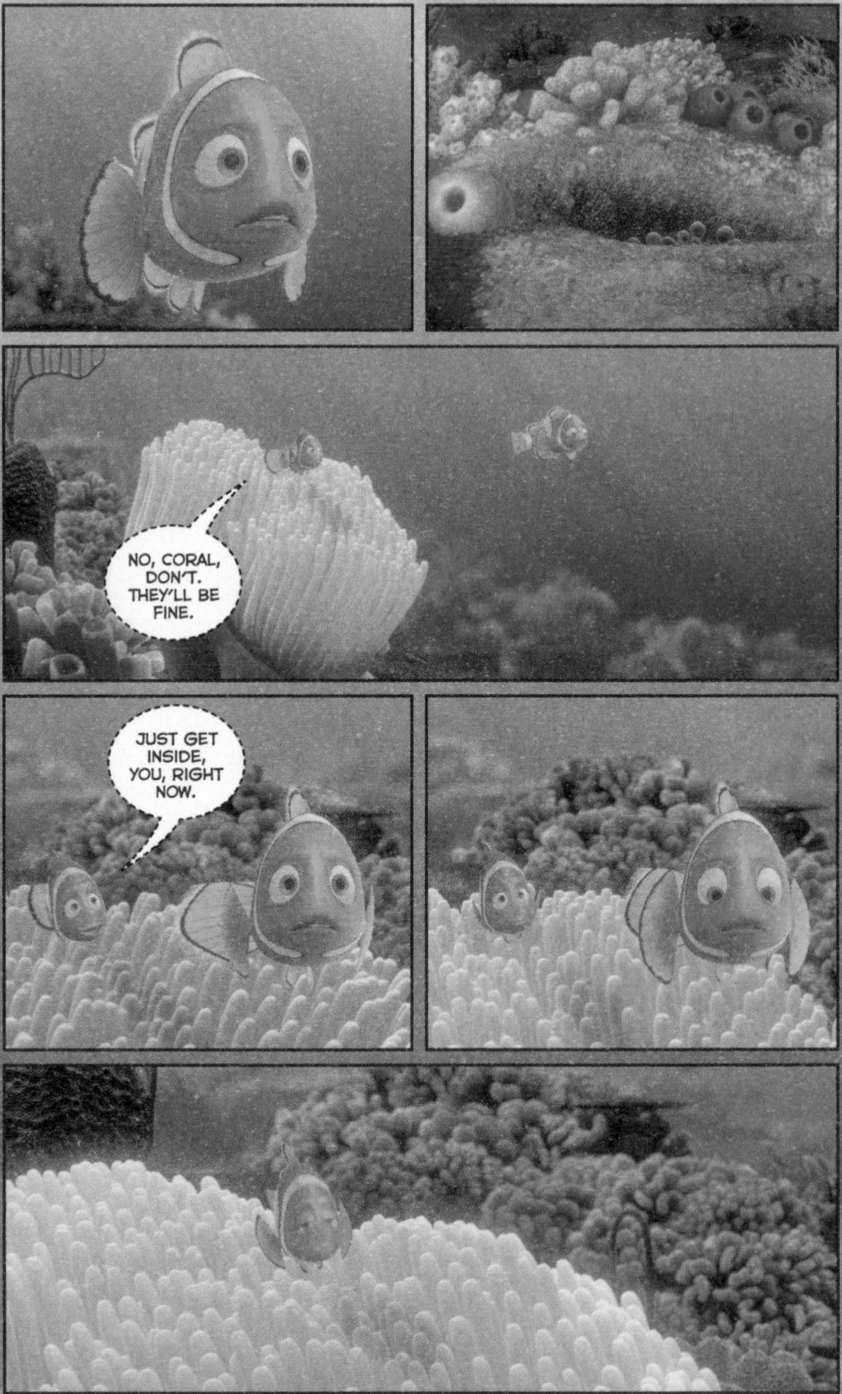
NO, CORAL, DON'T. THEY'LL BE FINE.
JUST GET INSIDE, YOU, RIGHT NOW.

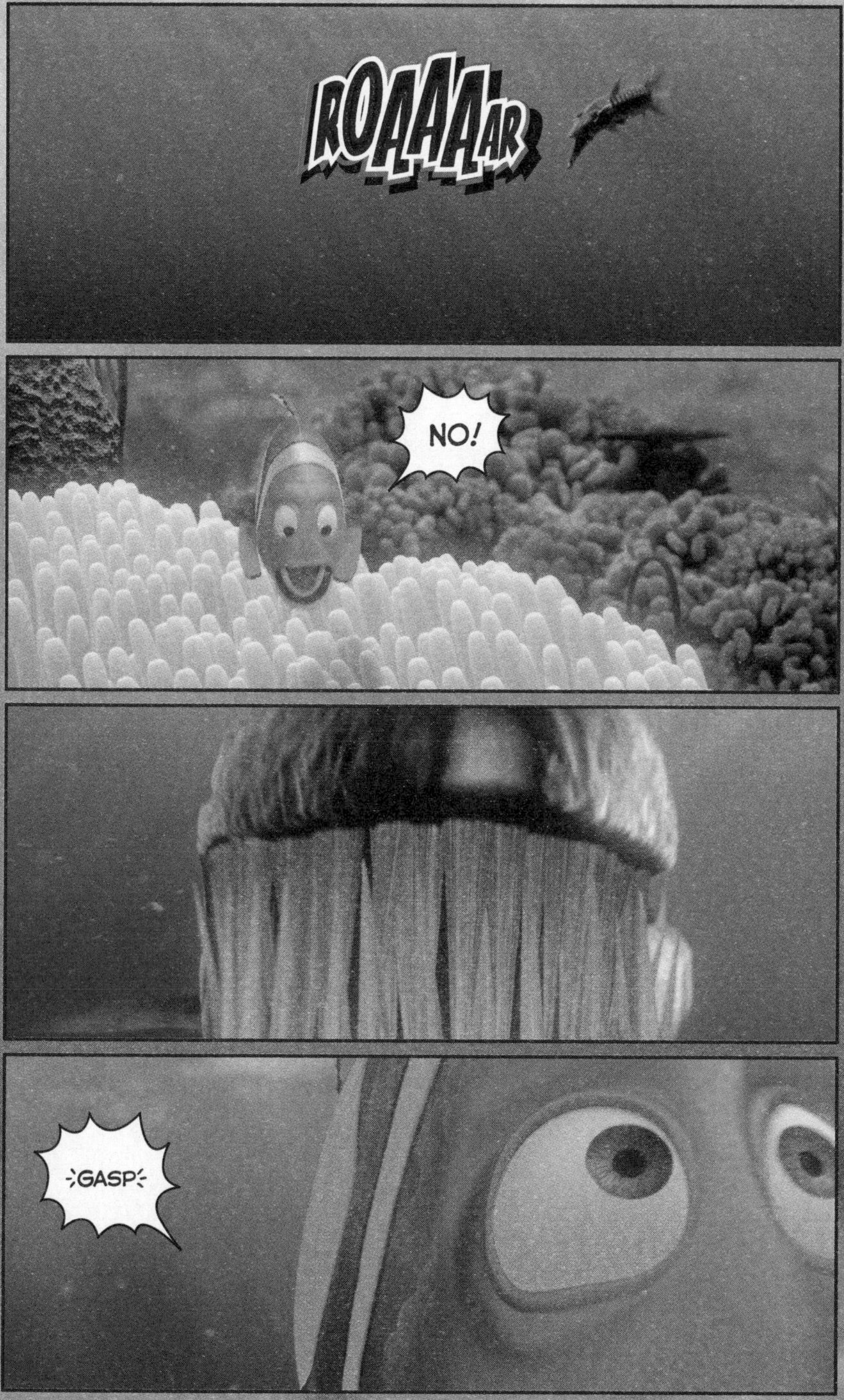
ROAAAAR
NO!
GASP

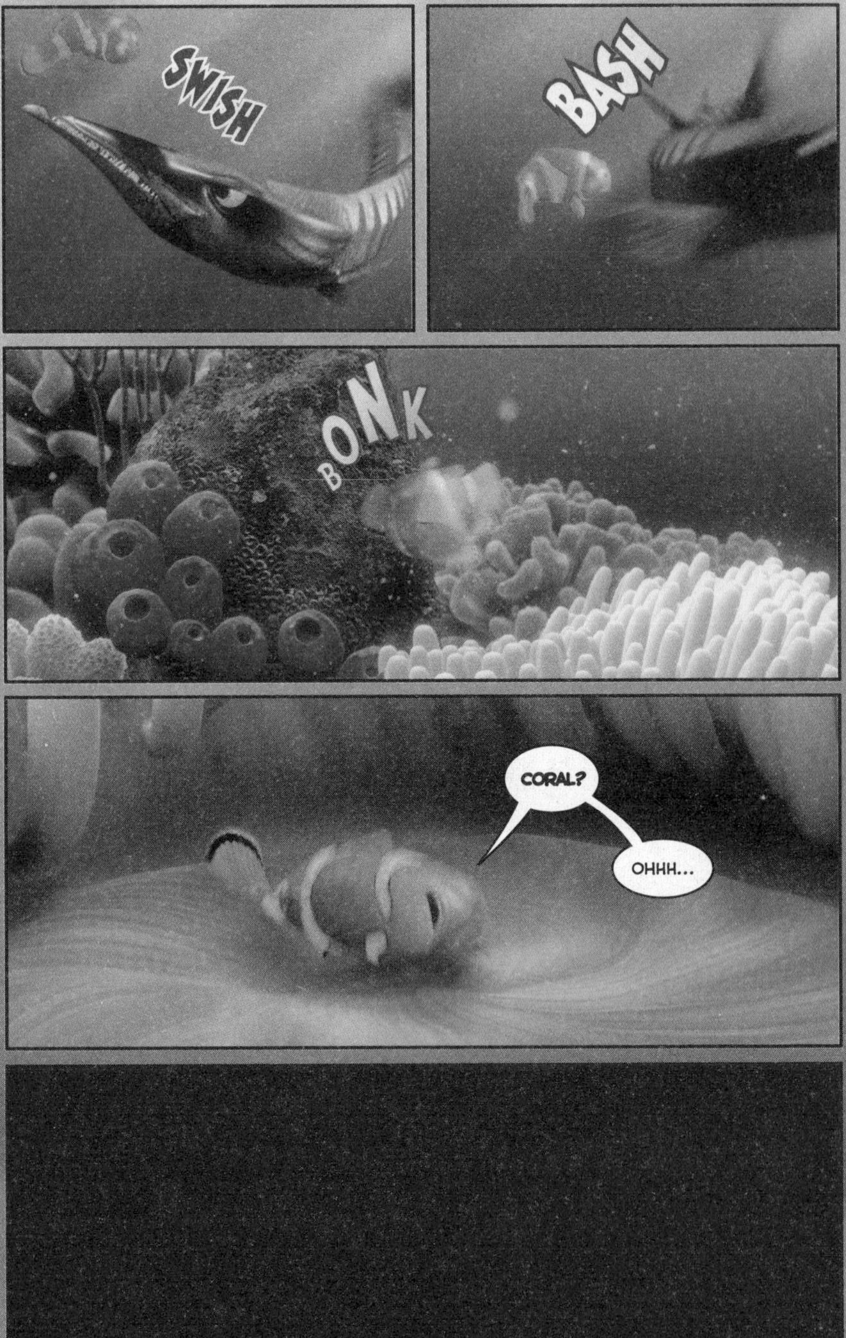
SWISH
BASH
BONK
CORAL?
OHHH...

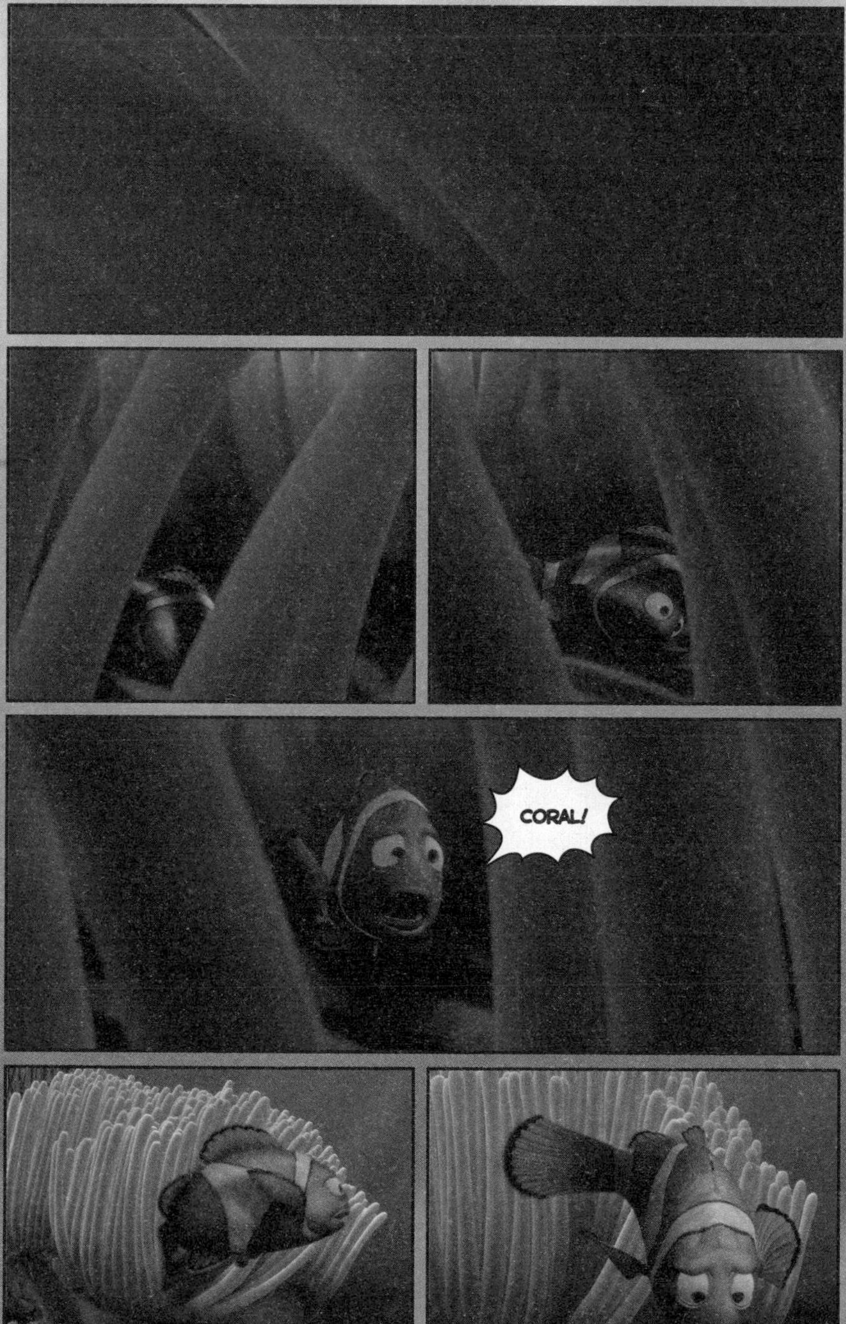
CORAL!

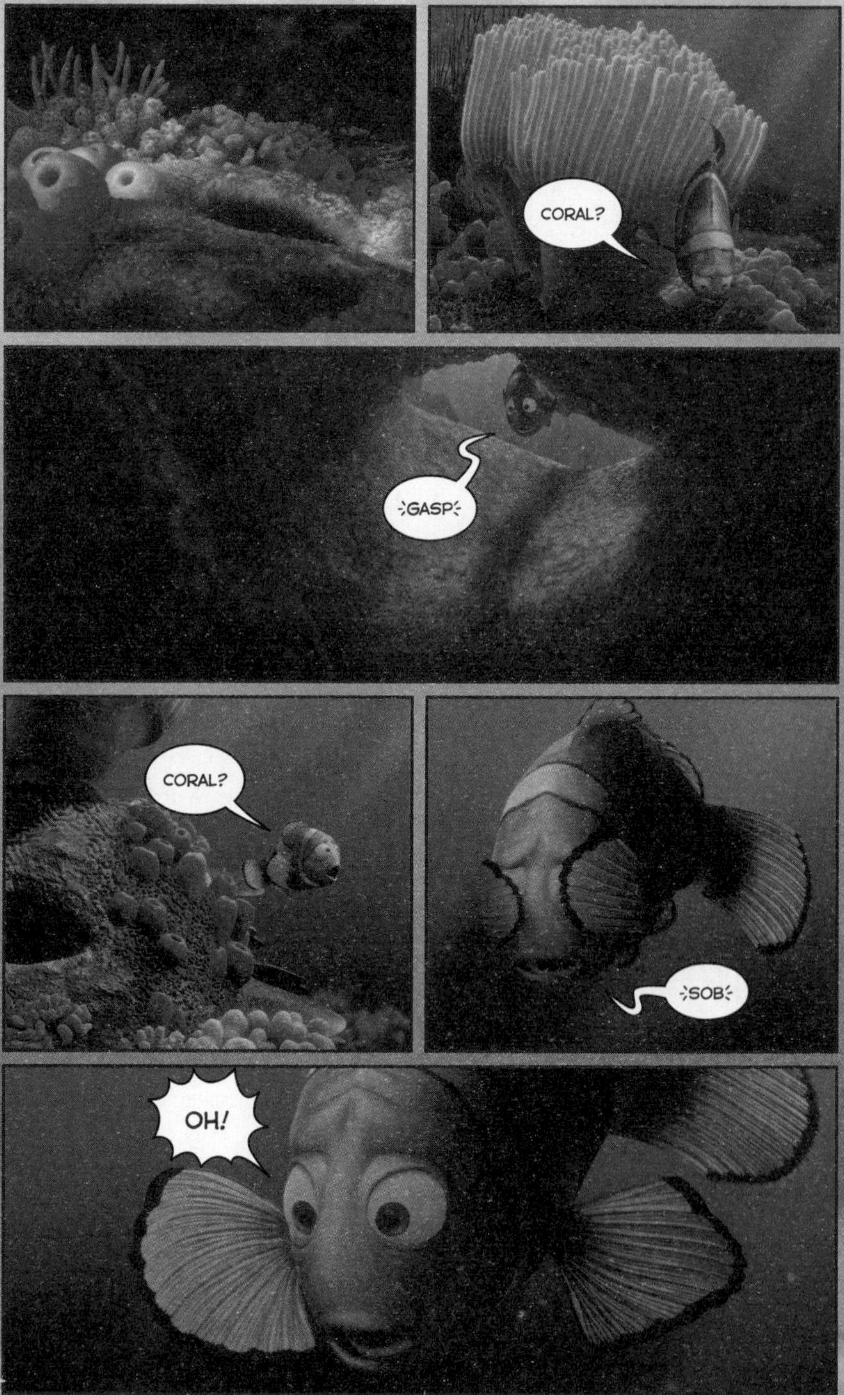
CORAL?
GASP
CORAL?
SOB
OH!

OHH...
THERE,
THERE,
THERE.

IT'S OKAY,
DADDY'S HERE.
DADDY'S GOT
YOU.

I
PROMISE, I
WILL NEVER LET
ANYTHING HAPPEN
TO YOU...
NEMO.

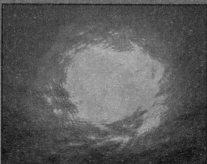

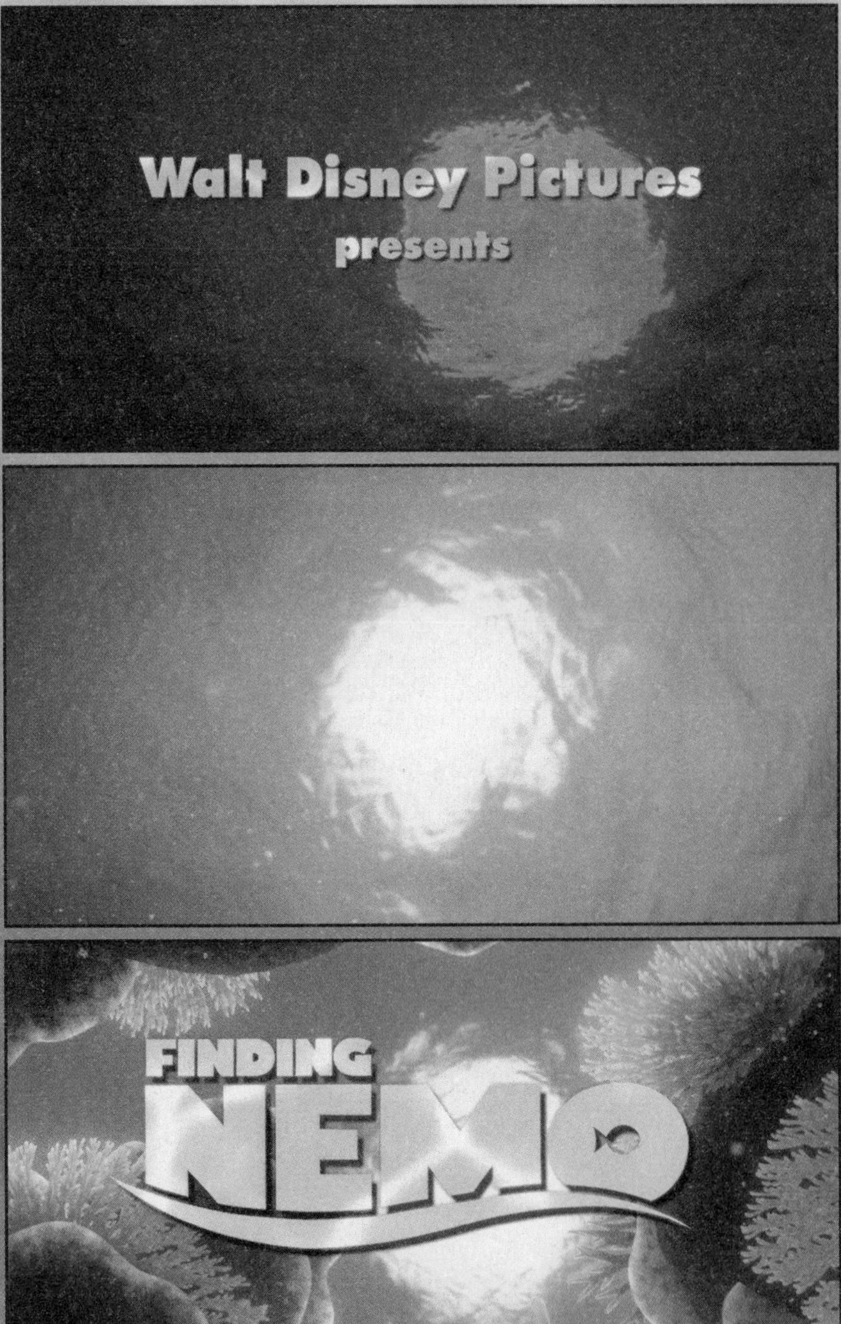

Walt Disney Pictures
presents

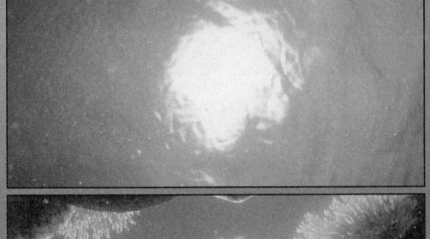

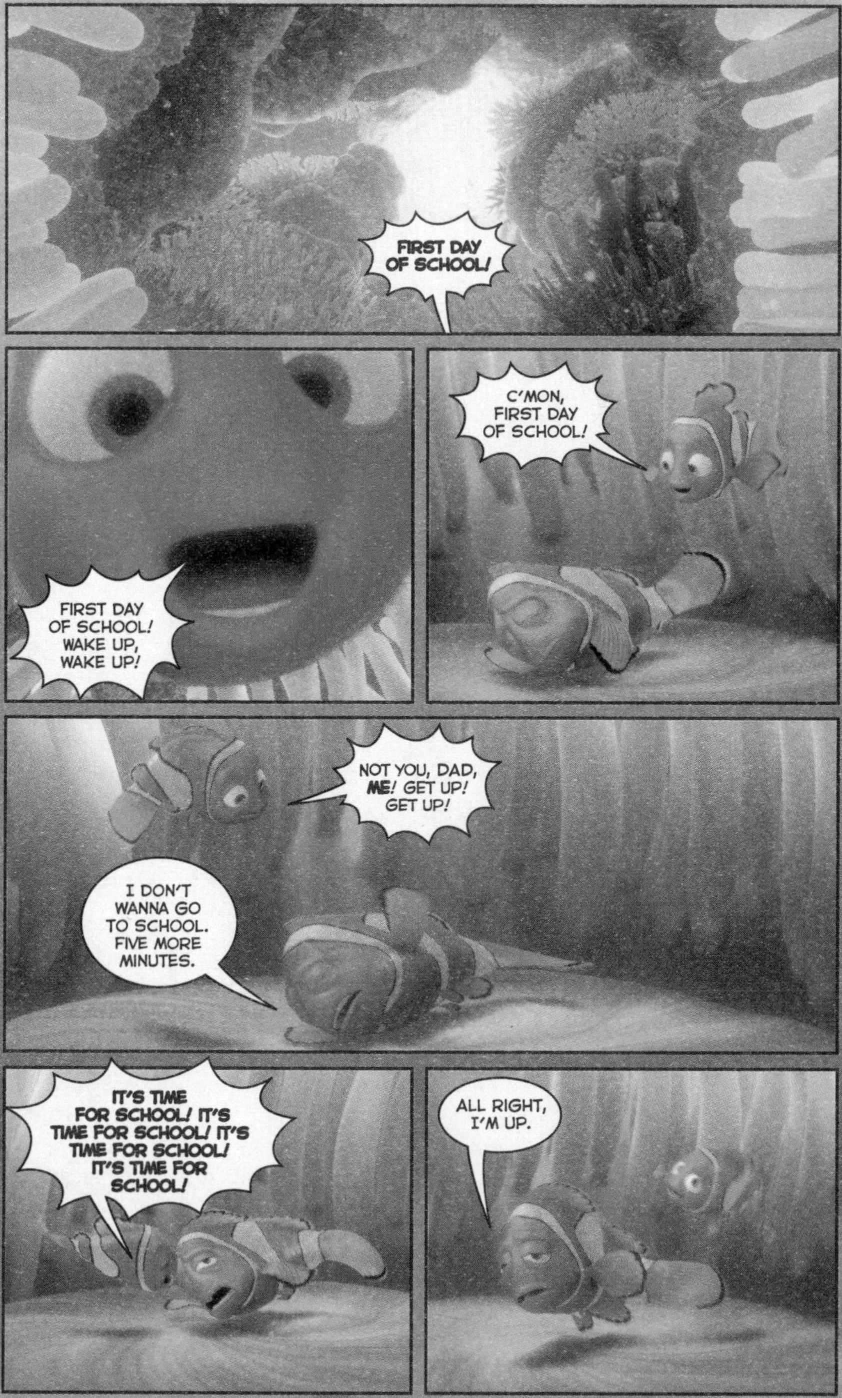

FIRST DAY OF SCHOOL!
FIRST DAY OF SCHOOL! WAKE UP, WAKE UP!
C'MON, FIRST DAY OF SCHOOL!
NOT YOU, DAD, ME! GET UP! GET UP!
I DON'T WANNA GO TO SCHOOL. FIVE MORE MINUTES.
IT'S TIME FOR SCHOOL! IT'S TIME FOR SCHOOL! IT'S TIME FOR SCHOOL! IT'S TIME FOR SCHOOL!
ALL RIGHT, I'M UP.

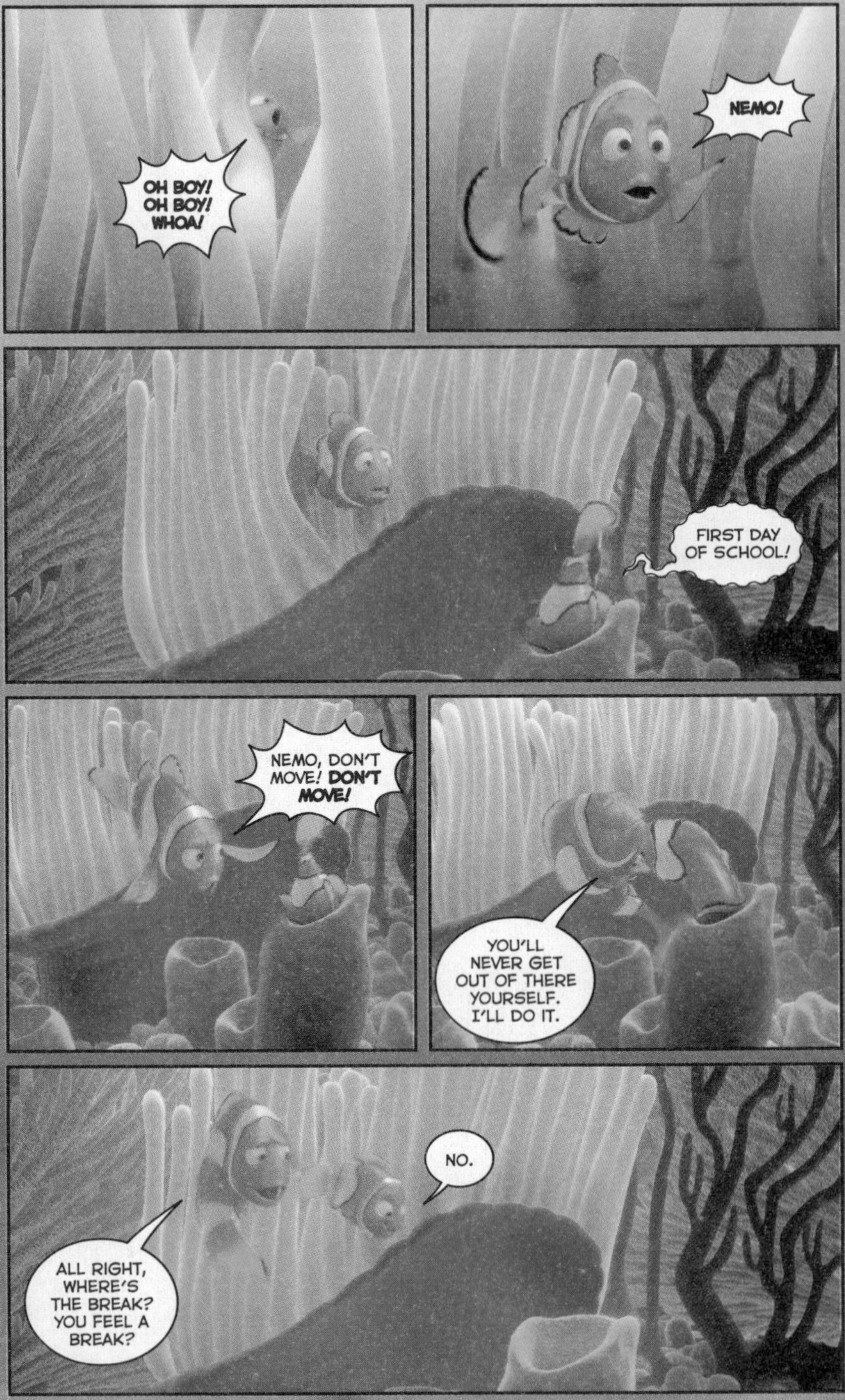
OH BOY! OH BOY! WHOA!
NEMO!
FIRST DAY OF SCHOOL!
NEMO, DON'T MOVE! DON'T MOVE!
YOU'LL NEVER GET OUT OF THERE YOURSELF. I'LL DO IT.
NO.
ALL RIGHT, WHERE'S THE BREAK? YOU FEEL A BREAK?

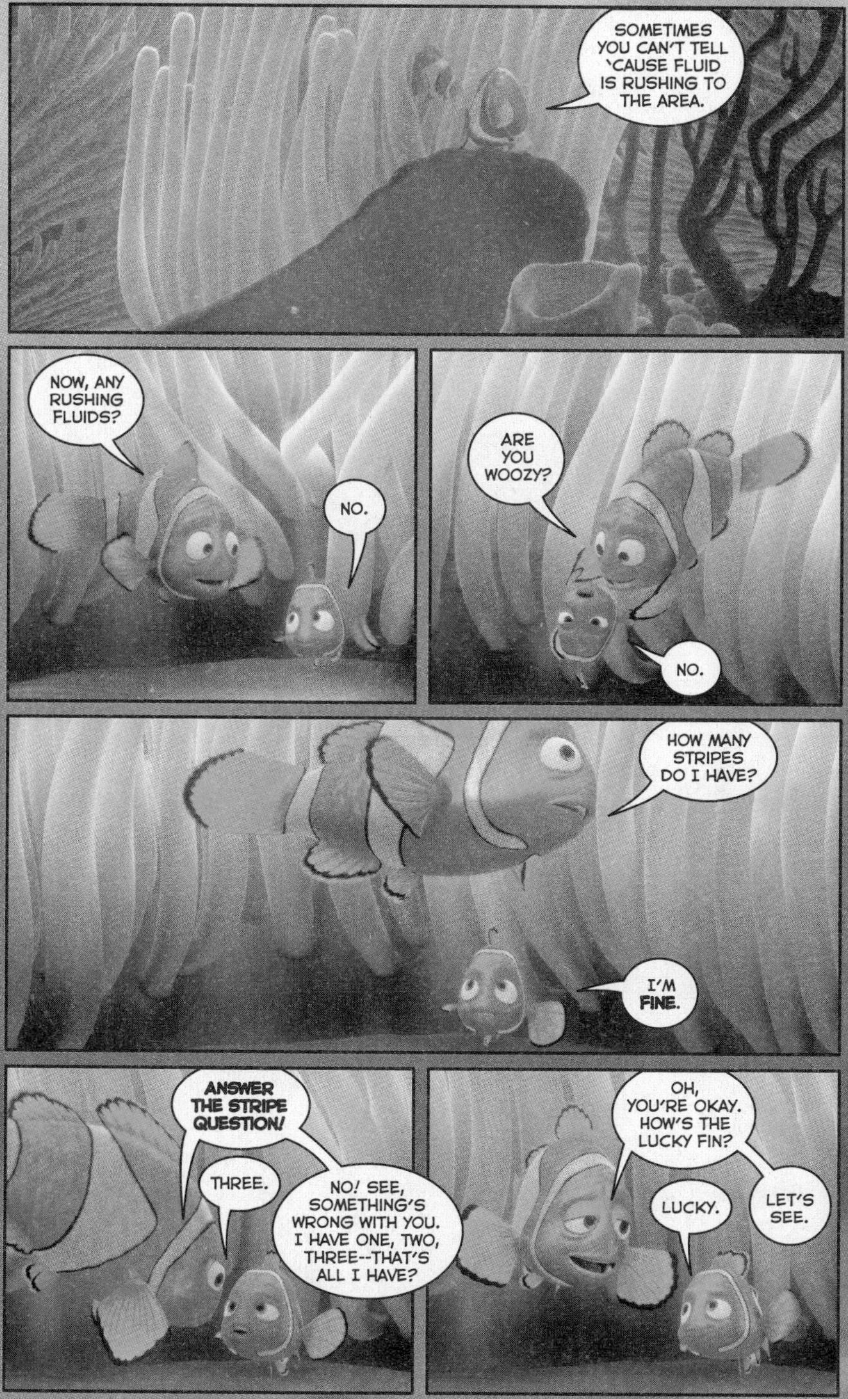
SOMETIMES YOU CAN'T TELL 'CAUSE FLUID IS RUSHING TO THE AREA.
NOW, ANY RUSHING FLUIDS?
NO.
ARE YOU WOOZY?
NO.
HOW MANY STRIPES DO I HAVE?
I'M **FINE.**
ANSWER THE STRIPE QUESTION!
THREE.
NO! SEE, SOMETHING'S WRONG WITH YOU. I HAVE ONE, TWO, THREE--THAT'S ALL I HAVE?
OH, YOU'RE OKAY. HOW'S THE LUCKY FIN?
LUCKY.
LET'S SEE.

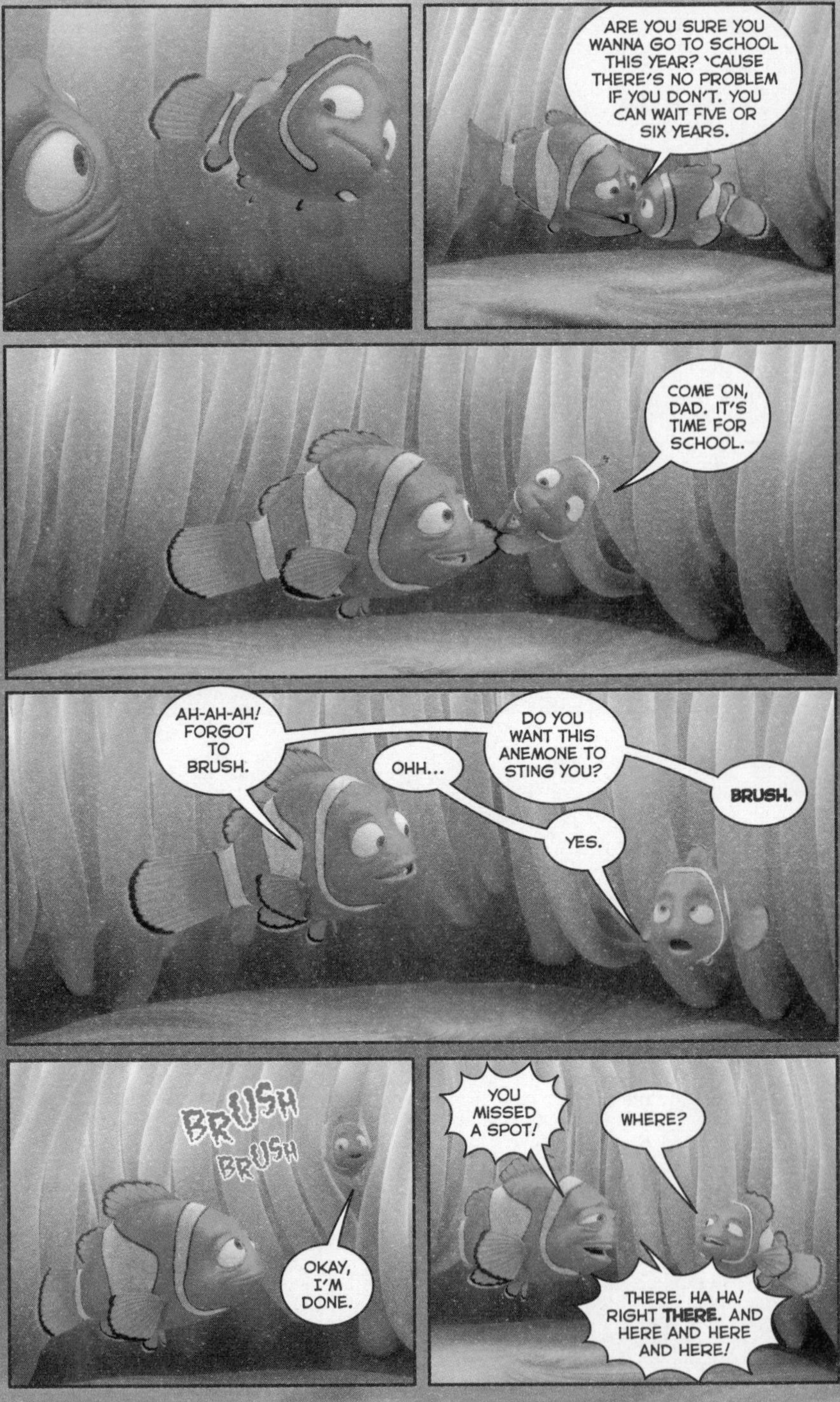
ARE YOU SURE YOU WANNA GO TO SCHOOL THIS YEAR? 'CAUSE THERE'S NO PROBLEM IF YOU DON'T. YOU CAN WAIT FIVE OR SIX YEARS.
COME ON, DAD. IT'S TIME FOR SCHOOL.
AH-AH-AH! FORGOT TO BRUSH.
DO YOU WANT THIS ANEMONE TO STING YOU?
OHH...
BRUSH.
YES.
BRUSH
BRUSH
OKAY, I'M DONE.
YOU MISSED A SPOT!
WHERE?
THERE. HA HA! RIGHT THERE. AND HERE AND HERE AND HERE!

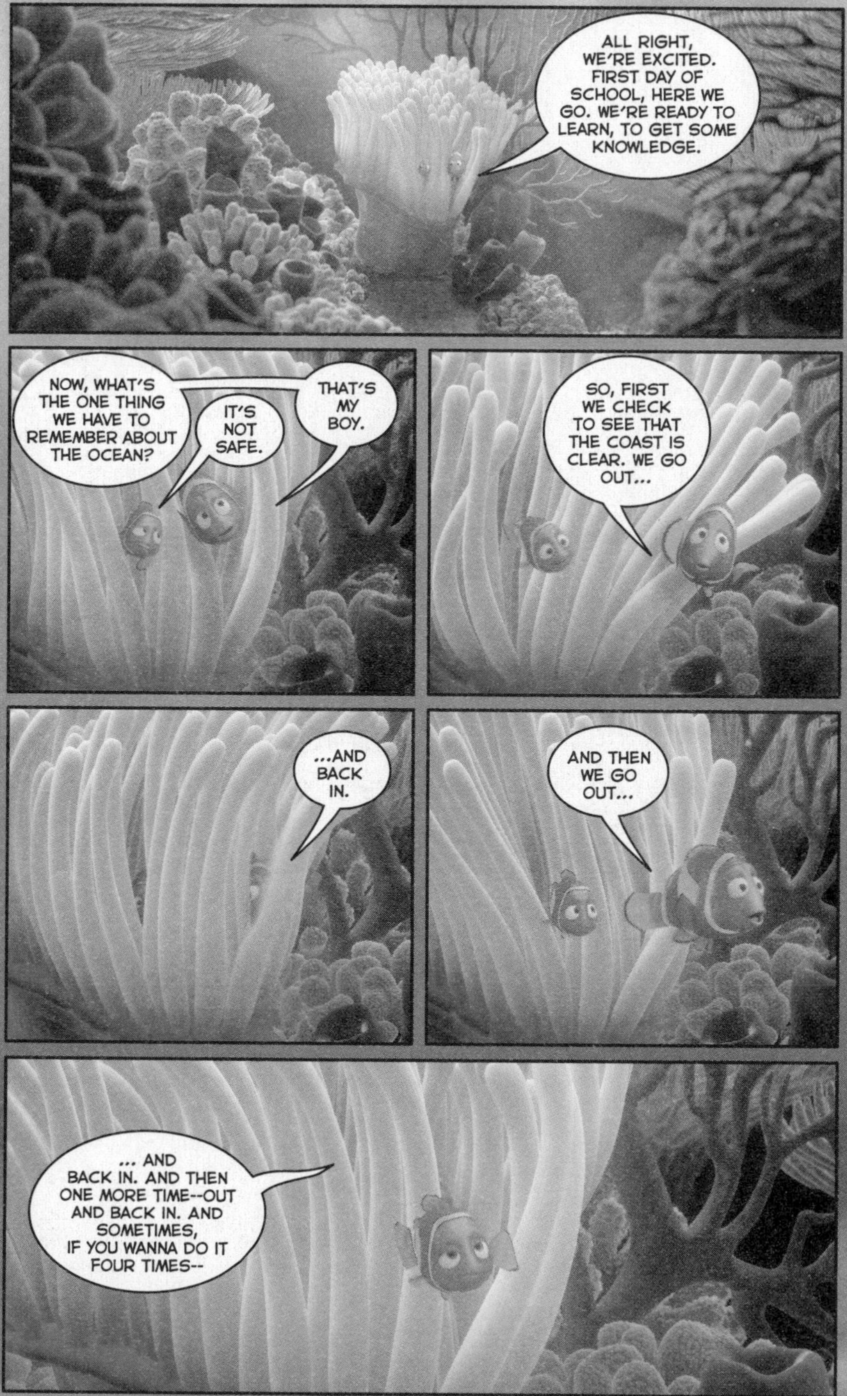
ALL RIGHT, WE'RE EXCITED. FIRST DAY OF SCHOOL, HERE WE GO. WE'RE READY TO LEARN, TO GET SOME KNOWLEDGE.
NOW, WHAT'S THE ONE THING WE HAVE TO REMEMBER ABOUT THE OCEAN?
IT'S NOT SAFE.
THAT'S MY BOY.
SO, FIRST WE CHECK TO SEE THAT THE COAST IS CLEAR. WE GO OUT...
...AND BACK IN.
AND THEN WE GO OUT...
... AND BACK IN. AND THEN ONE MORE TIME--OUT AND BACK IN. AND SOMETIMES, IF YOU WANNA DO IT FOUR TIMES--

DAD...

ALL RIGHT. COME ON, BOY.

DAD, MAYBE WHILE I'M AT SCHOOL, I'LL SEE A **SHARK**!

I HIGHLY DOUBT THAT.

HAVE YOU EVER **MET** A SHARK?

NO, AND I DON'T PLAN TO.

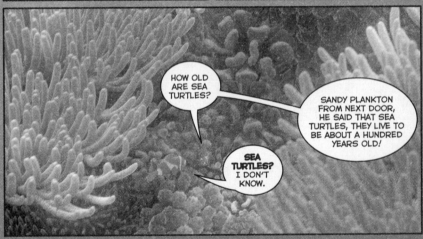

HOW OLD ARE SEA TURTLES?

SANDY PLANKTON FROM NEXT DOOR, HE SAID THAT SEA TURTLES, THEY LIVE TO BE ABOUT A HUNDRED YEARS OLD!

SEA TURTLES? I DON'T KNOW.

WELL, YOU KNOW WHAT, IF I EVER MEET A SEA TURTLE, I'LL ASK HIM. AFTER I'M DONE TALKING TO THE SHARK, OKAY?

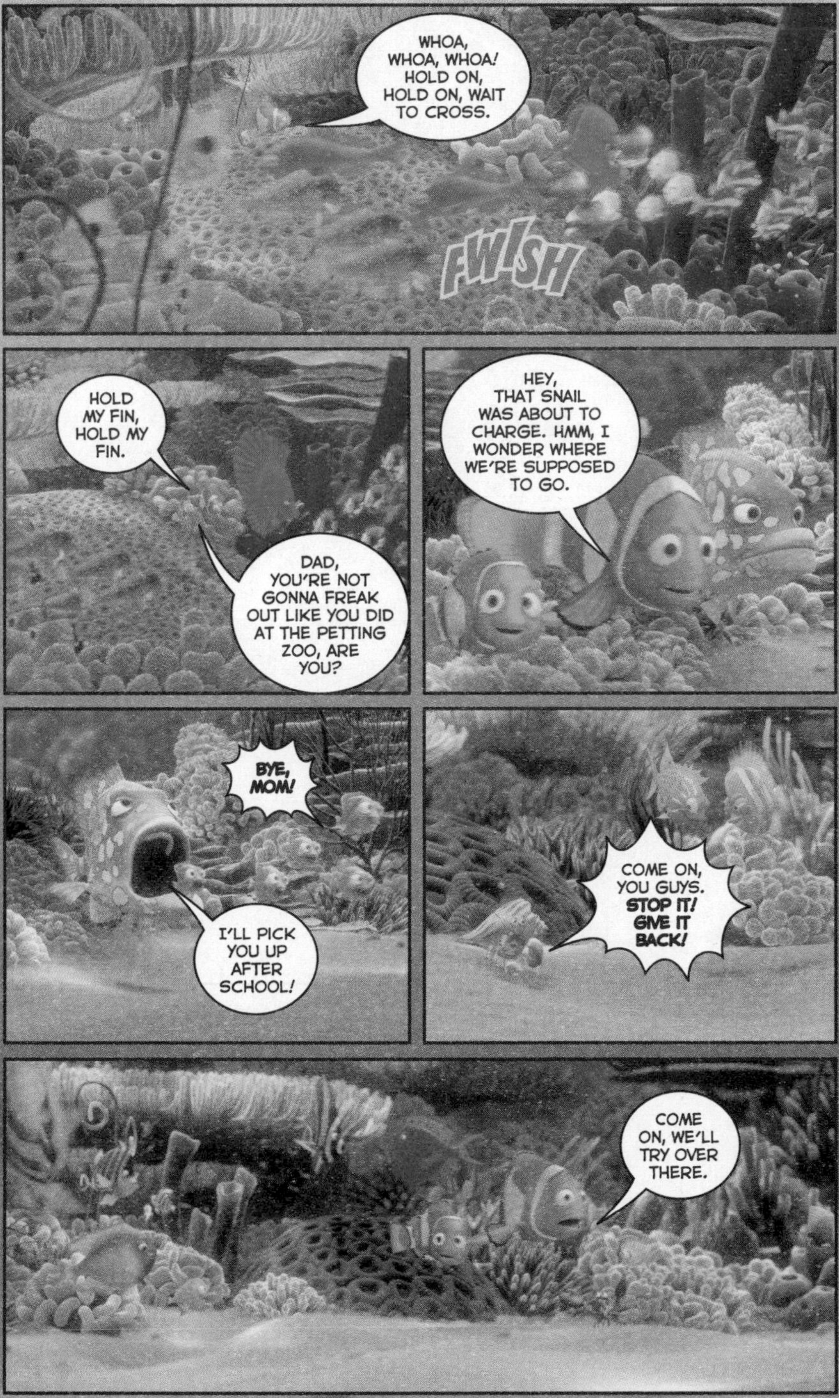
WHOA, WHOA, WHOA! HOLD ON, HOLD ON, WAIT TO CROSS.
FWISH
HOLD MY FIN, HOLD MY FIN.
DAD, YOU'RE NOT GONNA FREAK OUT LIKE YOU DID AT THE PETTING ZOO, ARE YOU?
HEY, THAT SNAIL WAS ABOUT TO CHARGE. HMM, I WONDER WHERE WE'RE SUPPOSED TO GO.
BYE, MOM!
I'LL PICK YOU UP AFTER SCHOOL!
COME ON, YOU GUYS. STOP IT! GIVE IT BACK!
COME ON, WE'LL TRY OVER THERE.

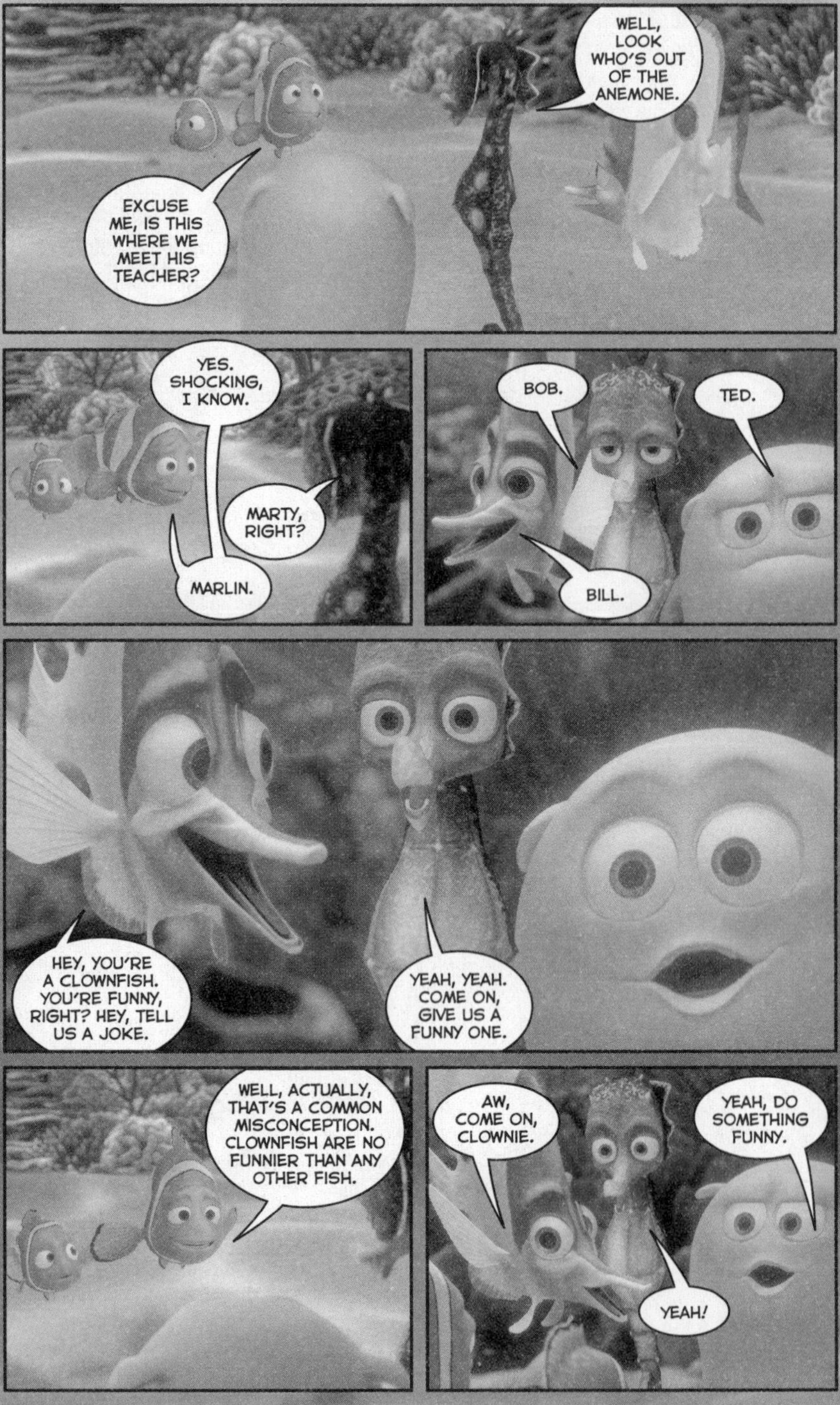
WELL, LOOK WHO'S OUT OF THE ANEMONE.
EXCUSE ME, IS THIS WHERE WE MEET HIS TEACHER?
YES. SHOCKING, I KNOW.
MARTY, RIGHT?
MARLIN.
BOB.
TED.
BILL.
HEY, YOU'RE A CLOWNFISH. YOU'RE FUNNY, RIGHT? HEY, TELL US A JOKE.
YEAH, YEAH. COME ON, GIVE US A FUNNY ONE.
WELL, ACTUALLY, THAT'S A COMMON MISCONCEPTION. CLOWNFISH ARE NO FUNNIER THAN ANY OTHER FISH.
AW, COME ON, CLOWNIE.
YEAH, DO SOMETHING FUNNY.
YEAH!

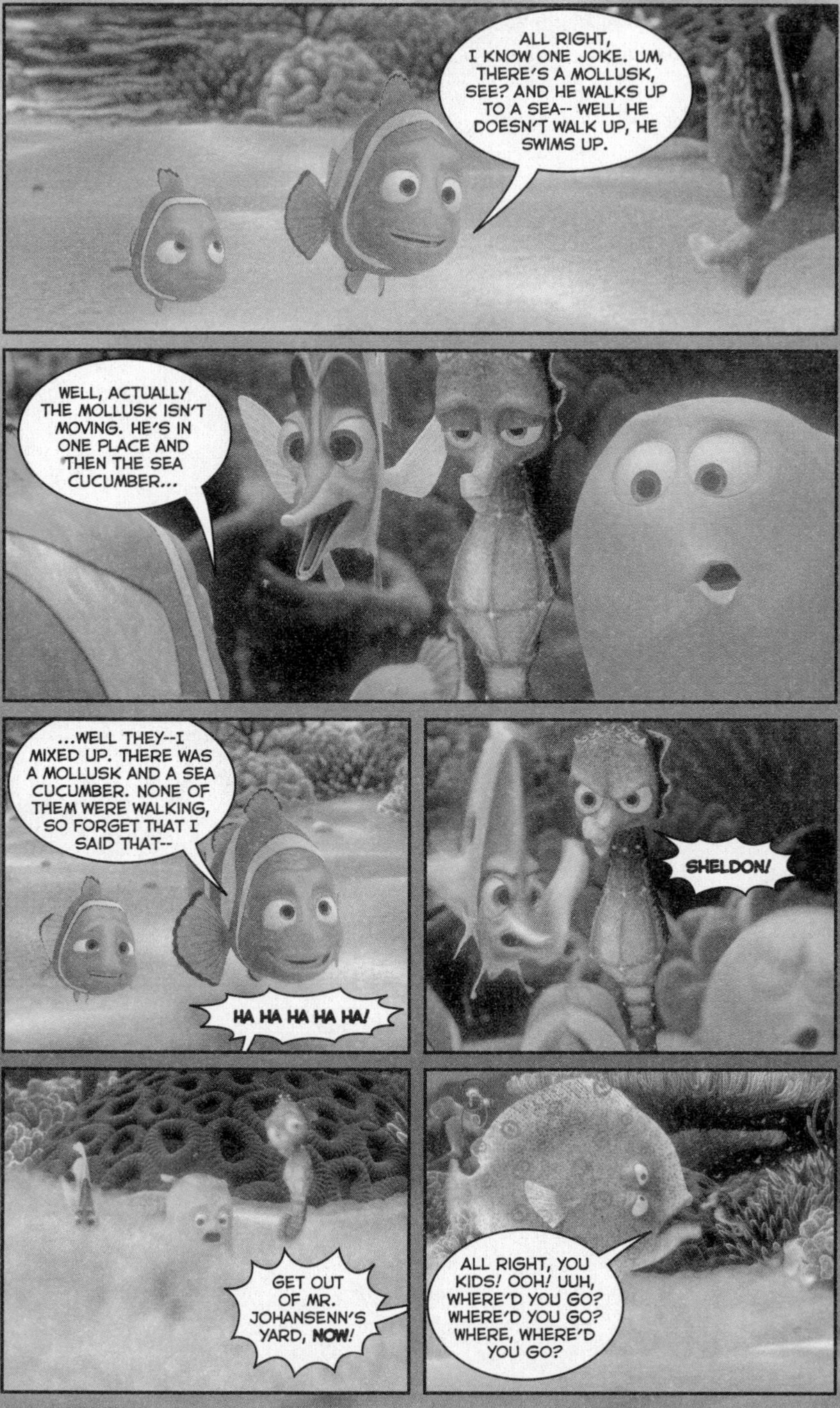
ALL RIGHT, I KNOW ONE JOKE. UM, THERE'S A MOLLUSK, SEE? AND HE WALKS UP TO A SEA-- WELL HE DOESN'T WALK UP, HE SWIMS UP.
WELL, ACTUALLY THE MOLLUSK ISN'T MOVING. HE'S IN ONE PLACE AND THEN THE SEA CUCUMBER...
...WELL THEY--I MIXED UP. THERE WAS A MOLLUSK AND A SEA CUCUMBER. NONE OF THEM WERE WALKING, SO FORGET THAT I SAID THAT--
HA HA HA HA HA!
SHELDON!
GET OUT OF MR. JOHANSENN'S YARD, NOW!
ALL RIGHT, YOU KIDS! OOH! UUH, WHERE'D YOU GO? WHERE'D YOU GO? WHERE, WHERE'D YOU GO?

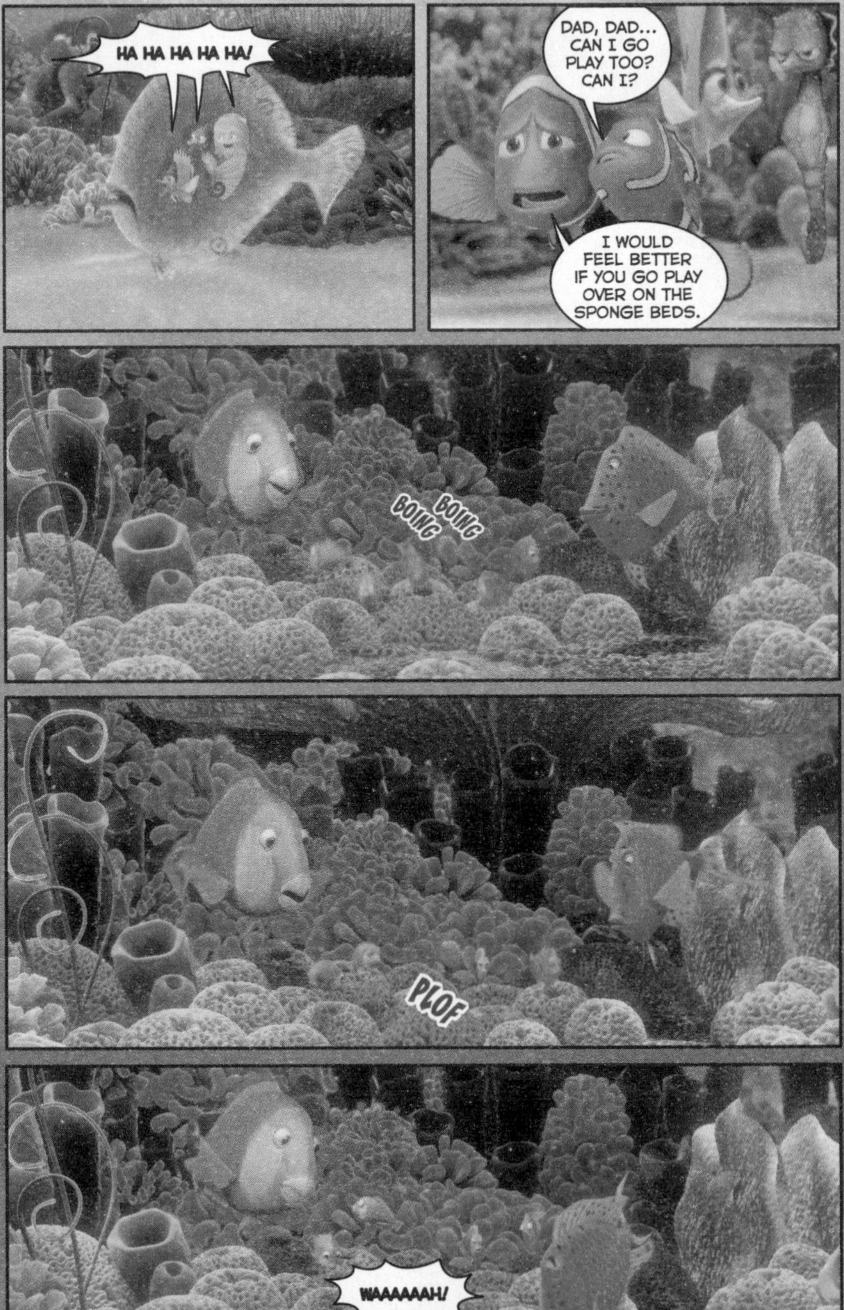
HA HA HA HA HA!
DAD, DAD... CAN I GO PLAY TOO? CAN I?
I WOULD FEEL BETTER IF YOU GO PLAY OVER ON THE SPONGE BEDS.
BOING BOING
PLOF
WAAAAAAH!

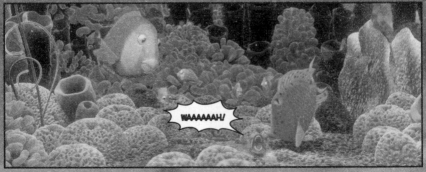

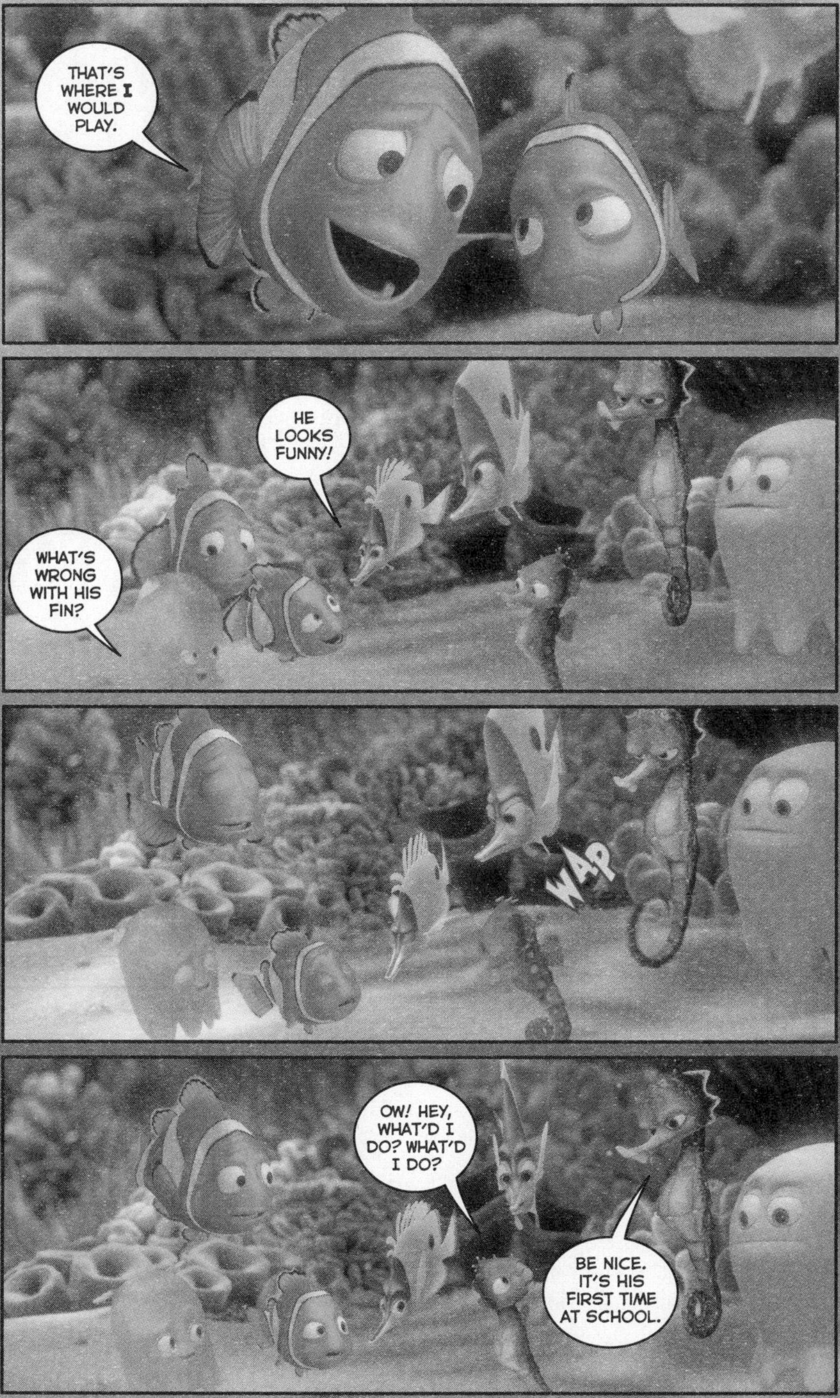
THAT'S WHERE **I** WOULD PLAY.
HE LOOKS FUNNY!
WHAT'S WRONG WITH HIS FIN?
WAP
OW! HEY, WHAT'D I DO? WHAT'D I DO?
BE NICE. IT'S HIS FIRST TIME AT SCHOOL.

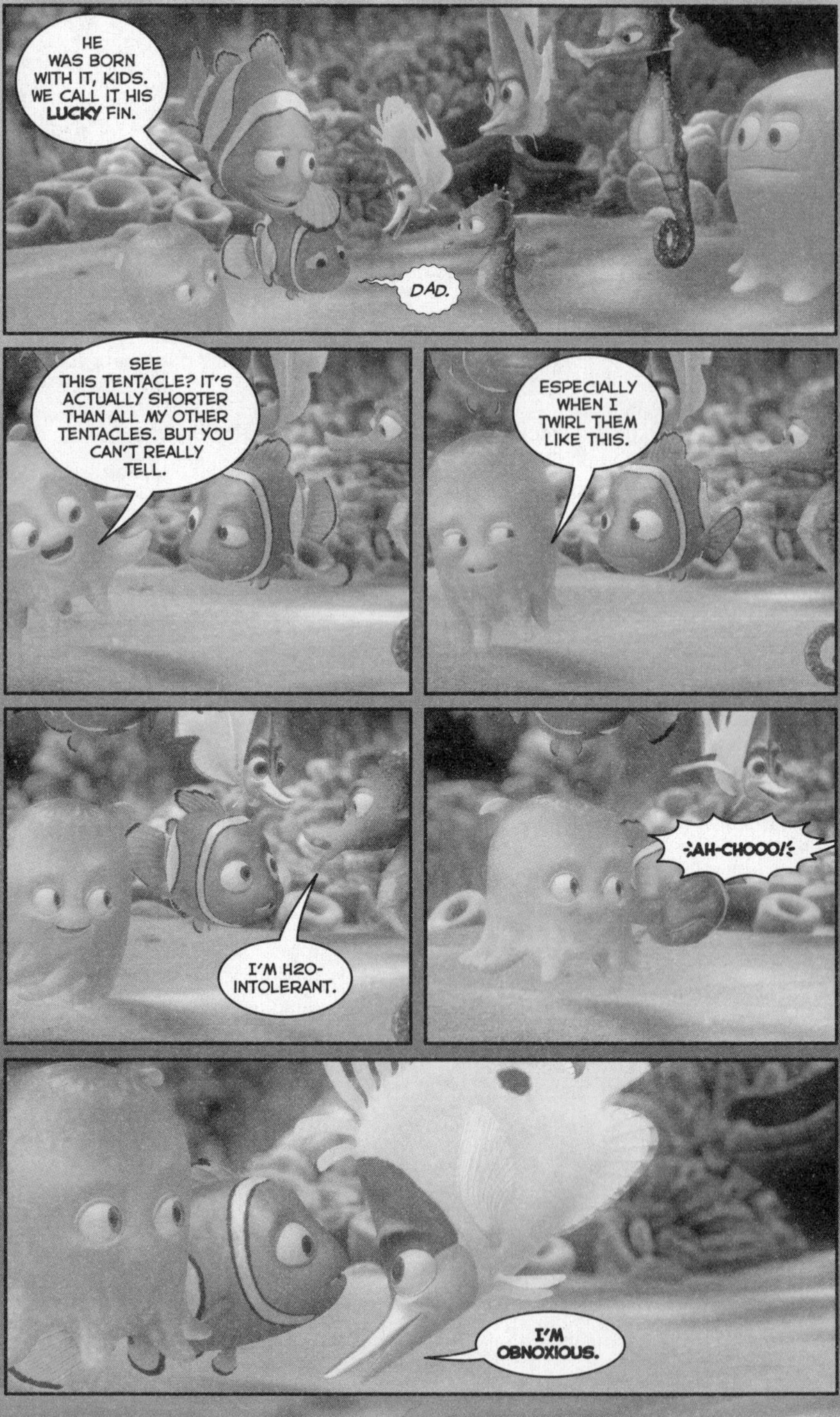
HE WAS BORN WITH IT, KIDS. WE CALL IT HIS LUCKY FIN.
DAD.
SEE THIS TENTACLE? IT'S ACTUALLY SHORTER THAN ALL MY OTHER TENTACLES. BUT YOU CAN'T REALLY TELL.
ESPECIALLY WHEN I TWIRL THEM LIKE THIS.
I'M H2O-INTOLERANT.
AH-CHOOO!
I'M OBNOXIOUS.

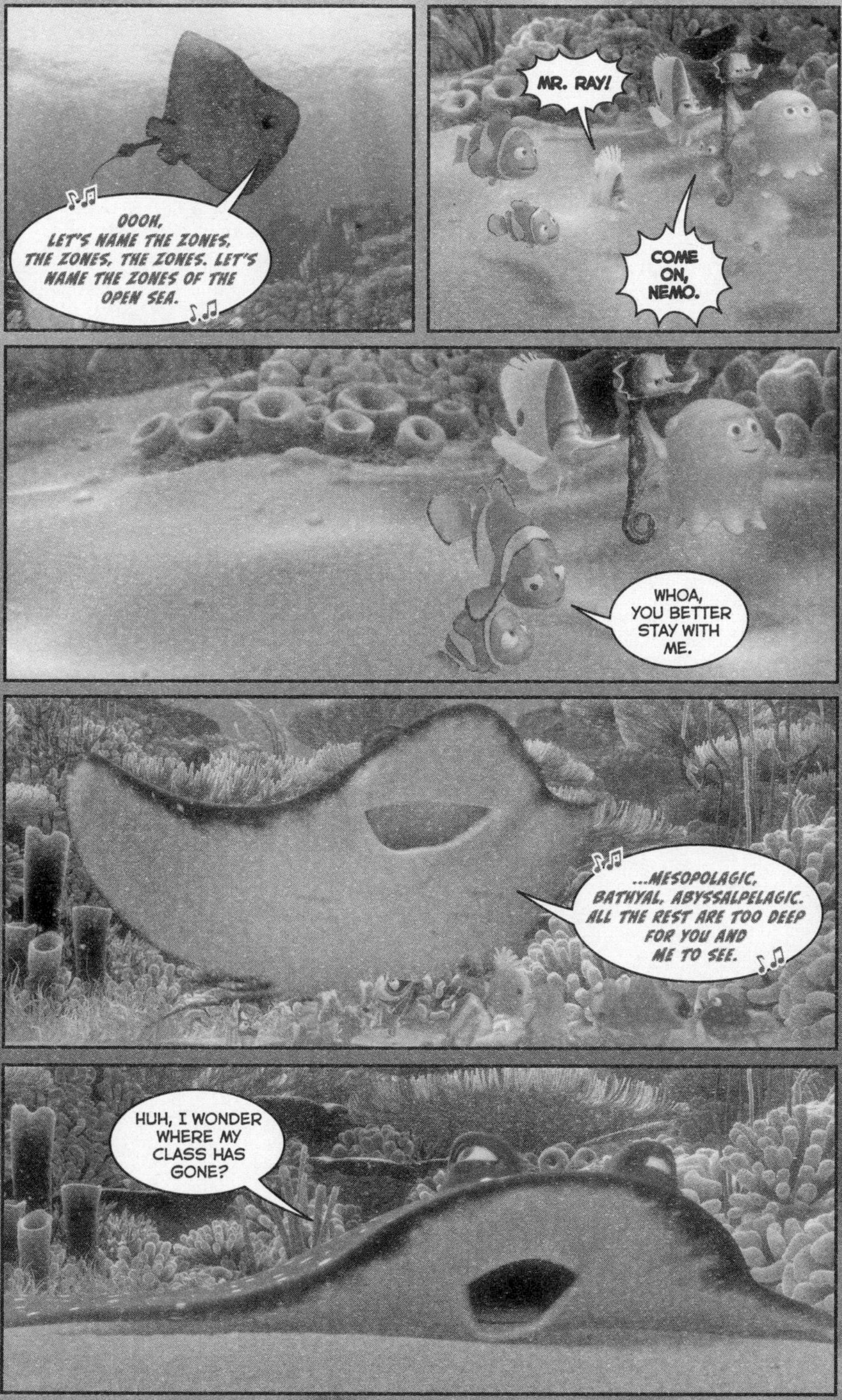
OOOH, LET'S NAME THE ZONES, THE ZONES, THE ZONES. LET'S NAME THE ZONES OF THE OPEN SEA.
MR. RAY!
COME ON, NEMO.
WHOA, YOU BETTER STAY WITH ME.
...MESOPOLAGIC, BATHYAL, ABYSSALPELAGIC. ALL THE REST ARE TOO DEEP FOR YOU AND ME TO SEE.
HUH, I WONDER WHERE MY CLASS HAS GONE?

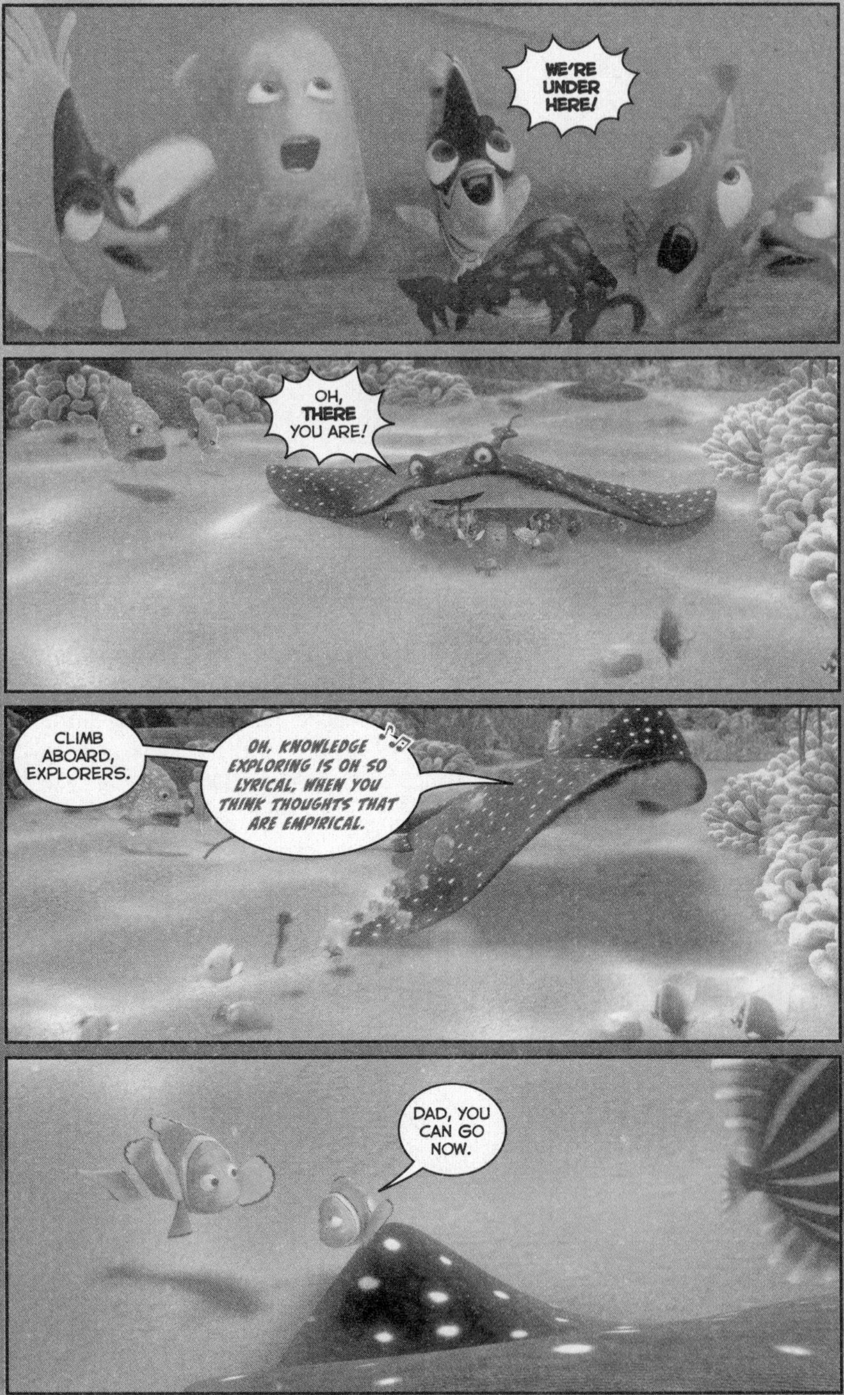
WE'RE UNDER HERE!
OH, THERE YOU ARE!
CLIMB ABOARD, EXPLORERS.
OH, KNOWLEDGE EXPLORING IS OH SO LYRICAL, WHEN YOU THINK THOUGHTS THAT ARE EMPIRICAL.
DAD, YOU CAN GO NOW.

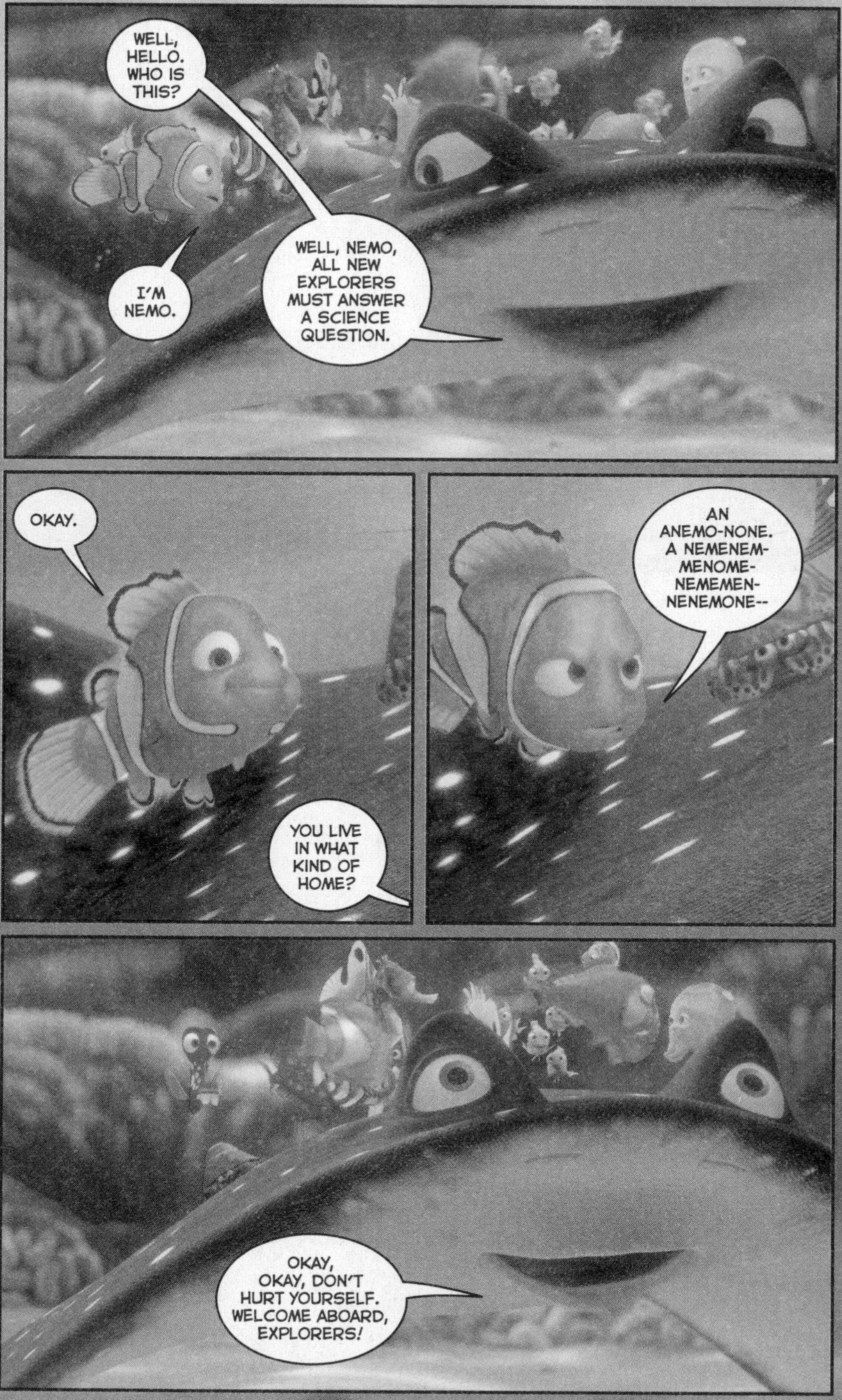
WELL, HELLO. WHO IS THIS?
I'M NEMO.
WELL, NEMO, ALL NEW EXPLORERS MUST ANSWER A SCIENCE QUESTION.
OKAY.
YOU LIVE IN WHAT KIND OF HOME?
AN ANEMO-NONE. A NEMENEM-MENOME-NEMEMEN-NENEMONE--
OKAY, OKAY, DON'T HURT YOURSELF. WELCOME ABOARD, EXPLORERS!

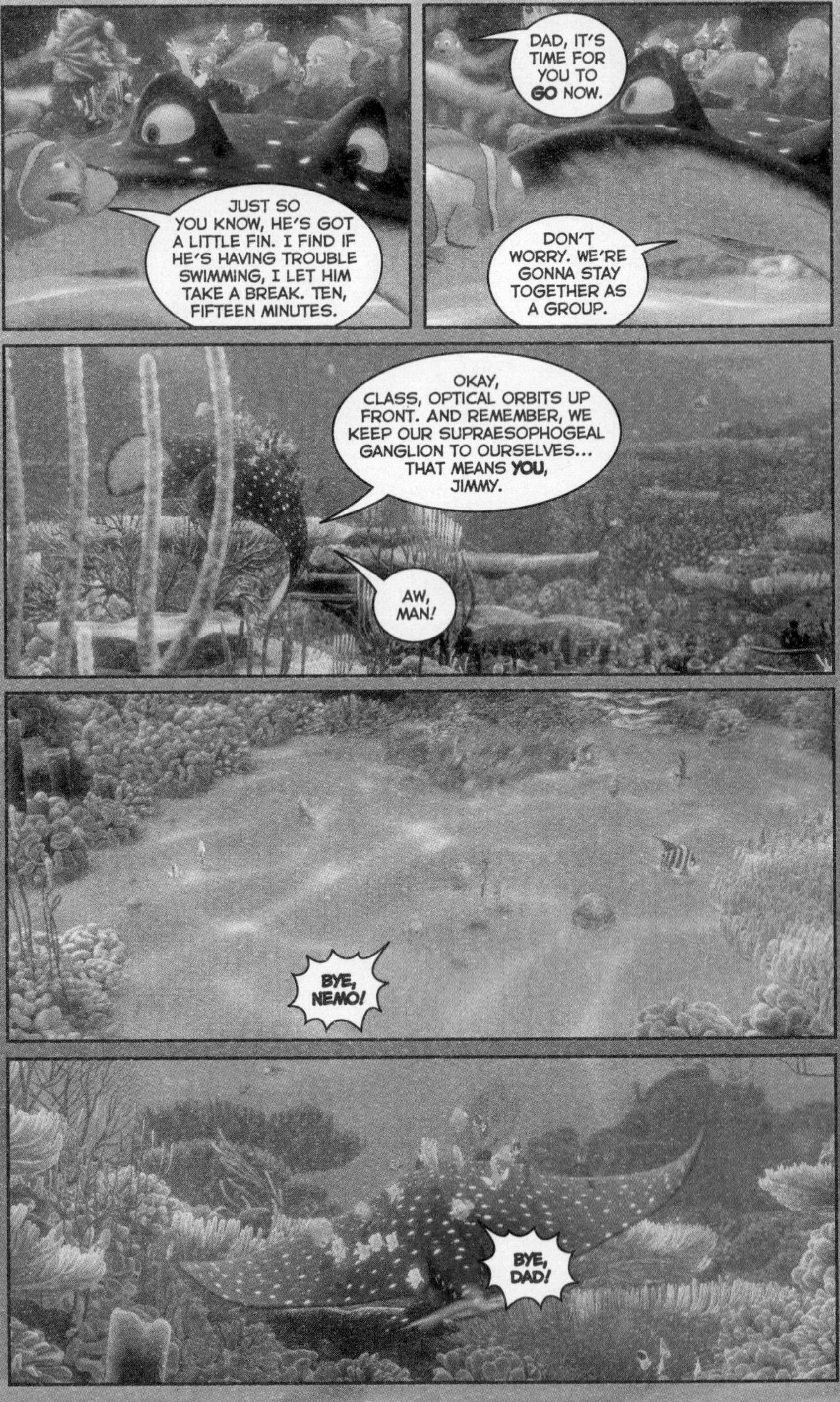
JUST SO YOU KNOW, HE'S GOT A LITTLE FIN. I FIND IF HE'S HAVING TROUBLE SWIMMING, I LET HIM TAKE A BREAK. TEN, FIFTEEN MINUTES.
DAD, IT'S TIME FOR YOU TO GO NOW.
DON'T WORRY. WE'RE GONNA STAY TOGETHER AS A GROUP.
OKAY, CLASS, OPTICAL ORBITS UP FRONT. AND REMEMBER, WE KEEP OUR SUPRAESOPHOGEAL GANGLION TO OURSELVES... THAT MEANS YOU, JIMMY.
AW, MAN!
BYE, NEMO!
BYE, DAD!

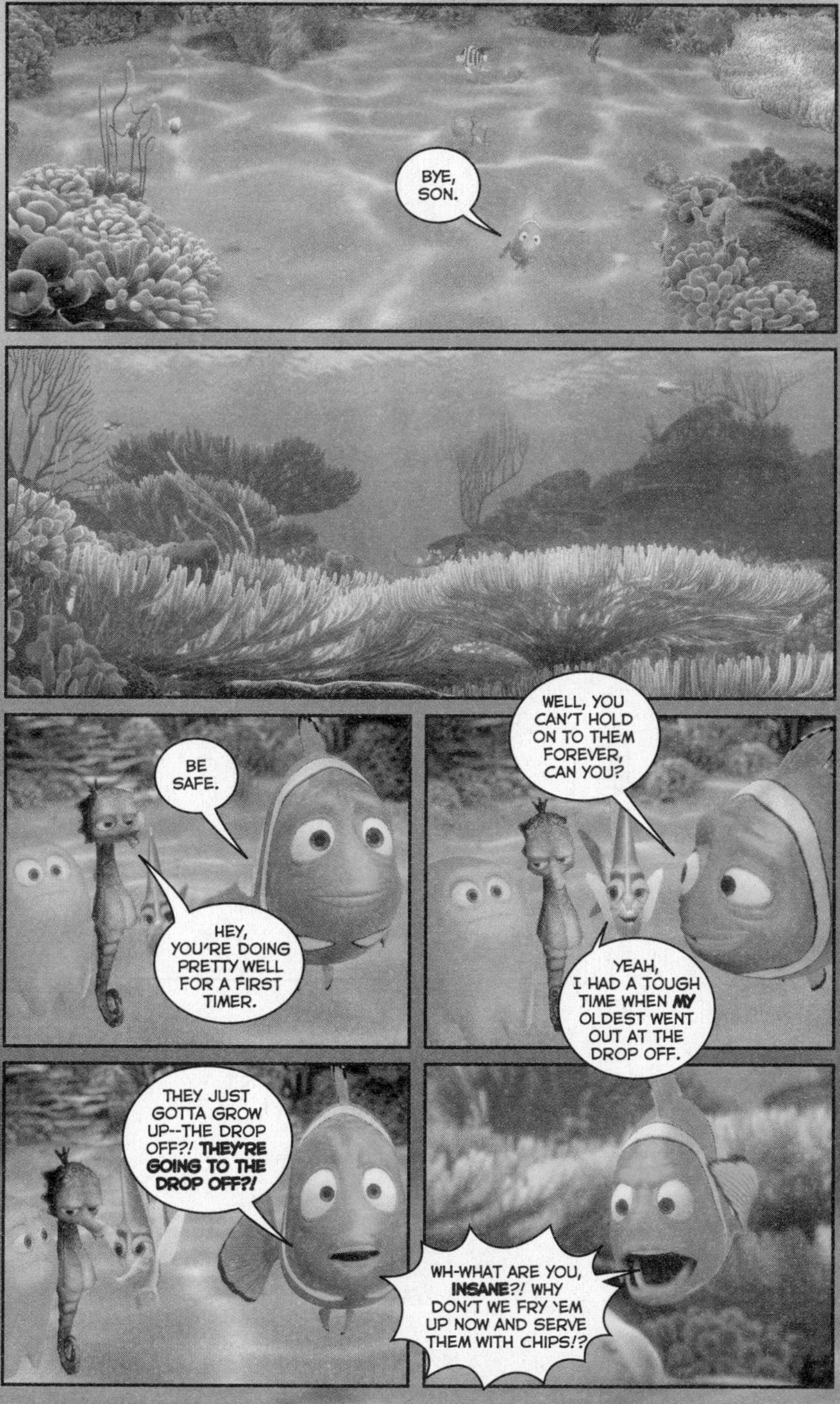
BYE, SON.
BE SAFE.
HEY, YOU'RE DOING PRETTY WELL FOR A FIRST TIMER.
WELL, YOU CAN'T HOLD ON TO THEM FOREVER, CAN YOU?
YEAH, I HAD A TOUGH TIME WHEN **MY** OLDEST WENT OUT AT THE DROP OFF.
THEY JUST GOTTA GROW UP--THE DROP OFF?! **THEY'RE GOING TO THE DROP OFF?!**
WH-WHAT ARE YOU, **INSANE**?! WHY DON'T WE FRY 'EM UP NOW AND SERVE THEM WITH CHIPS!?

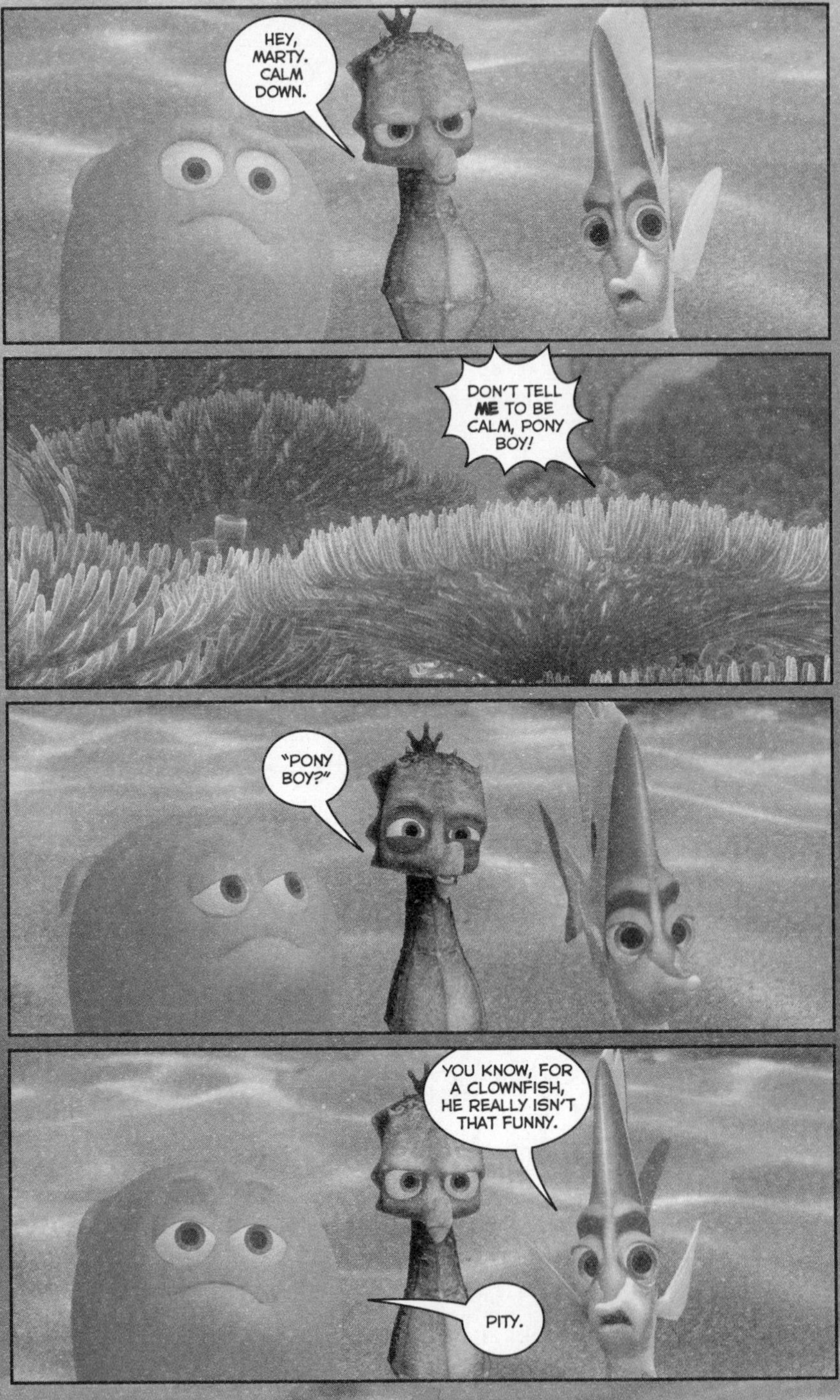
HEY, MARTY. CALM DOWN.
DON'T TELL **ME** TO BE CALM, PONY BOY!
"PONY BOY?"
YOU KNOW, FOR A CLOWNFISH, HE REALLY ISN'T THAT FUNNY.
PITY.

OH, LET'S NAME THE SPECIES, THE SPECIES, THE SPECIES. LET'S NAME THE SPECIES THAT LIVE IN THE SEA.

WHOA.

THERE'S PORIFERA, COELENTERATA, HYDROZOA, SCYPHOZOA, ANTHOZOA, CTENOPHORA, BRYOZOAS, THREE! GASTROPODA, ARTHROPODA, ECHINODERMA, AND SOME FISH LIKE YOU AND ME. COME ON, SING WITH ME. OH....!

JUST THE GIRLS THIS TIME.

OH, SEAWEED IS COOL. SEAWEED IS FUN. IT MAKES ITS FOOD FROM THE RAYS OF THE SUN......

OKAY, THE DROP OFF. ALL RIGHT, KIDS, FEEL FREE TO EXPLORE BUT STAY CLOSE.

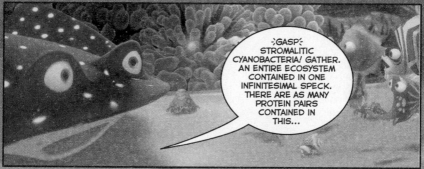

⸰GASP⸰ STROMALITIC CYANOBACTERIA! GATHER. AN ENTIRE ECOSYSTEM CONTAINED IN ONE INFINITESIMAL SPECK. THERE ARE AS MANY PROTEIN PAIRS CONTAINED IN THIS...

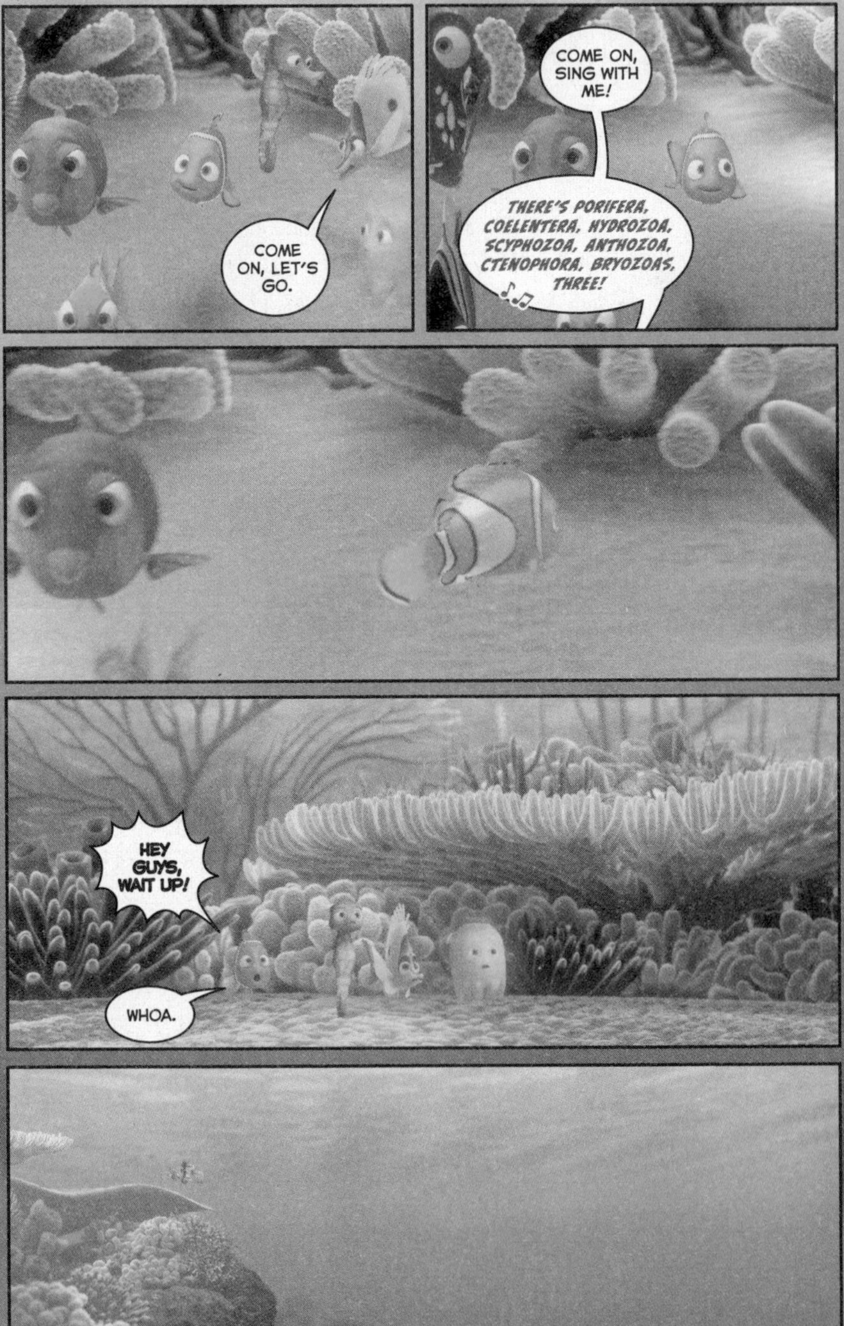
COME ON, LET'S GO.
COME ON, SING WITH ME!
THERE'S PORIFERA, COELENTERA, HYDROZOA, SCYPHOZOA, ANTHOZOA, CTENOPHORA, BRYOZOAS, THREE!
HEY GUYS, WAIT UP!
WHOA.

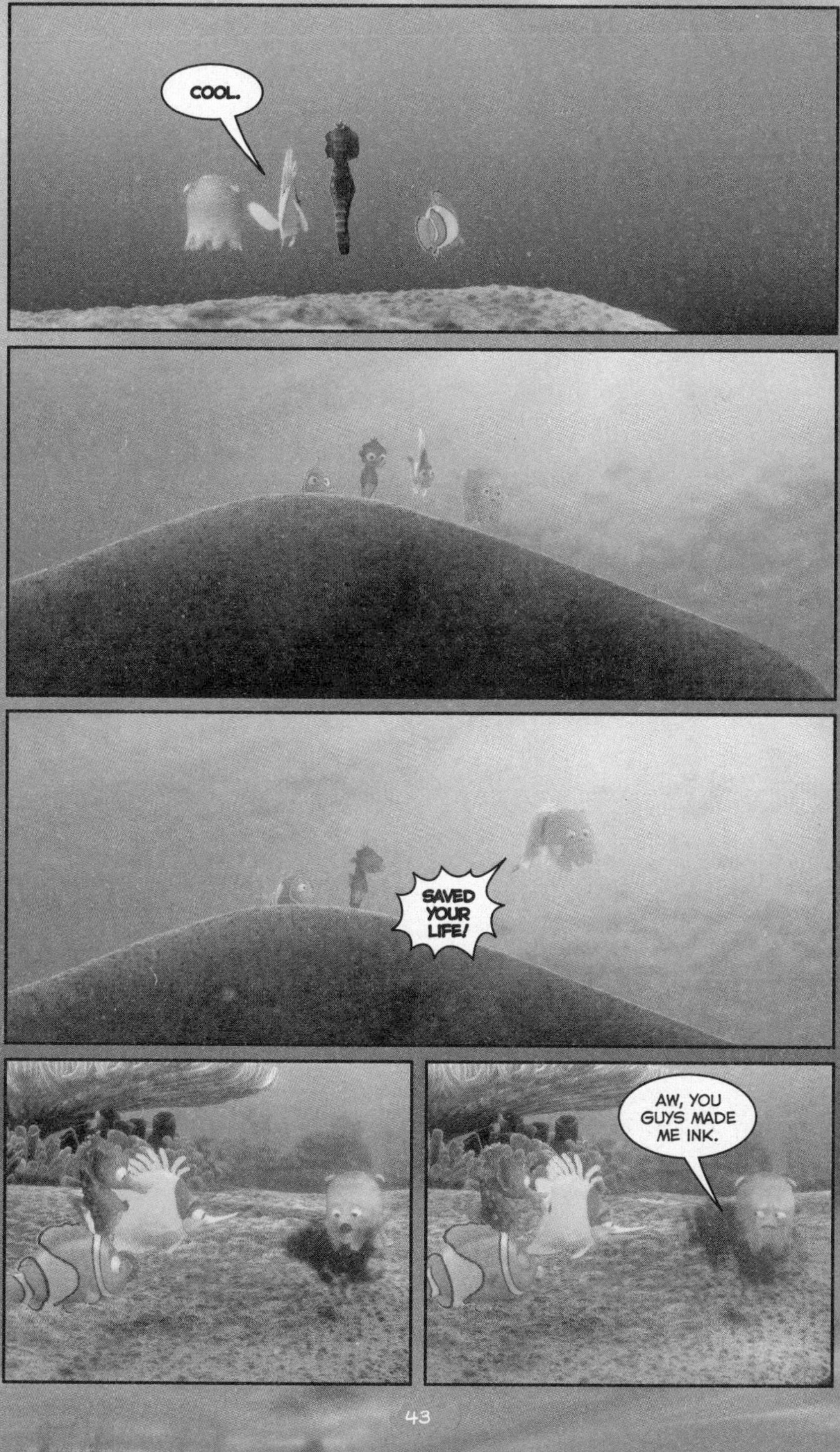
COOL.
SAVED YOUR LIFE!
AW, YOU GUYS MADE ME INK.

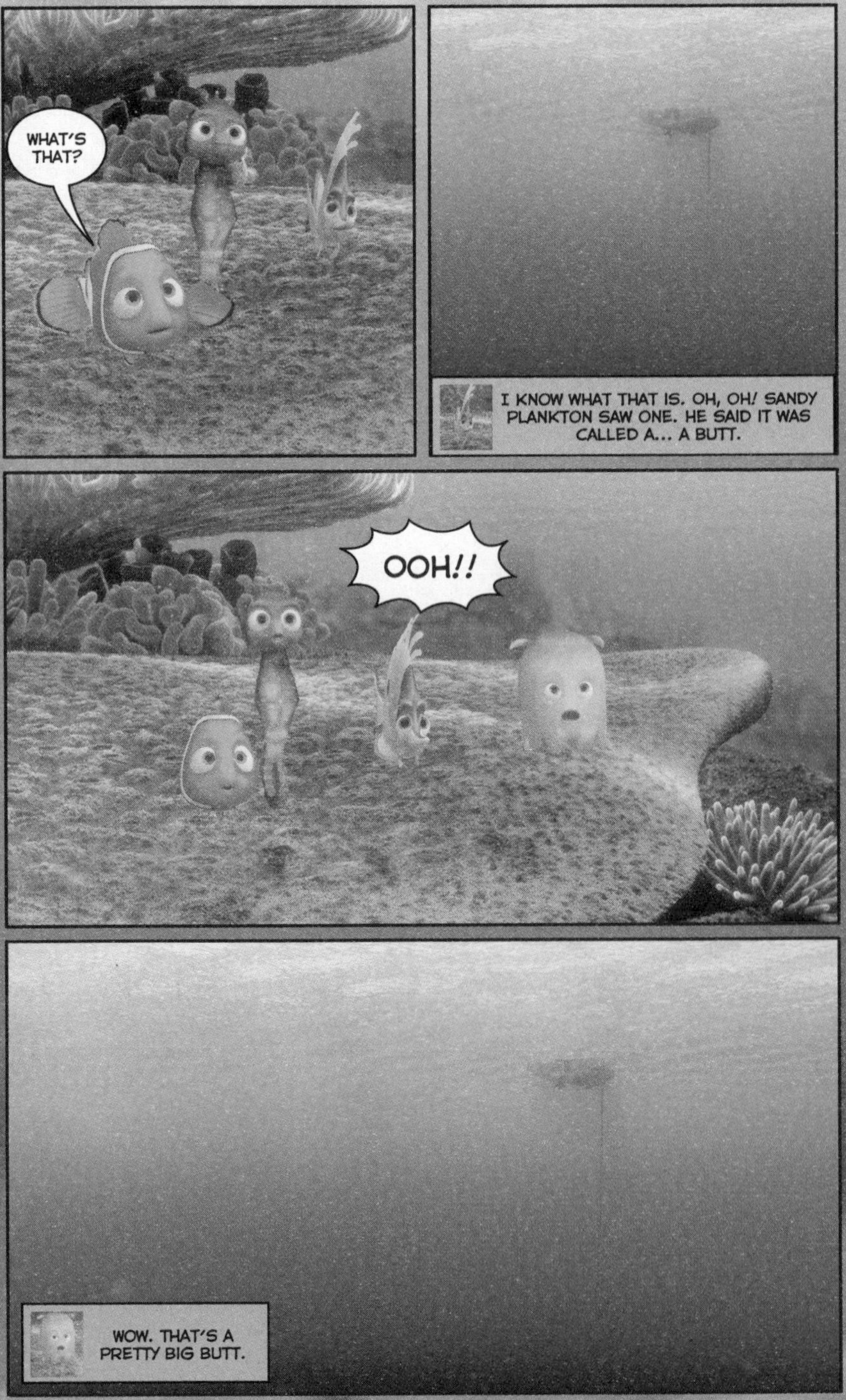
WHAT'S THAT?
I KNOW WHAT THAT IS. OH, OH! SANDY PLANKTON SAW ONE. HE SAID IT WAS CALLED A... A BUTT.
OOH!!
WOW. THAT'S A PRETTY BIG BUTT.

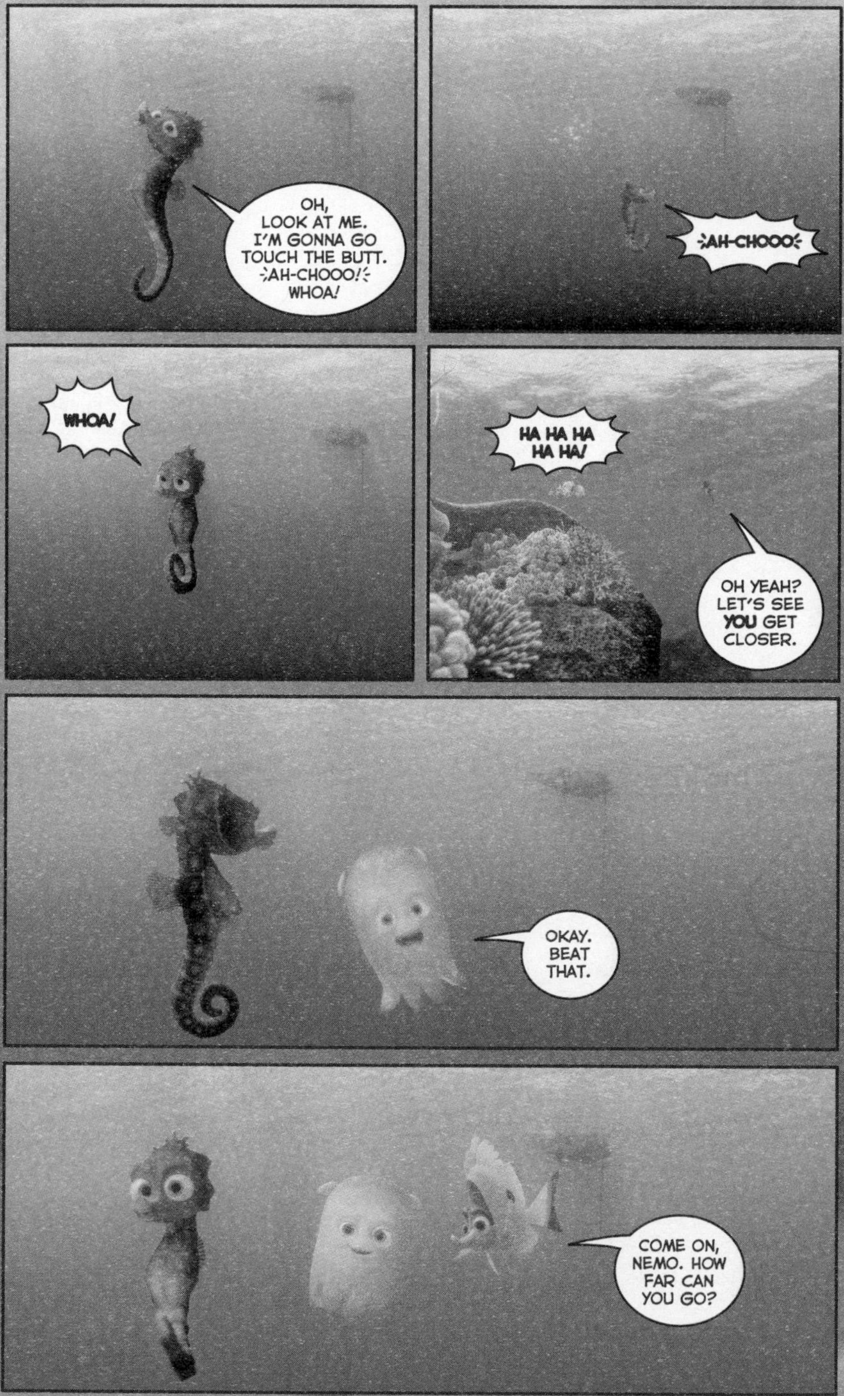
OH, LOOK AT ME. I'M GONNA GO TOUCH THE BUTT. AH-CHOOO! WHOA!
AH-CHOOO!
WHOA!
HA HA HA HA HA!
OH YEAH? LET'S SEE **YOU** GET CLOSER.
OKAY. BEAT THAT.
COME ON, NEMO. HOW FAR CAN YOU GO?

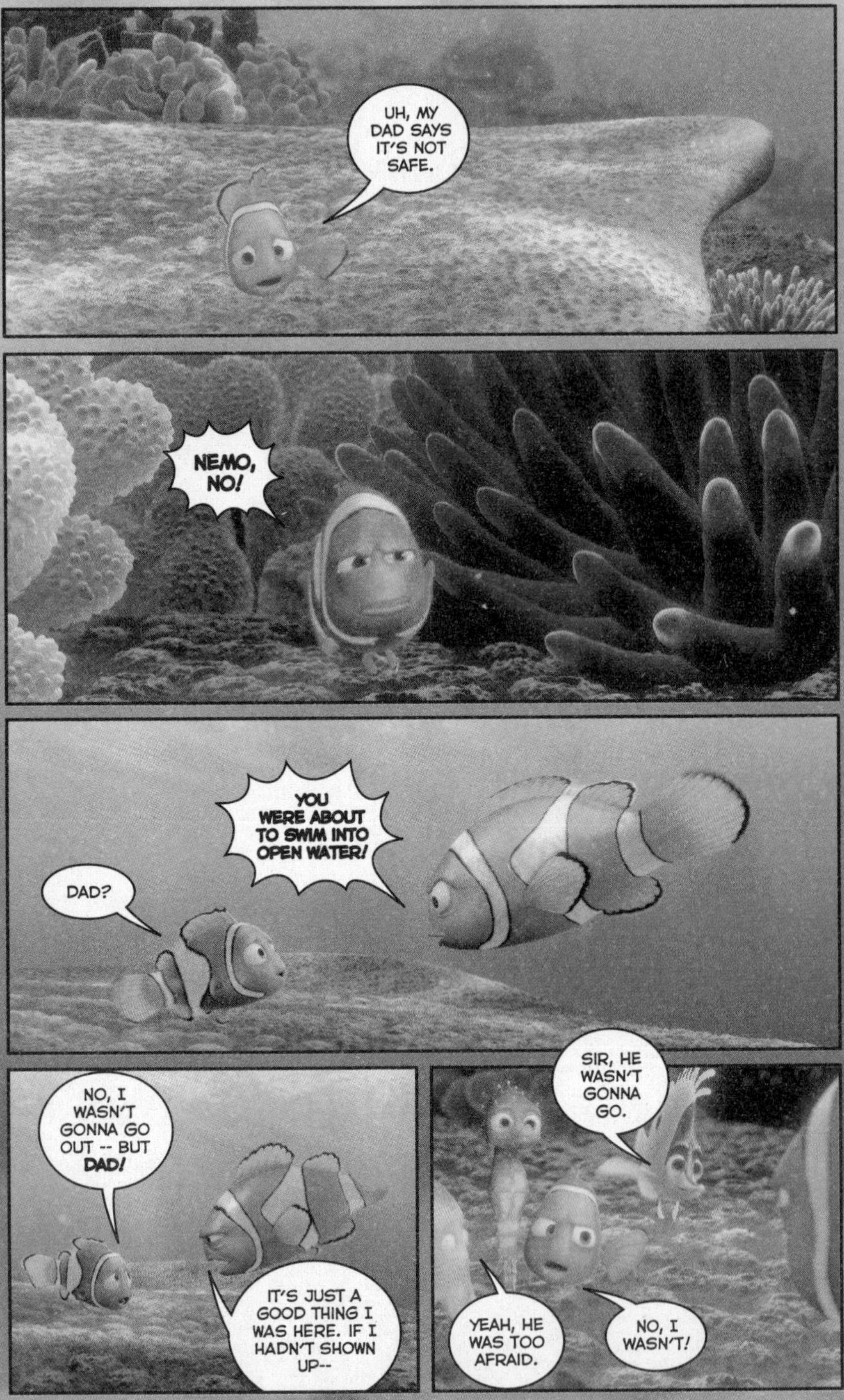
UH, MY DAD SAYS IT'S NOT SAFE.
NEMO, NO!
DAD?
YOU WERE ABOUT TO SWIM INTO OPEN WATER!
NO, I WASN'T GONNA GO OUT -- BUT **DAD!**
IT'S JUST A GOOD THING I WAS HERE. IF I HADN'T SHOWN UP--
SIR, HE WASN'T GONNA GO.
YEAH, HE WAS TOO AFRAID.
NO, I WASN'T!

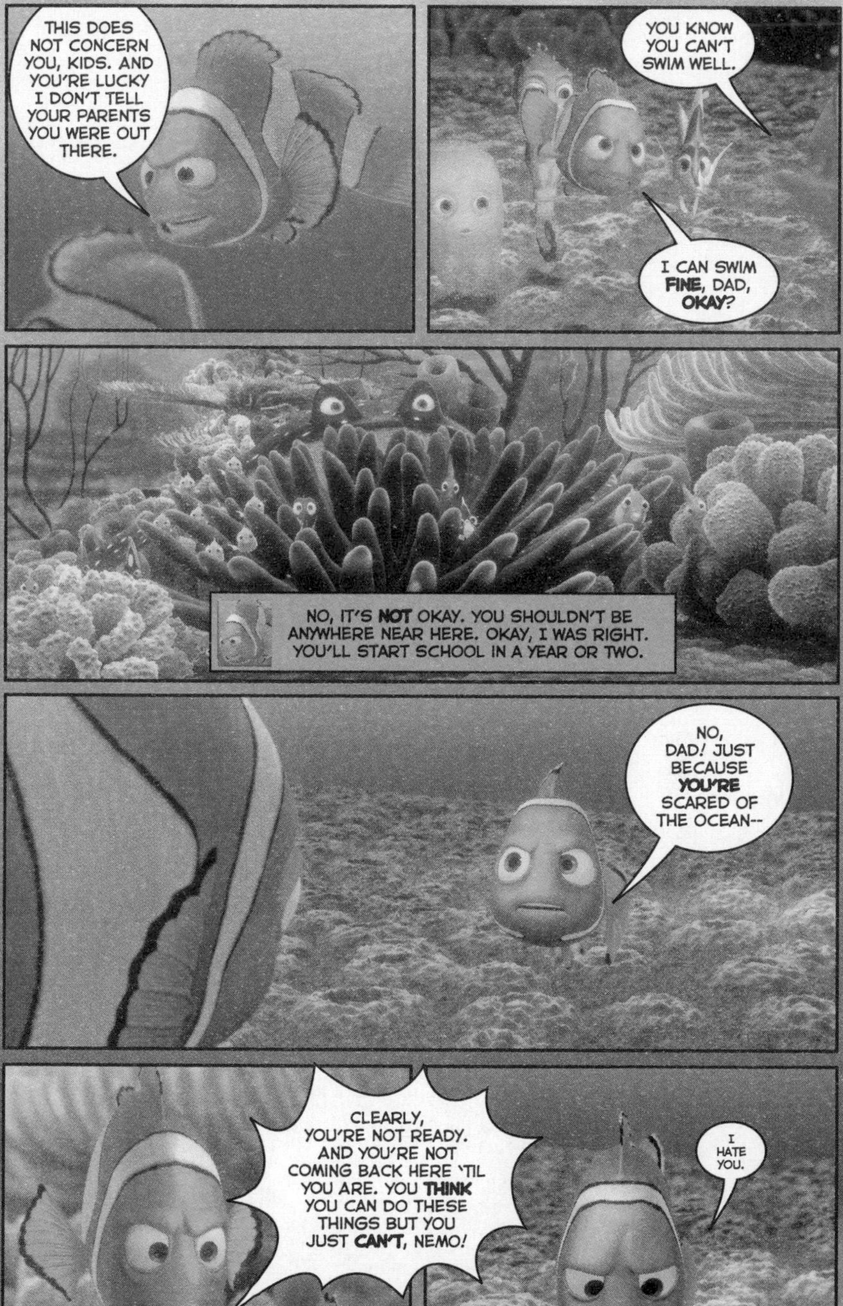
THIS DOES NOT CONCERN YOU, KIDS. AND YOU'RE LUCKY I DON'T TELL YOUR PARENTS YOU WERE OUT THERE.
YOU KNOW YOU CAN'T SWIM WELL.
I CAN SWIM FINE, DAD, OKAY?
NO, IT'S NOT OKAY. YOU SHOULDN'T BE ANYWHERE NEAR HERE. OKAY, I WAS RIGHT. YOU'LL START SCHOOL IN A YEAR OR TWO.
NO, DAD! JUST BECAUSE YOU'RE SCARED OF THE OCEAN--
CLEARLY, YOU'RE NOT READY. AND YOU'RE NOT COMING BACK HERE 'TIL YOU ARE. YOU THINK YOU CAN DO THESE THINGS BUT YOU JUST CAN'T, NEMO!
I HATE YOU.

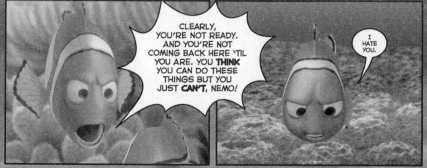

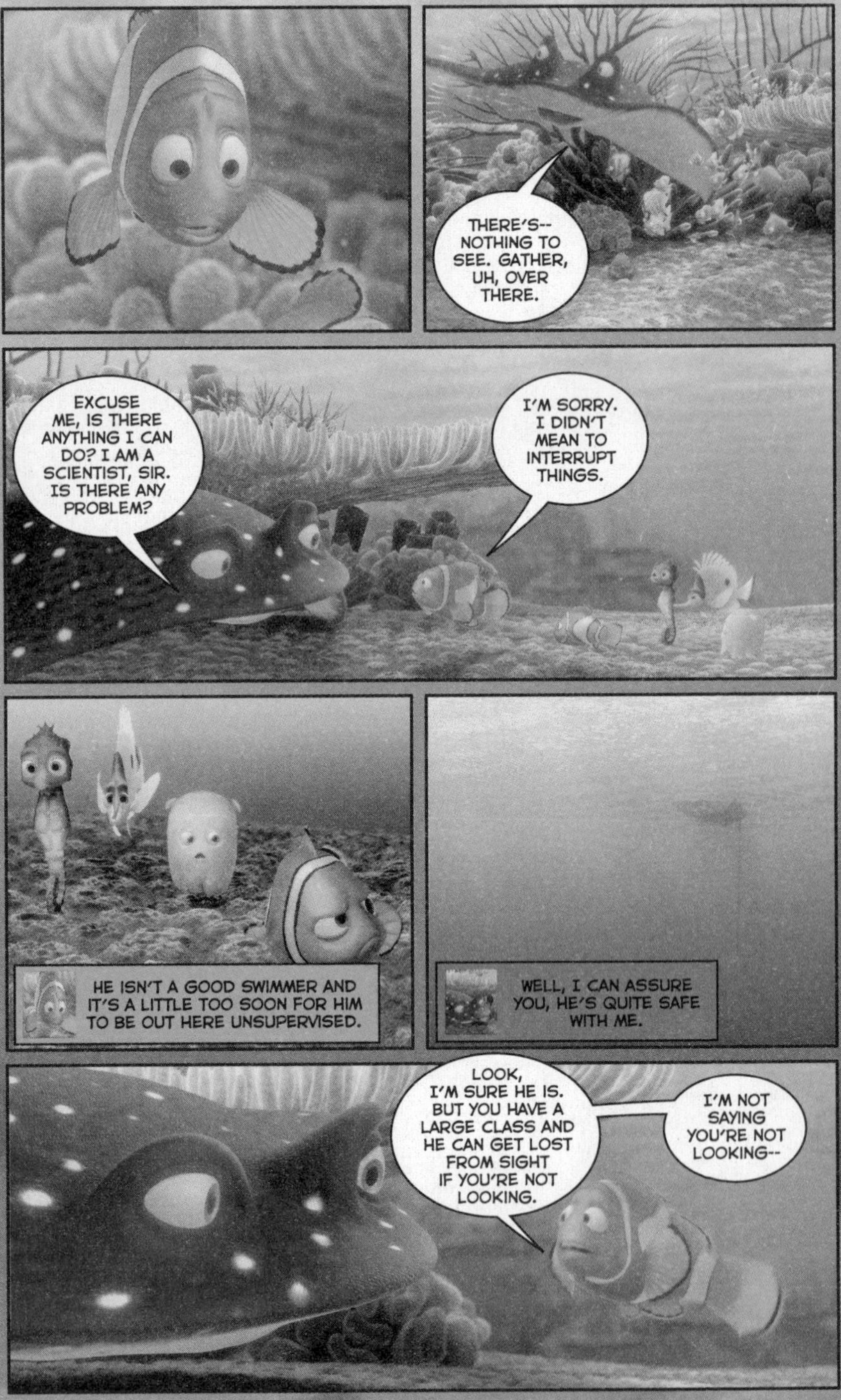
THERE'S--
NOTHING TO
SEE. GATHER,
UH, OVER
THERE.
EXCUSE
ME, IS THERE
ANYTHING I CAN
DO? I AM A
SCIENTIST, SIR.
IS THERE ANY
PROBLEM?
I'M SORRY.
I DIDN'T
MEAN TO
INTERRUPT
THINGS.
HE ISN'T A GOOD SWIMMER AND
IT'S A LITTLE TOO SOON FOR HIM
TO BE OUT HERE UNSUPERVISED.
WELL, I CAN ASSURE
YOU, HE'S QUITE SAFE
WITH ME.
LOOK,
I'M SURE HE IS.
BUT YOU HAVE A
LARGE CLASS AND
HE CAN GET LOST
FROM SIGHT
IF YOU'RE NOT
LOOKING.
I'M NOT
SAYING
YOU'RE NOT
LOOKING--

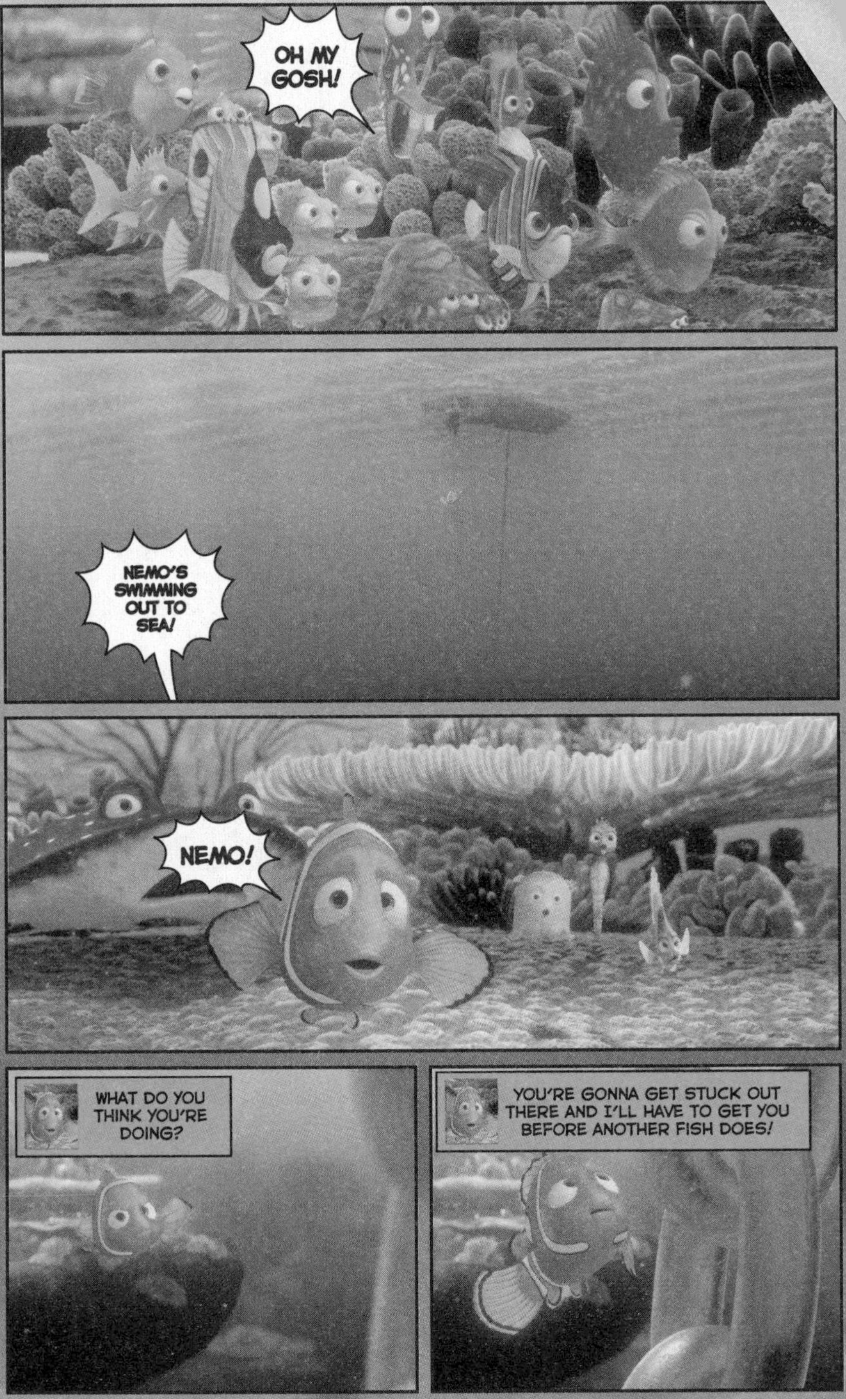
OH MY GOSH!
NEMO'S SWIMMING OUT TO SEA!
NEMO!
WHAT DO YOU THINK YOU'RE DOING?
YOU'RE GONNA GET STUCK OUT THERE AND I'LL HAVE TO GET YOU BEFORE ANOTHER FISH DOES!

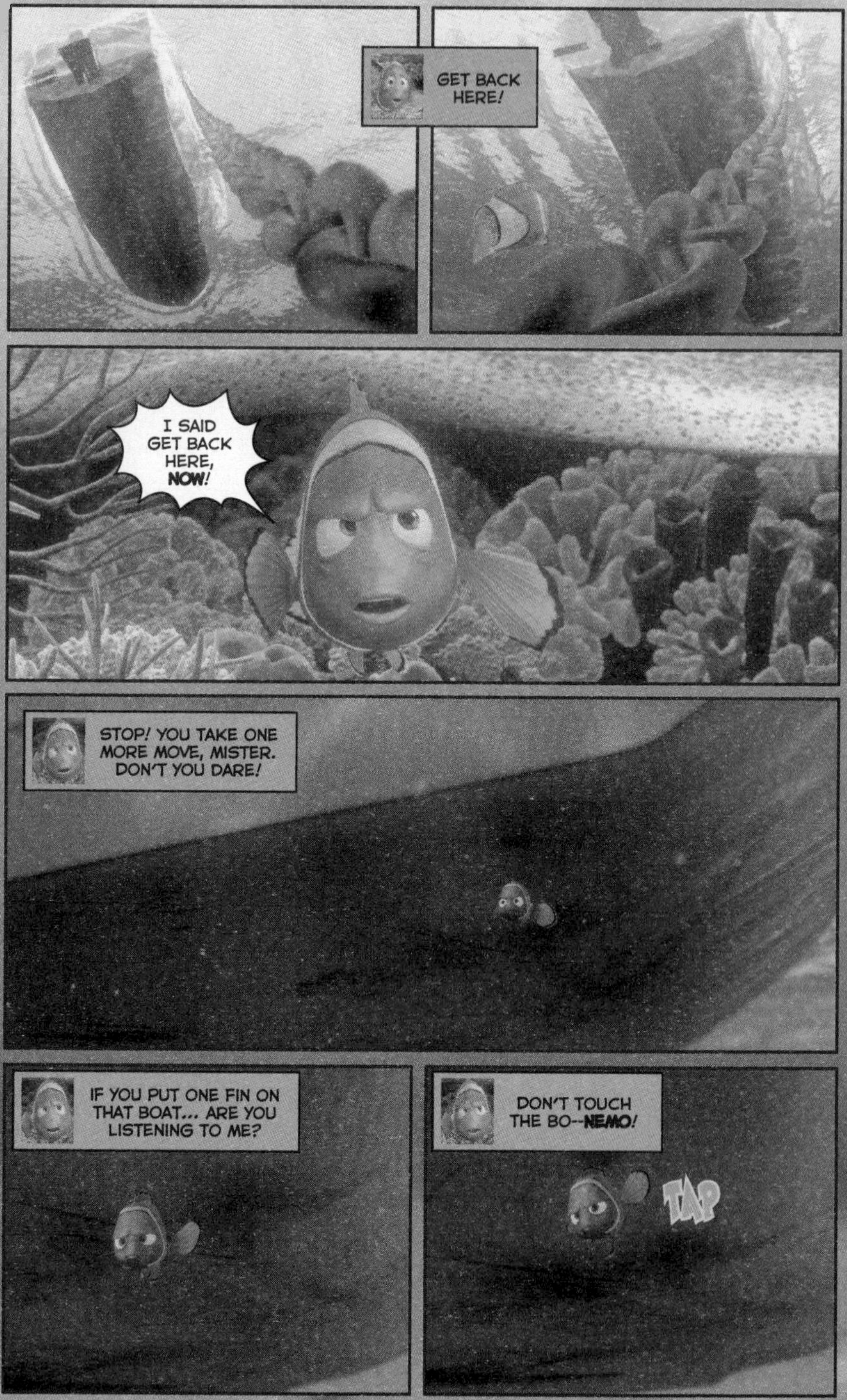
GET BACK HERE!
I SAID GET BACK HERE, **NOW**!
STOP! YOU TAKE ONE MORE MOVE, MISTER. DON'T YOU DARE!
IF YOU PUT ONE FIN ON THAT BOAT... ARE YOU LISTENING TO ME?
DON'T TOUCH THE BO--**NEMO**!
TAP

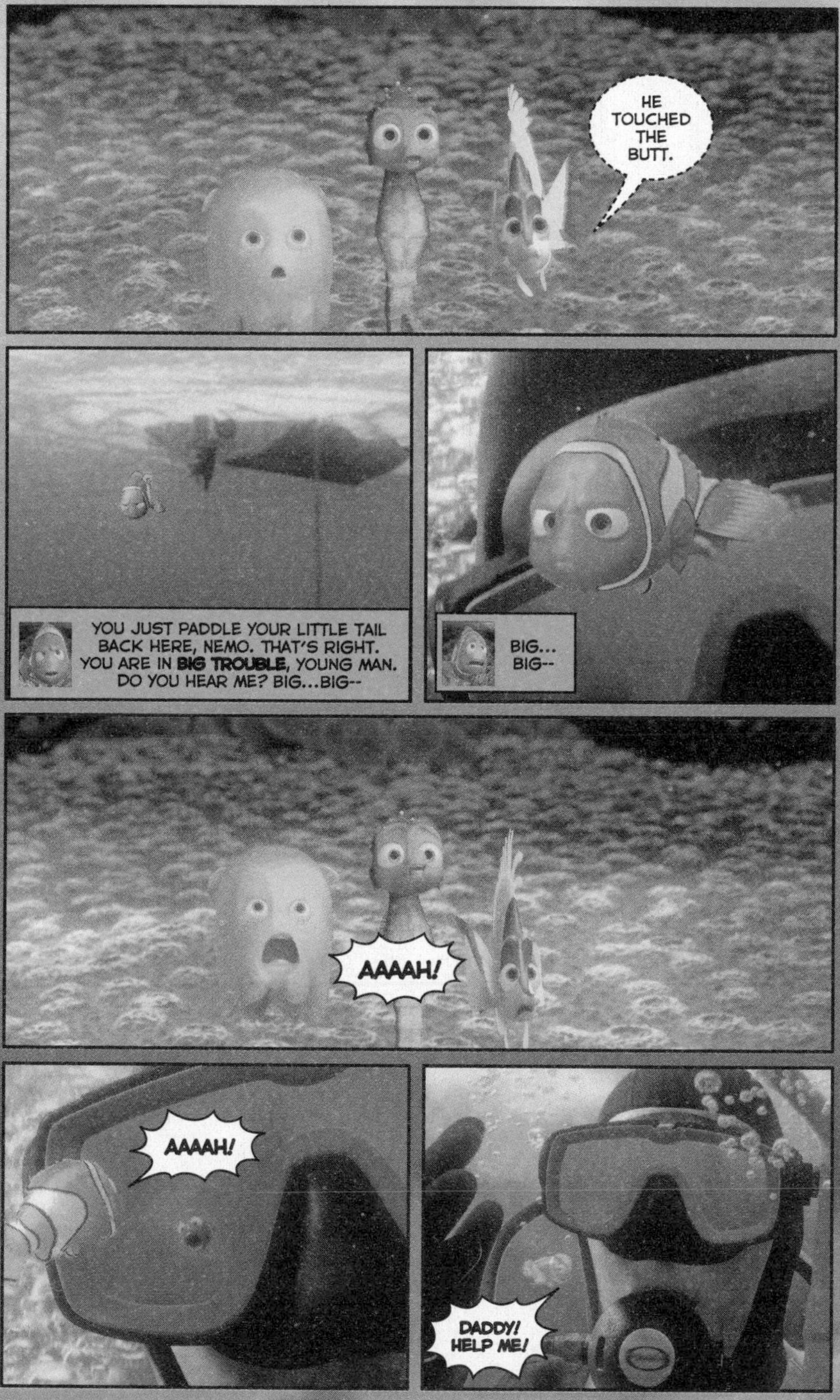
HE TOUCHED THE BUTT.
YOU JUST PADDLE YOUR LITTLE TAIL BACK HERE, NEMO. THAT'S RIGHT. YOU ARE IN **BIG TROUBLE**, YOUNG MAN. DO YOU HEAR ME? BIG...BIG--
BIG... BIG--
AAAAH!
AAAAH!
DADDY! HELP ME!

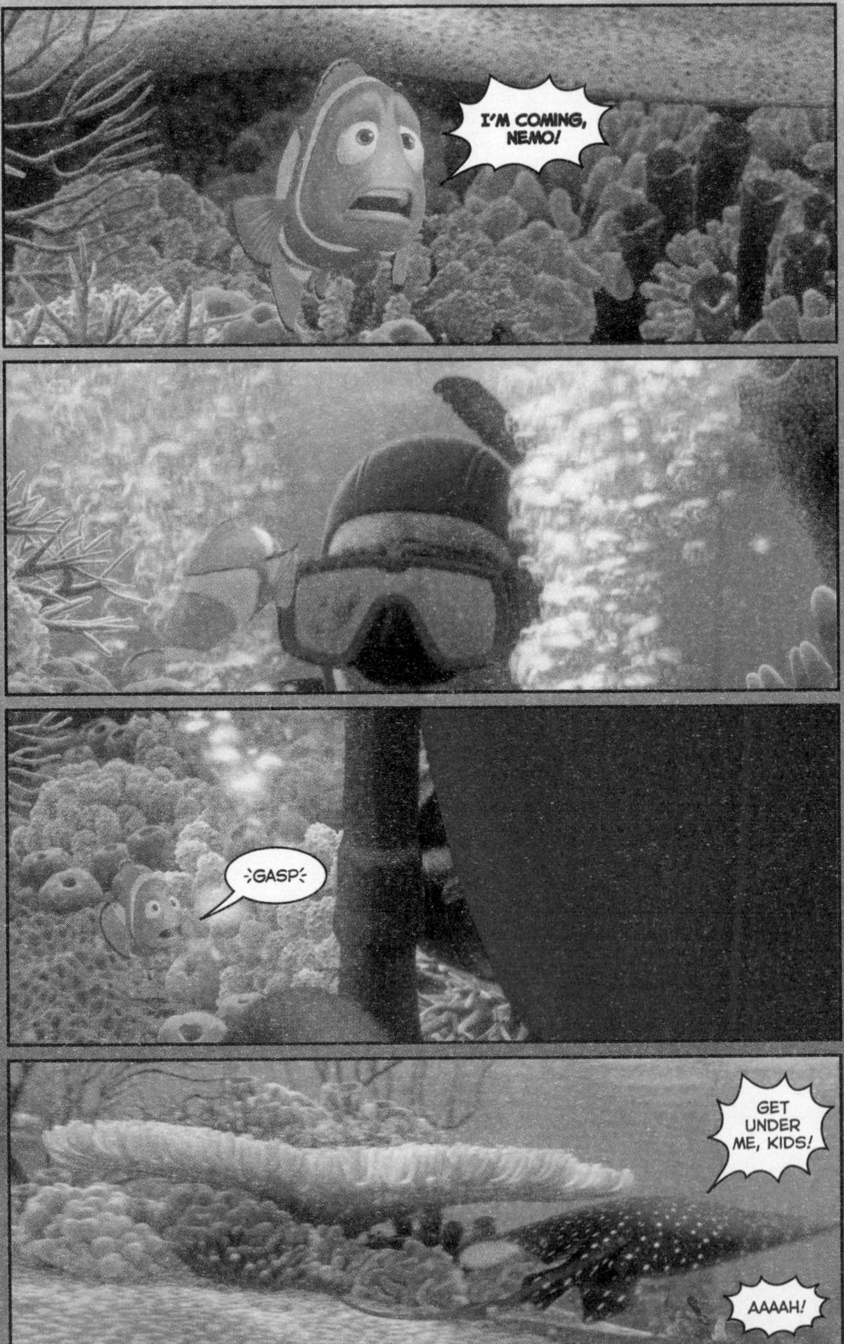
I'M COMING, NEMO!
GASP
GET UNDER ME, KIDS!
AAAAH!

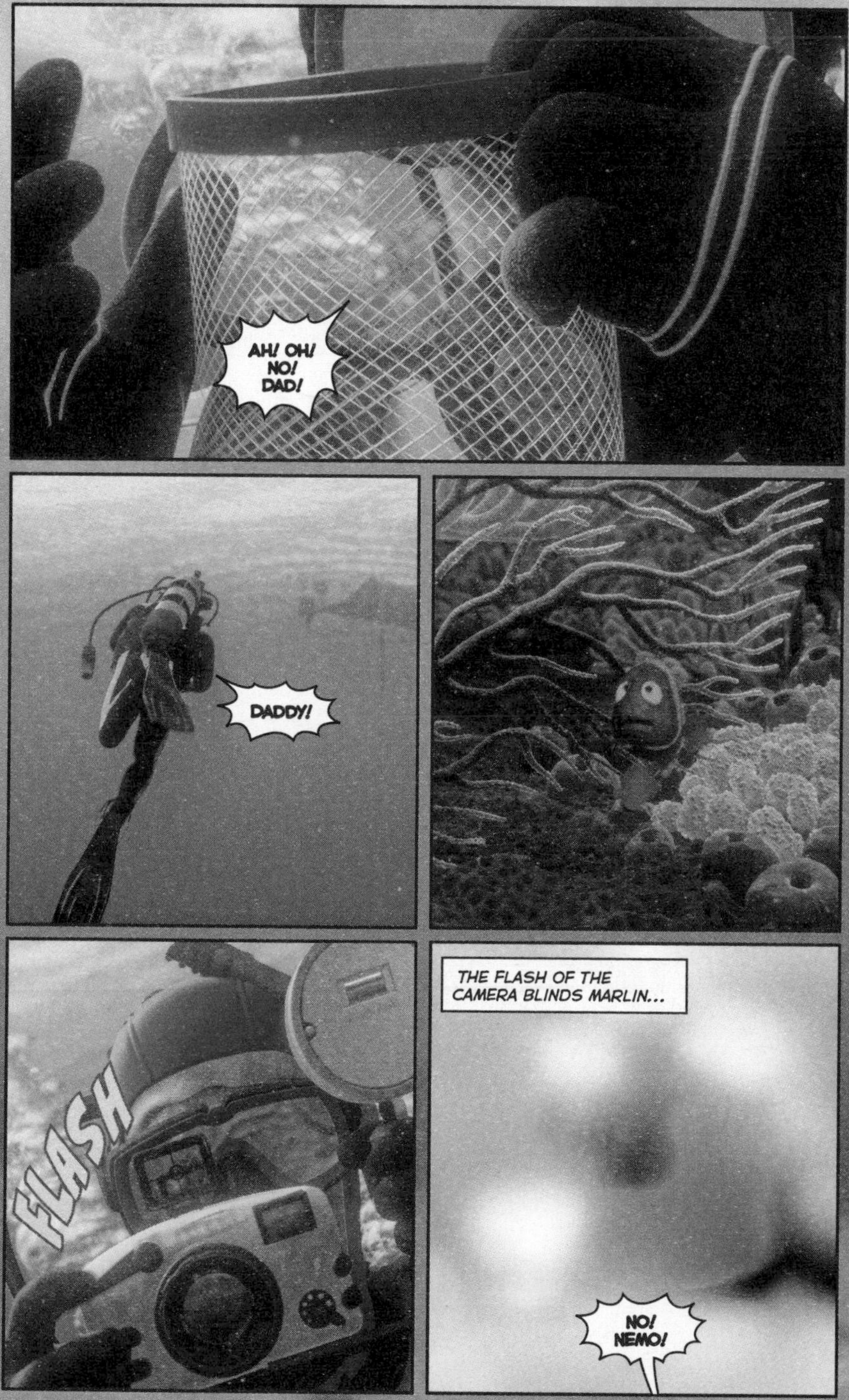
AH! OH! NO! DAD!
DADDY!
FLASH
THE FLASH OF THE CAMERA BLINDS MARLIN...
NO! NEMO!

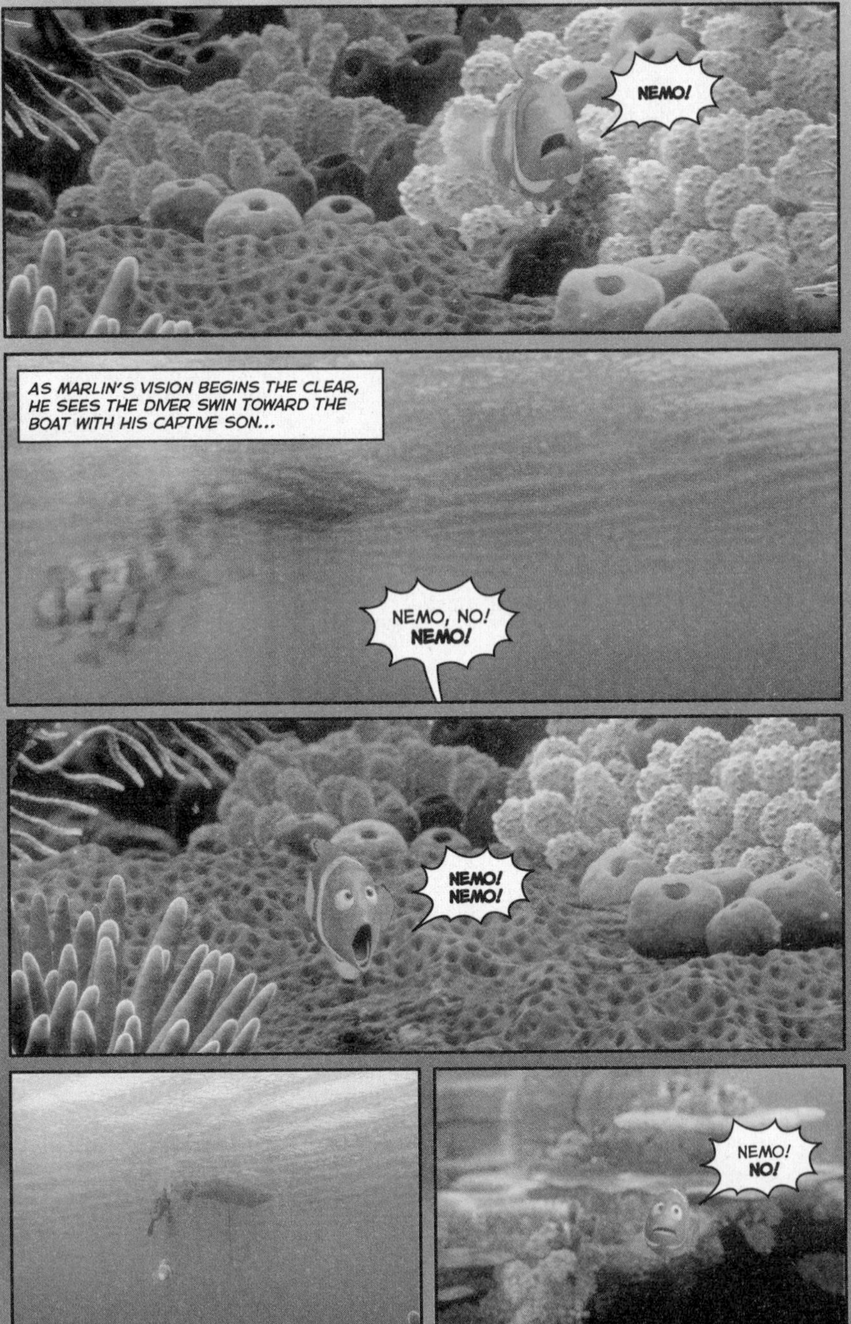
NEMO!
AS MARLIN'S VISION BEGINS THE CLEAR, HE SEES THE DIVER SWIN TOWARD THE BOAT WITH HIS CAPTIVE SON...
NEMO, NO! NEMO!
NEMO! NEMO!
NEMO! NO!

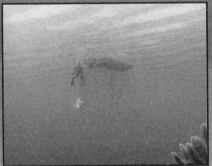

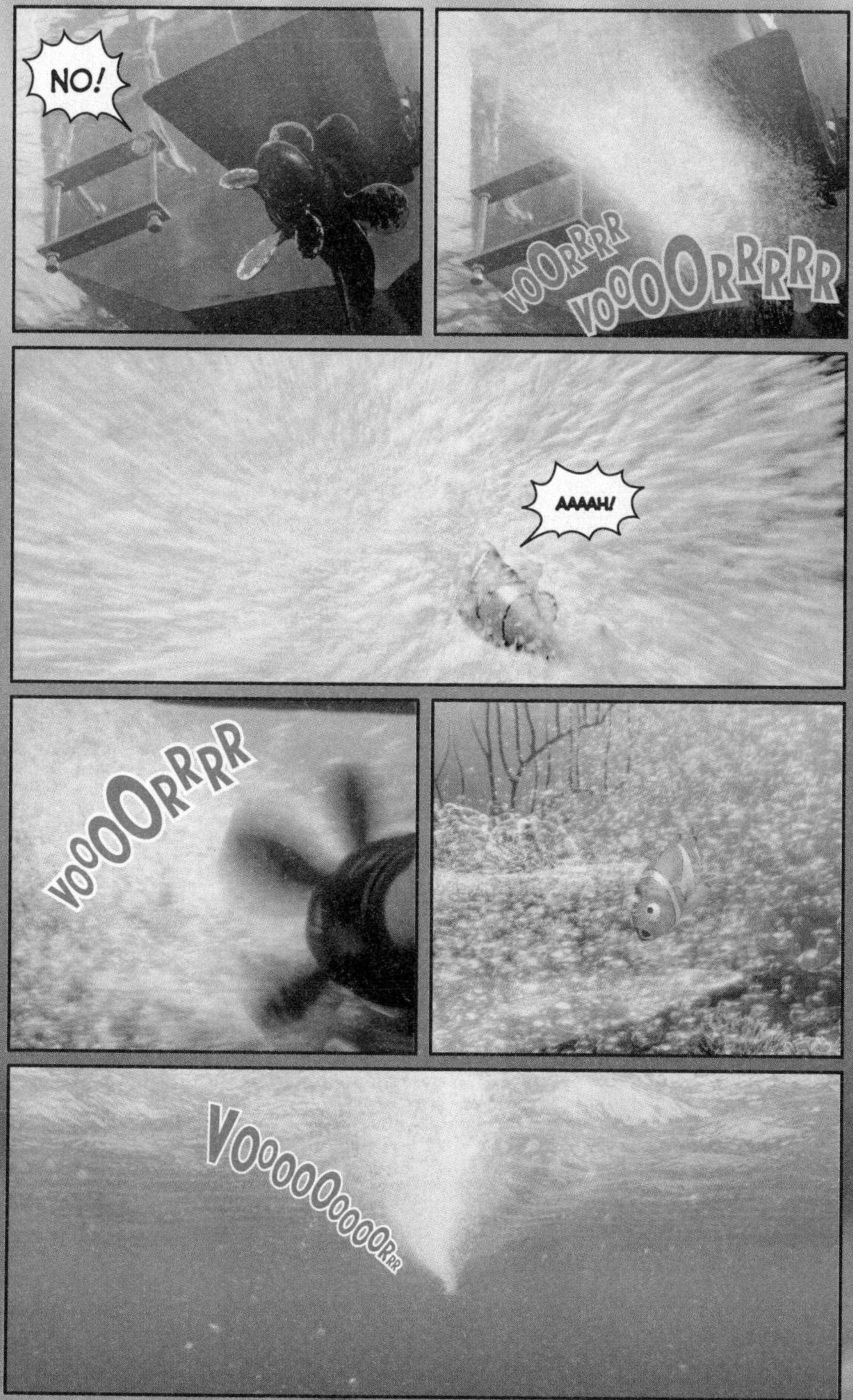
NO!
VOORRRR
VOOOORRRRR
AAAAH!
VOOORRR
VOOOOOOOORRR

NEMO! NEMO!
VRRRRRRRRMMM

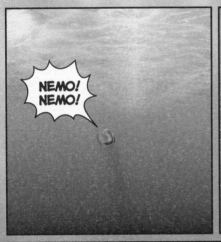

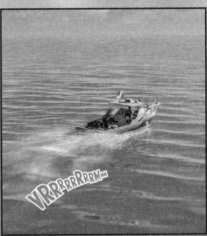

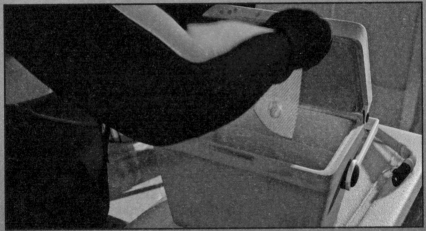

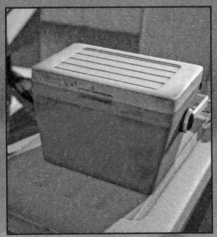

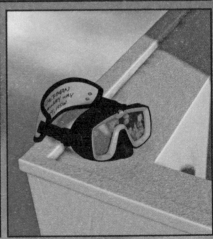

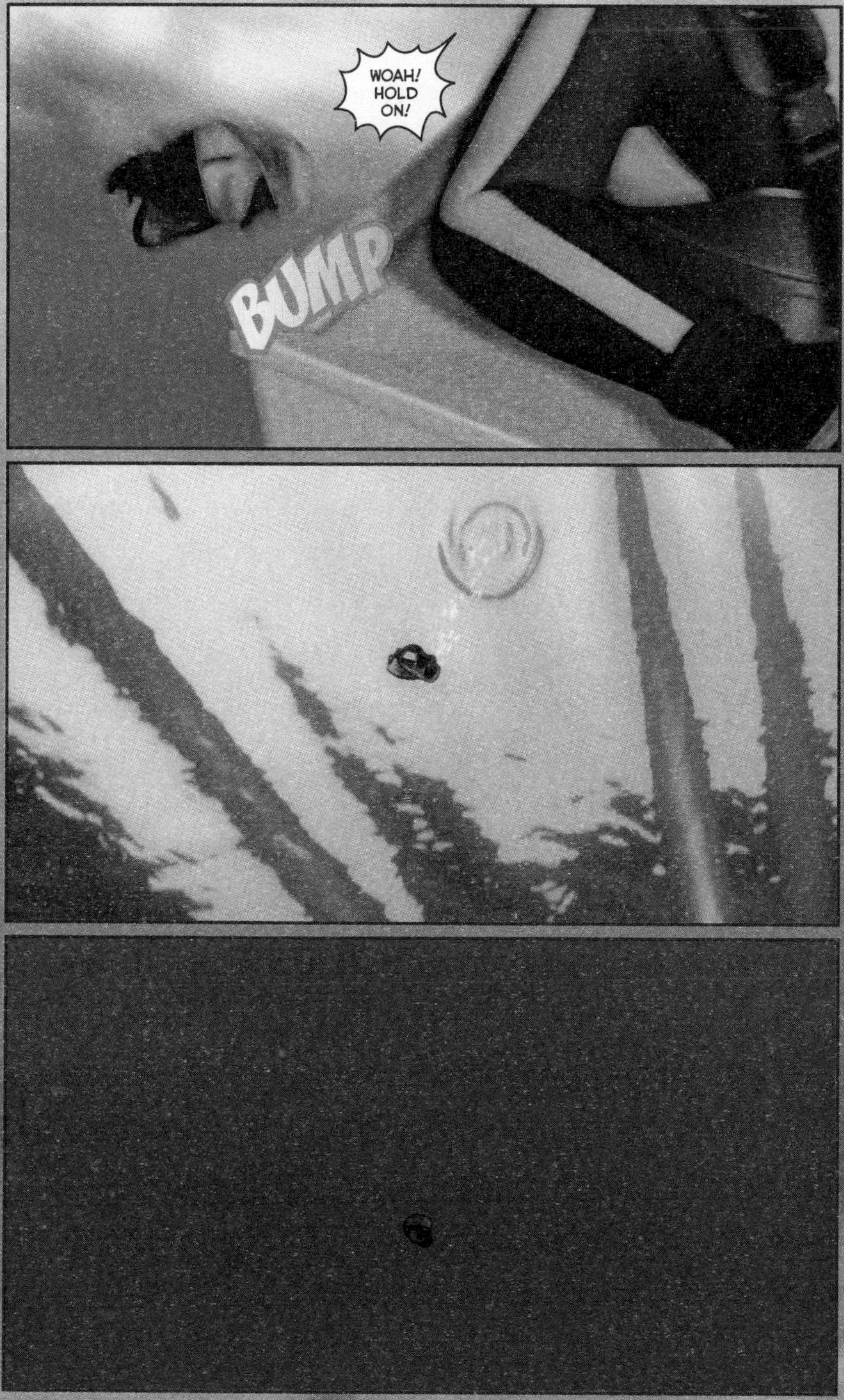
WOAH! HOLD ON!
BUMP

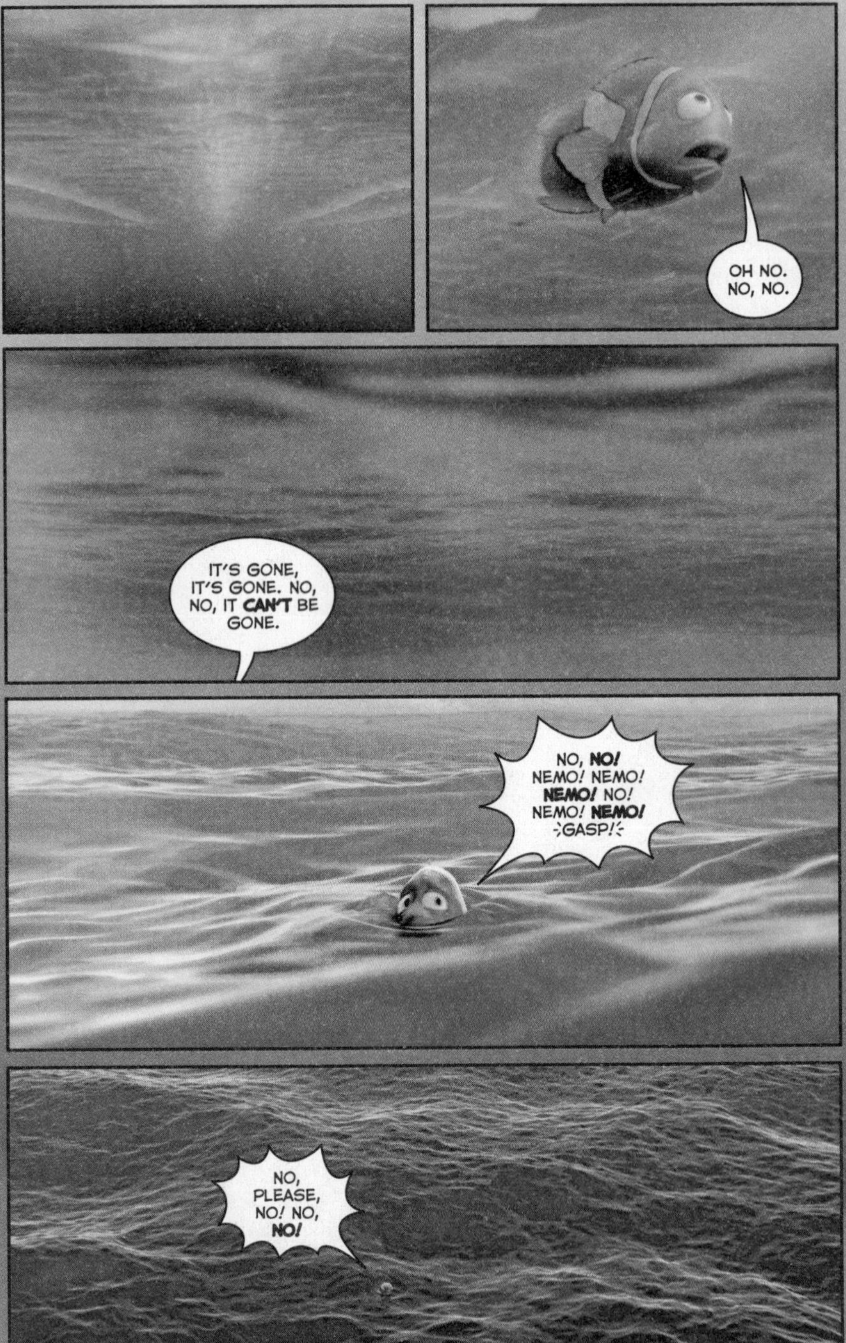
OH NO. NO, NO.
IT'S GONE, IT'S GONE. NO, NO, IT CAN'T BE GONE.
NO, NO! NEMO! NEMO! NEMO! NO! NEMO! NEMO! GASP!
NO, PLEASE, NO! NO, NO!

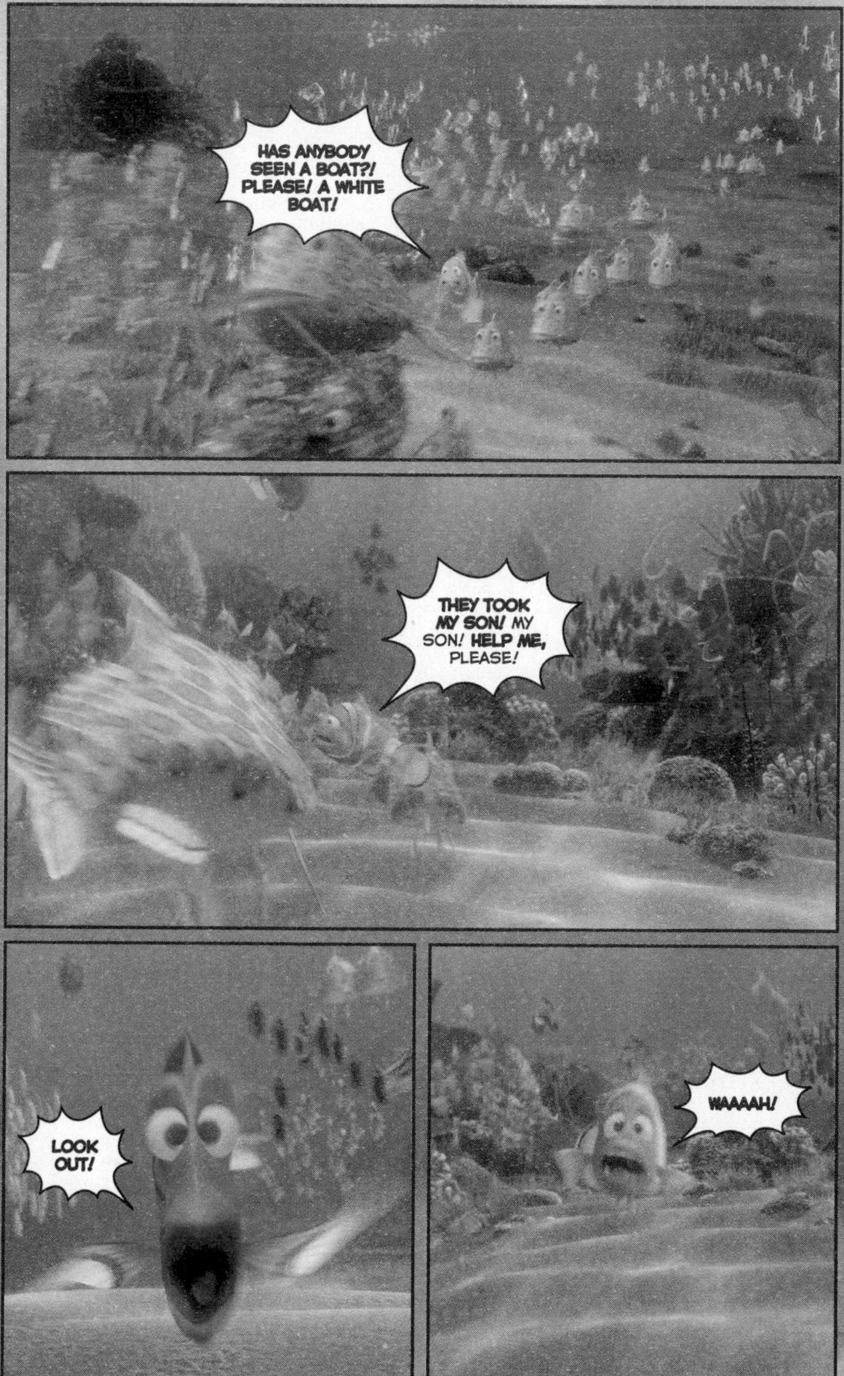
HAS ANYBODY SEEN A BOAT?! PLEASE! A WHITE BOAT!
THEY TOOK MY SON! MY SON! HELP ME, PLEASE!
LOOK OUT!
WAAAAH!

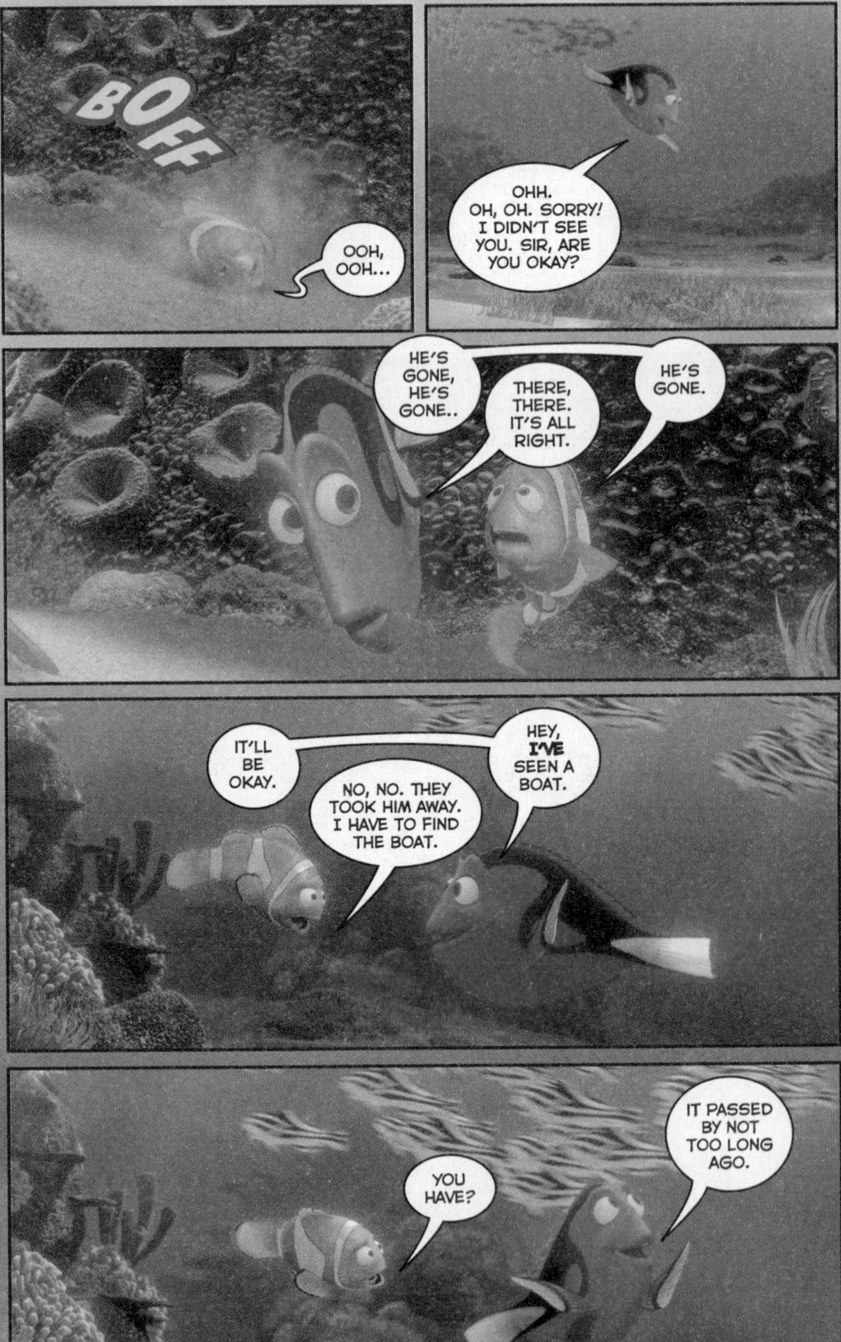
BOFF
OOH, OOH...
OHH. OH, OH. SORRY! I DIDN'T SEE YOU. SIR, ARE YOU OKAY?
HE'S GONE, HE'S GONE..
THERE, THERE. IT'S ALL RIGHT.
HE'S GONE.
IT'LL BE OKAY.
NO, NO. THEY TOOK HIM AWAY. I HAVE TO FIND THE BOAT.
HEY, **I'VE** SEEN A BOAT.
YOU HAVE?
IT PASSED BY NOT TOO LONG AGO.

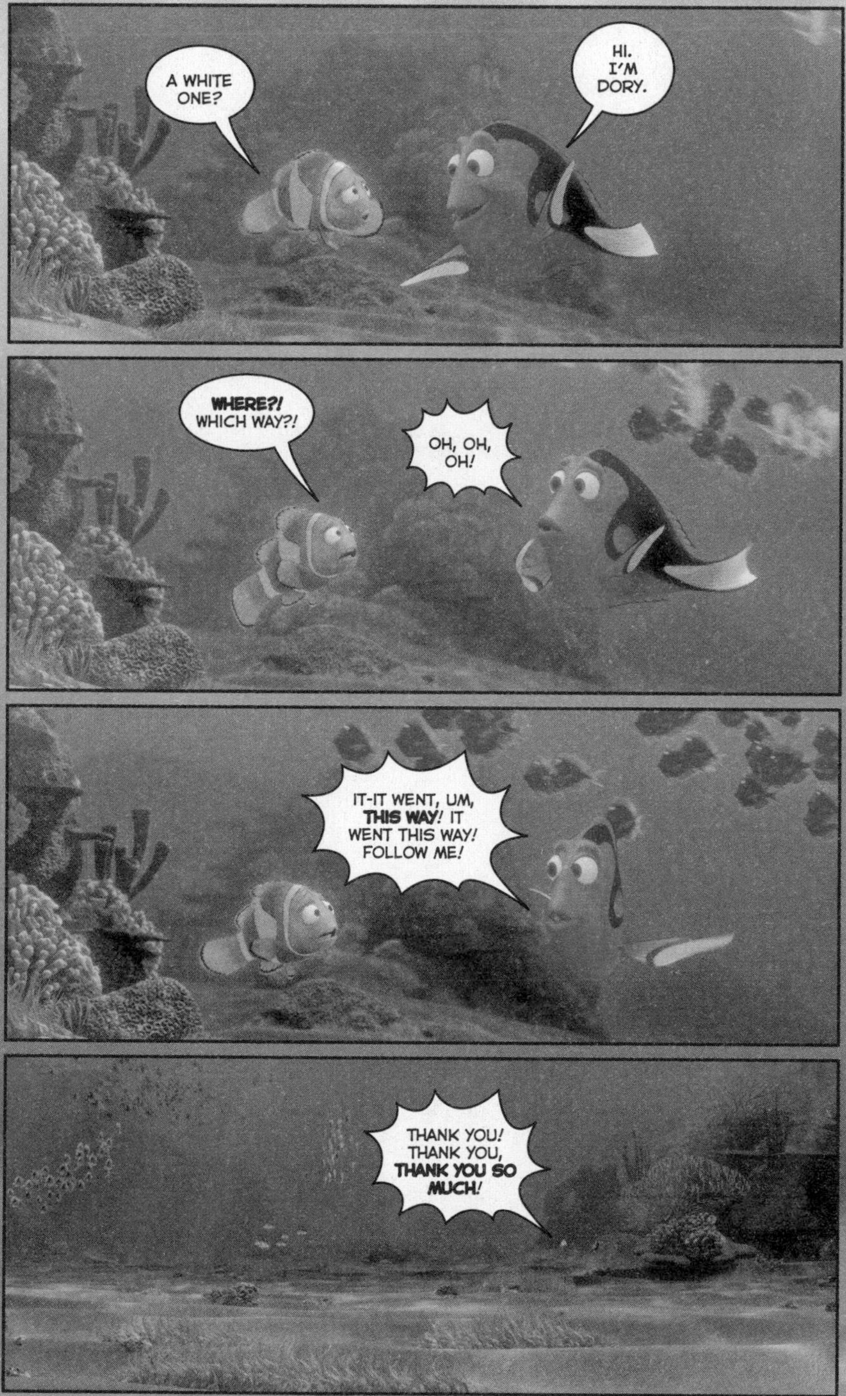
A WHITE ONE?
HI. I'M DORY.
WHERE?! WHICH WAY?!
OH, OH, OH!
IT-IT WENT, UM, **THIS WAY**! IT WENT THIS WAY! FOLLOW ME!
THANK YOU! THANK YOU, **THANK YOU SO MUCH**!

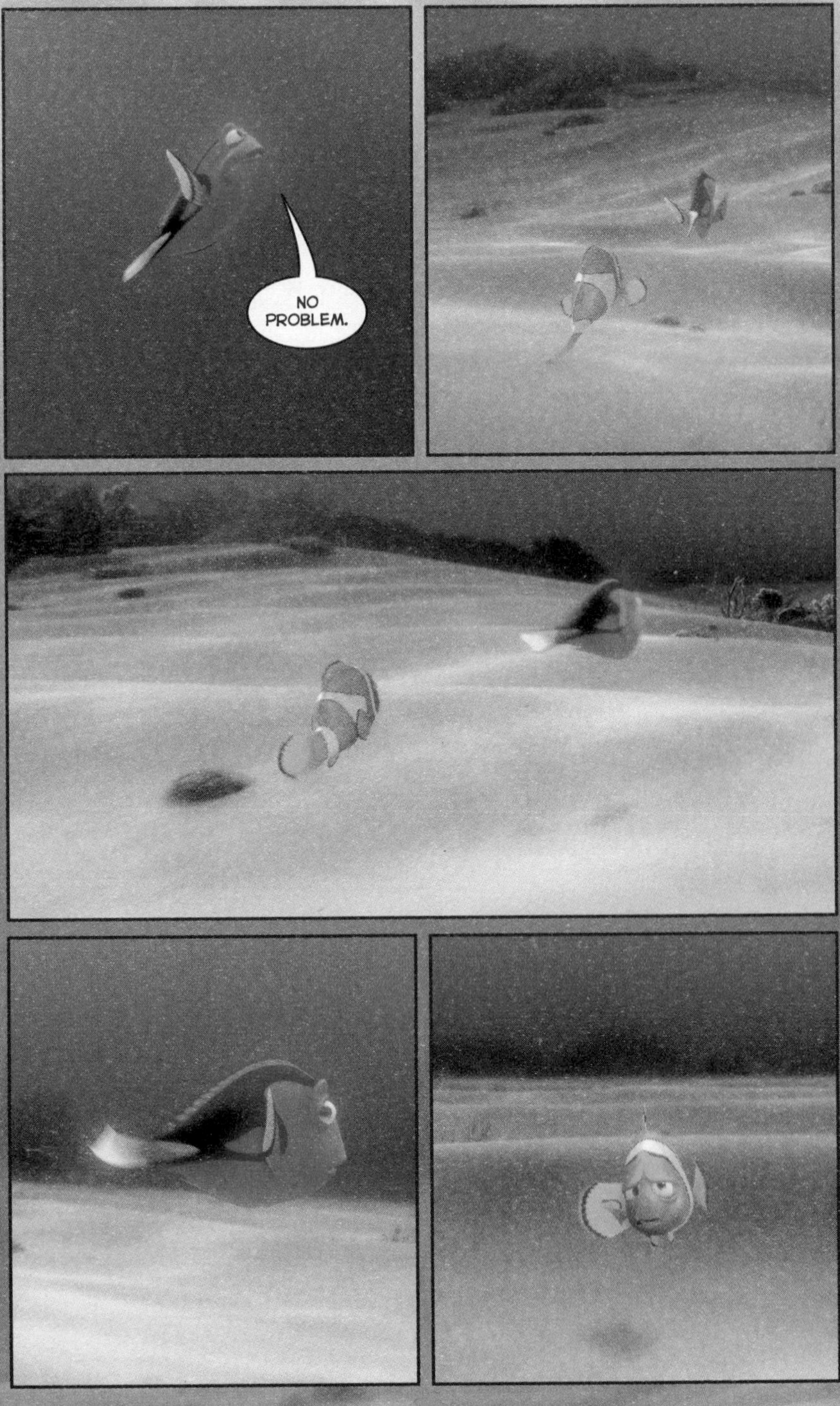
NO PROBLEM.

SUDDENLY, DORY DARTS AWAY!

SWOOOSH

HEY! WAIT!

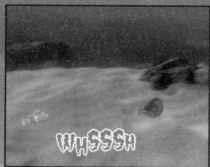

WHSSSH

WILL YOU QUIT IT?

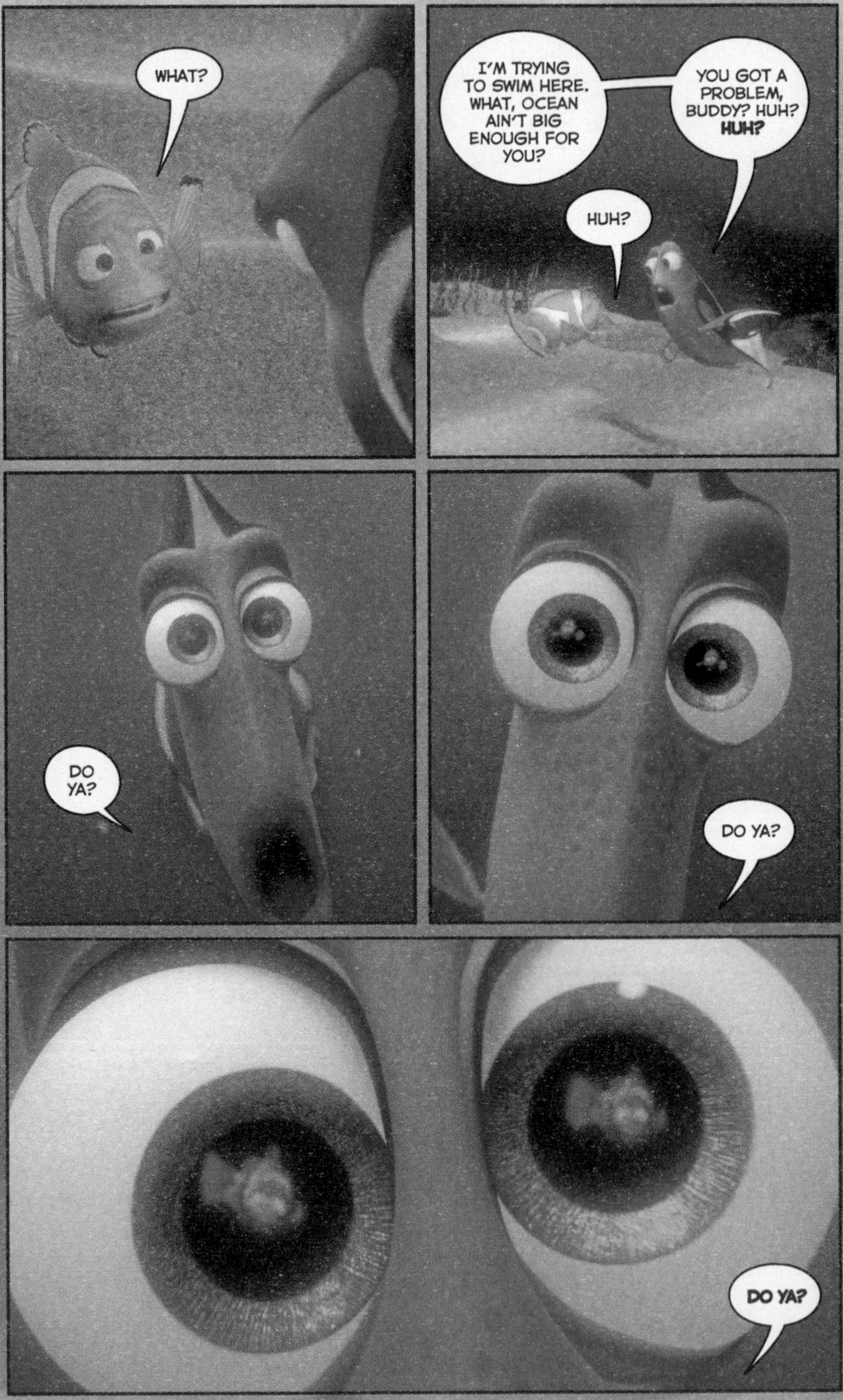
WHAT?
I'M TRYING TO SWIM HERE. WHAT, OCEAN AIN'T BIG ENOUGH FOR YOU?
YOU GOT A PROBLEM, BUDDY? HUH? **HUH?**
HUH?
DO YA?
DO YA?
DO YA?

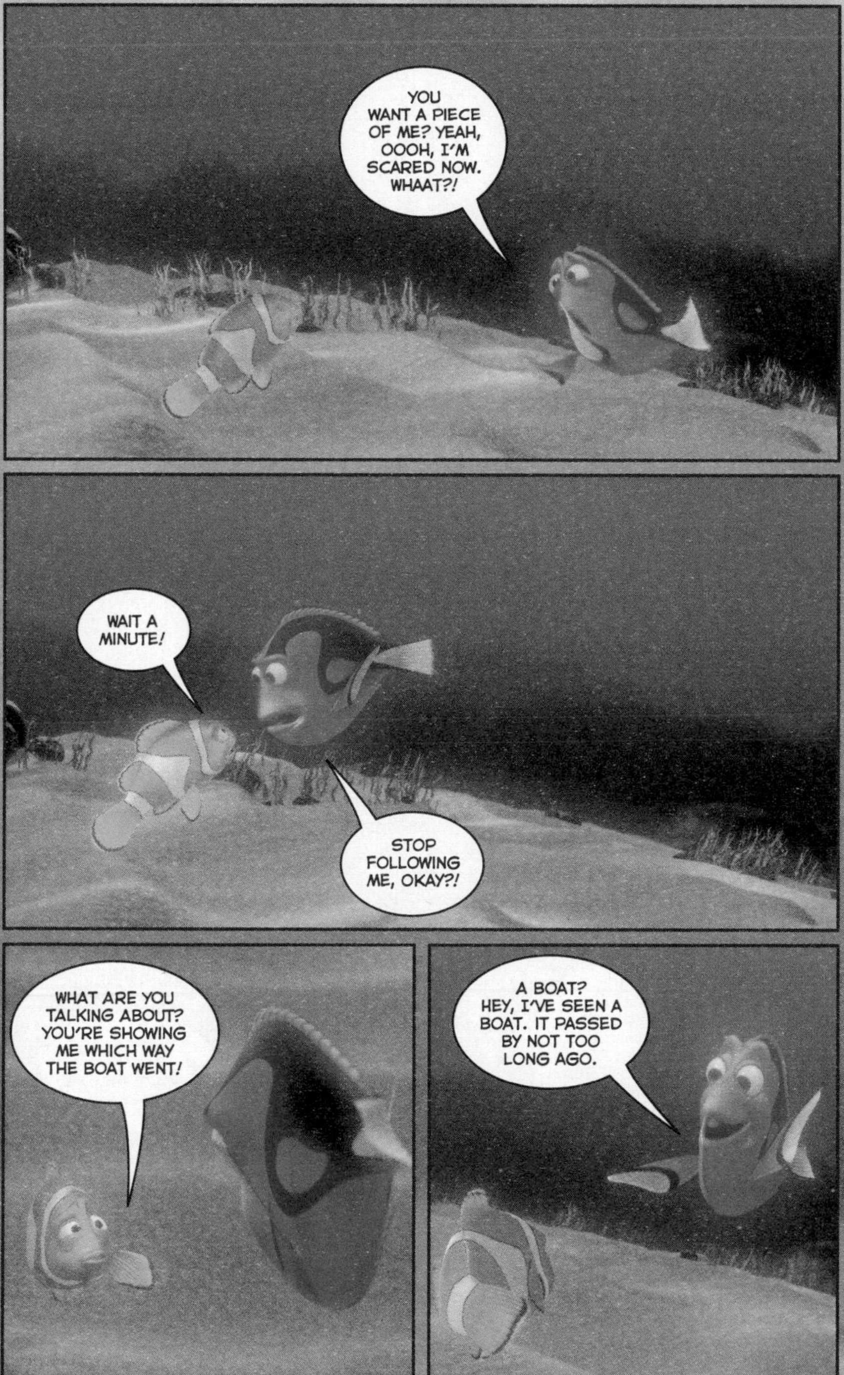
YOU WANT A PIECE OF ME? YEAH, OOOH, I'M SCARED NOW. WHAAT?!
WAIT A MINUTE!
STOP FOLLOWING ME, OKAY?!
WHAT ARE YOU TALKING ABOUT? YOU'RE SHOWING ME WHICH WAY THE BOAT WENT!
A BOAT? HEY, I'VE SEEN A BOAT. IT PASSED BY NOT TOO LONG AGO.

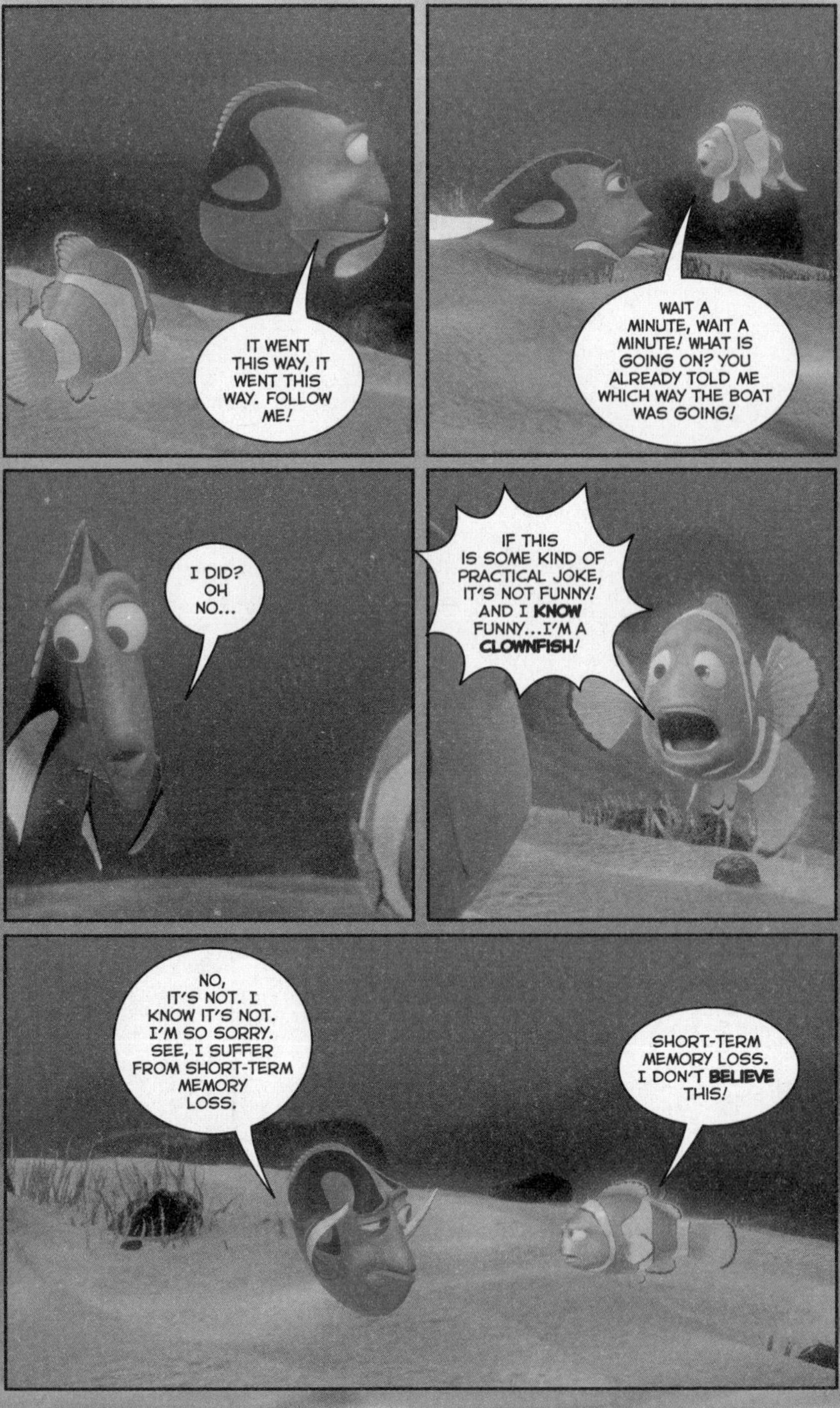
IT WENT THIS WAY, IT WENT THIS WAY. FOLLOW ME!
WAIT A MINUTE, WAIT A MINUTE! WHAT IS GOING ON? YOU ALREADY TOLD ME WHICH WAY THE BOAT WAS GOING!
I DID? OH NO...
IF THIS IS SOME KIND OF PRACTICAL JOKE, IT'S NOT FUNNY! AND I KNOW FUNNY...I'M A CLOWNFISH!
NO, IT'S NOT. I KNOW IT'S NOT. I'M SO SORRY. SEE, I SUFFER FROM SHORT-TERM MEMORY LOSS.
SHORT-TERM MEMORY LOSS. I DON'T BELIEVE THIS!

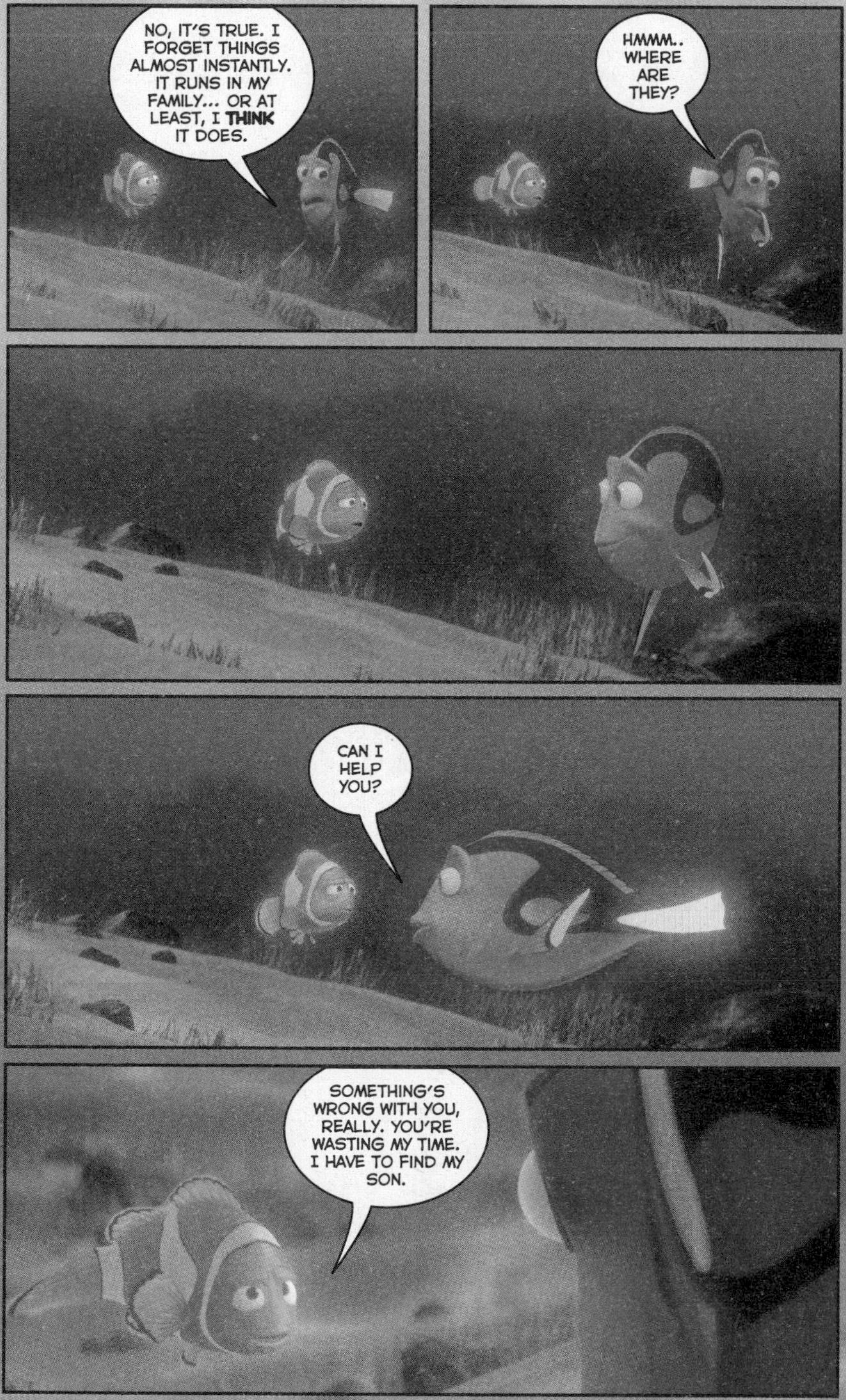
NO, IT'S TRUE. I FORGET THINGS ALMOST INSTANTLY. IT RUNS IN MY FAMILY... OR AT LEAST, I **THINK** IT DOES.
HMMM.. WHERE ARE THEY?
CAN I HELP YOU?
SOMETHING'S WRONG WITH YOU, REALLY. YOU'RE WASTING MY TIME. I HAVE TO FIND MY SON.

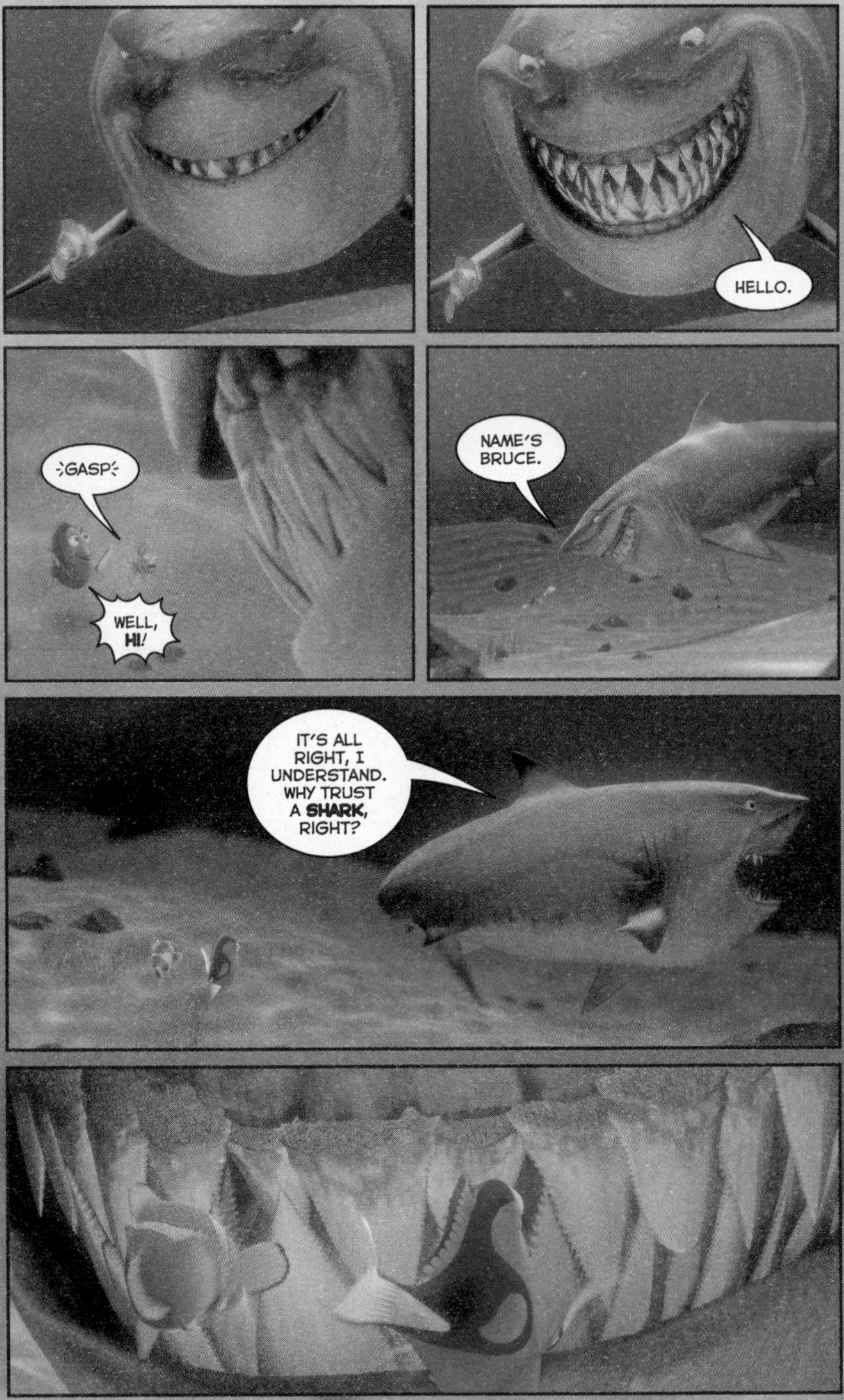
HELLO.
GASP
WELL, HI!
NAME'S BRUCE.
IT'S ALL RIGHT, I UNDERSTAND. WHY TRUST A SHARK, RIGHT?

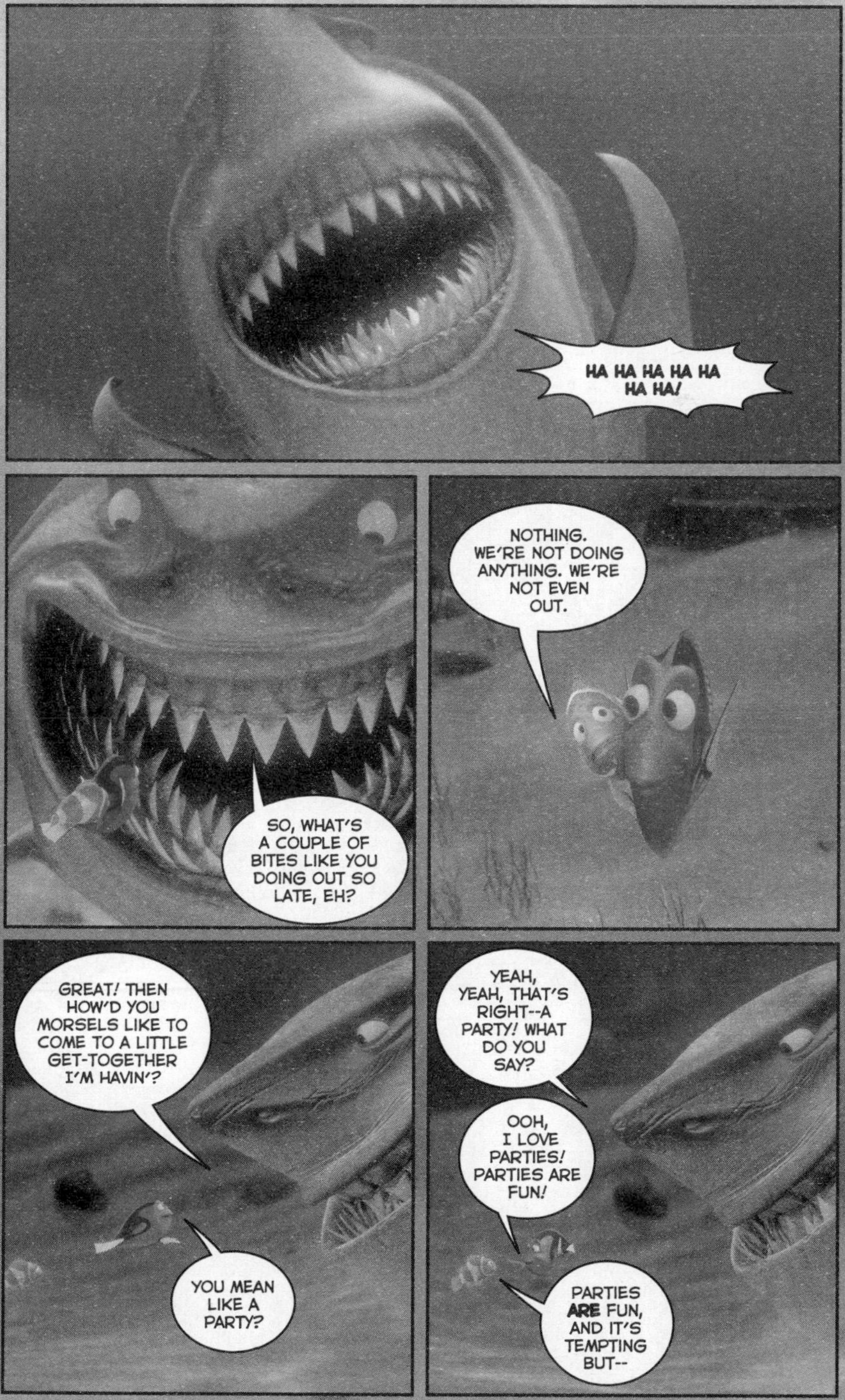
HA HA HA HA HA
HA HA!
SO, WHAT'S A COUPLE OF BITES LIKE YOU DOING OUT SO LATE, EH?
NOTHING. WE'RE NOT DOING ANYTHING. WE'RE NOT EVEN OUT.
GREAT! THEN HOW'D YOU MORSELS LIKE TO COME TO A LITTLE GET-TOGETHER I'M HAVIN'?
YOU MEAN LIKE A PARTY?
YEAH, YEAH, THAT'S RIGHT--A PARTY! WHAT DO YOU SAY?
OOH, I LOVE PARTIES! PARTIES ARE FUN!
PARTIES **ARE** FUN, AND IT'S TEMPTING BUT--

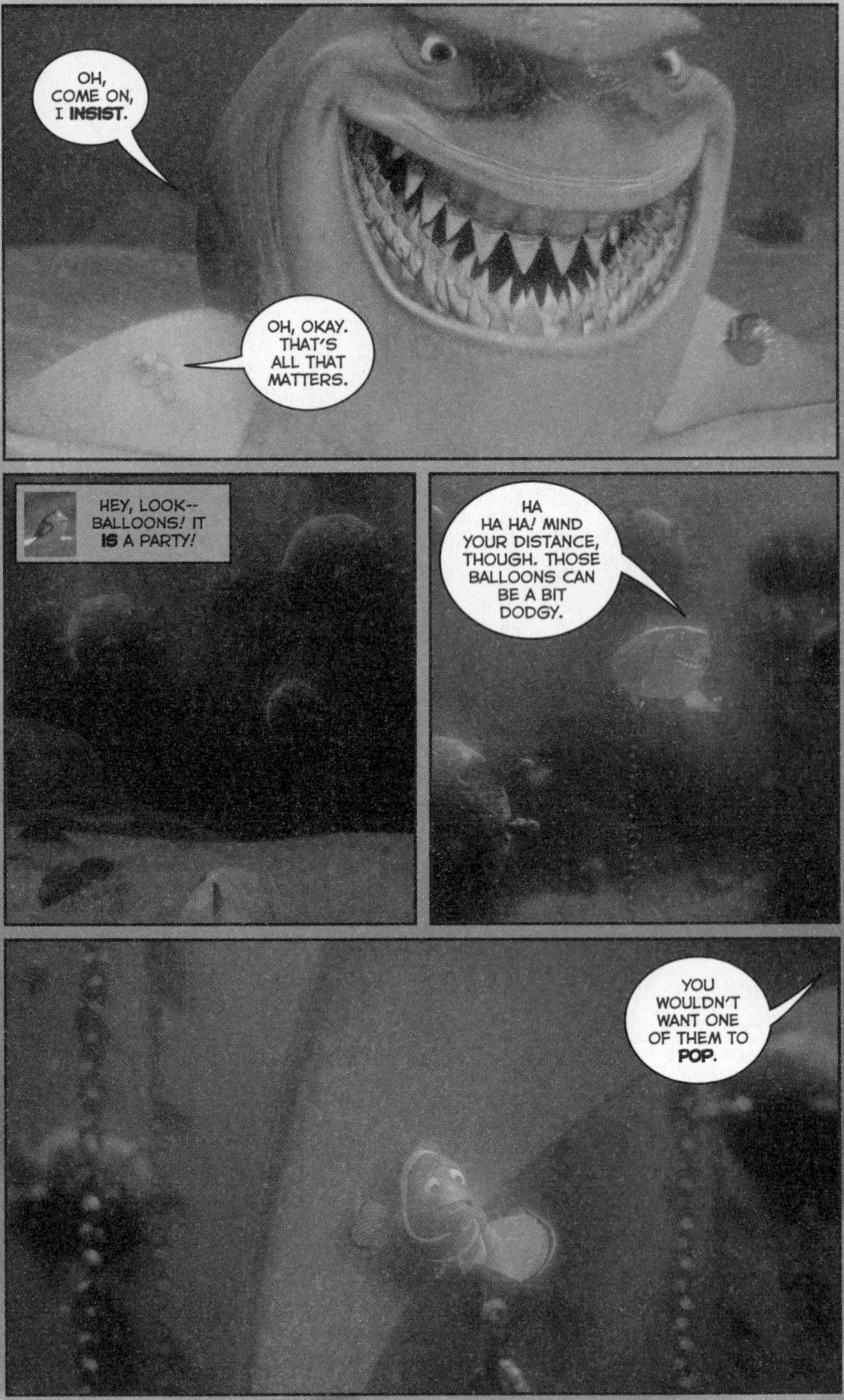
OH, COME ON, I INSIST.
OH, OKAY. THAT'S ALL THAT MATTERS.
HEY, LOOK-- BALLOONS! IT IS A PARTY!
HA HA HA! MIND YOUR DISTANCE, THOUGH. THOSE BALLOONS CAN BE A BIT DODGY.
YOU WOULDN'T WANT ONE OF THEM TO POP.

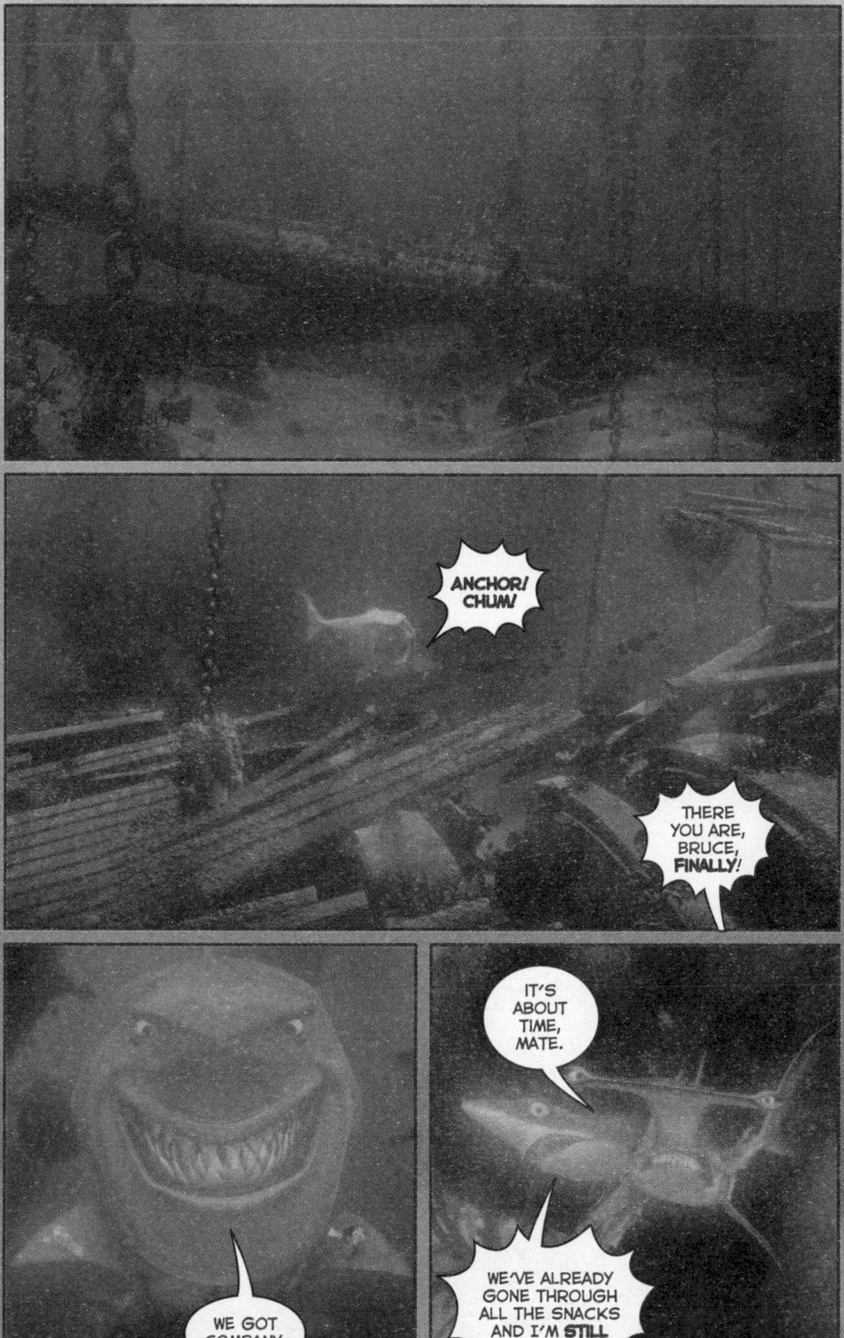
ANCHOR! CHUM!
THERE YOU ARE, BRUCE, FINALLY!
WE GOT COMPANY.
IT'S ABOUT TIME, MATE.
WE'VE ALREADY GONE THROUGH ALL THE SNACKS AND I'M STILL STARVIN'!

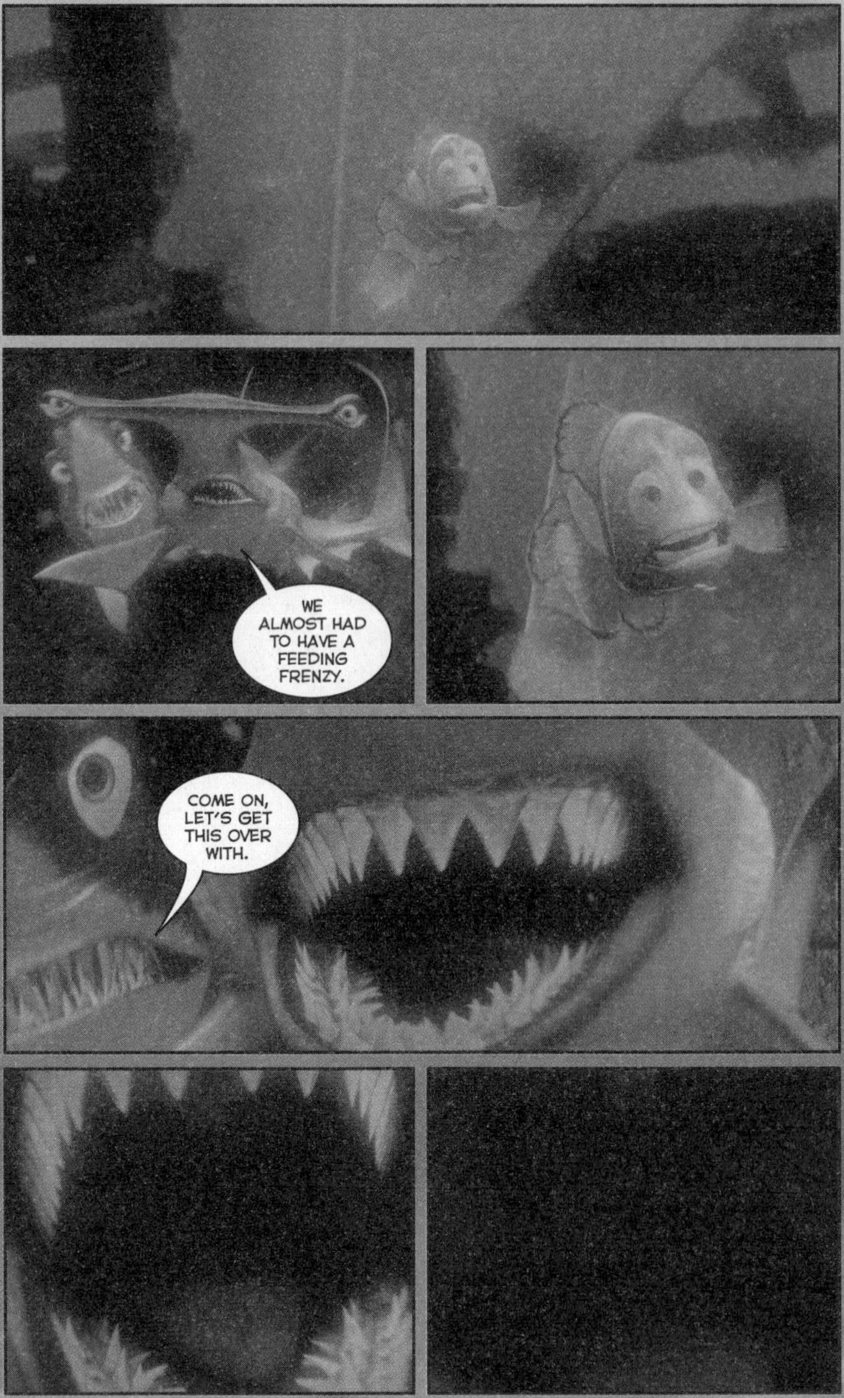
WE ALMOST HAD TO HAVE A FEEDING FRENZY.
COME ON, LET'S GET THIS OVER WITH.

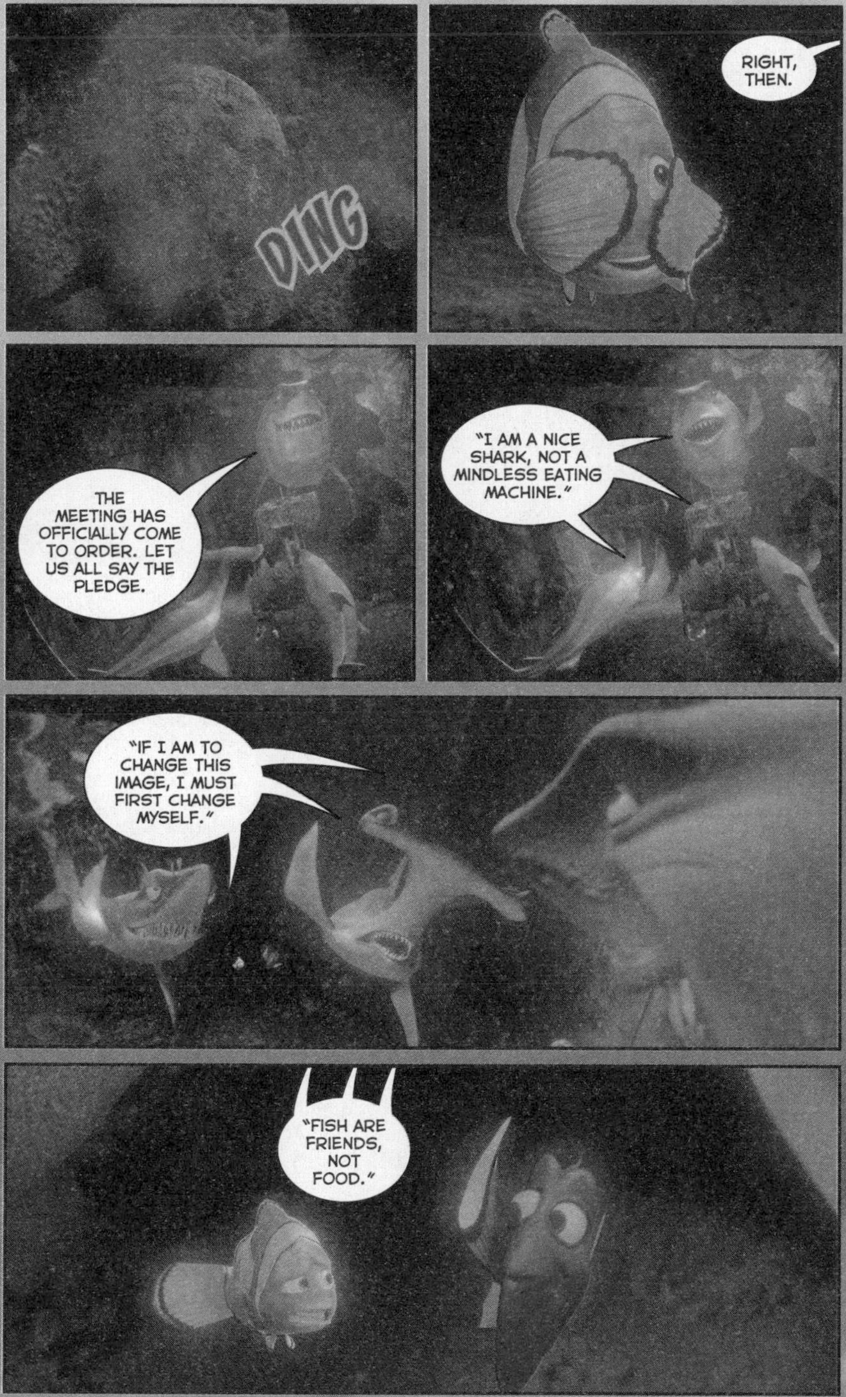
DING
RIGHT, THEN.
THE MEETING HAS OFFICIALLY COME TO ORDER. LET US ALL SAY THE PLEDGE.
"I AM A NICE SHARK, NOT A MINDLESS EATING MACHINE."
"IF I AM TO CHANGE THIS IMAGE, I MUST FIRST CHANGE MYSELF."
"FISH ARE FRIENDS, NOT FOOD."

EXCEPT STINKIN' DOLPHINS.
DOLPHINS! YEAH, THEY THINK THEY'RE **SOOO** CUTE!
"HEY, LOOK AT ME. I'M A FLIPPIN' LITTLE DOLPHIN!"
"LET ME FLIP FOR YA! AIN'T I SOMETHING!"

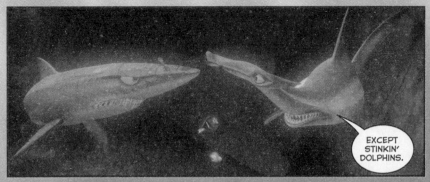

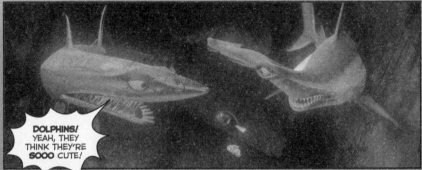

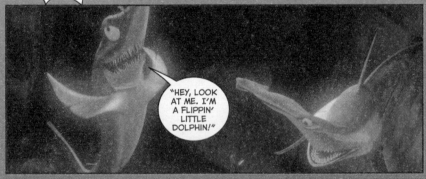

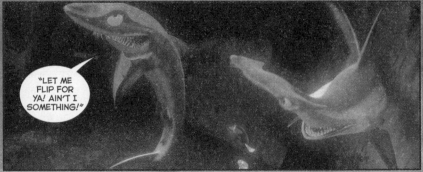

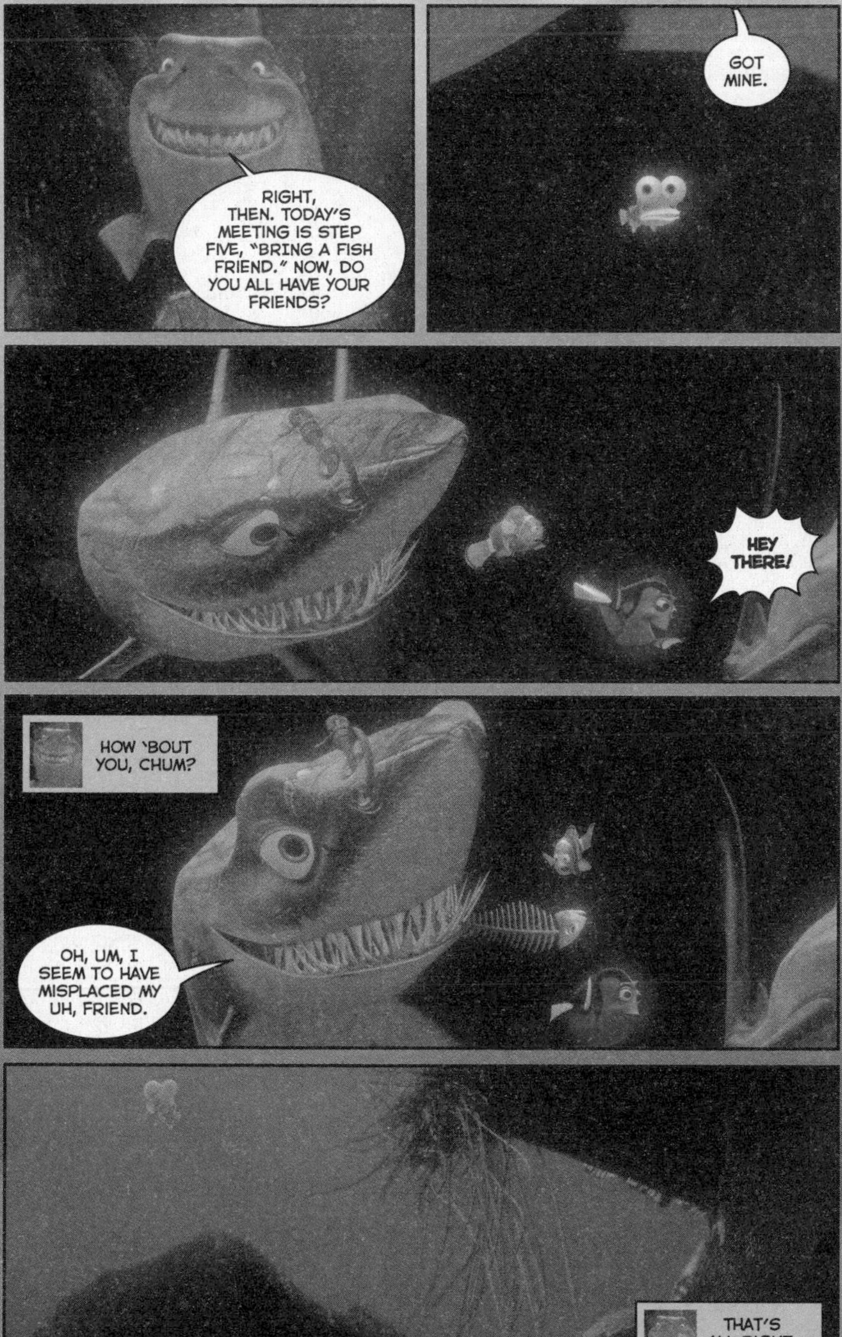
RIGHT, THEN. TODAY'S MEETING IS STEP FIVE, "BRING A FISH FRIEND." NOW, DO YOU ALL HAVE YOUR FRIENDS?
GOT MINE.
HEY THERE!
HOW 'BOUT YOU, CHUM?
OH, UM, I SEEM TO HAVE MISPLACED MY UH, FRIEND.
THAT'S ALL RIGHT, CHUM.

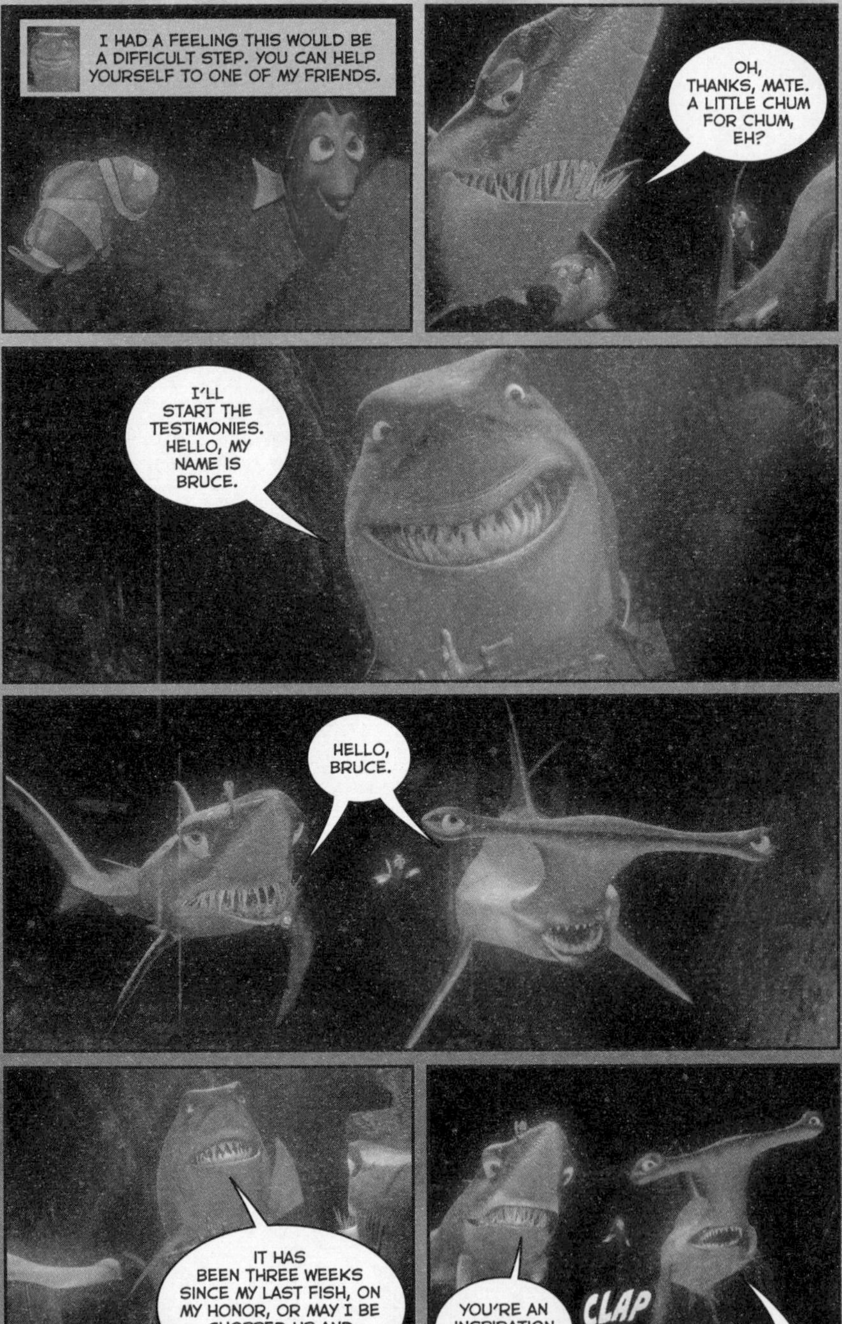
I HAD A FEELING THIS WOULD BE A DIFFICULT STEP. YOU CAN HELP YOURSELF TO ONE OF MY FRIENDS.
OH, THANKS, MATE. A LITTLE CHUM FOR CHUM, EH?
I'LL START THE TESTIMONIES. HELLO, MY NAME IS BRUCE.
HELLO, BRUCE.
IT HAS BEEN THREE WEEKS SINCE MY LAST FISH, ON MY HONOR, OR MAY I BE CHOPPED UP AND MADE INTO SOUP.
YOU'RE AN INSPIRATION TO ALL OF US.
CLAP
CLAP
AMEN.

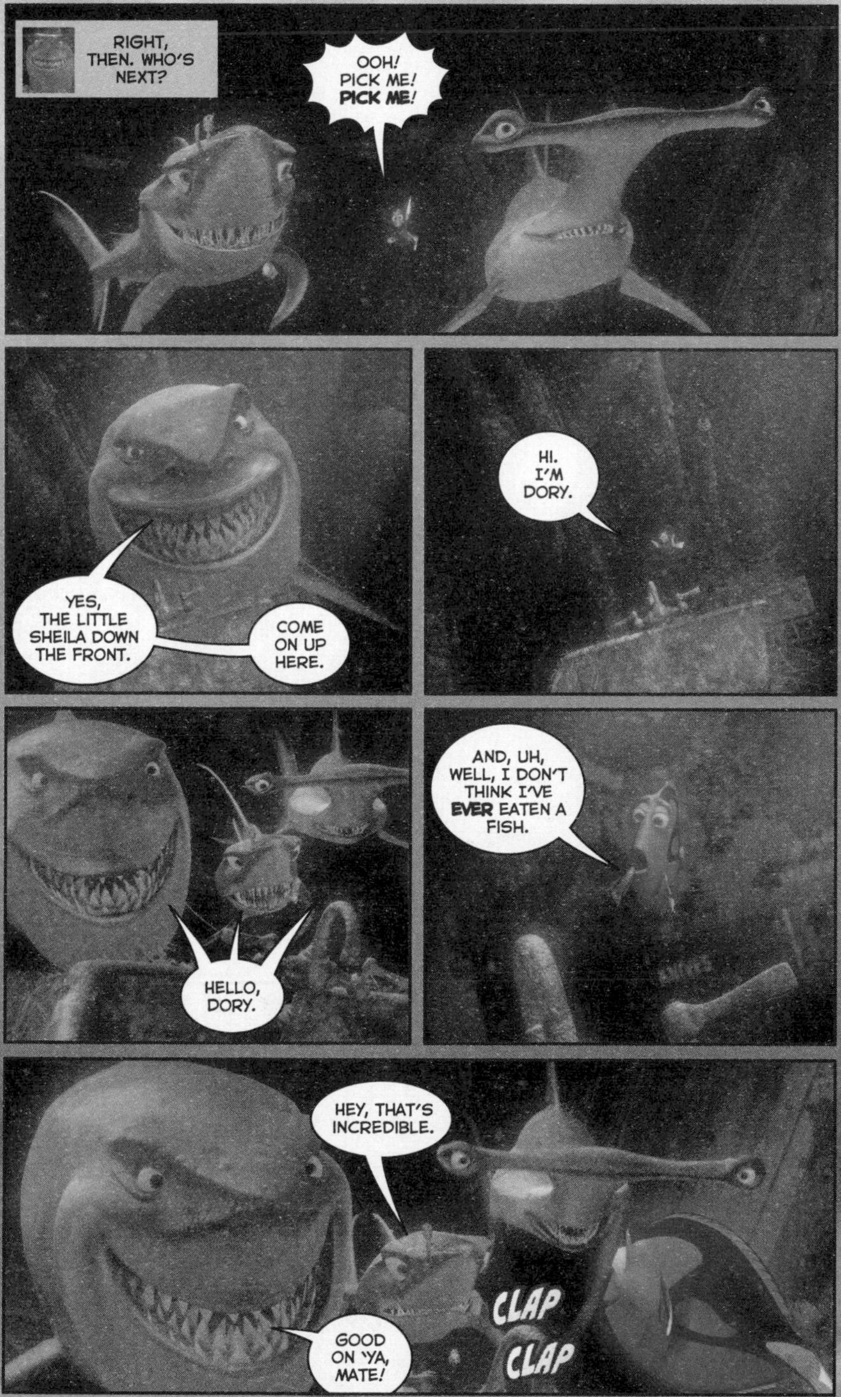
RIGHT, THEN. WHO'S NEXT?
OOH! PICK ME! **PICK ME!**
YES, THE LITTLE SHEILA DOWN THE FRONT.
COME ON UP HERE.
HI. I'M DORY.
HELLO, DORY.
AND, UH, WELL, I DON'T THINK I'VE **EVER** EATEN A FISH.
HEY, THAT'S INCREDIBLE.
GOOD ON 'YA, MATE!
CLAP
CLAP

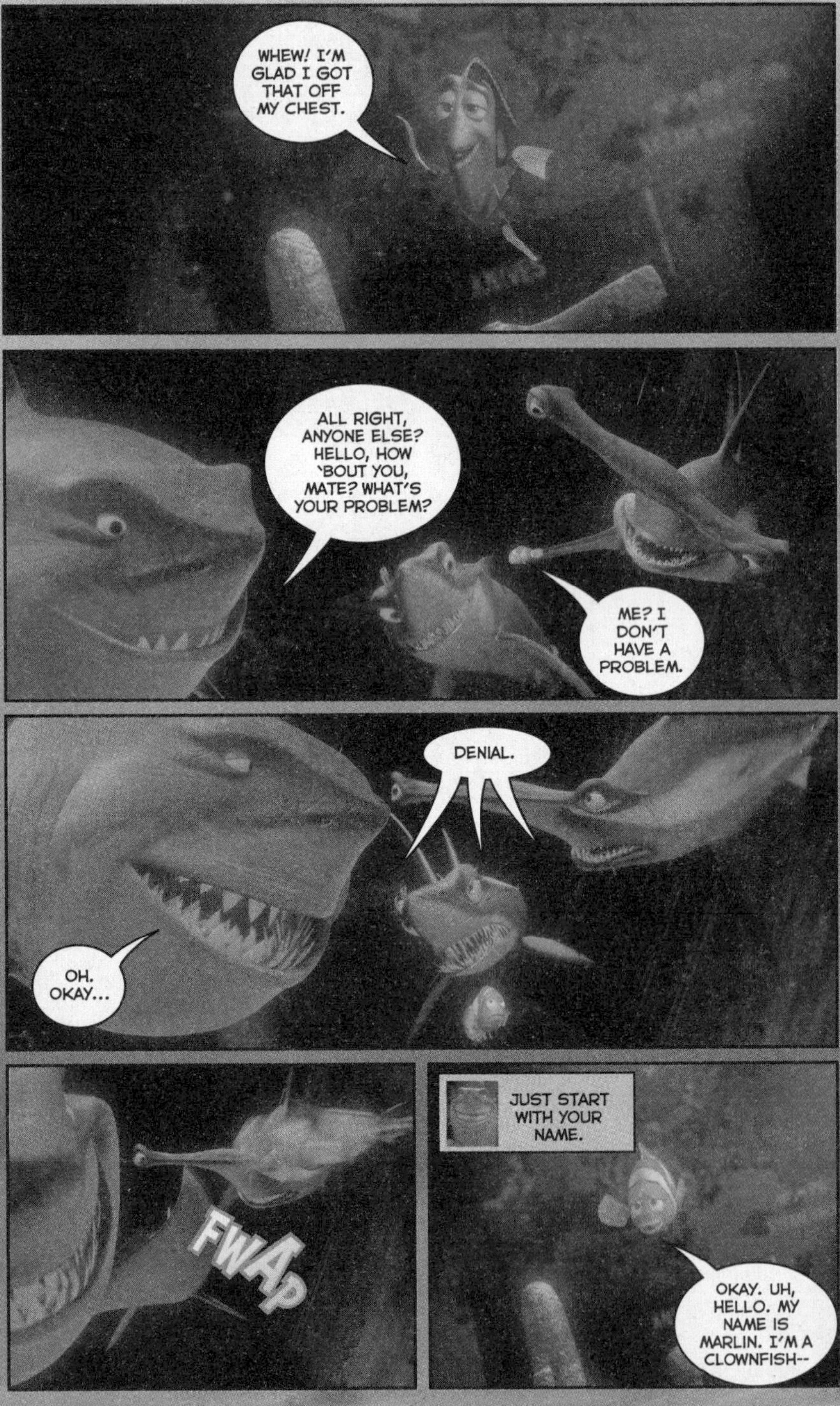
WHEW! I'M GLAD I GOT THAT OFF MY CHEST.
ALL RIGHT, ANYONE ELSE? HELLO, HOW 'BOUT YOU, MATE? WHAT'S YOUR PROBLEM?
ME? I DON'T HAVE A PROBLEM.
DENIAL.
OH. OKAY...
FWAP
JUST START WITH YOUR NAME.
OKAY. UH, HELLO. MY NAME IS MARLIN. I'M A CLOWNFISH--

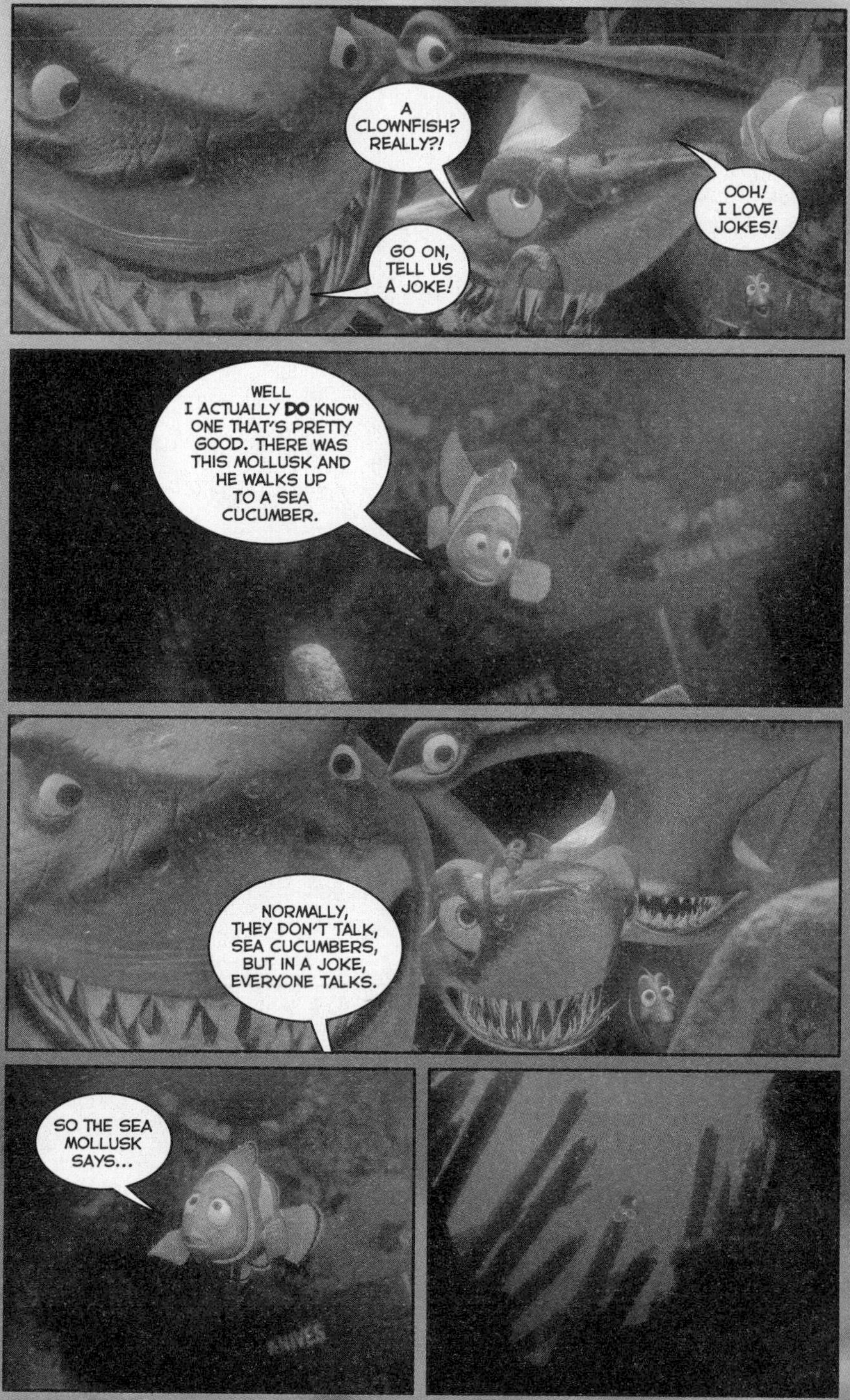

A CLOWNFISH? REALLY?!
OOH! I LOVE JOKES!
GO ON, TELL US A JOKE!
WELL I ACTUALLY **DO** KNOW ONE THAT'S PRETTY GOOD. THERE WAS THIS MOLLUSK AND HE WALKS UP TO A SEA CUCUMBER.
NORMALLY, THEY DON'T TALK, SEA CUCUMBERS, BUT IN A JOKE, EVERYONE TALKS.
SO THE SEA MOLLUSK SAYS...

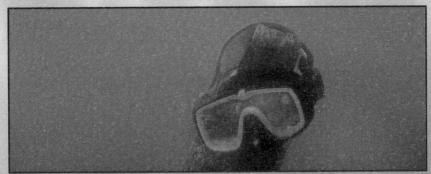

DADDY!

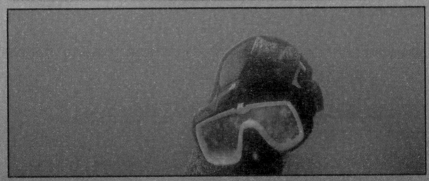

NEMO! NEMO!

FOR A CLOWNFISH, HE'S NOT THAT FUNNY.

NEMO! HA HA HA! NEMO! I DON'T GET IT.

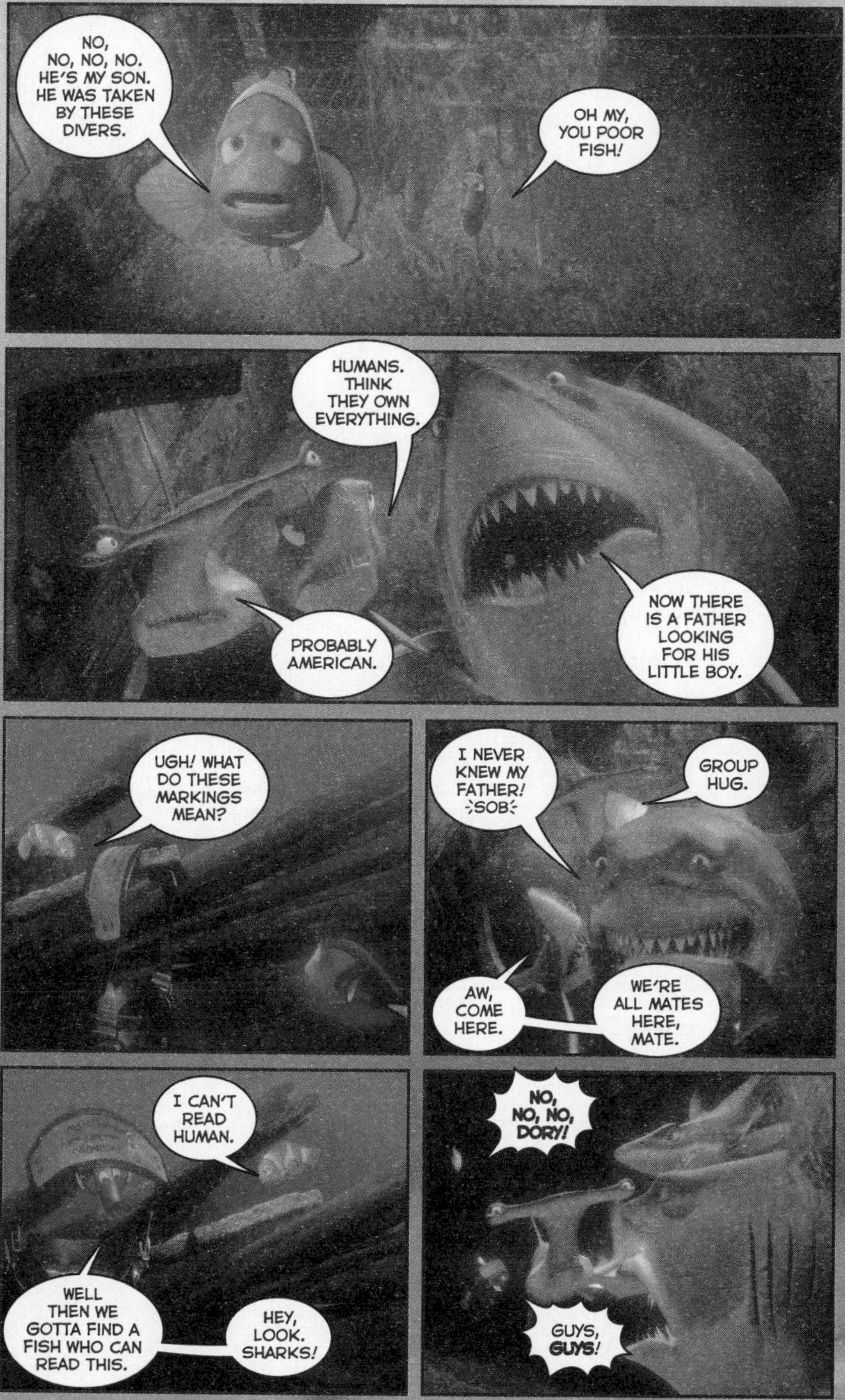
NO, NO, NO, NO. HE'S MY SON. HE WAS TAKEN BY THESE DIVERS.
OH MY, YOU POOR FISH!
HUMANS. THINK THEY OWN EVERYTHING.
PROBABLY AMERICAN.
NOW THERE IS A FATHER LOOKING FOR HIS LITTLE BOY.
UGH! WHAT DO THESE MARKINGS MEAN?
I NEVER KNEW MY FATHER! SOB
GROUP HUG.
AW, COME HERE.
WE'RE ALL MATES HERE, MATE.
I CAN'T READ HUMAN.
WELL THEN WE GOTTA FIND A FISH WHO CAN READ THIS.
HEY, LOOK. SHARKS!
NO, NO, NO, DORY!
GUYS, GUYS!

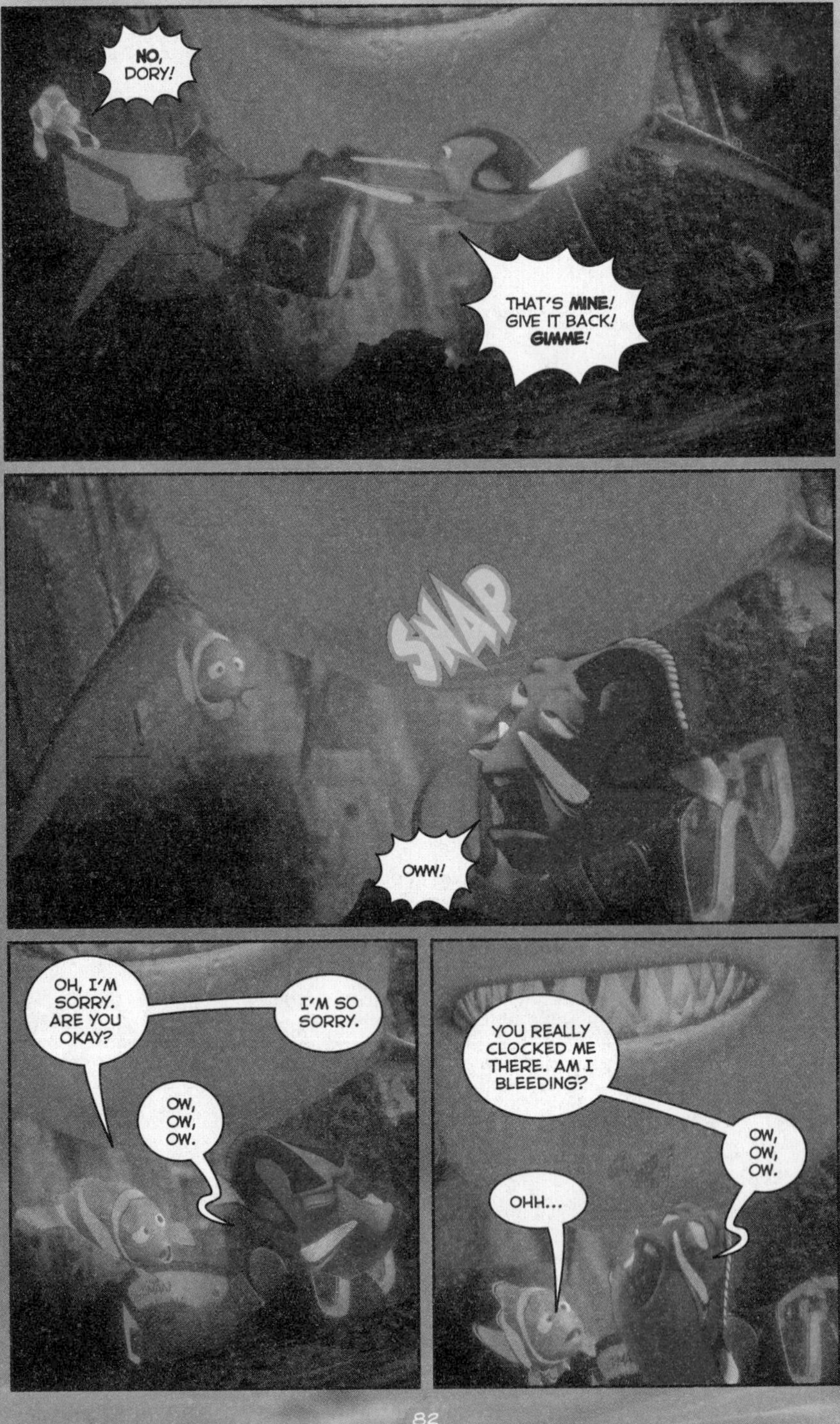
NO, DORY!
THAT'S MINE! GIVE IT BACK! GIMME!
SNAP
OWW!
OH, I'M SORRY. ARE YOU OKAY?
I'M SO SORRY.
OW, OW, OW.
YOU REALLY CLOCKED ME THERE. AM I BLEEDING?
OW, OW, OW.
OHH...

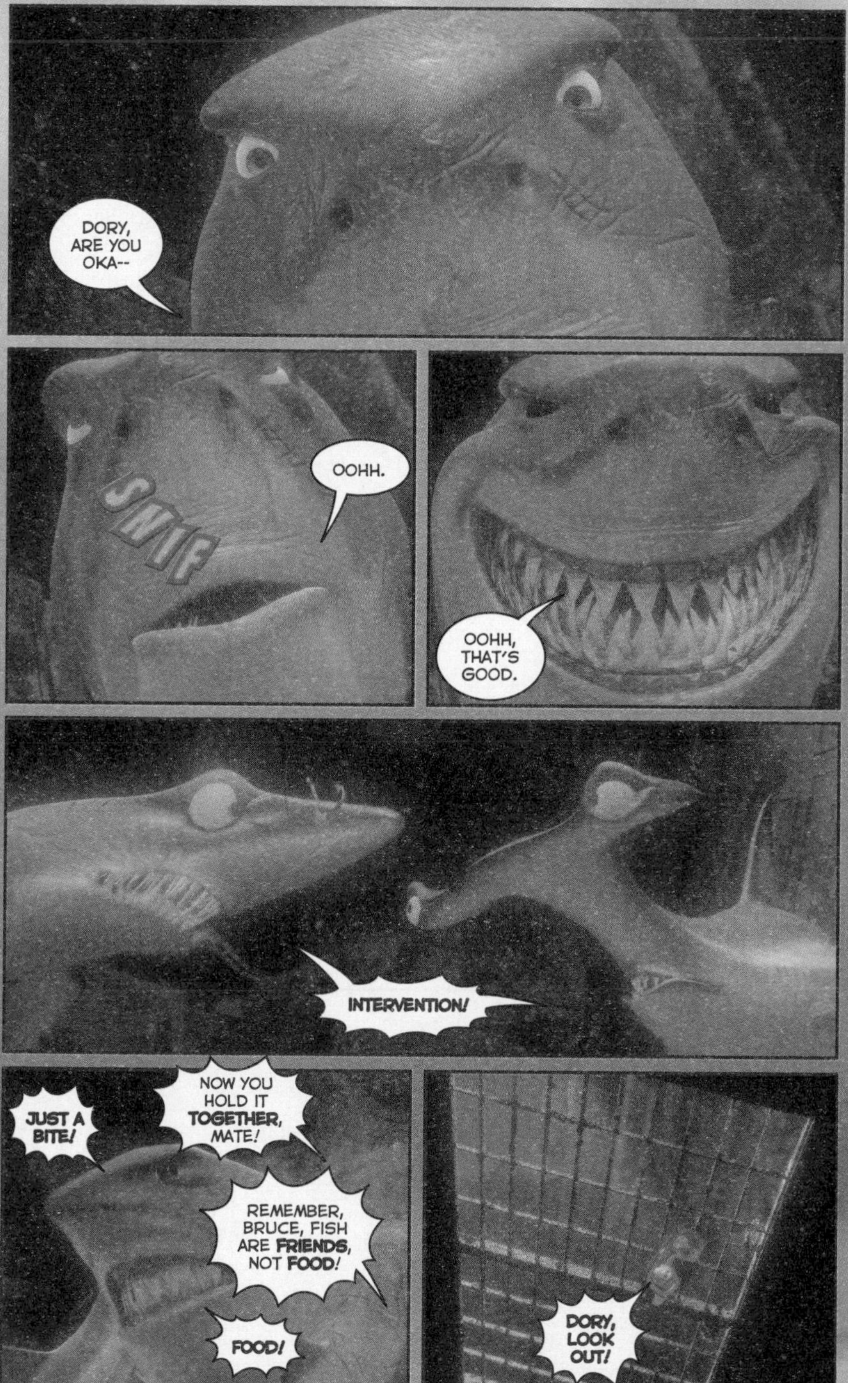
DORY, ARE YOU OKA--
SNIFF
OOHH.
OOHH, THAT'S GOOD.
INTERVENTION!
JUST A BITE!
NOW YOU HOLD IT TOGETHER, MATE!
REMEMBER, BRUCE, FISH ARE FRIENDS, NOT FOOD!
FOOD!
DORY, LOOK OUT!

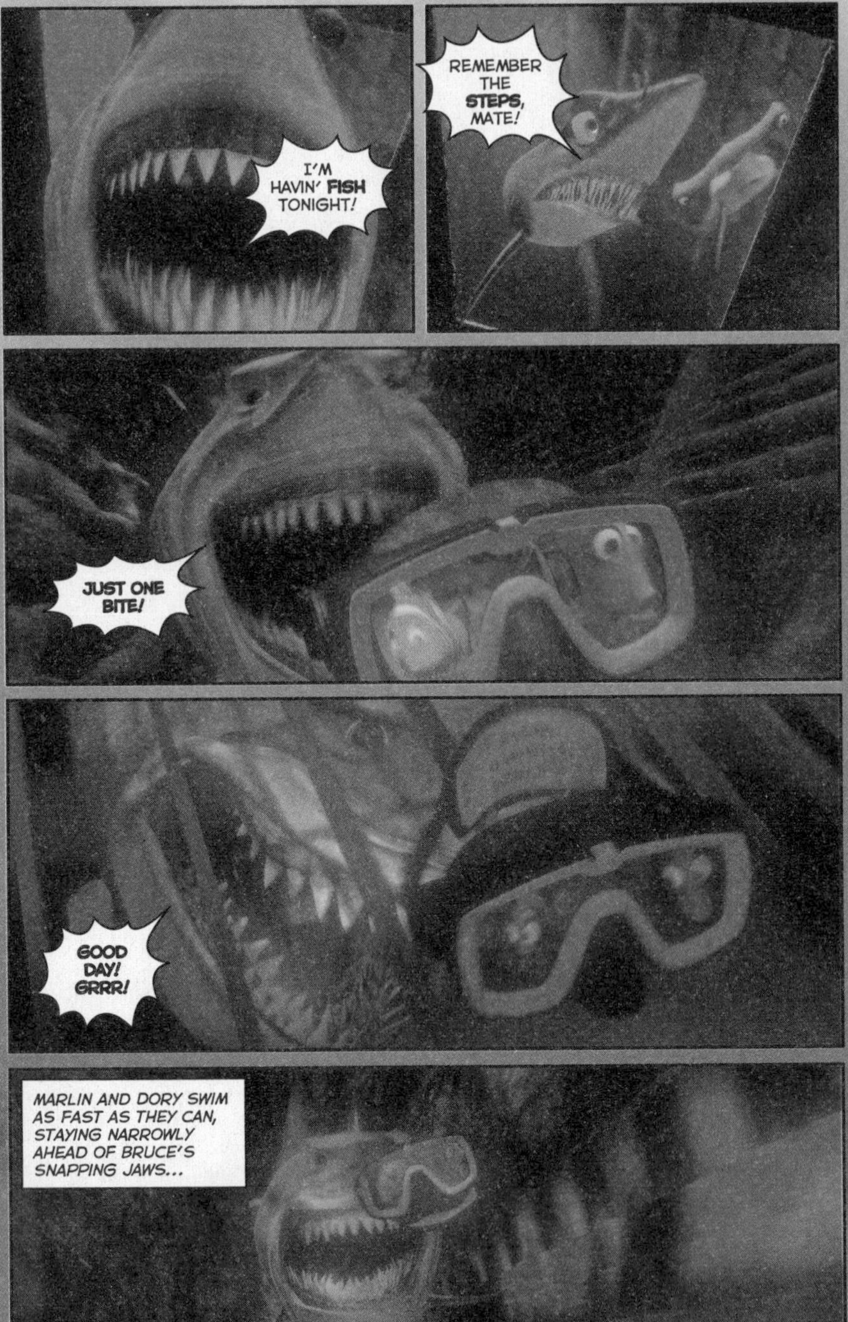
I'M HAVIN' FISH TONIGHT!
REMEMBER THE STEPS, MATE!
JUST ONE BITE!
GOOD DAY! GRRR!
MARLIN AND DORY SWIM AS FAST AS THEY CAN, STAYING NARROWLY AHEAD OF BRUCE'S SNAPPING JAWS...

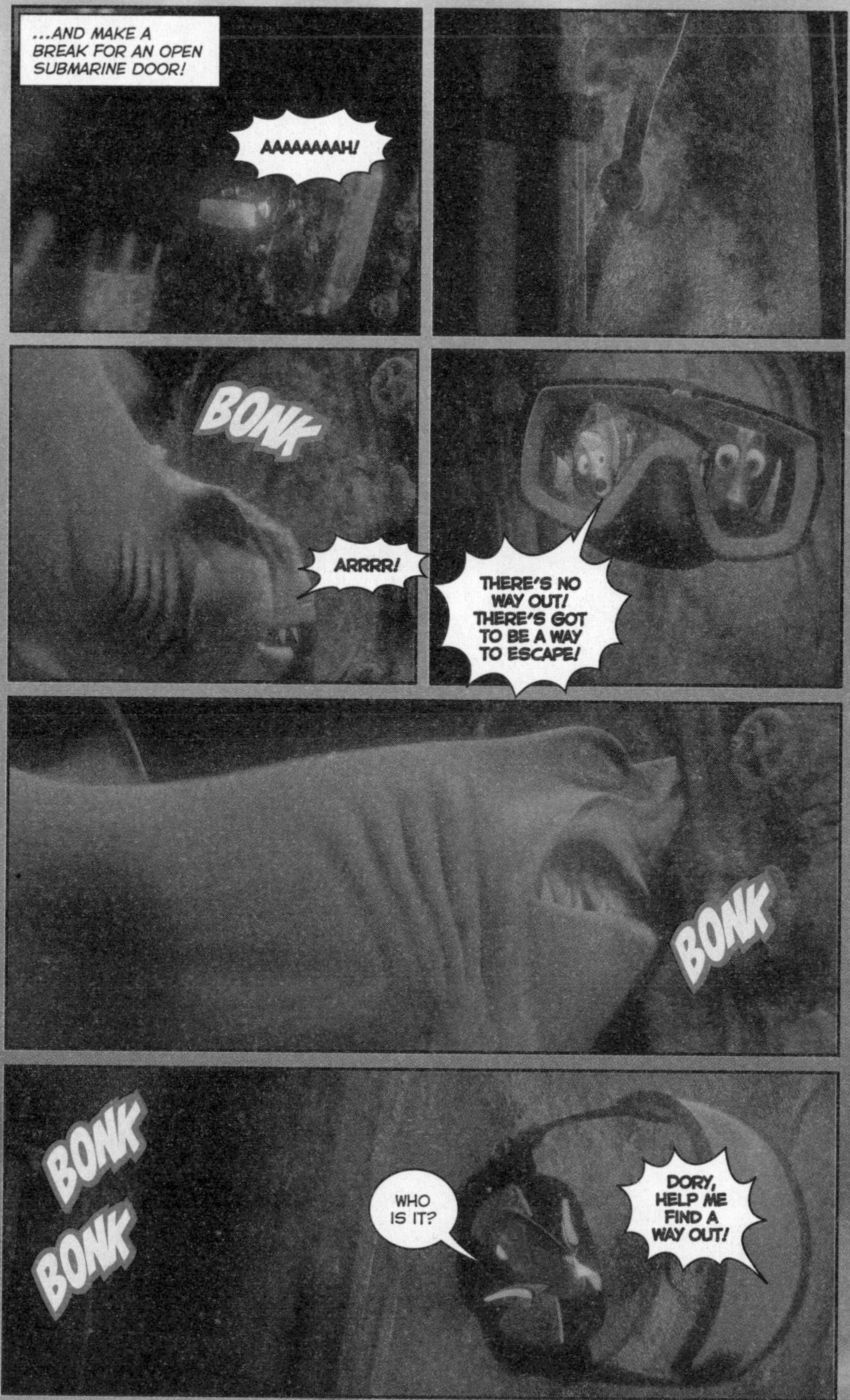
...AND MAKE A BREAK FOR AN OPEN SUBMARINE DOOR!
AAAAAAAAH!
BONK
ARRRR!
THERE'S NO WAY OUT! THERE'S GOT TO BE A WAY TO ESCAPE!
BONK
BONK
BONK
WHO IS IT?
DORY, HELP ME FIND A WAY OUT!

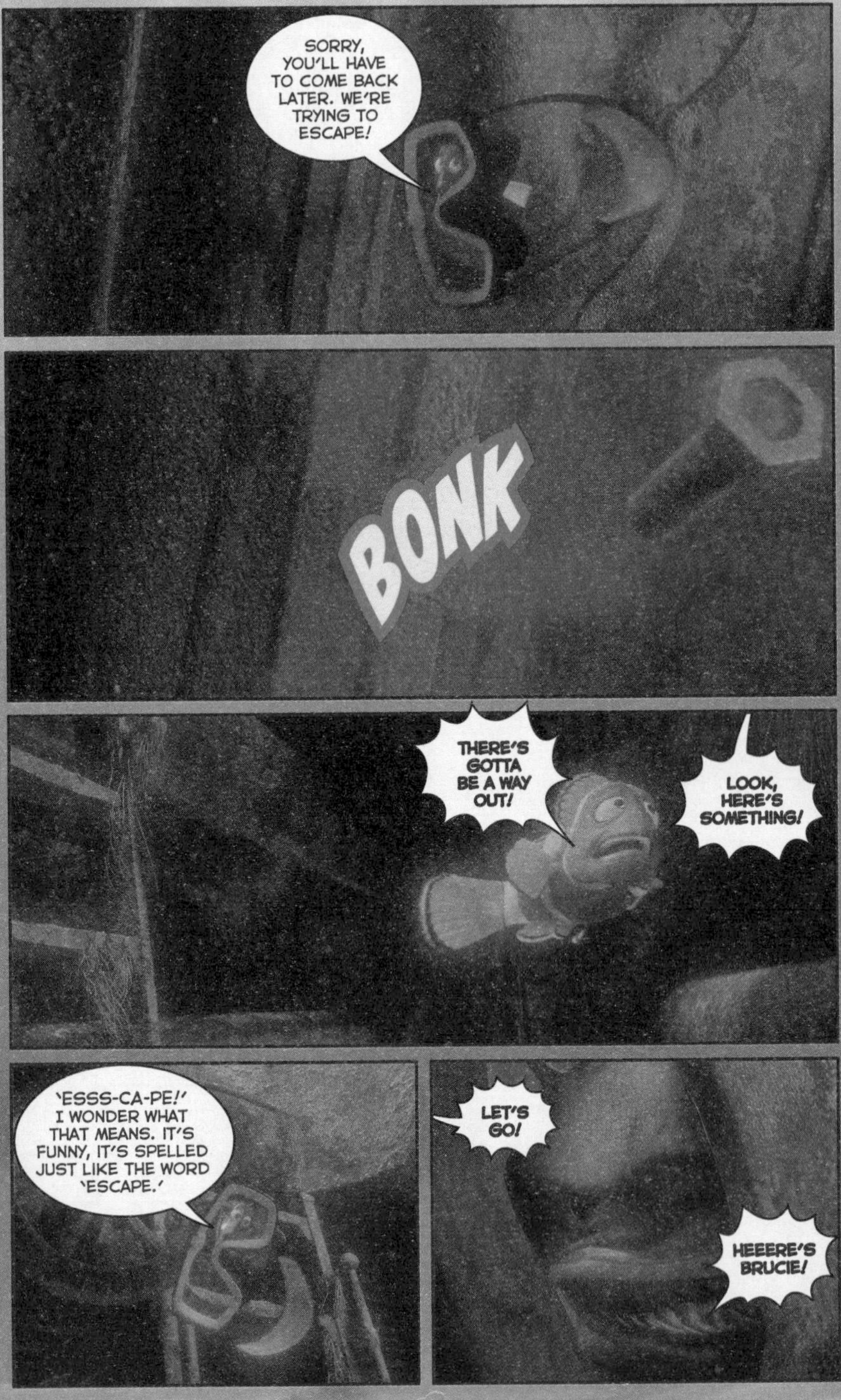
SORRY, YOU'LL HAVE TO COME BACK LATER. WE'RE TRYING TO ESCAPE!
BONK
THERE'S GOTTA BE A WAY OUT!
LOOK, HERE'S SOMETHING!
'ESSS-CA-PE!' I WONDER WHAT THAT MEANS. IT'S FUNNY, IT'S SPELLED JUST LIKE THE WORD 'ESCAPE.'
LET'S GO!
HEEERE'S BRUCIE!

WAIT A MINUTE... YOU CAN READ?
I CAN READ? THAT'S RIGHT, I CAN READ!
WELL, THEN HERE. READ THIS NOW!
CRASH
AAAAAAH!
HE REALLY DOESN'T MEAN IT, Y'KNOW! HE NEVER EVEN KNEW HIS FATHER!
DON'T FALL OFF THE WAGON!
AAAAAAH!
OH NO, IT'S BLOCKED!

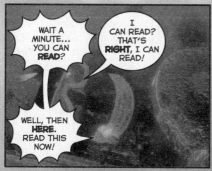

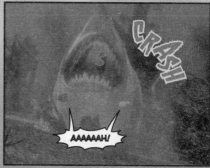

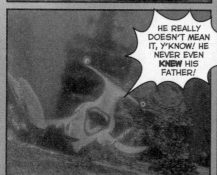

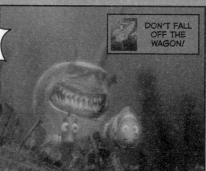

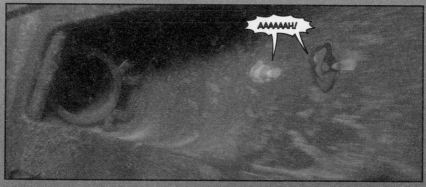

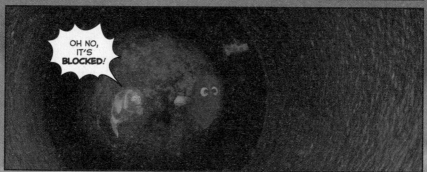

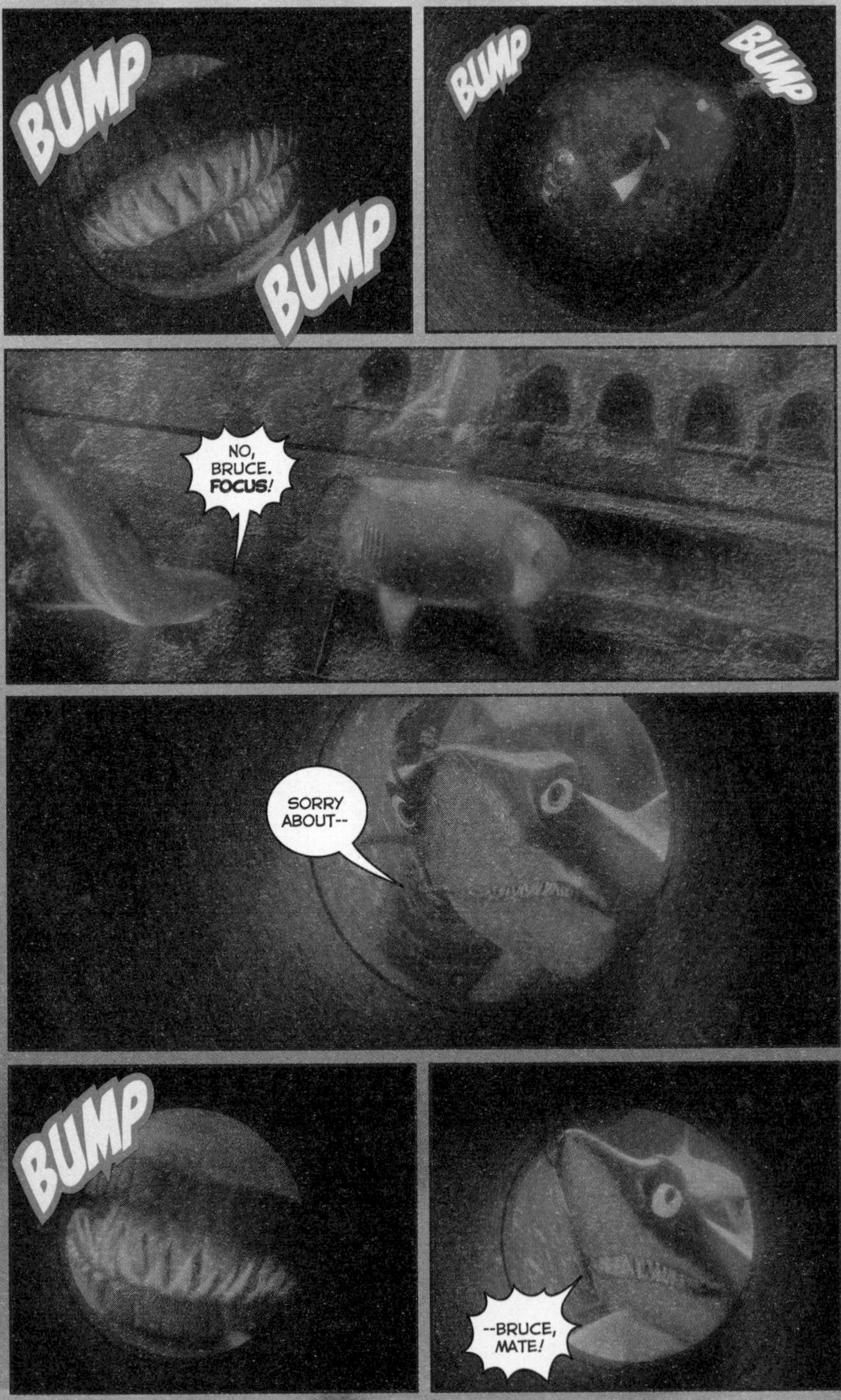

BUMP
BUMP
BUMP
BUMP
NO, BRUCE. **FOCUS!**
SORRY ABOUT--
BUMP
--BRUCE, MATE!

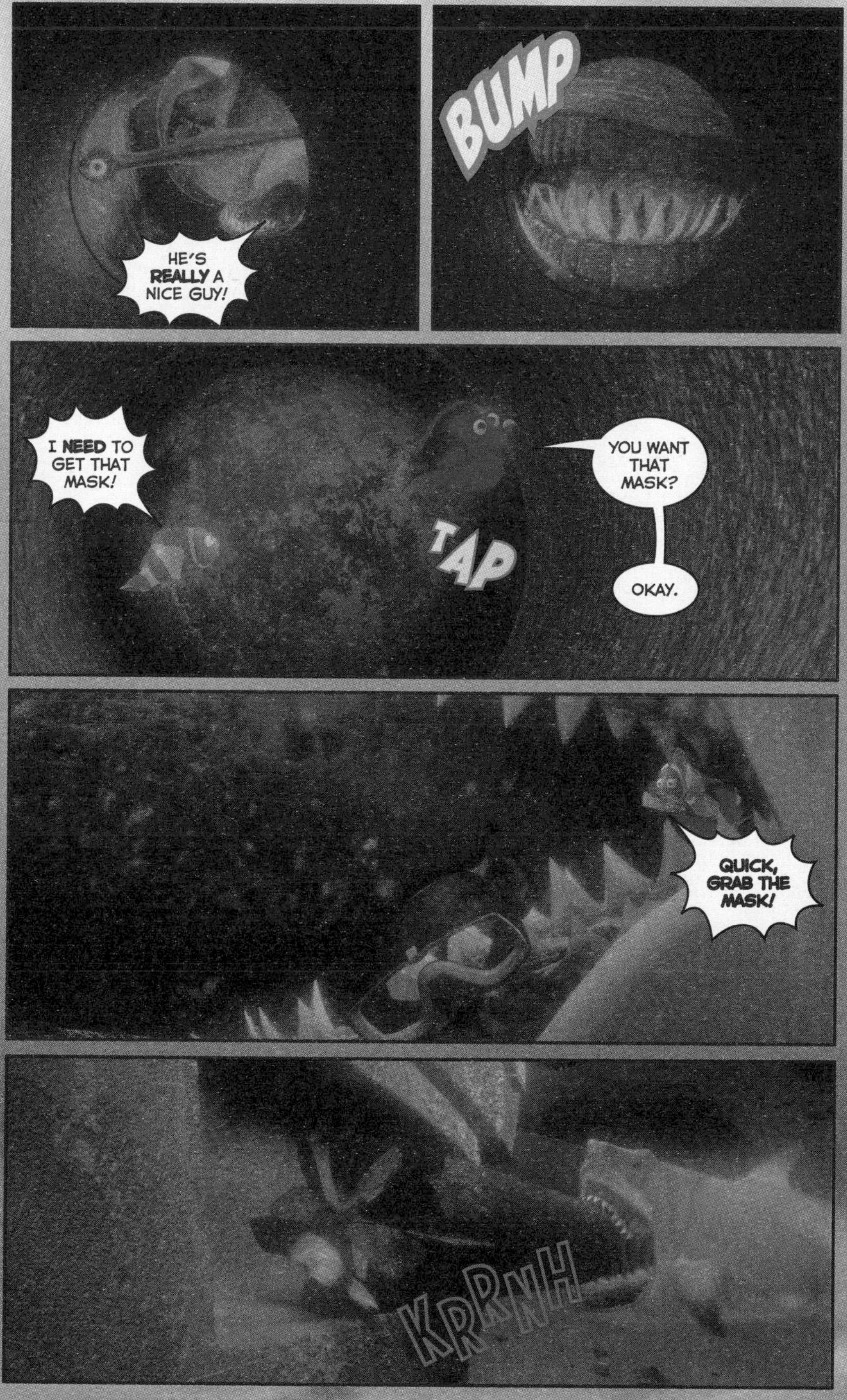
HE'S **REALLY** A NICE GUY!
BUMP
I **NEED** TO GET THAT MASK!
YOU WANT THAT MASK?
OKAY.
TAP
QUICK, GRAB THE MASK!
KRRNH

OH NO.
BRUCE?
WHAT?
SWIM AWAY!
SWIM AWAY!
AW, IS
THE PARTY
OVER?
CLANG

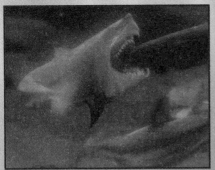

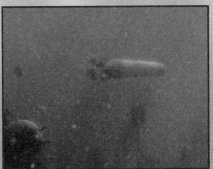

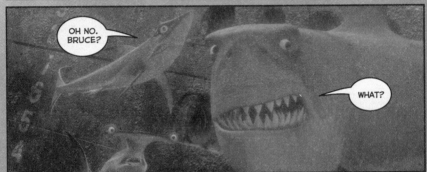

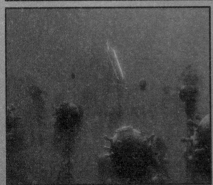

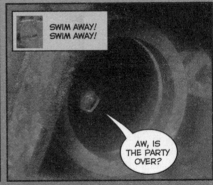

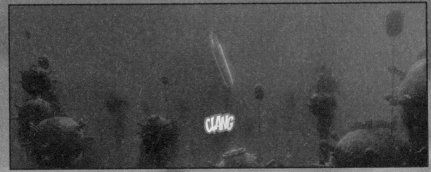

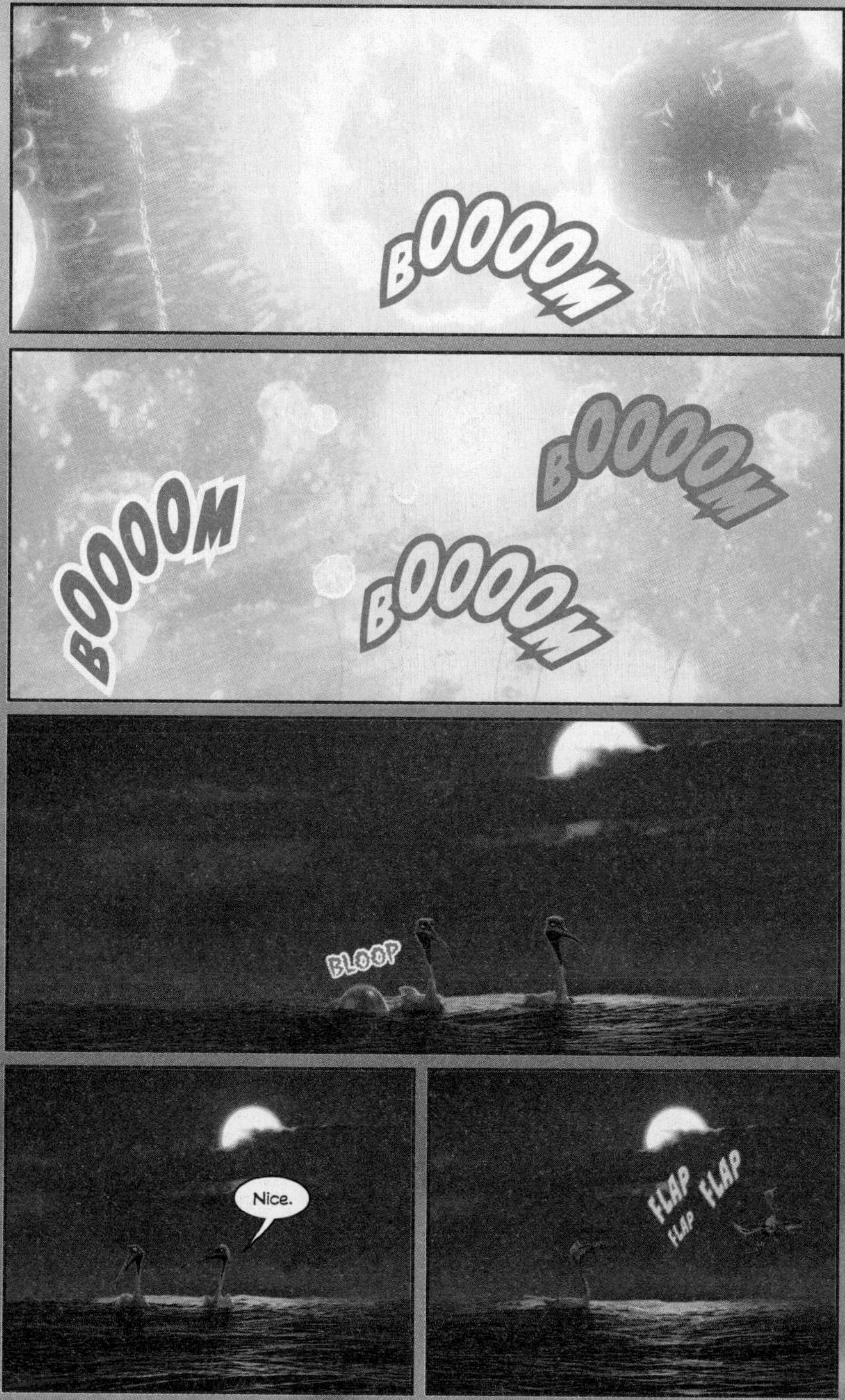
BOOOOM
BOOOOM
BOOOOM
BOOOOM
BLOOP
Nice.
FLAP
FLAP
FLAP

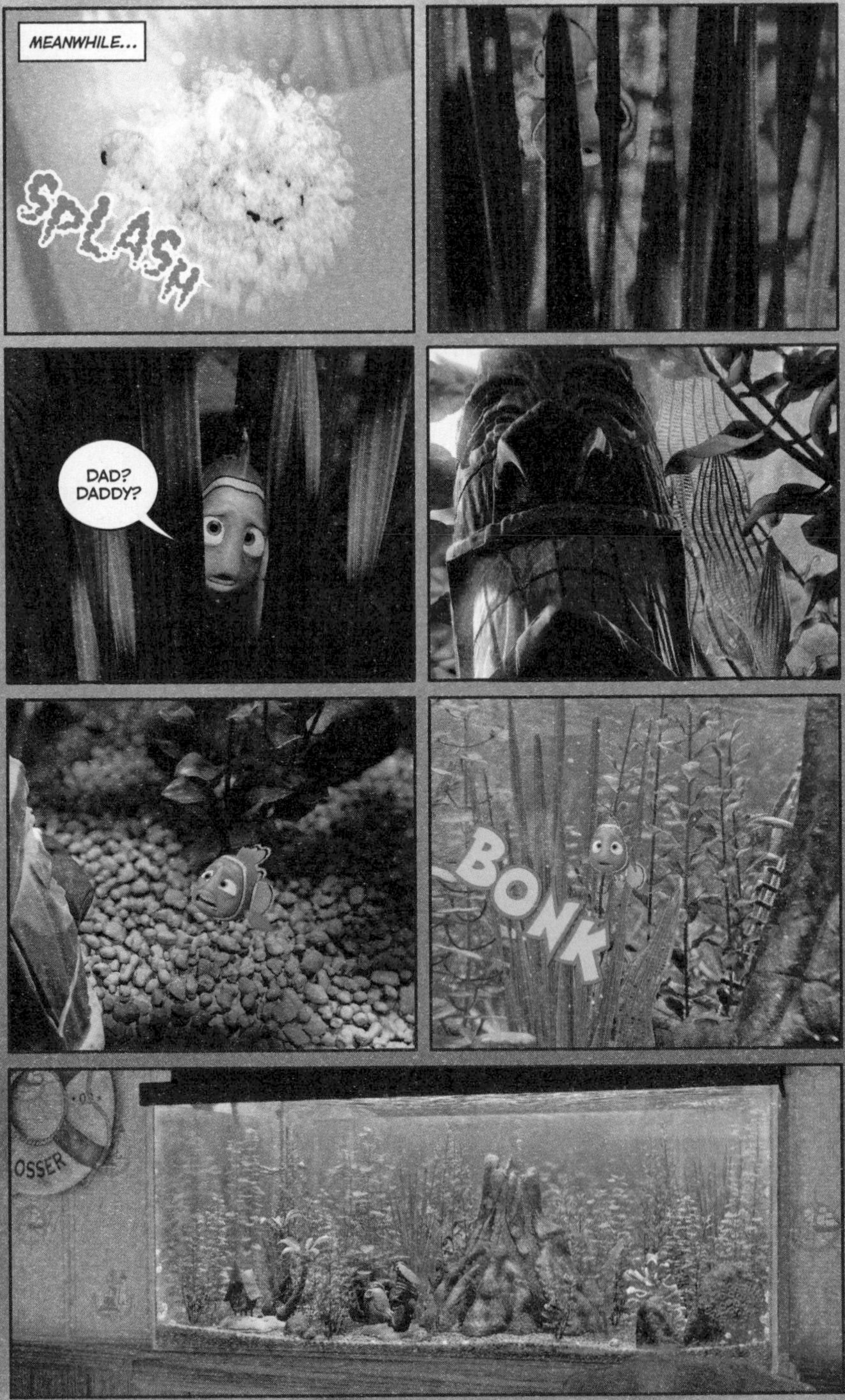
MEANWHILE...
SPLASH
DAD? DADDY?
BONK

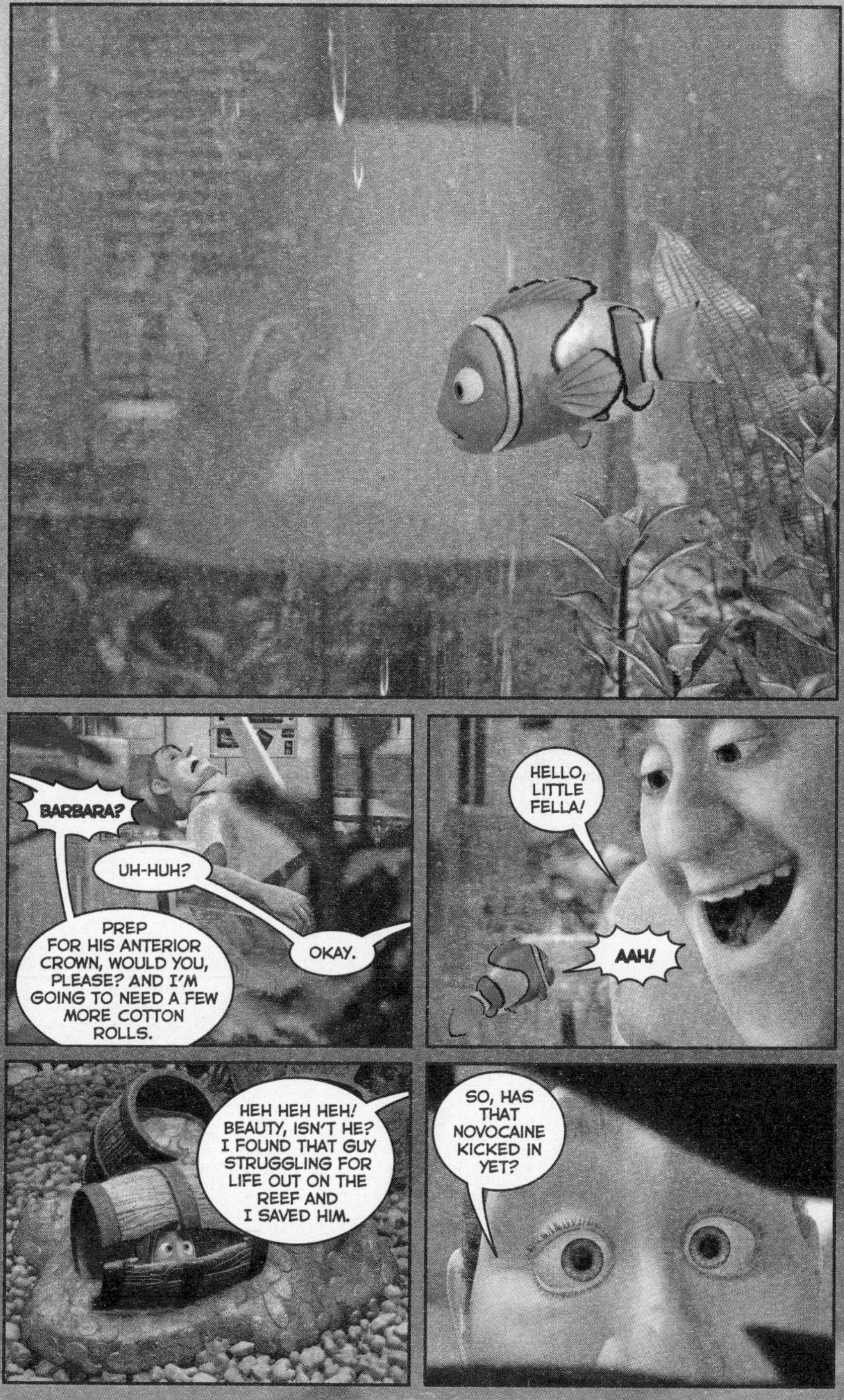
BARBARA?
UH-HUH?
PREP FOR HIS ANTERIOR CROWN, WOULD YOU, PLEASE? AND I'M GOING TO NEED A FEW MORE COTTON ROLLS.
OKAY.
HELLO, LITTLE FELLA!
AAH!
HEH HEH HEH! BEAUTY, ISN'T HE? I FOUND THAT GUY STRUGGLING FOR LIFE OUT ON THE REEF AND I SAVED HIM.
SO, HAS THAT NOVOCAINE KICKED IN YET?

BUBBLES!
BUBBLES! BUBBLES! BUBBLES!
BLOOP BLOOP BLOOP
MY BUBBLES.
HE LIKES BUBBLES.

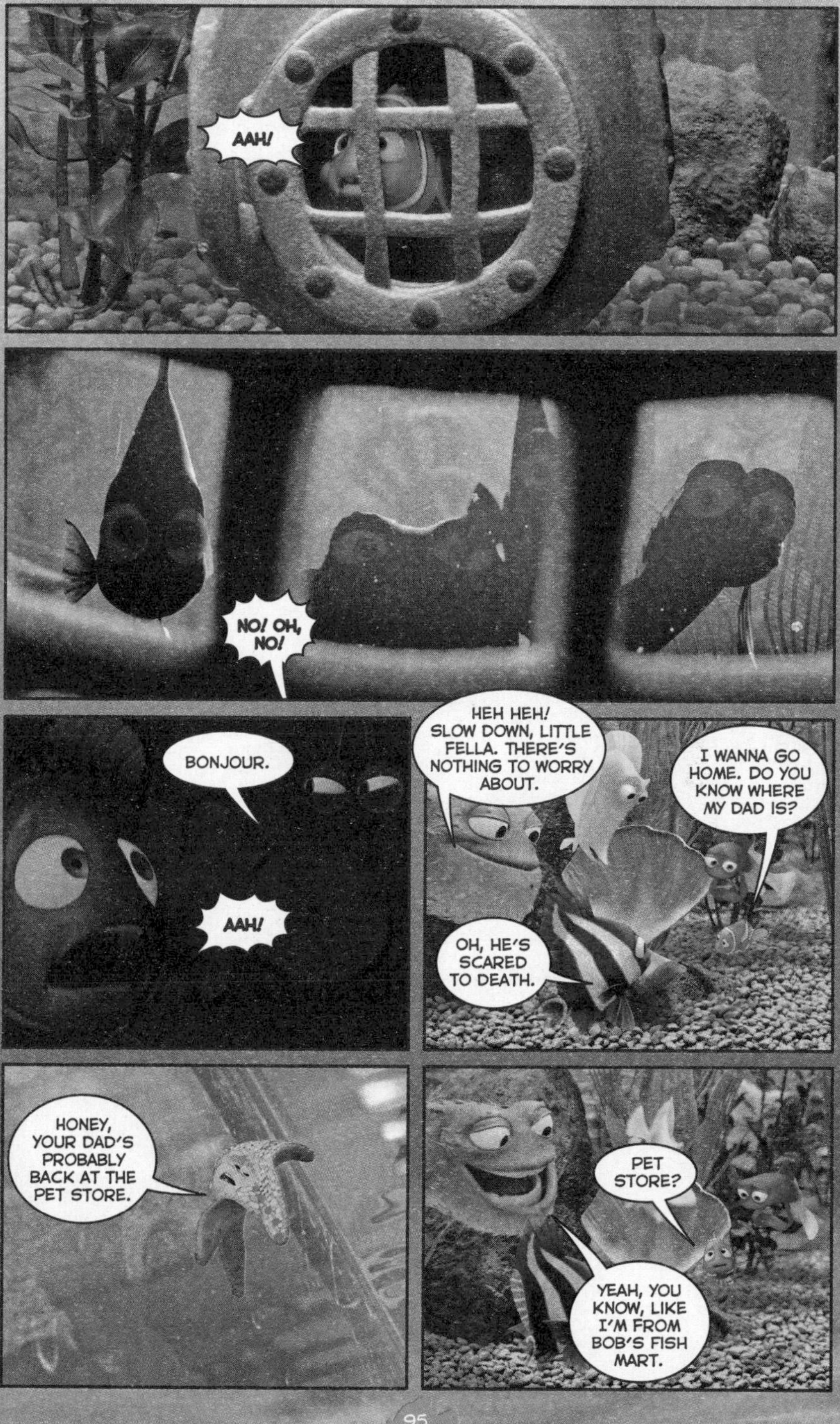
AAH!
NO! OH, NO!
BONJOUR.
AAH!
HEH HEH! SLOW DOWN, LITTLE FELLA. THERE'S NOTHING TO WORRY ABOUT.
I WANNA GO HOME. DO YOU KNOW WHERE MY DAD IS?
OH, HE'S SCARED TO DEATH.
HONEY, YOUR DAD'S PROBABLY BACK AT THE PET STORE.
PET STORE?
YEAH, YOU KNOW, LIKE I'M FROM BOB'S FISH MART.

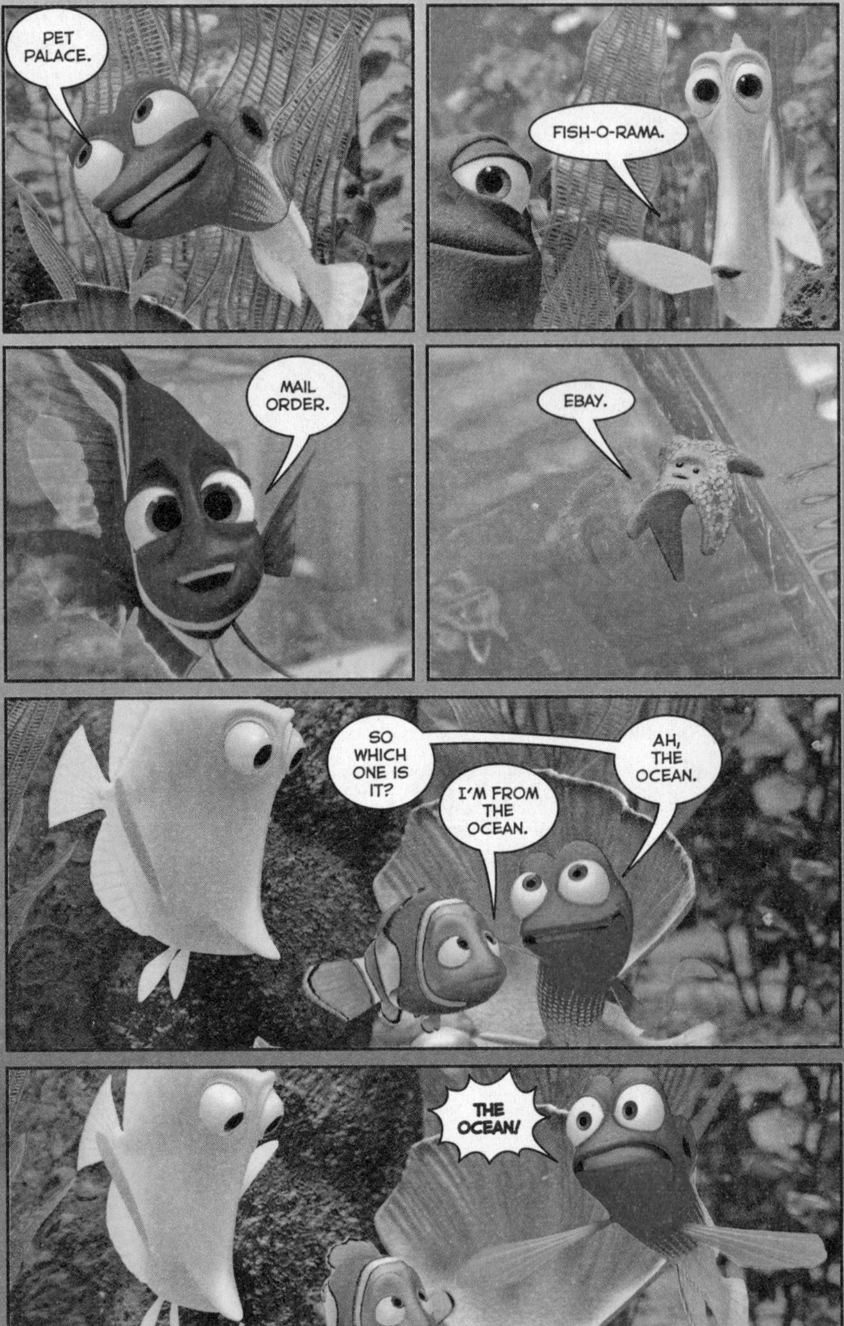
PET PALACE.
FISH-O-RAMA.
MAIL ORDER.
EBAY.
SO WHICH ONE IS IT?
AH, THE OCEAN.
I'M FROM THE OCEAN.
THE OCEAN!

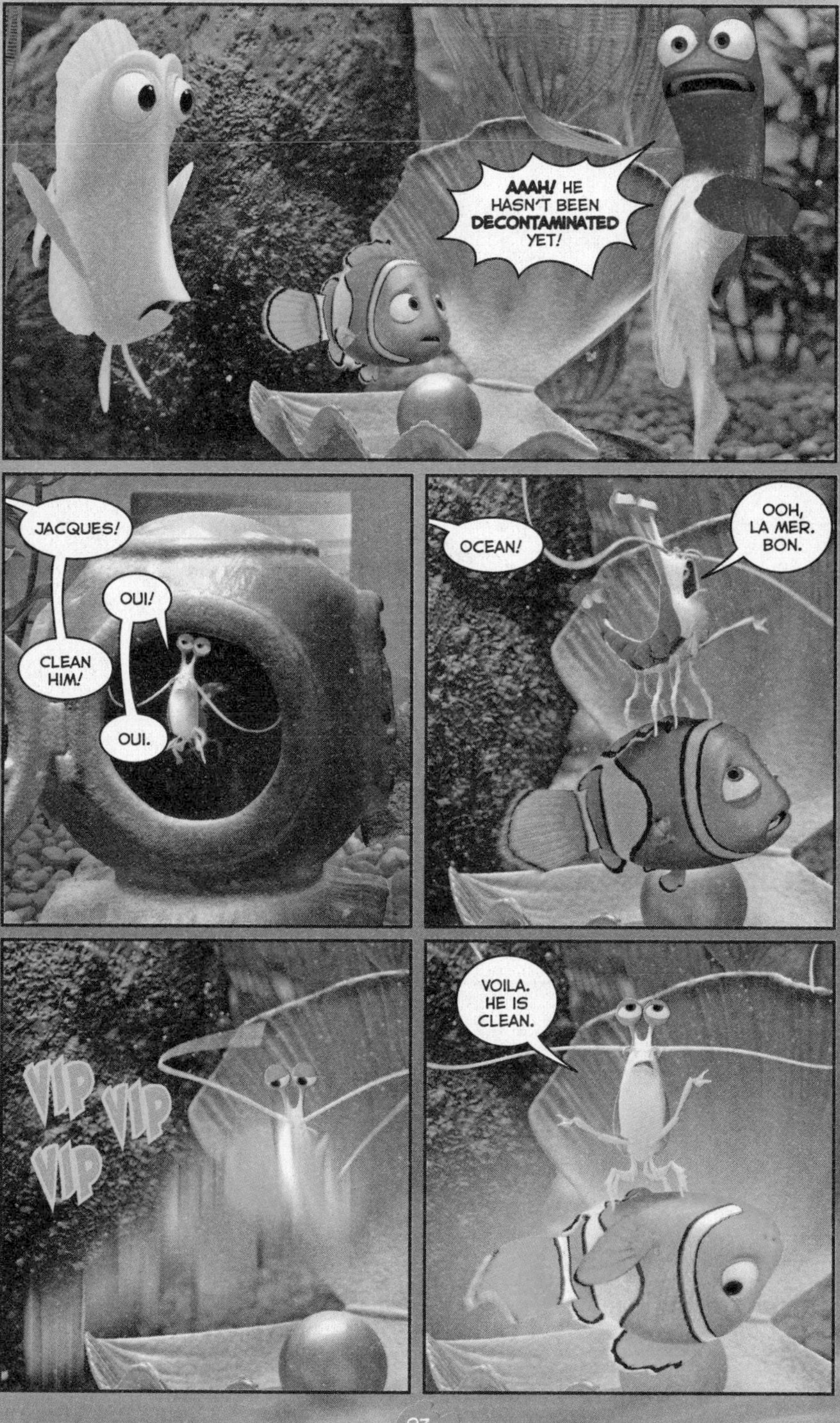
AAAH! HE HASN'T BEEN DECONTAMINATED YET!
JACQUES!
CLEAN HIM!
OUI!
OUI.
OCEAN!
OOH, LA MER. BON.
VIP VIP VIP
VOILA. HE IS CLEAN.

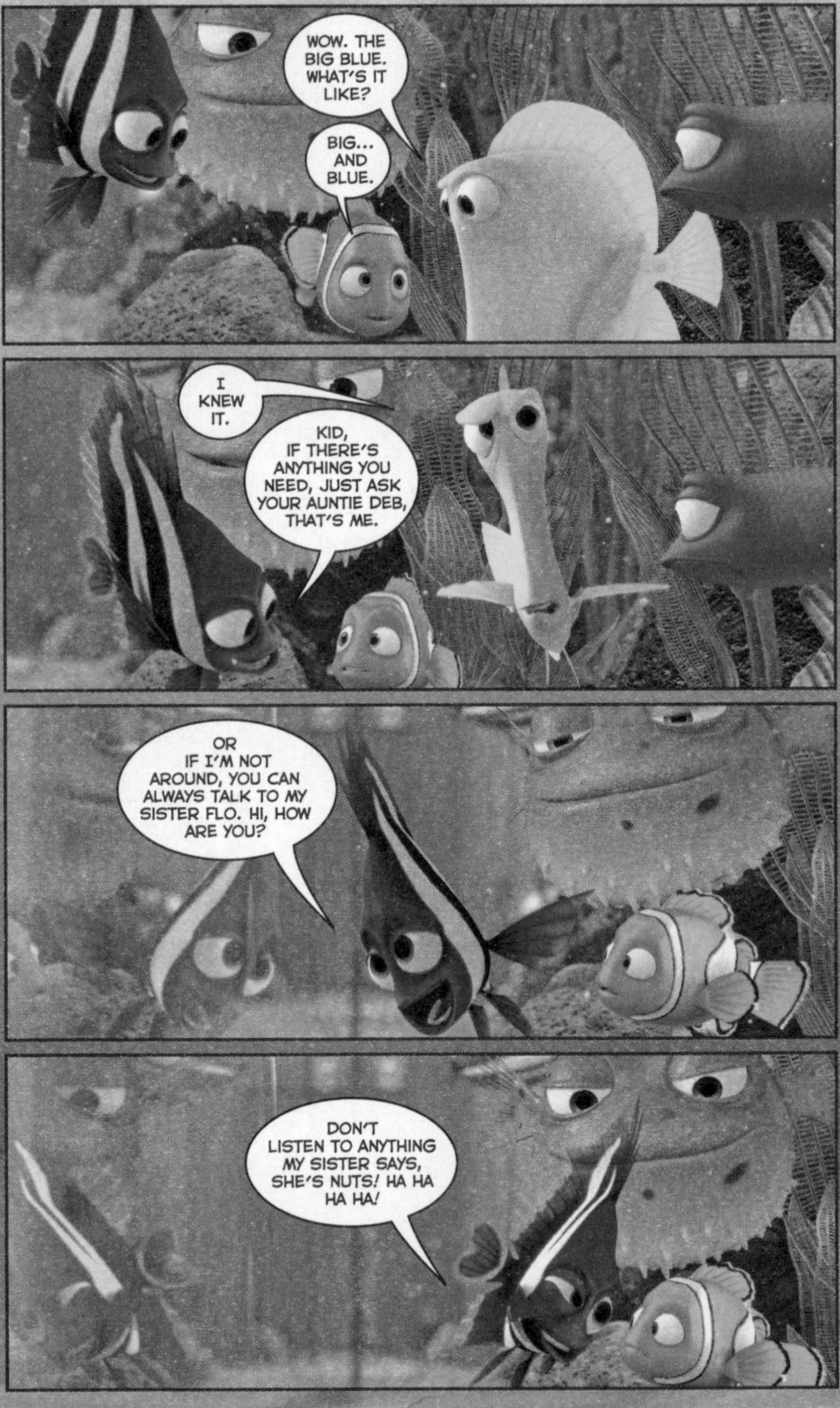
WOW. THE BIG BLUE. WHAT'S IT LIKE?
BIG... AND BLUE.
I KNEW IT.
KID, IF THERE'S ANYTHING YOU NEED, JUST ASK YOUR AUNTIE DEB, THAT'S ME.
OR IF I'M NOT AROUND, YOU CAN ALWAYS TALK TO MY SISTER FLO. HI, HOW ARE YOU?
DON'T LISTEN TO ANYTHING MY SISTER SAYS, SHE'S NUTS! HA HA HA HA!

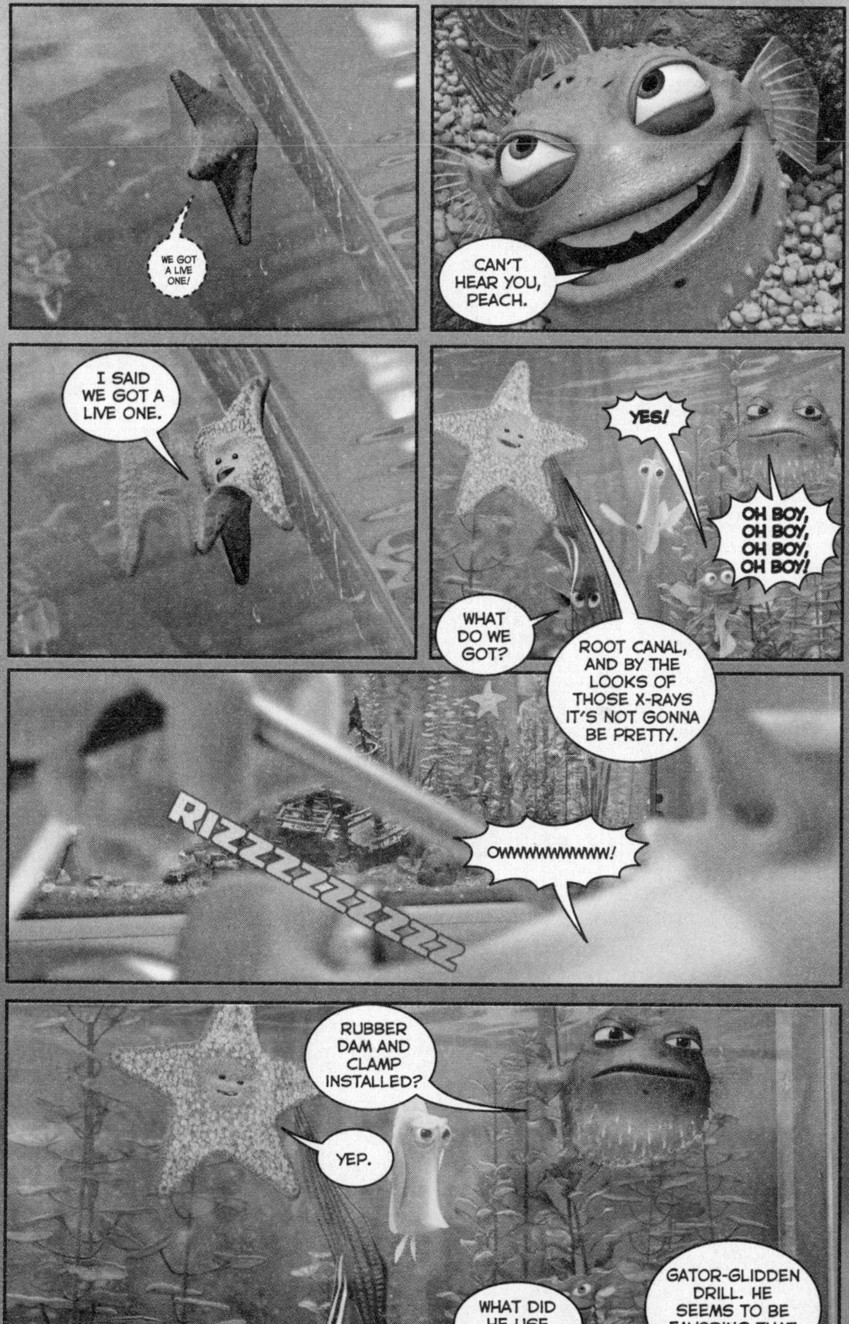

WE GOT A LIVE ONE!
CAN'T HEAR YOU, PEACH.
I SAID WE GOT A LIVE ONE.
YES!
OH BOY, OH BOY, OH BOY, OH BOY!
WHAT DO WE GOT?
ROOT CANAL, AND BY THE LOOKS OF THOSE X-RAYS IT'S NOT GONNA BE PRETTY.
RIZZZZZZZZZZZZ
OWWWWWWWWWW!
RUBBER DAM AND CLAMP INSTALLED?
YEP.
WHAT DID HE USE TO OPEN?
GATOR-GLIDDEN DRILL. HE SEEMS TO BE FAVORING THAT ONE LATELY.

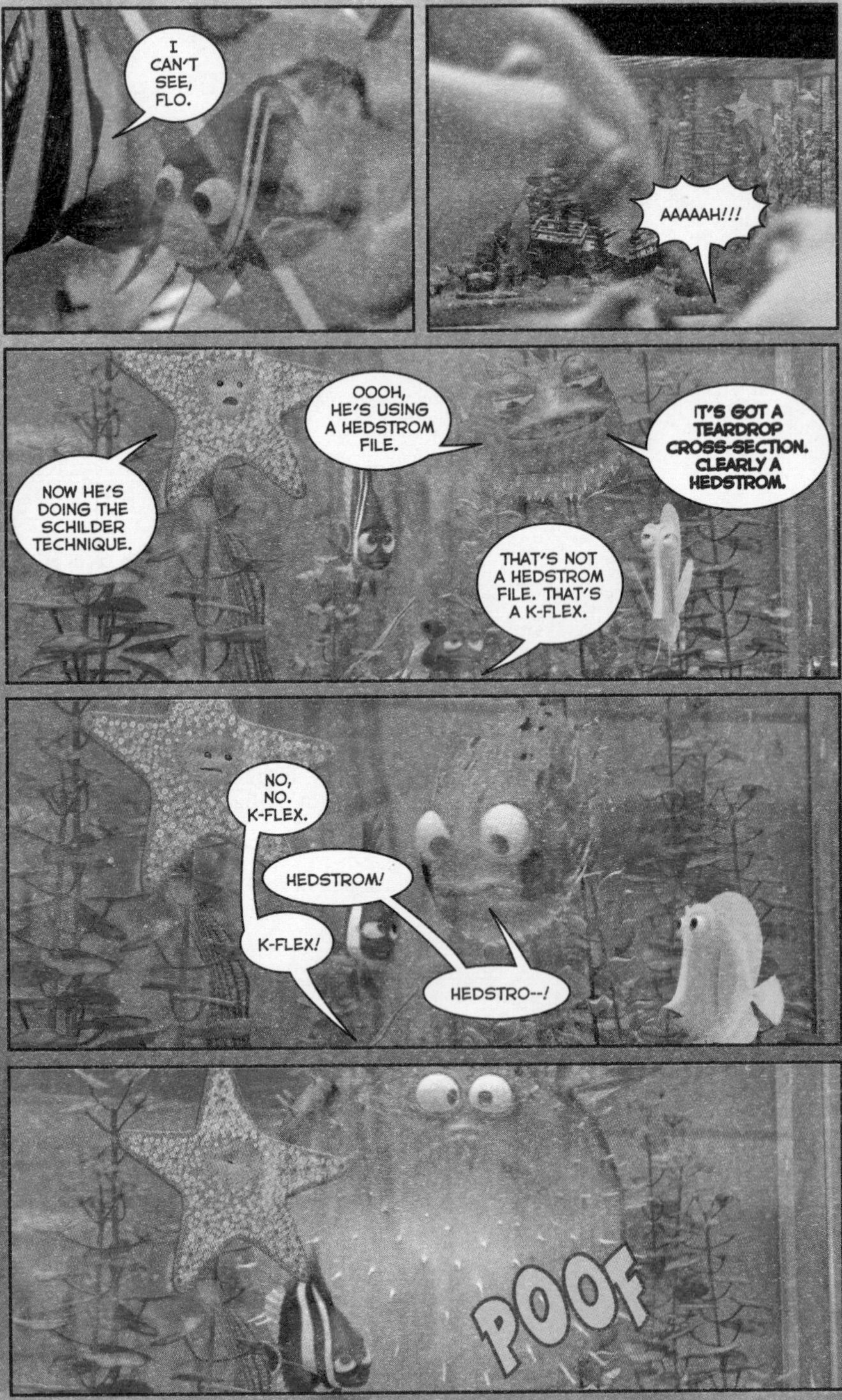
I CAN'T SEE, FLO.
AAAAAH!!!
NOW HE'S DOING THE SCHILDER TECHNIQUE.
OOOH, HE'S USING A HEDSTROM FILE.
IT'S GOT A TEARDROP CROSS-SECTION. CLEARLY A HEDSTROM.
THAT'S NOT A HEDSTROM FILE. THAT'S A K-FLEX.
NO, NO. K-FLEX.
HEDSTROM!
K-FLEX!
HEDSTRO--!
POOF

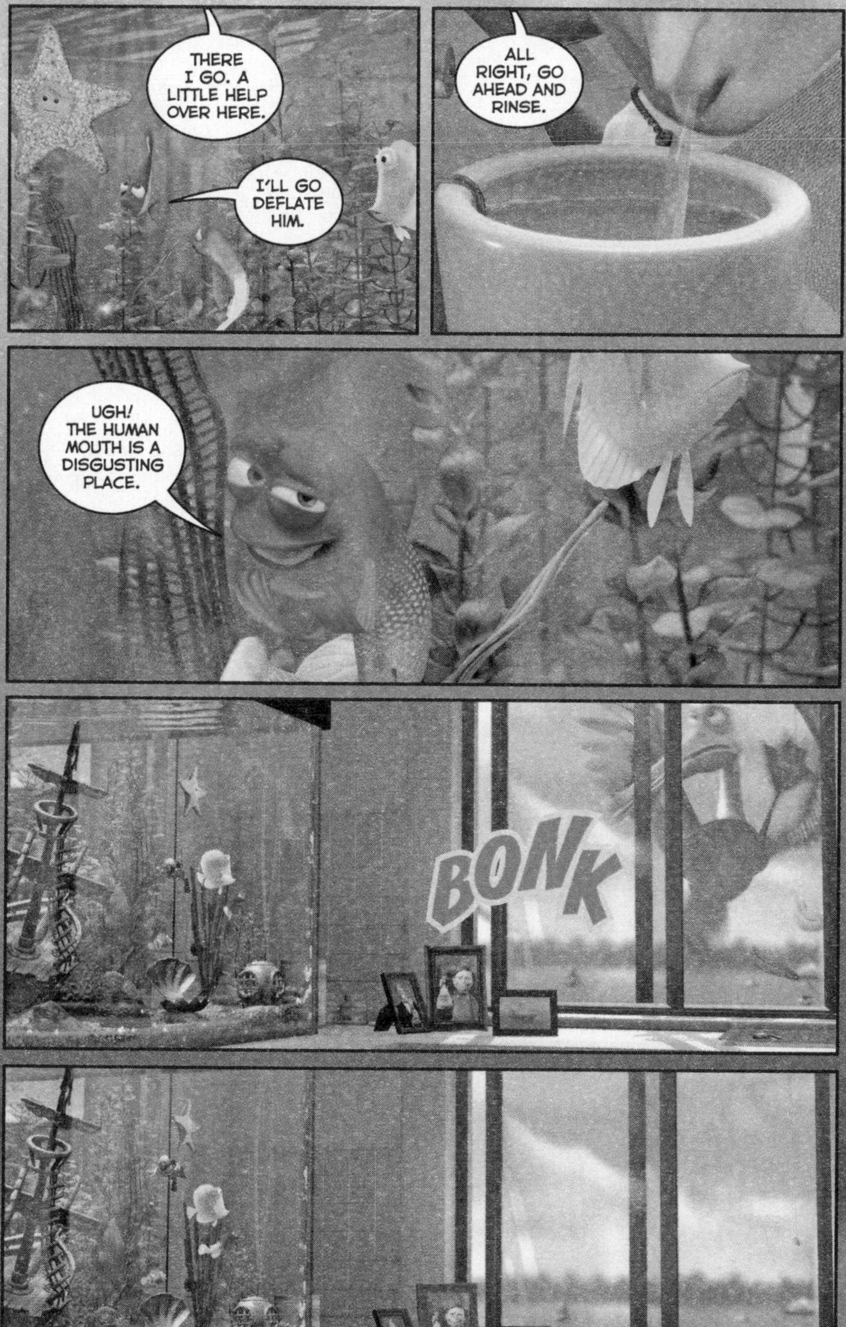
THERE I GO. A LITTLE HELP OVER HERE.
I'LL GO DEFLATE HIM.
ALL RIGHT, GO AHEAD AND RINSE.
UGH! THE HUMAN MOUTH IS A DISGUSTING PLACE.
BONK

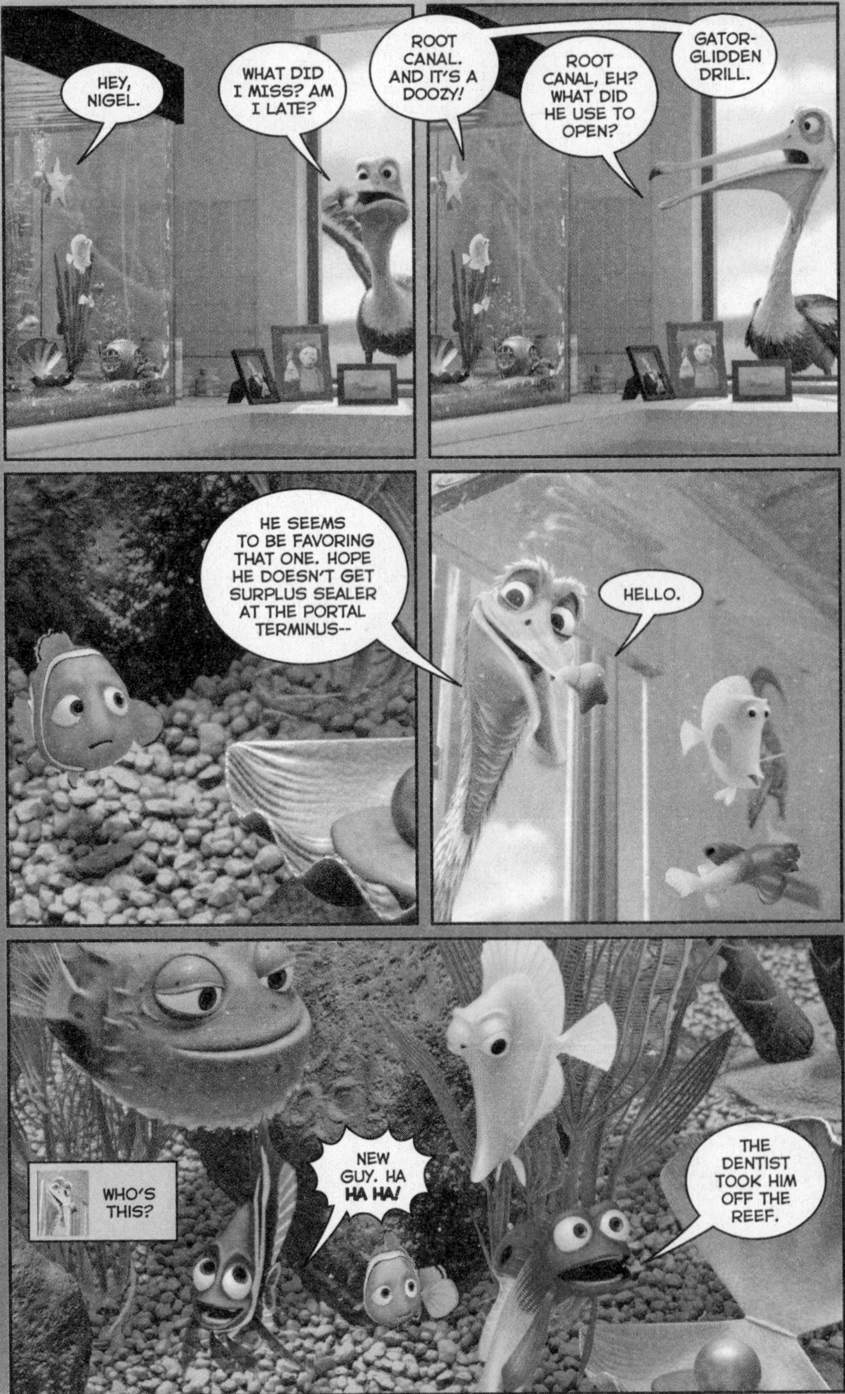
HEY, NIGEL.
WHAT DID I MISS? AM I LATE?
ROOT CANAL. AND IT'S A DOOZY!
ROOT CANAL, EH? WHAT DID HE USE TO OPEN?
GATOR-GLIDDEN DRILL.
HE SEEMS TO BE FAVORING THAT ONE. HOPE HE DOESN'T GET SURPLUS SEALER AT THE PORTAL TERMINUS--
HELLO.
WHO'S THIS?
NEW GUY. HA HA HA!
THE DENTIST TOOK HIM OFF THE REEF.

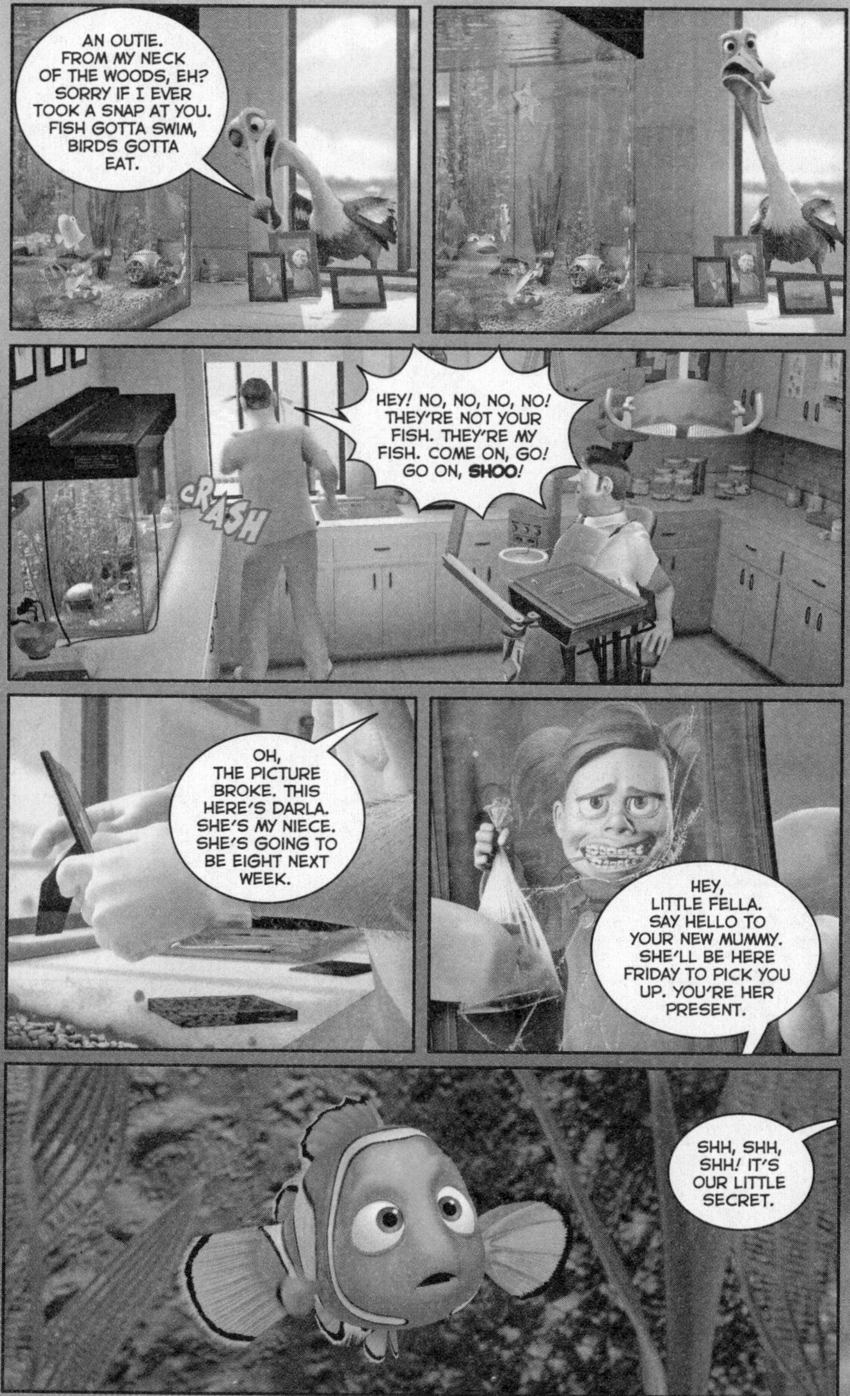
AN OUTIE. FROM MY NECK OF THE WOODS, EH? SORRY IF I EVER TOOK A SNAP AT YOU. FISH GOTTA SWIM, BIRDS GOTTA EAT.
HEY! NO, NO, NO, NO! THEY'RE NOT YOUR FISH. THEY'RE MY FISH. COME ON, GO! GO ON, SHOO!
CRASH
OH, THE PICTURE BROKE. THIS HERE'S DARLA. SHE'S MY NIECE. SHE'S GOING TO BE EIGHT NEXT WEEK.
HEY, LITTLE FELLA. SAY HELLO TO YOUR NEW MUMMY. SHE'LL BE HERE FRIDAY TO PICK YOU UP. YOU'RE HER PRESENT.
SHH, SHH, SHH! IT'S OUR LITTLE SECRET.

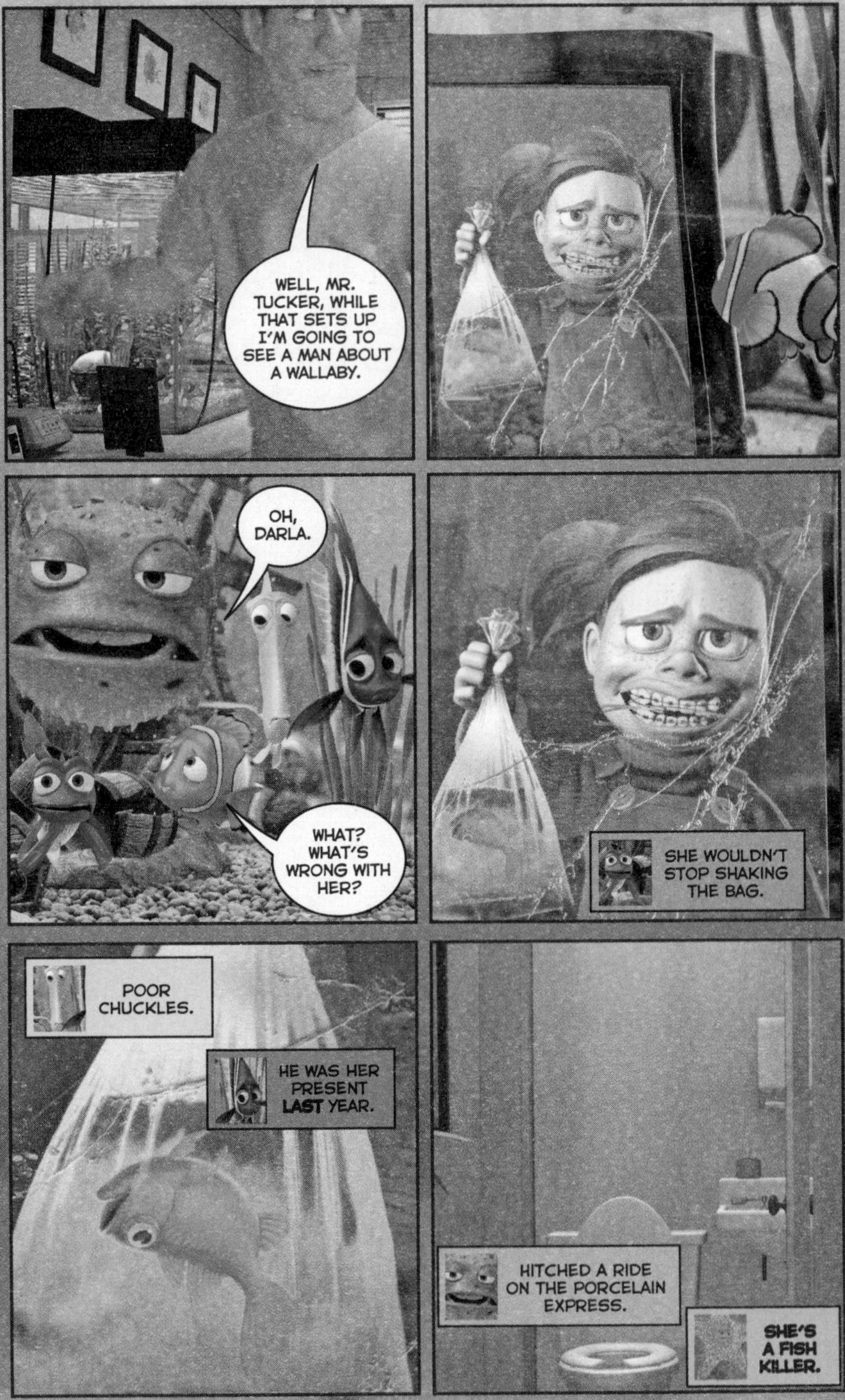
WELL, MR. TUCKER, WHILE THAT SETS UP I'M GOING TO SEE A MAN ABOUT A WALLABY.
OH, DARLA.
WHAT? WHAT'S WRONG WITH HER?
SHE WOULDN'T STOP SHAKING THE BAG.
POOR CHUCKLES.
HE WAS HER PRESENT LAST YEAR.
HITCHED A RIDE ON THE PORCELAIN EXPRESS.
SHE'S A FISH KILLER.

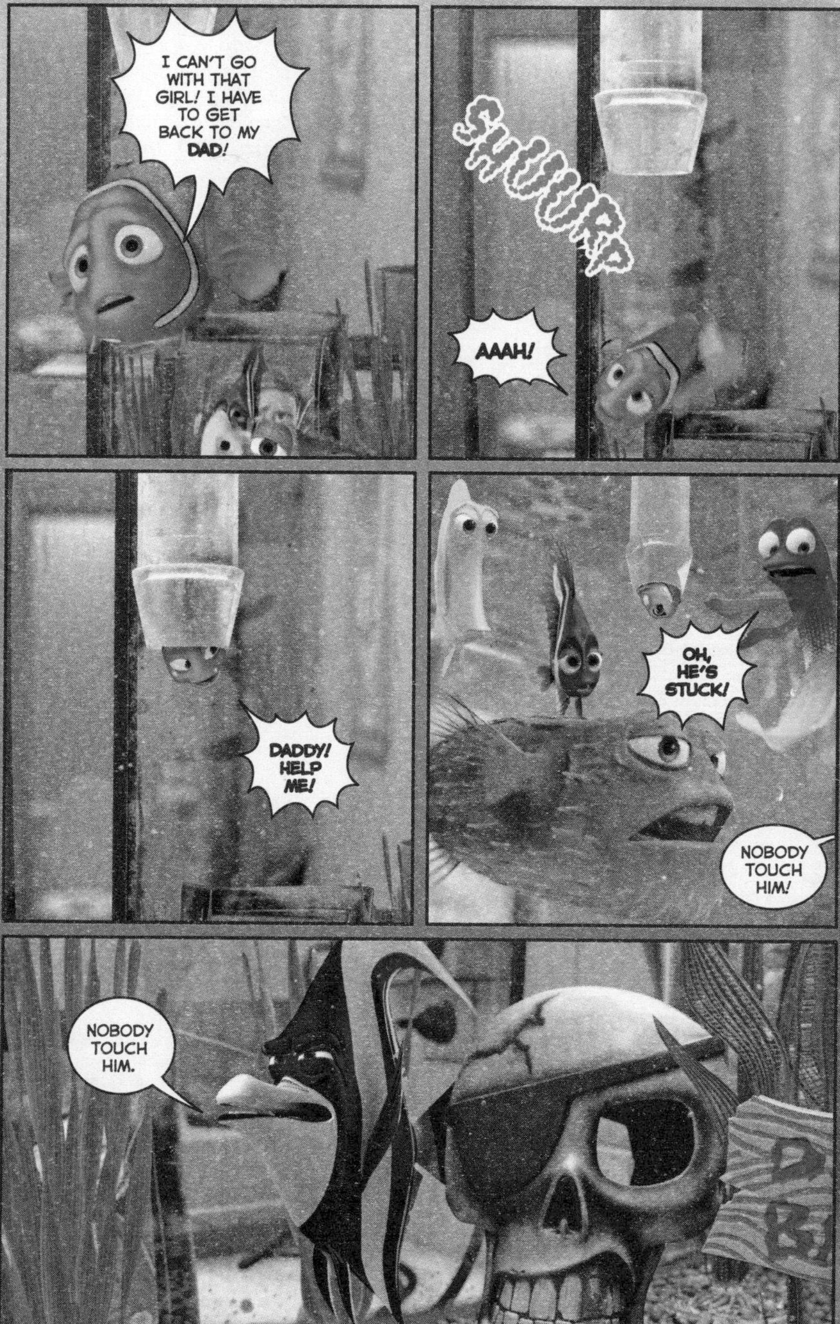

I CAN'T GO WITH THAT GIRL! I HAVE TO GET BACK TO MY DAD!
SHUURP
AAAH!
DADDY! HELP ME!
OH, HE'S STUCK!
NOBODY TOUCH HIM!
NOBODY TOUCH HIM.

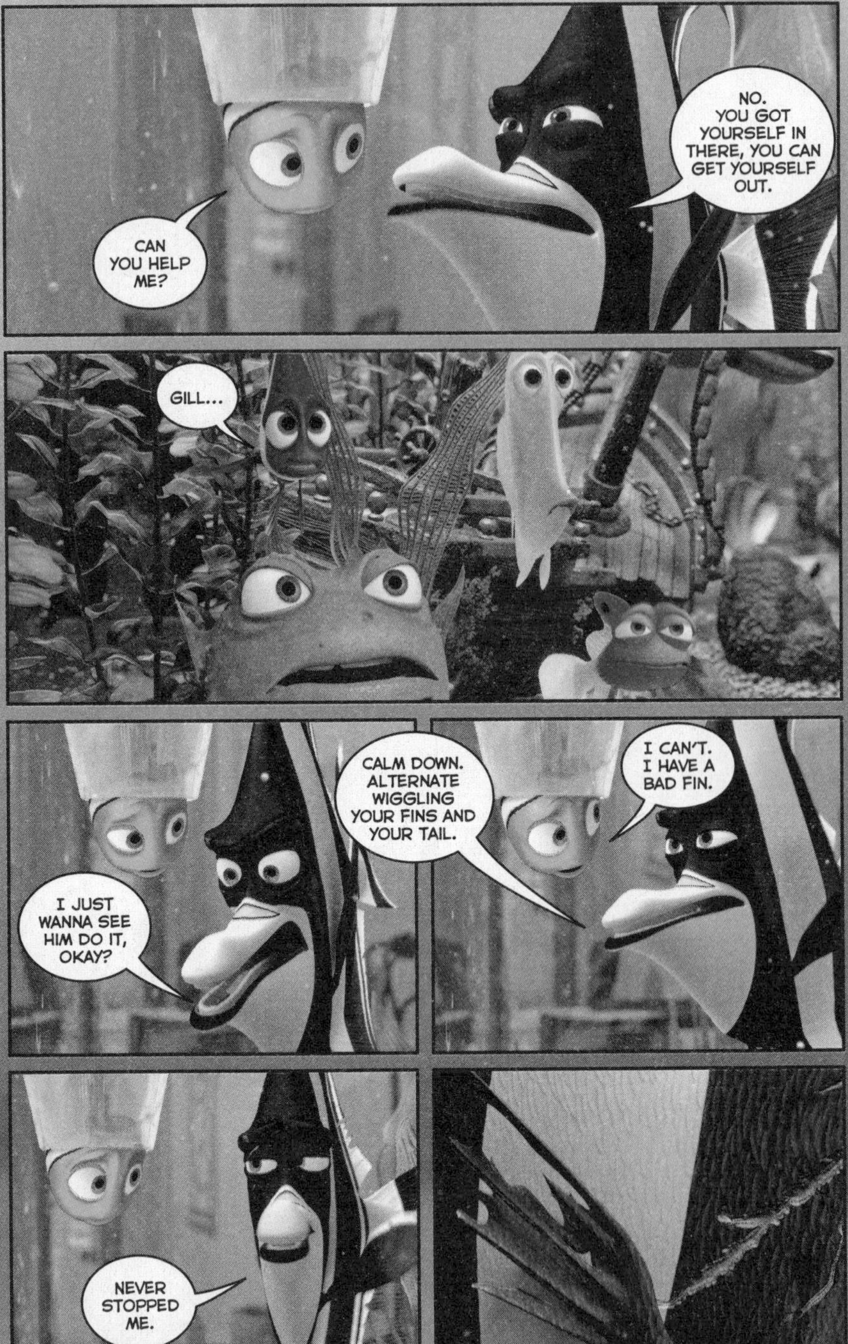
CAN YOU HELP ME?
NO. YOU GOT YOURSELF IN THERE, YOU CAN GET YOURSELF OUT.
GILL...
I JUST WANNA SEE HIM DO IT, OKAY?
CALM DOWN. ALTERNATE WIGGLING YOUR FINS AND YOUR TAIL.
I CAN'T. I HAVE A BAD FIN.
NEVER STOPPED ME.

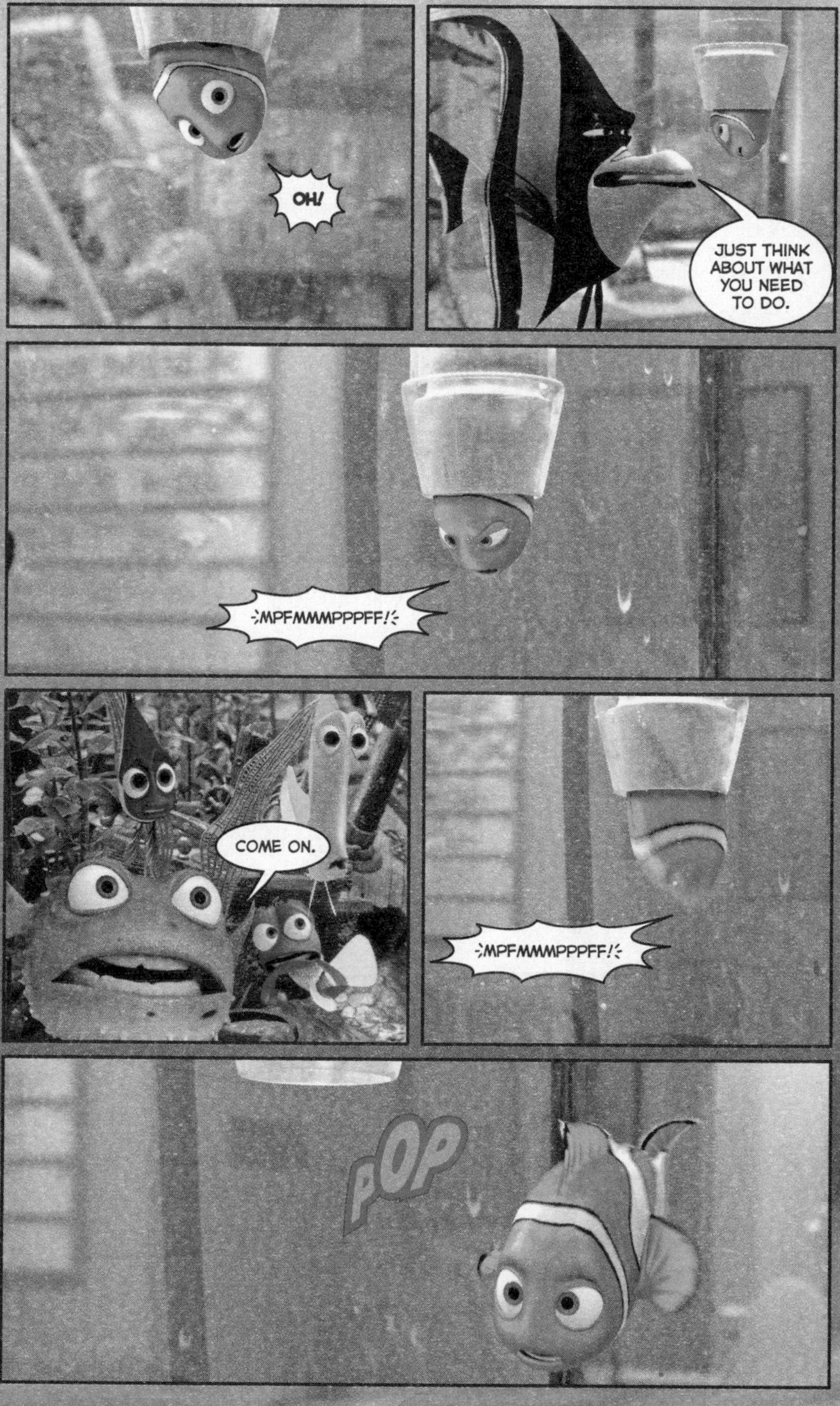
OH!
JUST THINK ABOUT WHAT YOU NEED TO DO.
MPFMMMPPPFF!
COME ON.
MPFMMMPPPFF!
POP

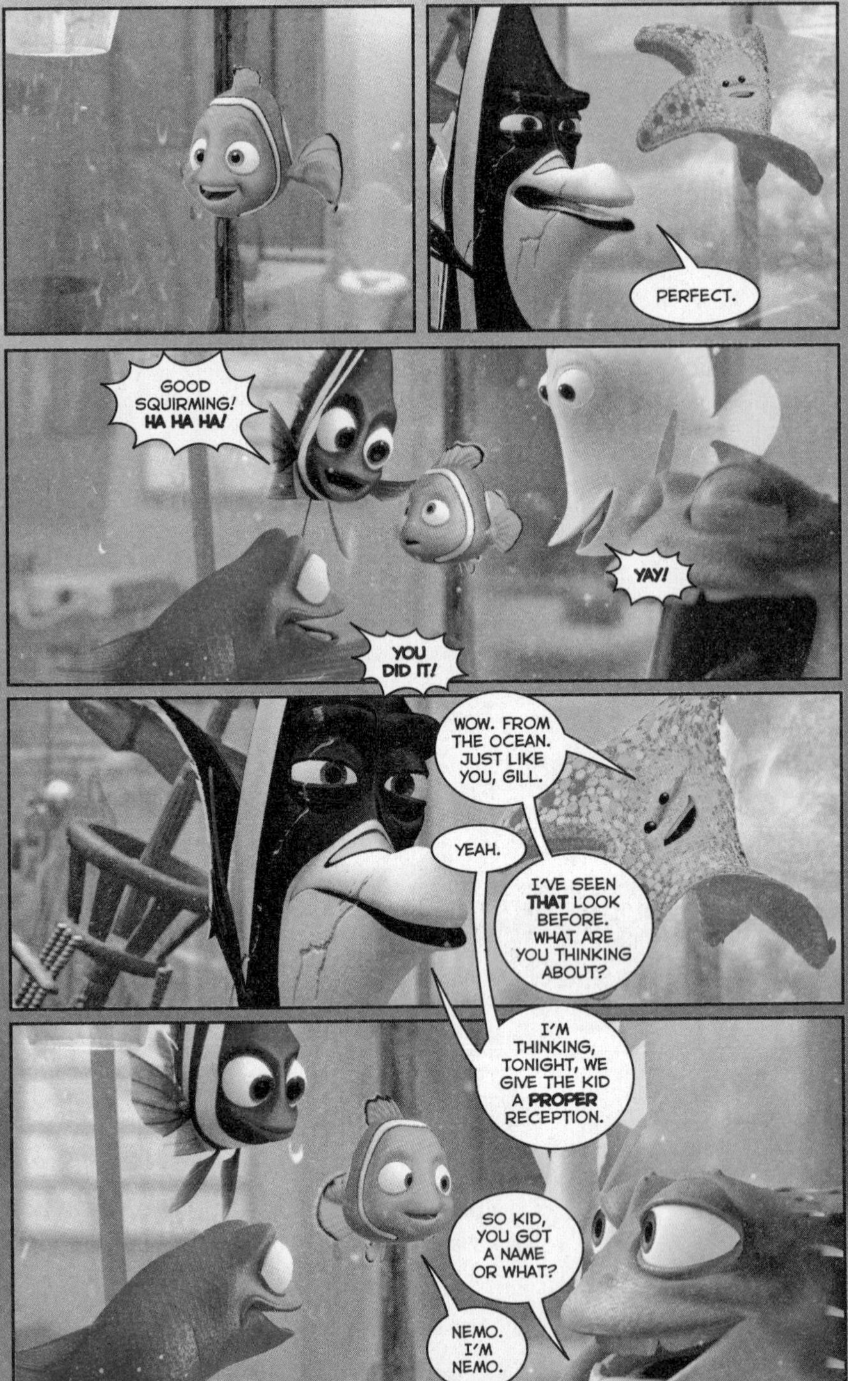
PERFECT.
GOOD SQUIRMING! HA HA HA!
YAY!
YOU DID IT!
WOW. FROM THE OCEAN. JUST LIKE YOU, GILL.
YEAH.
I'VE SEEN THAT LOOK BEFORE. WHAT ARE YOU THINKING ABOUT?
I'M THINKING, TONIGHT, WE GIVE THE KID A PROPER RECEPTION.
SO KID, YOU GOT A NAME OR WHAT?
NEMO. I'M NEMO.

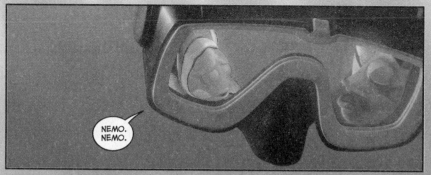

NEMO.
NEMO.

ARE YOU GONNA EAT THAT?

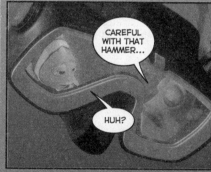

CAREFUL WITH THAT HAMMER...

HUH?

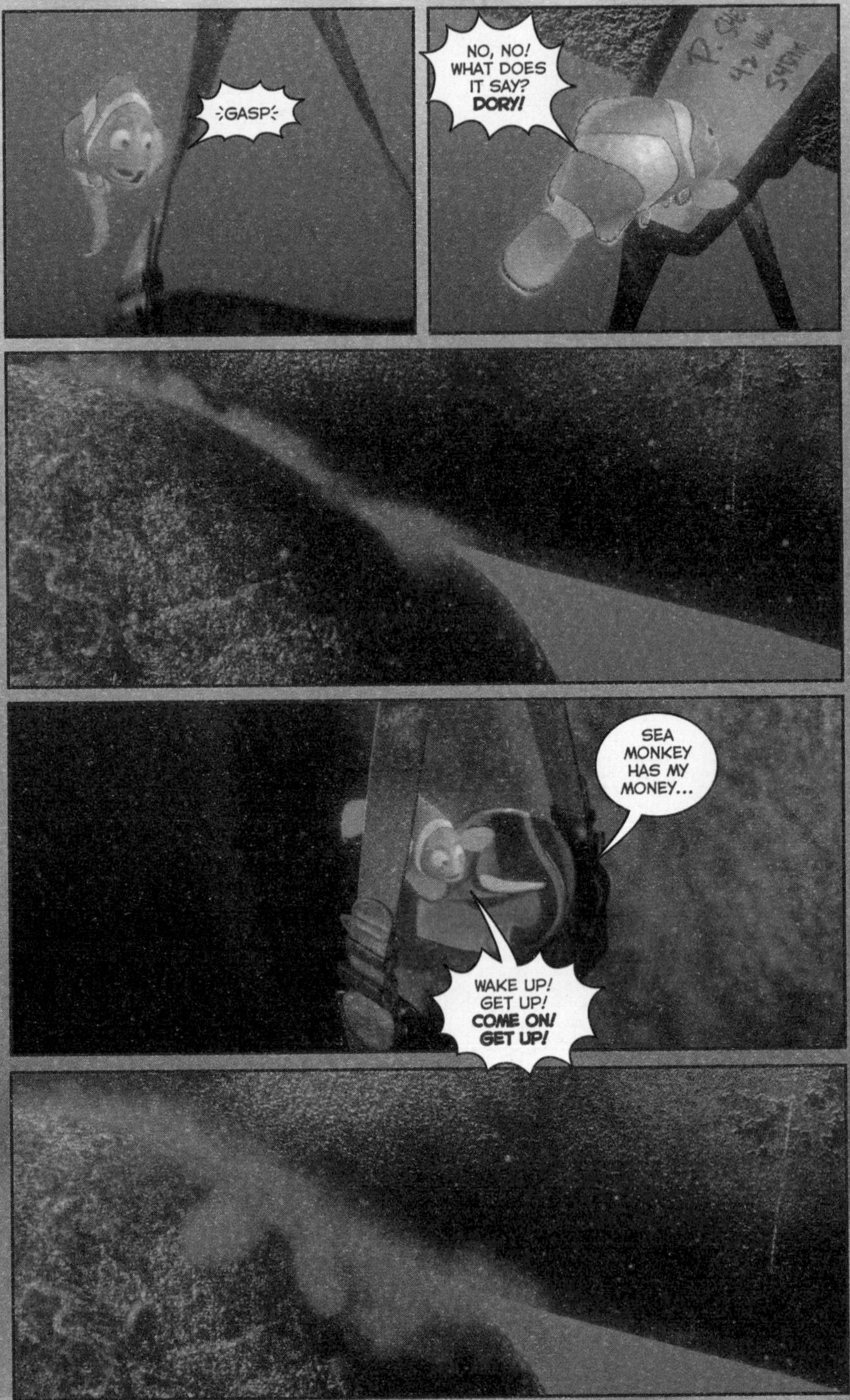

GASP
NO, NO! WHAT DOES IT SAY? DORY!
SEA MONKEY HAS MY MONEY...
WAKE UP! GET UP! COME ON! GET UP!

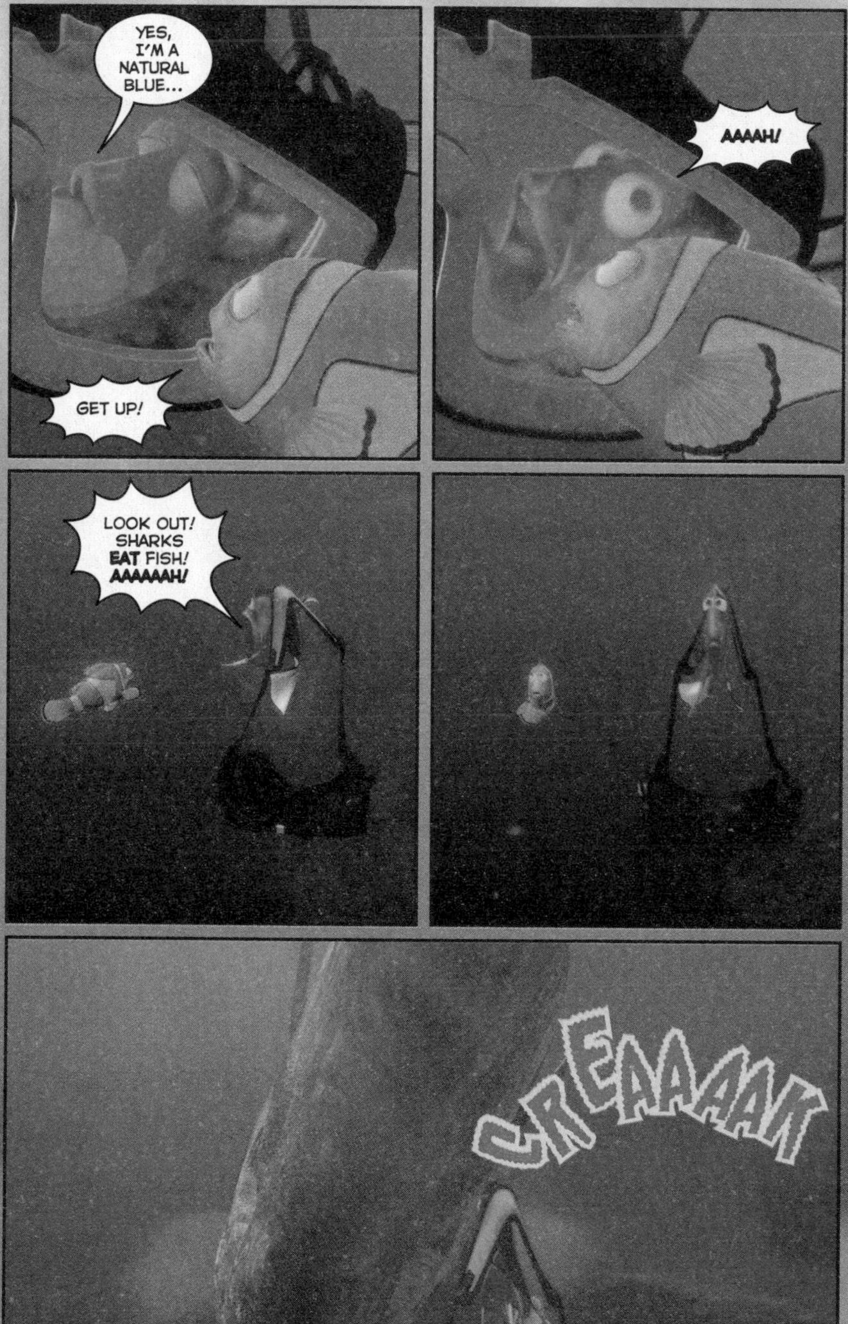
YES, I'M A NATURAL BLUE...
GET UP!
AAAAH!
LOOK OUT! SHARKS EAT FISH! AAAAAAH!
CREAAAAK

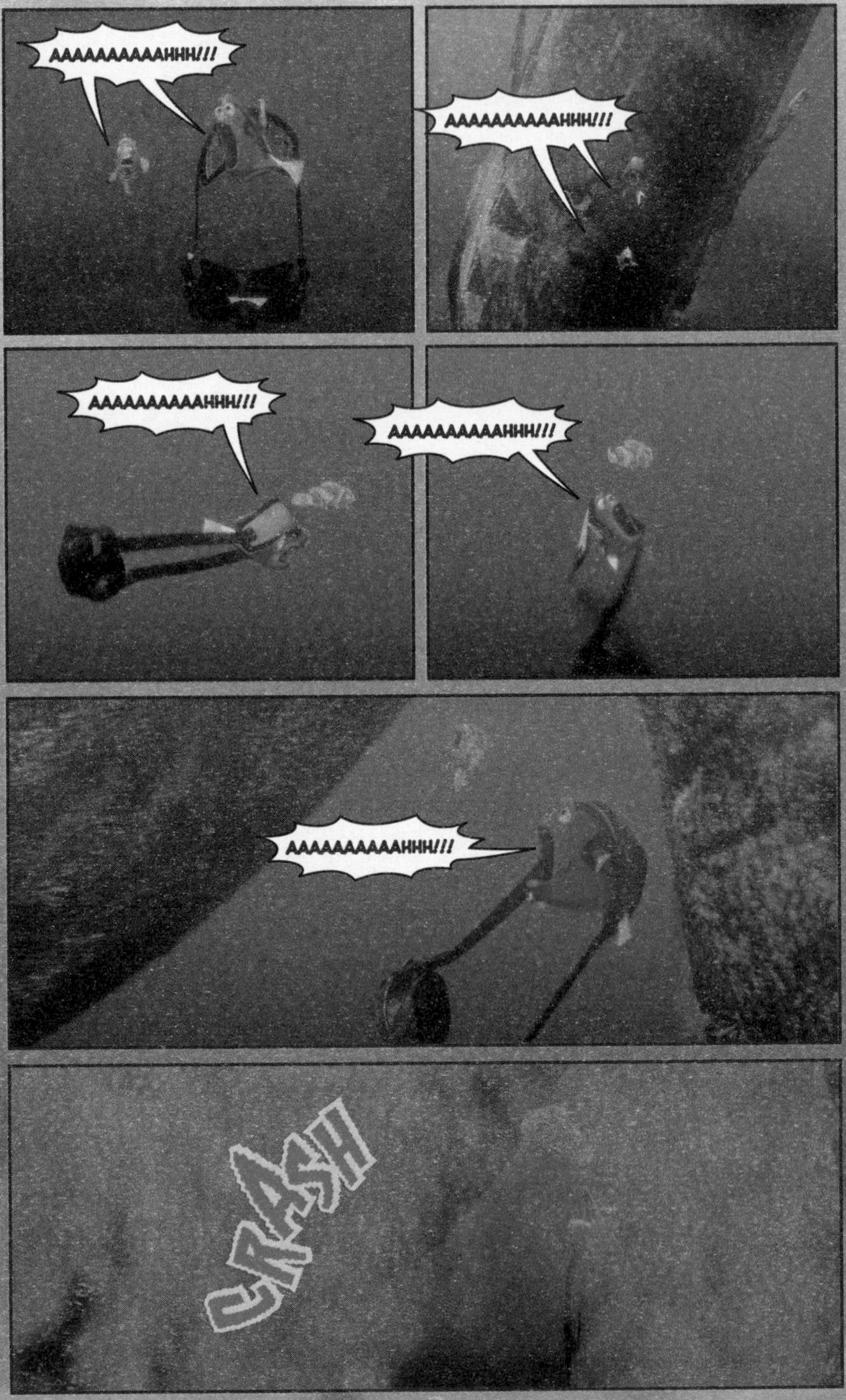
AAAAAAAAAAAHHH!!!
AAAAAAAAAAAHHH!!!
AAAAAAAAAAAHHH!!!
AAAAAAAAAAAHHH!!!
AAAAAAAAAAAHHH!!!
CRASH

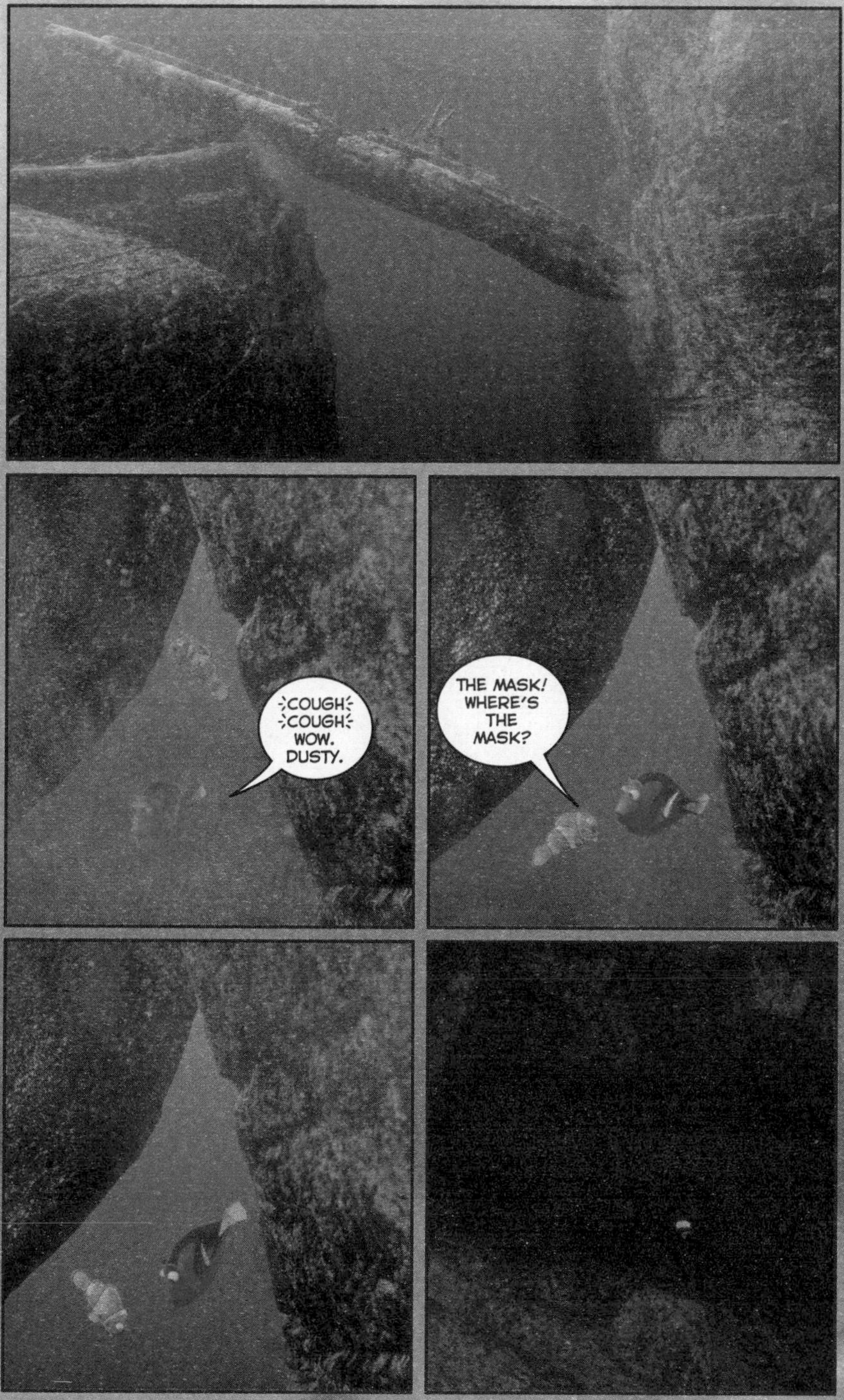
COUGH COUGH WOW. DUSTY.
THE MASK! WHERE'S THE MASK?

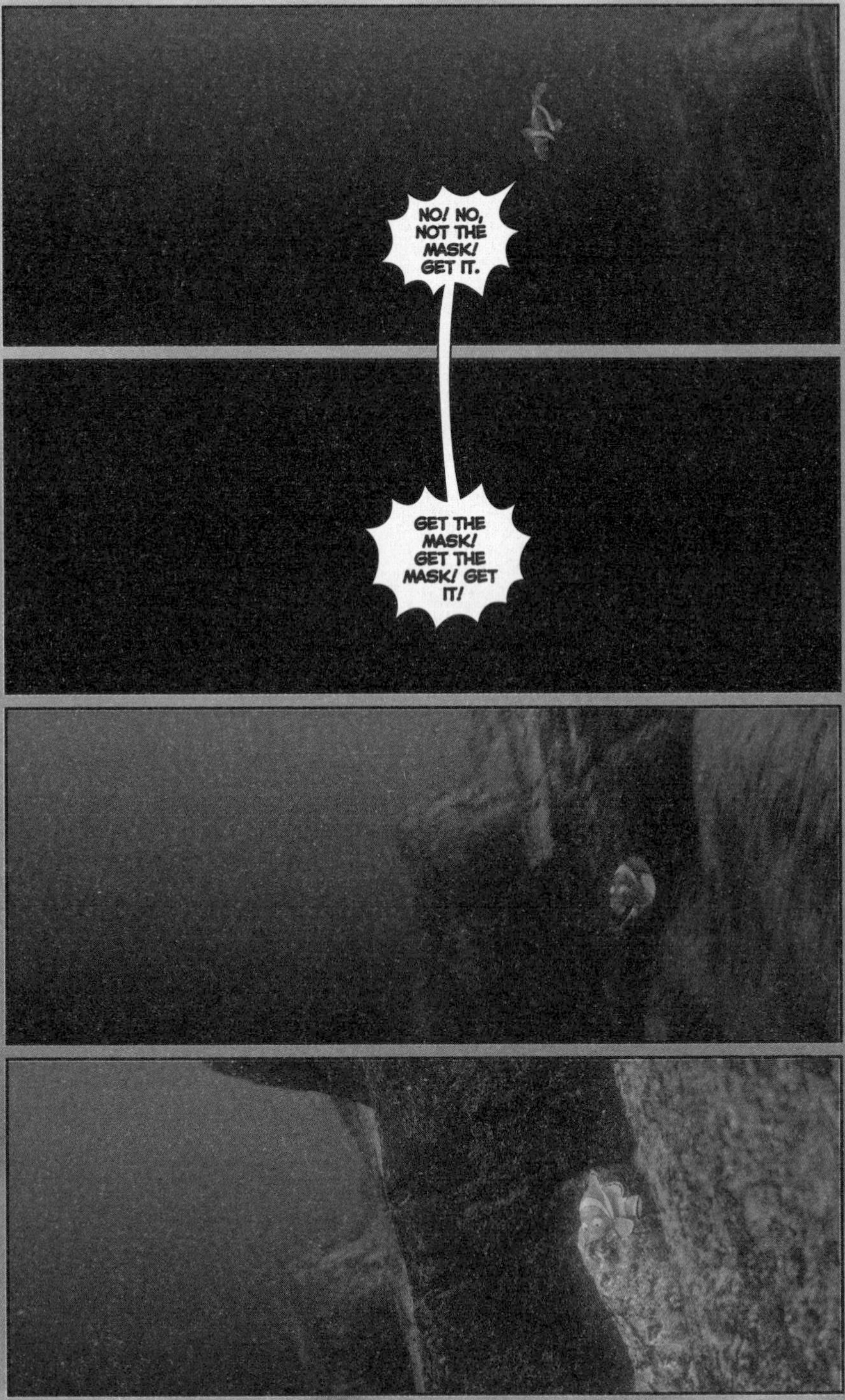
NO! NO, NOT THE MASK! GET IT.
GET THE MASK! GET THE MASK! GET IT!

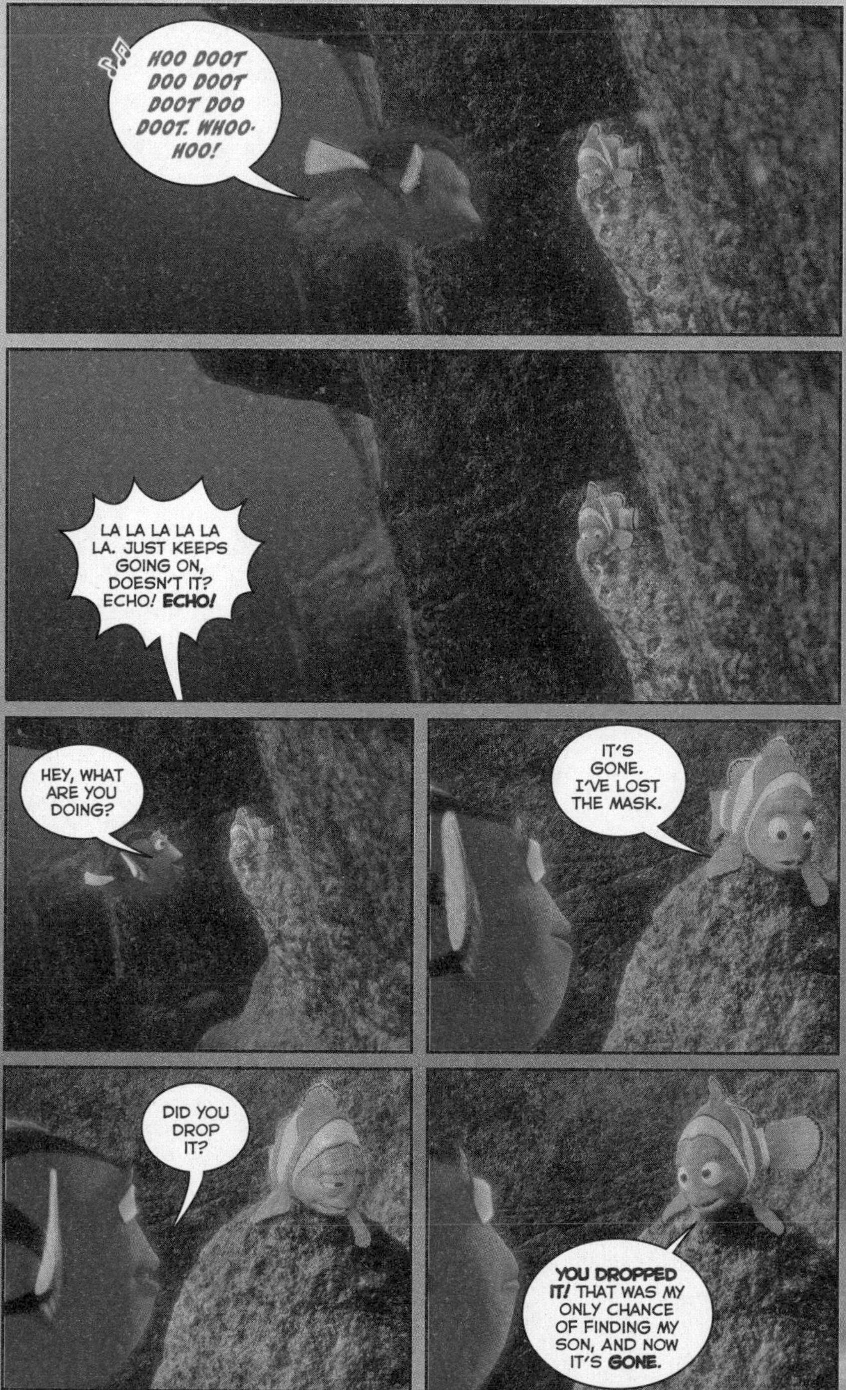
HOO DOOT DOO DOOT DOOT DOO DOOT. WHOO-HOO!
LA LA LA LA LA LA. JUST KEEPS GOING ON, DOESN'T IT? ECHO! **ECHO!**
HEY, WHAT ARE YOU DOING?
IT'S GONE. I'VE LOST THE MASK.
DID YOU DROP IT?
YOU DROPPED IT! THAT WAS MY ONLY CHANCE OF FINDING MY SON, AND NOW IT'S **GONE**.

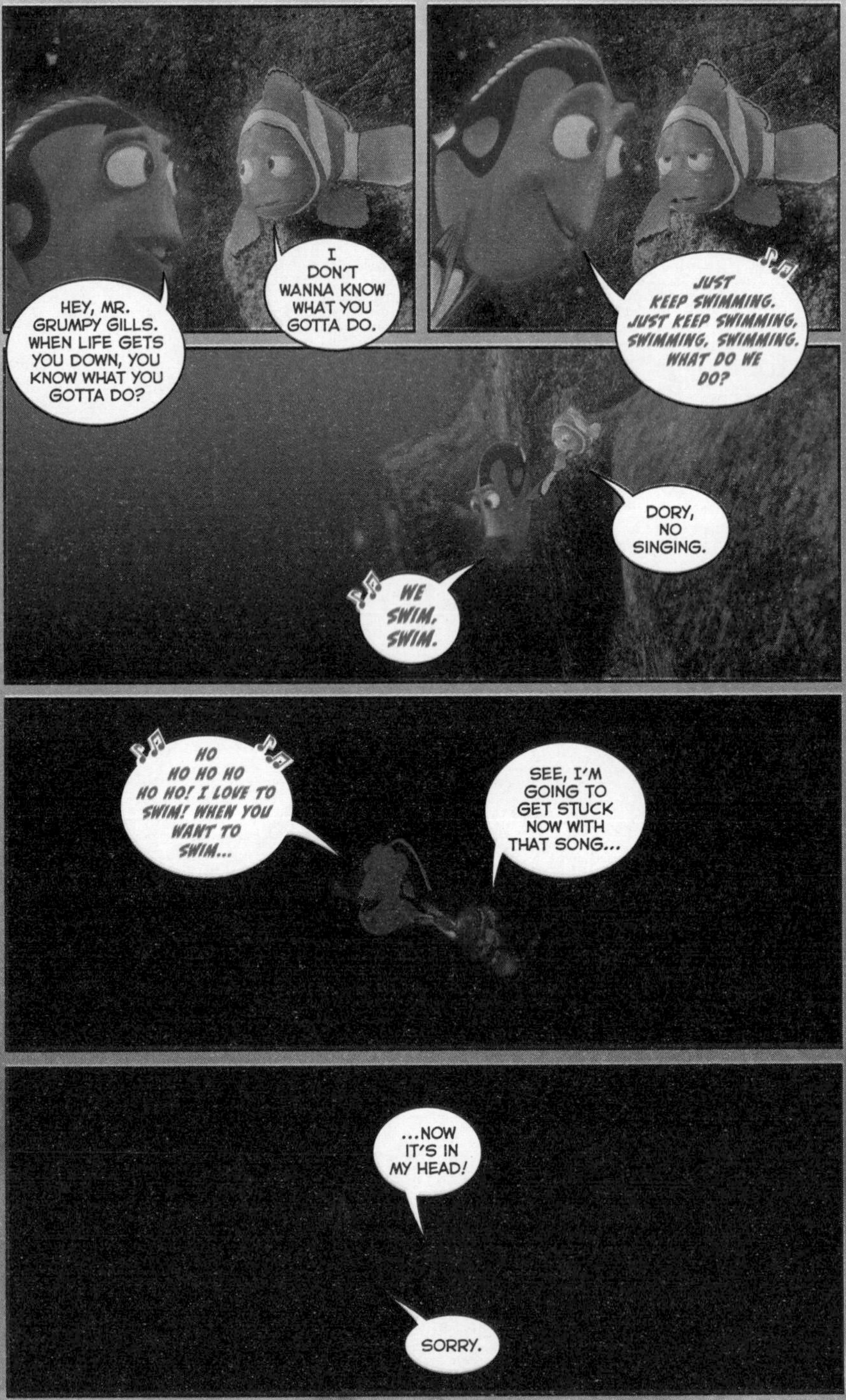
HEY, MR. GRUMPY GILLS. WHEN LIFE GETS YOU DOWN, YOU KNOW WHAT YOU GOTTA DO?
I DON'T WANNA KNOW WHAT YOU GOTTA DO.
JUST KEEP SWIMMING. JUST KEEP SWIMMING, SWIMMING, SWIMMING. WHAT DO WE DO?
DORY, NO SINGING.
WE SWIM, SWIM.
HO HO HO HO HO HO! I LOVE TO SWIM! WHEN YOU WANT TO SWIM...
SEE, I'M GOING TO GET STUCK NOW WITH THAT SONG...
...NOW IT'S IN MY HEAD!
SORRY.

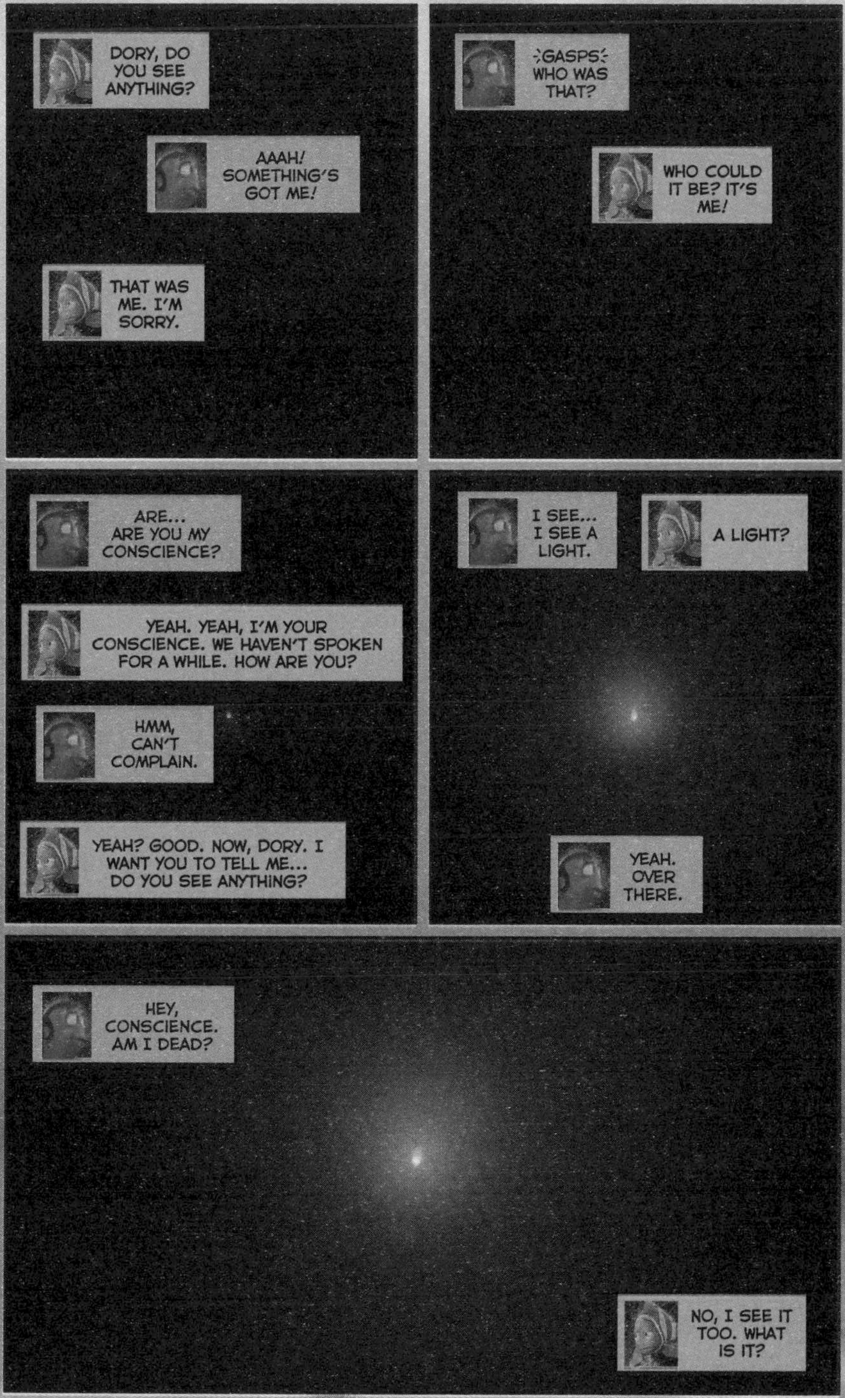
DORY, DO YOU SEE ANYTHING?
AAAH! SOMETHING'S GOT ME!
THAT WAS ME. I'M SORRY.
-GASPS- WHO WAS THAT?
WHO COULD IT BE? IT'S ME!
ARE... ARE YOU MY CONSCIENCE?
YEAH. YEAH, I'M YOUR CONSCIENCE. WE HAVEN'T SPOKEN FOR A WHILE. HOW ARE YOU?
HMM, CAN'T COMPLAIN.
YEAH? GOOD. NOW, DORY. I WANT YOU TO TELL ME... DO YOU SEE ANYTHING?
I SEE... I SEE A LIGHT.
A LIGHT?
YEAH. OVER THERE.
HEY, CONSCIENCE. AM I DEAD?
NO, I SEE IT TOO. WHAT IS IT?

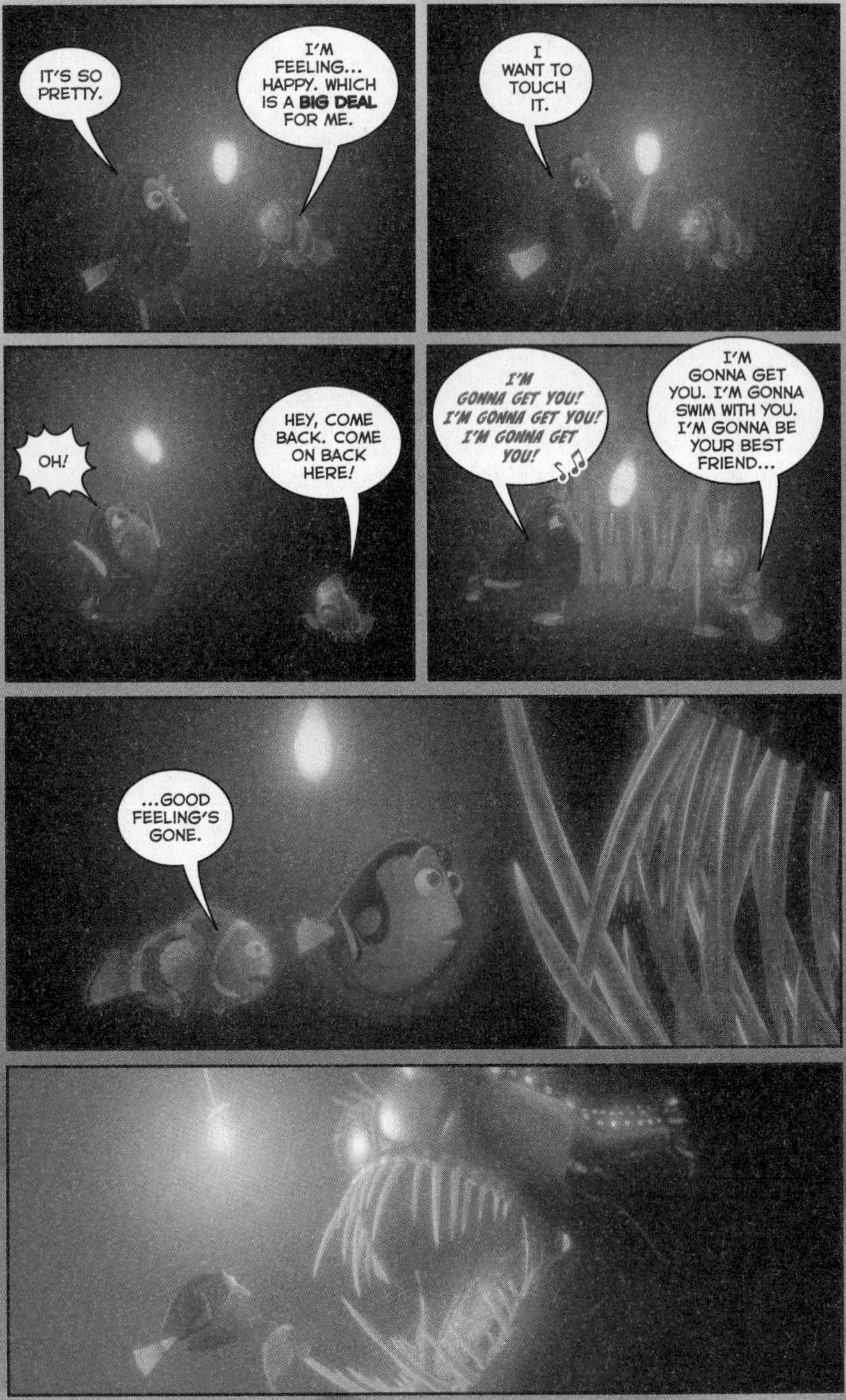
IT'S SO PRETTY.
I'M FEELING... HAPPY. WHICH IS A BIG DEAL FOR ME.
I WANT TO TOUCH IT.
OH!
HEY, COME BACK. COME ON BACK HERE!
I'M GONNA GET YOU! I'M GONNA GET YOU! I'M GONNA GET YOU!
I'M GONNA GET YOU. I'M GONNA SWIM WITH YOU. I'M GONNA BE YOUR BEST FRIEND...
...GOOD FEELING'S GONE.

AAAAAAAAAAHHH!!!

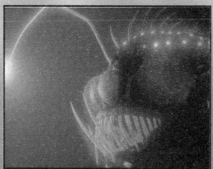

I CAN'T SEE! I DON'T KNOW WHERE I'M GOING!

AAH!

THE MASK!

WHAT MASK?

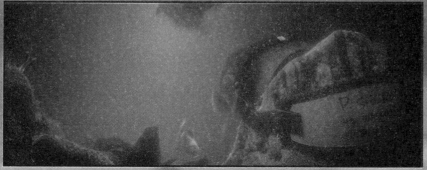

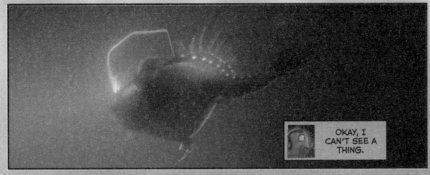

OKAY, I CAN'T SEE A THING.

OH, GEE!

HEY, LOOK! A MASK!

READ IT!

I'M SORRY, BUT IF YOU COULD JUST BRING IT A LITTLE CLOSER, I KIND OF NEED THE LIGHT.

THAT'S GREAT, KEEP IT RIGHT THERE.

OKAY, OKAY. MR. BOSSY.

JUST READ IT!

UH, 'P.' OKAY, P.

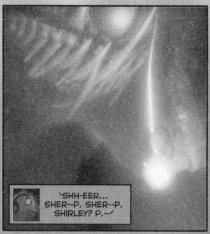

'SHH-EER... SHER--P. SHER--P. SHIRLEY? P.--'

OH! THE FIRST LINE'S 'P. SHERMAN!'

DON'T EAT ME! DON'T EAT ME! AAAAH!

P. SHERMAN DOESN'T MAKE ANY SENSE!

OKAY, SECOND LINE. '42.'

LIGHT, PLEASE.

'WALLA--WALLA-- WALLA-BEEE...'

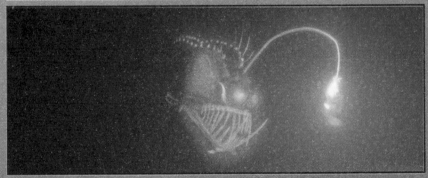

CHOMP

WAAH! WAAAH! WAAAAH!

THE SECOND LINE'S '42 WALLABY WAY!'

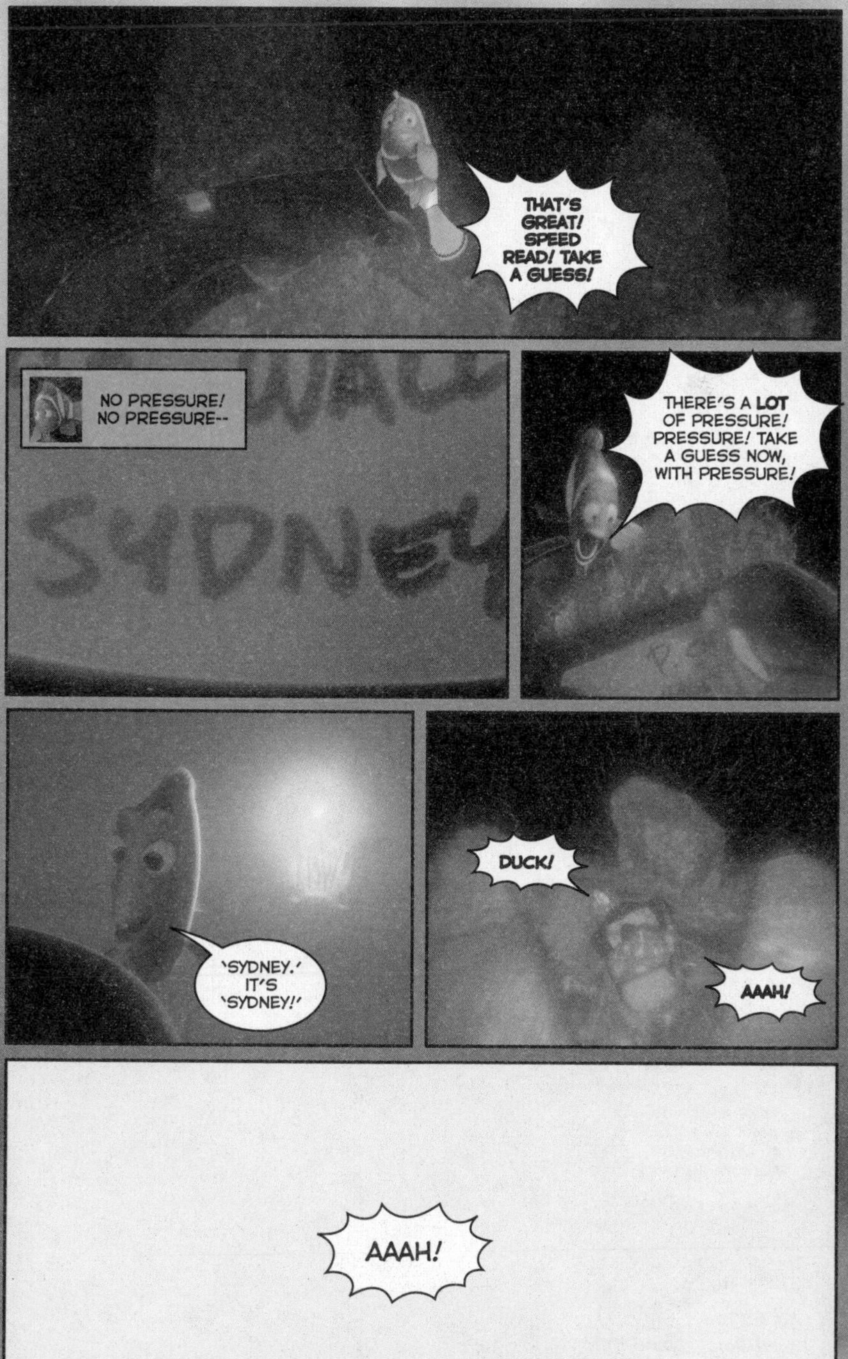
THAT'S GREAT! SPEED READ! TAKE A GUESS!
NO PRESSURE! NO PRESSURE--
SYDNEY
THERE'S A **LOT** OF PRESSURE! PRESSURE! TAKE A GUESS NOW, WITH PRESSURE!
'SYDNEY.' IT'S 'SYDNEY!'
DUCK!
AAAH!
AAAH!

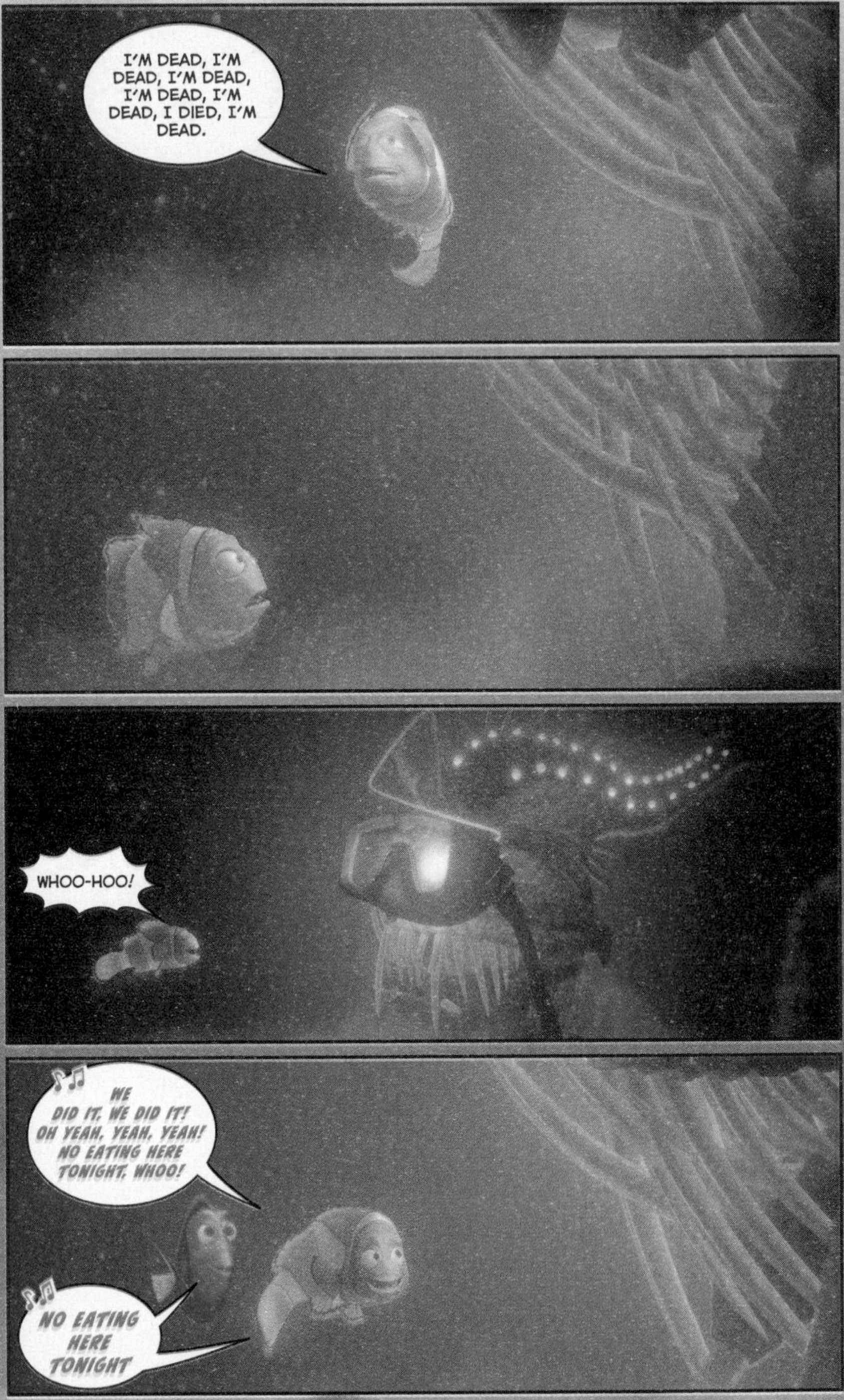
I'M DEAD, I'M DEAD, I'M DEAD, I'M DEAD, I'M DEAD, I DIED, I'M DEAD.
WHOO-HOO!
WE DID IT, WE DID IT! OH YEAH, YEAH, YEAH! NO EATING HERE TONIGHT, WHOO!
NO EATING HERE TONIGHT

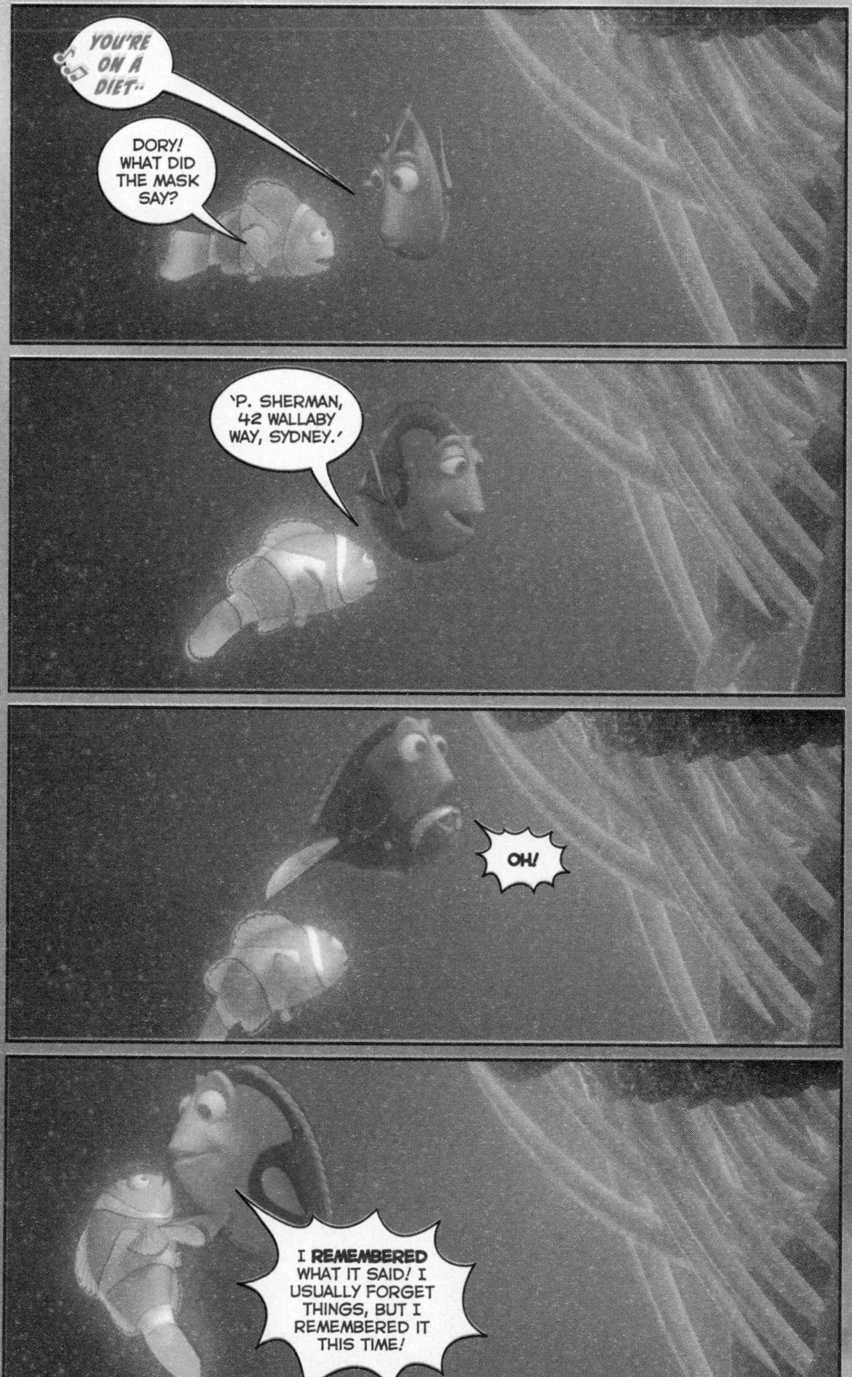
YOU'RE ON A DIET..
DORY! WHAT DID THE MASK SAY?
'P. SHERMAN, 42 WALLABY WAY, SYDNEY.'
OH!
I REMEMBERED WHAT IT SAID! I USUALLY FORGET THINGS, BUT I REMEMBERED IT THIS TIME!

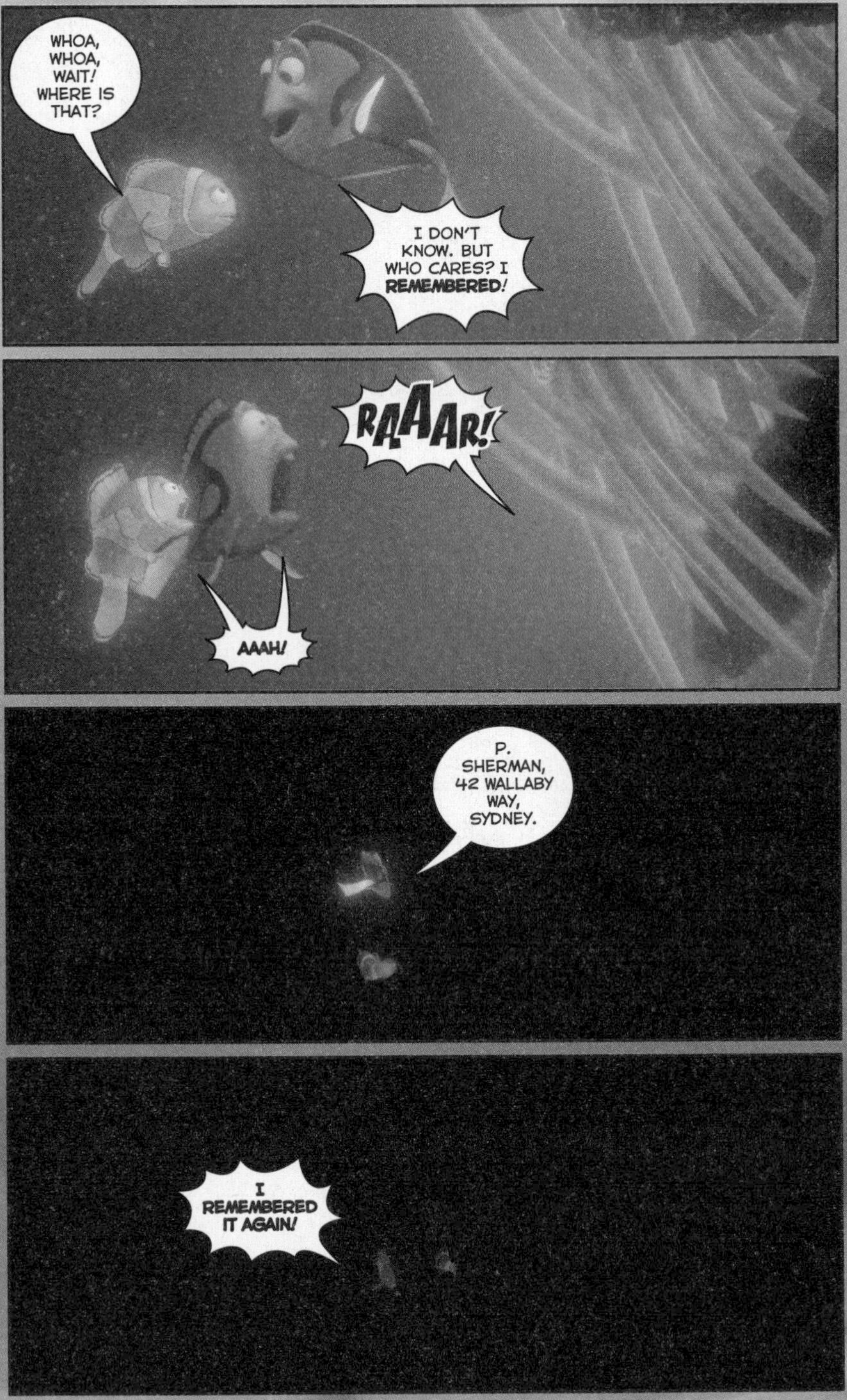
WHOA, WHOA, WAIT! WHERE IS THAT?
I DON'T KNOW. BUT WHO CARES? I REMEMBERED!
RAAAR!
AAAH!
P. SHERMAN, 42 WALLABY WAY, SYDNEY.
I REMEMBERED IT AGAIN!

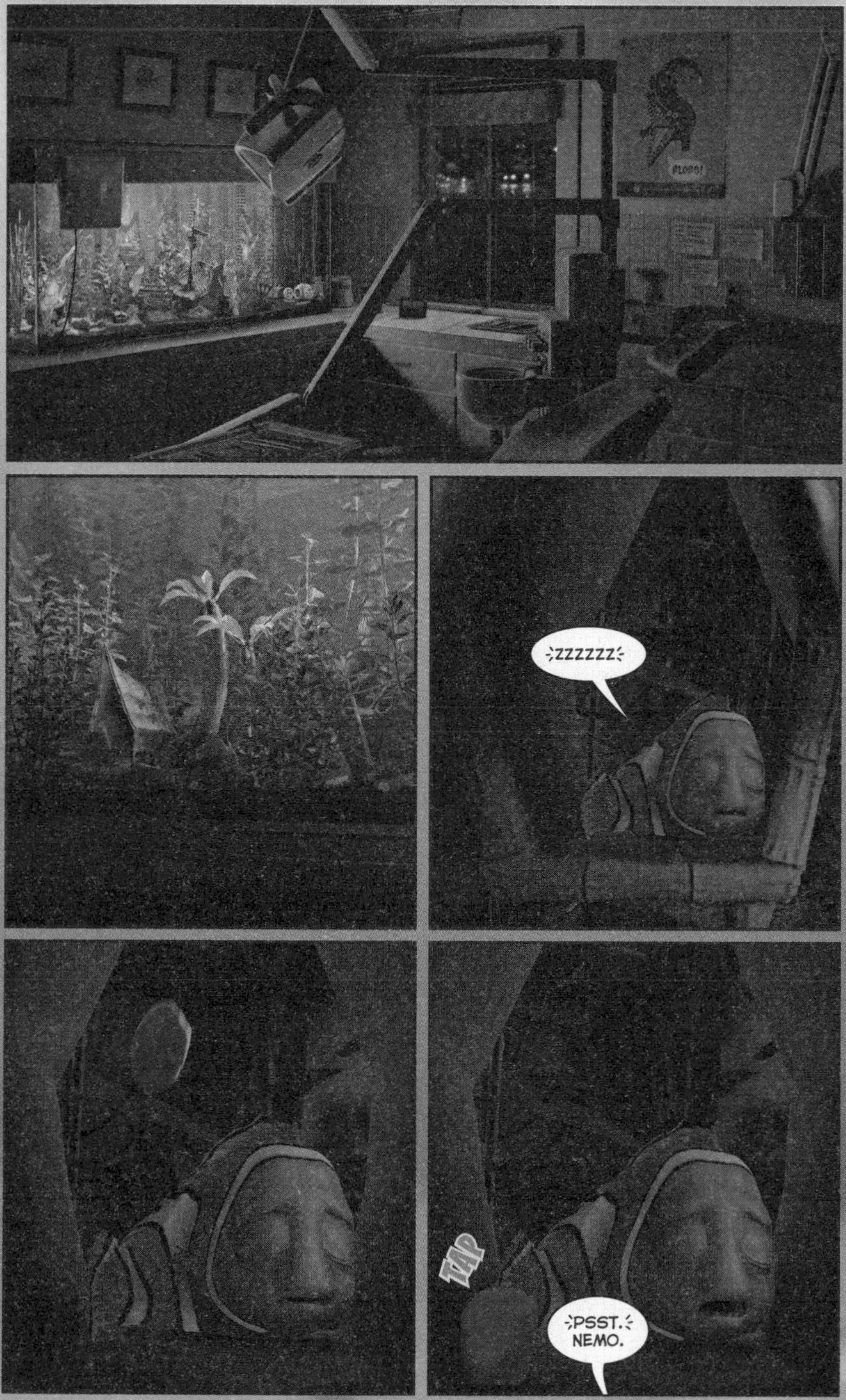
ZZZZZZ
ZAP
PSST. NEMO.

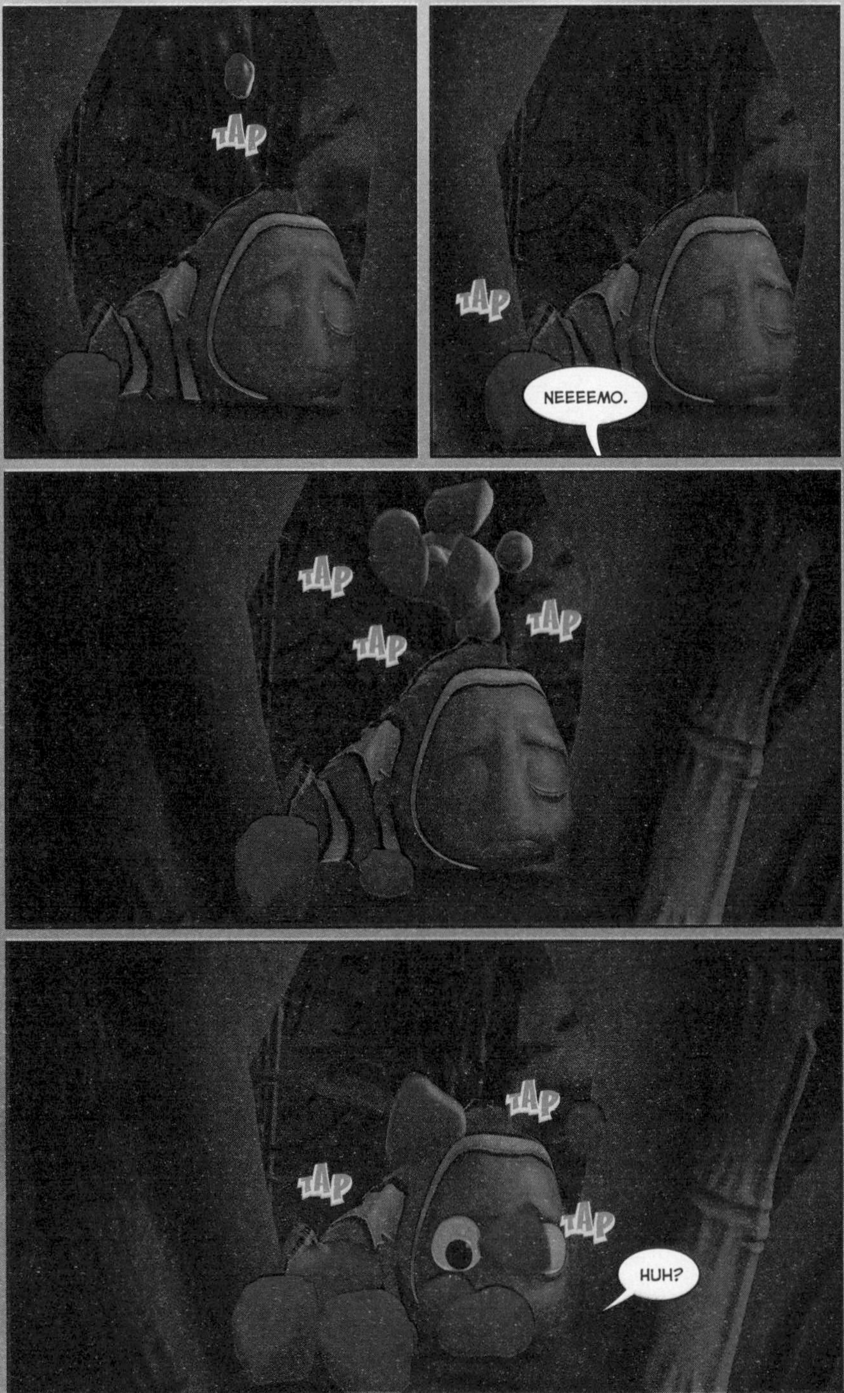
TAP
TAP
NEEEEMO.
TAP
TAP
TAP
TAP
TAP
TAP
HUH?

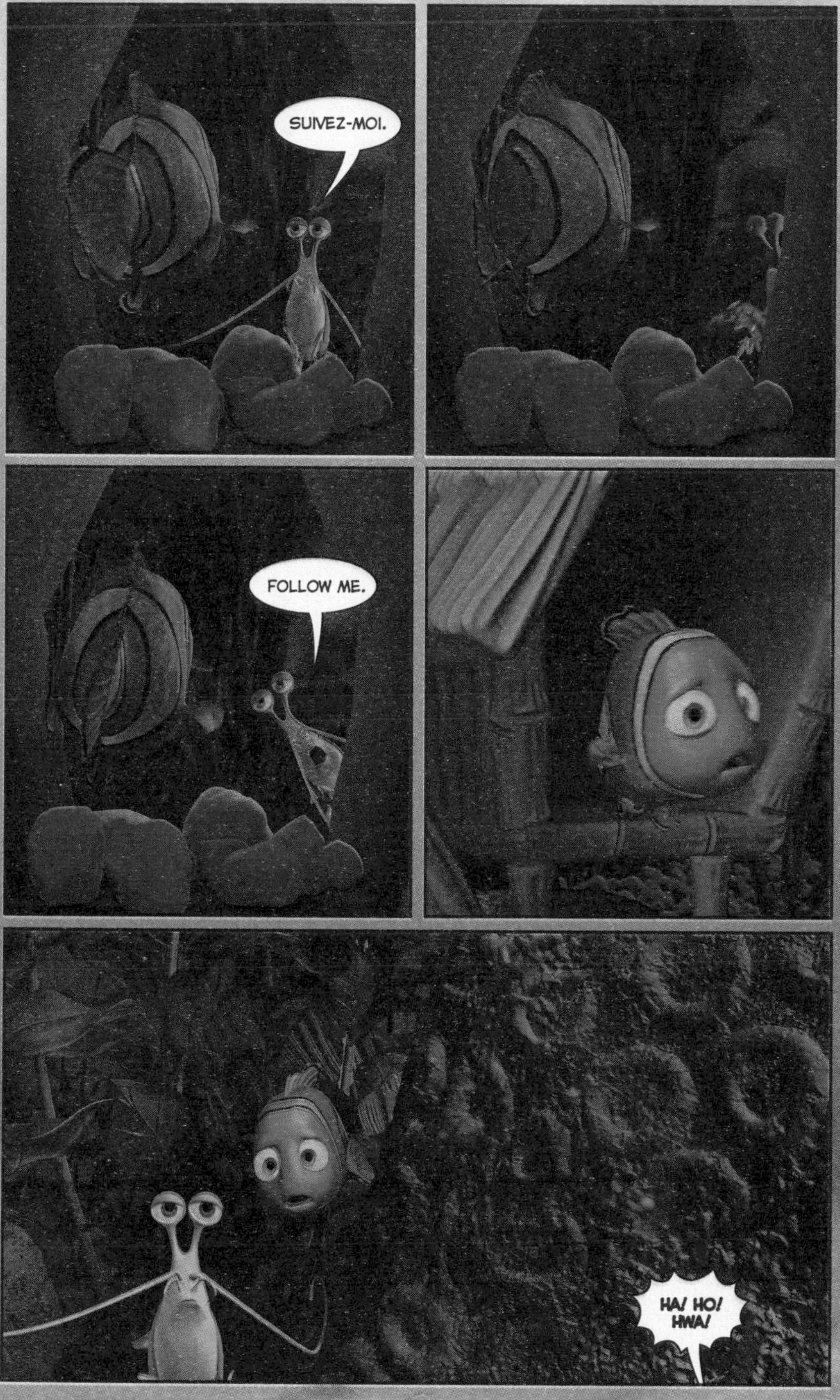
SUIVEZ-MOI.
FOLLOW ME.
HA! HO! HWA!

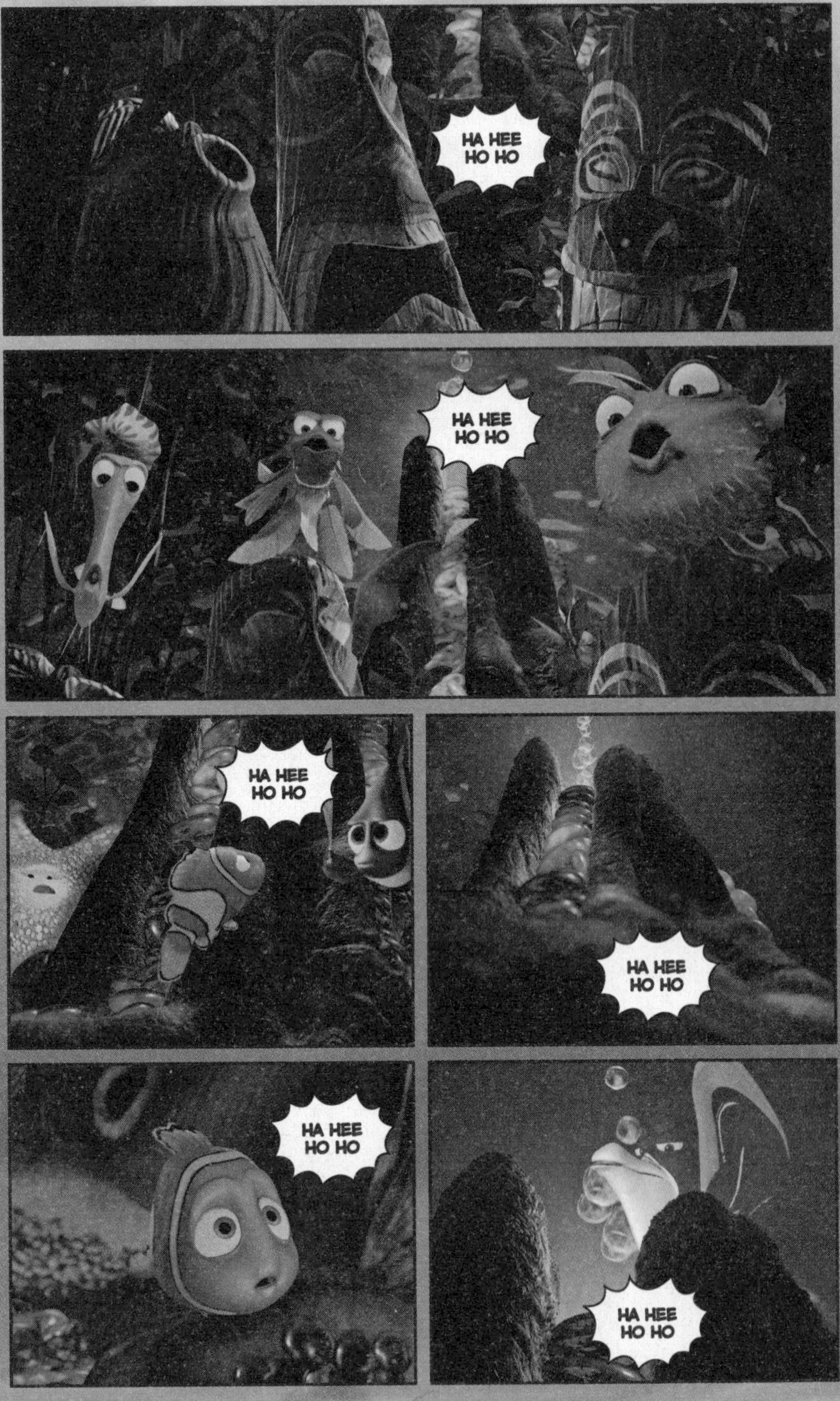
HA HEE HO HO
HA HEE HO HO
HA HEE HO HO
HA HEE HO HO
HA HEE HO HO
HA HEE HO HO

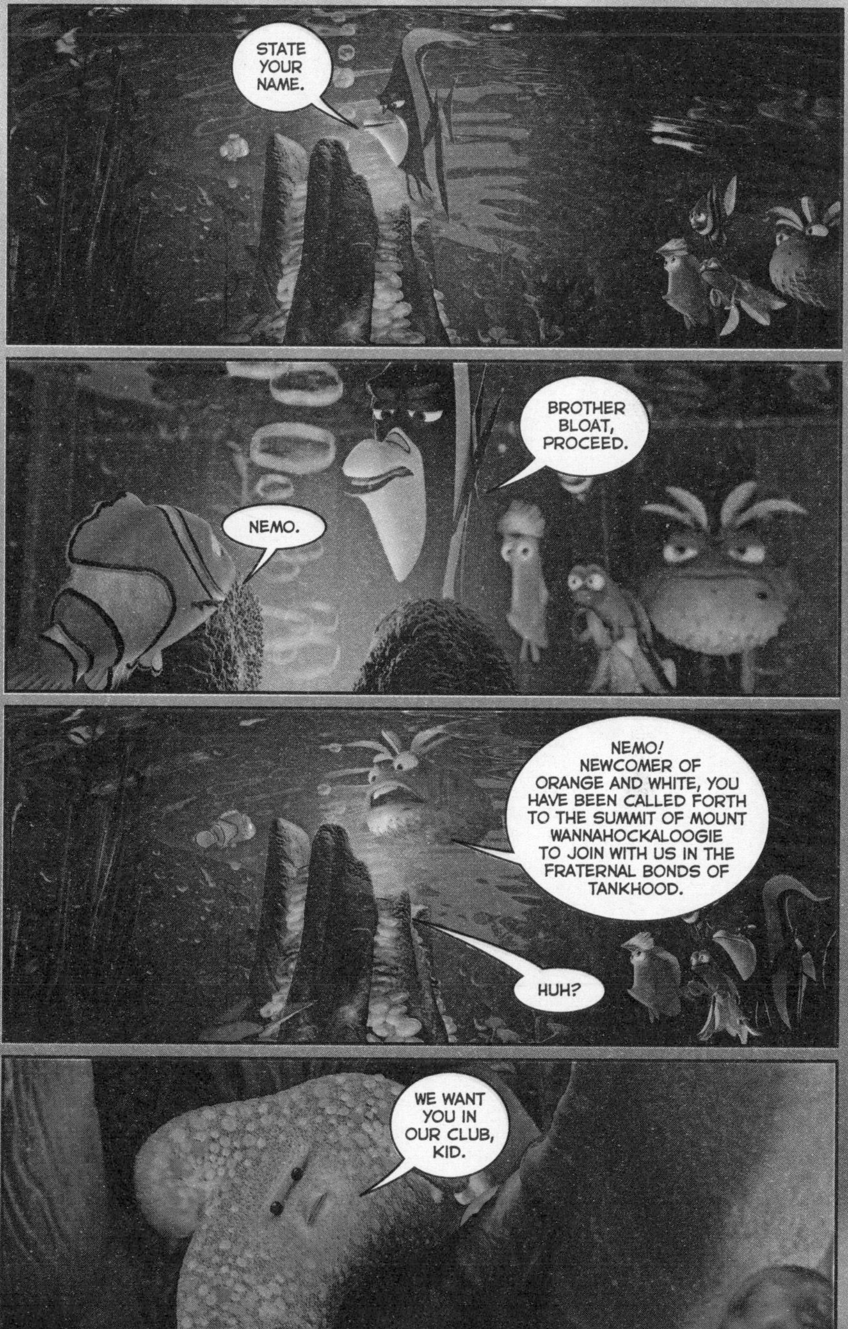
STATE YOUR NAME.
NEMO.
BROTHER BLOAT, PROCEED.
NEMO! NEWCOMER OF ORANGE AND WHITE, YOU HAVE BEEN CALLED FORTH TO THE SUMMIT OF MOUNT WANNAHOCKALOOGIE TO JOIN WITH US IN THE FRATERNAL BONDS OF TANKHOOD.
HUH?
WE WANT YOU IN OUR CLUB, KID.

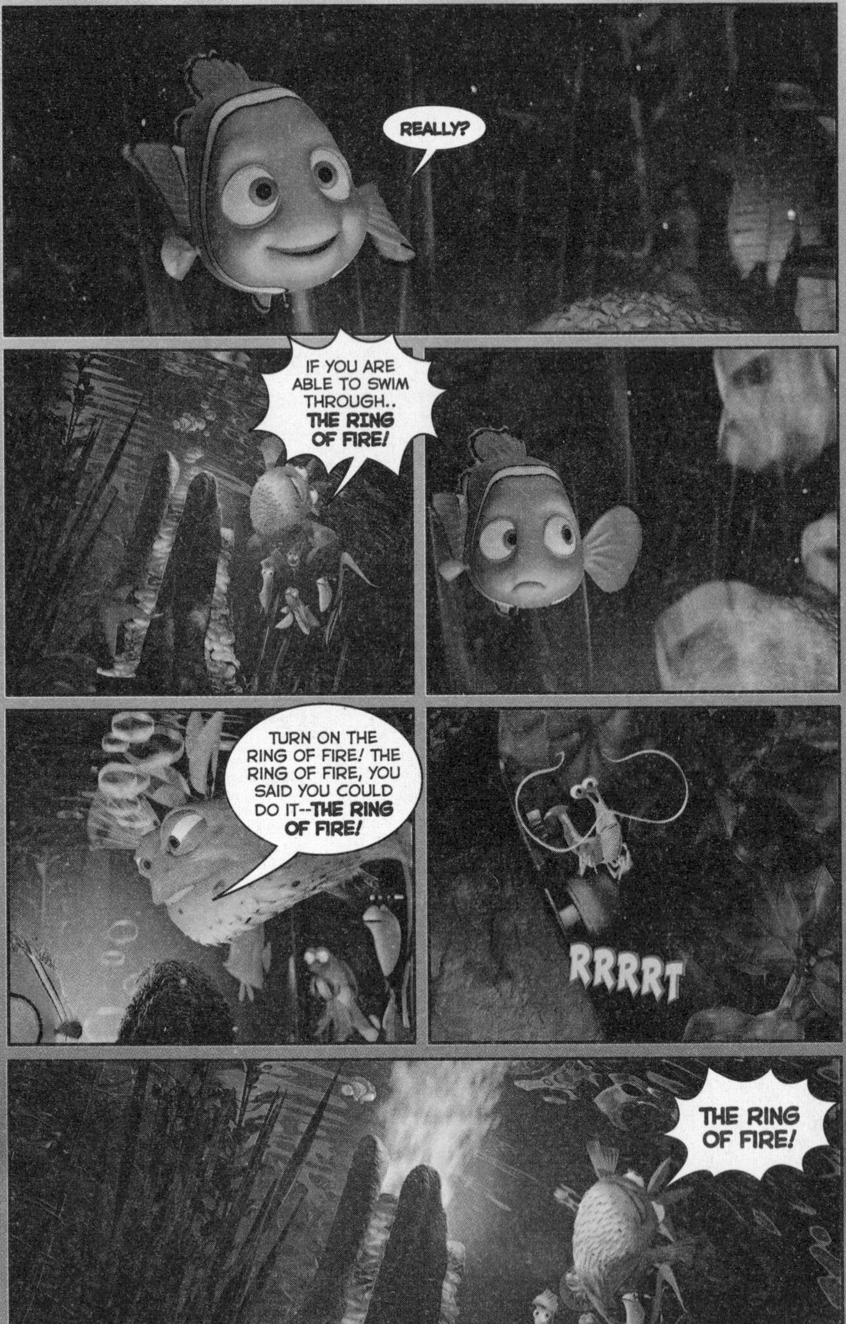
REALLY?
IF YOU ARE ABLE TO SWIM THROUGH.. THE RING OF FIRE!
TURN ON THE RING OF FIRE! THE RING OF FIRE, YOU SAID YOU COULD DO IT--THE RING OF FIRE!
RRRRT
THE RING OF FIRE!

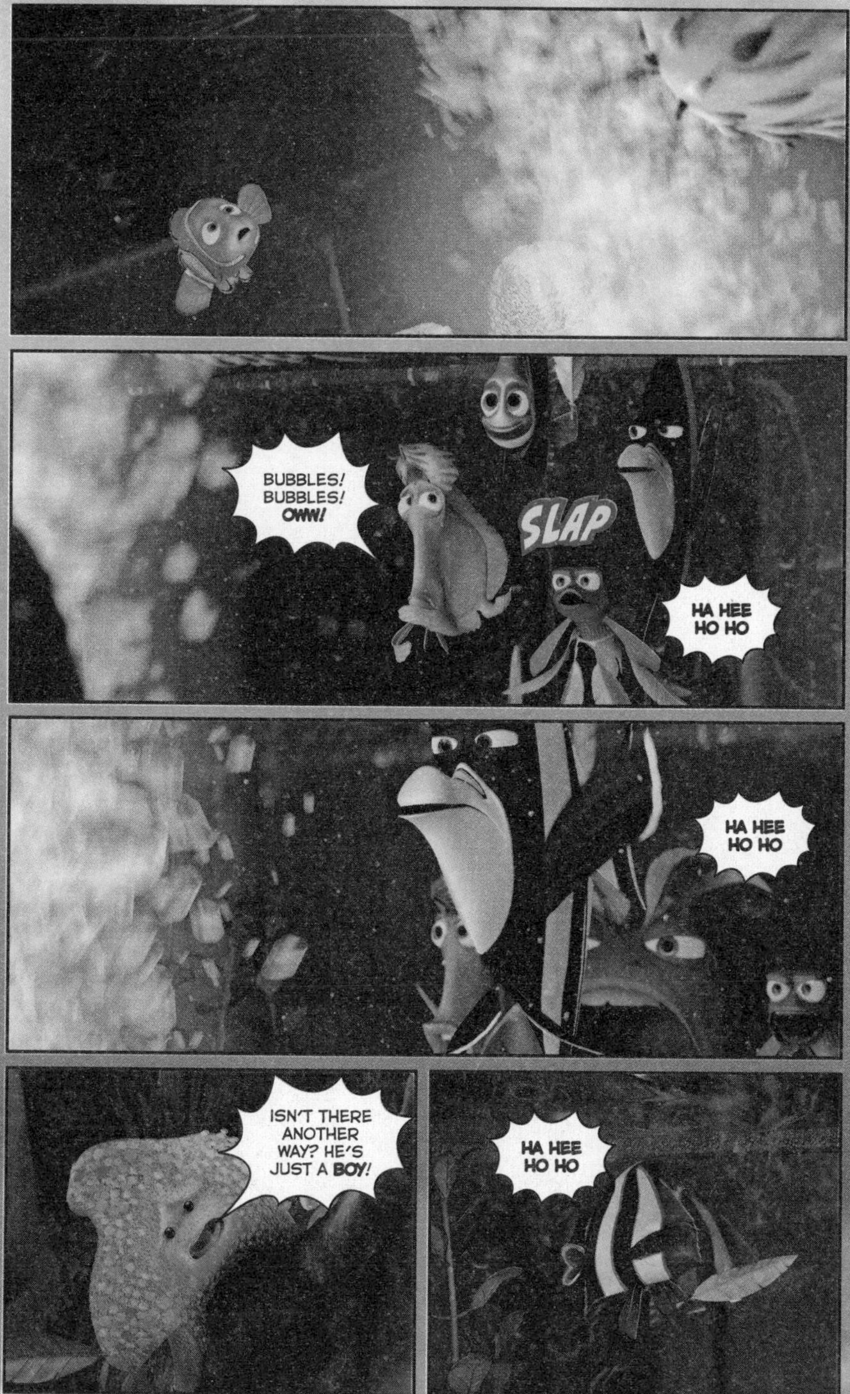
BUBBLES! BUBBLES! OWW!
SLAP
HA HEE HO HO
HA HEE HO HO
ISN'T THERE ANOTHER WAY? HE'S JUST A BOY!
HA HEE HO HO

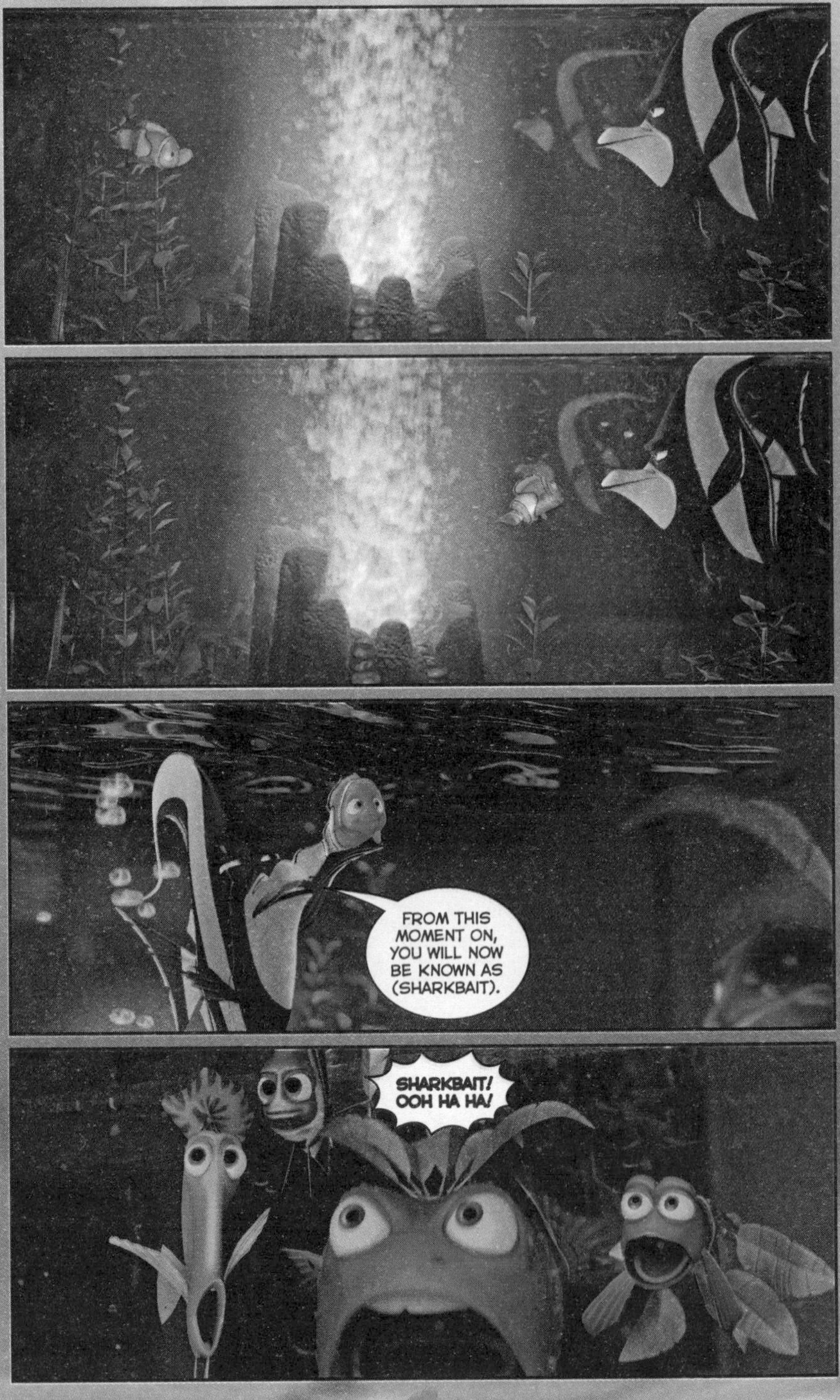
FROM THIS MOMENT ON, YOU WILL NOW BE KNOWN AS (SHARKBAIT).
SHARKBAIT! OOH HA HA!

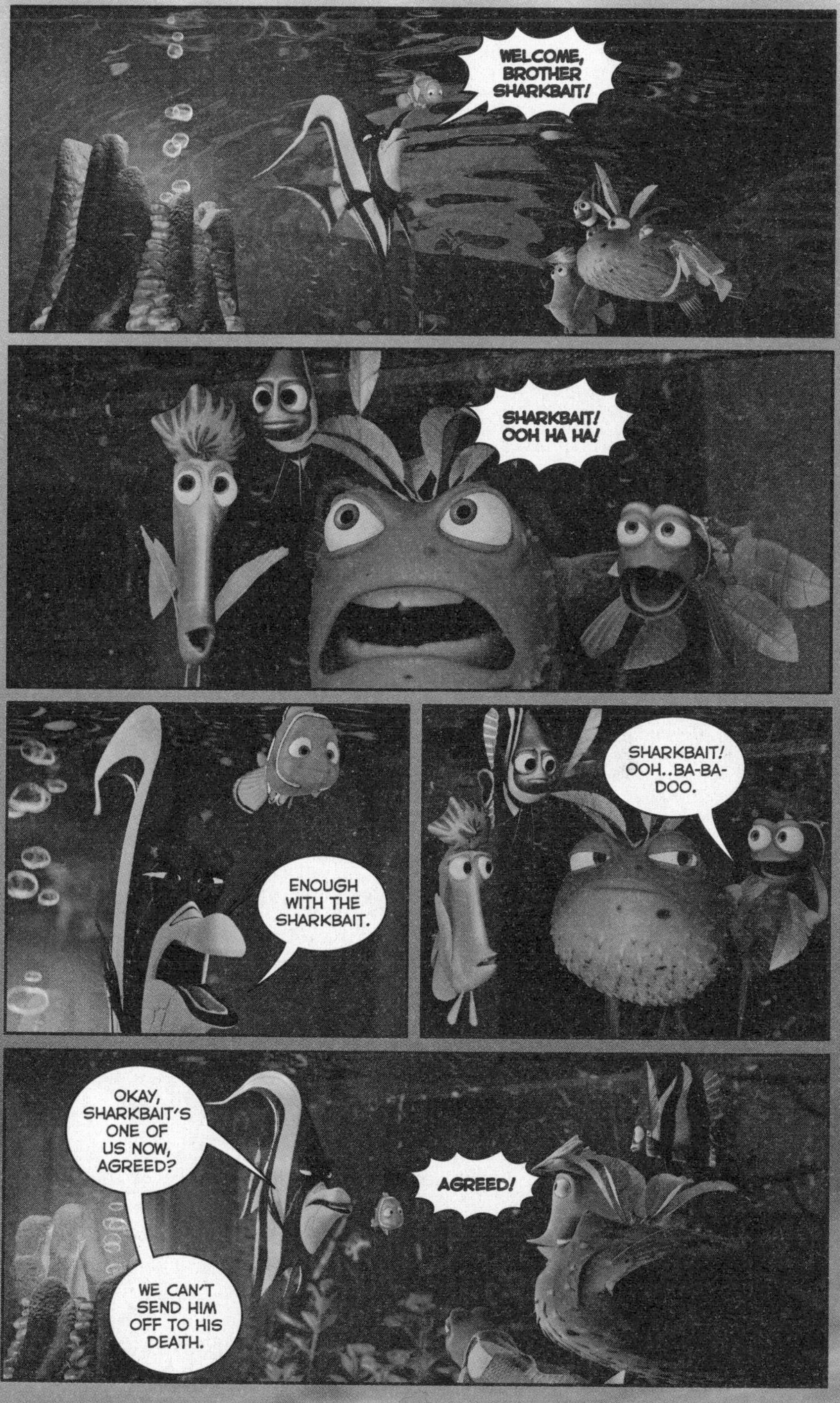
WELCOME, BROTHER SHARKBAIT!
SHARKBAIT! OOH HA HA!
ENOUGH WITH THE SHARKBAIT.
SHARKBAIT! OOH..BA-BA-DOO.
OKAY, SHARKBAIT'S ONE OF US NOW, AGREED?
AGREED!
WE CAN'T SEND HIM OFF TO HIS DEATH.

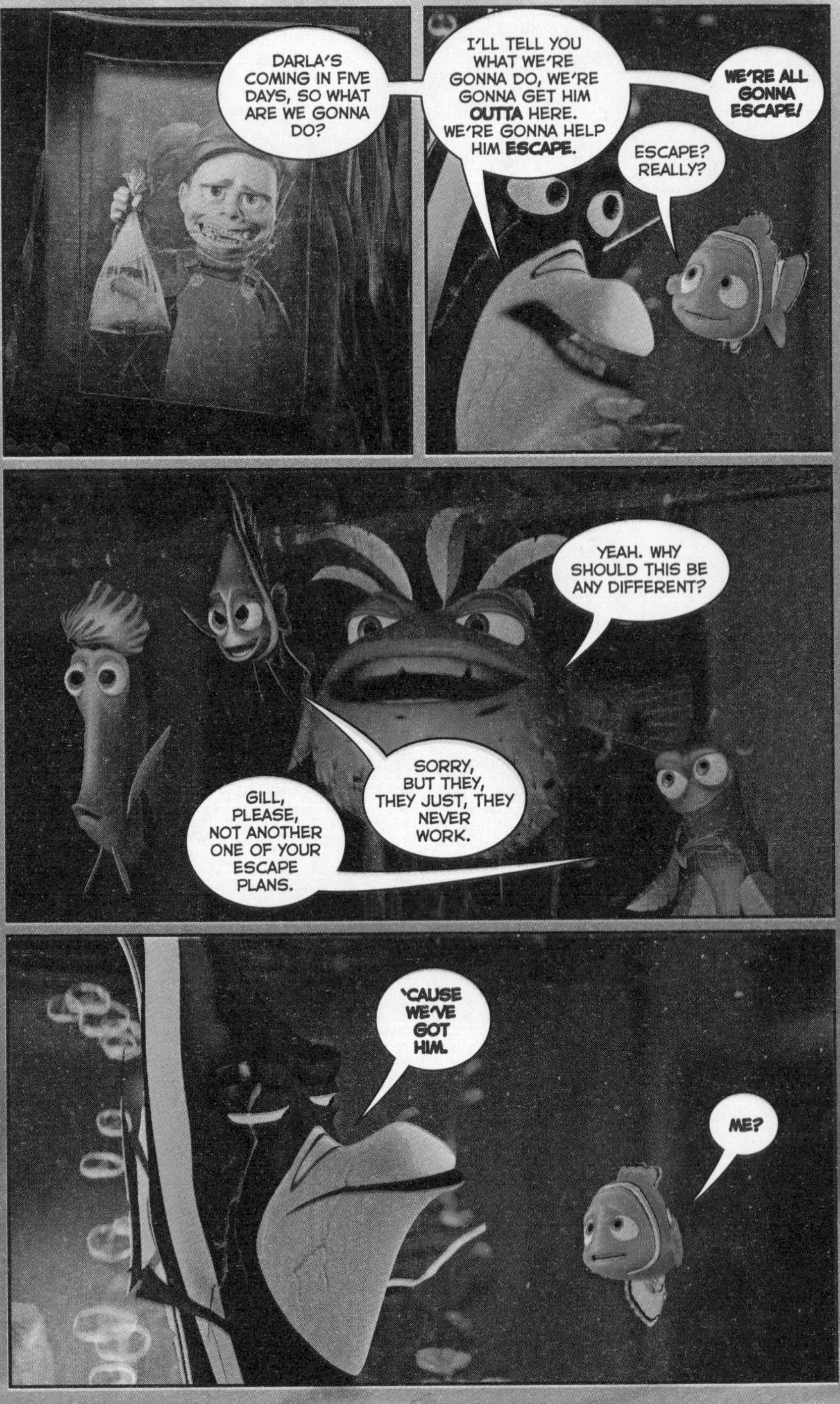
DARLA'S COMING IN FIVE DAYS, SO WHAT ARE WE GONNA DO?
I'LL TELL YOU WHAT WE'RE GONNA DO, WE'RE GONNA GET HIM OUTTA HERE. WE'RE GONNA HELP HIM ESCAPE.
WE'RE ALL GONNA ESCAPE!
ESCAPE? REALLY?
GILL, PLEASE, NOT ANOTHER ONE OF YOUR ESCAPE PLANS.
SORRY, BUT THEY, THEY JUST, THEY NEVER WORK.
YEAH. WHY SHOULD THIS BE ANY DIFFERENT?
'CAUSE WE'VE GOT HIM.
ME?

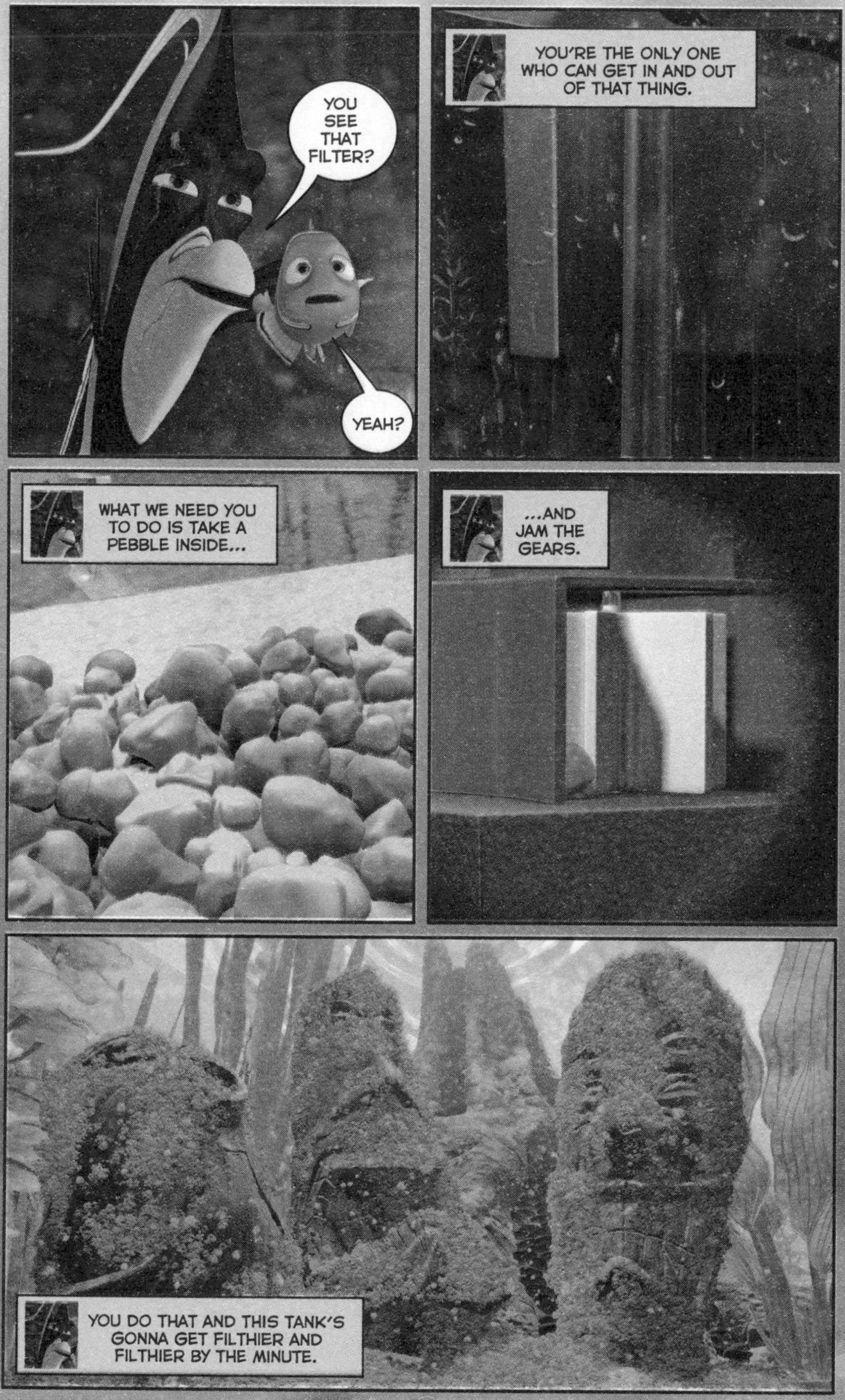
YOU SEE THAT FILTER?
YEAH?
YOU'RE THE ONLY ONE WHO CAN GET IN AND OUT OF THAT THING.
WHAT WE NEED YOU TO DO IS TAKE A PEBBLE INSIDE...
...AND JAM THE GEARS.
YOU DO THAT AND THIS TANK'S GONNA GET FILTHIER AND FILTHIER BY THE MINUTE.

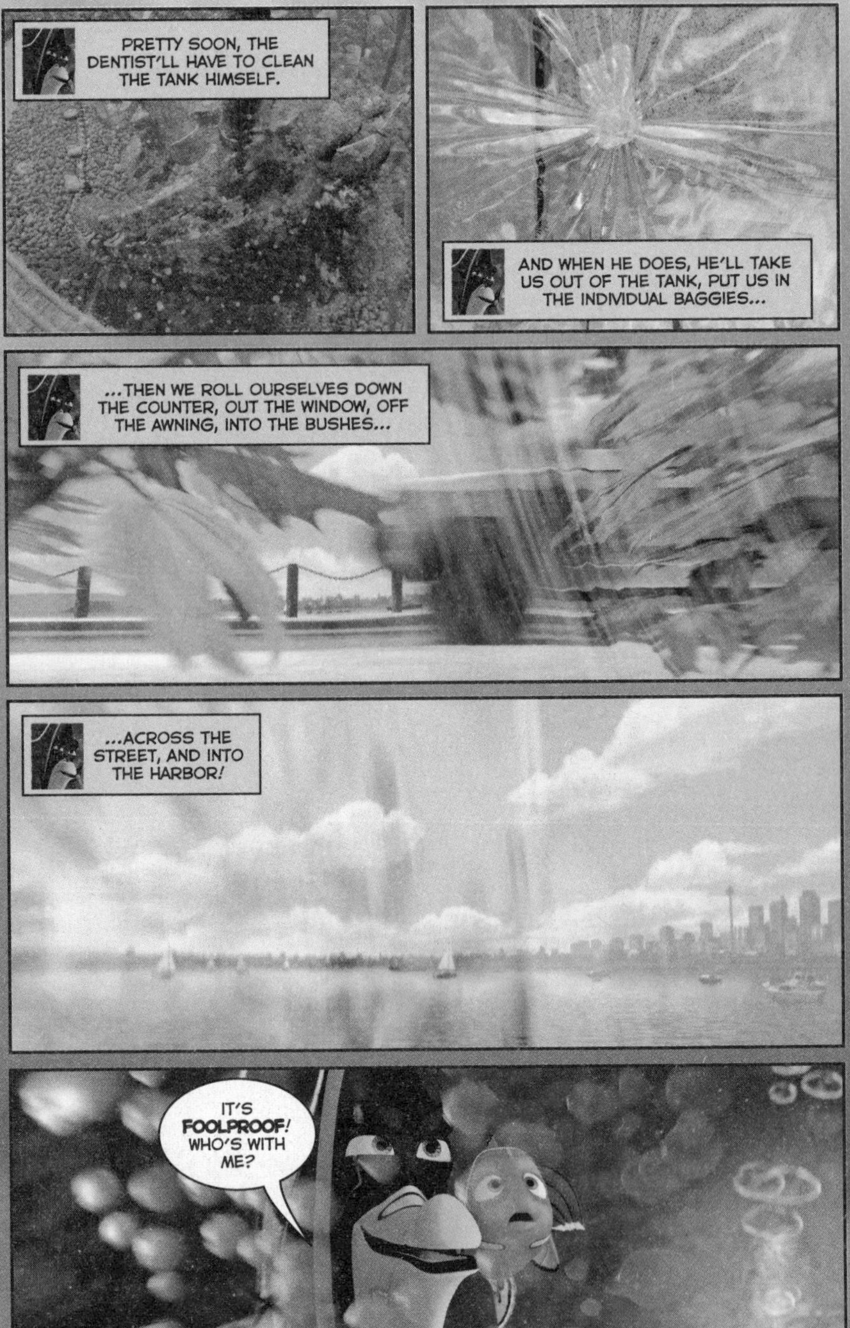
PRETTY SOON, THE DENTIST'LL HAVE TO CLEAN THE TANK HIMSELF.
AND WHEN HE DOES, HE'LL TAKE US OUT OF THE TANK, PUT US IN THE INDIVIDUAL BAGGIES...
...THEN WE ROLL OURSELVES DOWN THE COUNTER, OUT THE WINDOW, OFF THE AWNING, INTO THE BUSHES...
...ACROSS THE STREET, AND INTO THE HARBOR!
IT'S **FOOLPROOF**! WHO'S WITH ME?

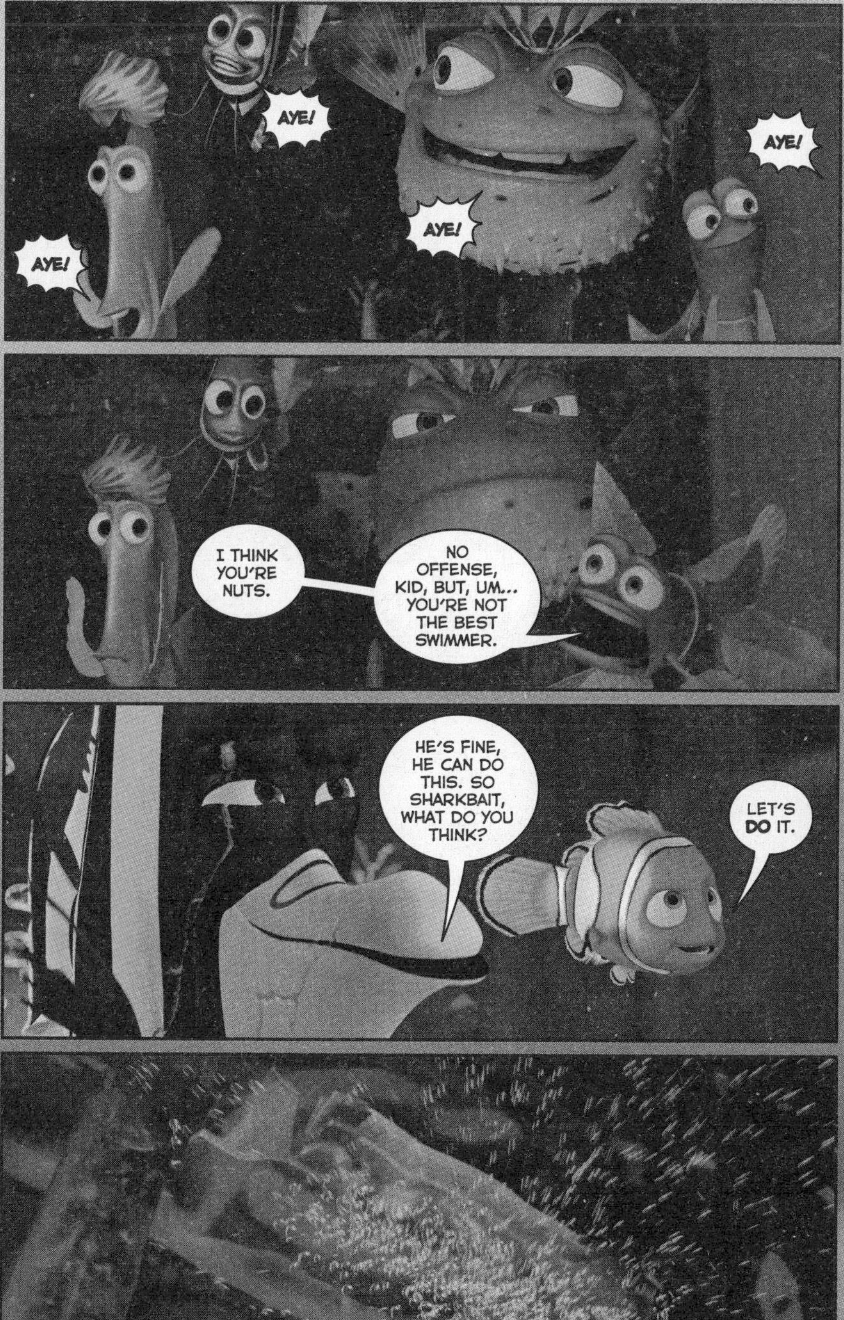
AYE!
AYE!
AYE!
AYE!
I THINK YOU'RE NUTS.
NO OFFENSE, KID, BUT, UM... YOU'RE NOT THE BEST SWIMMER.
HE'S FINE, HE CAN DO THIS. SO SHARKBAIT, WHAT DO YOU THINK?
LET'S **DO** IT.

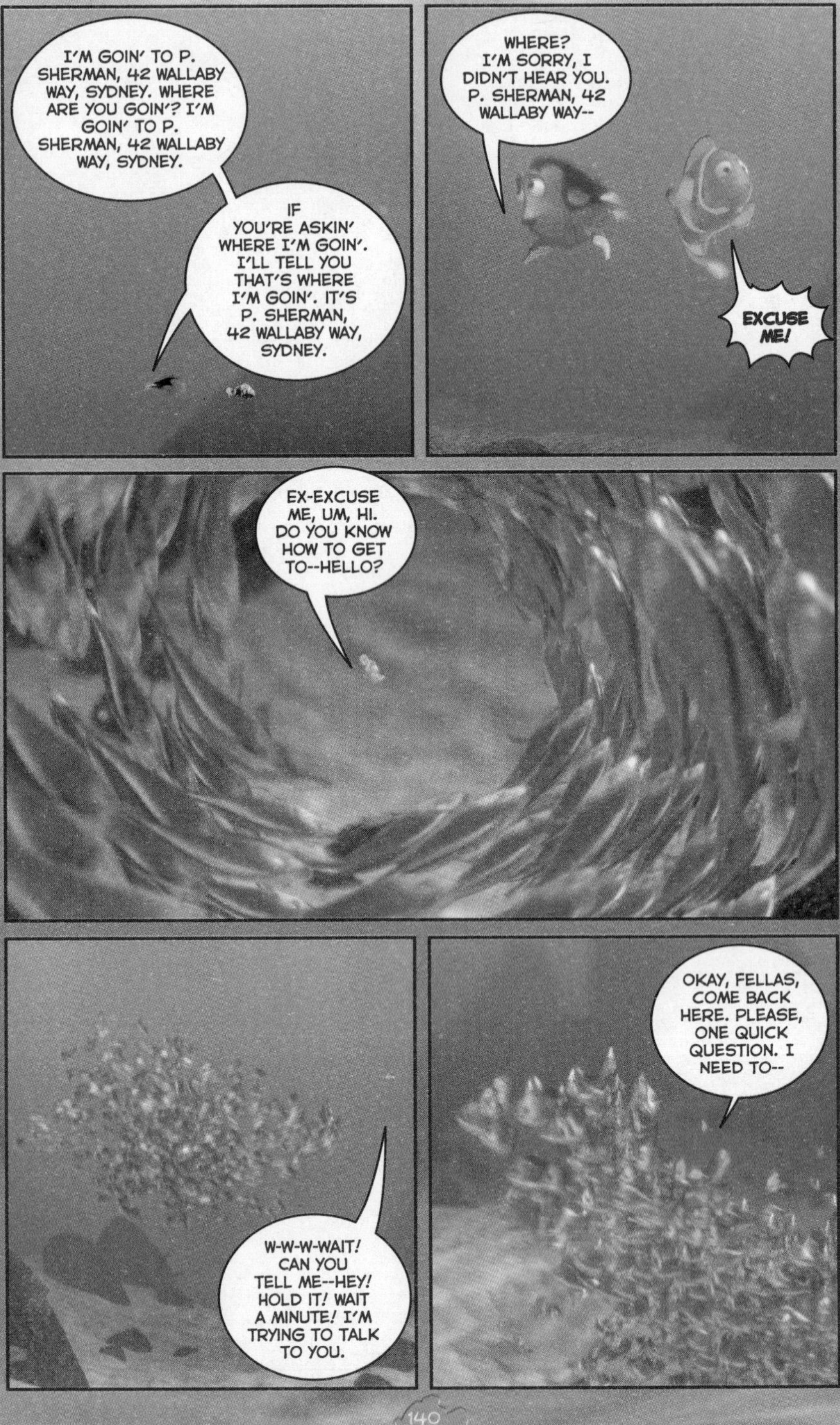
I'M GOIN' TO P. SHERMAN, 42 WALLABY WAY, SYDNEY. WHERE ARE YOU GOIN'? I'M GOIN' TO P. SHERMAN, 42 WALLABY WAY, SYDNEY.
IF YOU'RE ASKIN' WHERE I'M GOIN'. I'LL TELL YOU THAT'S WHERE I'M GOIN'. IT'S P. SHERMAN, 42 WALLABY WAY, SYDNEY.
WHERE? I'M SORRY, I DIDN'T HEAR YOU. P. SHERMAN, 42 WALLABY WAY--
EXCUSE ME!
EX-EXCUSE ME, UM, HI. DO YOU KNOW HOW TO GET TO--HELLO?
W-W-W-WAIT! CAN YOU TELL ME--HEY! HOLD IT! WAIT A MINUTE! I'M TRYING TO TALK TO YOU.
OKAY, FELLAS, COME BACK HERE. PLEASE, ONE QUICK QUESTION. I NEED TO--

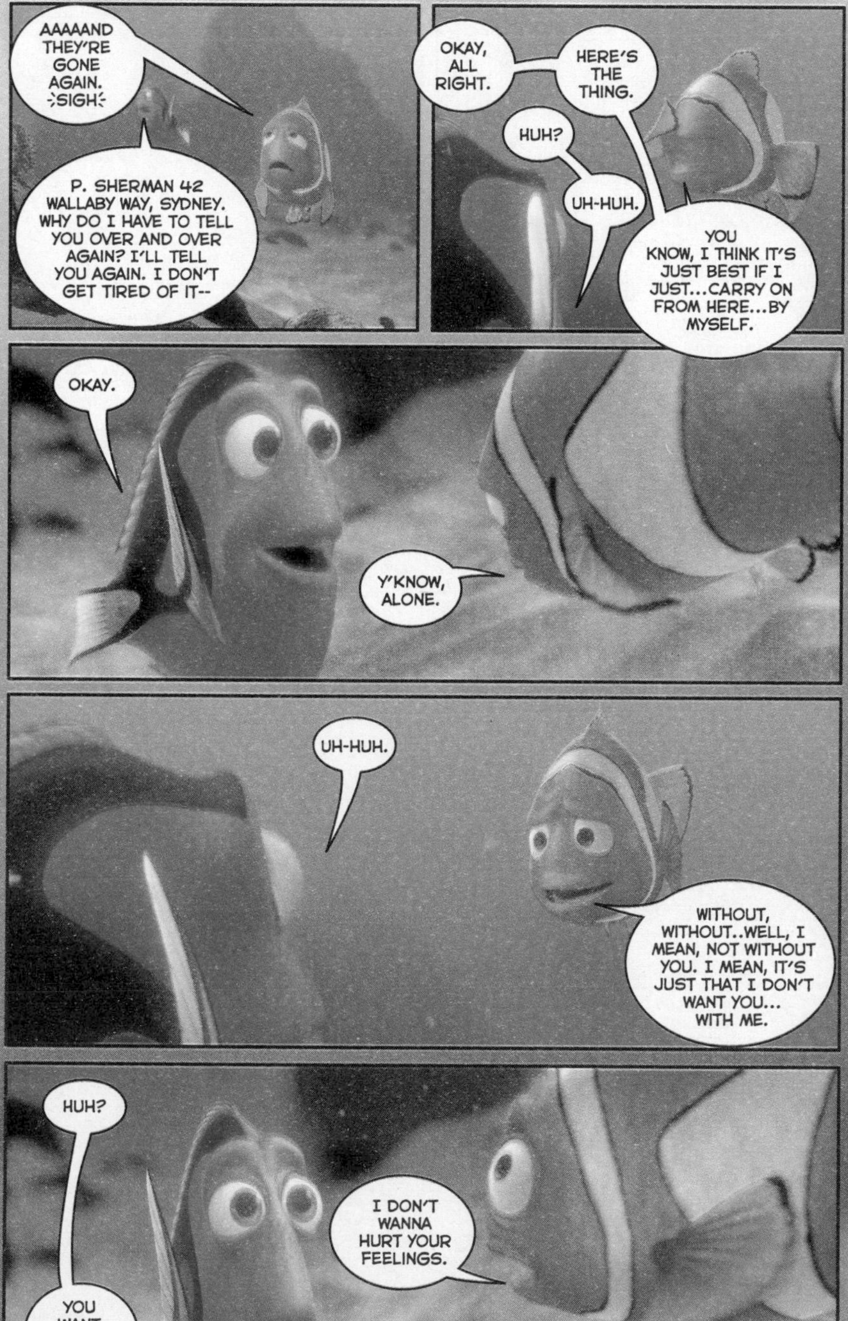
AAAAAND THEY'RE GONE AGAIN. ⁘SIGH⁘
P. SHERMAN 42 WALLABY WAY, SYDNEY. WHY DO I HAVE TO TELL YOU OVER AND OVER AGAIN? I'LL TELL YOU AGAIN. I DON'T GET TIRED OF IT--
OKAY, ALL RIGHT.
HERE'S THE THING.
HUH?
UH-HUH.
YOU KNOW, I THINK IT'S JUST BEST IF I JUST...CARRY ON FROM HERE...BY MYSELF.
OKAY.
Y'KNOW, ALONE.
UH-HUH.
WITHOUT, WITHOUT..WELL, I MEAN, NOT WITHOUT YOU. I MEAN, IT'S JUST THAT I DON'T WANT YOU... WITH ME.
HUH?
YOU WANT ME TO LEAVE?
I DON'T WANNA HURT YOUR FEELINGS.

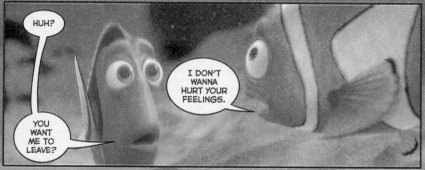

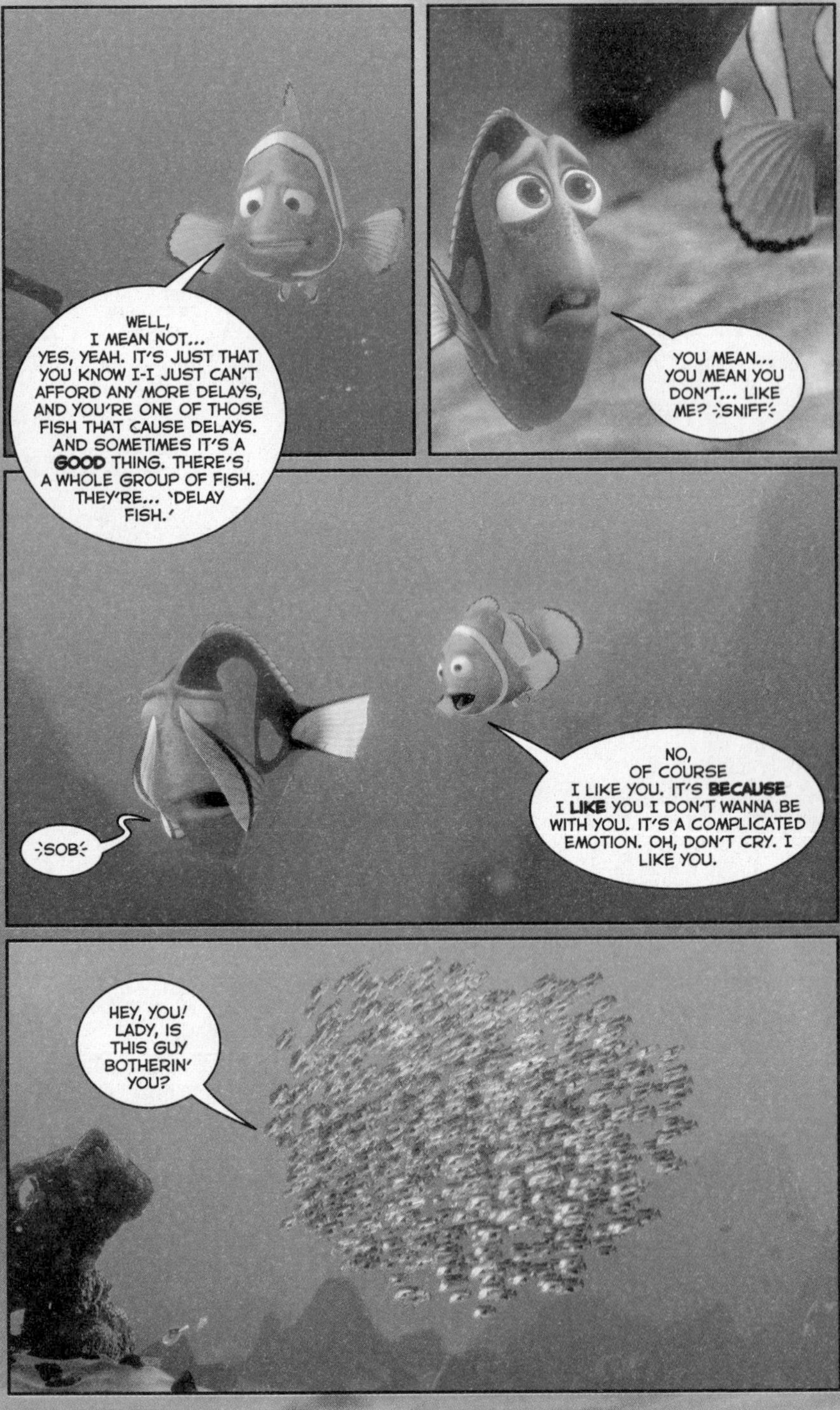
WELL, I MEAN NOT... YES, YEAH. IT'S JUST THAT YOU KNOW I-I JUST CAN'T AFFORD ANY MORE DELAYS, AND YOU'RE ONE OF THOSE FISH THAT CAUSE DELAYS. AND SOMETIMES IT'S A **GOOD** THING. THERE'S A WHOLE GROUP OF FISH. THEY'RE... 'DELAY FISH.'
YOU MEAN... YOU MEAN YOU DON'T... LIKE ME? *SNIFF*
SOB
NO, OF COURSE I LIKE YOU. IT'S **BECAUSE** I **LIKE** YOU I DON'T WANNA BE WITH YOU. IT'S A COMPLICATED EMOTION. OH, DON'T CRY. I LIKE YOU.
HEY, YOU! LADY, IS THIS GUY BOTHERIN' YOU?

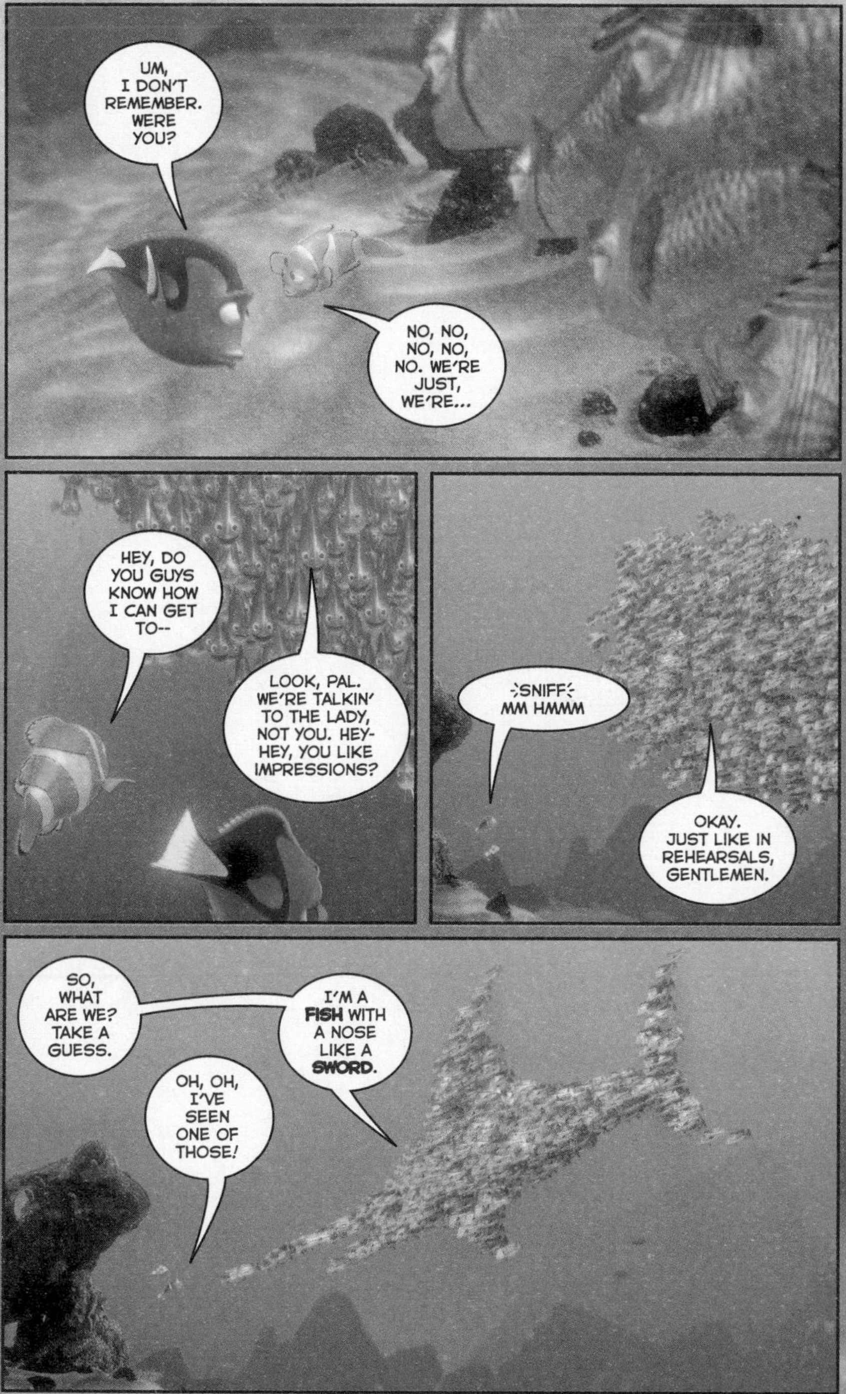
UM, I DON'T REMEMBER. WERE YOU?
NO, NO, NO, NO, NO. WE'RE JUST, WE'RE...
HEY, DO YOU GUYS KNOW HOW I CAN GET TO--
LOOK, PAL. WE'RE TALKIN' TO THE LADY, NOT YOU. HEY-HEY, YOU LIKE IMPRESSIONS?
-SNIFF- MM HMMM
OKAY. JUST LIKE IN REHEARSALS, GENTLEMEN.
SO, WHAT ARE WE? TAKE A GUESS.
I'M A **FISH** WITH A NOSE LIKE A **SWORD**.
OH, OH, I'VE SEEN ONE OF THOSE!

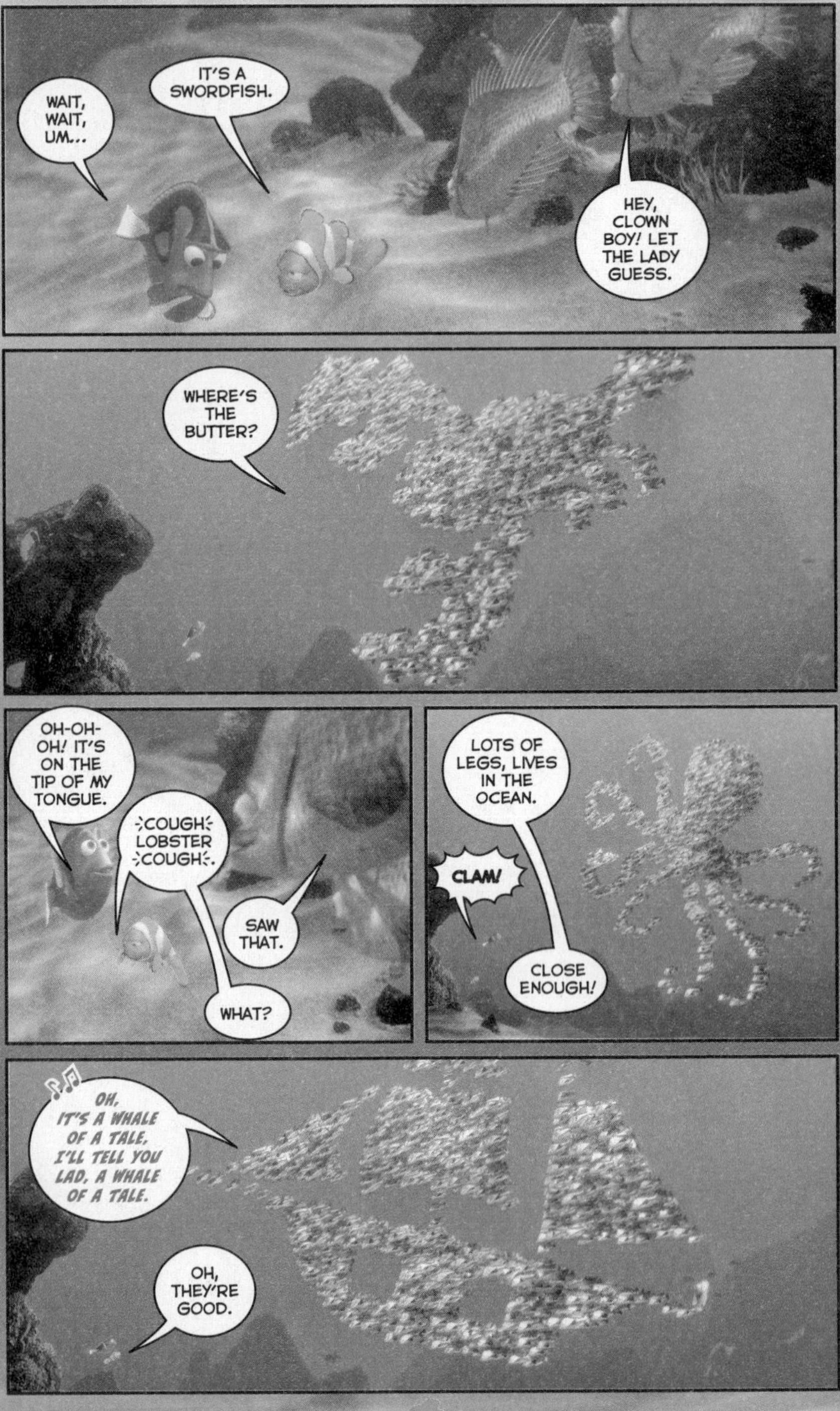
WAIT, WAIT, UM...
IT'S A SWORDFISH.
HEY, CLOWN BOY! LET THE LADY GUESS.
WHERE'S THE BUTTER?
OH-OH-OH! IT'S ON THE TIP OF MY TONGUE.
COUGH LOBSTER COUGH.
SAW THAT.
WHAT?
LOTS OF LEGS, LIVES IN THE OCEAN.
CLAM!
CLOSE ENOUGH!
OH, IT'S A WHALE OF A TALE, I'LL TELL YOU LAD, A WHALE OF A TALE.
OH, THEY'RE GOOD.

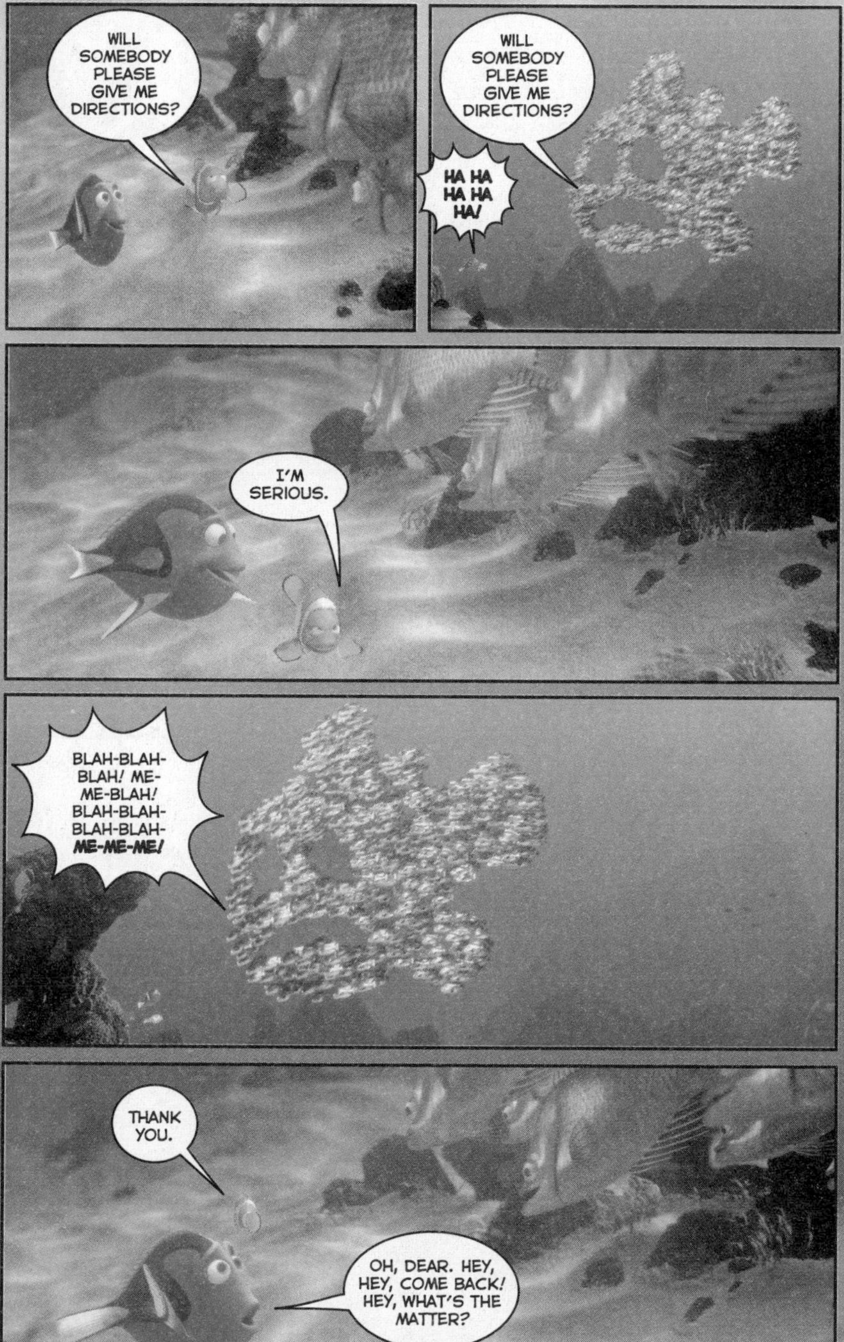
WILL SOMEBODY PLEASE GIVE ME DIRECTIONS?
WILL SOMEBODY PLEASE GIVE ME DIRECTIONS?
HA HA HA HA HA!
I'M SERIOUS.
BLAH-BLAH-BLAH! ME-ME-BLAH! BLAH-BLAH-BLAH-BLAH-ME-ME-ME!
THANK YOU.
OH, DEAR. HEY, HEY, COME BACK! HEY, WHAT'S THE MATTER?

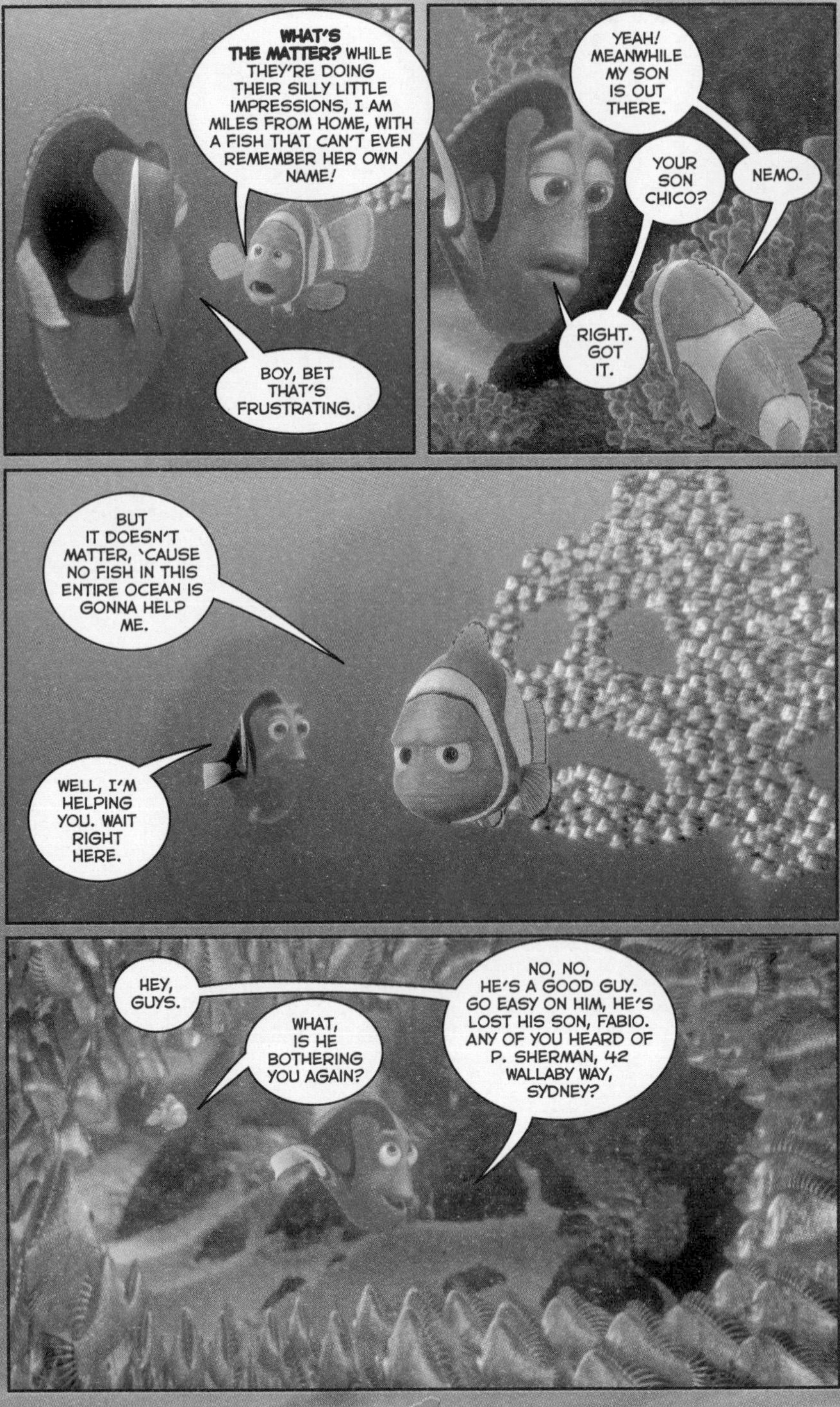

WHAT'S THE MATTER? WHILE THEY'RE DOING THEIR SILLY LITTLE IMPRESSIONS, I AM MILES FROM HOME, WITH A FISH THAT CAN'T EVEN REMEMBER HER OWN NAME!
BOY, BET THAT'S FRUSTRATING.
YEAH! MEANWHILE MY SON IS OUT THERE.
YOUR SON CHICO?
NEMO.
RIGHT. GOT IT.
BUT IT DOESN'T MATTER, 'CAUSE NO FISH IN THIS ENTIRE OCEAN IS GONNA HELP ME.
WELL, I'M HELPING YOU. WAIT RIGHT HERE.
HEY, GUYS.
WHAT, IS HE BOTHERING YOU AGAIN?
NO, NO, HE'S A GOOD GUY. GO EASY ON HIM, HE'S LOST HIS SON, FABIO. ANY OF YOU HEARD OF P. SHERMAN, 42 WALLABY WAY, SYDNEY?

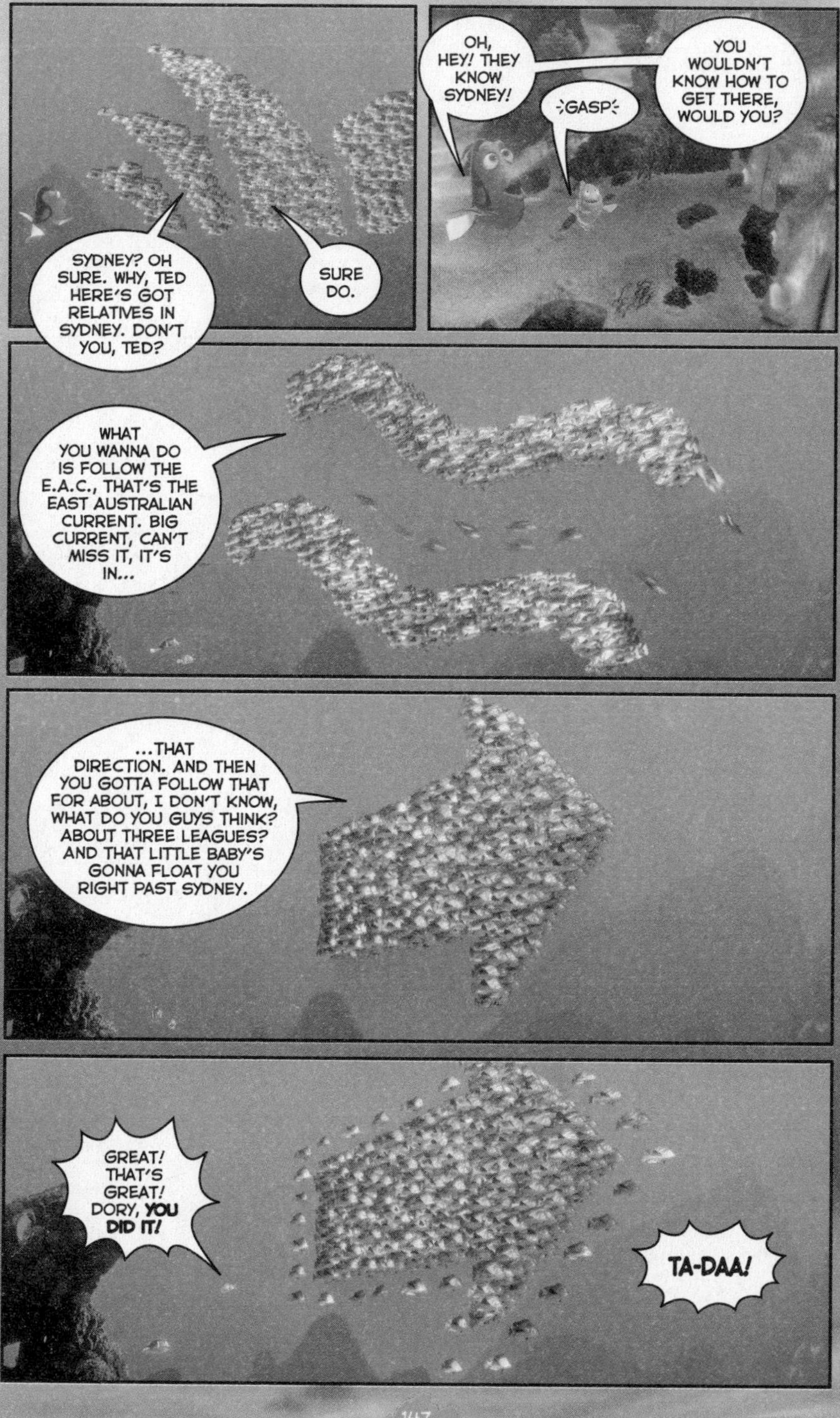
SYDNEY? OH SURE. WHY, TED HERE'S GOT RELATIVES IN SYDNEY. DON'T YOU, TED?
SURE DO.
OH, HEY! THEY KNOW SYDNEY!
GASP
YOU WOULDN'T KNOW HOW TO GET THERE, WOULD YOU?
WHAT YOU WANNA DO IS FOLLOW THE E.A.C., THAT'S THE EAST AUSTRALIAN CURRENT. BIG CURRENT, CAN'T MISS IT, IT'S IN...
...THAT DIRECTION. AND THEN YOU GOTTA FOLLOW THAT FOR ABOUT, I DON'T KNOW, WHAT DO YOU GUYS THINK? ABOUT THREE LEAGUES? AND THAT LITTLE BABY'S GONNA FLOAT YOU RIGHT PAST SYDNEY.
GREAT! THAT'S GREAT! DORY, **YOU DID IT!**
TA-DAA!

OH, PLEASE. I'M JUST YOUR LITTLE HELPER. HELPING ALONG, THAT'S ME.

WELL, LISTEN FELLAS, THANK YOU.

DON'T MENTION IT. AND, UH, LOOSEN UP. OKAY, BUDDY?

OH, YOU GUYS. YOU REALLY NAILED HIM. BYE.

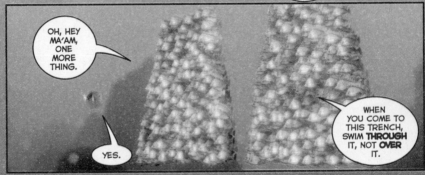

OH, HEY MA'AM, ONE MORE THING.

YES.

WHEN YOU COME TO THIS TRENCH, SWIM **THROUGH** IT, NOT **OVER** IT.

TRENCH, THROUGH IT, NOT OVER IT. I'LL REMEMBER.

HEY, HEY! HEY! HEY! HEY, WAIT UP, PARTNER. HOLD ON. WAIT! WAIT-WAIT! I GOT, I GOTTA TELL YOU SOMETHING...

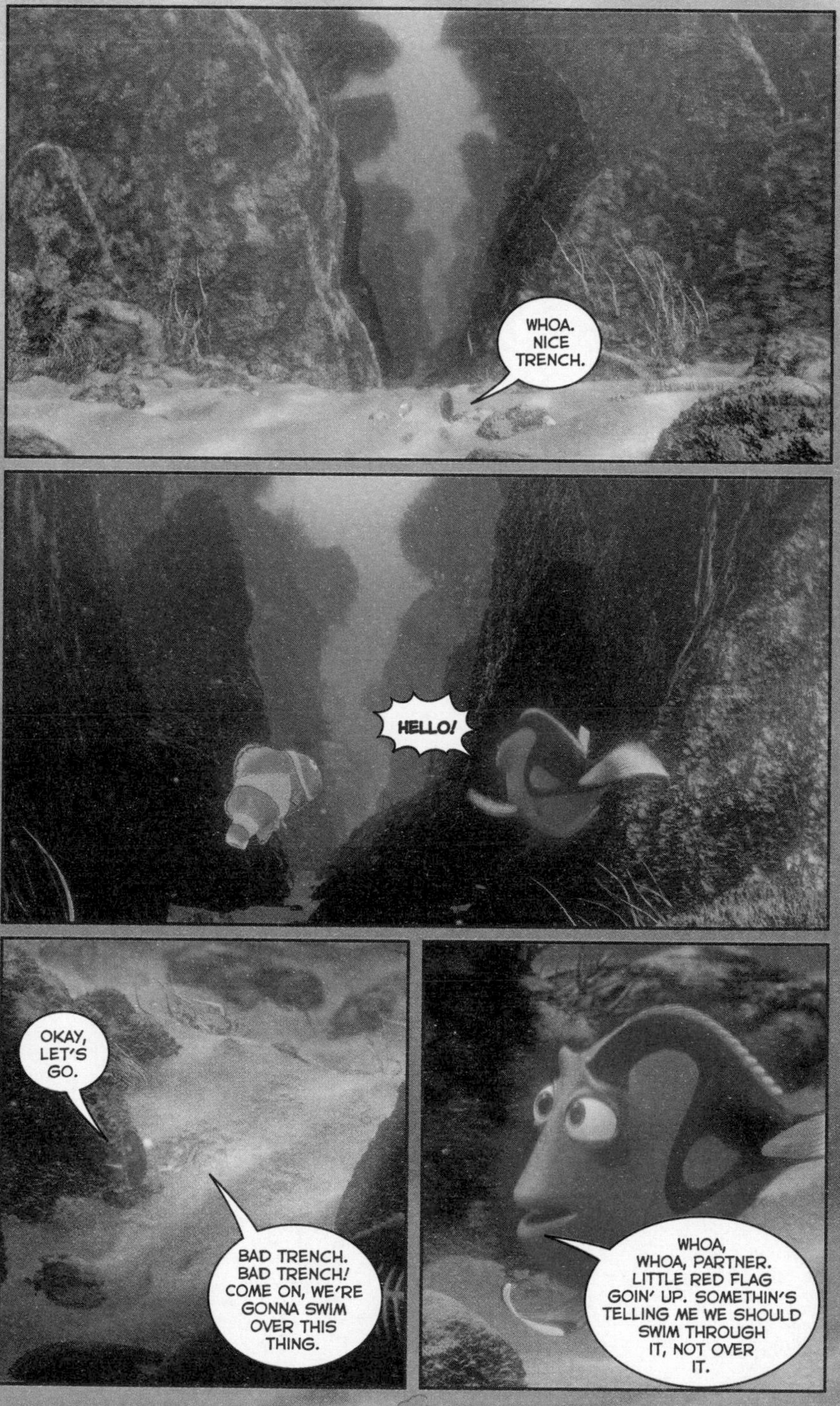
WHOA. NICE TRENCH.
HELLO!
OKAY, LET'S GO.
BAD TRENCH. BAD TRENCH! COME ON, WE'RE GONNA SWIM OVER THIS THING.
WHOA, WHOA, PARTNER. LITTLE RED FLAG GOIN' UP. SOMETHIN'S TELLING ME WE SHOULD SWIM THROUGH IT, NOT OVER IT.

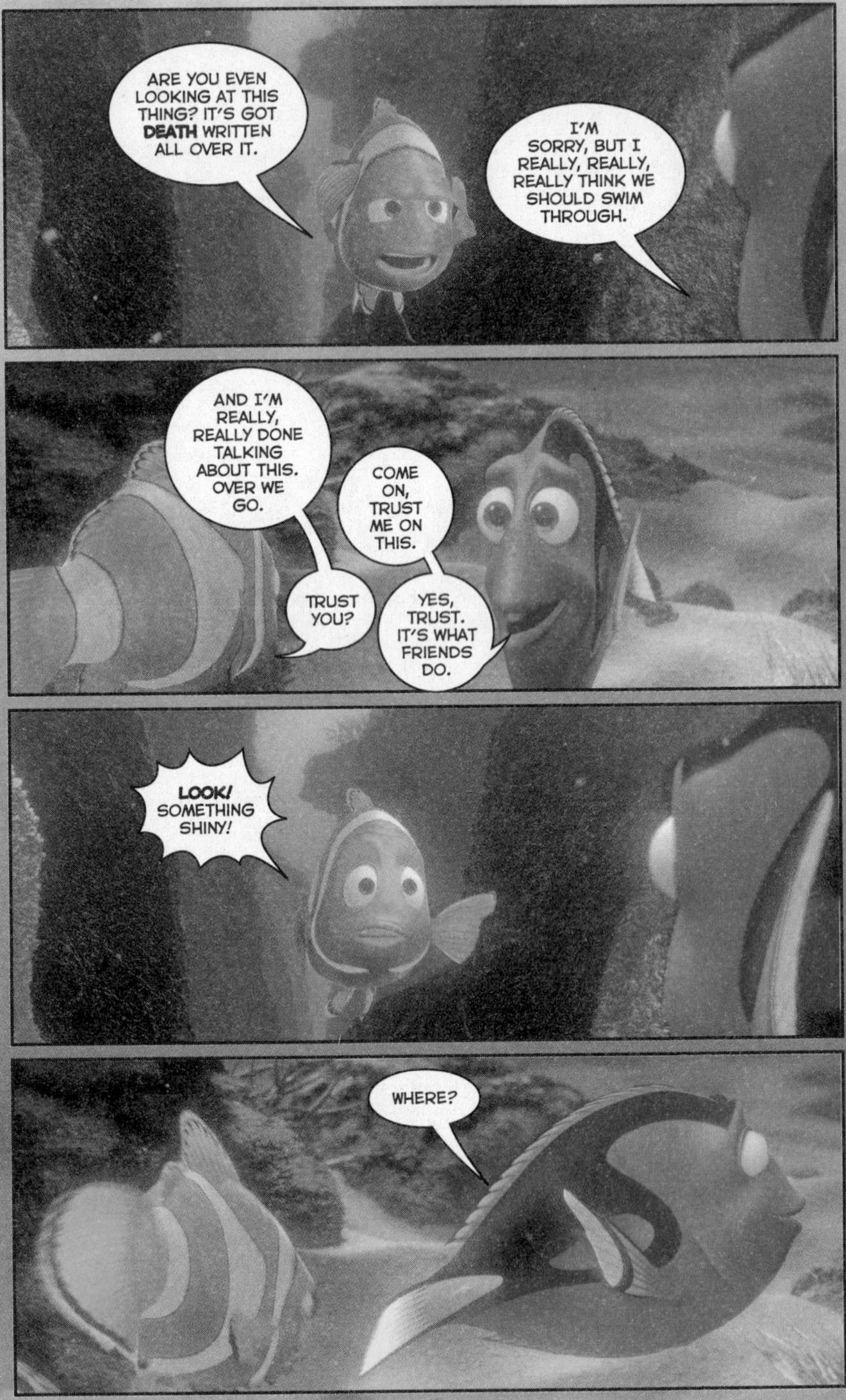
ARE YOU EVEN LOOKING AT THIS THING? IT'S GOT **DEATH** WRITTEN ALL OVER IT.
I'M SORRY, BUT I REALLY, REALLY, REALLY THINK WE SHOULD SWIM THROUGH.
AND I'M REALLY, REALLY DONE TALKING ABOUT THIS. OVER WE GO.
COME ON, TRUST ME ON THIS.
TRUST YOU?
YES, TRUST. IT'S WHAT FRIENDS DO.
LOOK! SOMETHING SHINY!
WHERE?

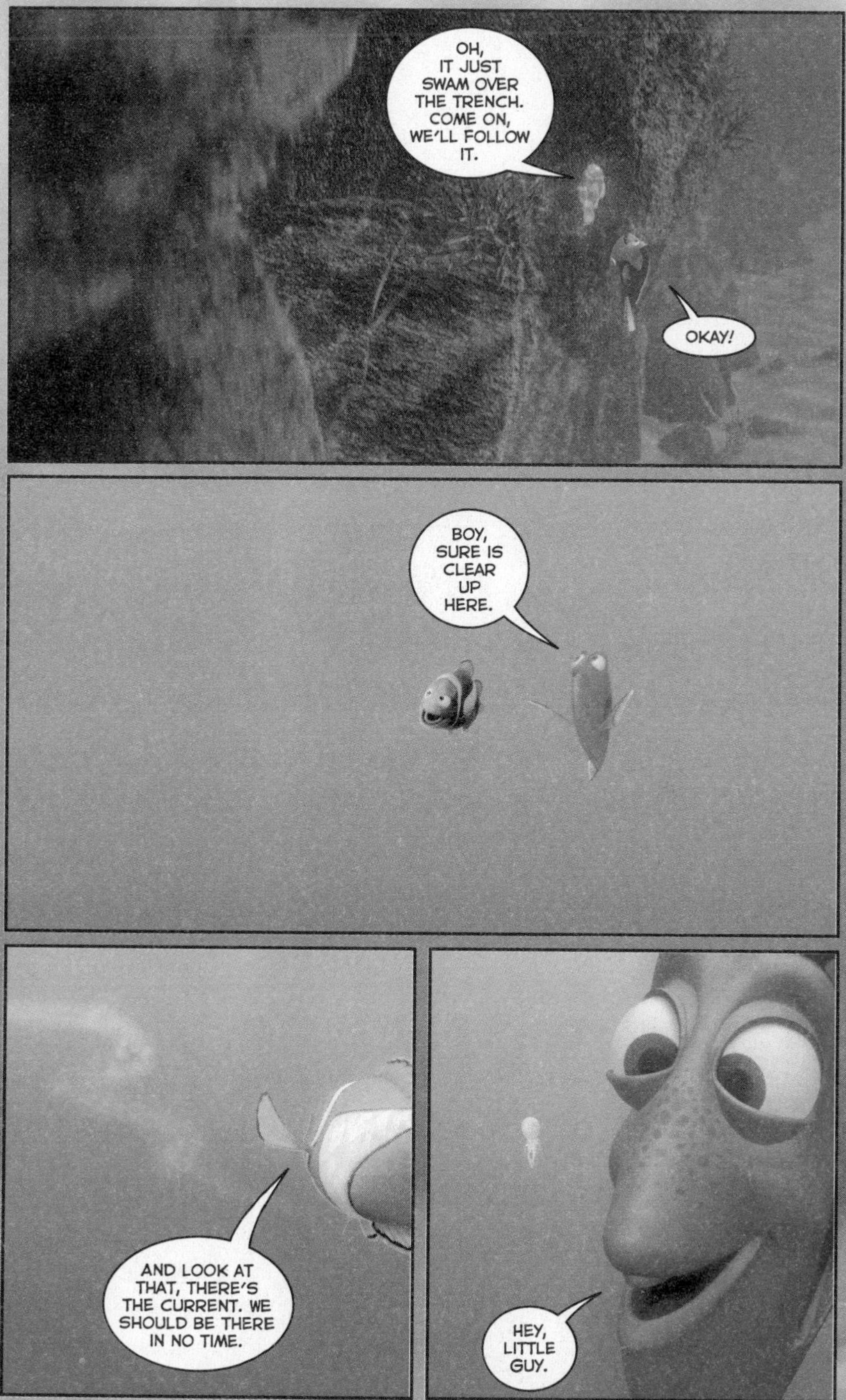
OH, IT JUST SWAM OVER THE TRENCH. COME ON, WE'LL FOLLOW IT.
OKAY!
BOY, SURE IS CLEAR UP HERE.
AND LOOK AT THAT, THERE'S THE CURRENT. WE SHOULD BE THERE IN NO TIME.
HEY, LITTLE GUY.

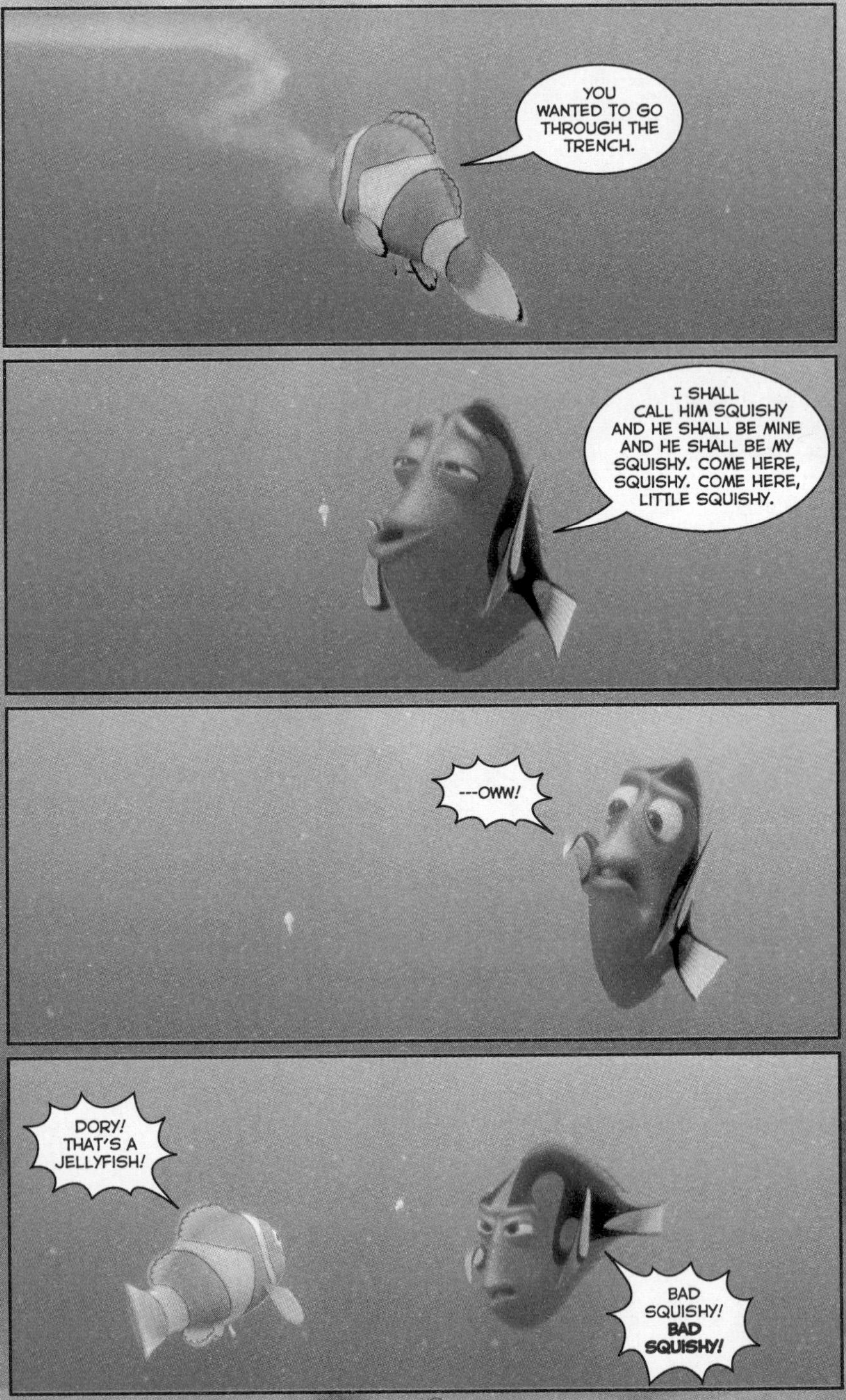

YOU WANTED TO GO THROUGH THE TRENCH.
I SHALL CALL HIM SQUISHY AND HE SHALL BE MINE AND HE SHALL BE MY SQUISHY. COME HERE, SQUISHY. COME HERE, LITTLE SQUISHY.
---OWW!
DORY! THAT'S A JELLYFISH!
BAD SQUISHY! **BAD SQUISHY!**

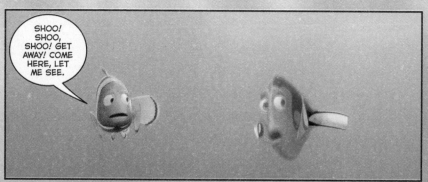

SHOO! SHOO, SHOO! GET AWAY! COME HERE, LET ME SEE.

DON'T TOUCH IT! DON'T **TOUCH** IT!

I'M NOT GONNA TOUCH IT. I JUST WANNA LOOK.

HEEEY, HOW COME IT DIDN'T STING YOU?

IT DID. IT'S JUST THAT...

OW! OW, OWW!

...HOLD STILL. I LIVE IN THIS ANEMONE AND I'M, I'M, I'M USED TO THESE KIND OF STINGS. COME HERE.

OW! OW, OWW!

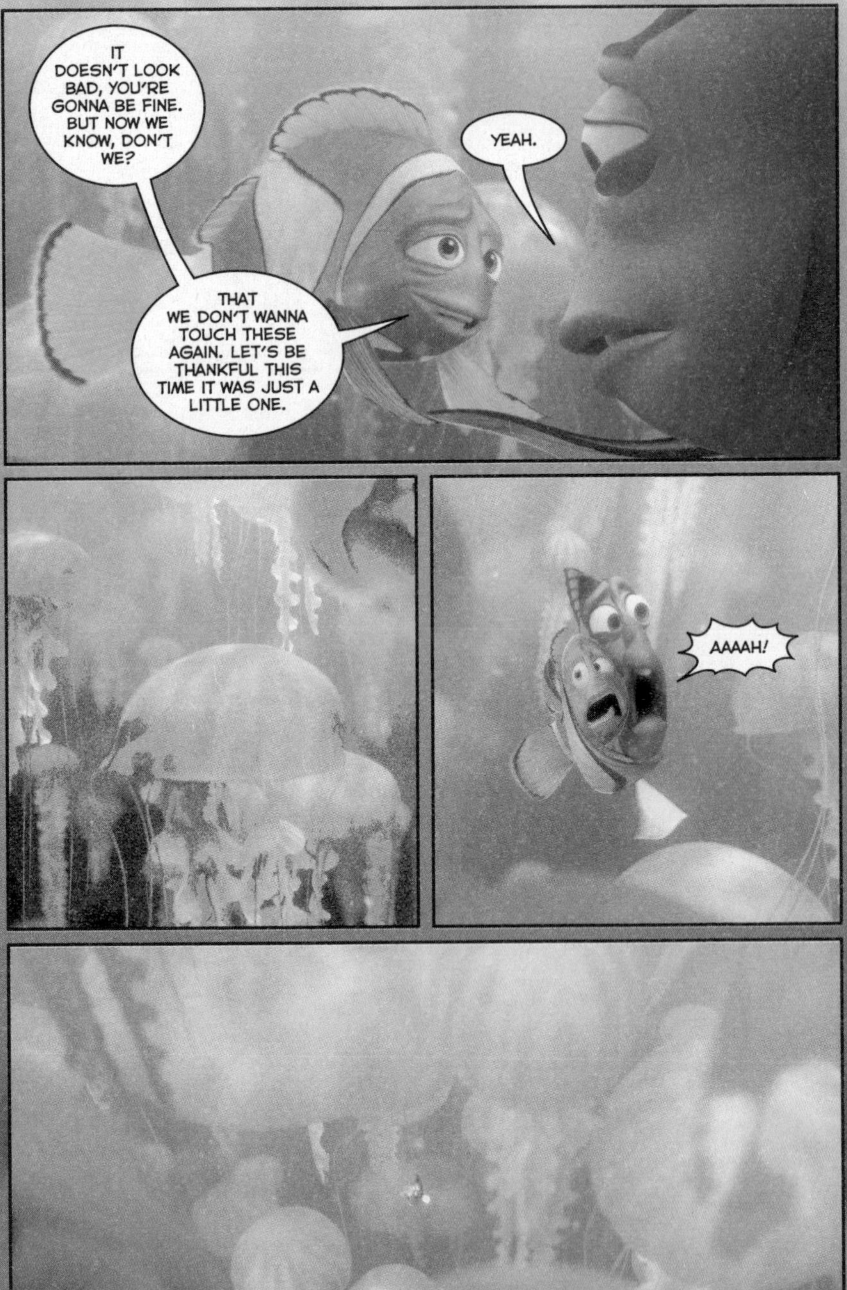
IT DOESN'T LOOK BAD, YOU'RE GONNA BE FINE. BUT NOW WE KNOW, DON'T WE?
YEAH.
THAT WE DON'T WANNA TOUCH THESE AGAIN. LET'S BE THANKFUL THIS TIME IT WAS JUST A LITTLE ONE.
AAAAH!

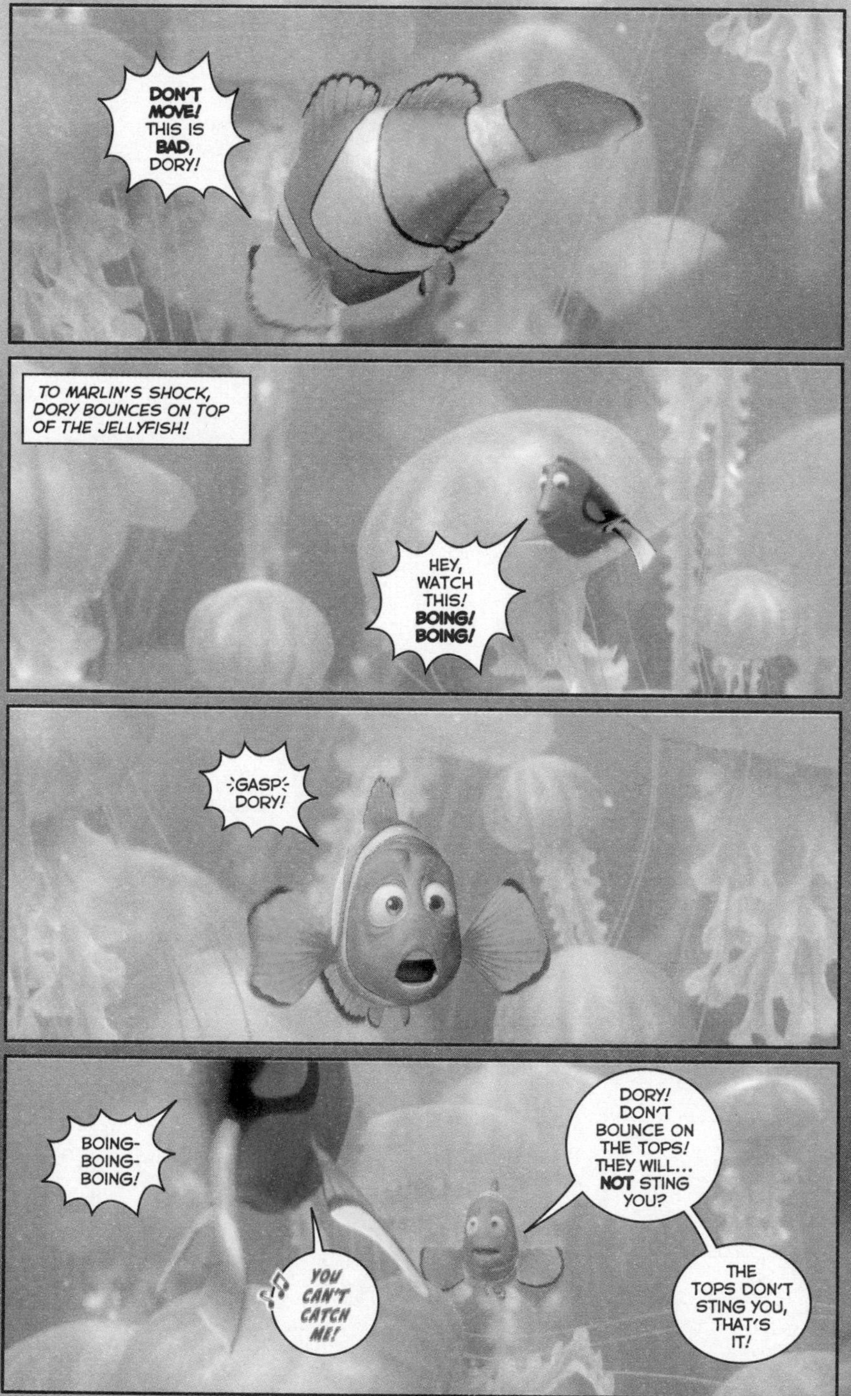
DON'T MOVE! THIS IS BAD, DORY!
TO MARLIN'S SHOCK, DORY BOUNCES ON TOP OF THE JELLYFISH!
HEY, WATCH THIS! BOING! BOING!
GASP DORY!
BOING-BOING-BOING!
YOU CAN'T CATCH ME!
DORY! DON'T BOUNCE ON THE TOPS! THEY WILL... NOT STING YOU?
THE TOPS DON'T STING YOU, THAT'S IT!

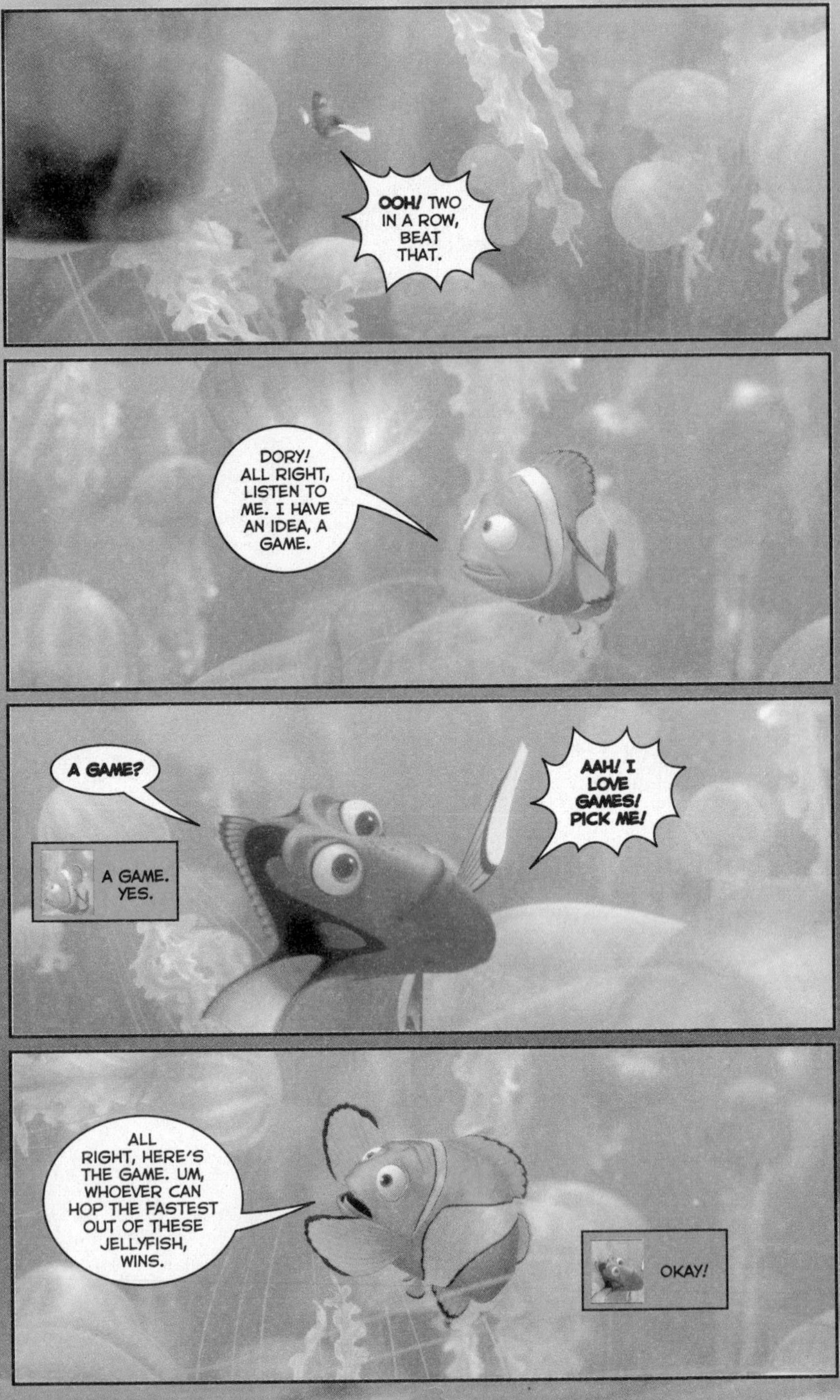
OOH! TWO IN A ROW, BEAT THAT.
DORY! ALL RIGHT, LISTEN TO ME. I HAVE AN IDEA, A GAME.
A GAME?
AAH! I LOVE GAMES! PICK ME!
A GAME. YES.
ALL RIGHT, HERE'S THE GAME. UM, WHOEVER CAN HOP THE FASTEST OUT OF THESE JELLYFISH, WINS.
OKAY!

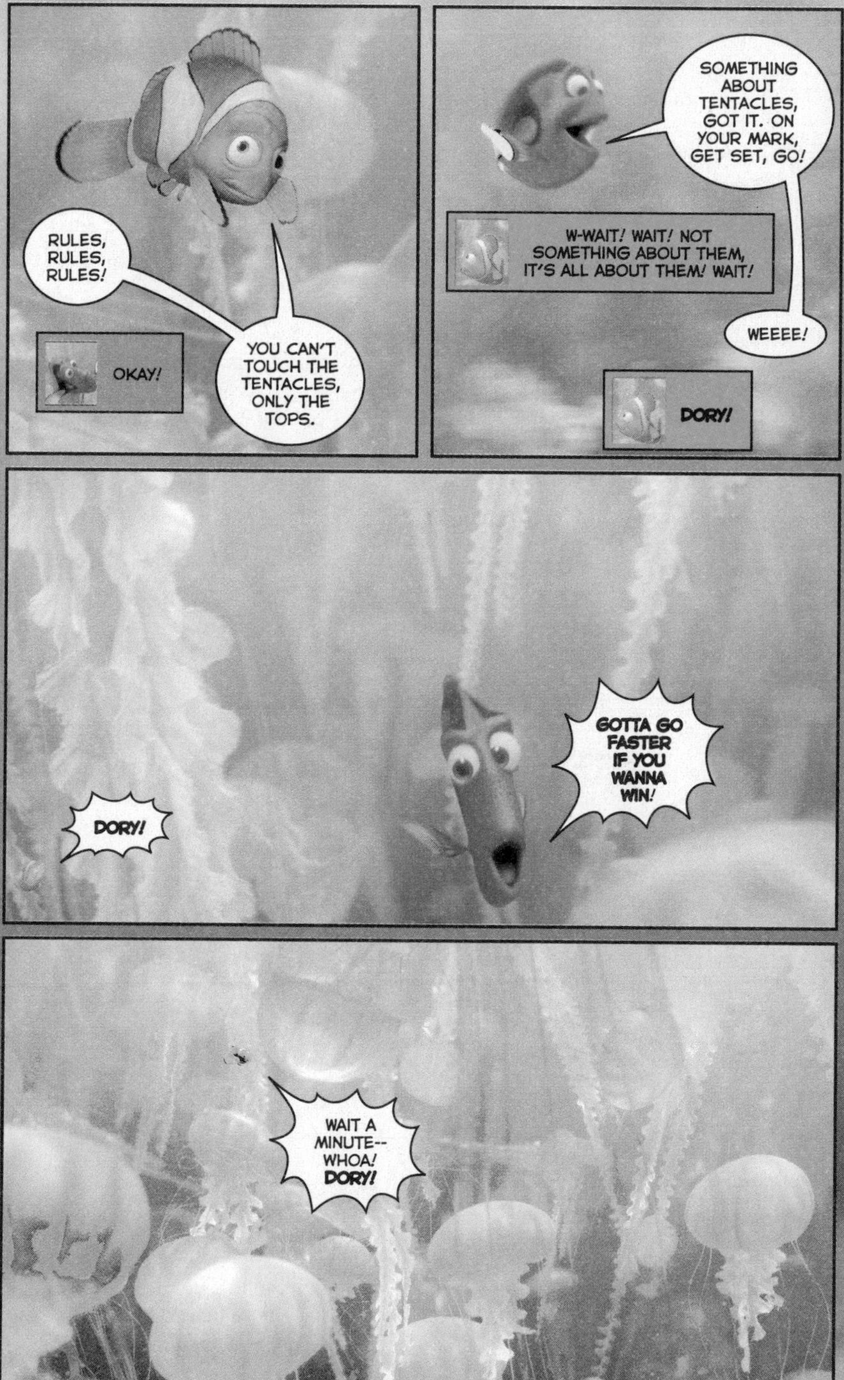
RULES, RULES, RULES!
YOU CAN'T TOUCH THE TENTACLES, ONLY THE TOPS.
OKAY!
SOMETHING ABOUT TENTACLES, GOT IT. ON YOUR MARK, GET SET, GO!
W-WAIT! WAIT! NOT SOMETHING ABOUT THEM, IT'S ALL ABOUT THEM! WAIT!
WEEEE!
DORY!
GOTTA GO FASTER IF YOU WANNA WIN!
DORY!
WAIT A MINUTE-- WHOA! DORY!

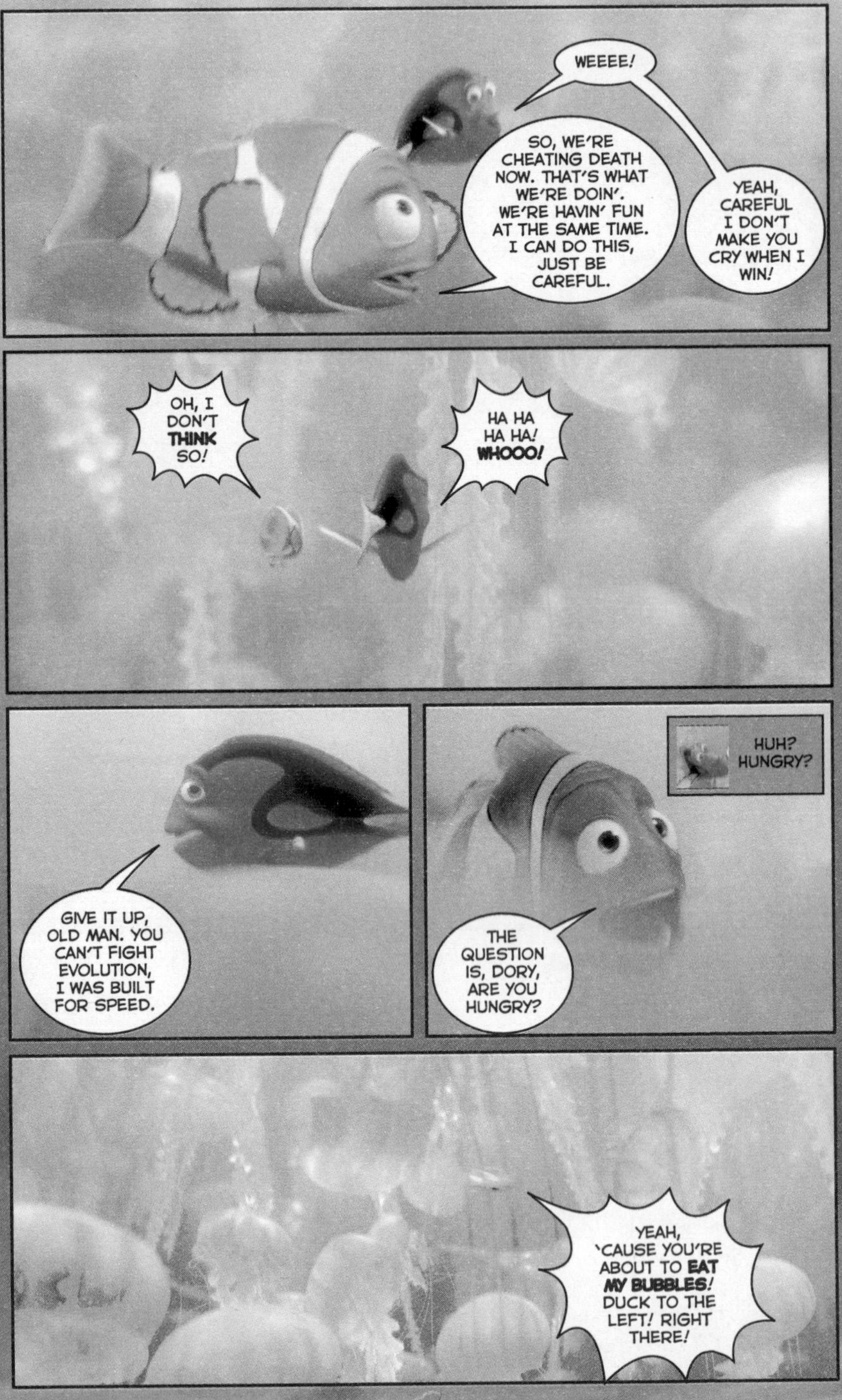
WEEEE!
SO, WE'RE CHEATING DEATH NOW. THAT'S WHAT WE'RE DOIN'. WE'RE HAVIN' FUN AT THE SAME TIME. I CAN DO THIS, JUST BE CAREFUL.
YEAH, CAREFUL I DON'T MAKE YOU CRY WHEN I WIN!
OH, I DON'T **THINK** SO!
HA HA HA HA! **WHOOO!**
GIVE IT UP, OLD MAN. YOU CAN'T FIGHT EVOLUTION, I WAS BUILT FOR SPEED.
HUH? HUNGRY?
THE QUESTION IS, DORY, ARE YOU HUNGRY?
YEAH, 'CAUSE YOU'RE ABOUT TO **EAT MY BUBBLES**! DUCK TO THE LEFT! RIGHT THERE!

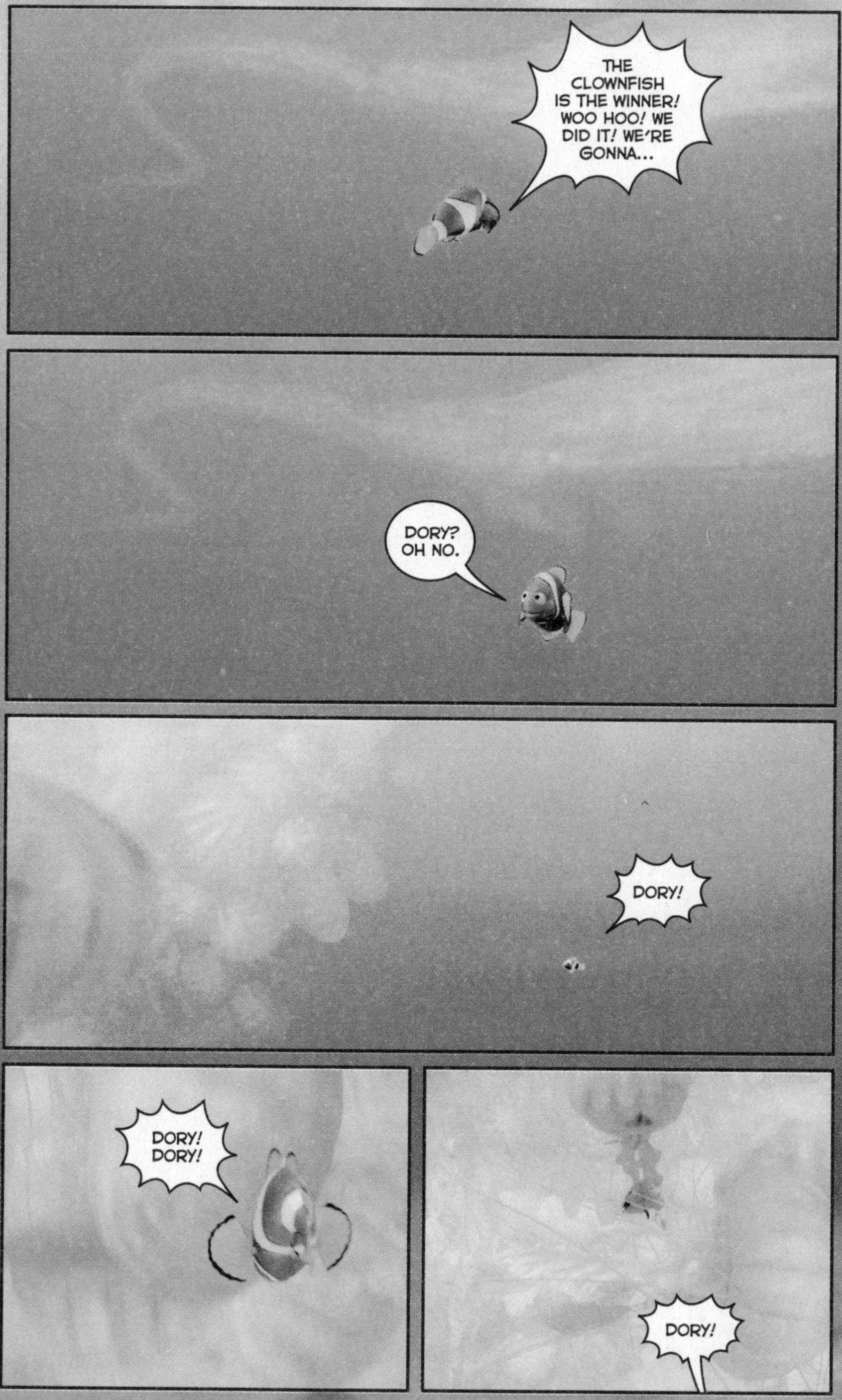
THE CLOWNFISH IS THE WINNER! WOO HOO! WE DID IT! WE'RE GONNA...
DORY? OH NO.
DORY!
DORY! DORY!
DORY!

OUCH!
UGGGHHH!
UGH...AM I DISQUALIFIED?
NO, YOU'RE DOING FINE! YOU'RE, YOU'RE ACTUALLY WINNING! BUT YOU GOTTA STAY AWAKE. UH, WHERE DOES P. SHERMAN LIVE?
P... SHERMAN... WALLABY WAY... SYDNEY...
THAT'S IT!

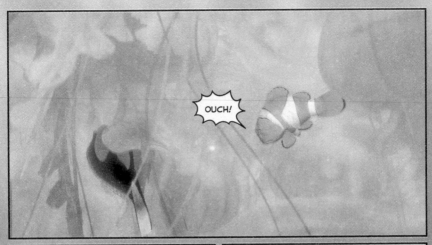

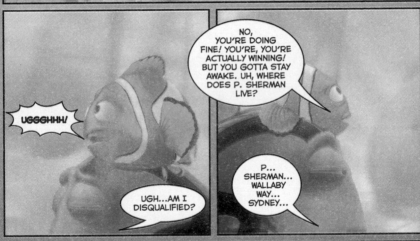

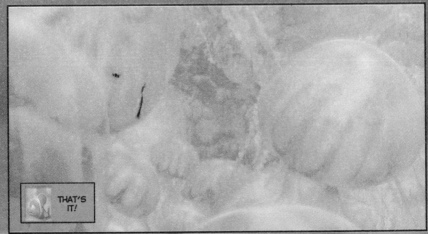

OWW! OW! STAY AWAKE! STAY AWAKE!

OW! STAY AWAKE!

AWAKE...P... SHERMAN...

STAY-- AWAKE!

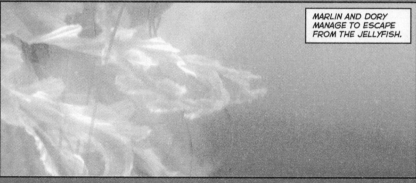

MARLIN AND DORY MANAGE TO ESCAPE FROM THE JELLYFISH.

AWAKE...

...42 WALLABY WAY...

AWAKE... WAKE UP... NEMO...

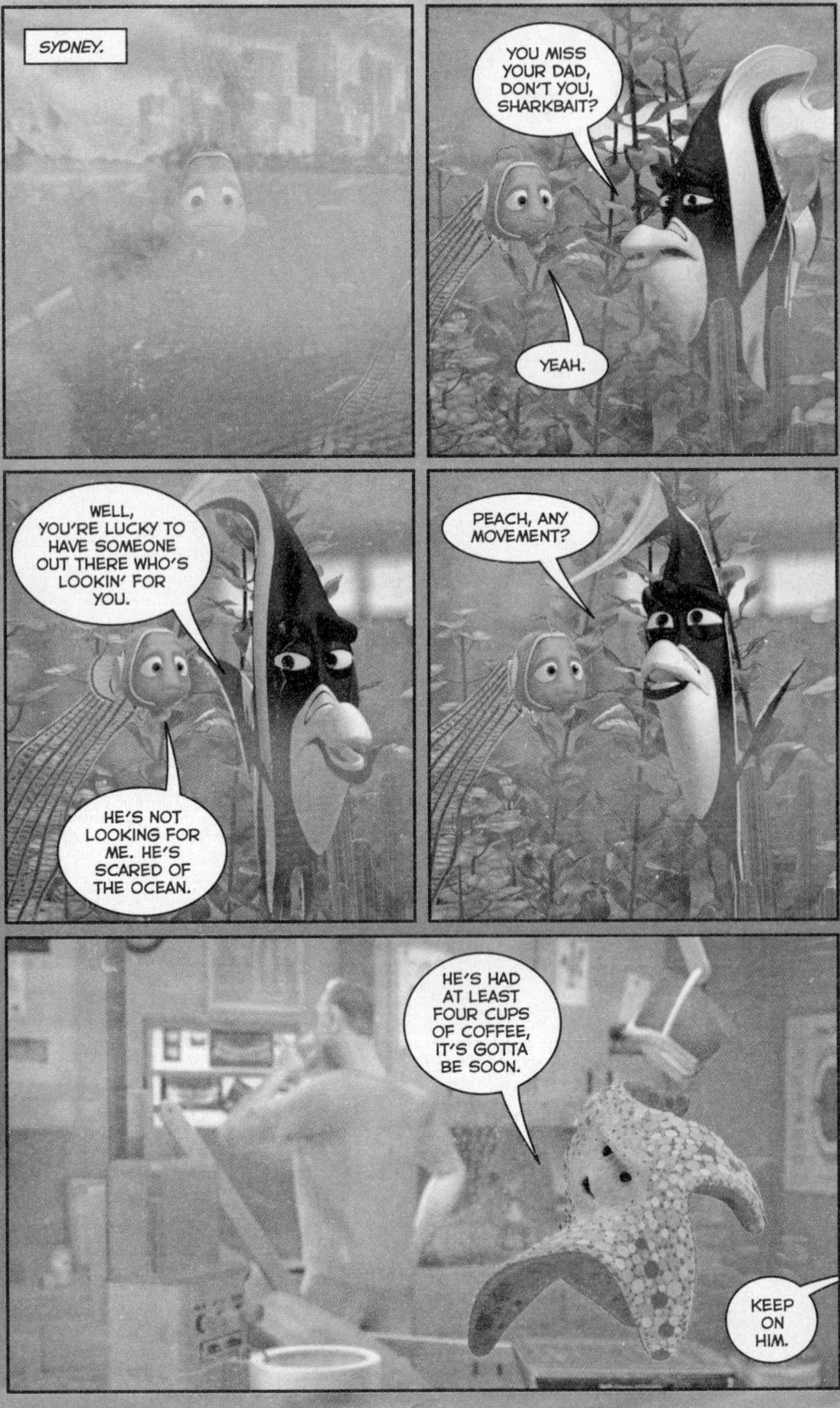
SYDNEY.
YOU MISS YOUR DAD, DON'T YOU, SHARKBAIT?
YEAH.
WELL, YOU'RE LUCKY TO HAVE SOMEONE OUT THERE WHO'S LOOKIN' FOR YOU.
HE'S NOT LOOKING FOR ME. HE'S SCARED OF THE OCEAN.
PEACH, ANY MOVEMENT?
HE'S HAD AT LEAST FOUR CUPS OF COFFEE, IT'S GOTTA BE SOON.
KEEP ON HIM.

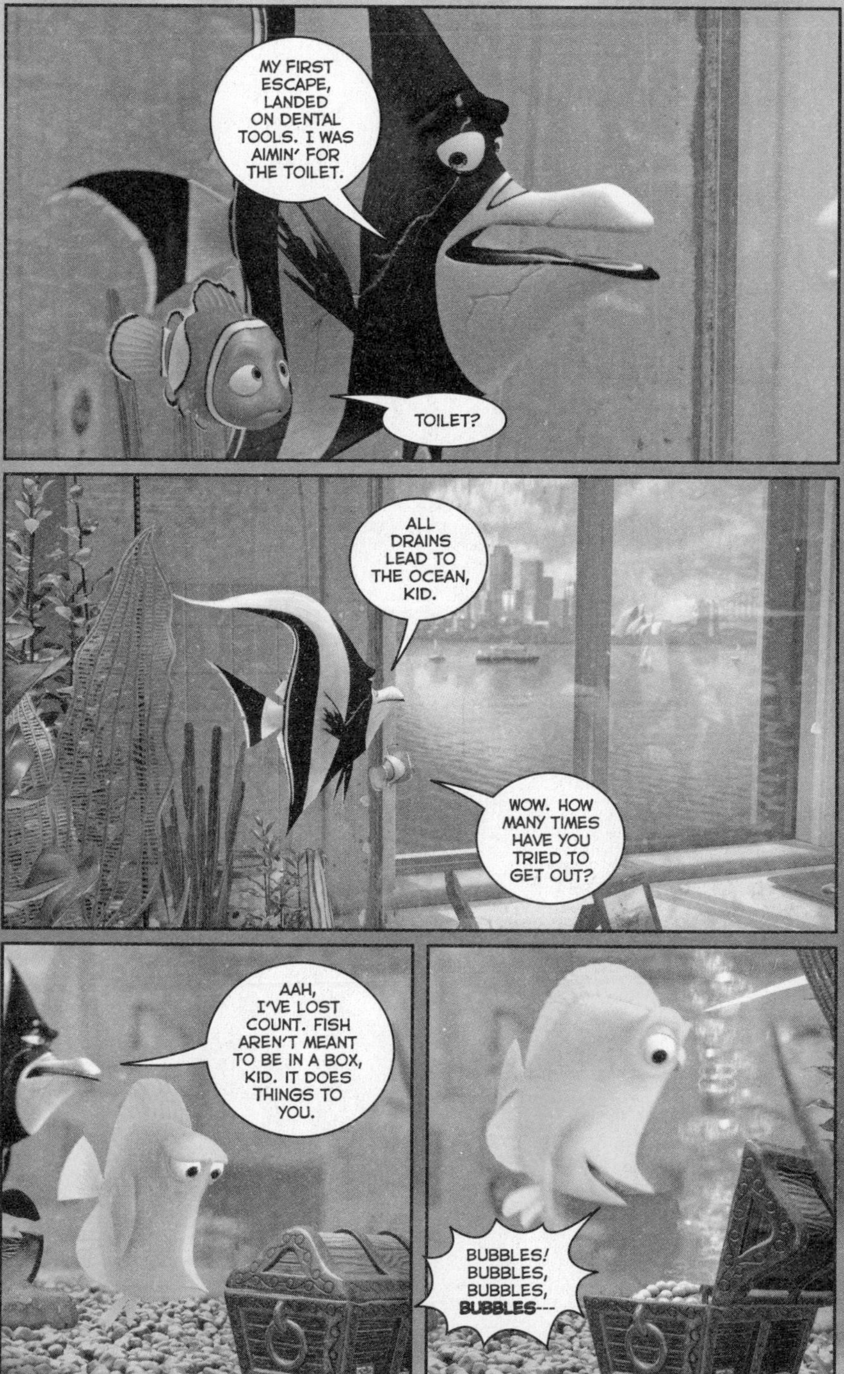
MY FIRST ESCAPE, LANDED ON DENTAL TOOLS. I WAS AIMIN' FOR THE TOILET.
TOILET?
ALL DRAINS LEAD TO THE OCEAN, KID.
WOW. HOW MANY TIMES HAVE YOU TRIED TO GET OUT?
AAH, I'VE LOST COUNT. FISH AREN'T MEANT TO BE IN A BOX, KID. IT DOES THINGS TO YOU.
BUBBLES! BUBBLES, BUBBLES, BUBBLES---

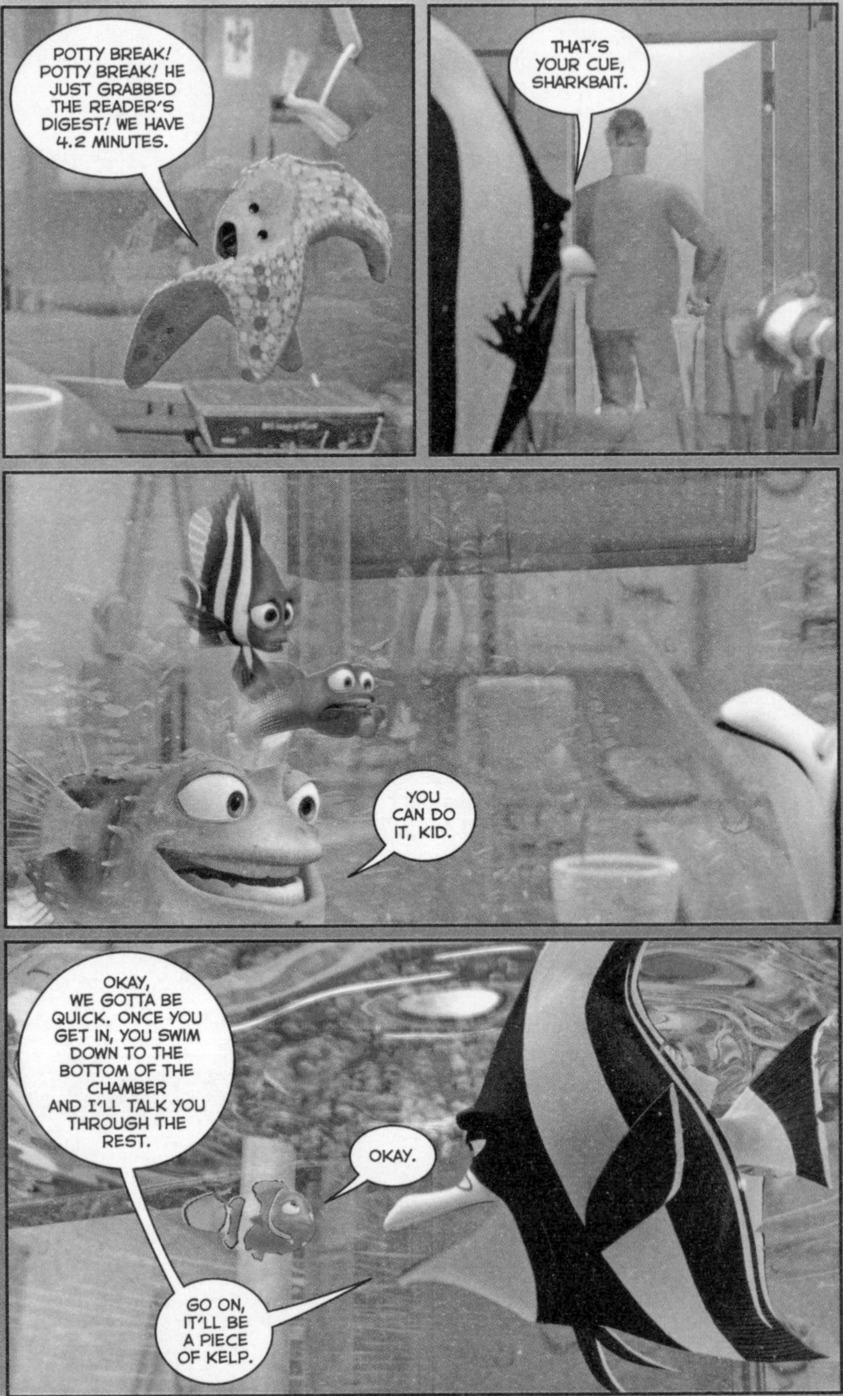
POTTY BREAK! POTTY BREAK! HE JUST GRABBED THE READER'S DIGEST! WE HAVE 4.2 MINUTES.
THAT'S YOUR CUE, SHARKBAIT.
YOU CAN DO IT, KID.
OKAY, WE GOTTA BE QUICK. ONCE YOU GET IN, YOU SWIM DOWN TO THE BOTTOM OF THE CHAMBER AND I'LL TALK YOU THROUGH THE REST.
OKAY.
GO ON, IT'LL BE A PIECE OF KELP.

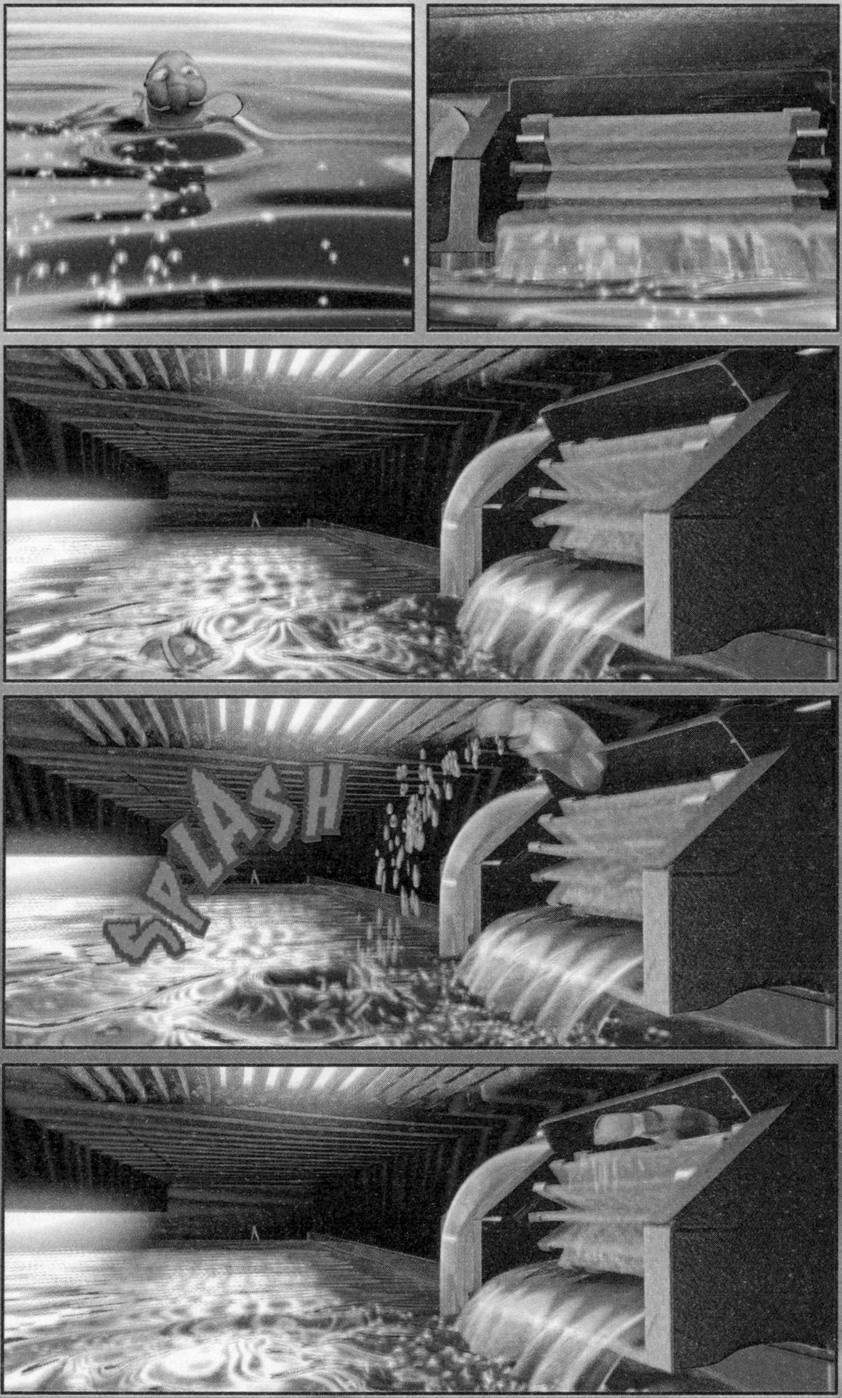
SPLASH

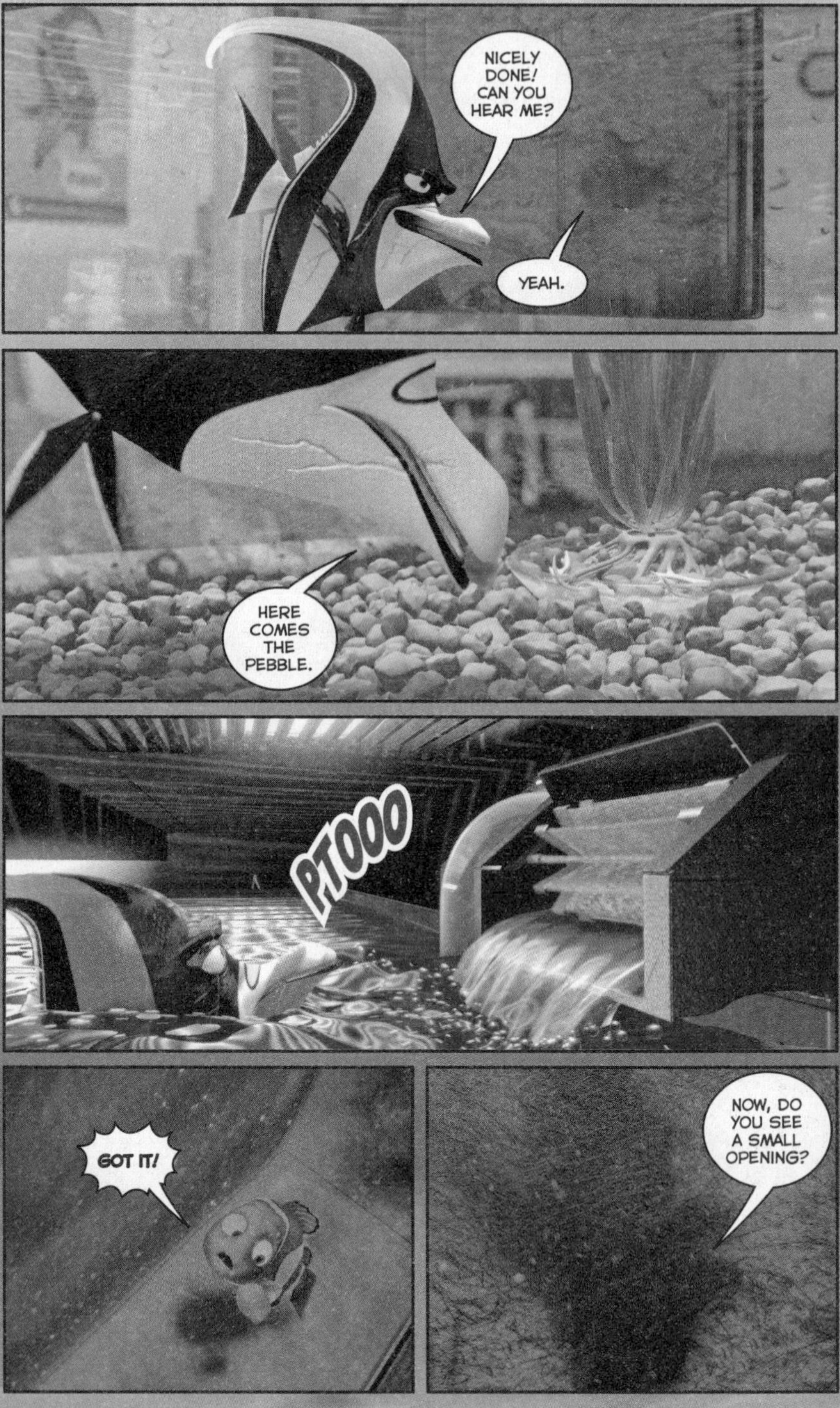
NICELY DONE! CAN YOU HEAR ME?
YEAH.
HERE COMES THE PEBBLE.
PTOOO
GOT IT!
NOW, DO YOU SEE A SMALL OPENING?

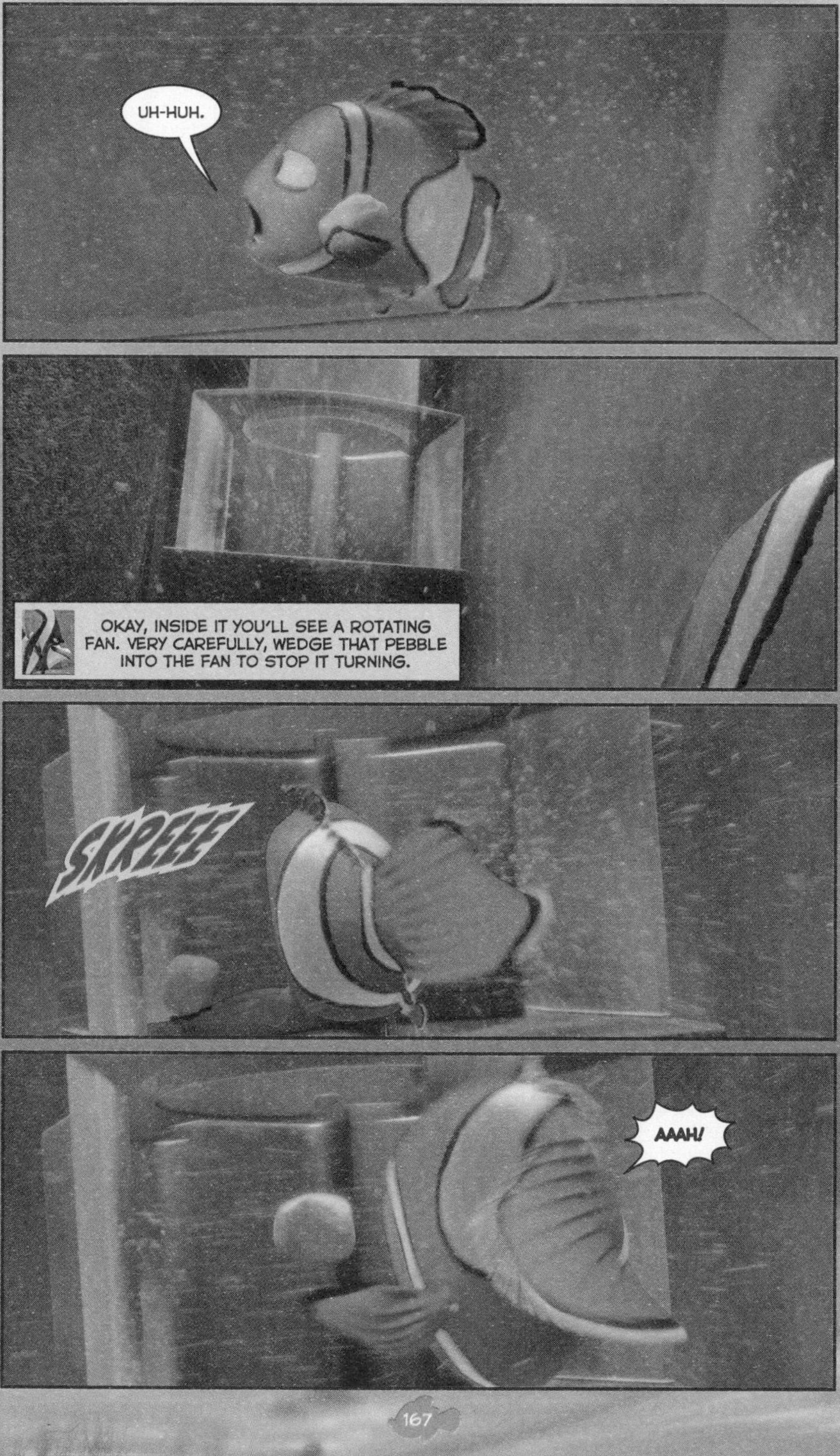
UH-HUH.
OKAY, INSIDE IT YOU'LL SEE A ROTATING FAN. VERY CAREFULLY, WEDGE THAT PEBBLE INTO THE FAN TO STOP IT TURNING.
SKREEE
AAAH!

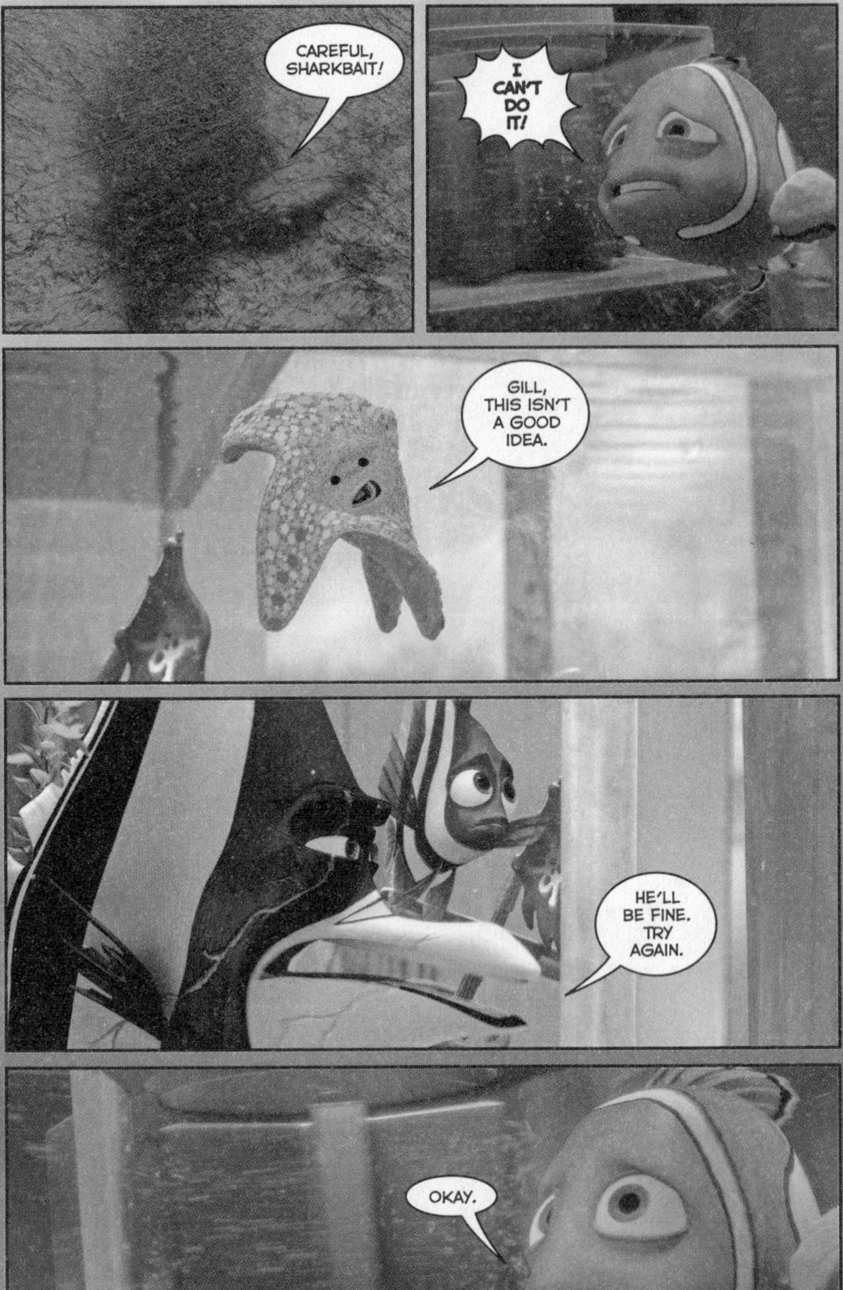
CAREFUL, SHARKBAIT!
I CAN'T DO IT!
GILL, THIS ISN'T A GOOD IDEA.
HE'LL BE FINE. TRY AGAIN.
OKAY.

THAT'S IT,
SHARKBAIT. NICE
AND STEADY.

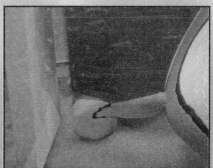

CLANK

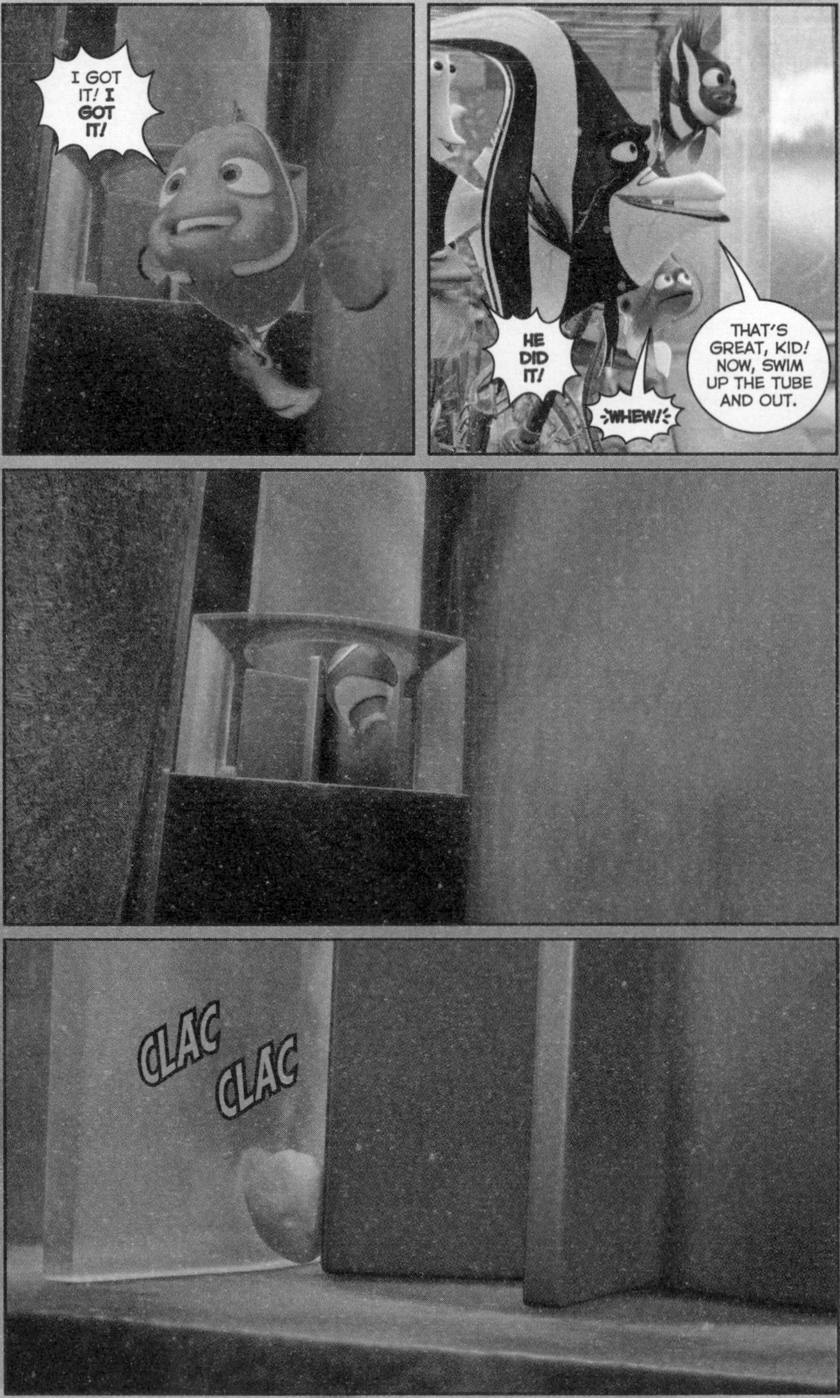
I GOT IT! I GOT IT!
HE DID IT!
WHEW!
THAT'S GREAT, KID! NOW, SWIM UP THE TUBE AND OUT.
CLAC
CLAC

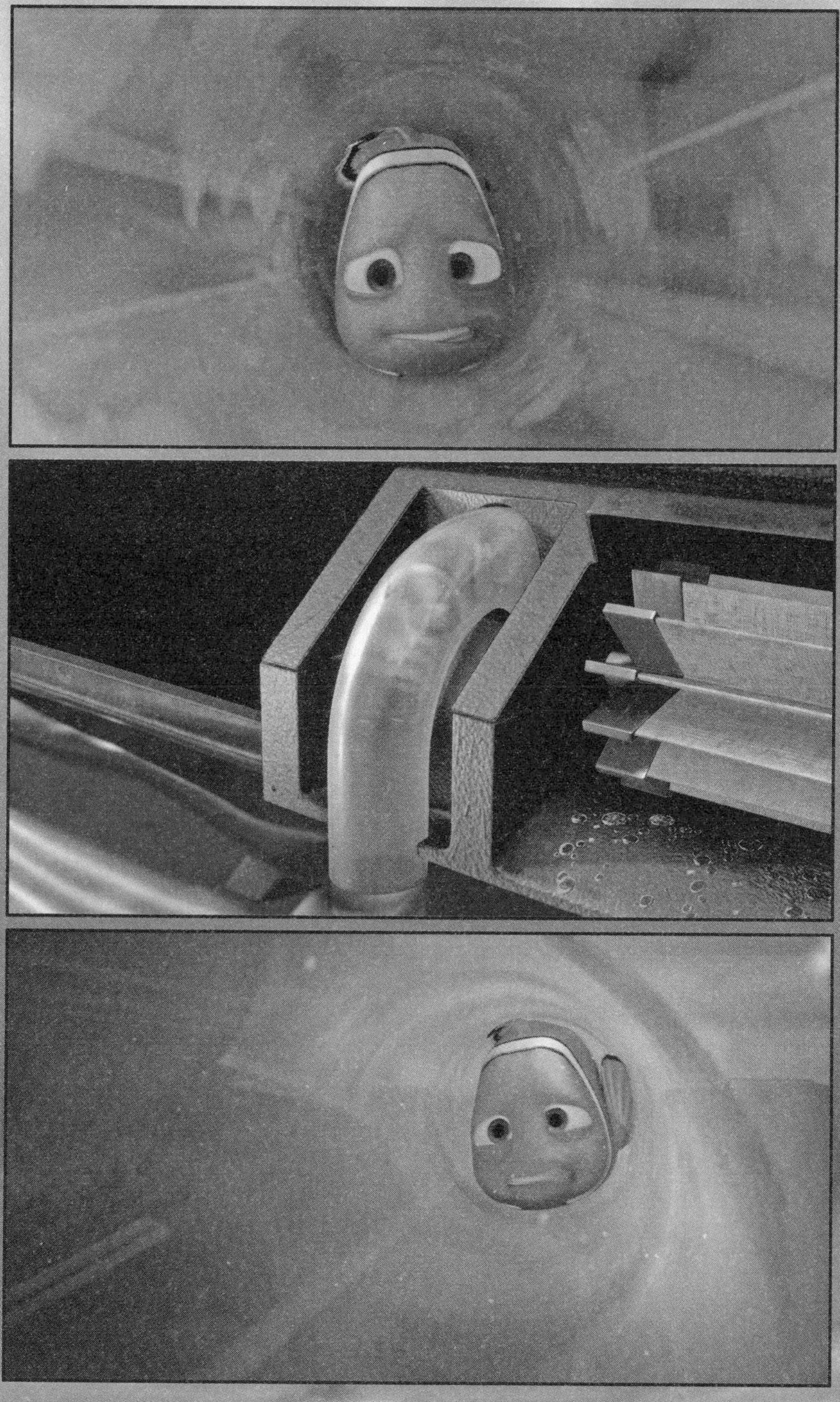

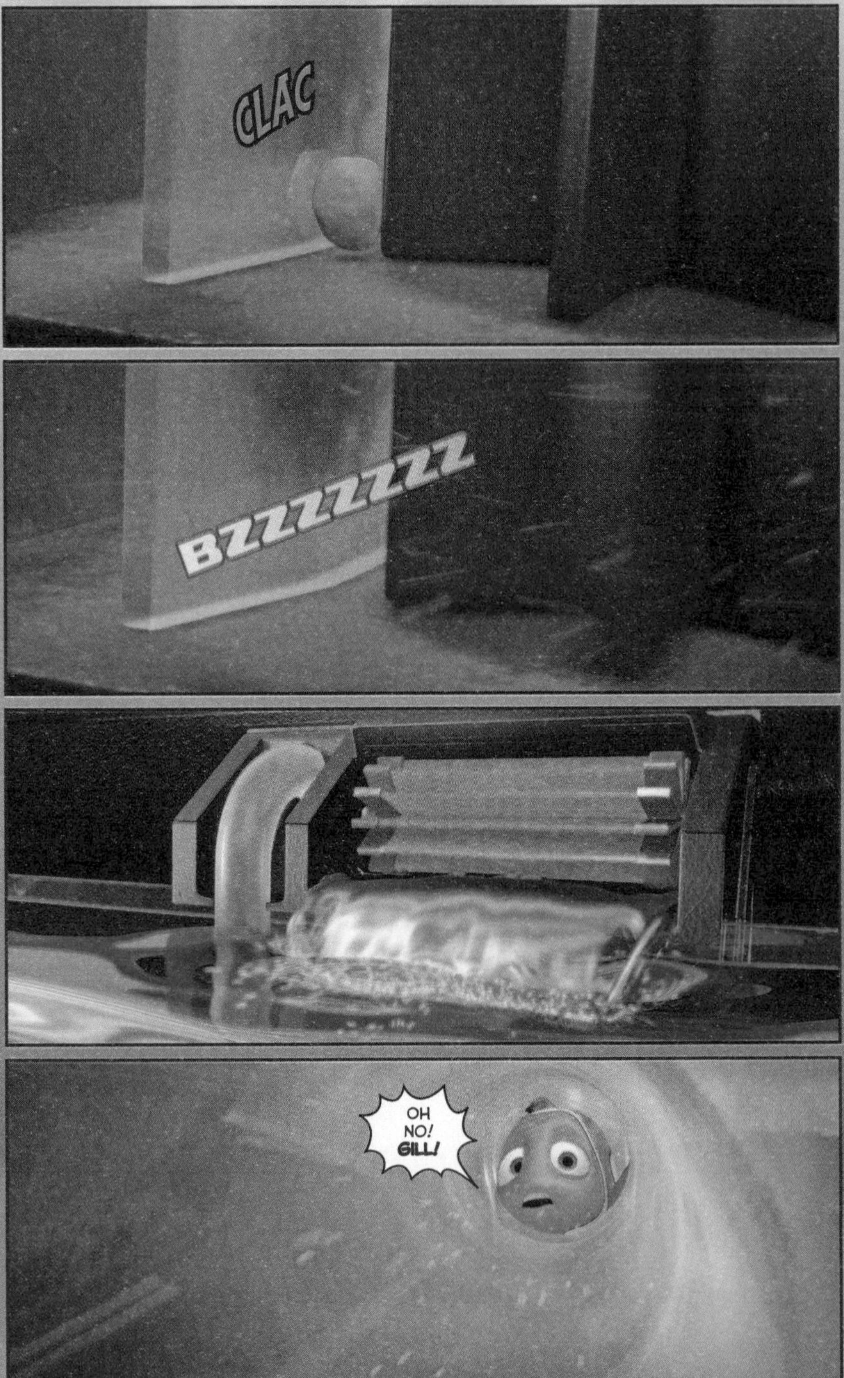
CLAC
BZZZZZZZ
OH NO! GILL!

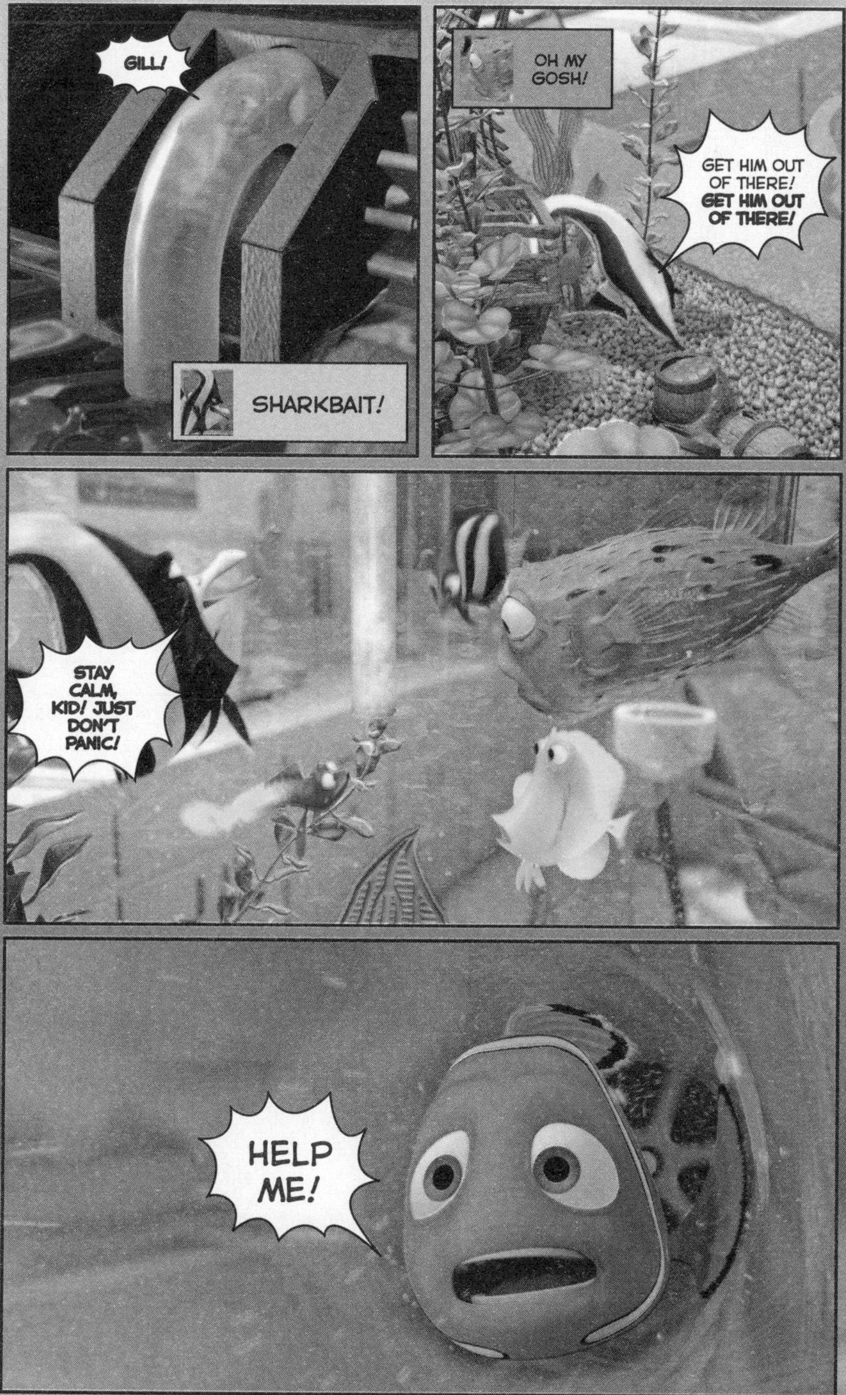
GILL!
SHARKBAIT!
OH MY GOSH!
GET HIM OUT OF THERE! GET HIM OUT OF THERE!
STAY CALM, KID! JUST DON'T PANIC!
HELP ME!

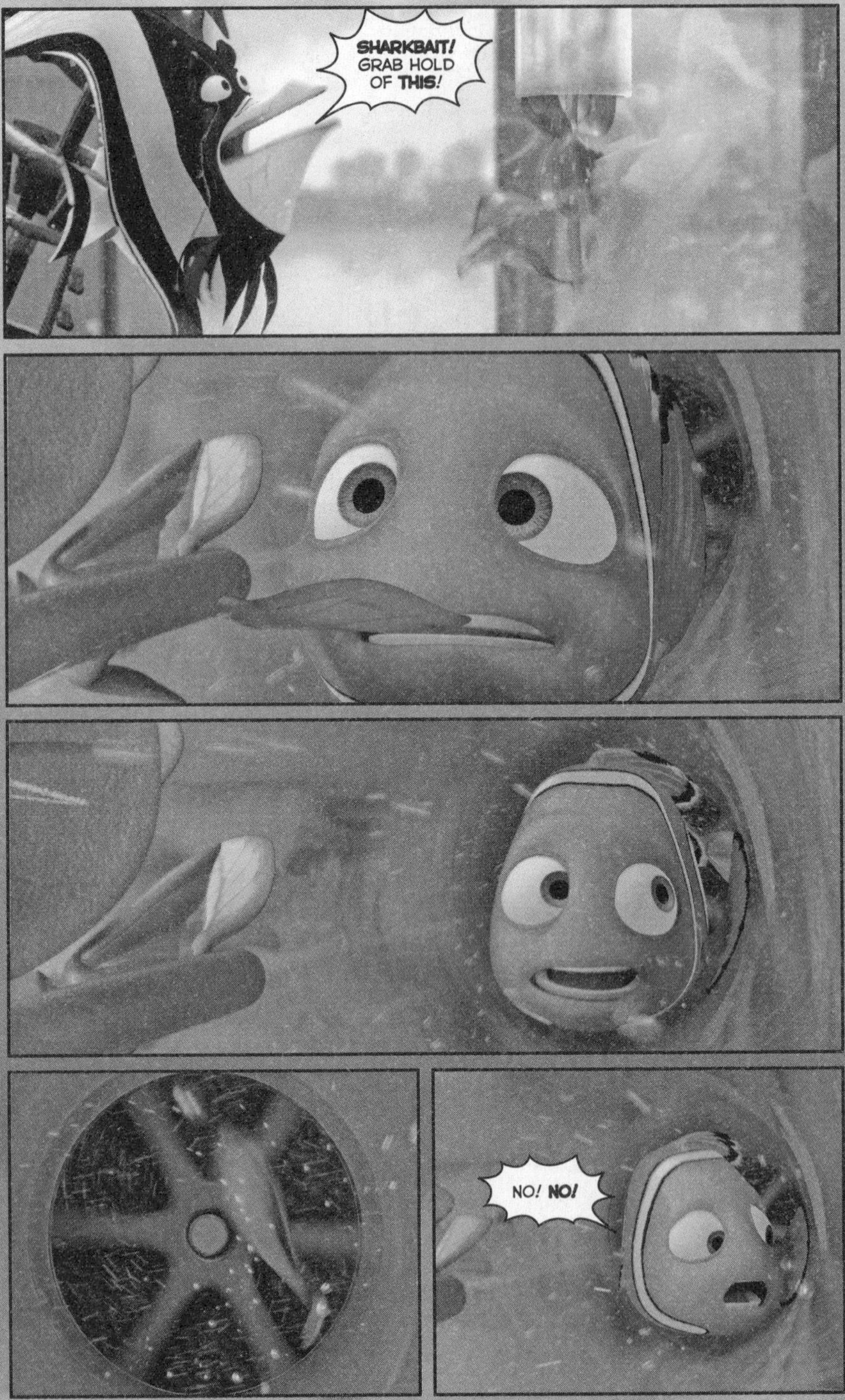
SHARKBAIT! GRAB HOLD OF THIS!
NO! NO!

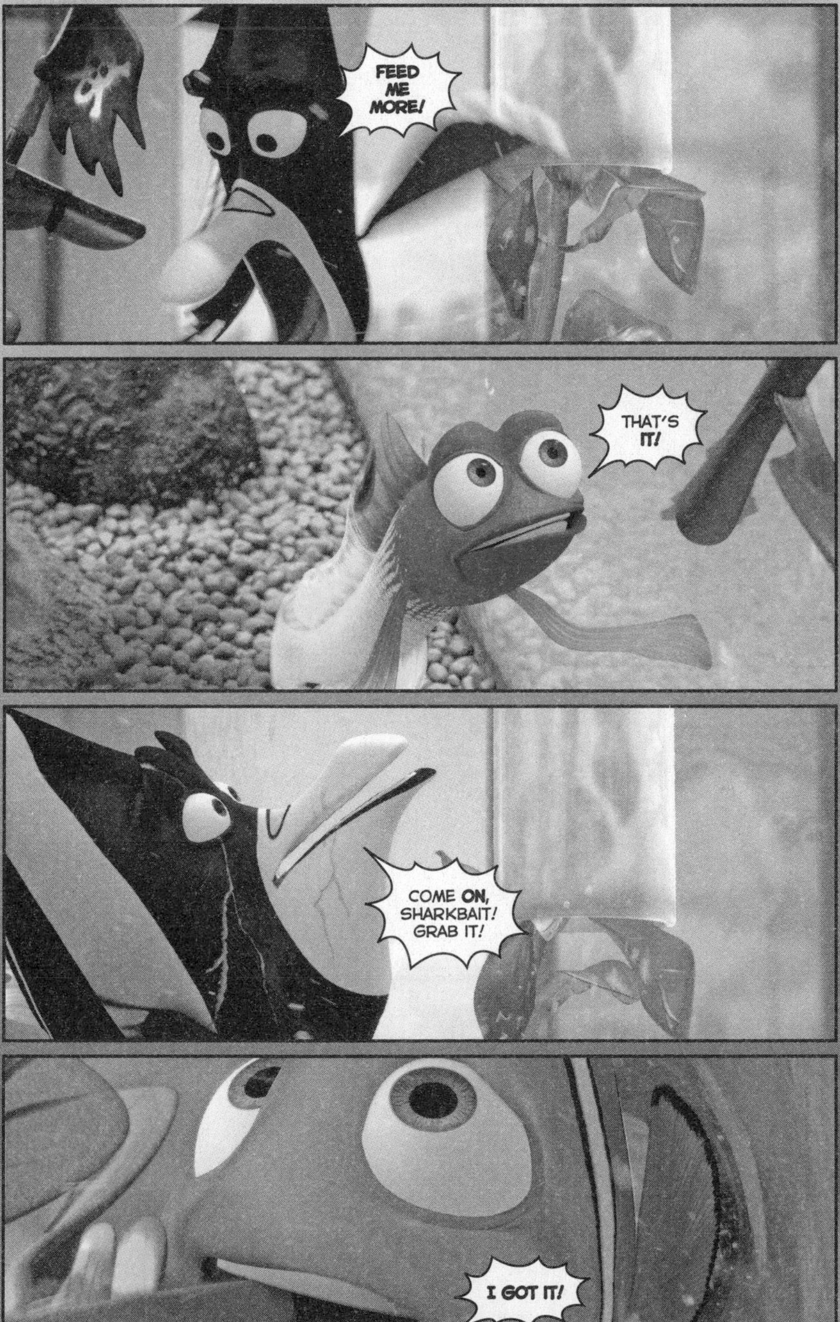
FEED ME MORE!
THAT'S IT!
COME ON, SHARKBAIT! GRAB IT!
I GOT IT!

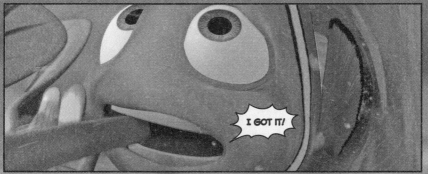

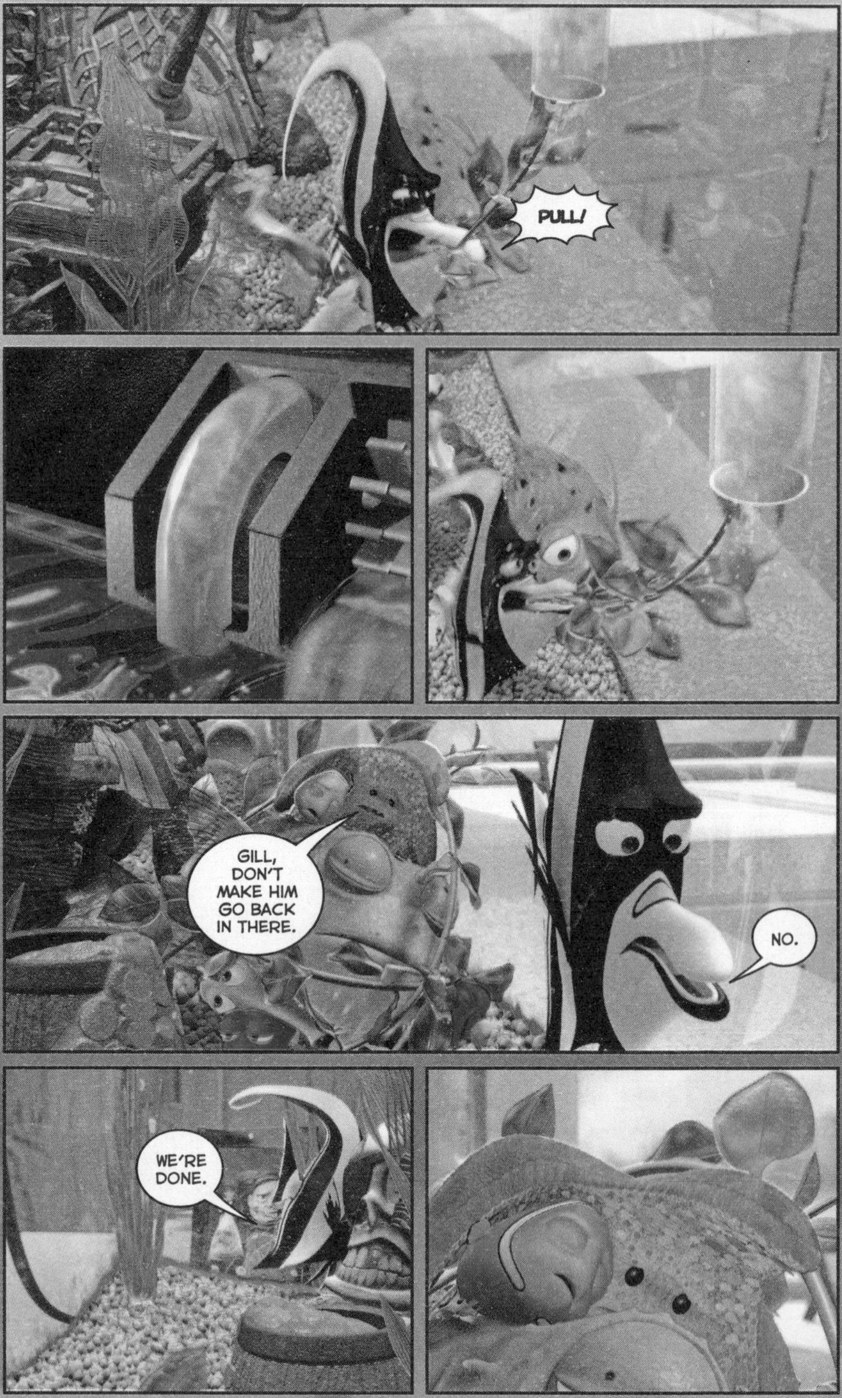
PULL!
GILL, DON'T MAKE HIM GO BACK IN THERE.
NO.
WE'RE DONE.

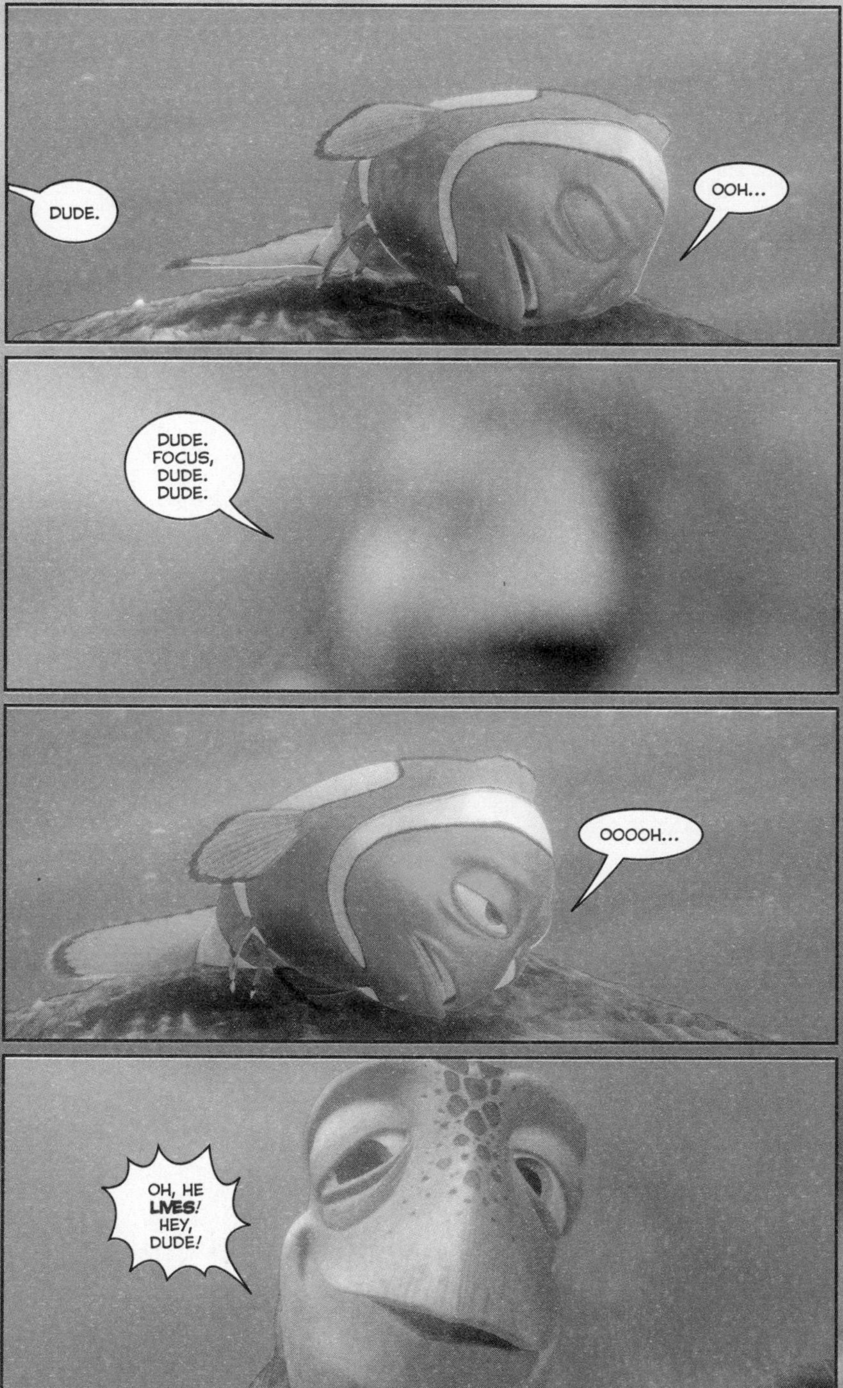
DUDE.
OOH...
DUDE. FOCUS, DUDE. DUDE.
OOOOH...
OH, HE LIVES! HEY, DUDE!

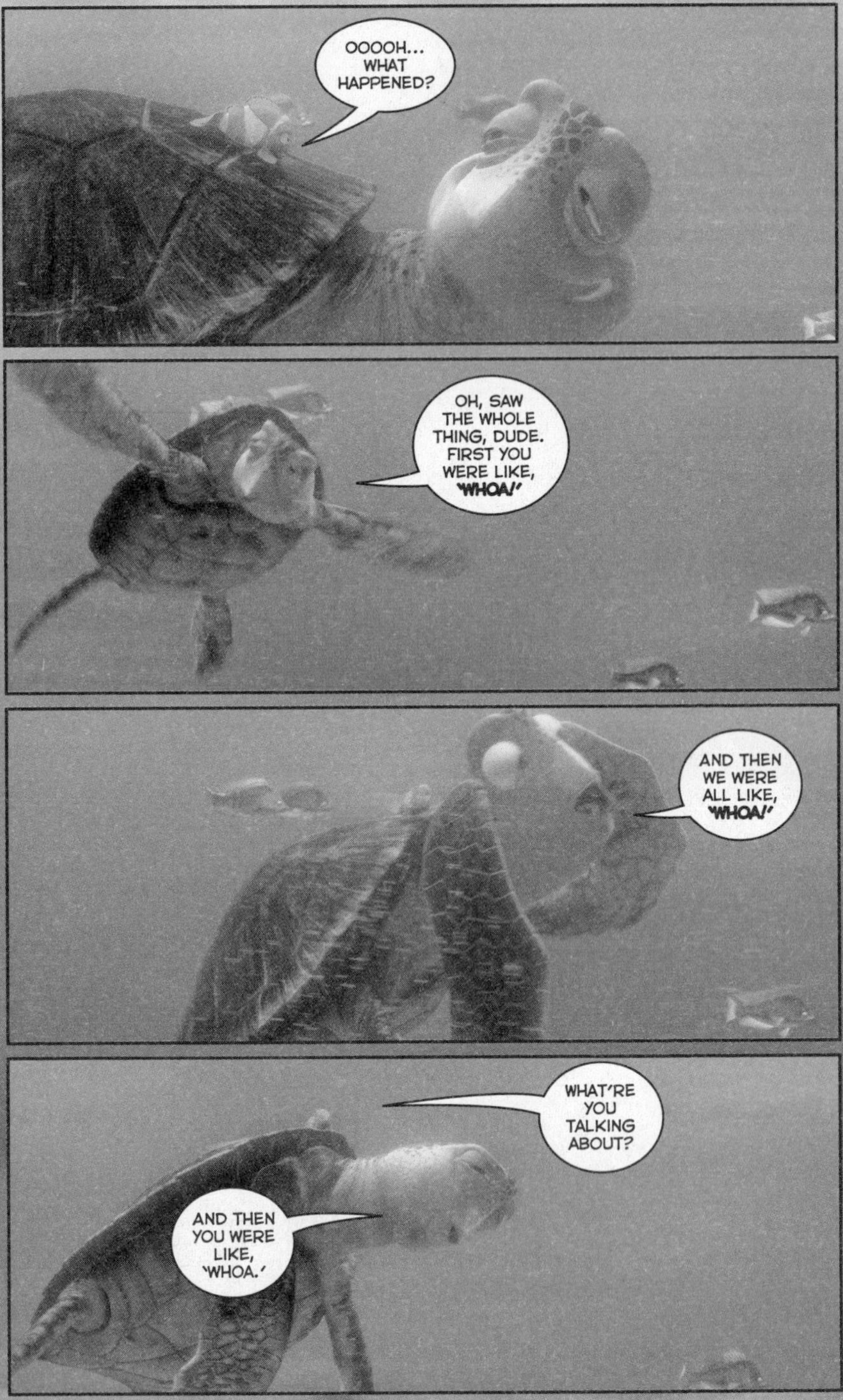
OOOOH... WHAT HAPPENED?
OH, SAW THE WHOLE THING, DUDE. FIRST YOU WERE LIKE, 'WHOA!'
AND THEN WE WERE ALL LIKE, 'WHOA!'
WHAT'RE YOU TALKING ABOUT?
AND THEN YOU WERE LIKE, 'WHOA.'

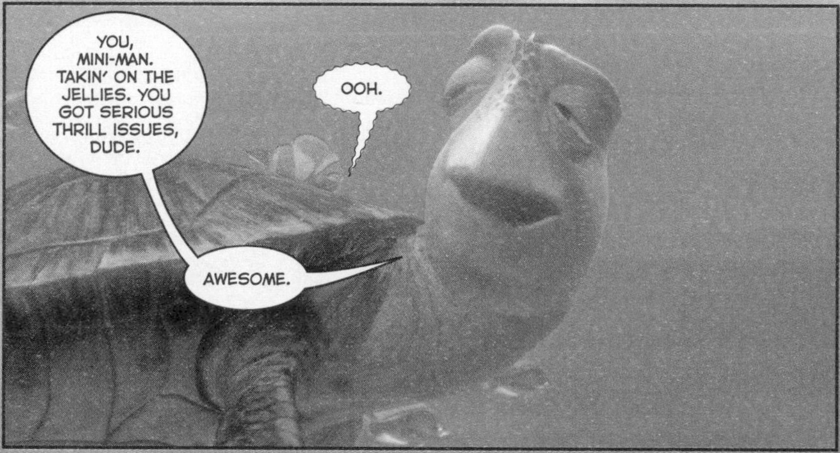
YOU, MINI-MAN. TAKIN' ON THE JELLIES. YOU GOT SERIOUS THRILL ISSUES, DUDE.
OOH.
AWESOME.

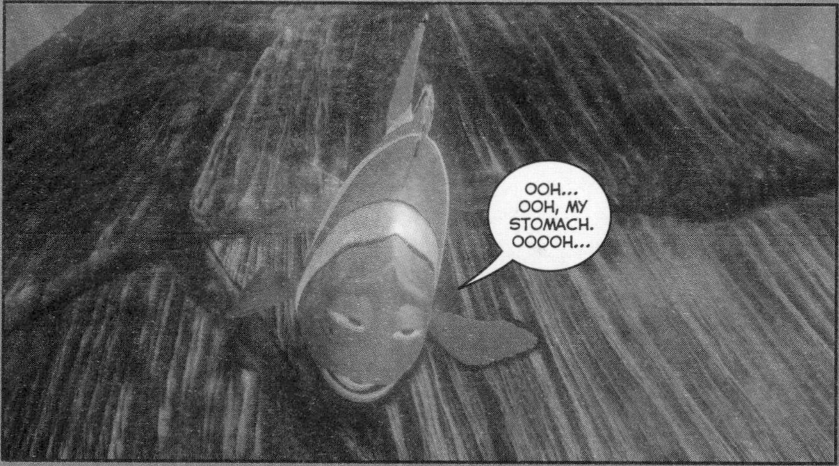
OOH... OOH, MY STOMACH. OOOOH...

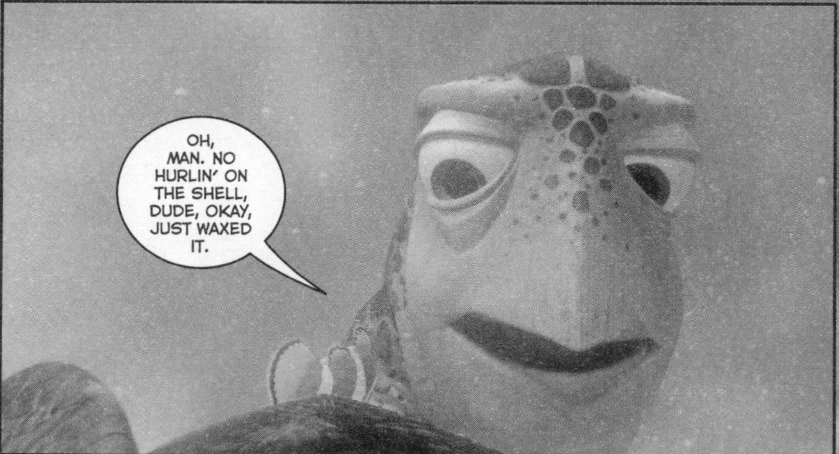
OH, MAN. NO HURLIN' ON THE SHELL, DUDE, OKAY, JUST WAXED IT.

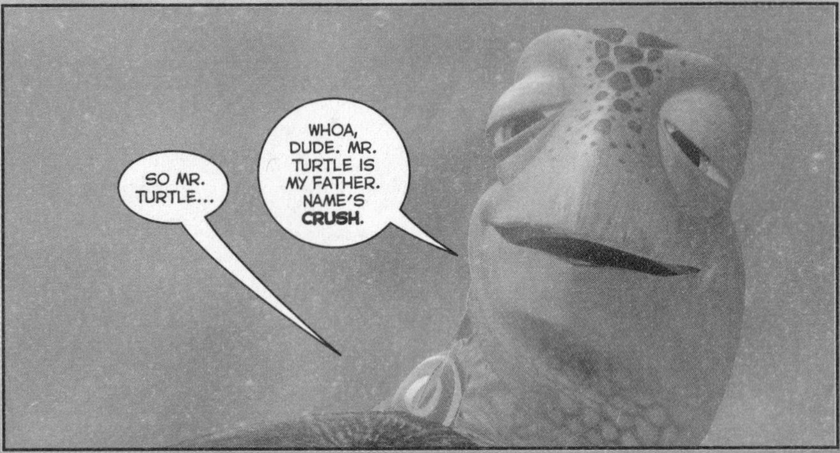
SO MR. TURTLE...
WHOA, DUDE. MR. TURTLE IS MY FATHER. NAME'S **CRUSH**.

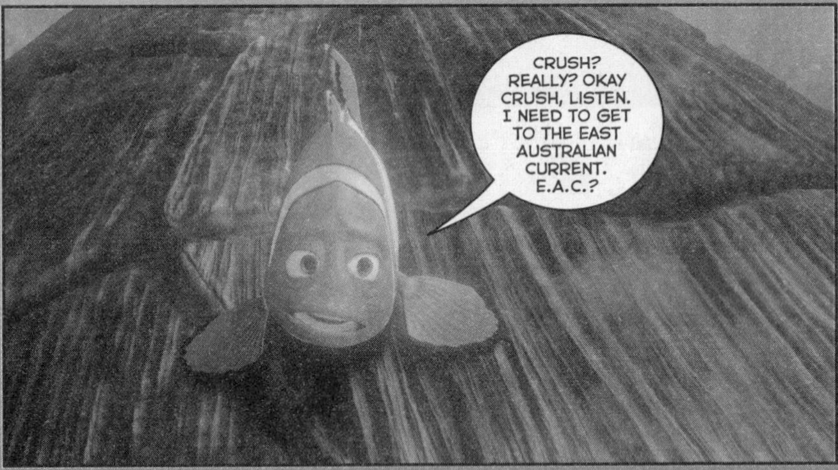
CRUSH? REALLY? OKAY CRUSH, LISTEN. I NEED TO GET TO THE EAST AUSTRALIAN CURRENT. E.A.C.?

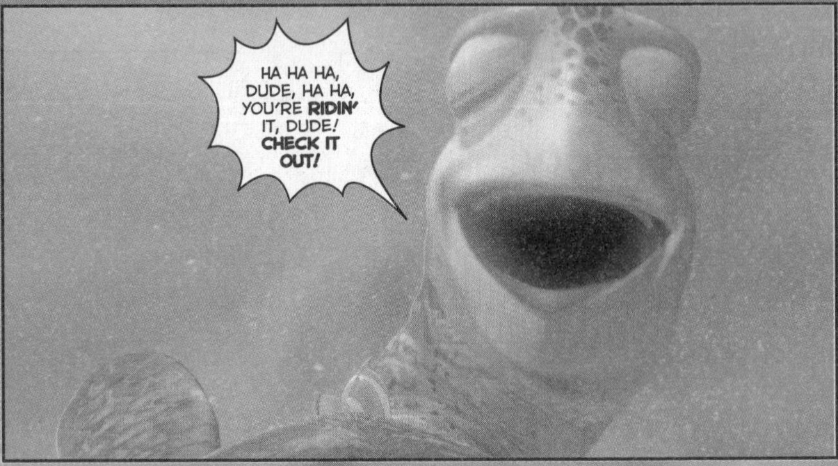
HA HA HA, DUDE, HA HA, YOU'RE **RIDIN'** IT, DUDE! **CHECK IT OUT!**

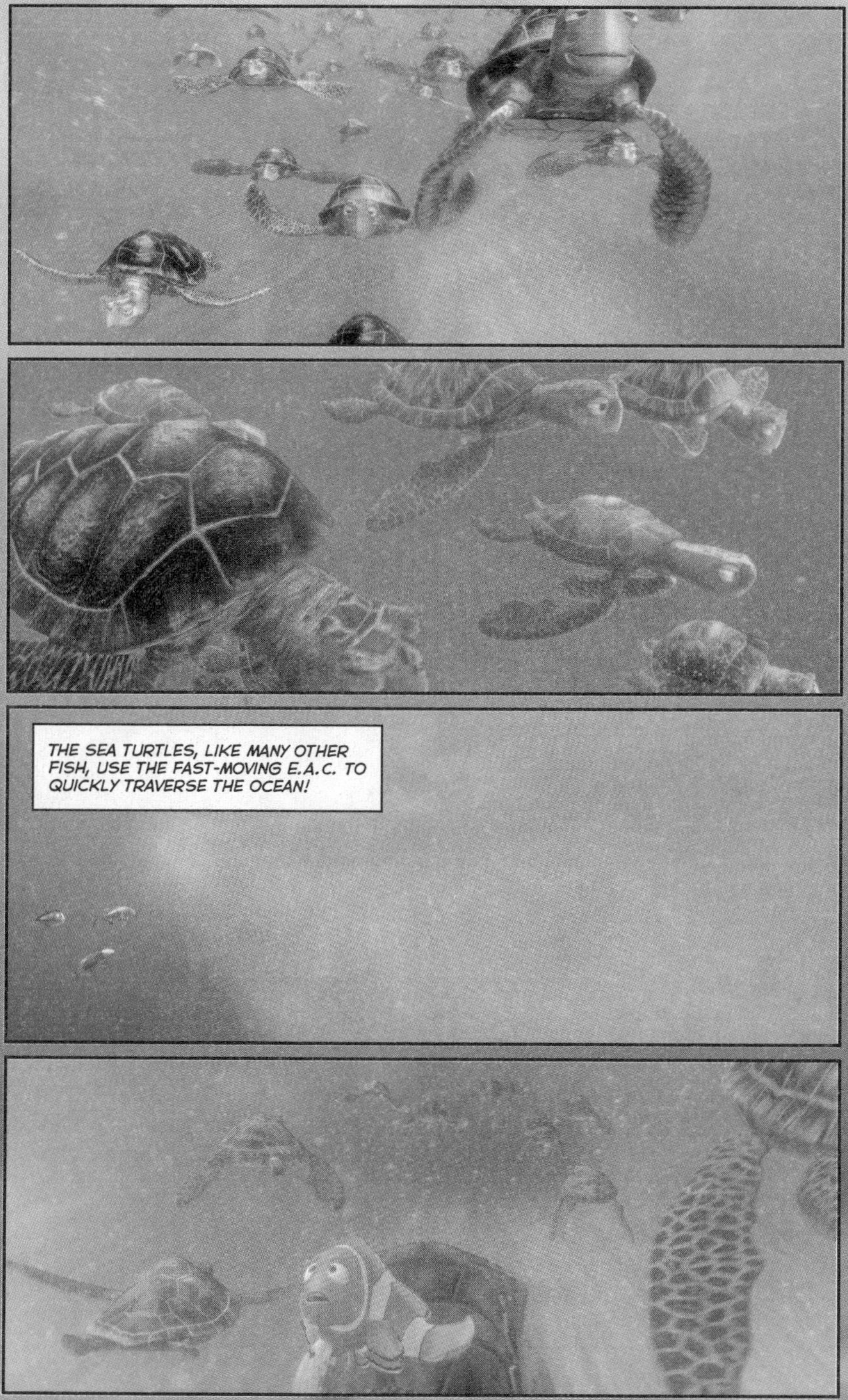
THE SEA TURTLES, LIKE MANY OTHER FISH, USE THE FAST-MOVING E.A.C. TO QUICKLY TRAVERSE THE OCEAN!

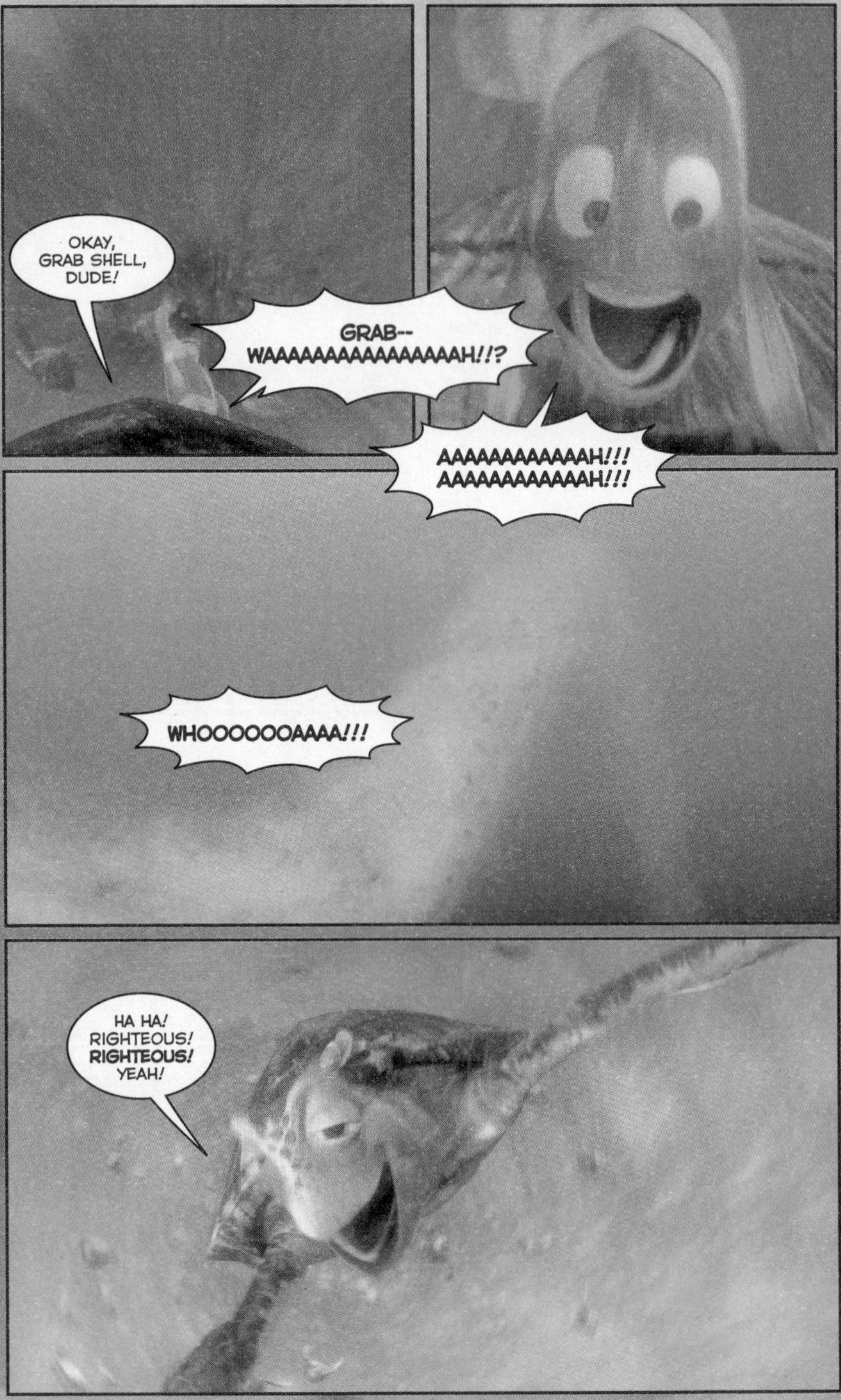
OKAY, GRAB SHELL, DUDE!
GRAB-- WAAAAAAAAAAAAAAAAAH!!?
AAAAAAAAAAAAAH!!! AAAAAAAAAAAAAH!!!
WHOOOOOOAAAA!!!
HA HA! RIGHTEOUS! RIGHTEOUS! YEAH!

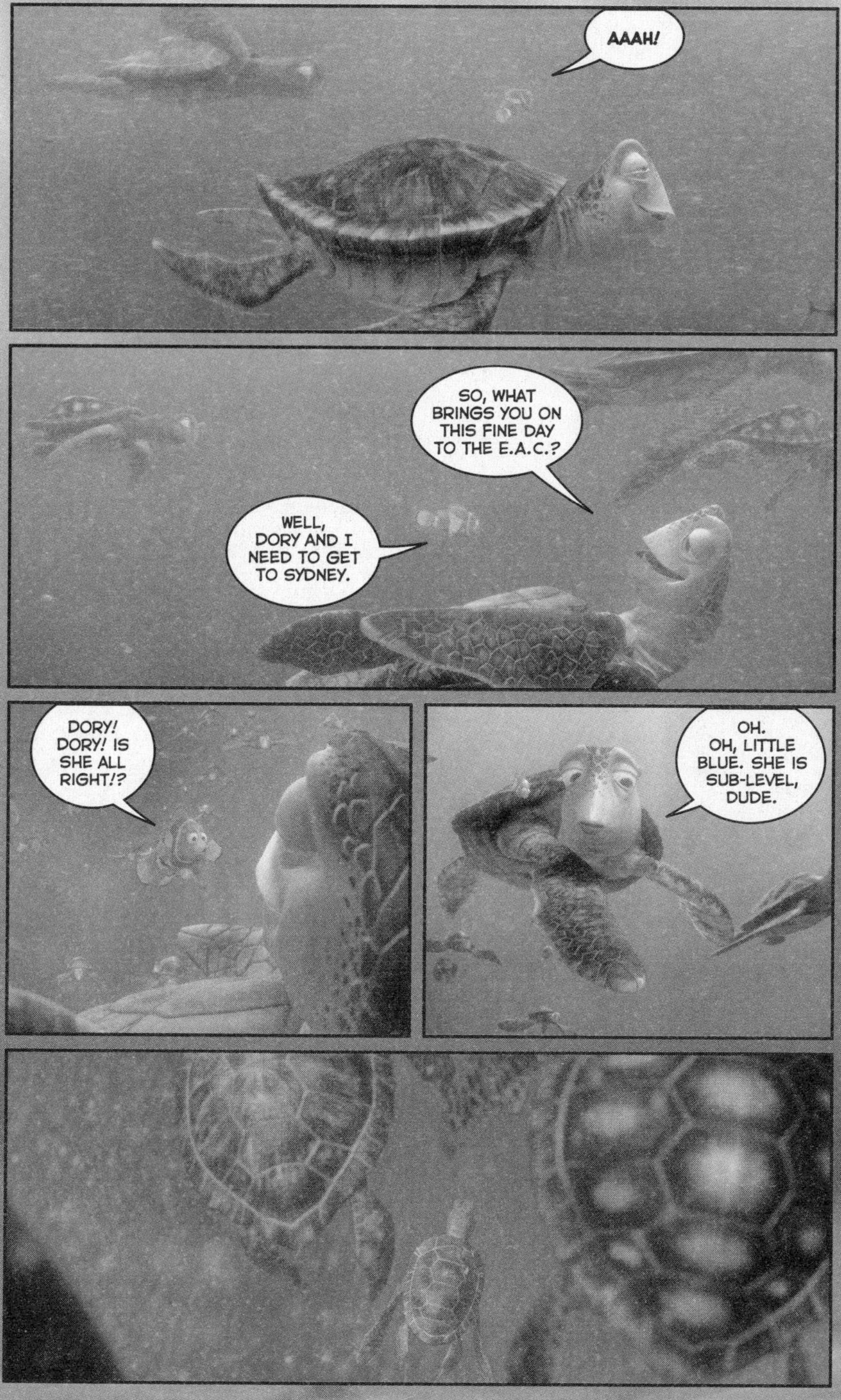

AAAH!
SO, WHAT BRINGS YOU ON THIS FINE DAY TO THE E.A.C.?
WELL, DORY AND I NEED TO GET TO SYDNEY.
DORY! DORY! IS SHE ALL RIGHT!?
OH. OH, LITTLE BLUE. SHE IS SUB-LEVEL, DUDE.

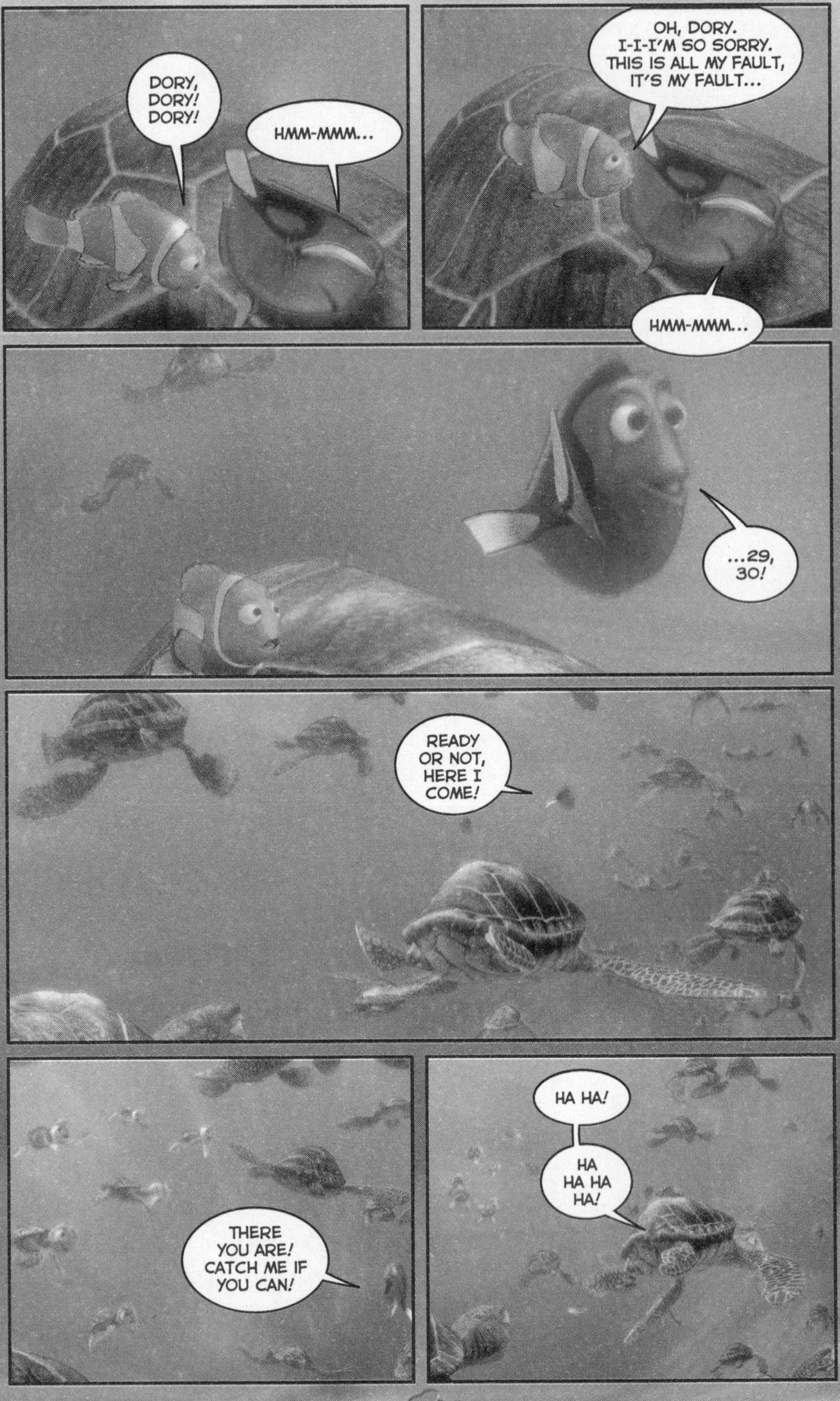
DORY, DORY! DORY!
HMM-MMM...
OH, DORY. I-I-I'M SO SORRY. THIS IS ALL MY FAULT, IT'S MY FAULT...
HMM-MMM...
...29, 30!
READY OR NOT, HERE I COME!
THERE YOU ARE! CATCH ME IF YOU CAN!
HA HA!
HA HA HA HA!

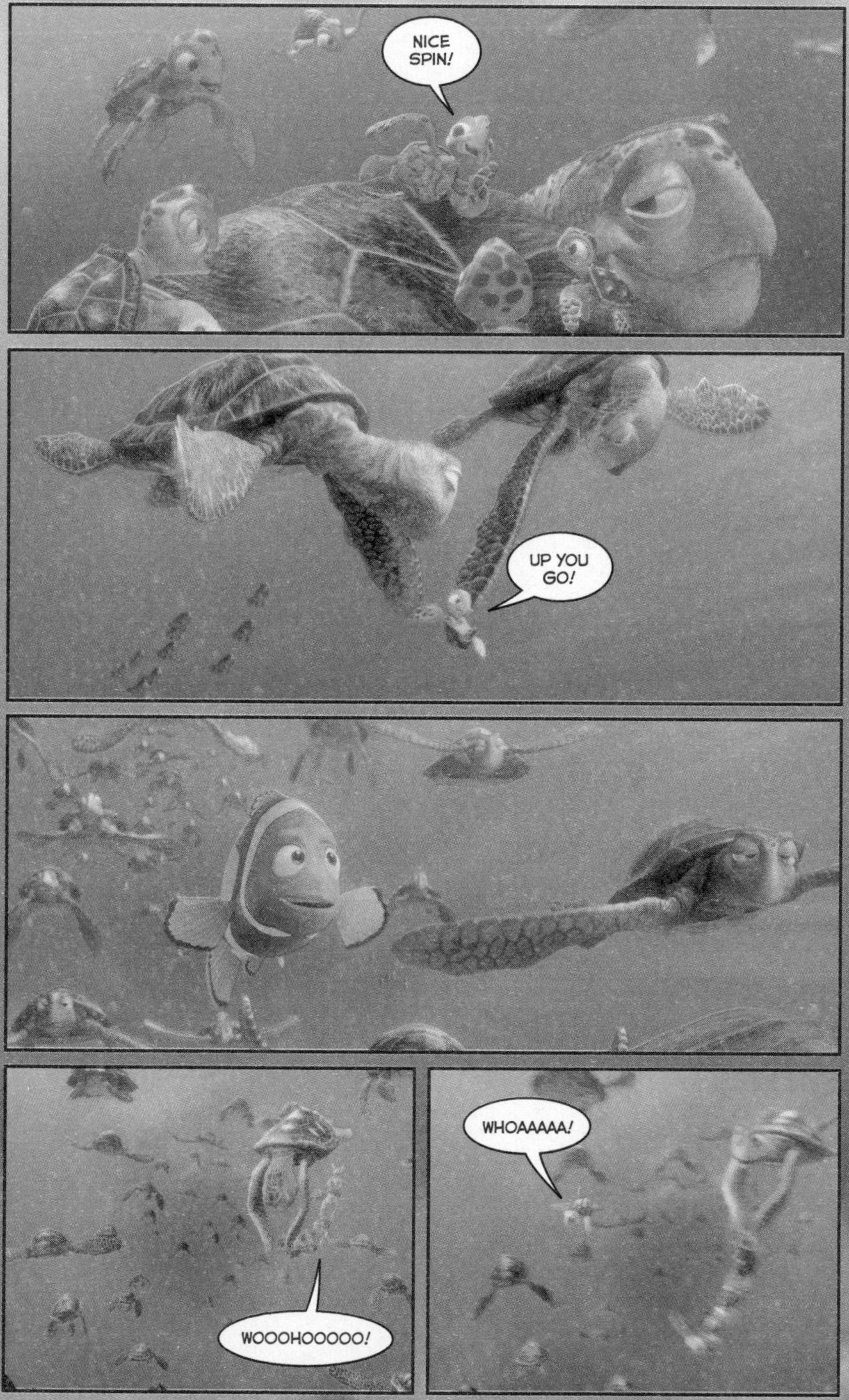
NICE SPIN!
UP YOU GO!
WOOOHOOOOO!
WHOAAAAA!

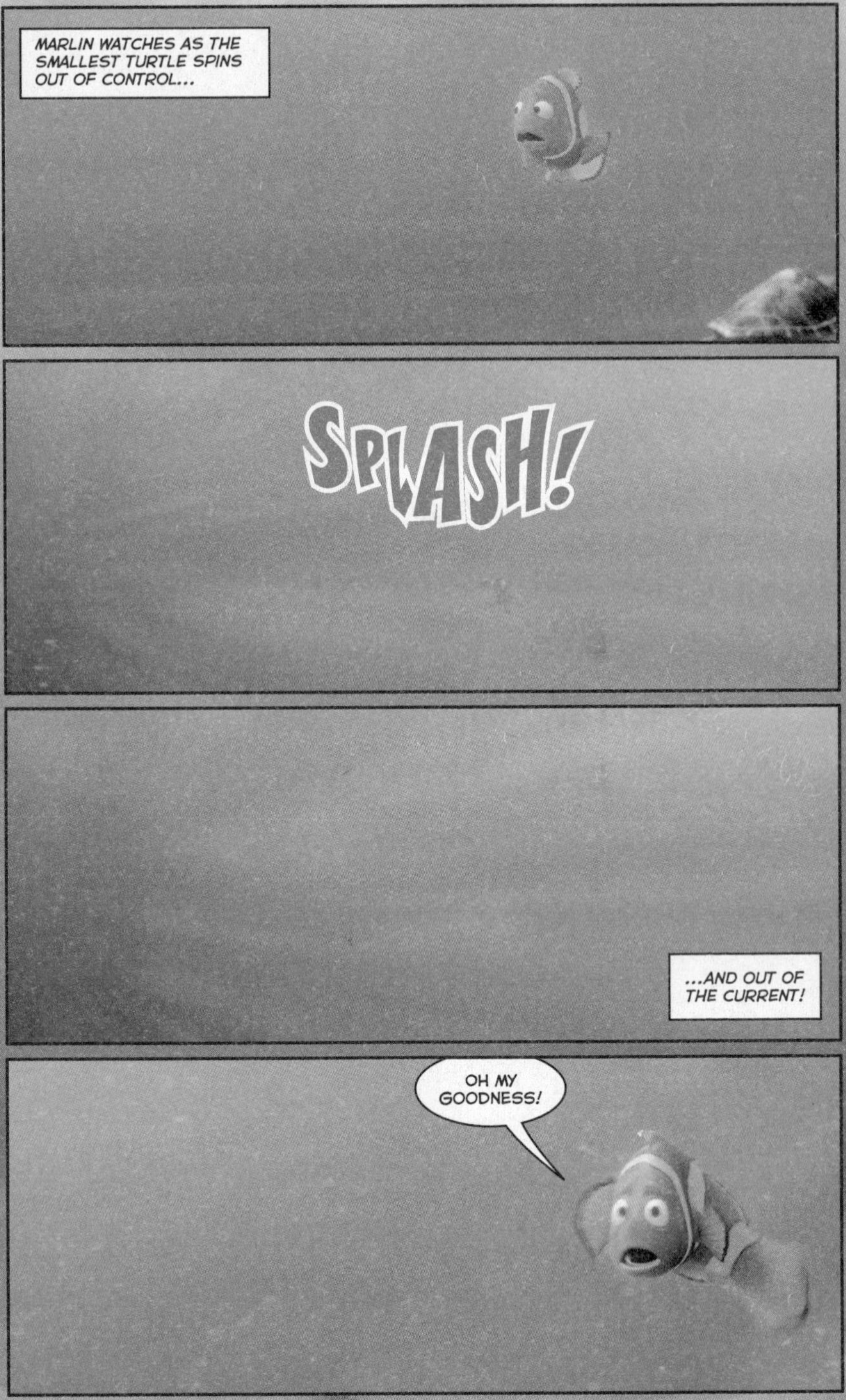
MARLIN WATCHES AS THE SMALLEST TURTLE SPINS OUT OF CONTROL...
SPLASH!
...AND OUT OF THE CURRENT!
OH MY GOODNESS!

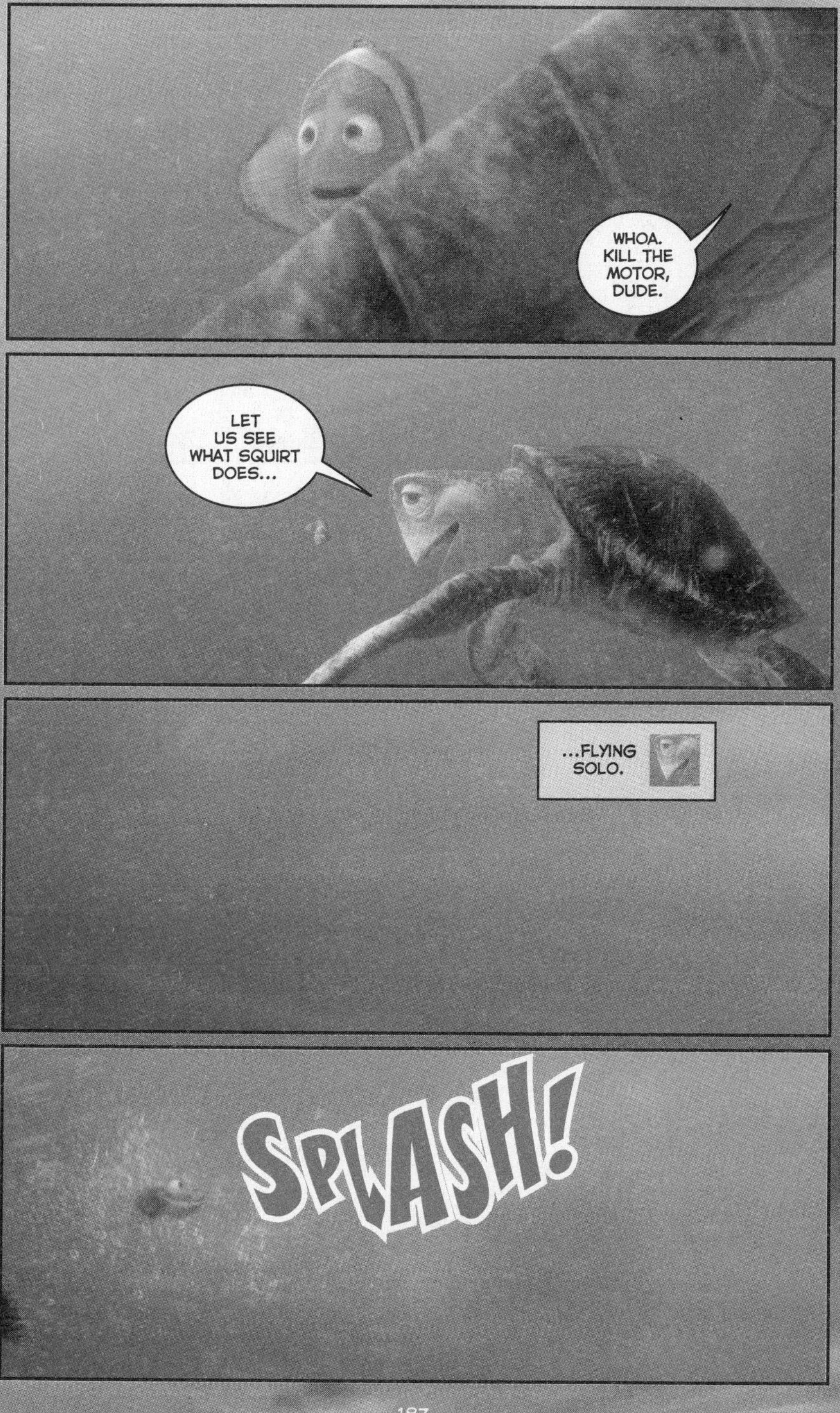
WHOA. KILL THE MOTOR, DUDE.
LET US SEE WHAT SQUIRT DOES...
...FLYING SOLO.
SPLASH!

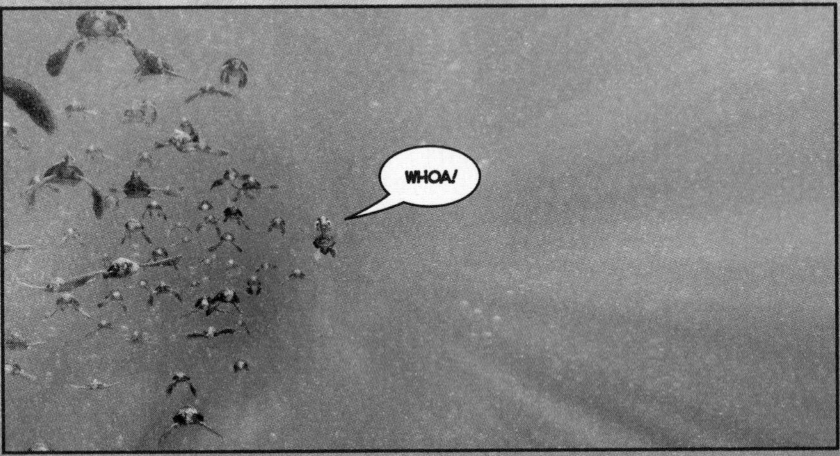
WHOA!

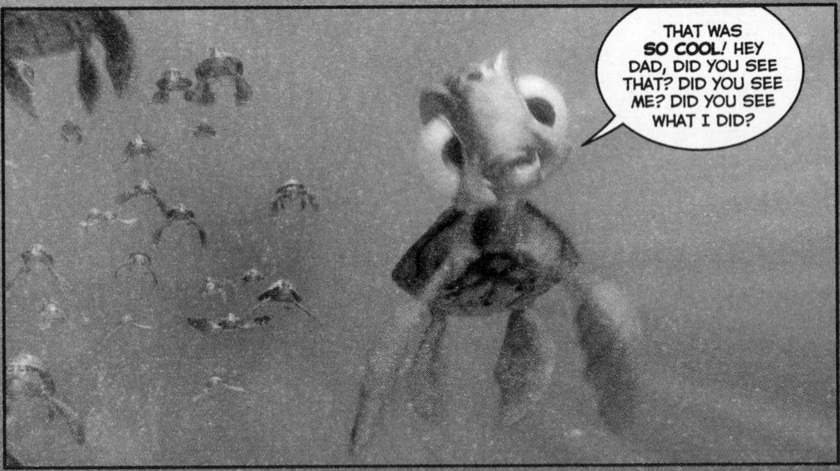
THAT WAS SO COOL! HEY DAD, DID YOU SEE THAT? DID YOU SEE ME? DID YOU SEE WHAT I DID?

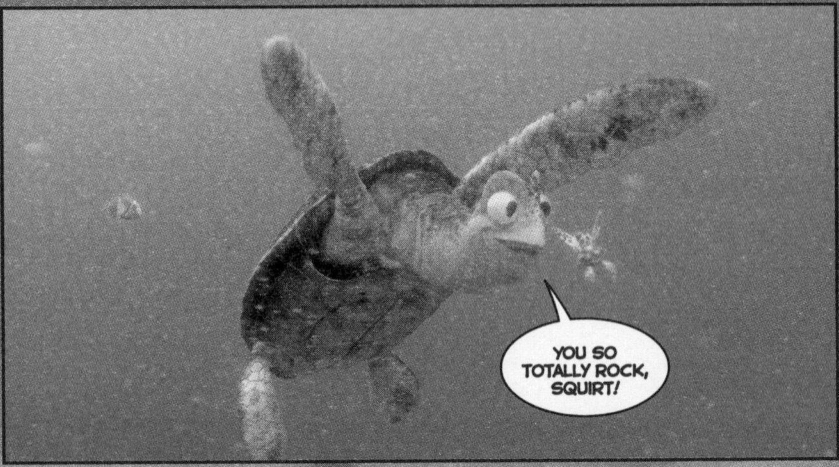
YOU SO TOTALLY ROCK, SQUIRT!

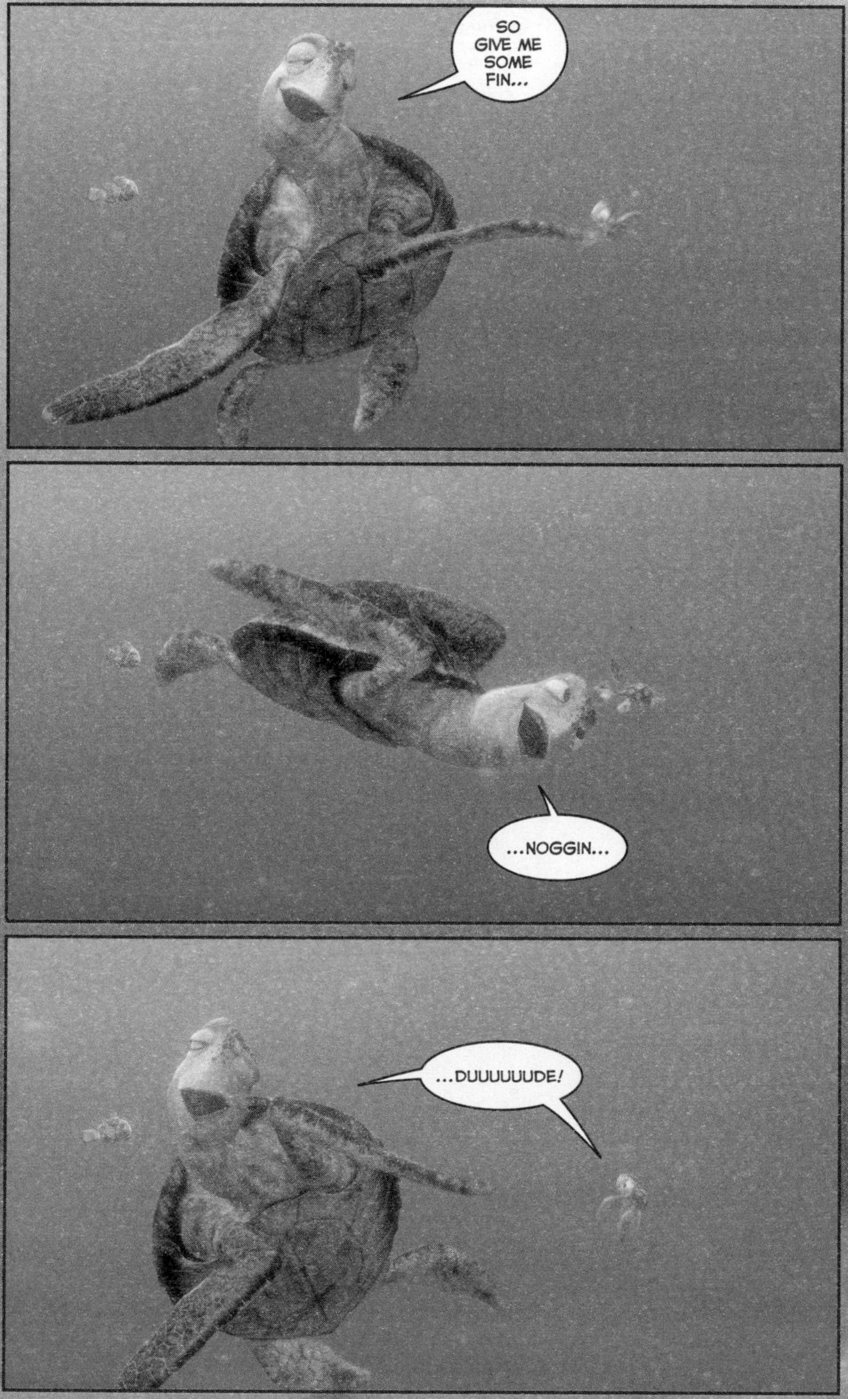
SO GIVE ME SOME FIN...
...NOGGIN...
...DUUUUUUDE!

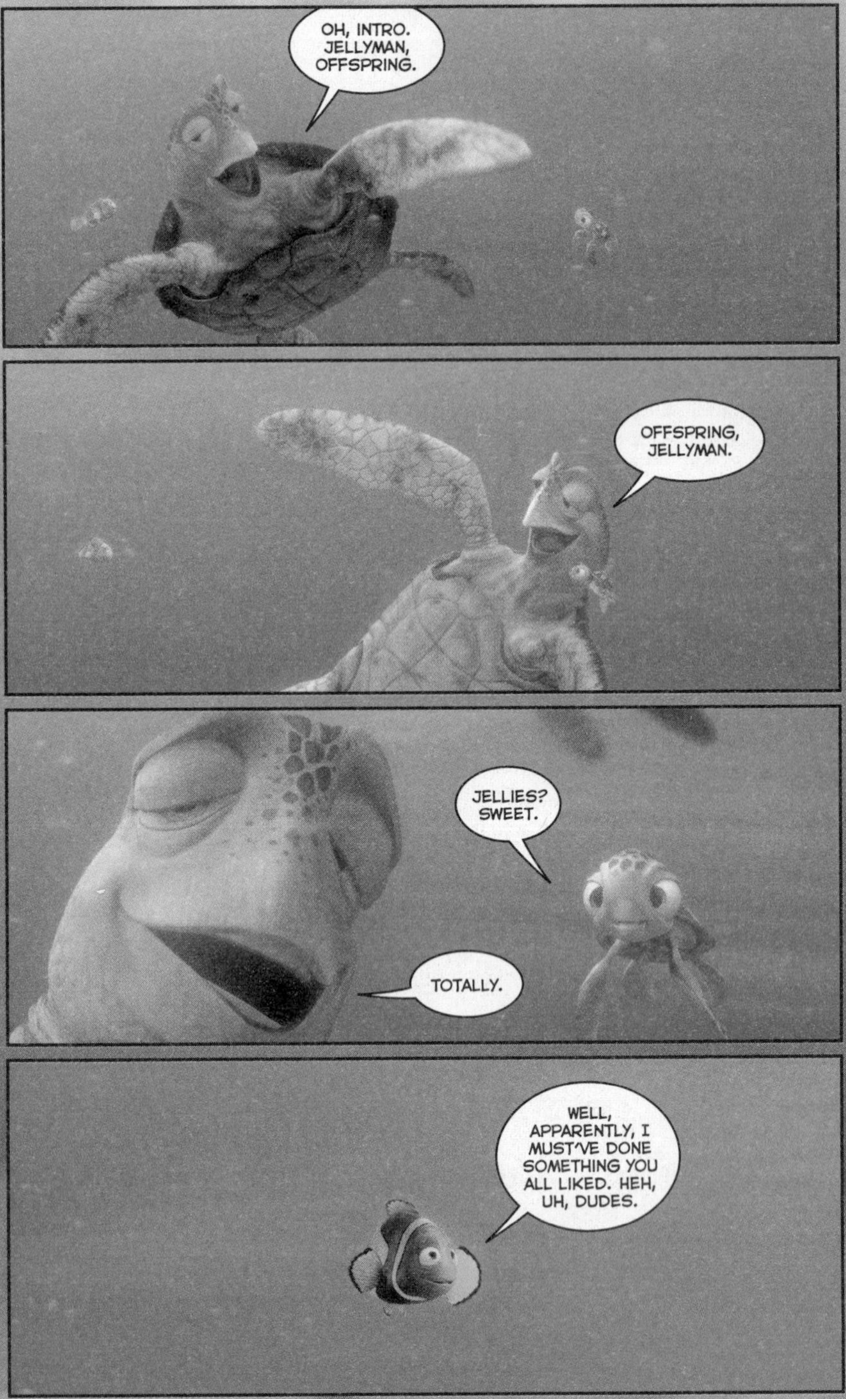
OH, INTRO. JELLYMAN, OFFSPRING.
OFFSPRING, JELLYMAN.
JELLIES? SWEET.
TOTALLY.
WELL, APPARENTLY, I MUST'VE DONE SOMETHING YOU ALL LIKED. HEH, UH, DUDES.

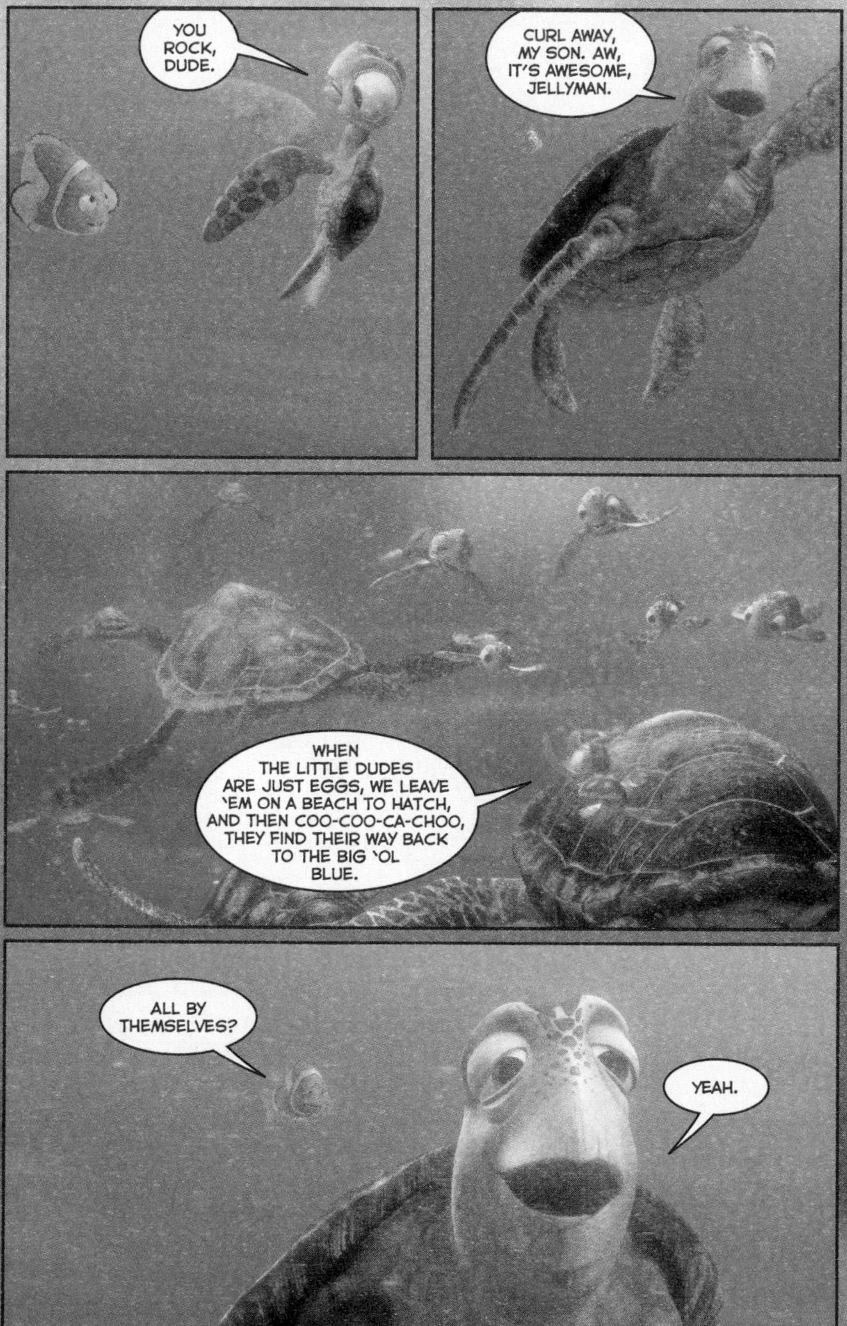
YOU ROCK, DUDE.
CURL AWAY, MY SON. AW, IT'S AWESOME, JELLYMAN.
WHEN THE LITTLE DUDES ARE JUST EGGS, WE LEAVE 'EM ON A BEACH TO HATCH, AND THEN COO-COO-CA-CHOO, THEY FIND THEIR WAY BACK TO THE BIG 'OL BLUE.
ALL BY THEMSELVES?
YEAH.

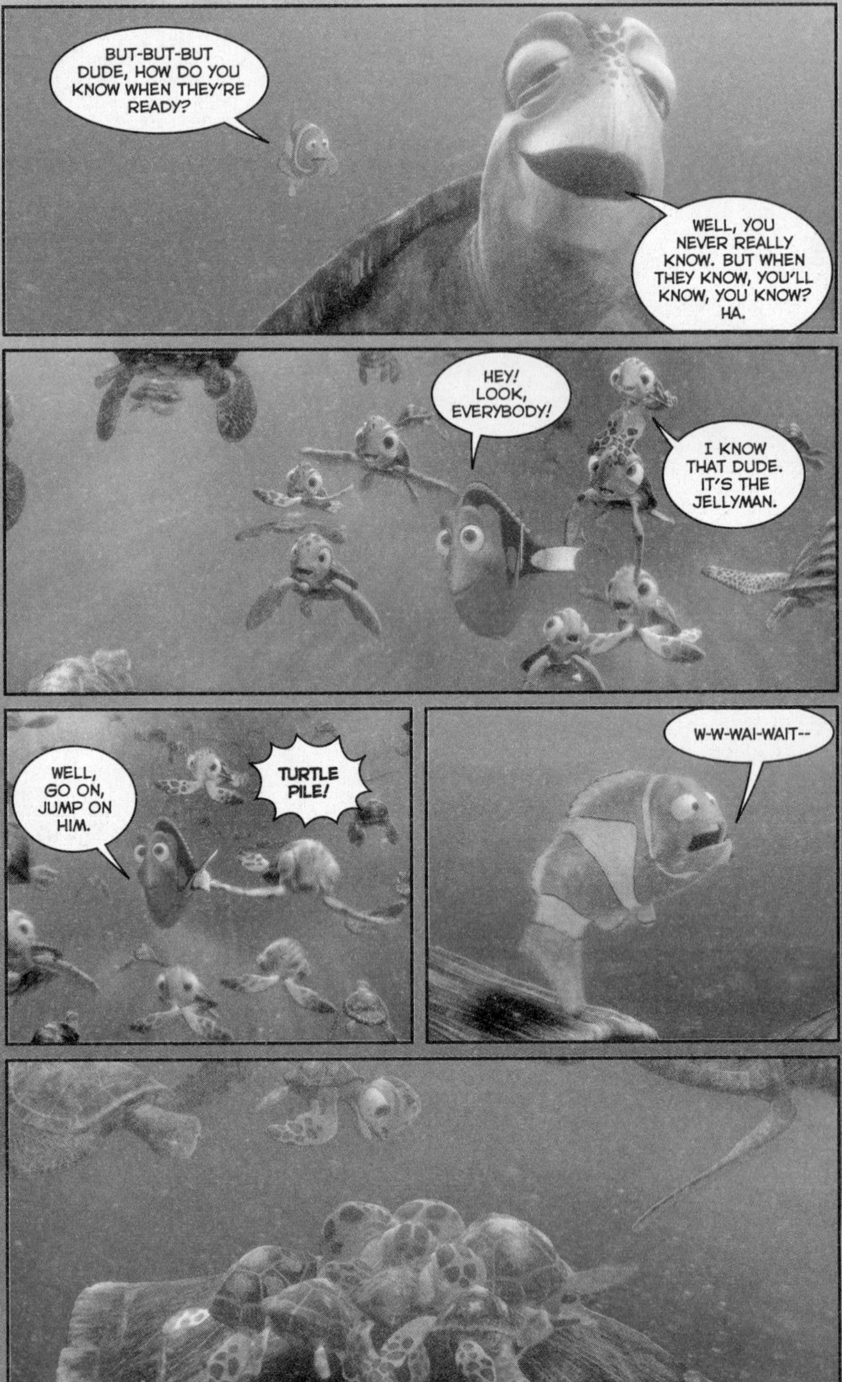
BUT-BUT-BUT DUDE, HOW DO YOU KNOW WHEN THEY'RE READY?
WELL, YOU NEVER REALLY KNOW. BUT WHEN THEY KNOW, YOU'LL KNOW, YOU KNOW? HA.
HEY! LOOK, EVERYBODY!
I KNOW THAT DUDE. IT'S THE JELLYMAN.
WELL, GO ON, JUMP ON HIM.
TURTLE PILE!
W-W-WAI-WAIT--

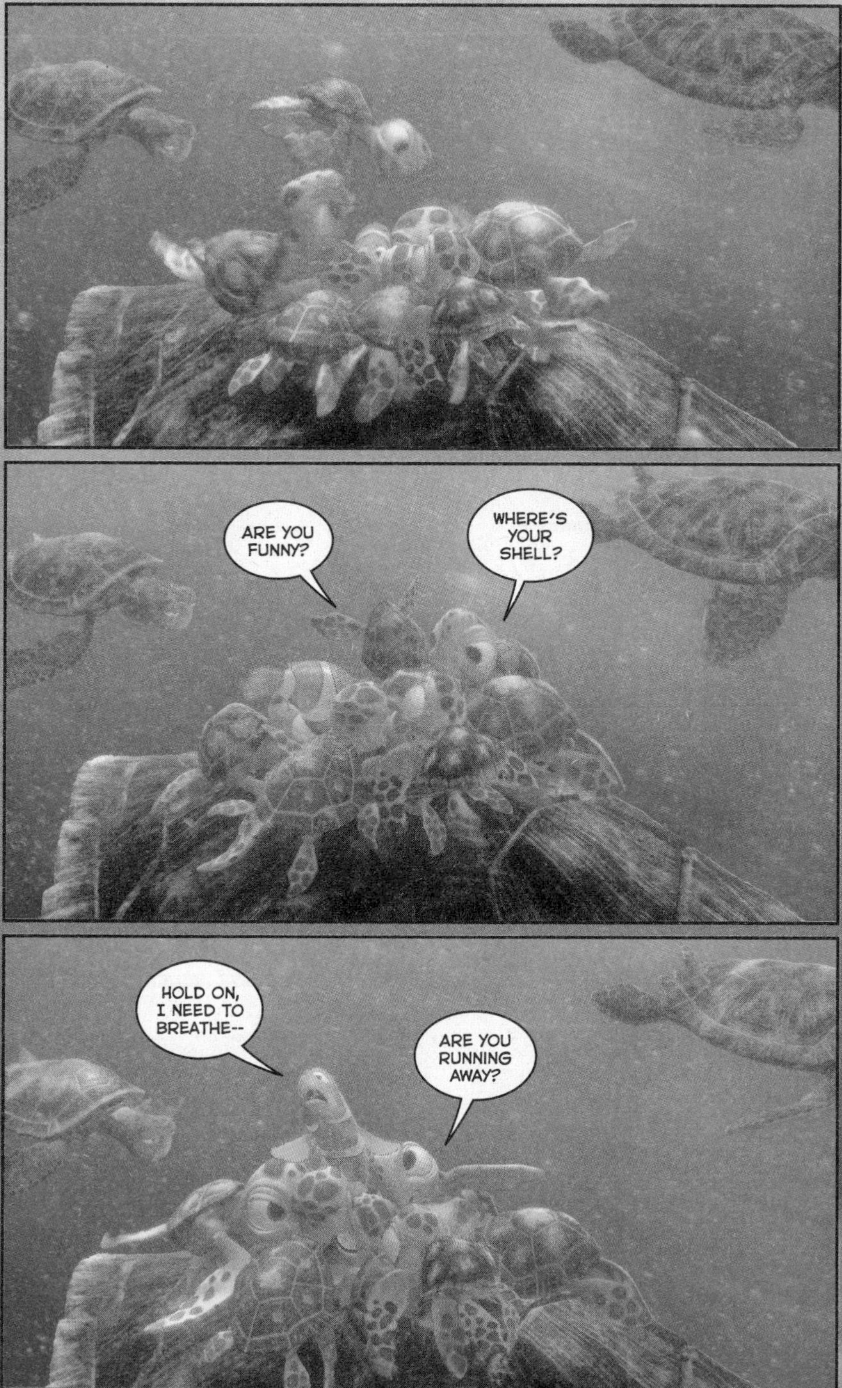
ARE YOU FUNNY?
WHERE'S YOUR SHELL?
HOLD ON, I NEED TO BREATHE--
ARE YOU RUNNING AWAY?

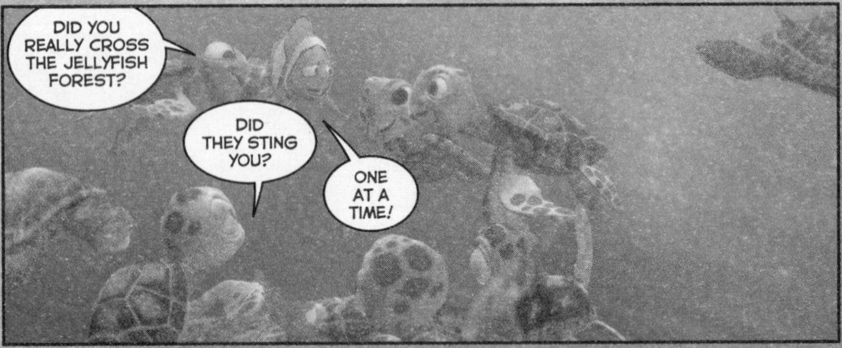
DID YOU REALLY CROSS THE JELLYFISH FOREST?
DID THEY STING YOU?
ONE AT A TIME!

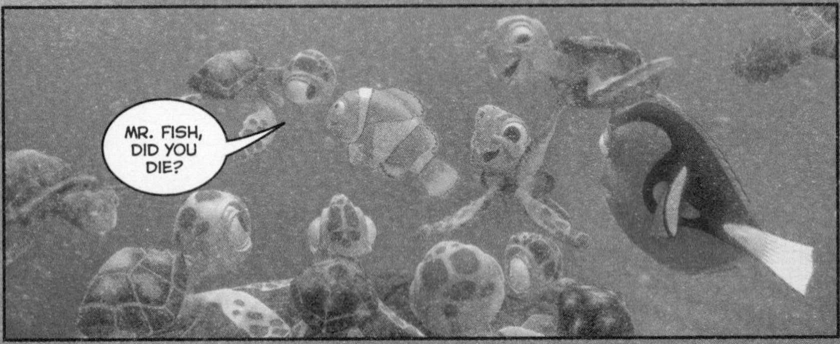
MR. FISH, DID YOU DIE?

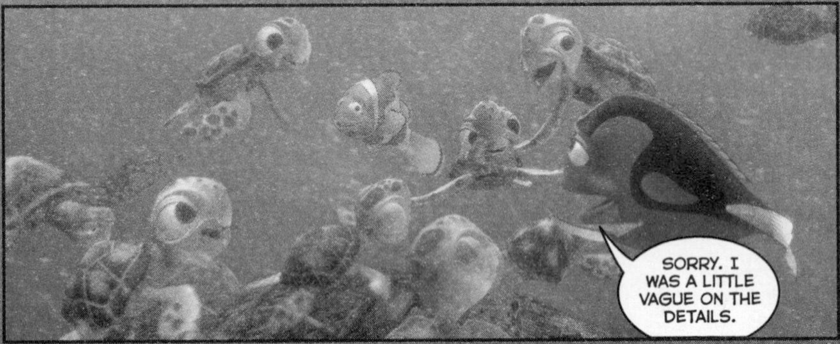
SORRY. I WAS A LITTLE VAGUE ON THE DETAILS.

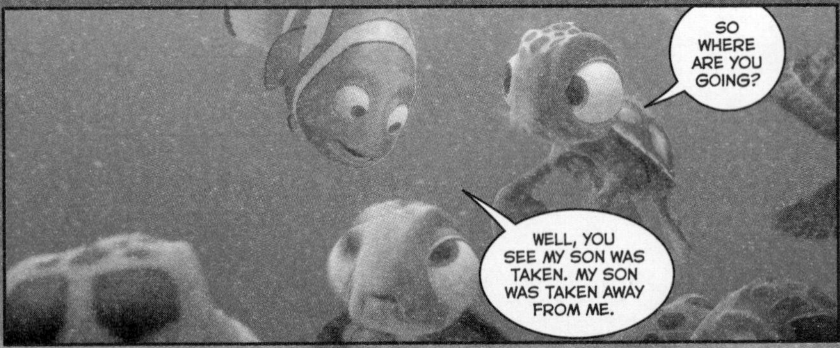
SO WHERE ARE YOU GOING?
WELL, YOU SEE MY SON WAS TAKEN. MY SON WAS TAKEN AWAY FROM ME.

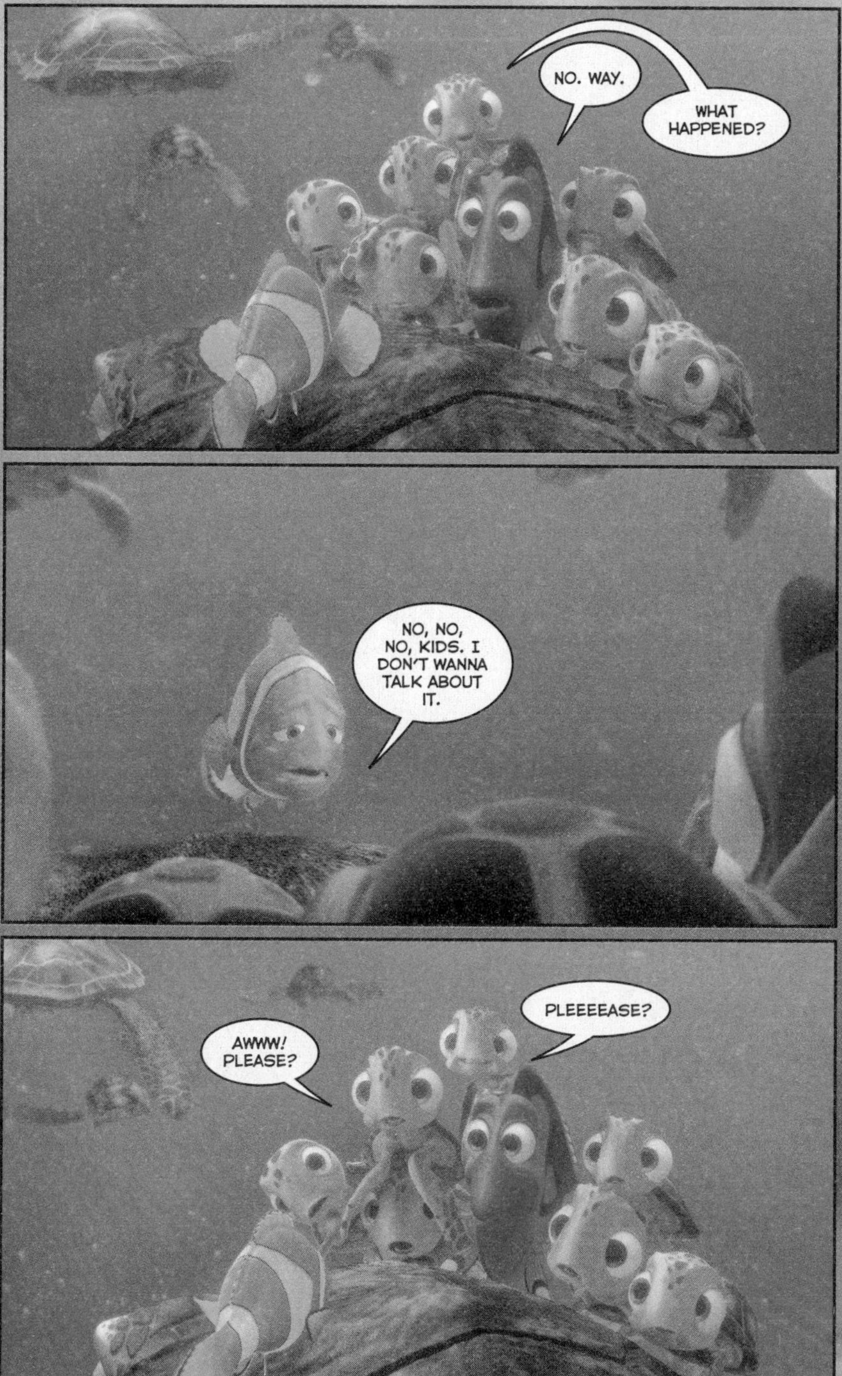
NO. WAY.
WHAT HAPPENED?
NO, NO, NO, KIDS. I DON'T WANNA TALK ABOUT IT.
AWWW! PLEASE?
PLEEEEASE?

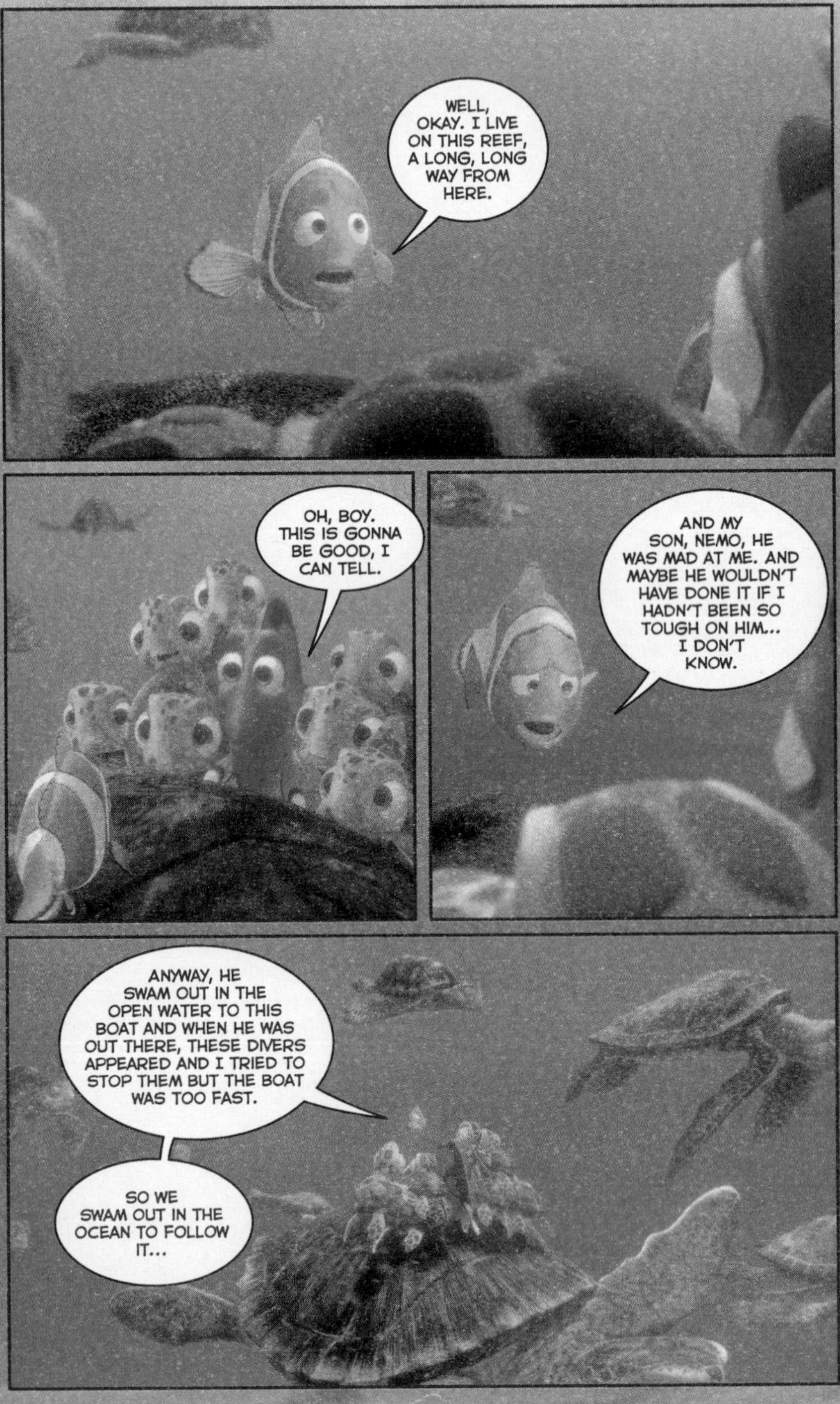
WELL, OKAY. I LIVE ON THIS REEF, A LONG, LONG WAY FROM HERE.
OH, BOY. THIS IS GONNA BE GOOD, I CAN TELL.
AND MY SON, NEMO, HE WAS MAD AT ME. AND MAYBE HE WOULDN'T HAVE DONE IT IF I HADN'T BEEN SO TOUGH ON HIM... I DON'T KNOW.
ANYWAY, HE SWAM OUT IN THE OPEN WATER TO THIS BOAT AND WHEN HE WAS OUT THERE, THESE DIVERS APPEARED AND I TRIED TO STOP THEM BUT THE BOAT WAS TOO FAST.
SO WE SWAM OUT IN THE OCEAN TO FOLLOW IT...

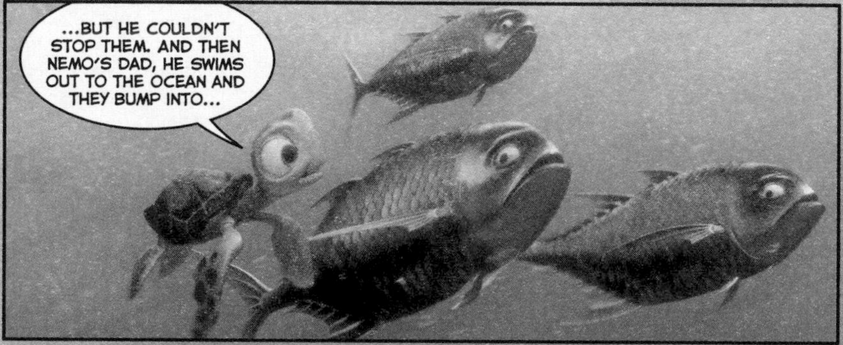
...BUT HE COULDN'T STOP THEM. AND THEN NEMO'S DAD, HE SWIMS OUT TO THE OCEAN AND THEY BUMP INTO...

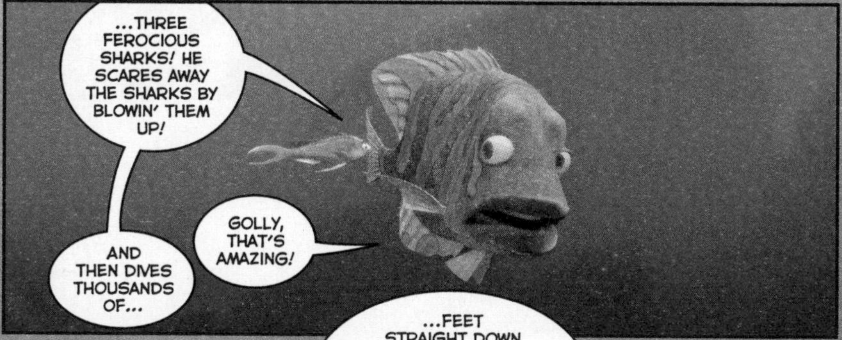
...THREE FEROCIOUS SHARKS! HE SCARES AWAY THE SHARKS BY BLOWIN' THEM UP!
AND THEN DIVES THOUSANDS OF...
GOLLY, THAT'S AMAZING!

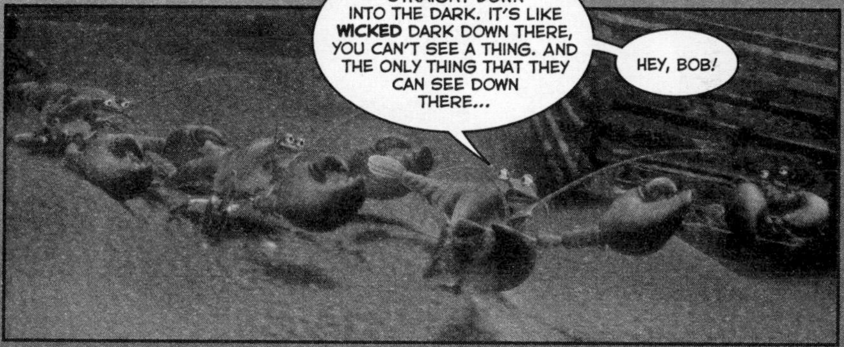
...FEET STRAIGHT DOWN INTO THE DARK. IT'S LIKE **WICKED** DARK DOWN THERE, YOU CAN'T SEE A THING. AND THE ONLY THING THAT THEY CAN SEE DOWN THERE...
HEY, BOB!

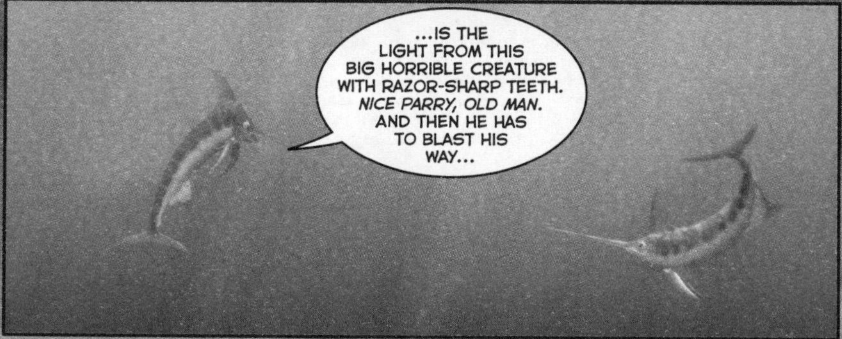
...IS THE LIGHT FROM THIS BIG HORRIBLE CREATURE WITH RAZOR-SHARP TEETH. *NICE PARRY, OLD MAN.* AND THEN HE HAS TO BLAST HIS WAY...

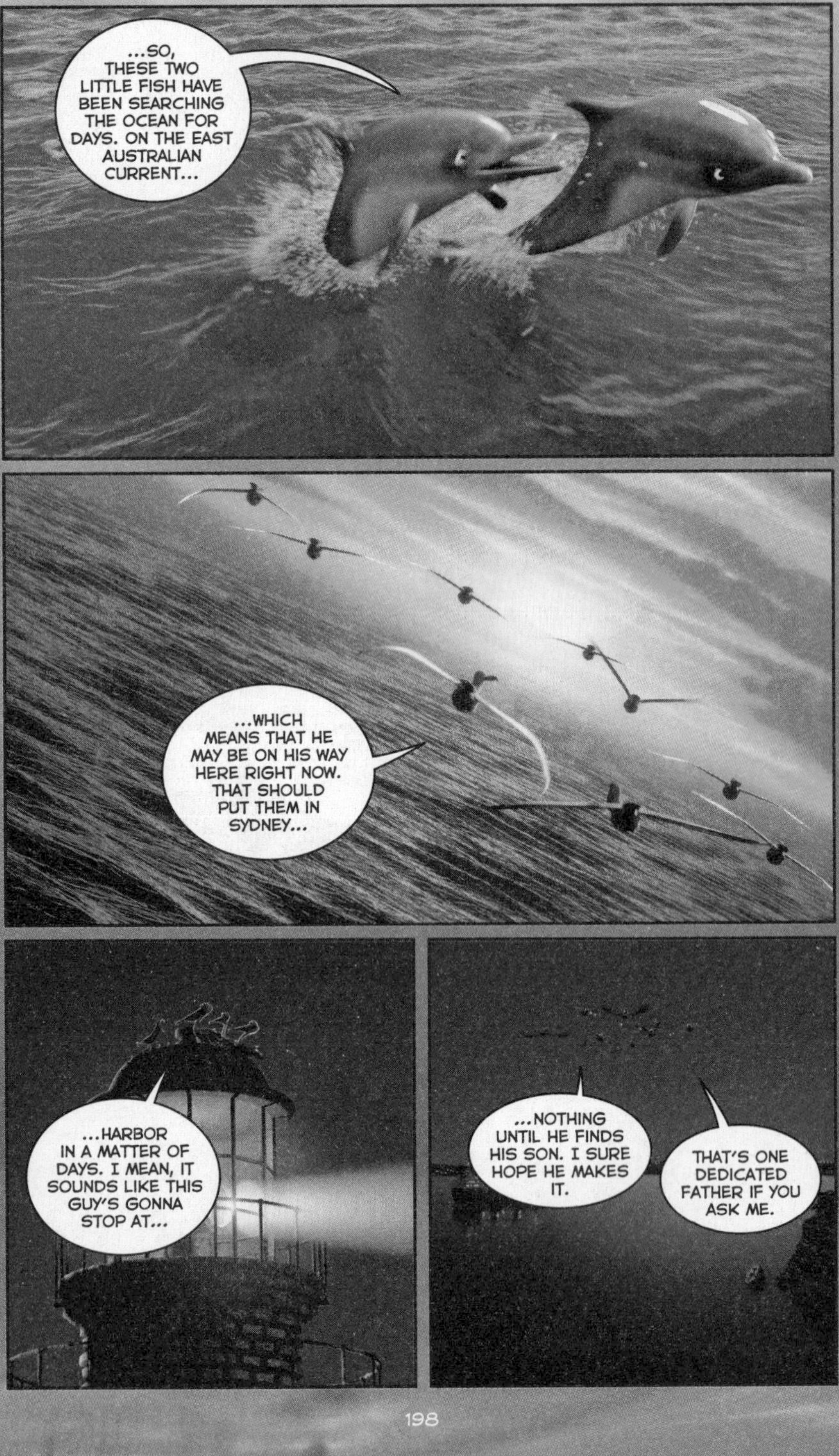
...SO, THESE TWO LITTLE FISH HAVE BEEN SEARCHING THE OCEAN FOR DAYS. ON THE EAST AUSTRALIAN CURRENT...
...WHICH MEANS THAT HE MAY BE ON HIS WAY HERE RIGHT NOW. THAT SHOULD PUT THEM IN SYDNEY...
...HARBOR IN A MATTER OF DAYS. I MEAN, IT SOUNDS LIKE THIS GUY'S GONNA STOP AT...
...NOTHING UNTIL HE FINDS HIS SON. I SURE HOPE HE MAKES IT.
THAT'S ONE DEDICATED FATHER IF YOU ASK ME.

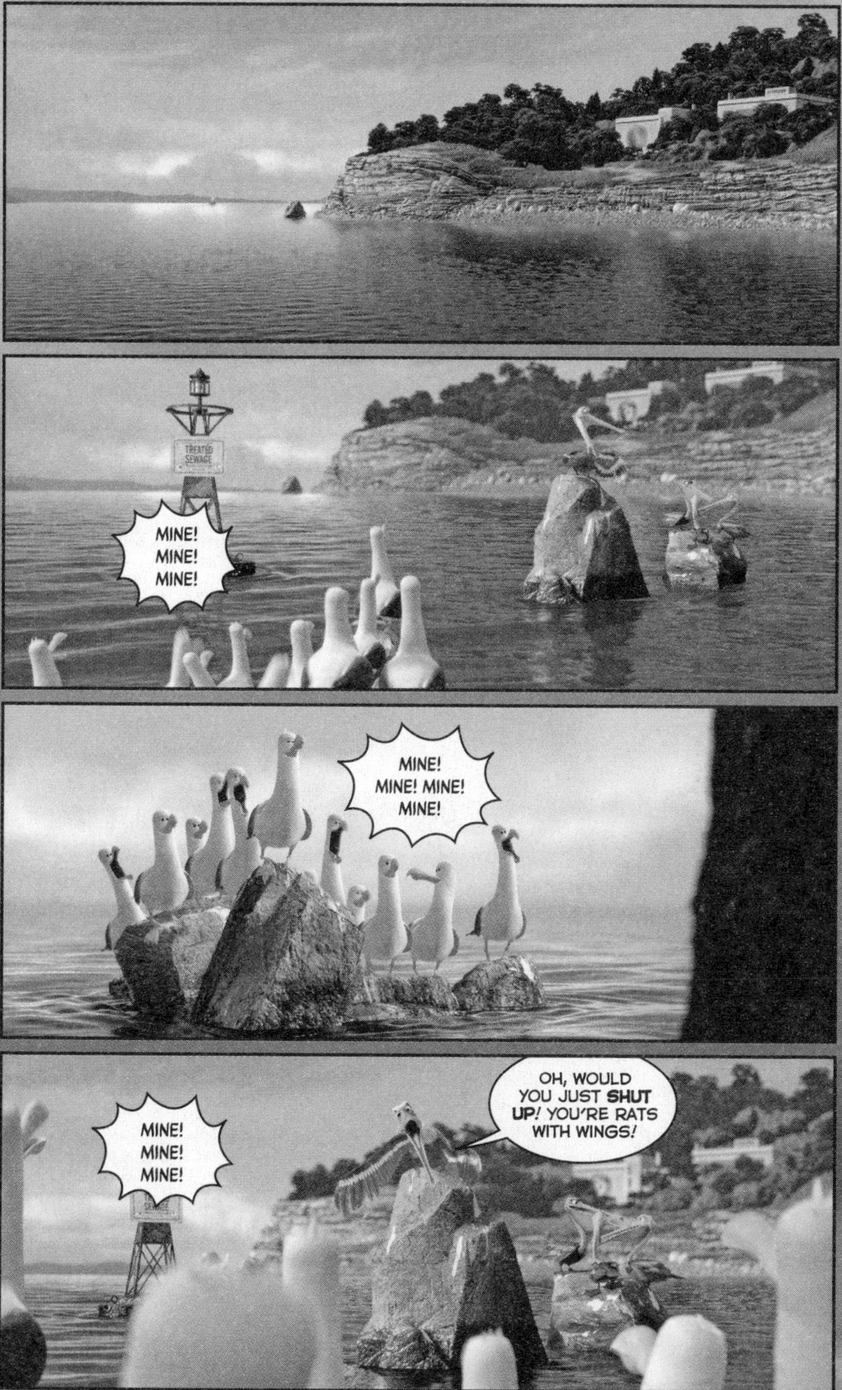
TREATED SEWAGE
MINE! MINE! MINE!
MINE! MINE! MINE! MINE!
MINE! MINE! MINE!
OH, WOULD YOU JUST **SHUT UP**! YOU'RE RATS WITH WINGS!

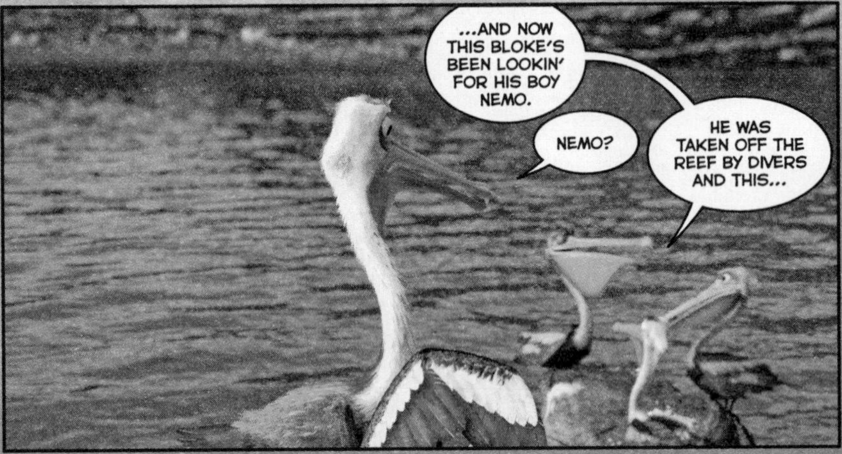
...AND NOW THIS BLOKE'S BEEN LOOKIN' FOR HIS BOY NEMO.
NEMO?
HE WAS TAKEN OFF THE REEF BY DIVERS AND THIS...

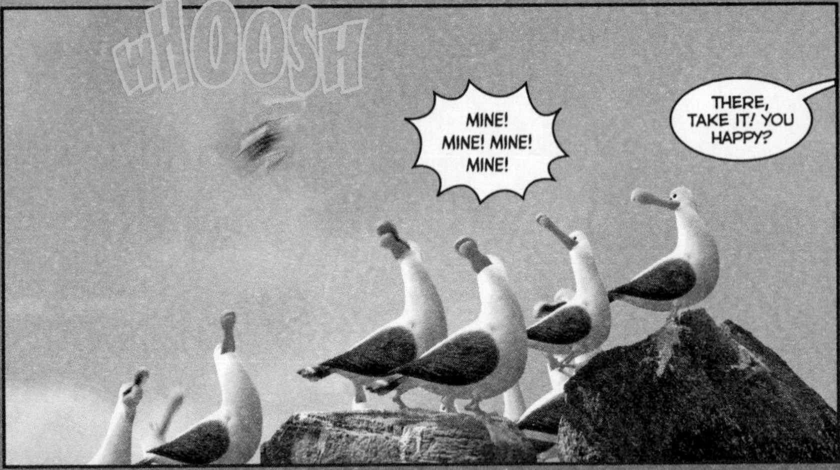
WHOOSH
MINE! MINE! MINE! MINE!
THERE, TAKE IT! YOU HAPPY?

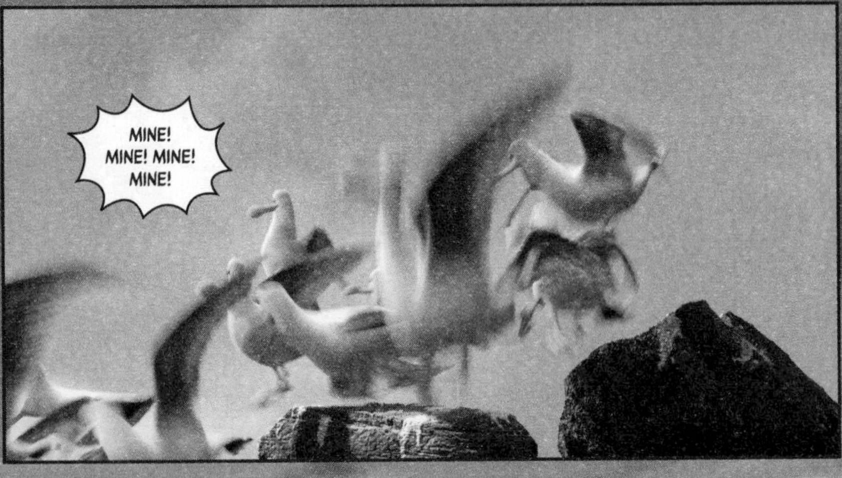
MINE! MINE! MINE! MINE!

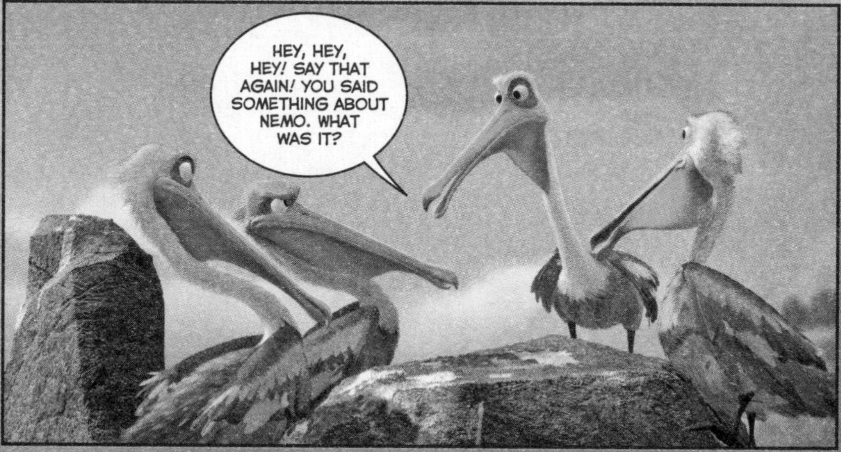
HEY, HEY, HEY! SAY THAT AGAIN! YOU SAID SOMETHING ABOUT NEMO. WHAT WAS IT?

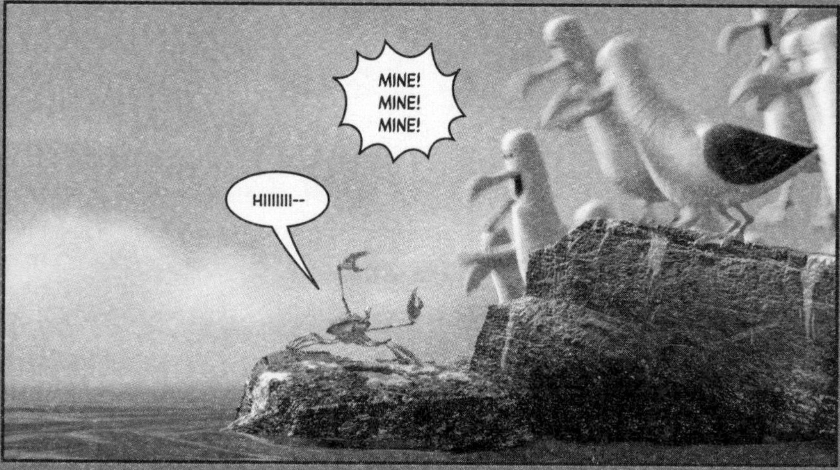
MINE! MINE! MINE!
HIIIIIII--

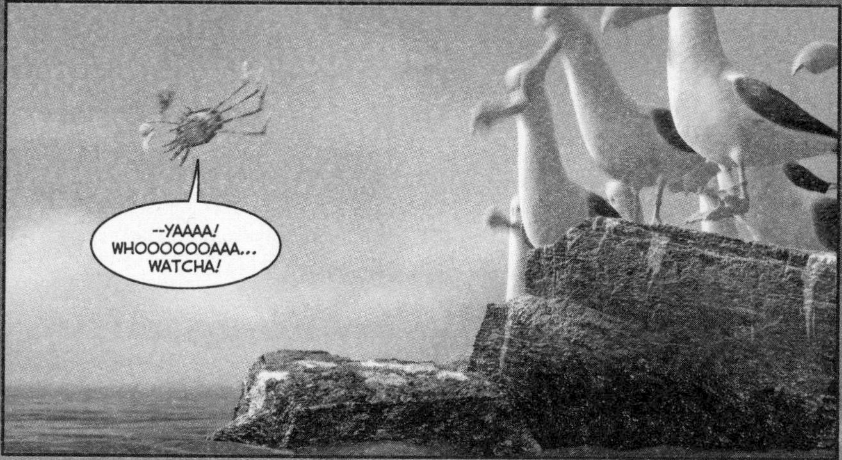
--YAAAA! WHOOOOOOAAA... WATCHA!

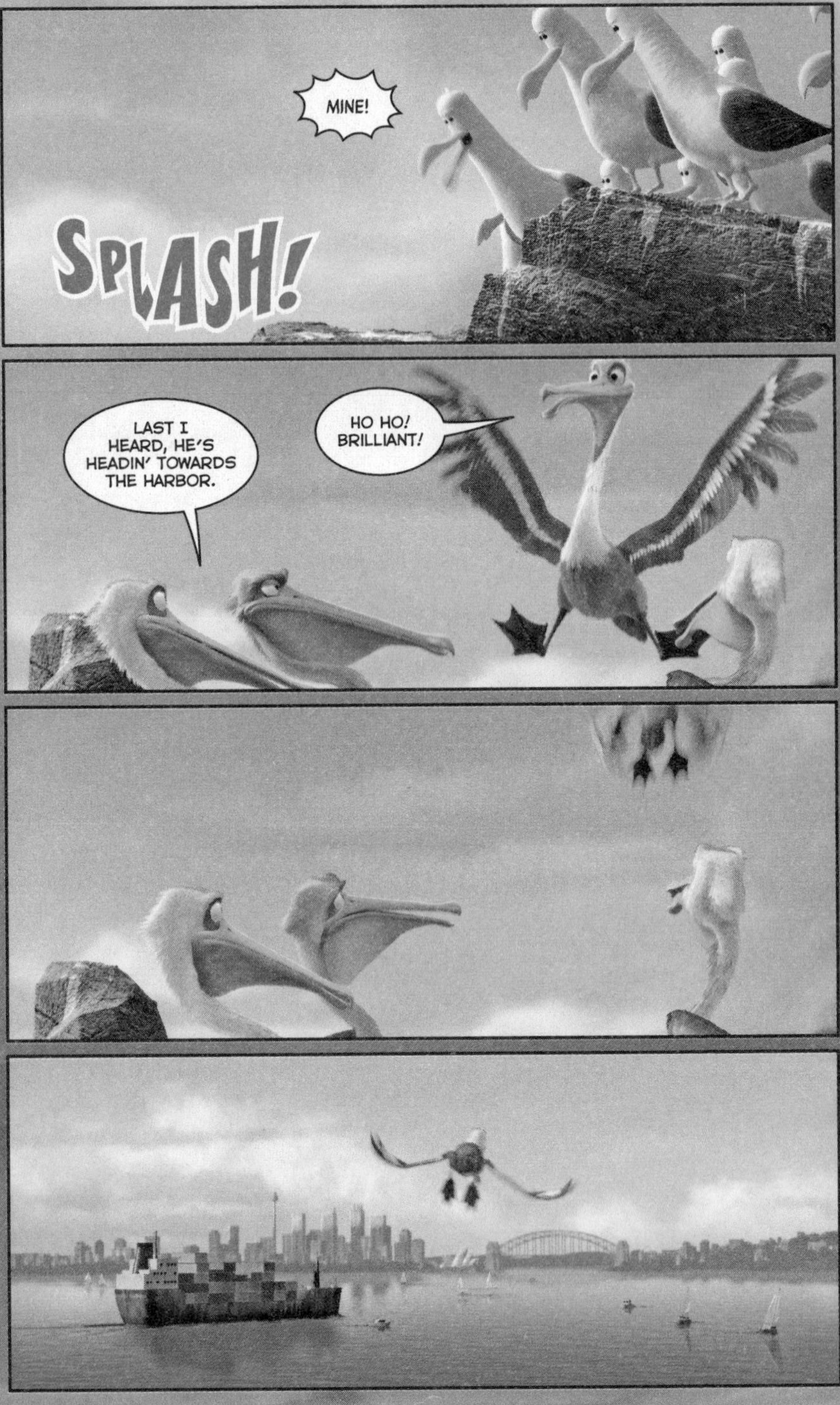
MINE!
SPLASH!
LAST I HEARD, HE'S HEADIN' TOWARDS THE HARBOR.
HO HO! BRILLIANT!

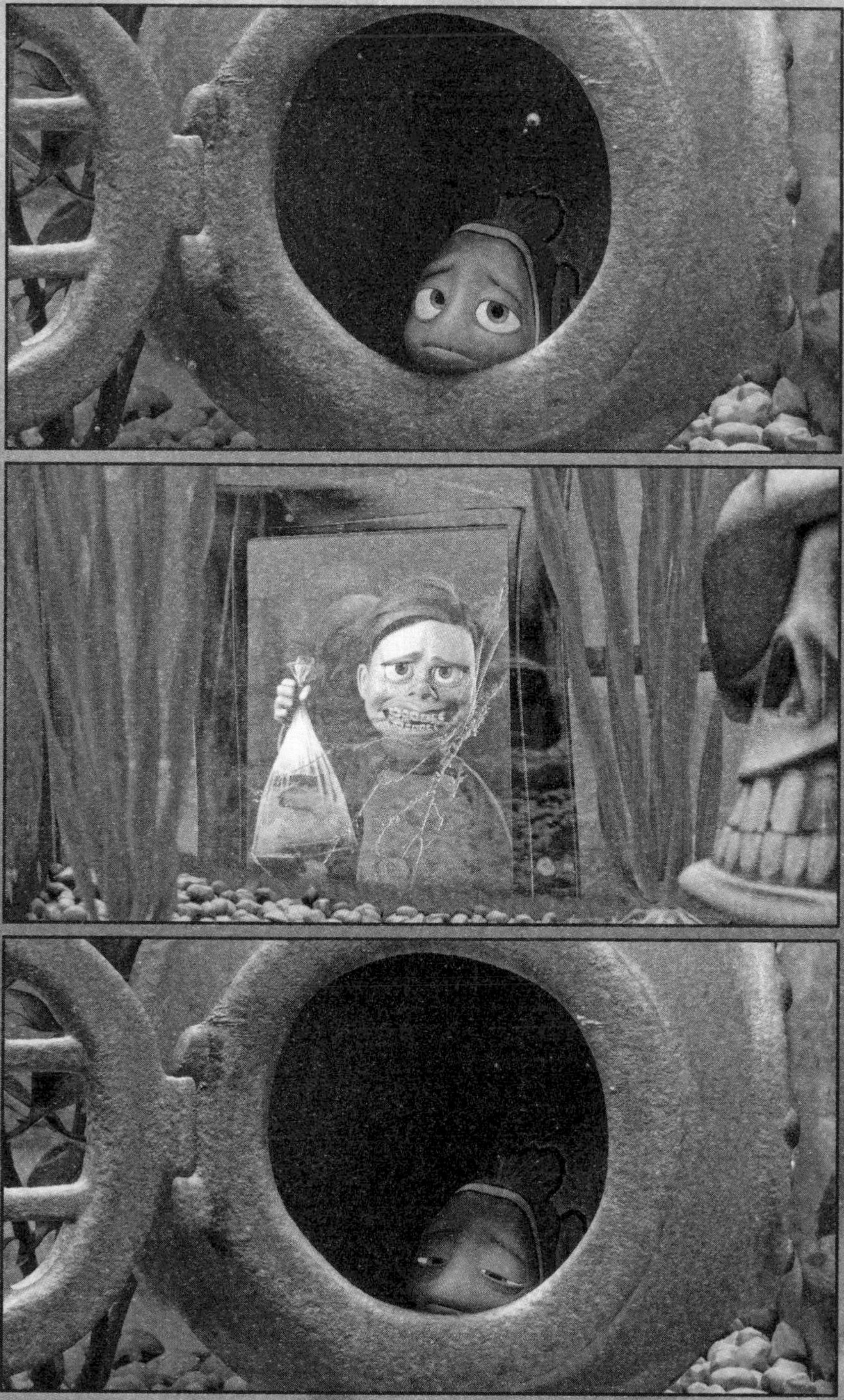

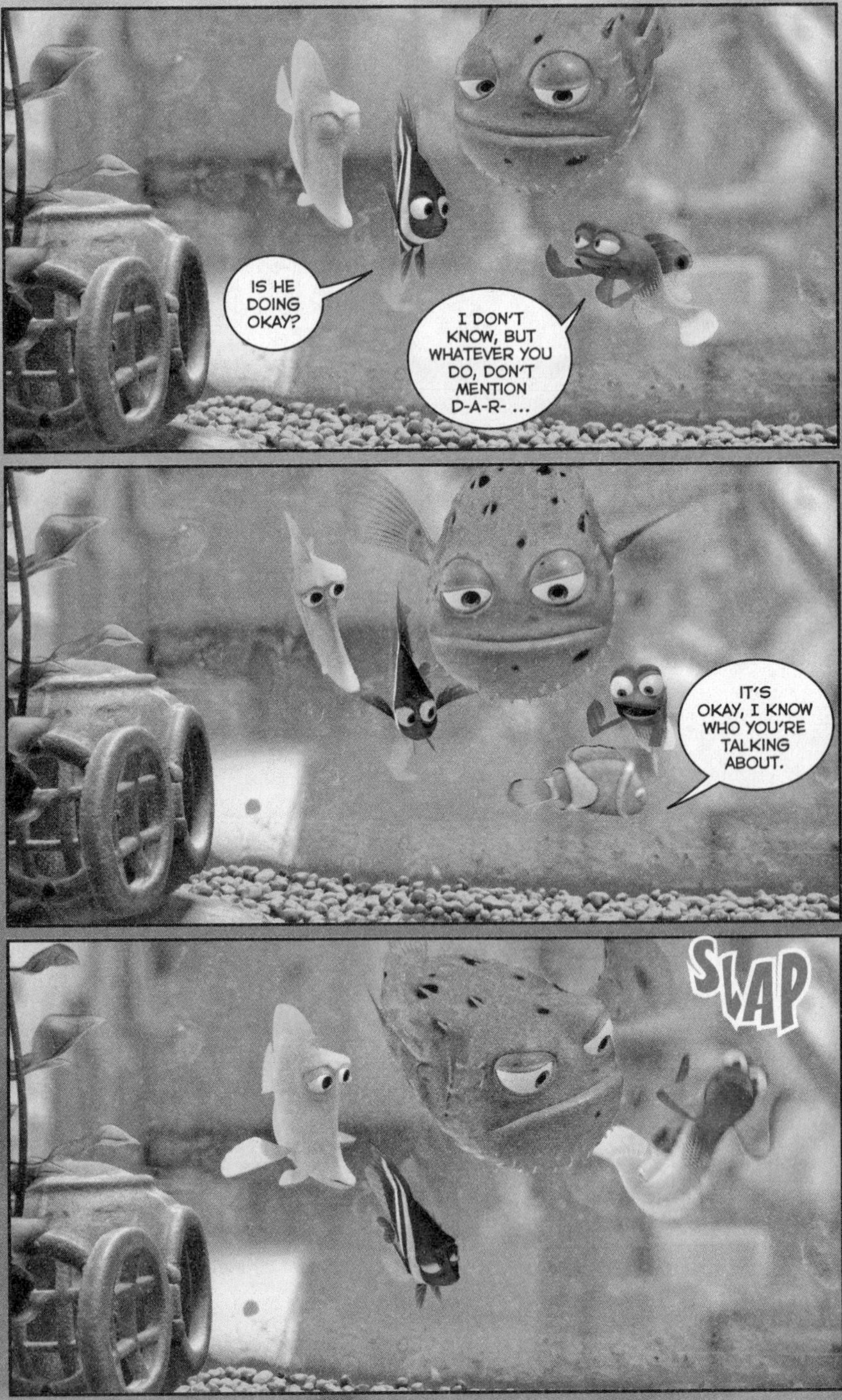
IS HE DOING OKAY?
I DON'T KNOW, BUT WHATEVER YOU DO, DON'T MENTION D-A-R- ...
IT'S OKAY, I KNOW WHO YOU'RE TALKING ABOUT.
SLAP

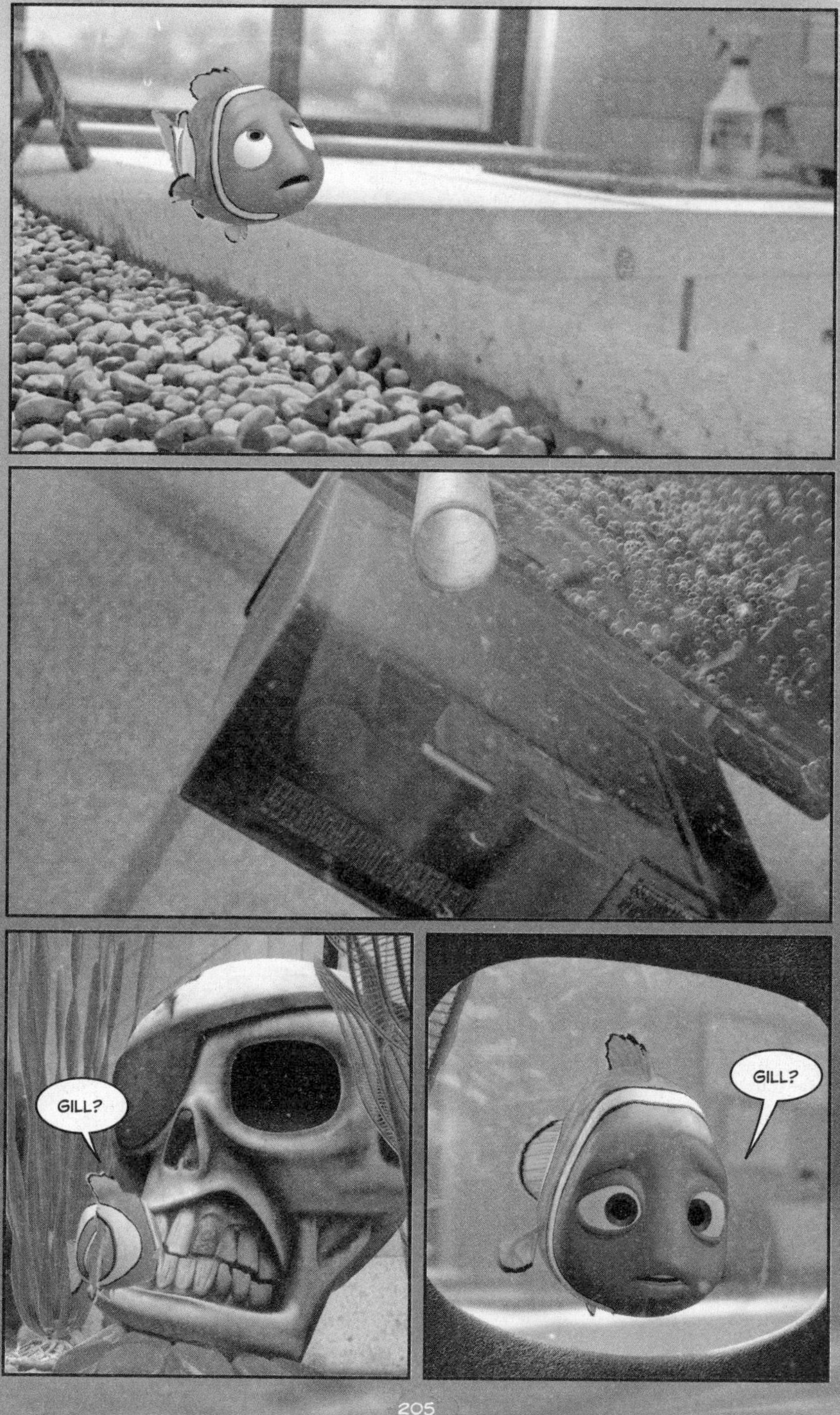
GILL?
GILL?

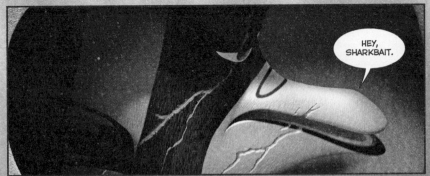

HEY, SHARKBAIT.

I'M SORRY I COULDN'T STOP THE--

NO, I'M THE ONE WHO SHOULD BE SORRY. I WAS SO READY TO GET OUT, SO READY TO TASTE THAT OCEAN. I WAS WILLING TO PUT YOU IN HARM'S WAY TO GET THERE.

NOTHING SHOULD BE WORTH THAT. I'M SORRY I COULDN'T GET YOU BACK TO YOUR FATHER, KID.

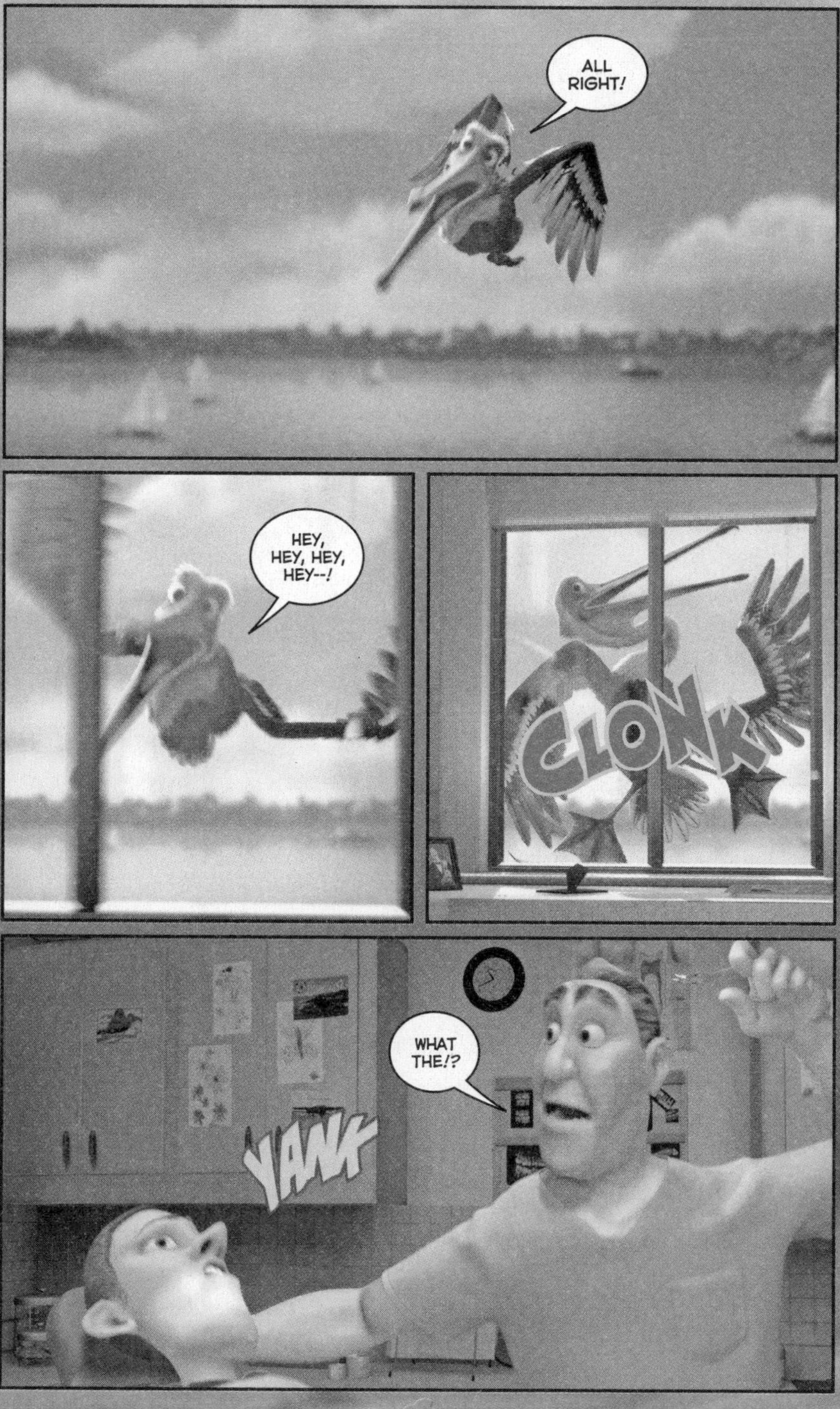
ALL RIGHT!
HEY, HEY, HEY, HEY--!
CLONK
WHAT THE!?
YANK

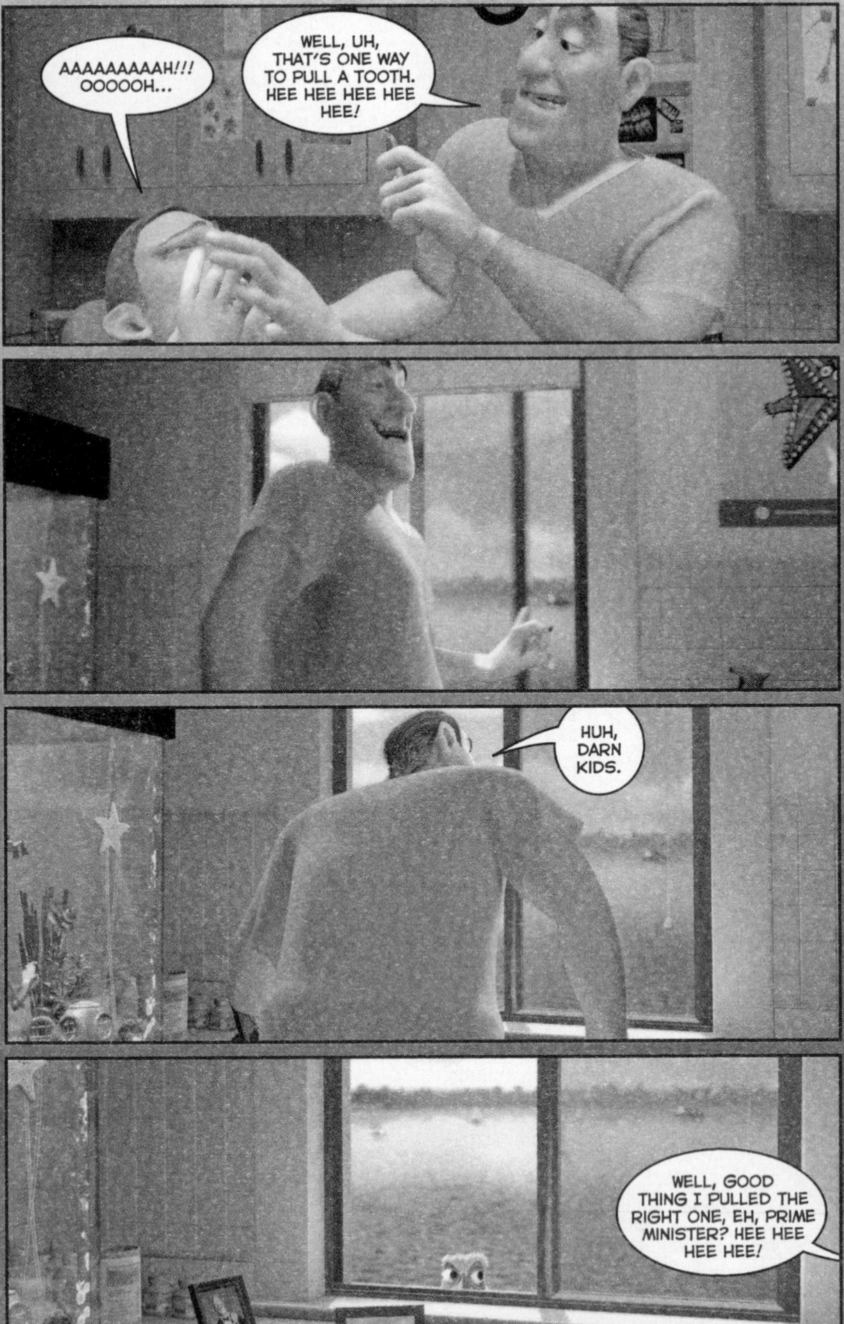
AAAAAAAAAH!!! OOOOOH...
WELL, UH, THAT'S ONE WAY TO PULL A TOOTH. HEE HEE HEE HEE HEE!
HUH, DARN KIDS.
WELL, GOOD THING I PULLED THE RIGHT ONE, EH, PRIME MINISTER? HEE HEE HEE HEE!

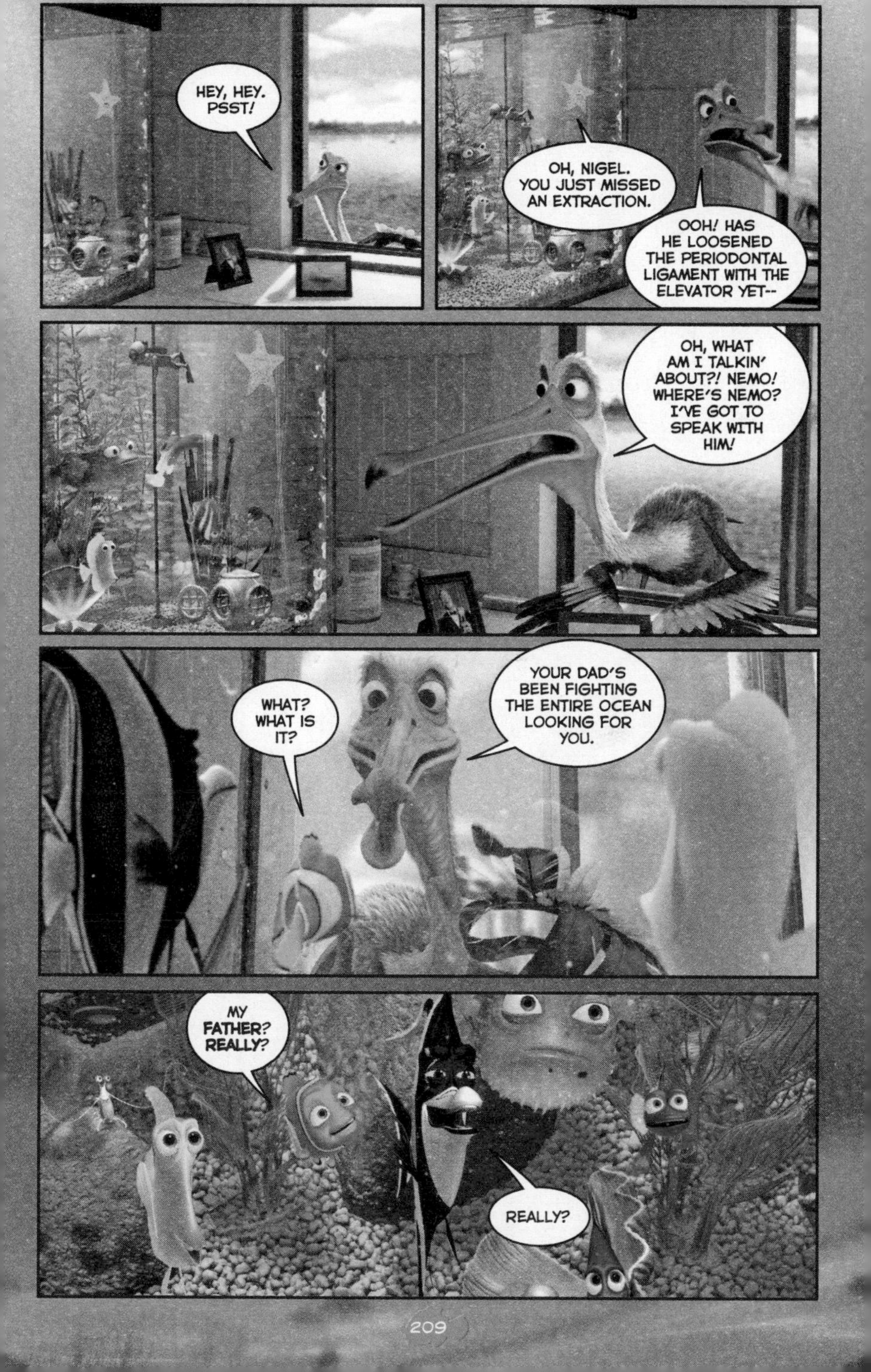
HEY, HEY. PSST!
OH, NIGEL. YOU JUST MISSED AN EXTRACTION.
OOH! HAS HE LOOSENED THE PERIODONTAL LIGAMENT WITH THE ELEVATOR YET--
OH, WHAT AM I TALKIN' ABOUT?! NEMO! WHERE'S NEMO? I'VE GOT TO SPEAK WITH HIM!
WHAT? WHAT IS IT?
YOUR DAD'S BEEN FIGHTING THE ENTIRE OCEAN LOOKING FOR YOU.
MY FATHER? REALLY?
REALLY?

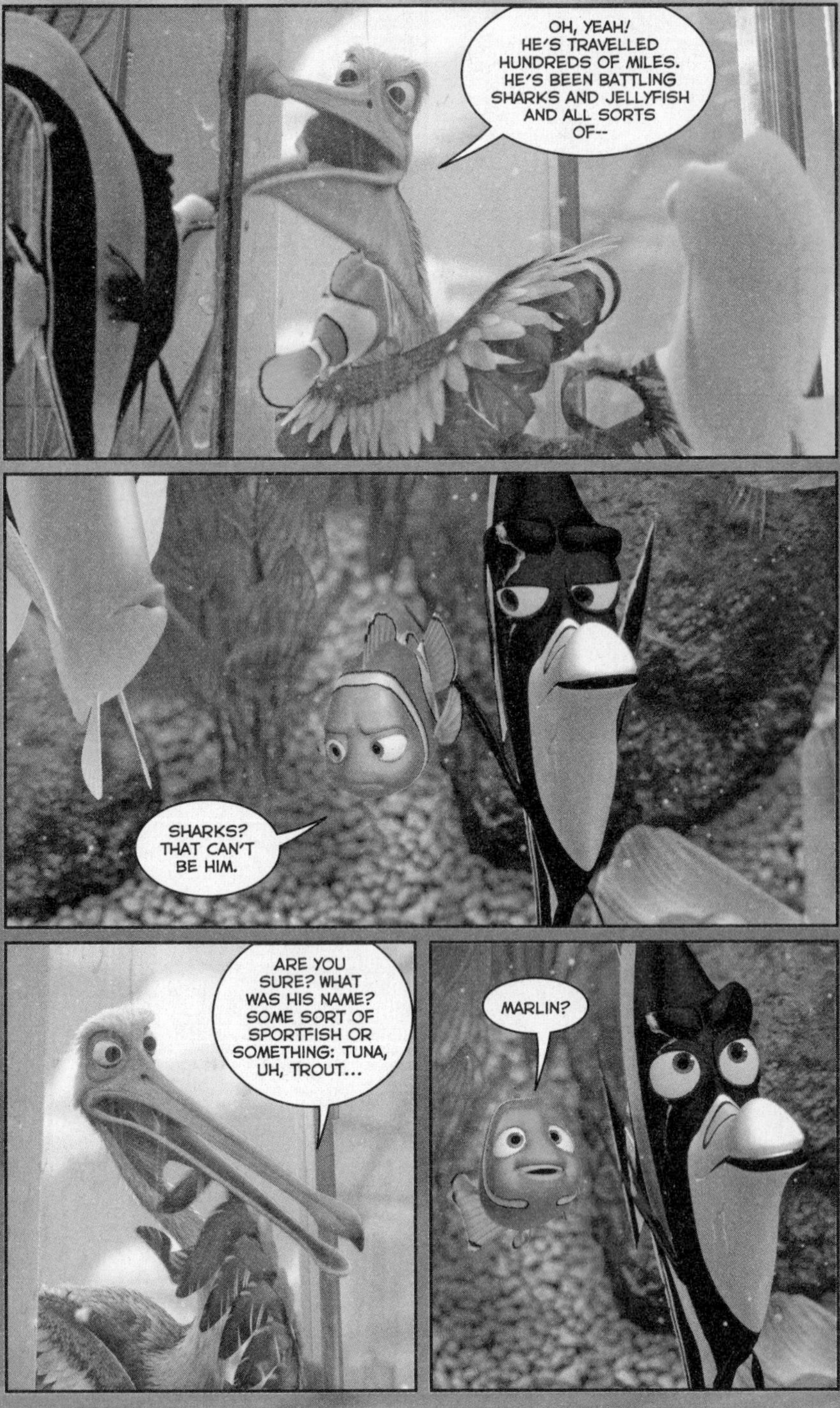
OH, YEAH! HE'S TRAVELLED HUNDREDS OF MILES. HE'S BEEN BATTLING SHARKS AND JELLYFISH AND ALL SORTS OF--
SHARKS? THAT CAN'T BE HIM.
ARE YOU SURE? WHAT WAS HIS NAME? SOME SORT OF SPORTFISH OR SOMETHING: TUNA, UH, TROUT...
MARLIN?

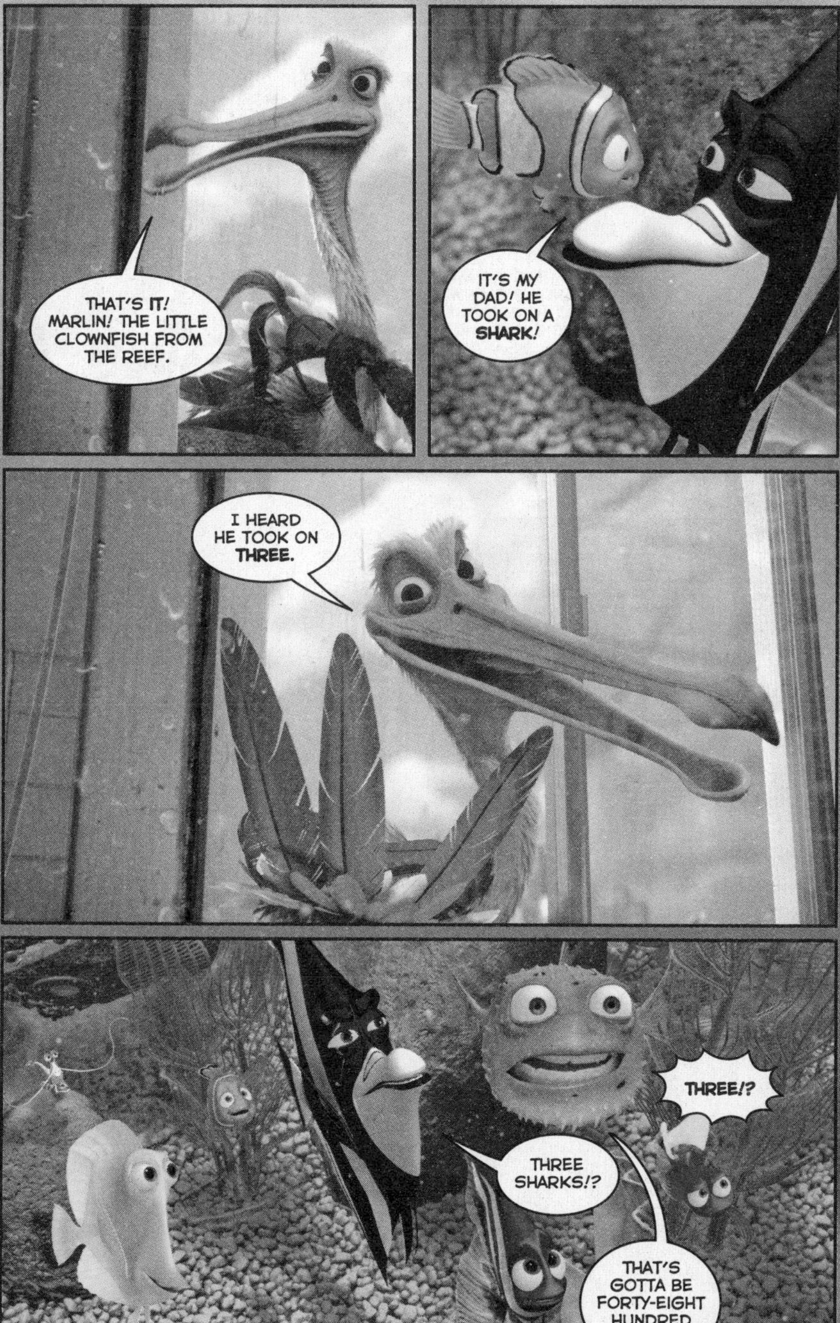
THAT'S IT! MARLIN! THE LITTLE CLOWNFISH FROM THE REEF.
IT'S MY DAD! HE TOOK ON A SHARK!
I HEARD HE TOOK ON THREE.
THREE!?
THREE SHARKS!?
THAT'S GOTTA BE FORTY-EIGHT HUNDRED TEETH!

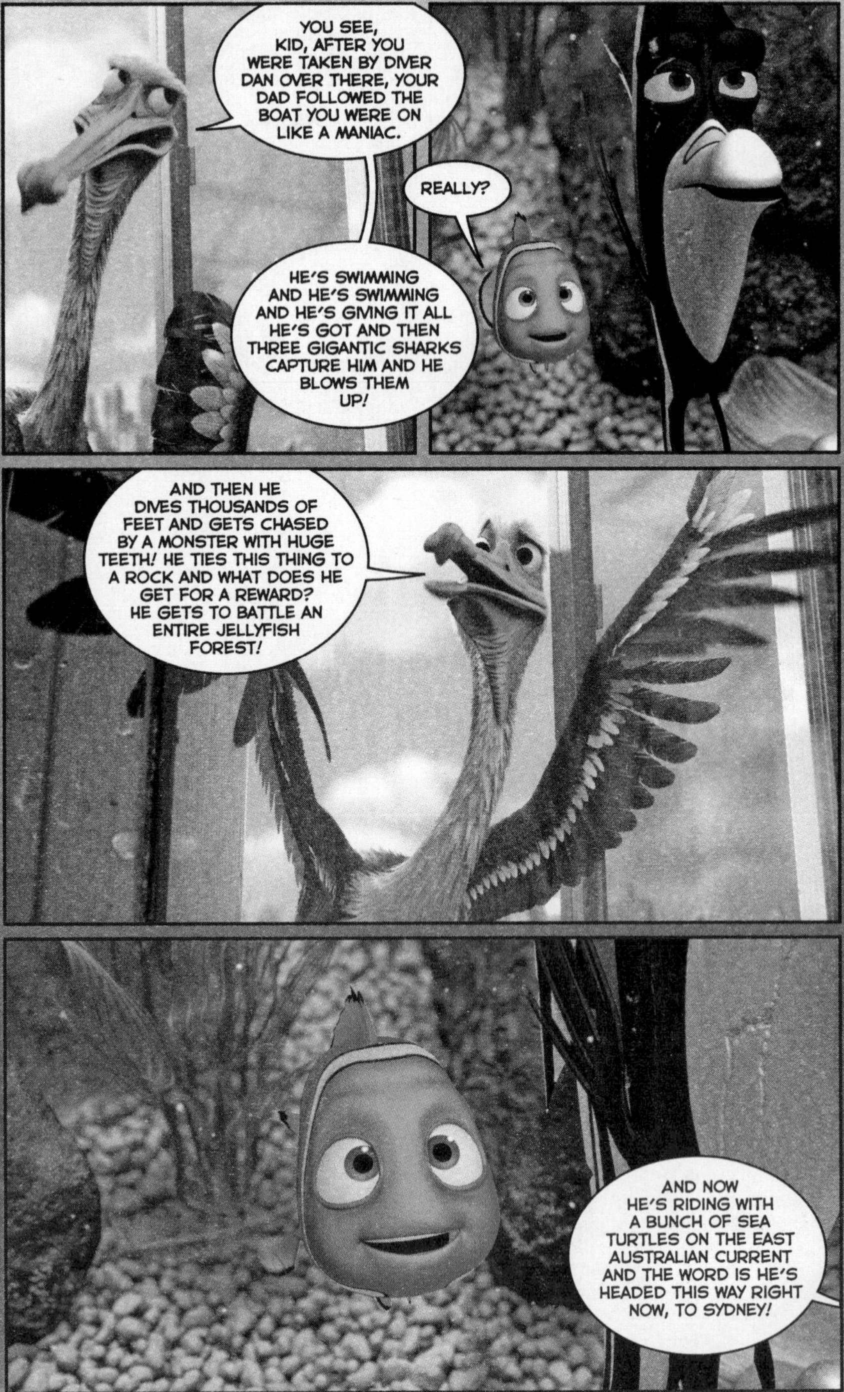
YOU SEE, KID, AFTER YOU WERE TAKEN BY DIVER DAN OVER THERE, YOUR DAD FOLLOWED THE BOAT YOU WERE ON LIKE A MANIAC.
REALLY?
HE'S SWIMMING AND HE'S SWIMMING AND HE'S GIVING IT ALL HE'S GOT AND THEN THREE GIGANTIC SHARKS CAPTURE HIM AND HE BLOWS THEM UP!
AND THEN HE DIVES THOUSANDS OF FEET AND GETS CHASED BY A MONSTER WITH HUGE TEETH! HE TIES THIS THING TO A ROCK AND WHAT DOES HE GET FOR A REWARD? HE GETS TO BATTLE AN ENTIRE JELLYFISH FOREST!
AND NOW HE'S RIDING WITH A BUNCH OF SEA TURTLES ON THE EAST AUSTRALIAN CURRENT AND THE WORD IS HE'S HEADED THIS WAY RIGHT NOW, TO SYDNEY!

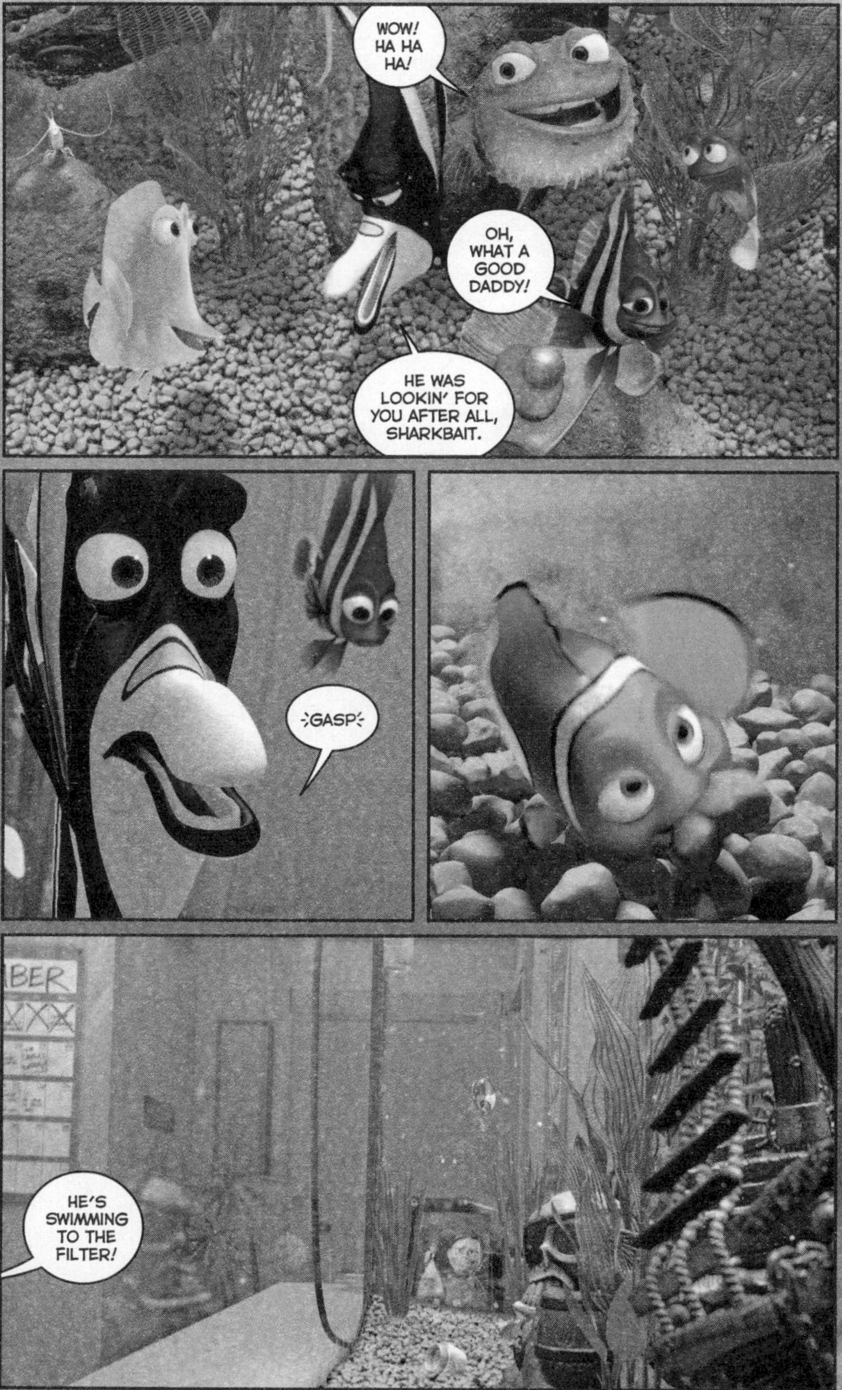
WOW! HA HA HA!
OH, WHAT A GOOD DADDY!
HE WAS LOOKIN' FOR YOU AFTER ALL, SHARKBAIT.
-GASP-
HE'S SWIMMING TO THE FILTER!

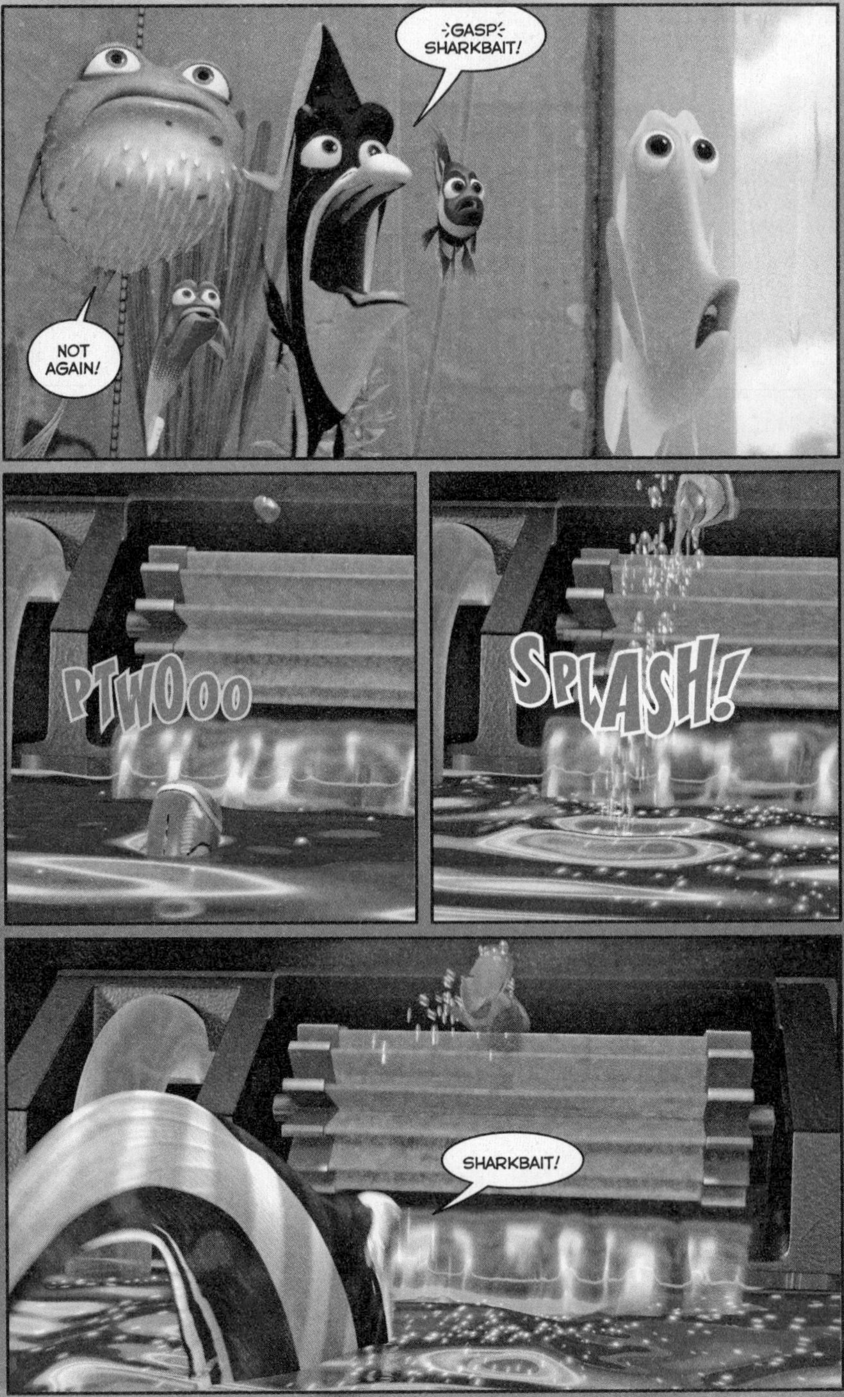
-GASP-
SHARKBAIT!
NOT AGAIN!
PTWOOO
SPLASH!
SHARKBAIT!

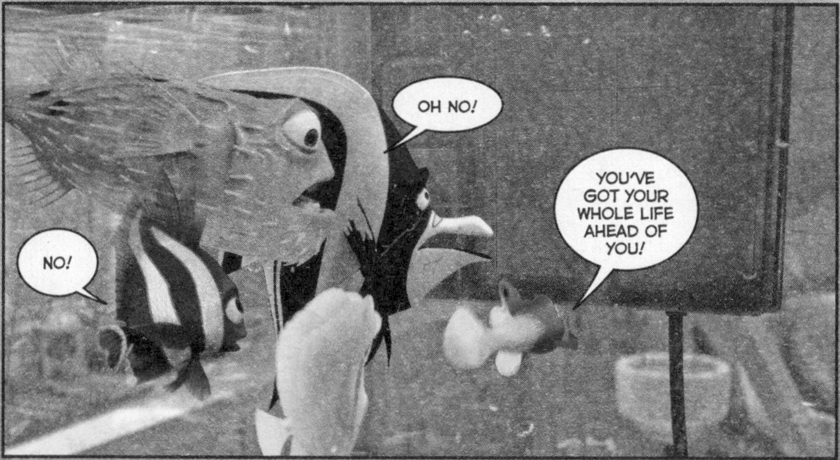
OH NO!
YOU'VE GOT YOUR WHOLE LIFE AHEAD OF YOU!
NO!

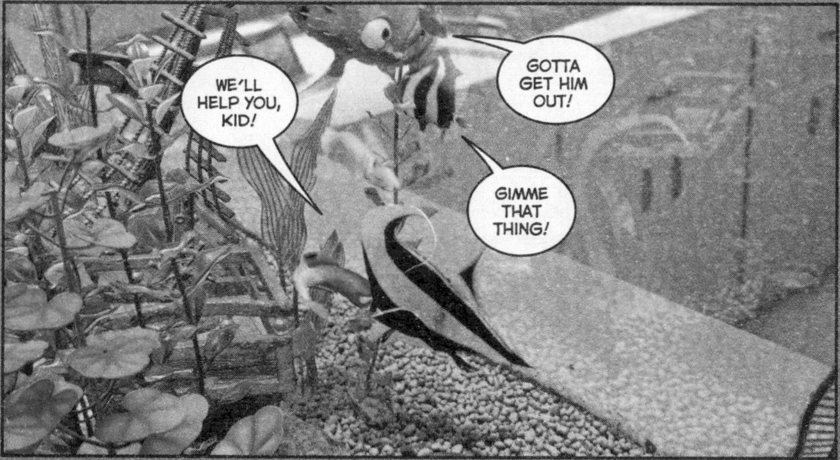
WE'LL HELP YOU, KID!
GOTTA GET HIM OUT!
GIMME THAT THING!

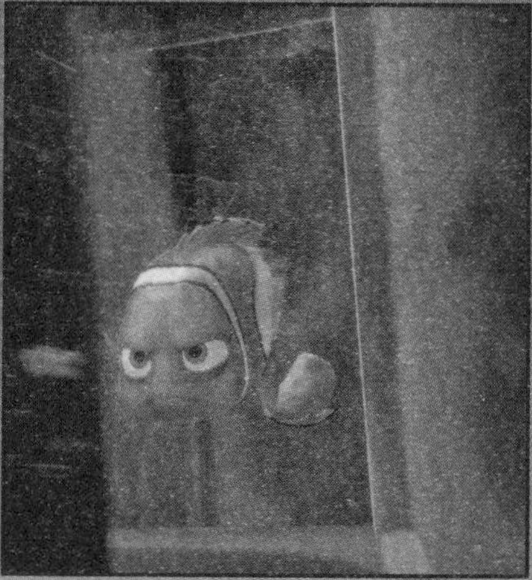

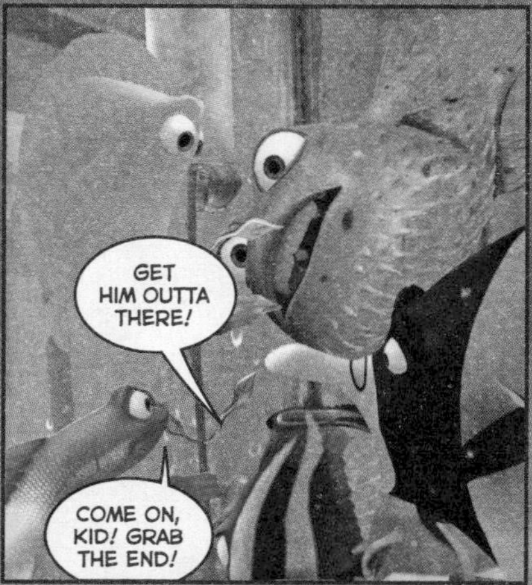
GET HIM OUTTA THERE!
COME ON, KID! GRAB THE END!

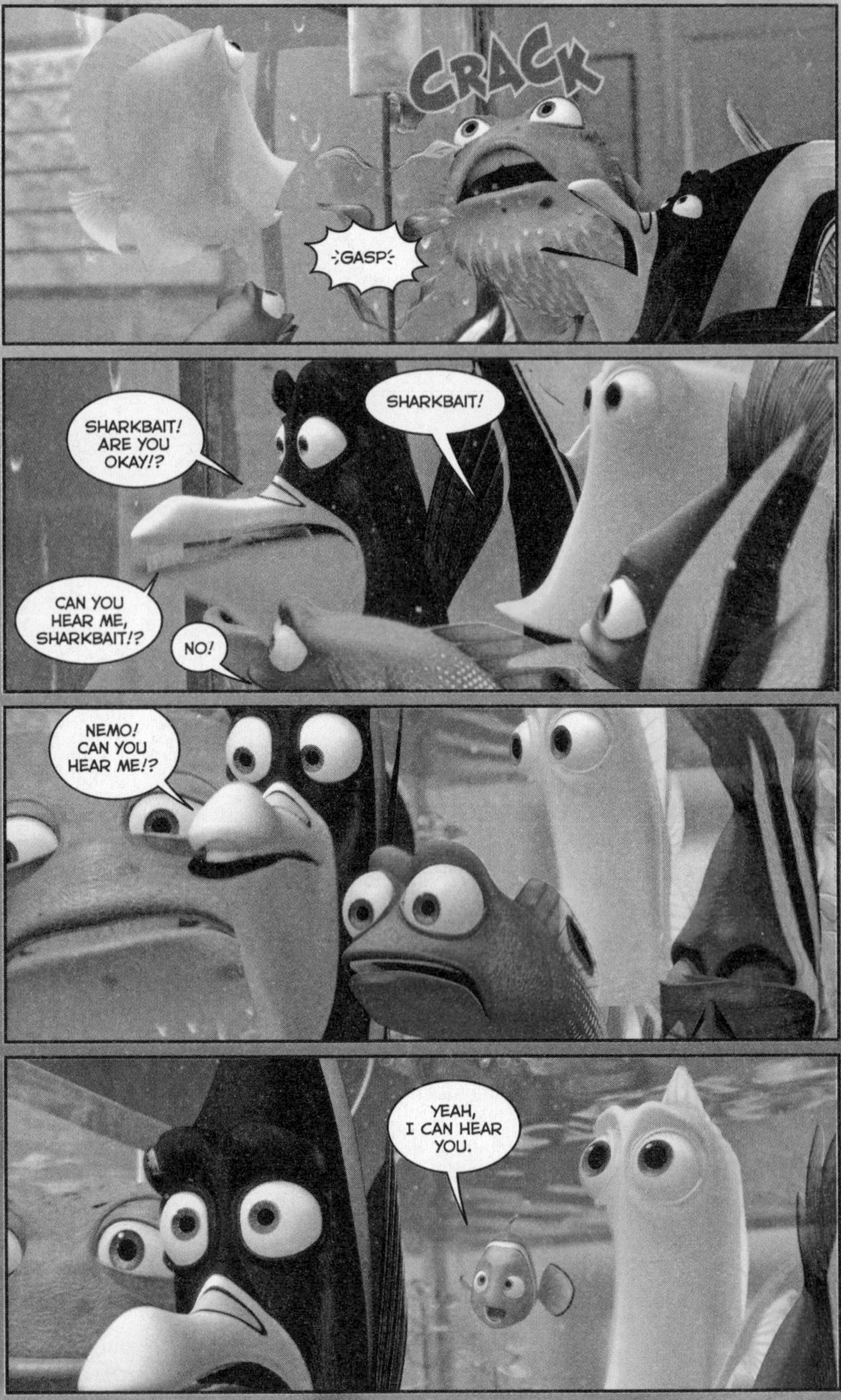
CRACK
GASP
SHARKBAIT! ARE YOU OKAY!?
SHARKBAIT!
CAN YOU HEAR ME, SHARKBAIT!?
NO!
NEMO! CAN YOU HEAR ME!?
YEAH, I CAN HEAR YOU.

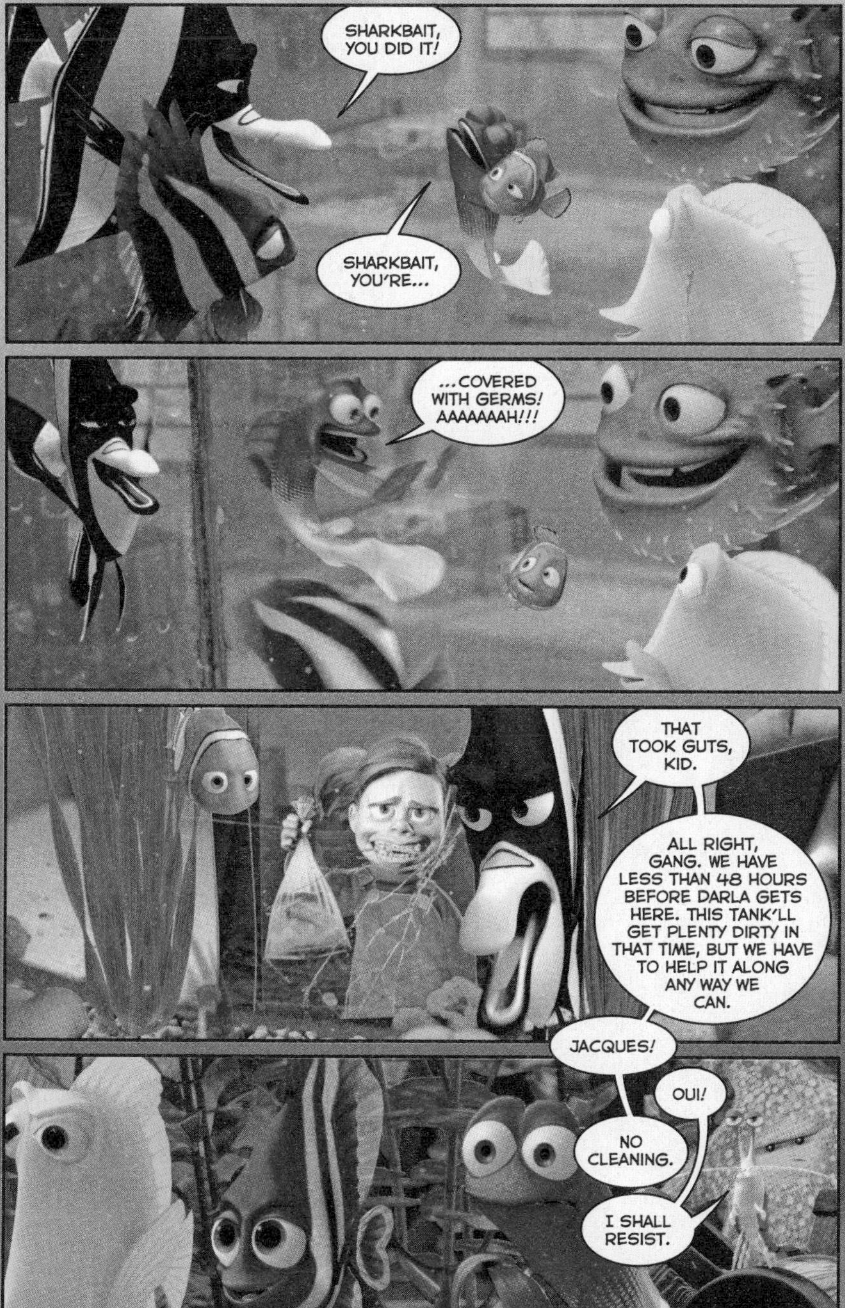
SHARKBAIT, YOU DID IT!
SHARKBAIT, YOU'RE...
...COVERED WITH GERMS! AAAAAAAH!!!
THAT TOOK GUTS, KID.
ALL RIGHT, GANG. WE HAVE LESS THAN 48 HOURS BEFORE DARLA GETS HERE. THIS TANK'LL GET PLENTY DIRTY IN THAT TIME, BUT WE HAVE TO HELP IT ALONG ANY WAY WE CAN.
JACQUES!
OUI!
NO CLEANING.
I SHALL RESIST.

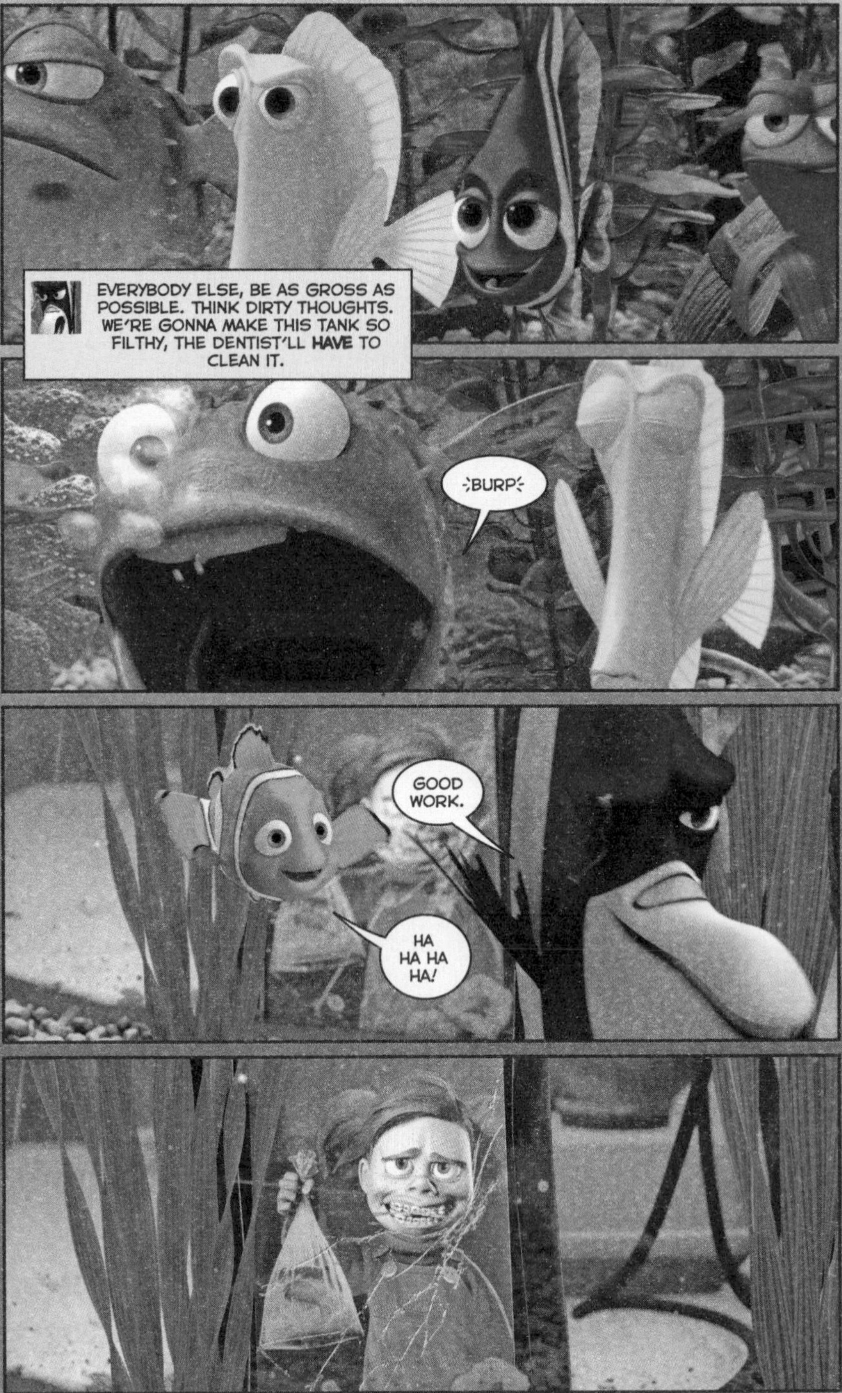
EVERYBODY ELSE, BE AS GROSS AS POSSIBLE. THINK DIRTY THOUGHTS. WE'RE GONNA MAKE THIS TANK SO FILTHY, THE DENTIST'LL **HAVE** TO CLEAN IT.
BURP
GOOD WORK.
HA HA HA HA!

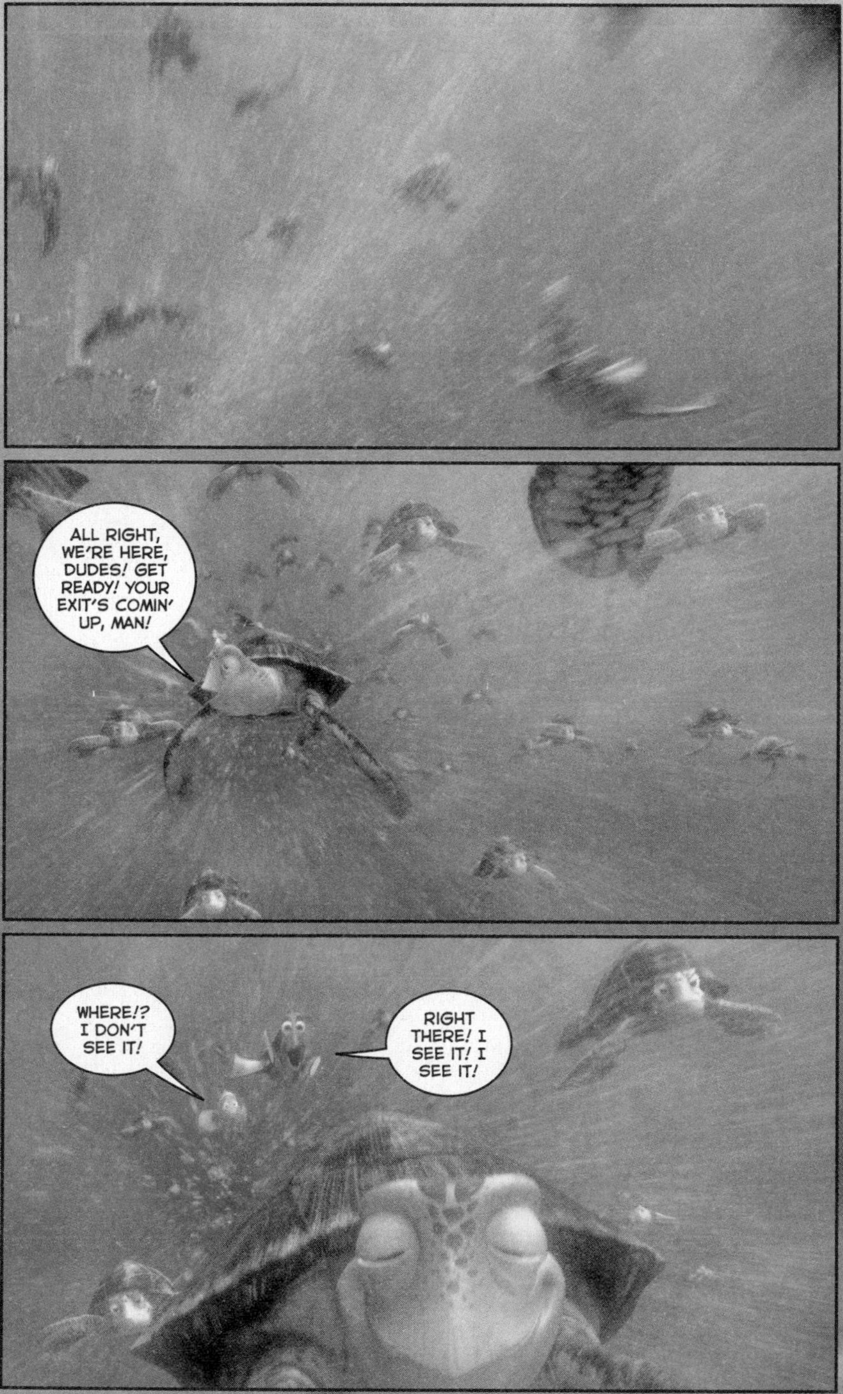
ALL RIGHT, WE'RE HERE, DUDES! GET READY! YOUR EXIT'S COMIN' UP, MAN!
WHERE!? I DON'T SEE IT!
RIGHT THERE! I SEE IT! I SEE IT!

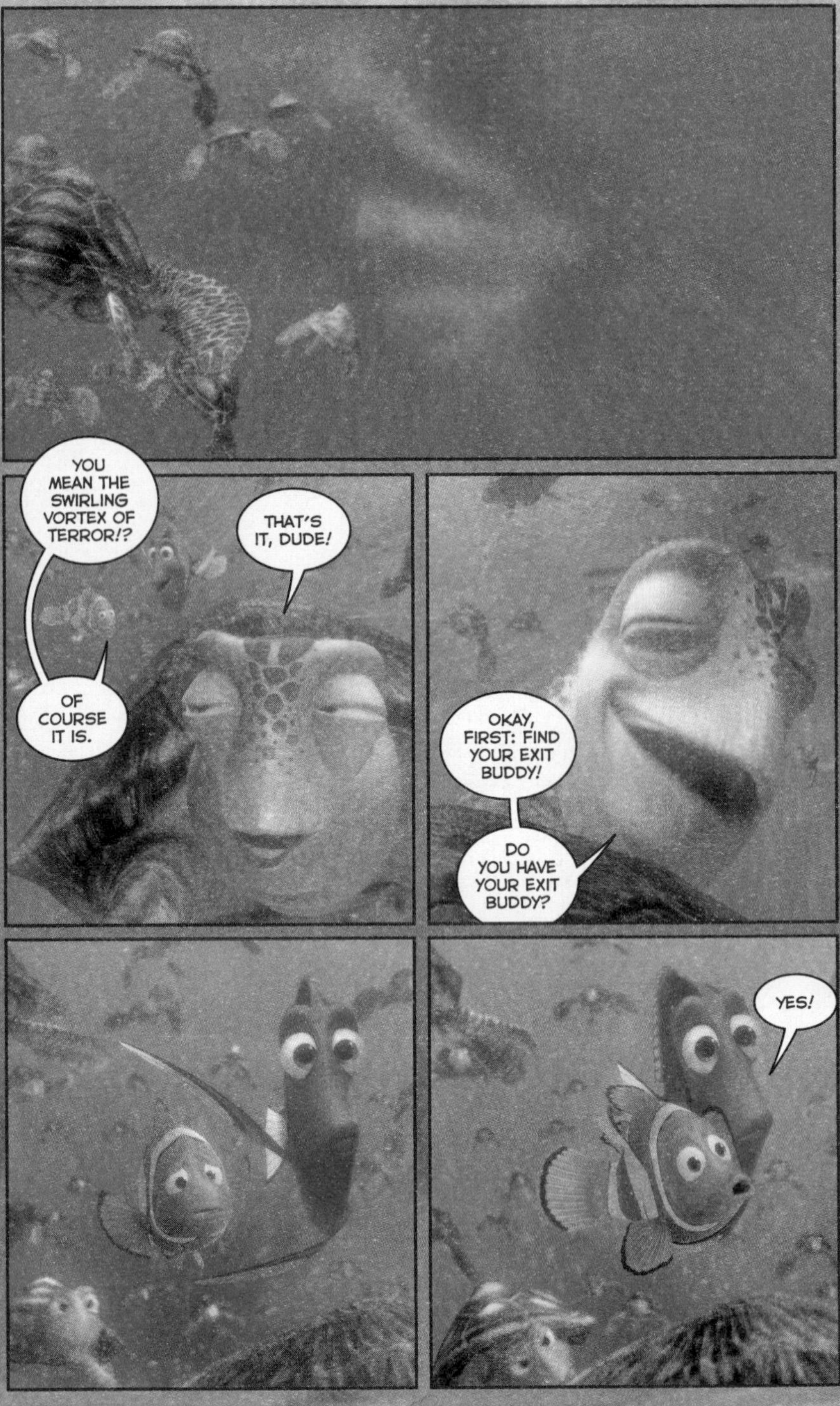
YOU MEAN THE SWIRLING VORTEX OF TERROR!?
THAT'S IT, DUDE!
OF COURSE IT IS.
OKAY, FIRST: FIND YOUR EXIT BUDDY!
DO YOU HAVE YOUR EXIT BUDDY?
YES!

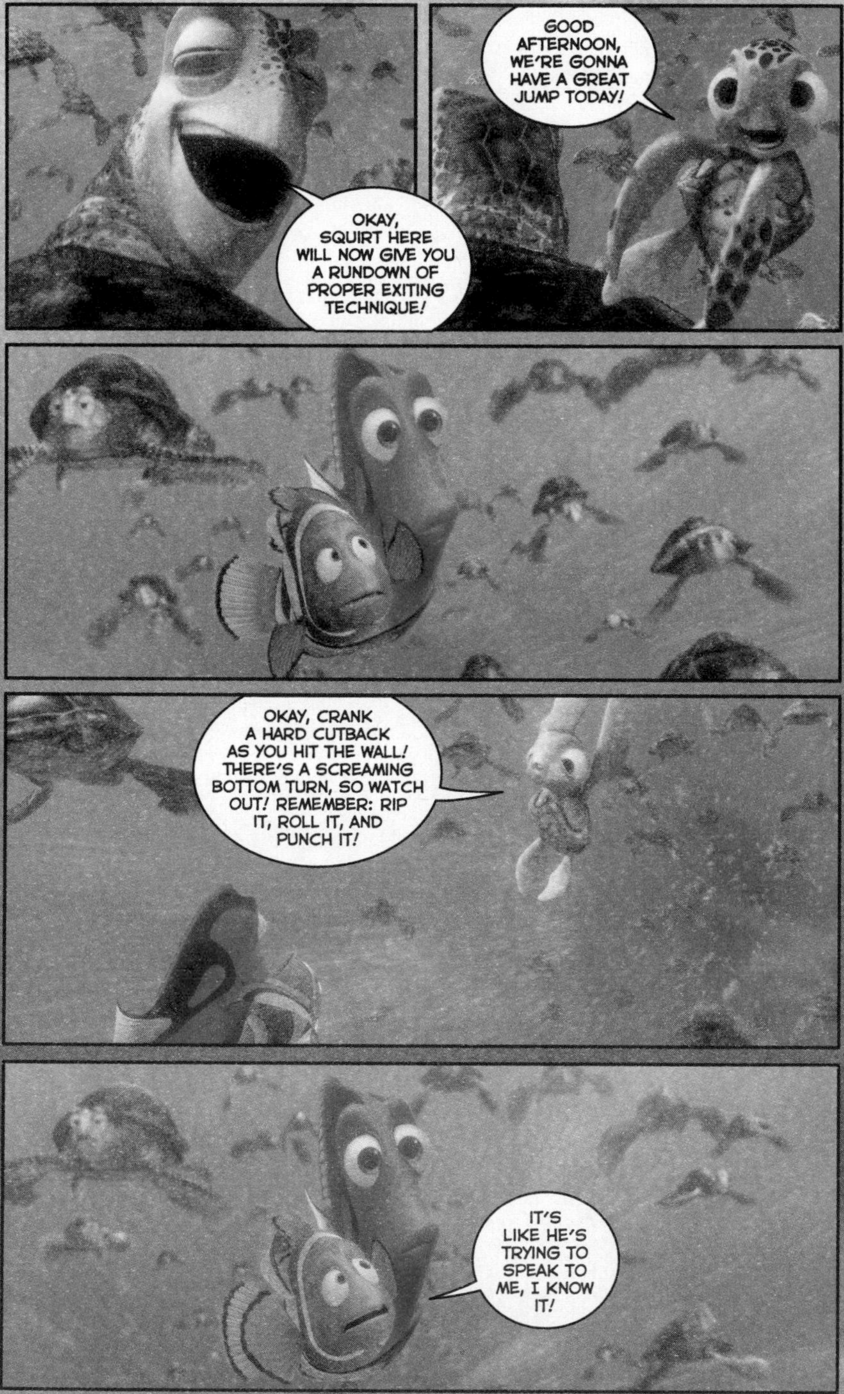
OKAY, SQUIRT HERE WILL NOW GIVE YOU A RUNDOWN OF PROPER EXITING TECHNIQUE!
GOOD AFTERNOON, WE'RE GONNA HAVE A GREAT JUMP TODAY!
OKAY, CRANK A HARD CUTBACK AS YOU HIT THE WALL! THERE'S A SCREAMING BOTTOM TURN, SO WATCH OUT! REMEMBER: RIP IT, ROLL IT, AND PUNCH IT!
IT'S LIKE HE'S TRYING TO SPEAK TO ME, I KNOW IT!

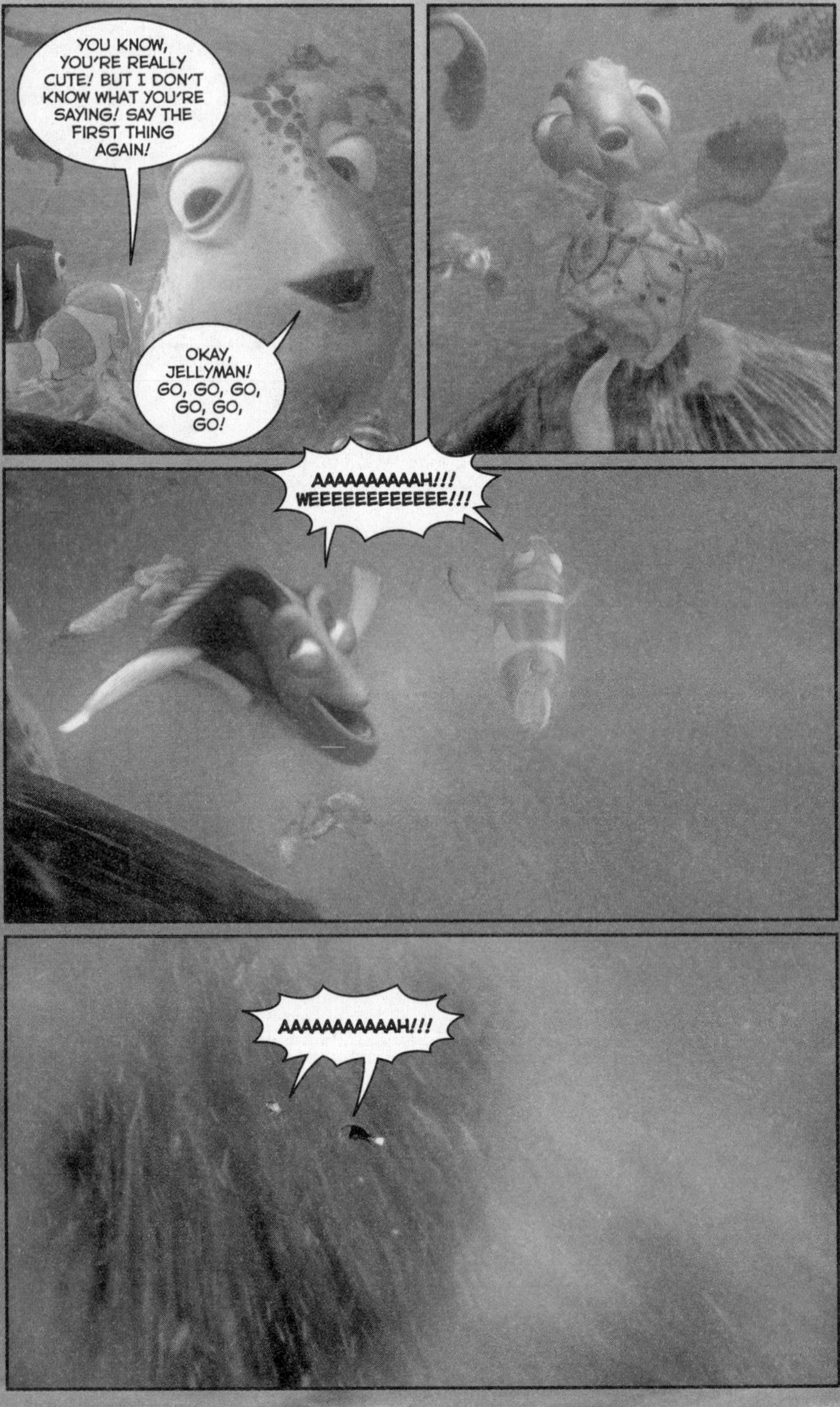
YOU KNOW, YOU'RE REALLY CUTE! BUT I DON'T KNOW WHAT YOU'RE SAYING! SAY THE FIRST THING AGAIN!
OKAY, JELLYMAN! GO, GO, GO, GO, GO, GO!
AAAAAAAAAAH!!! WEEEEEEEEEEEE!!!
AAAAAAAAAAAH!!!

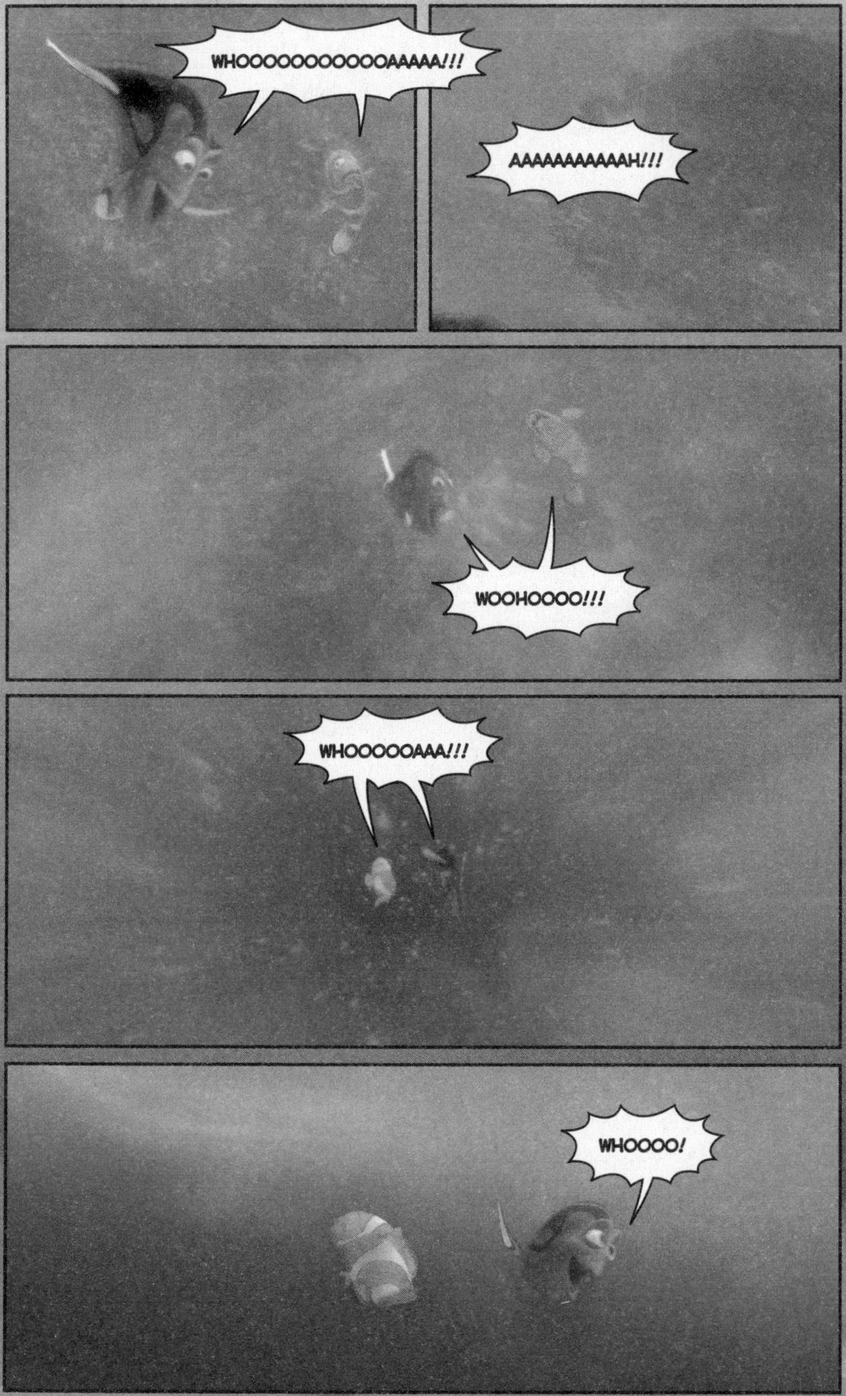
WHOOOOOOOOOOOOAAAAA!!!
AAAAAAAAAAAAH!!!
WOOHOOOO!!!
WHOOOOOAAA!!!
WHOOOO!

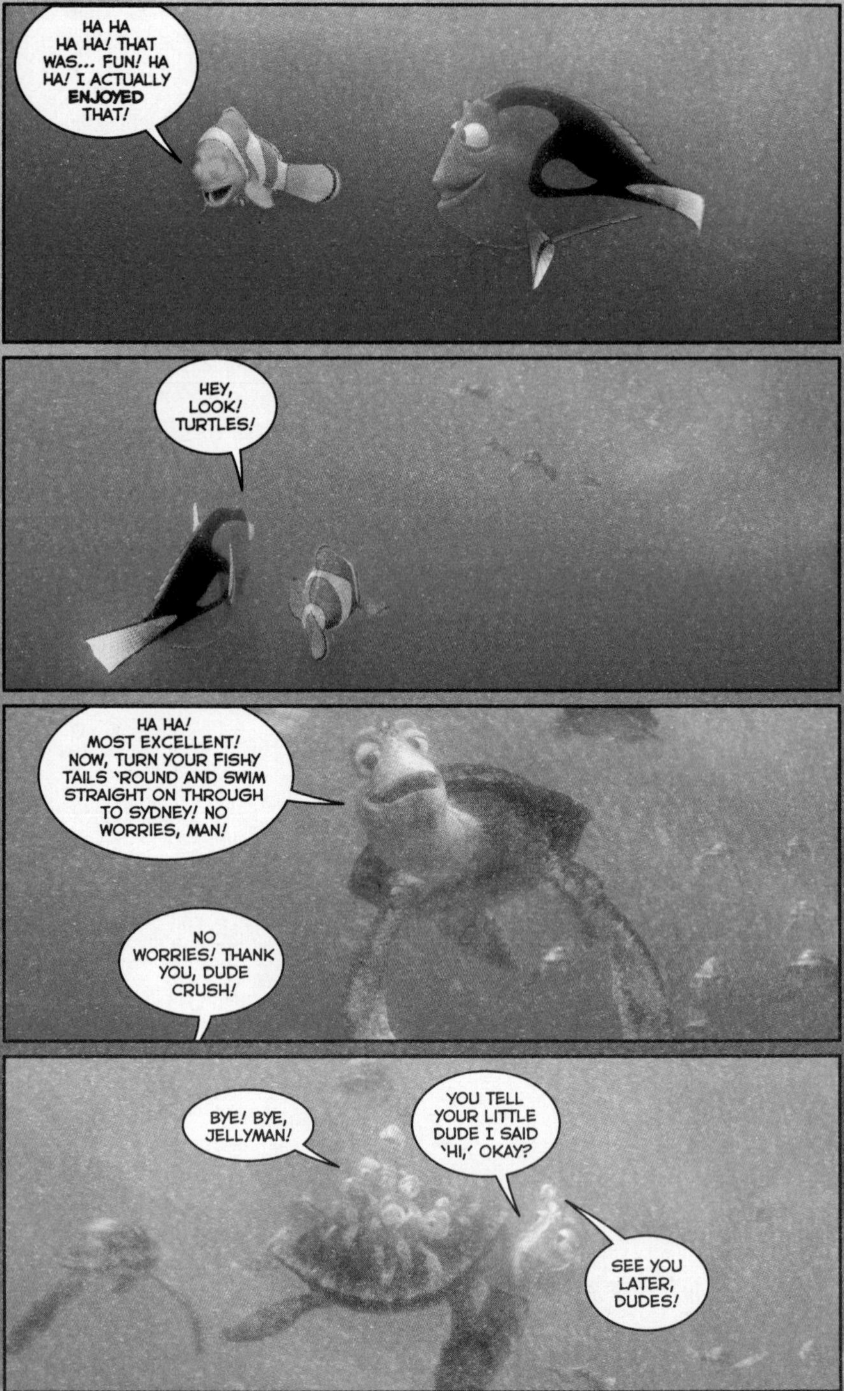
HA HA HA HA! THAT WAS... FUN! HA HA! I ACTUALLY **ENJOYED** THAT!
HEY, LOOK! TURTLES!
HA HA! MOST EXCELLENT! NOW, TURN YOUR FISHY TAILS 'ROUND AND SWIM STRAIGHT ON THROUGH TO SYDNEY! NO WORRIES, MAN!
NO WORRIES! THANK YOU, DUDE CRUSH!
BYE! BYE, JELLYMAN!
YOU TELL YOUR LITTLE DUDE I SAID 'HI,' OKAY?
SEE YOU LATER, DUDES!

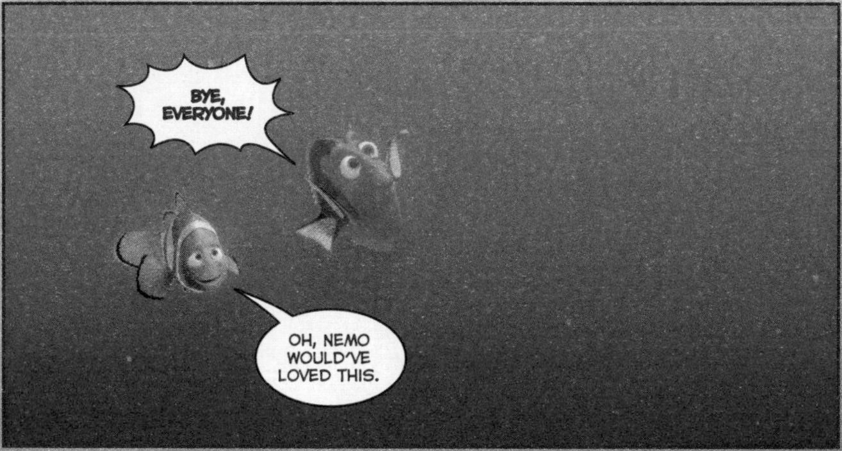
BYE, EVERYONE!
OH, NEMO WOULD'VE LOVED THIS.

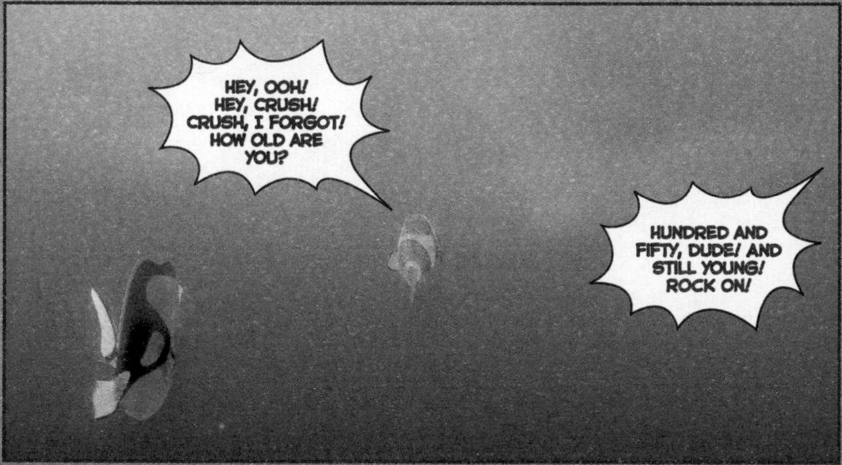
HEY, OOH! HEY, CRUSH! CRUSH, I FORGOT! HOW OLD ARE YOU?
HUNDRED AND FIFTY, DUDE! AND STILL YOUNG! ROCK ON!

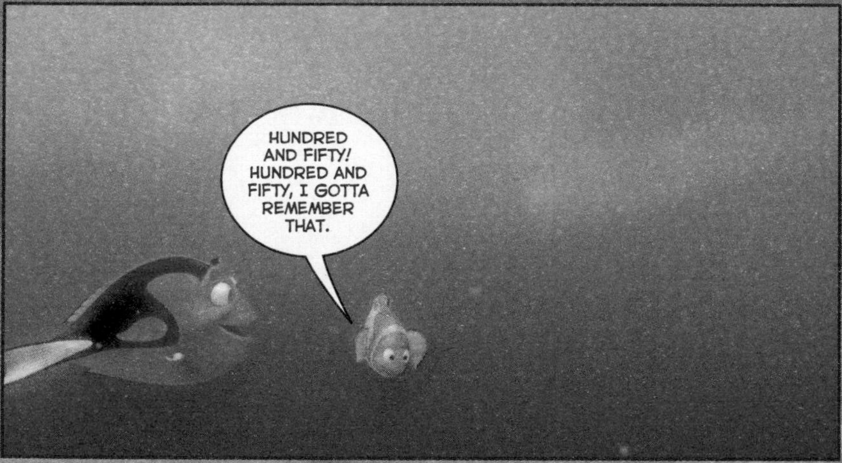
HUNDRED AND FIFTY! HUNDRED AND FIFTY, I GOTTA REMEMBER THAT.

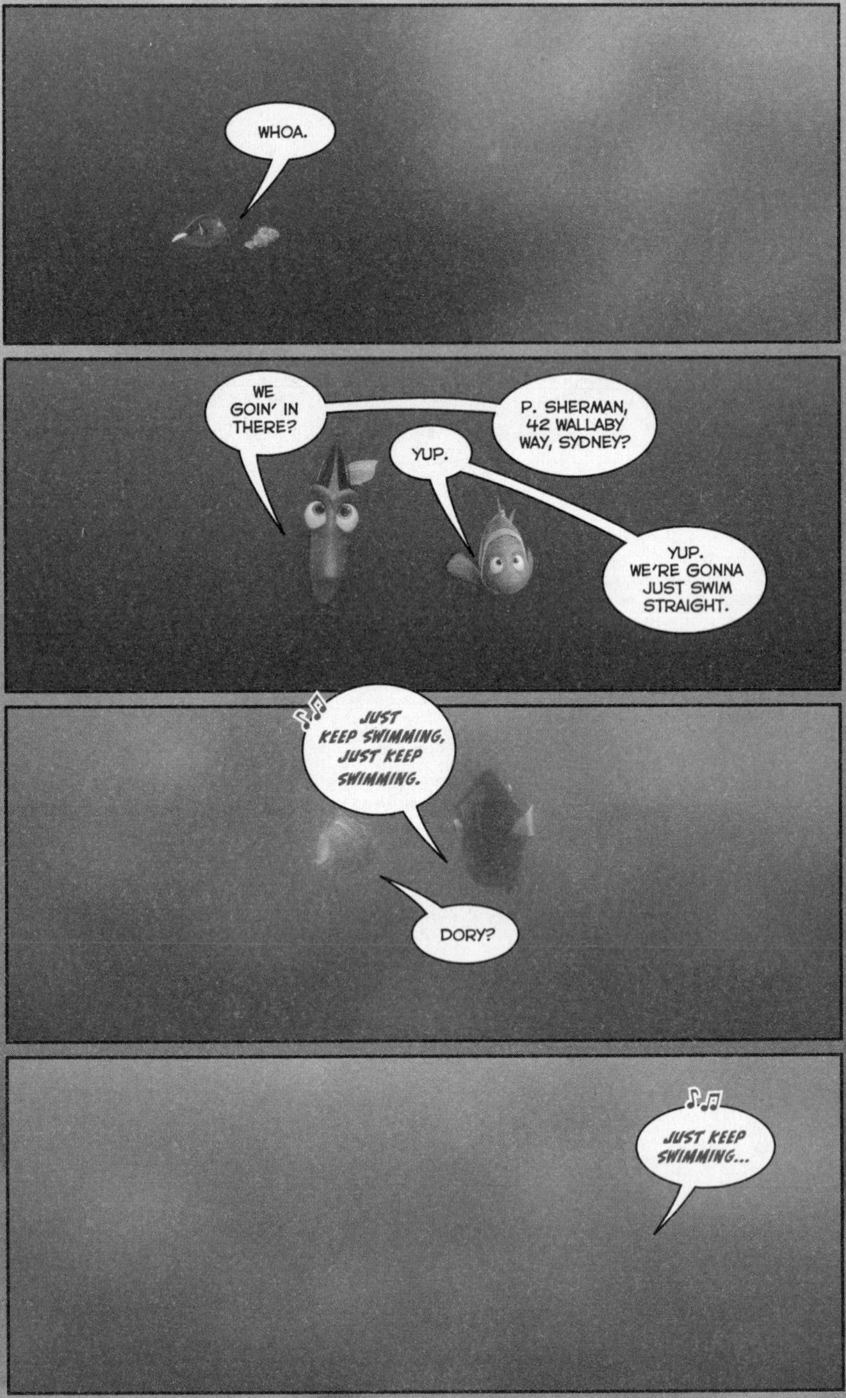
WHOA.
WE GOIN' IN THERE?
P. SHERMAN, 42 WALLABY WAY, SYDNEY?
YUP.
YUP. WE'RE GONNA JUST SWIM STRAIGHT.
JUST KEEP SWIMMING, JUST KEEP SWIMMING.
DORY?
JUST KEEP SWIMMING...

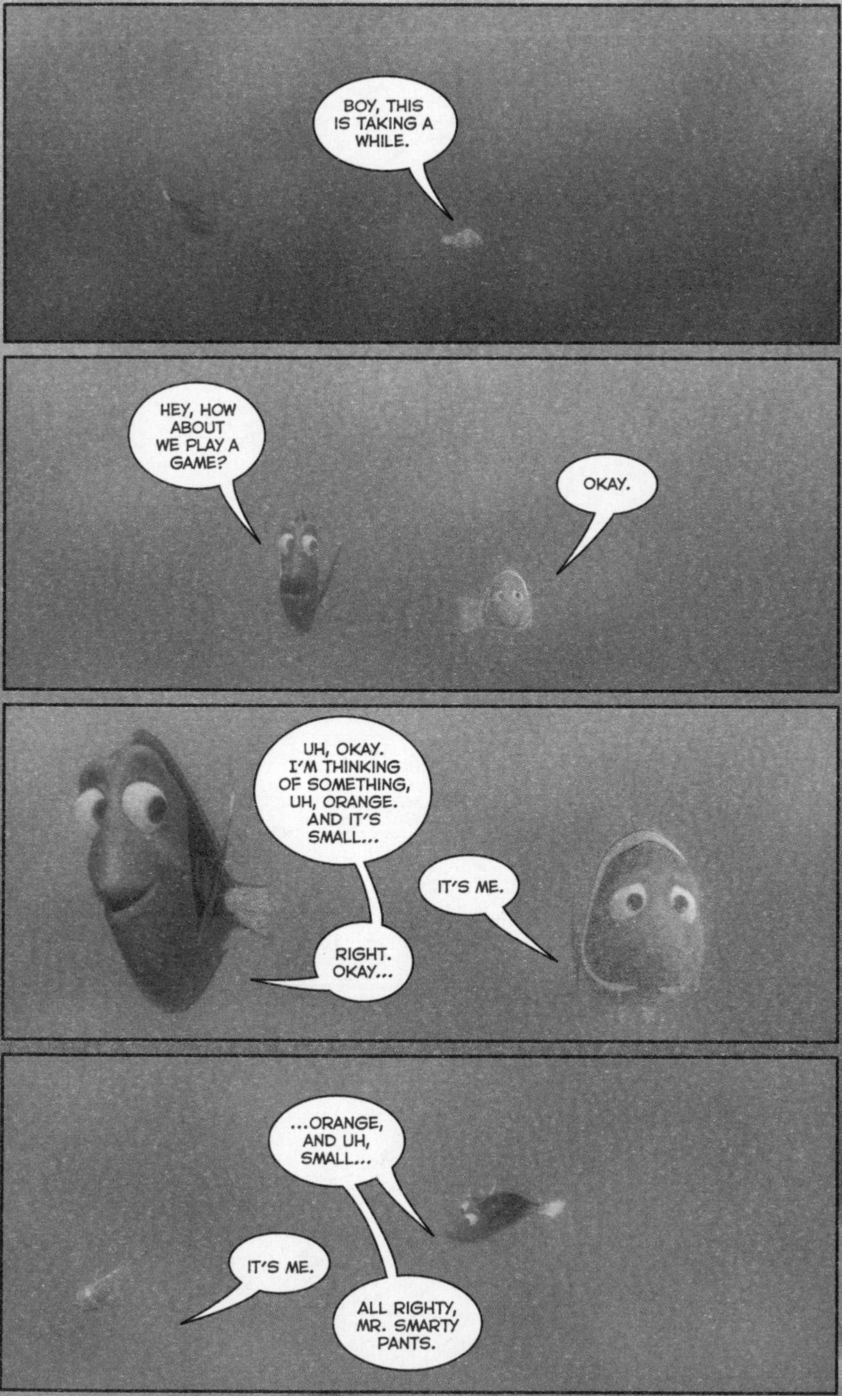
BOY, THIS IS TAKING A WHILE.
HEY, HOW ABOUT WE PLAY A GAME?
OKAY.
UH, OKAY. I'M THINKING OF SOMETHING, UH, ORANGE. AND IT'S SMALL...
IT'S ME.
RIGHT. OKAY...
...ORANGE, AND UH, SMALL...
IT'S ME.
ALL RIGHTY, MR. SMARTY PANTS.

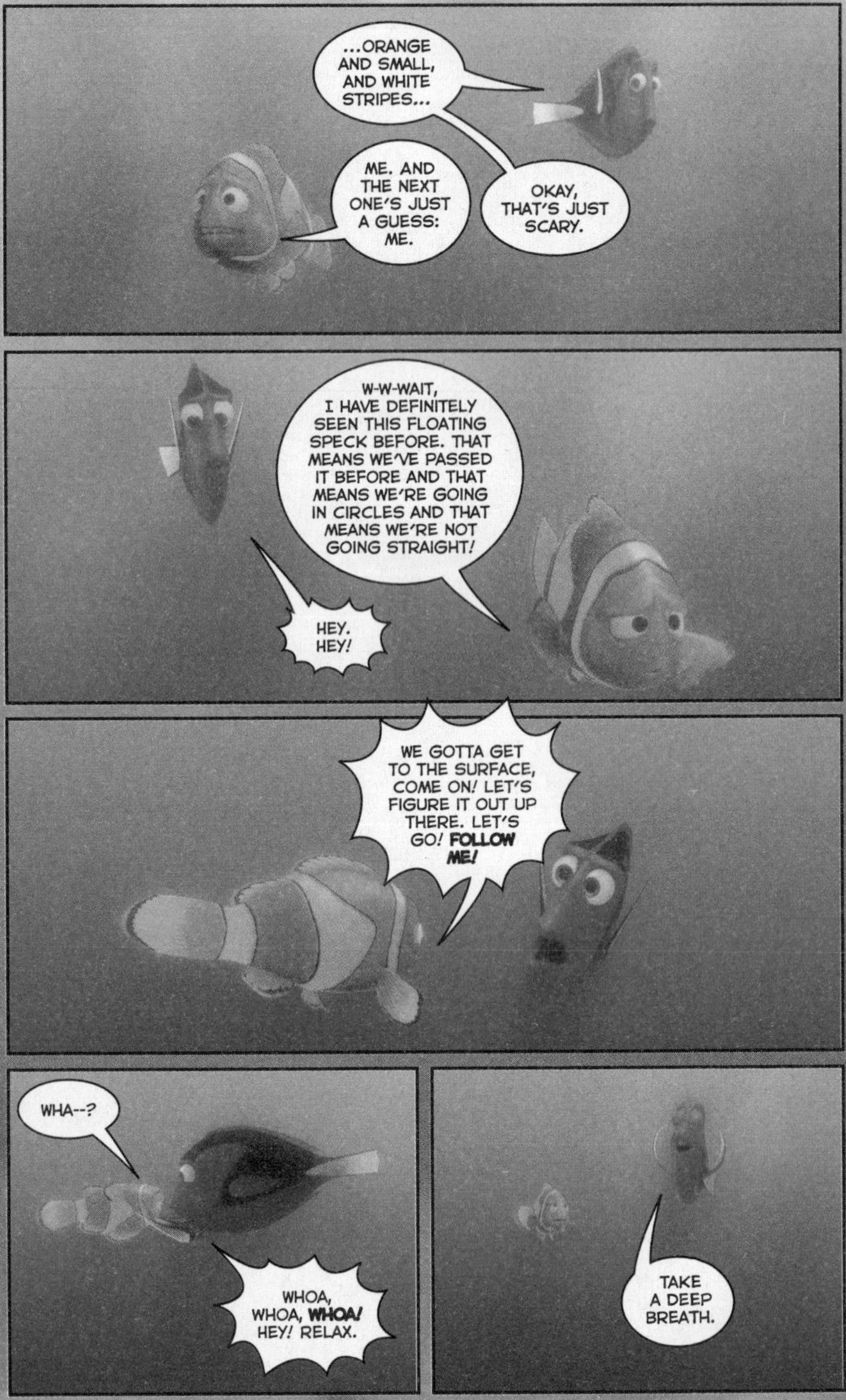
...ORANGE AND SMALL, AND WHITE STRIPES...
ME. AND THE NEXT ONE'S JUST A GUESS: ME.
OKAY, THAT'S JUST SCARY.
W-W-WAIT, I HAVE DEFINITELY SEEN THIS FLOATING SPECK BEFORE. THAT MEANS WE'VE PASSED IT BEFORE AND THAT MEANS WE'RE GOING IN CIRCLES AND THAT MEANS WE'RE NOT GOING STRAIGHT!
HEY. HEY!
WE GOTTA GET TO THE SURFACE, COME ON! LET'S FIGURE IT OUT UP THERE. LET'S GO! **FOLLOW ME!**
WHA--?
WHOA, WHOA, **WHOA!** HEY! RELAX.
TAKE A DEEP BREATH.

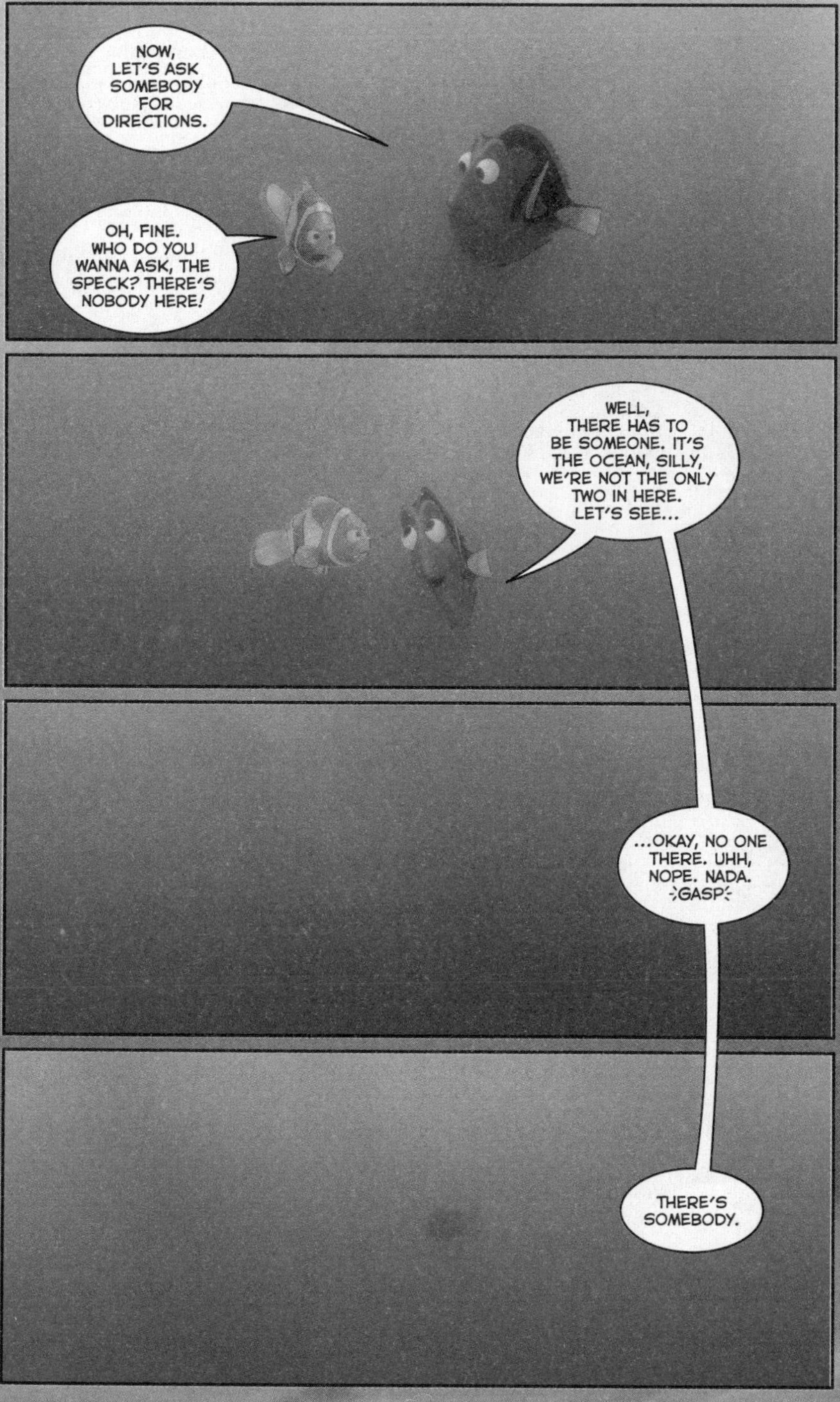
NOW, LET'S ASK SOMEBODY FOR DIRECTIONS.
OH, FINE. WHO DO YOU WANNA ASK, THE SPECK? THERE'S NOBODY HERE!
WELL, THERE HAS TO BE SOMEONE. IT'S THE OCEAN, SILLY, WE'RE NOT THE ONLY TWO IN HERE. LET'S SEE...
...OKAY, NO ONE THERE. UHH, NOPE. NADA. GASP
THERE'S SOMEBODY.

HEY! EXCUSE--

DORY! DORY! DORY! OKAY, NOW IT'S MY TURN. I'M THINKING OF SOMETHING DARK AND MYSTERIOUS. IT'S A FISH WE DON'T KNOW. AND IF WE ASK IT DIRECTIONS, IT COULD INGEST US AND SPIT OUT OUR BONES!

WHAT IS IT WITH MEN AND ASKING FOR DIRECTIONS?

LOOK, I DON'T WANNA PLAY THE GENDER CARD RIGHT NOW. YOU WANNA PLAY A CARD? LET'S PLAY THE 'LET'S NOT DIE' CARD.

YOU WANNA GET OUTTA HERE, DON'T YOU?

OF COURSE, I DO.

WELL THEN, HOW ARE WE GONNA DO THAT UNLESS WE GIVE IT A SHOT AND HOPE FOR THE BEST? HMMM? HMMMM!?

COME ON, TRUST ME ON THIS.

DORY, YOU DON'T FULLY UNDERSTAND...

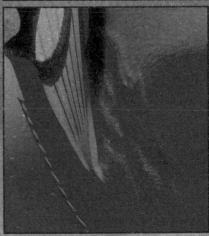

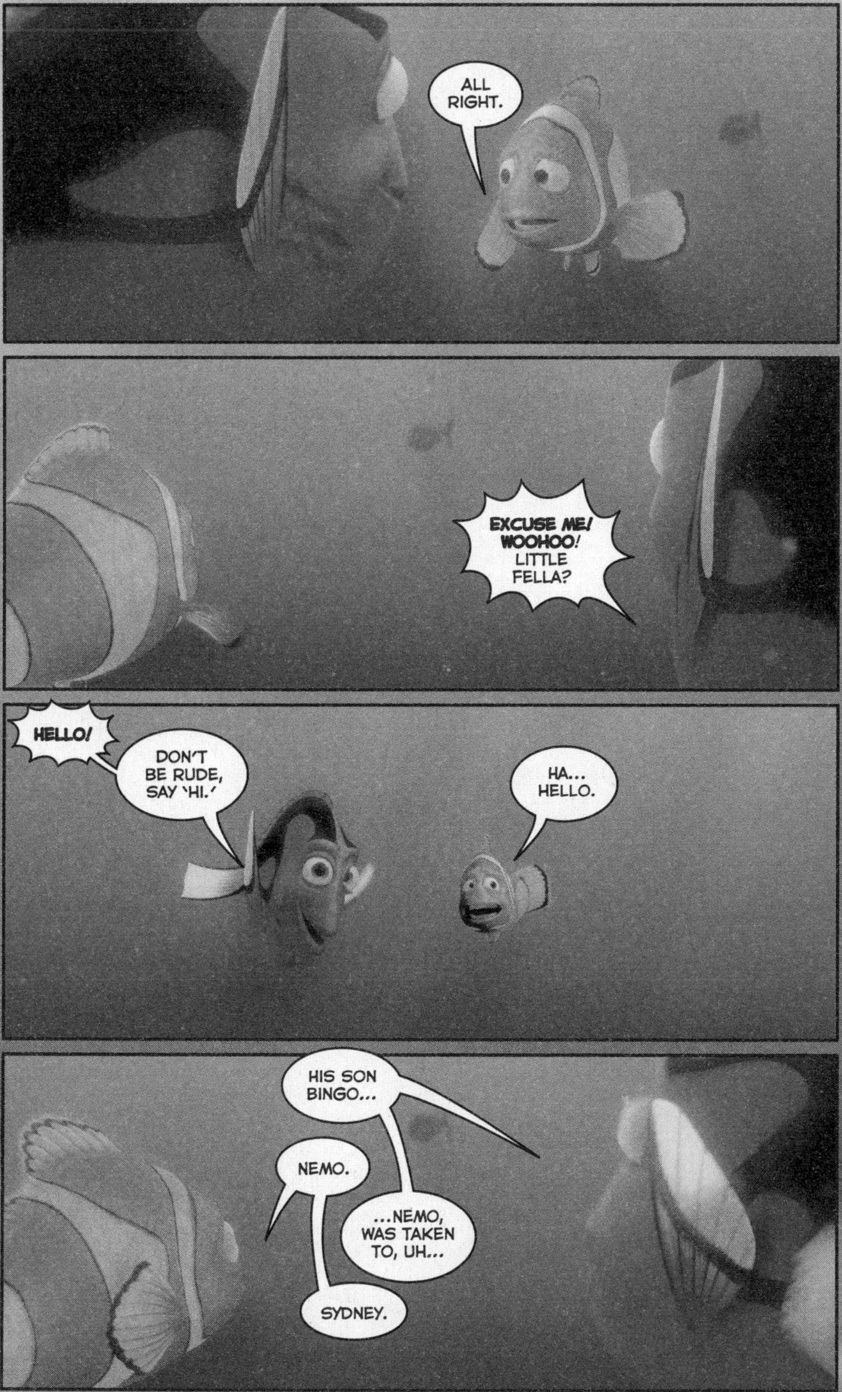
ALL RIGHT.
EXCUSE ME! WOOHOO! LITTLE FELLA?
HELLO!
DON'T BE RUDE, SAY 'HI.'
HA... HELLO.
HIS SON BINGO...
NEMO.
...NEMO, WAS TAKEN TO, UH...
SYDNEY.

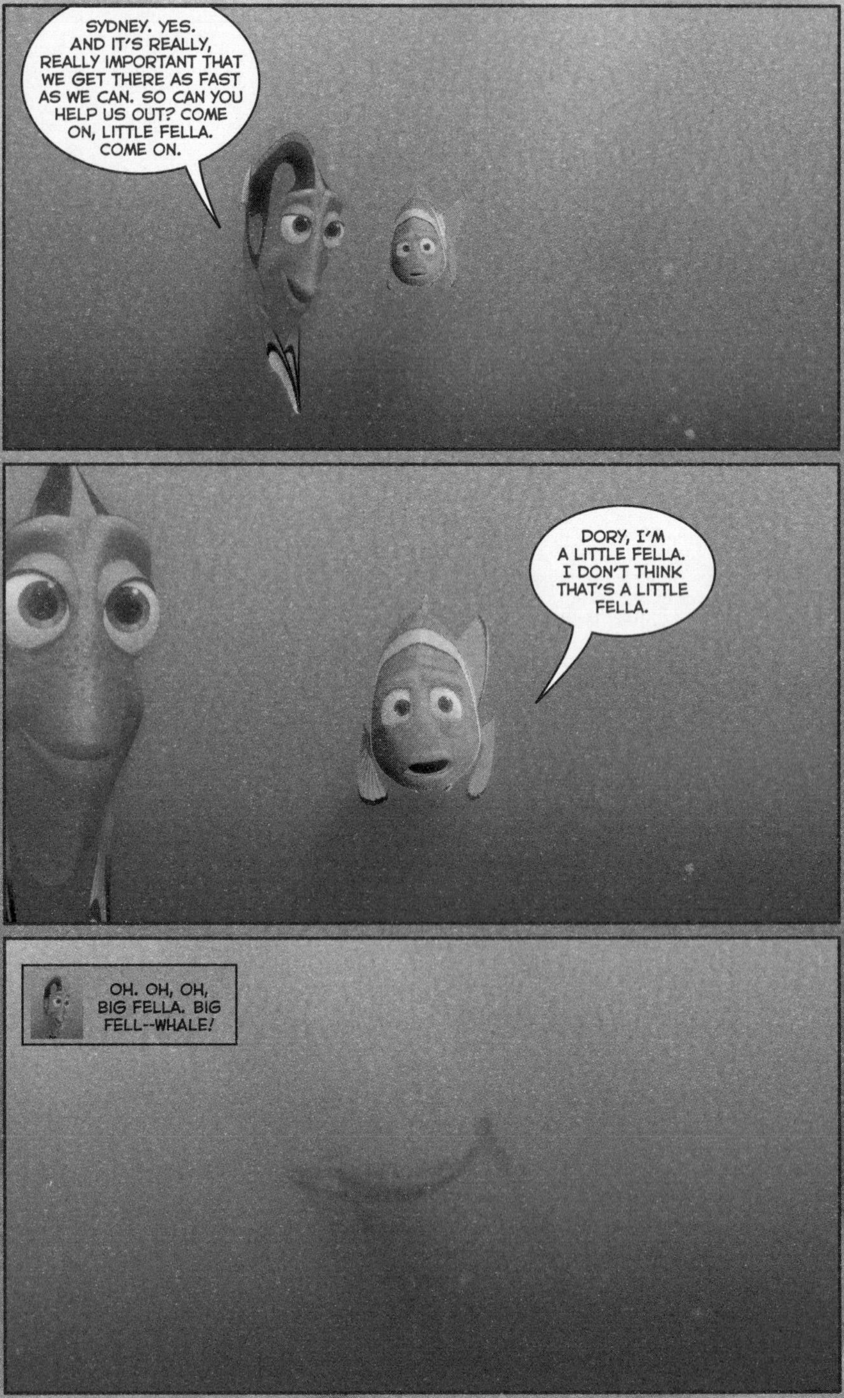
SYDNEY. YES. AND IT'S REALLY, REALLY IMPORTANT THAT WE GET THERE AS FAST AS WE CAN. SO CAN YOU HELP US OUT? COME ON, LITTLE FELLA. COME ON.
DORY, I'M A LITTLE FELLA. I DON'T THINK THAT'S A LITTLE FELLA.
OH. OH, OH, BIG FELLA. BIG FELL--WHALE!

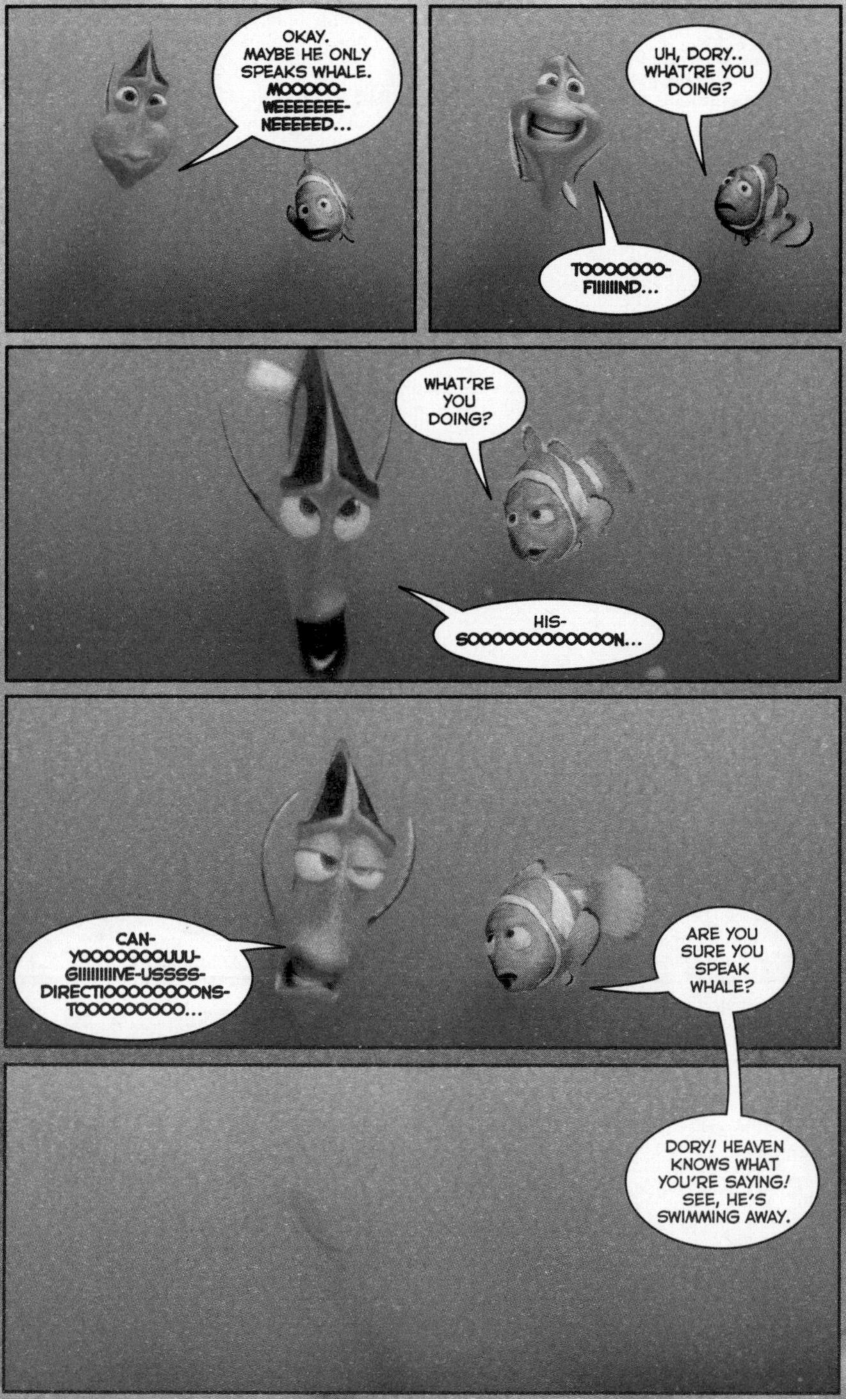
OKAY. MAYBE HE ONLY SPEAKS WHALE. MOOOOO-WEEEEEEE-NEEEEED...
UH, DORY.. WHAT'RE YOU DOING?
TOOOOOOO-FIIIIIND...
WHAT'RE YOU DOING?
HIS-SOOOOOOOOOOOON...
CAN-YOOOOOOOUUU-GIIIIIIIVE-USSSS-DIRECTIOOOOOOOONS-TOOOOOOOOO...
ARE YOU SURE YOU SPEAK WHALE?
DORY! HEAVEN KNOWS WHAT YOU'RE SAYING! SEE, HE'S SWIMMING AWAY.

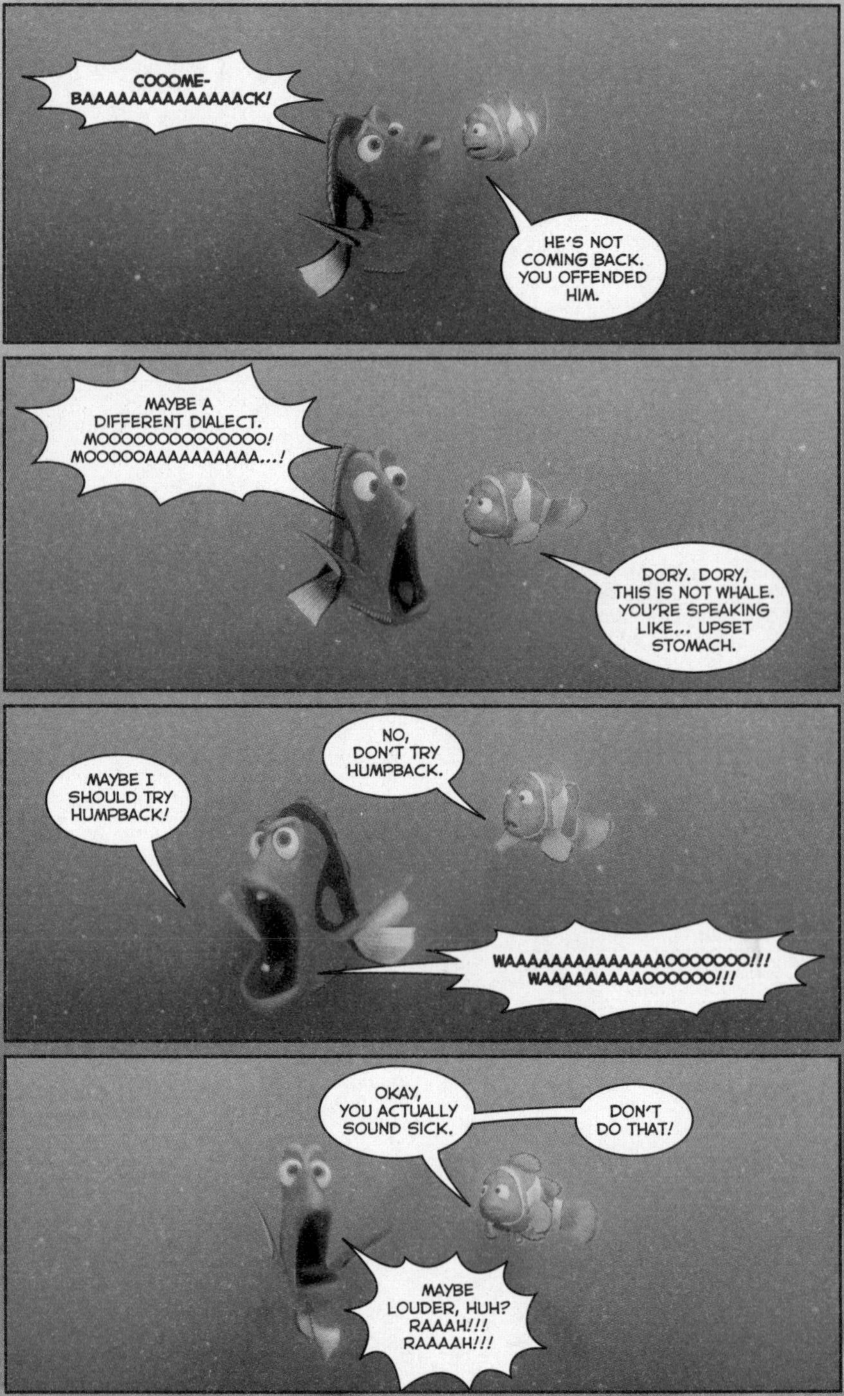
COOOME-BAAAAAAAAAAAAAAACK!
HE'S NOT COMING BACK. YOU OFFENDED HIM.
MAYBE A DIFFERENT DIALECT. MOOOOOOOOOOOOOO! MOOOOOAAAAAAAAAA...!
DORY. DORY, THIS IS NOT WHALE. YOU'RE SPEAKING LIKE... UPSET STOMACH.
MAYBE I SHOULD TRY HUMPBACK!
NO, DON'T TRY HUMPBACK.
WAAAAAAAAAAAAAAAOOOOOOO!!! WAAAAAAAAAOOOOOO!!!
OKAY, YOU ACTUALLY SOUND SICK.
DON'T DO THAT!
MAYBE LOUDER, HUH? RAAAH!!! RAAAAH!!!

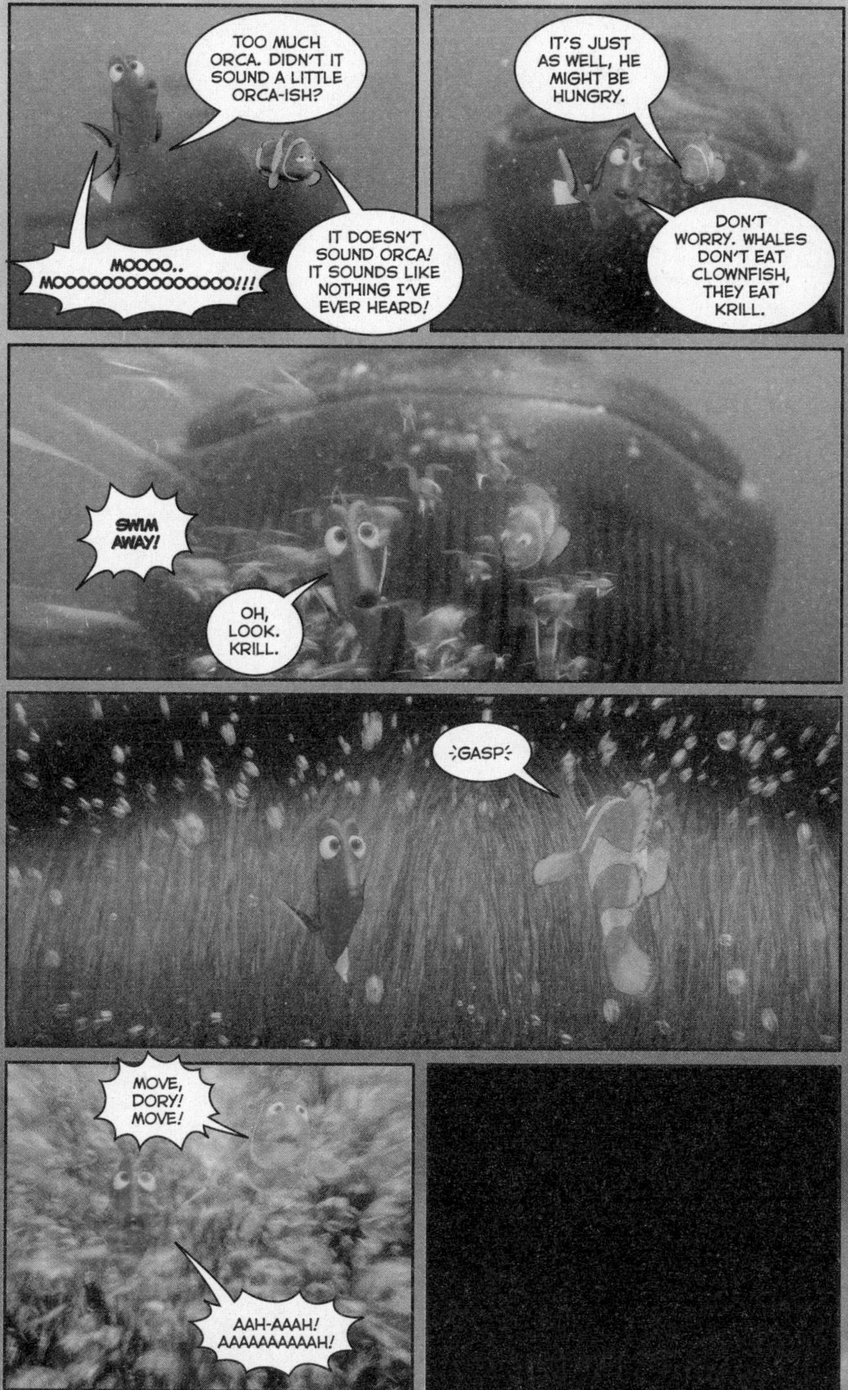
TOO MUCH ORCA. DIDN'T IT SOUND A LITTLE ORCA-ISH?
MOOOO.. MOOOOOOOOOOOOOOOO!!!
IT DOESN'T SOUND ORCA! IT SOUNDS LIKE NOTHING I'VE EVER HEARD!
IT'S JUST AS WELL, HE MIGHT BE HUNGRY.
DON'T WORRY. WHALES DON'T EAT CLOWNFISH, THEY EAT KRILL.
SWIM AWAY!
OH, LOOK. KRILL.
GASP
MOVE, DORY! MOVE!
AAH-AAAH! AAAAAAAAAAH!

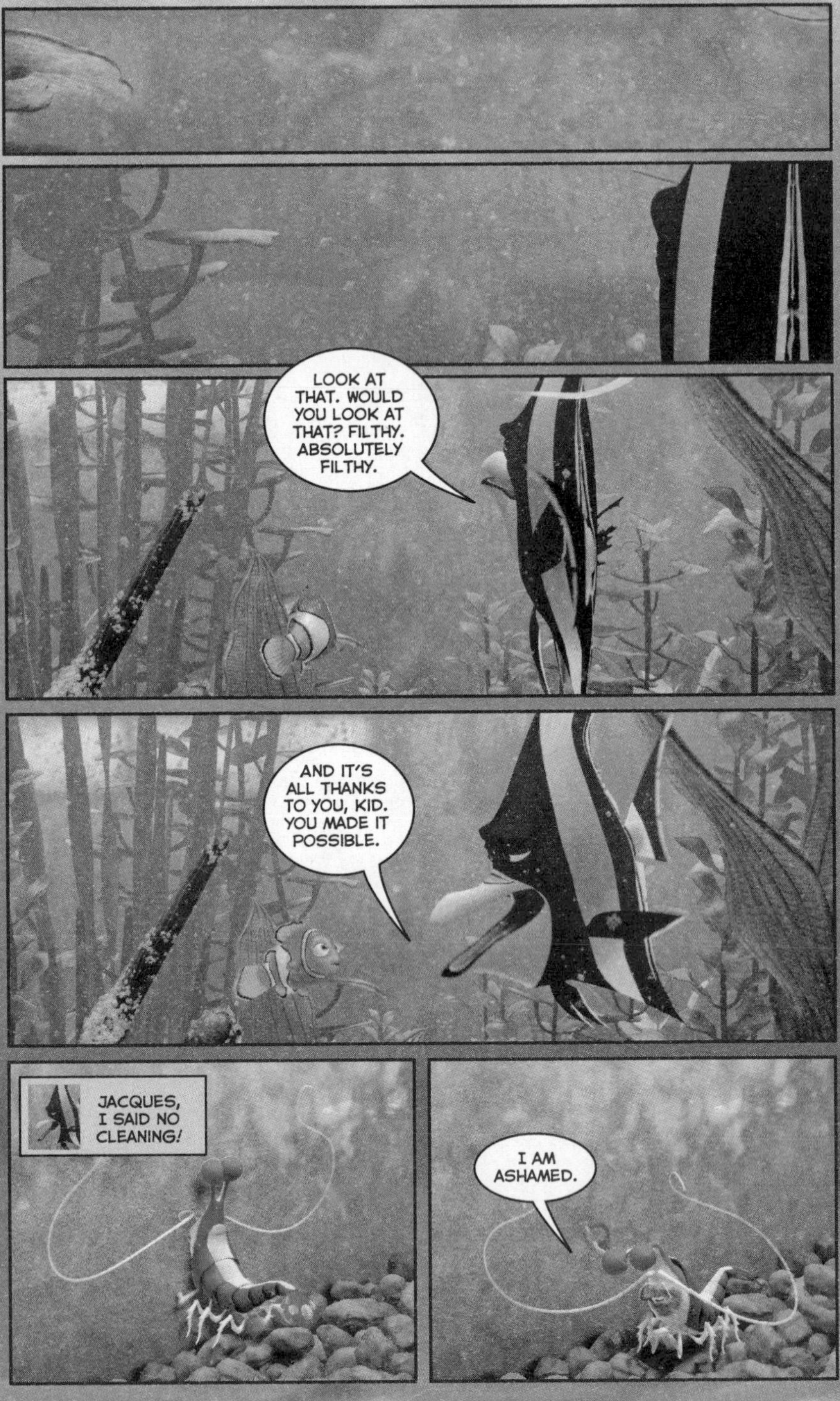
LOOK AT THAT. WOULD YOU LOOK AT THAT? FILTHY. ABSOLUTELY FILTHY.
AND IT'S ALL THANKS TO YOU, KID. YOU MADE IT POSSIBLE.
JACQUES, I SAID NO CLEANING!
I AM ASHAMED.

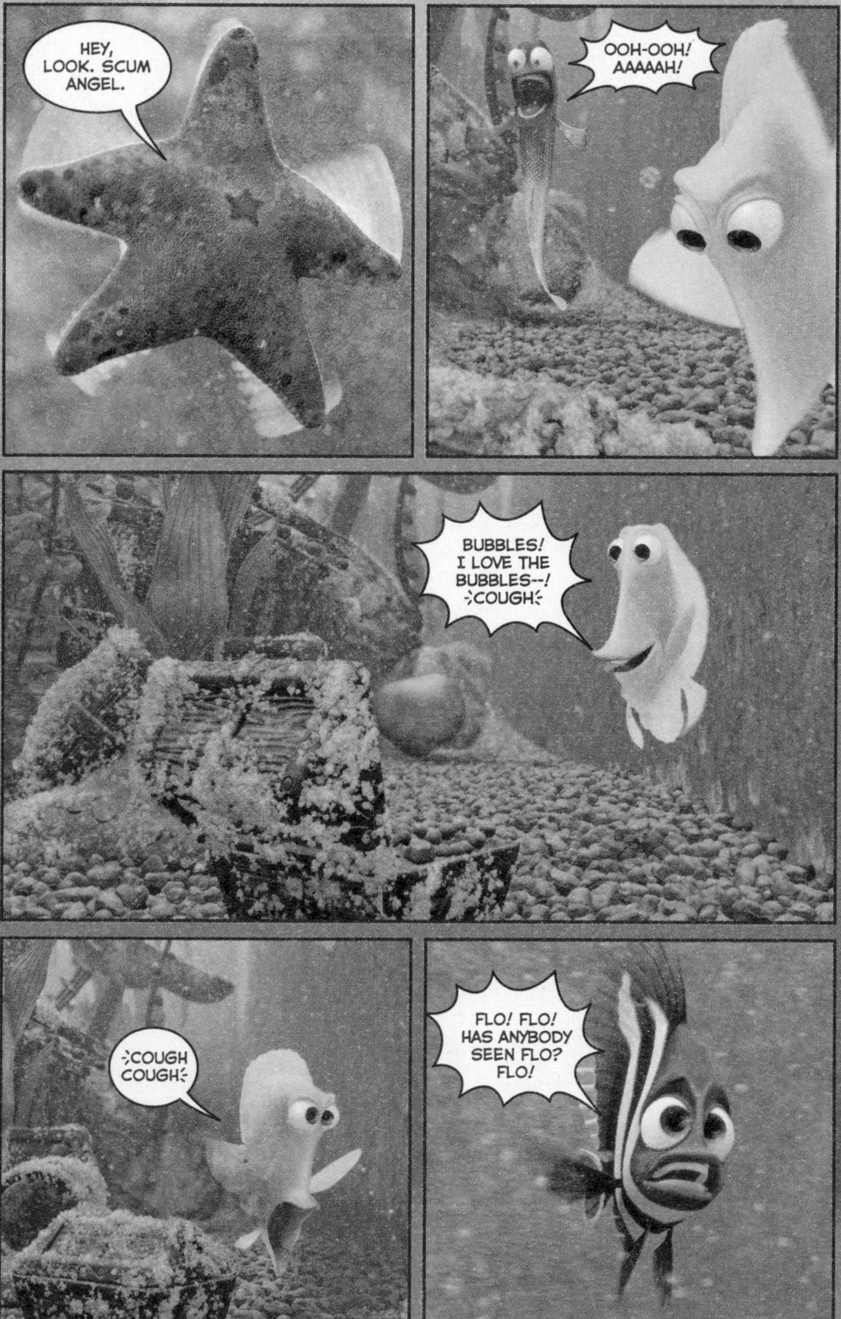
HEY, LOOK. SCUM ANGEL.
OOH-OOH! AAAAAH!
BUBBLES! I LOVE THE BUBBLES--! -COUGH-
-COUGH COUGH-
FLO! FLO! HAS ANYBODY SEEN FLO? FLO!

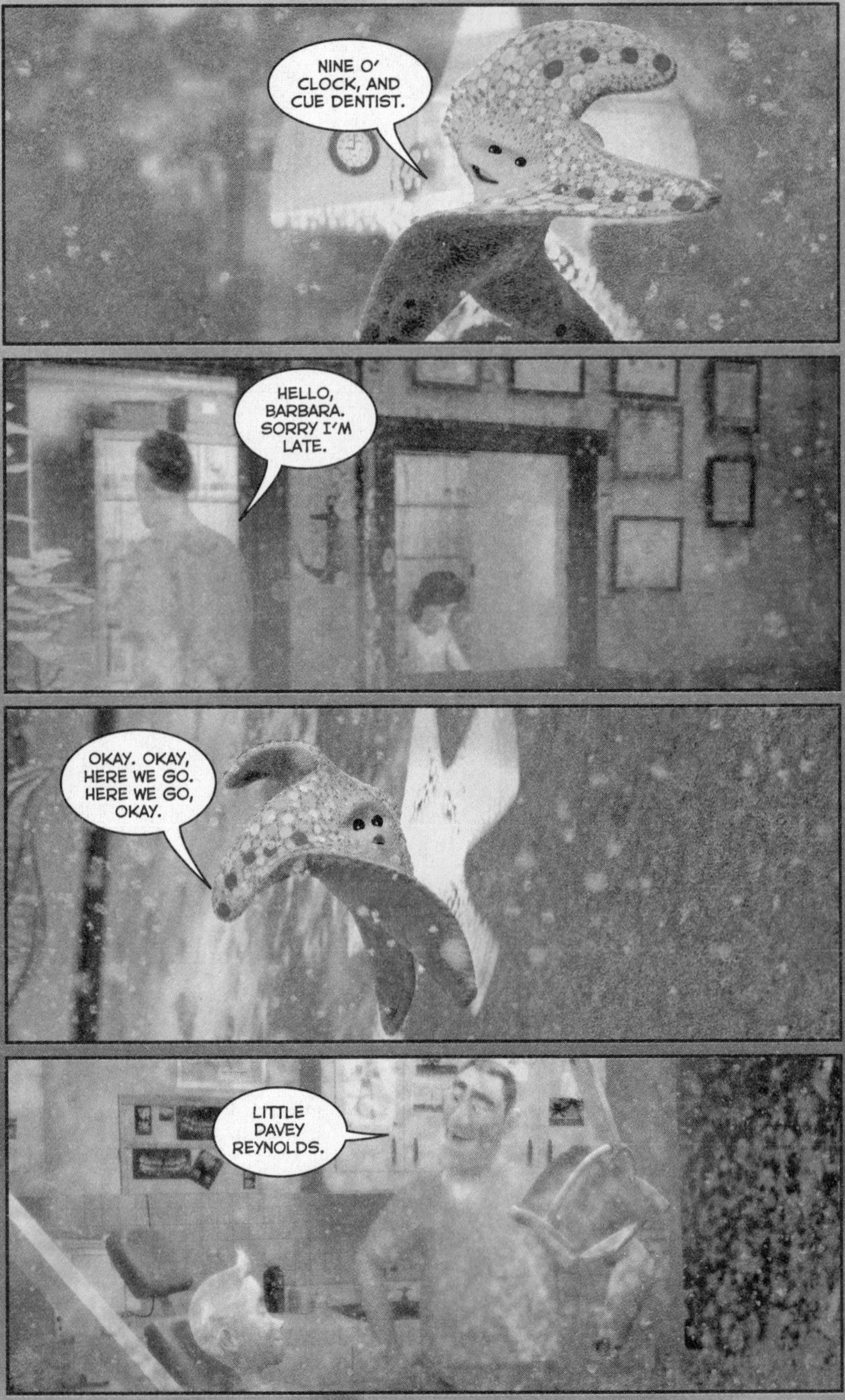
NINE O' CLOCK, AND CUE DENTIST.
HELLO, BARBARA. SORRY I'M LATE.
OKAY. OKAY, HERE WE GO. HERE WE GO, OKAY.
LITTLE DAVEY REYNOLDS.

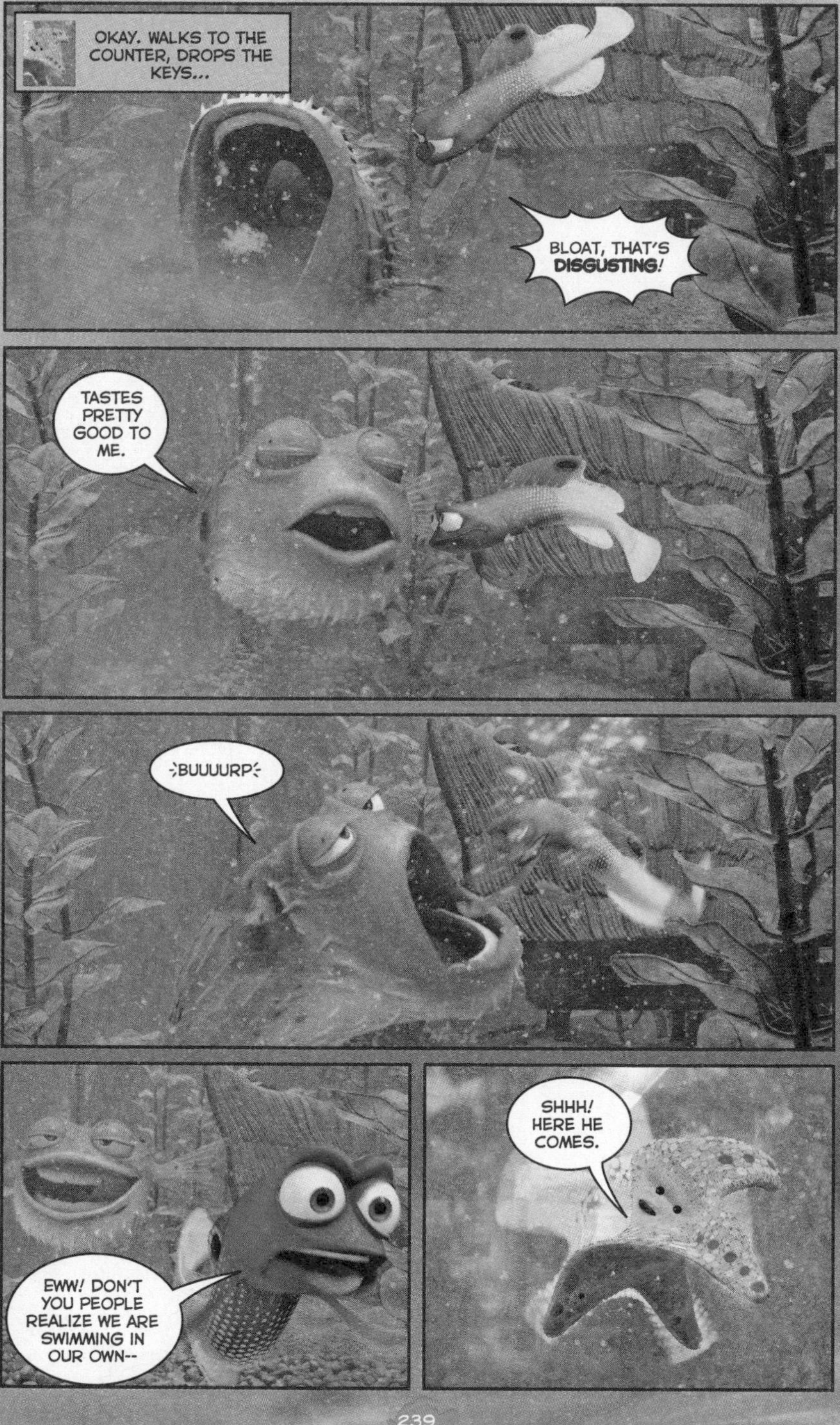
OKAY. WALKS TO THE COUNTER, DROPS THE KEYS...
BLOAT, THAT'S **DISGUSTING**!
TASTES PRETTY GOOD TO ME.
BUUUURP
EWW! DON'T YOU PEOPLE REALIZE WE ARE SWIMMING IN OUR OWN--
SHHH! HERE HE COMES.

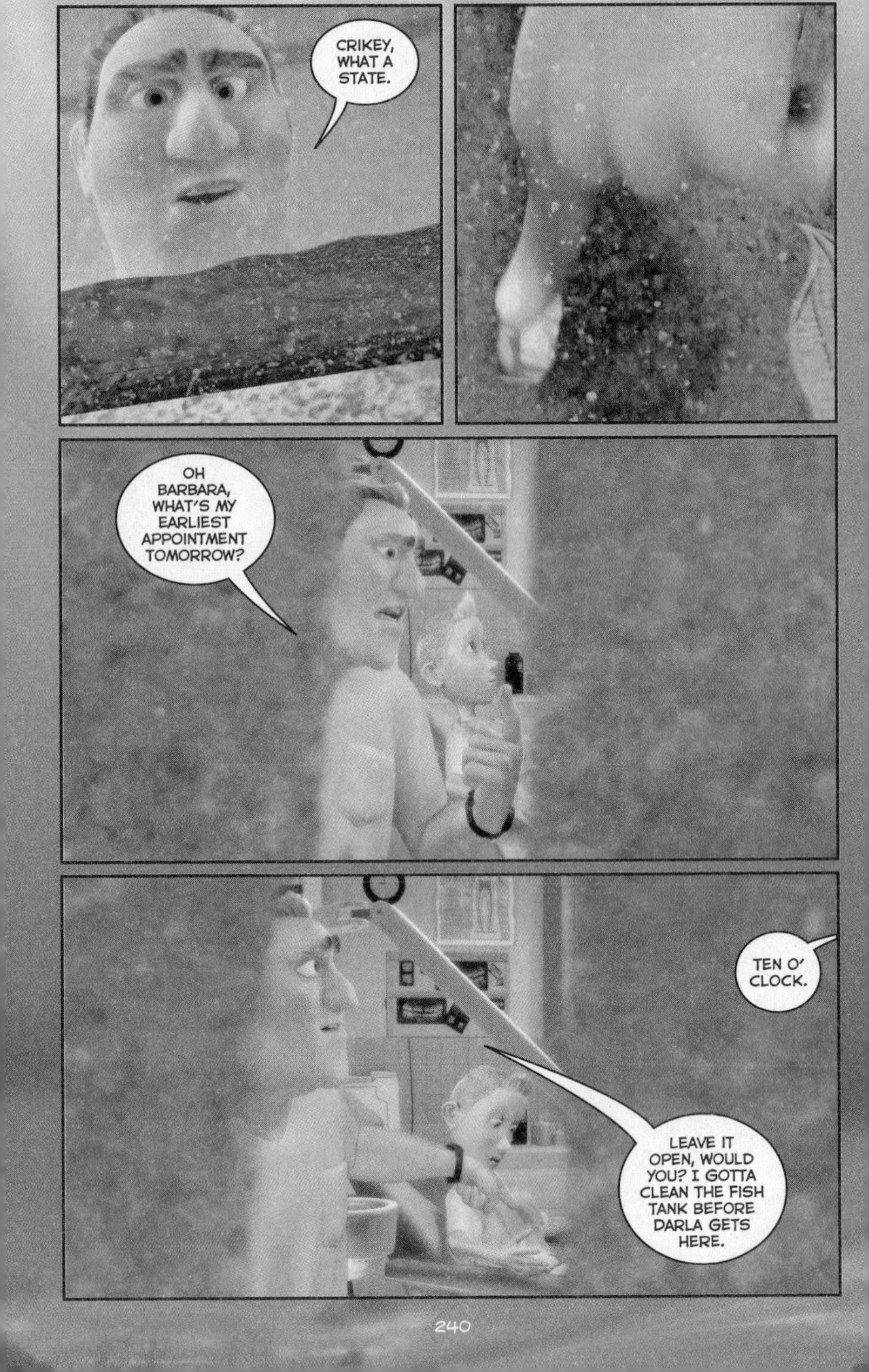
CRIKEY, WHAT A STATE.
OH BARBARA, WHAT'S MY EARLIEST APPOINTMENT TOMORROW?
TEN O' CLOCK.
LEAVE IT OPEN, WOULD YOU? I GOTTA CLEAN THE FISH TANK BEFORE DARLA GETS HERE.

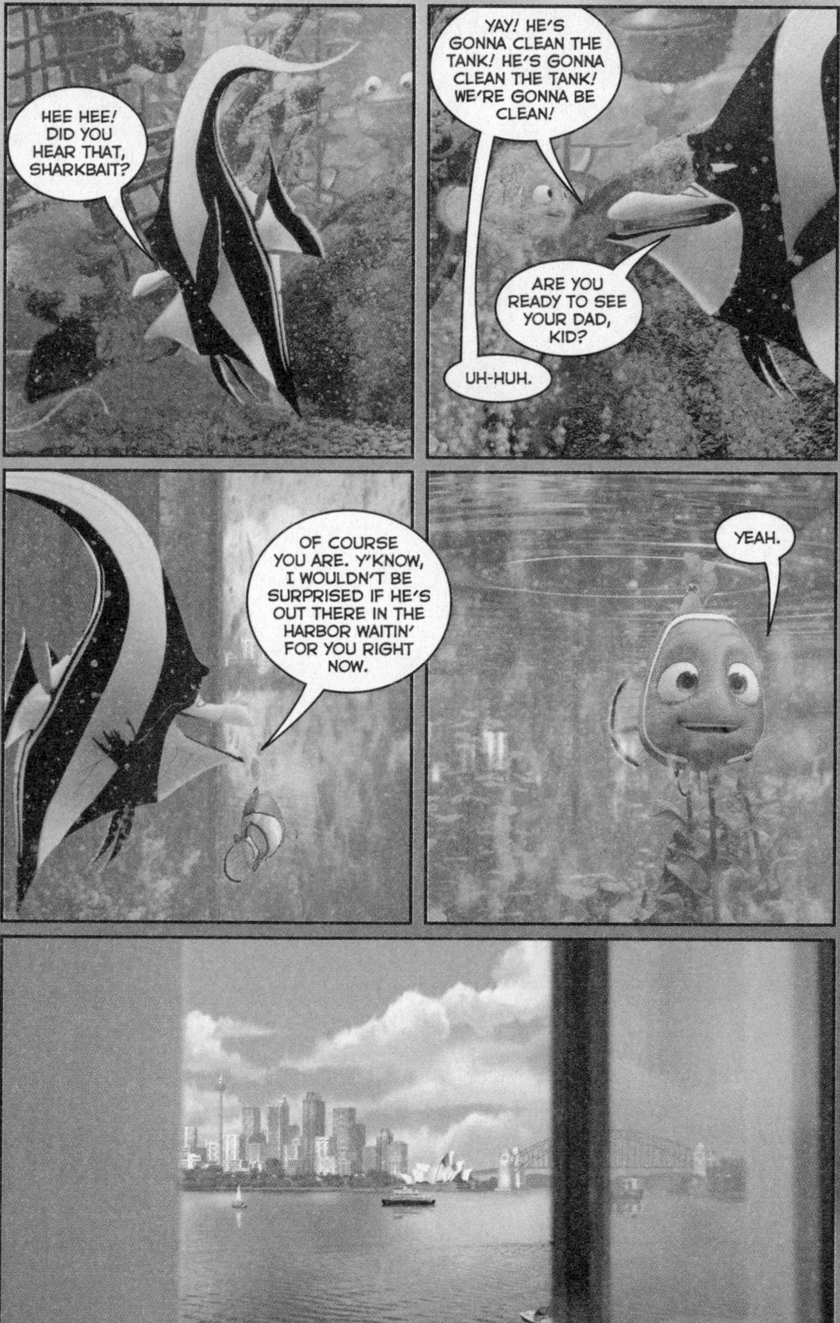
HEE HEE! DID YOU HEAR THAT, SHARKBAIT?
YAY! HE'S GONNA CLEAN THE TANK! HE'S GONNA CLEAN THE TANK! WE'RE GONNA BE CLEAN!
ARE YOU READY TO SEE YOUR DAD, KID?
UH-HUH.
OF COURSE YOU ARE. Y'KNOW, I WOULDN'T BE SURPRISED IF HE'S OUT THERE IN THE HARBOR WAITIN' FOR YOU RIGHT NOW.
YEAH.

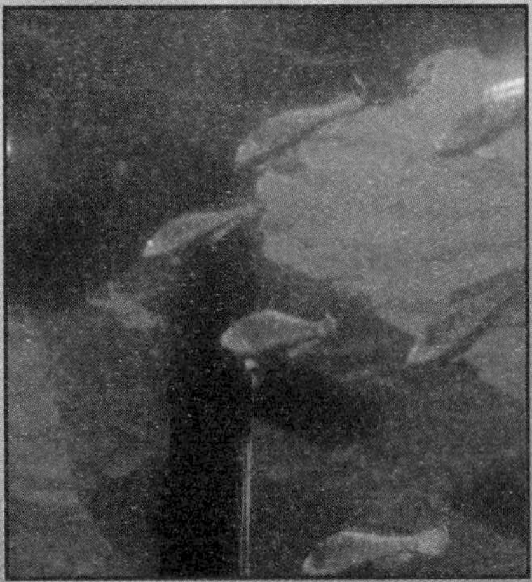
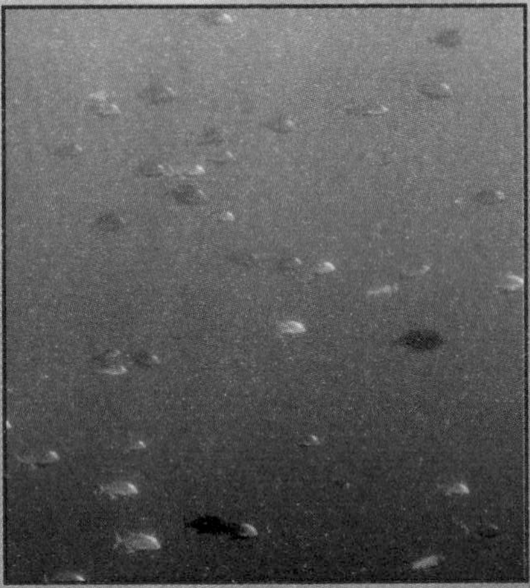
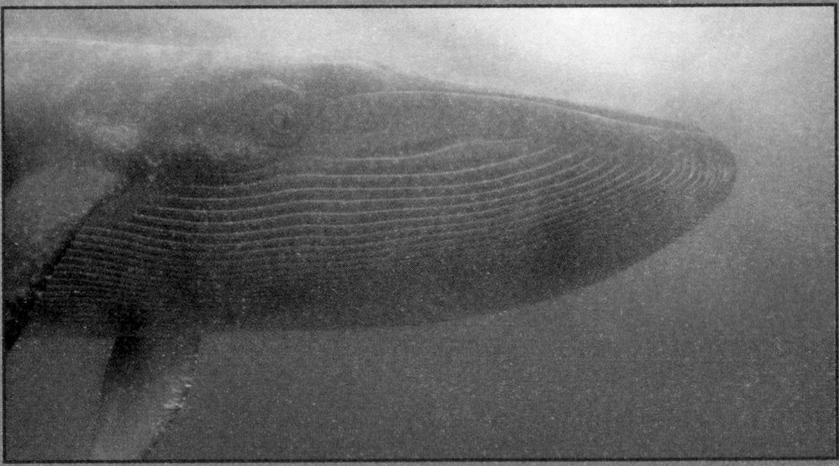
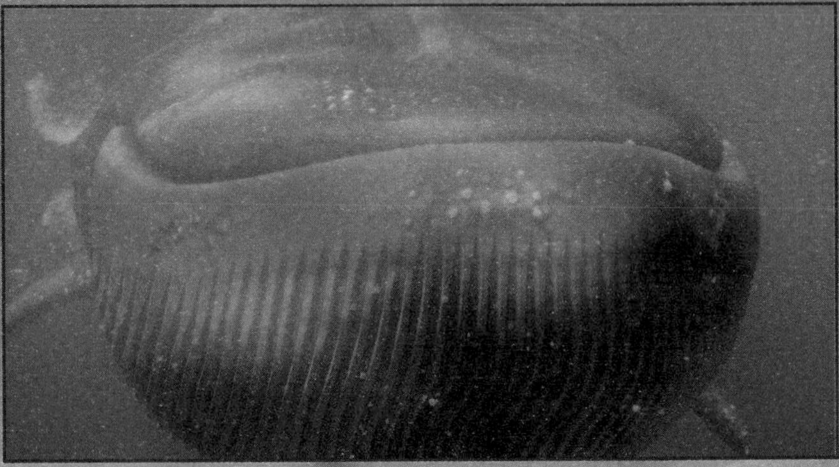

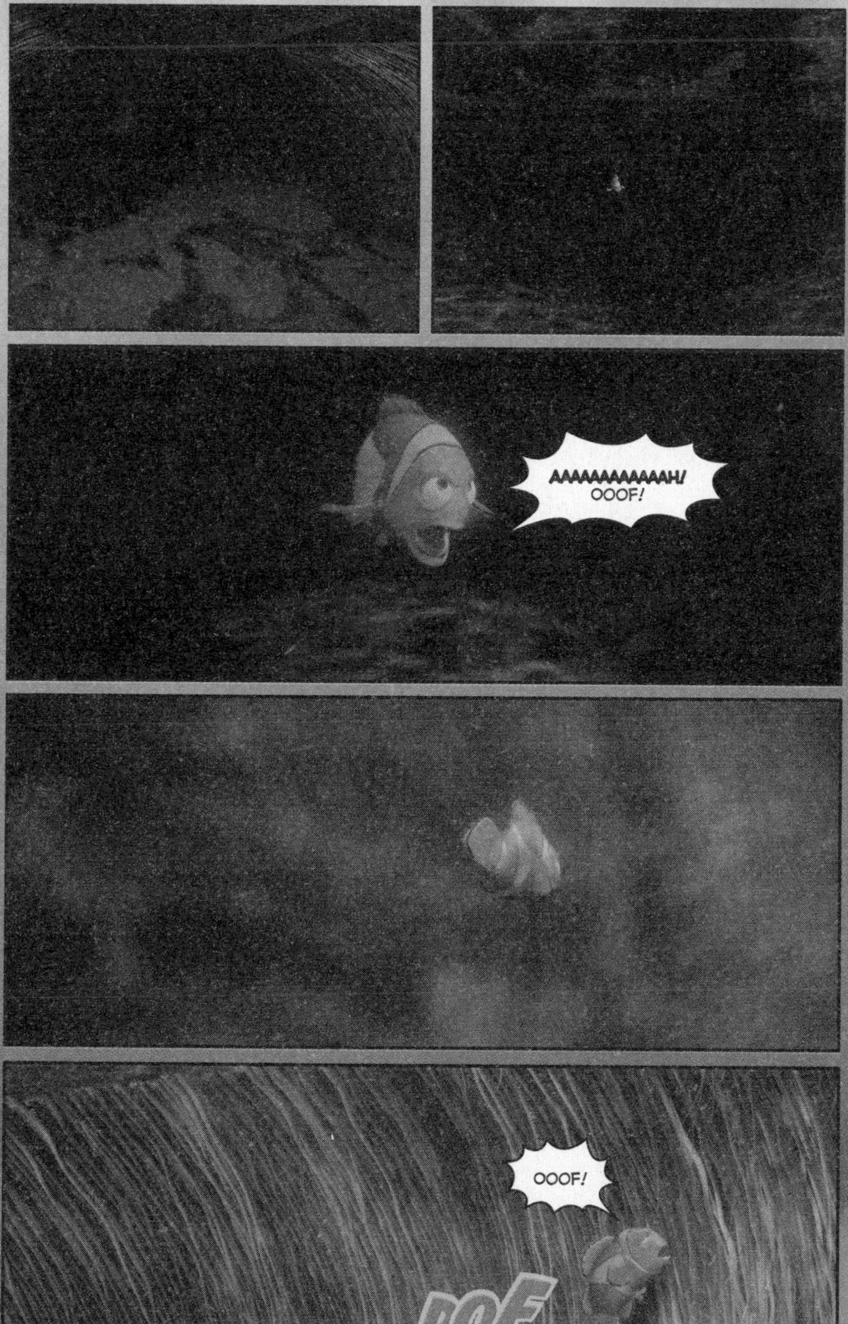
AAAAAAAAAAAAAH!
OOOF!
OOOF!
POF

HA--HAAA--HAAAAAAAH!
WHOOO!
AAAAAAAAAAAAAH!
POF

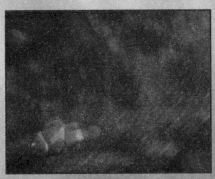

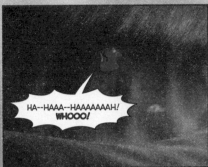

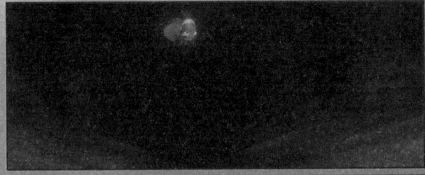

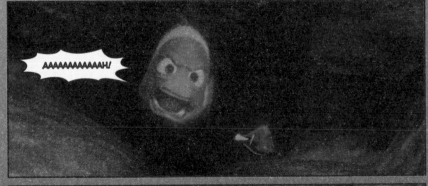

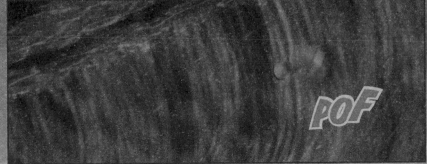

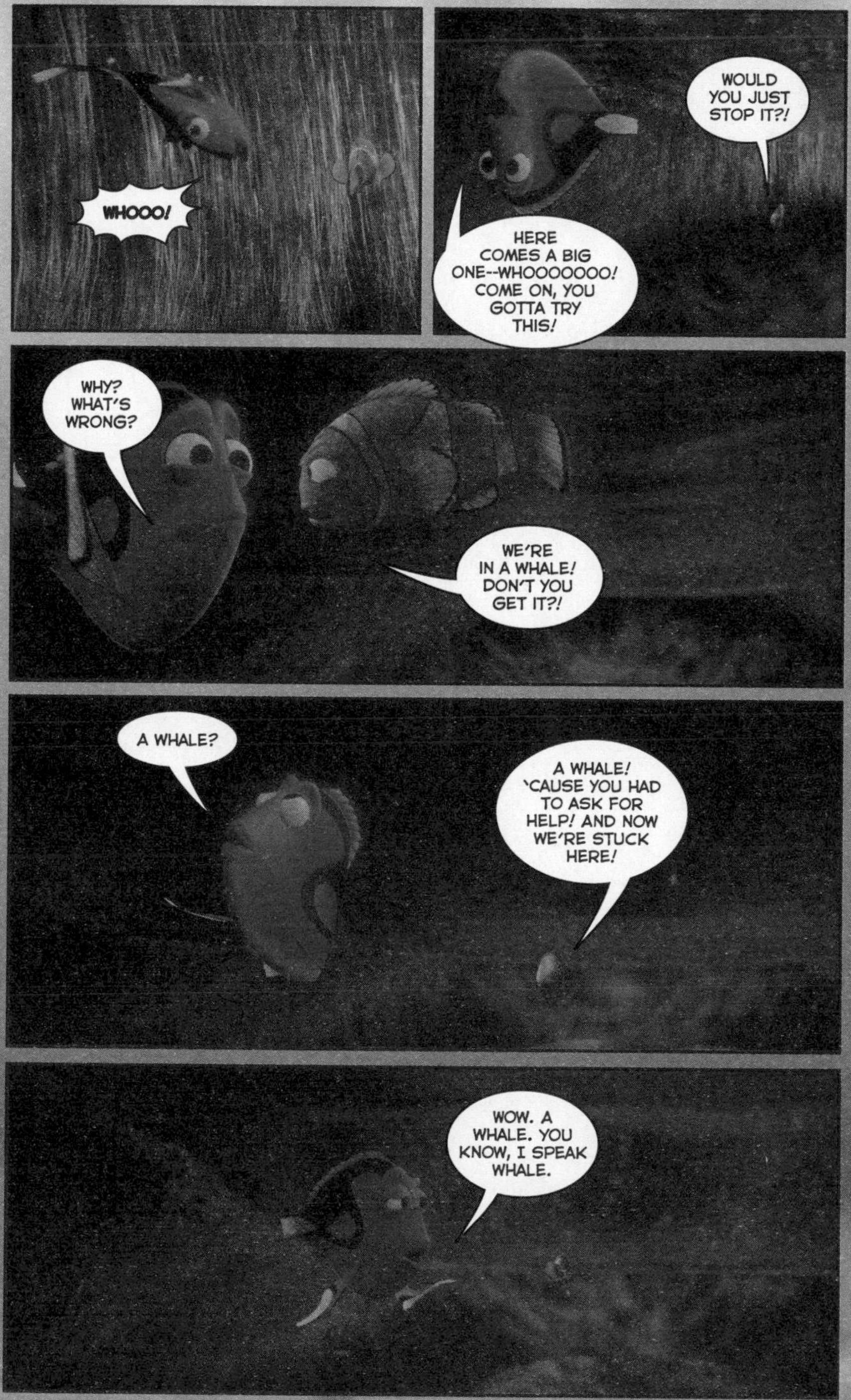
WHOOO!
WOULD YOU JUST STOP IT?!
HERE COMES A BIG ONE--WHOOOOOOO! COME ON, YOU GOTTA TRY THIS!
WHY? WHAT'S WRONG?
WE'RE IN A WHALE! DON'T YOU GET IT?!
A WHALE?
A WHALE! 'CAUSE YOU HAD TO ASK FOR HELP! AND NOW WE'RE STUCK HERE!
WOW. A WHALE. YOU KNOW, I SPEAK WHALE.

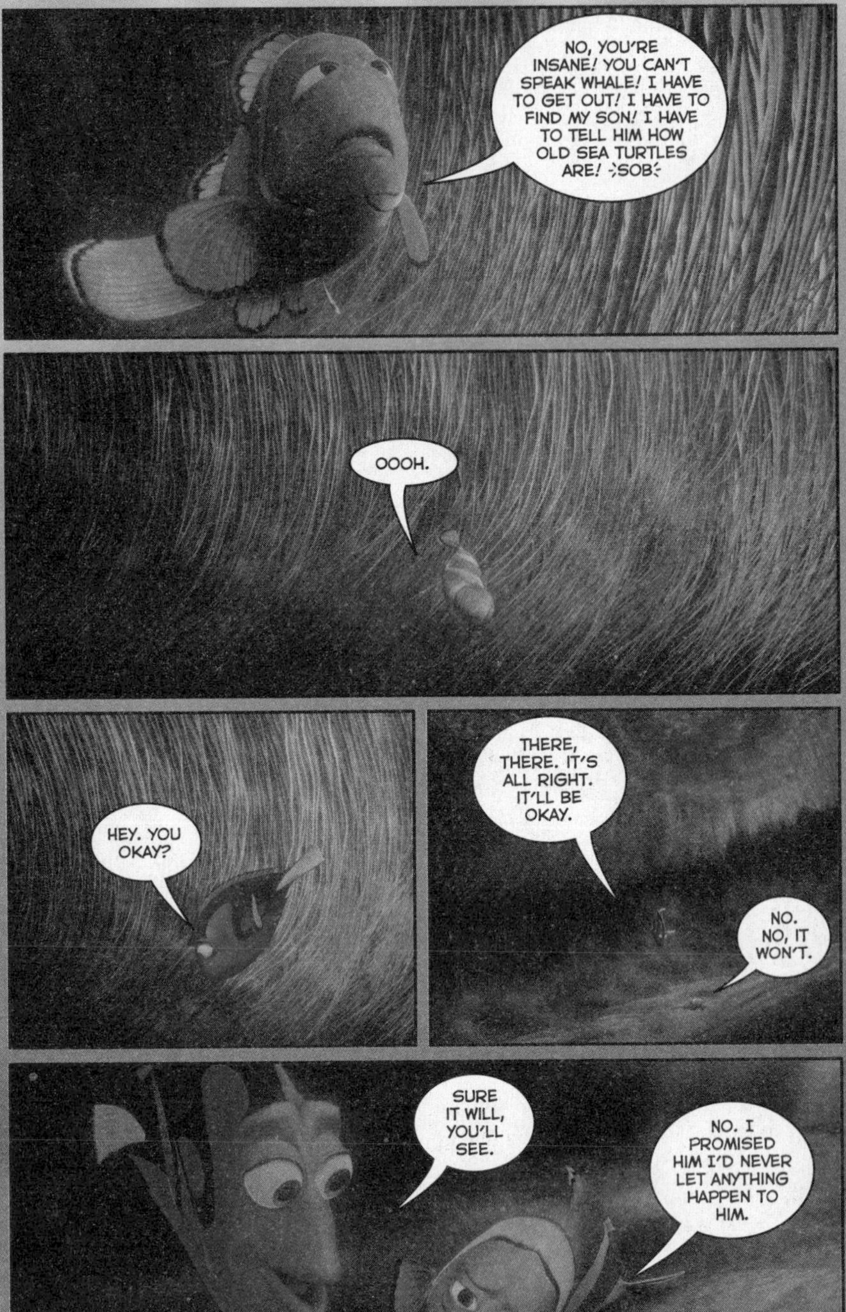
NO, YOU'RE INSANE! YOU CAN'T SPEAK WHALE! I HAVE TO GET OUT! I HAVE TO FIND MY SON! I HAVE TO TELL HIM HOW OLD SEA TURTLES ARE! SOB
OOOH.
HEY. YOU OKAY?
THERE, THERE. IT'S ALL RIGHT. IT'LL BE OKAY.
NO. NO, IT WON'T.
SURE IT WILL, YOU'LL SEE.
NO. I PROMISED HIM I'D NEVER LET ANYTHING HAPPEN TO HIM.

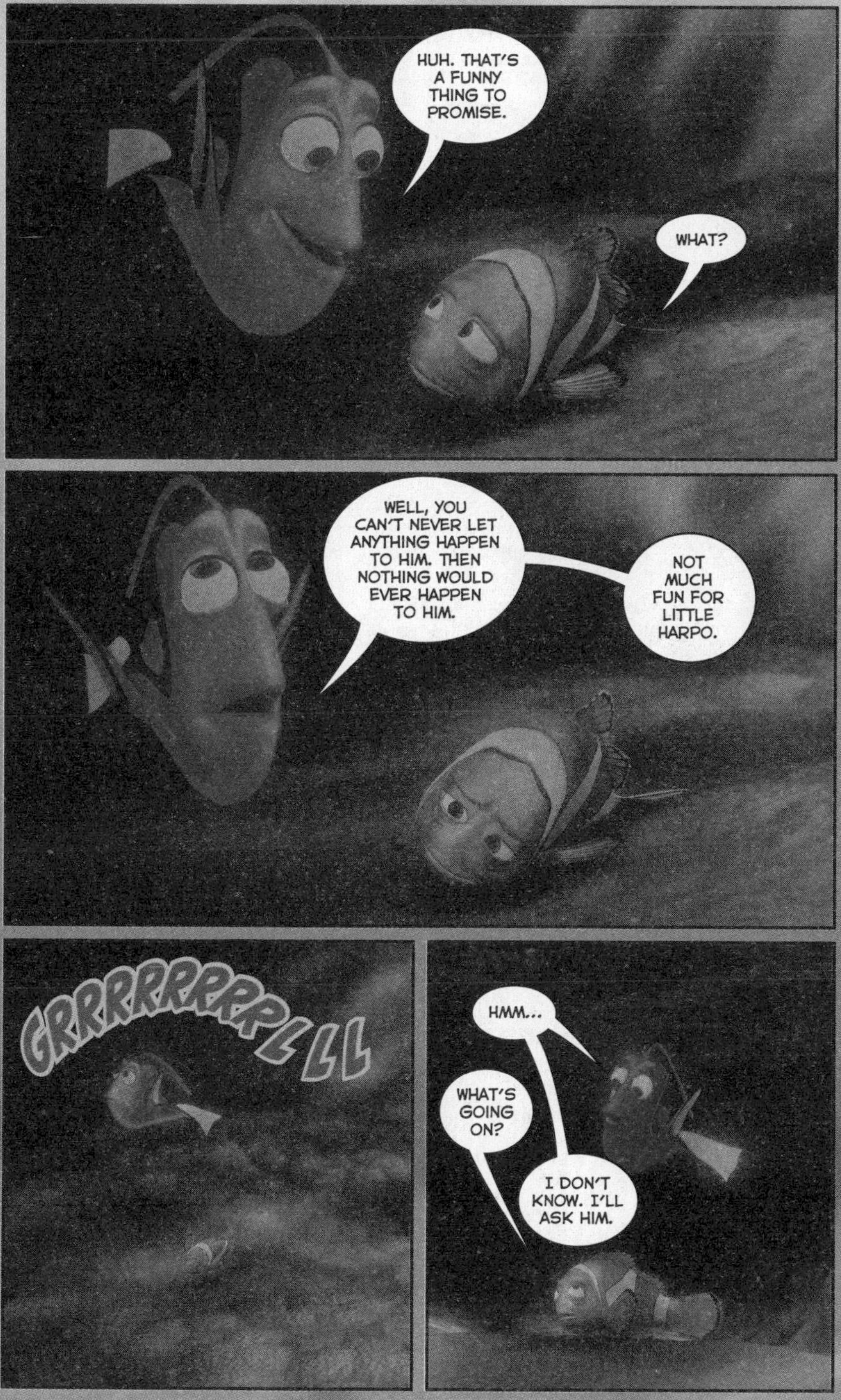
HUH. THAT'S A FUNNY THING TO PROMISE.
WHAT?
WELL, YOU CAN'T NEVER LET ANYTHING HAPPEN TO HIM. THEN NOTHING WOULD EVER HAPPEN TO HIM.
NOT MUCH FUN FOR LITTLE HARPO.
GRRRRRRRRLLL
HMM...
WHAT'S GOING ON?
I DON'T KNOW. I'LL ASK HIM.

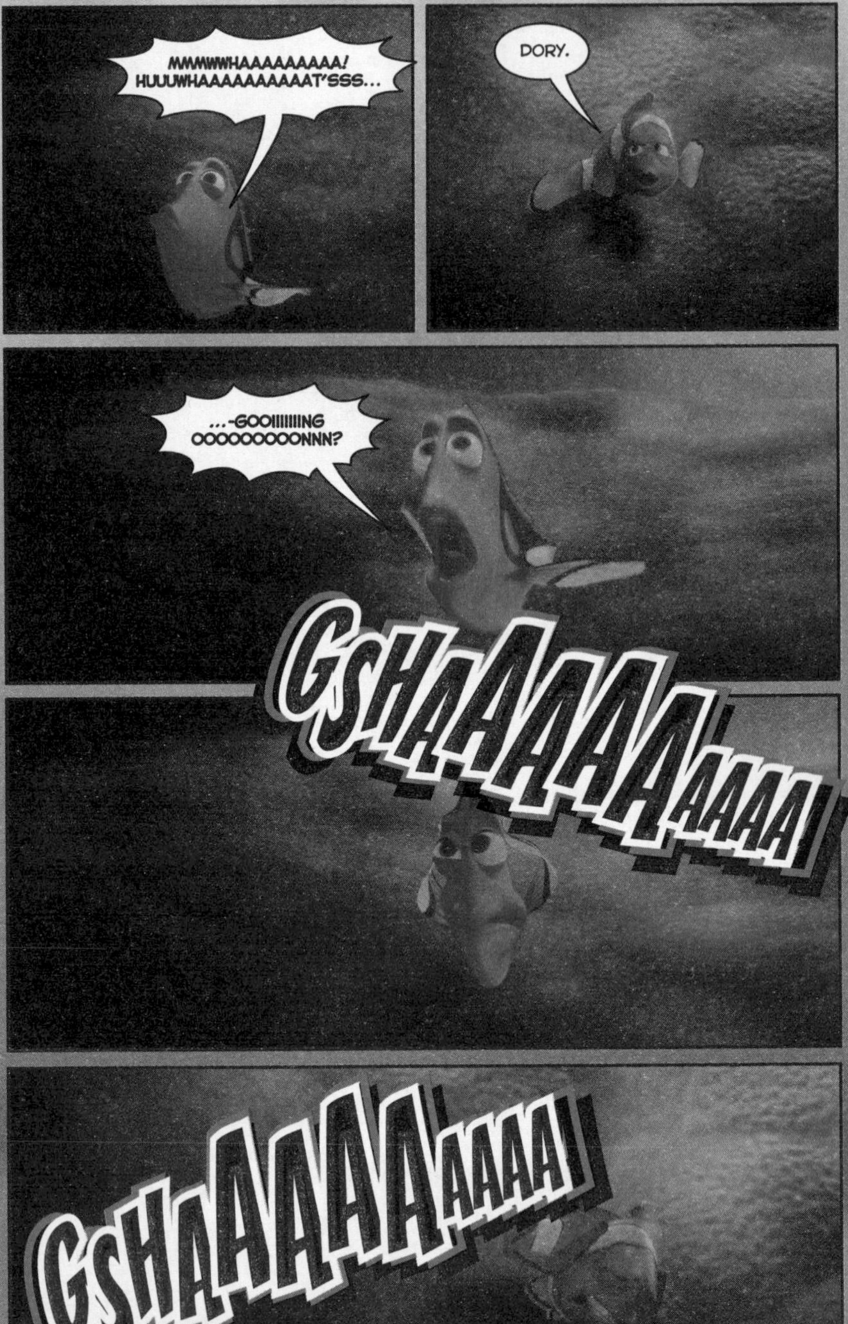
MMMWWHAAAAAAAAA!
HUUUWHAAAAAAAAAAT'SSS...
DORY.
...-GOOIIIIIIING
OOOOOOOOOONNN?
GSHAAAAAAaaaa
GSHAAAAAaaaa

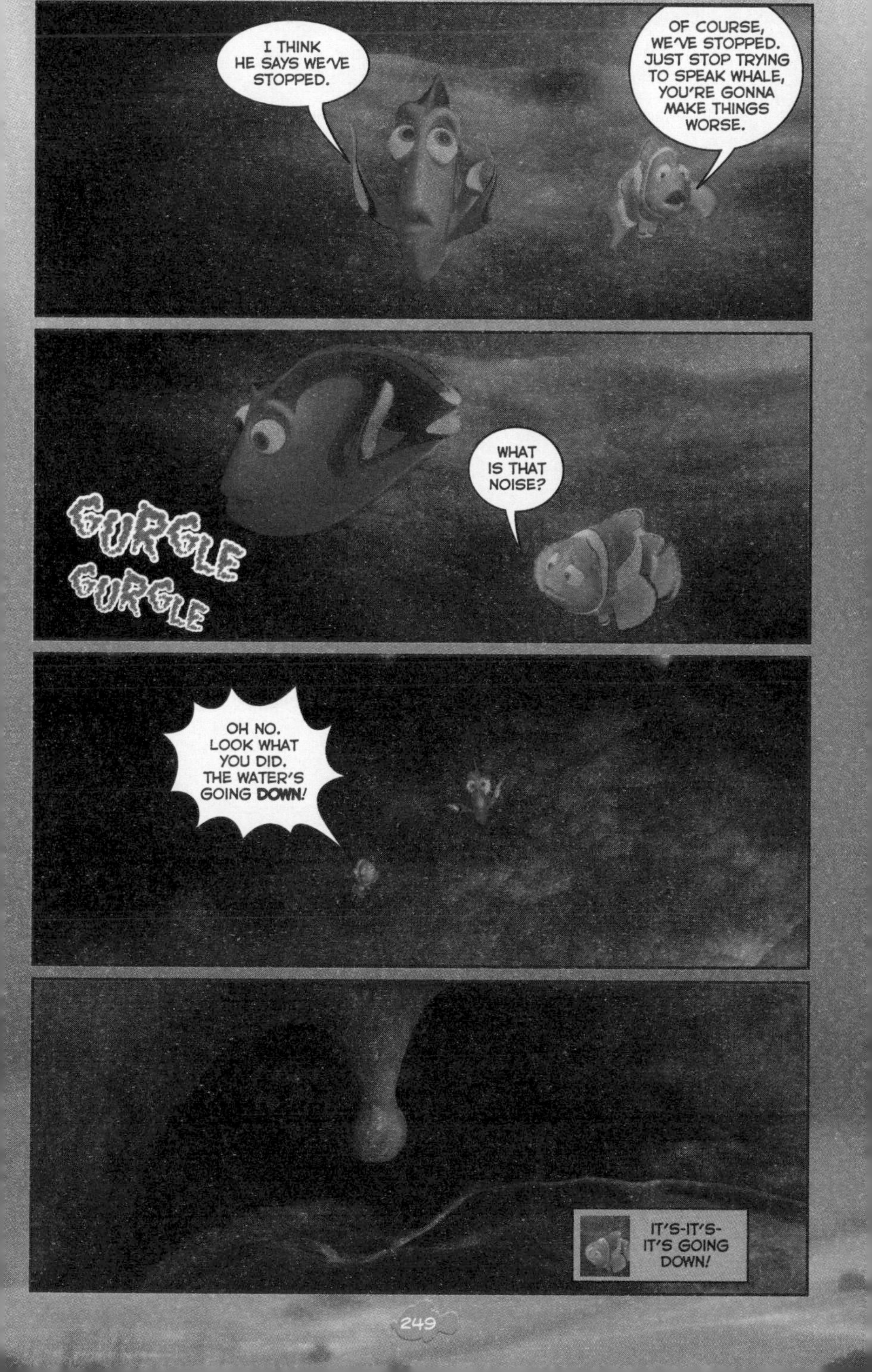
I THINK HE SAYS WE'VE STOPPED.
OF COURSE, WE'VE STOPPED. JUST STOP TRYING TO SPEAK WHALE, YOU'RE GONNA MAKE THINGS WORSE.
GURGLE
GURGLE
WHAT IS THAT NOISE?
OH NO. LOOK WHAT YOU DID. THE WATER'S GOING **DOWN**!
IT'S-IT'S-IT'S GOING DOWN!

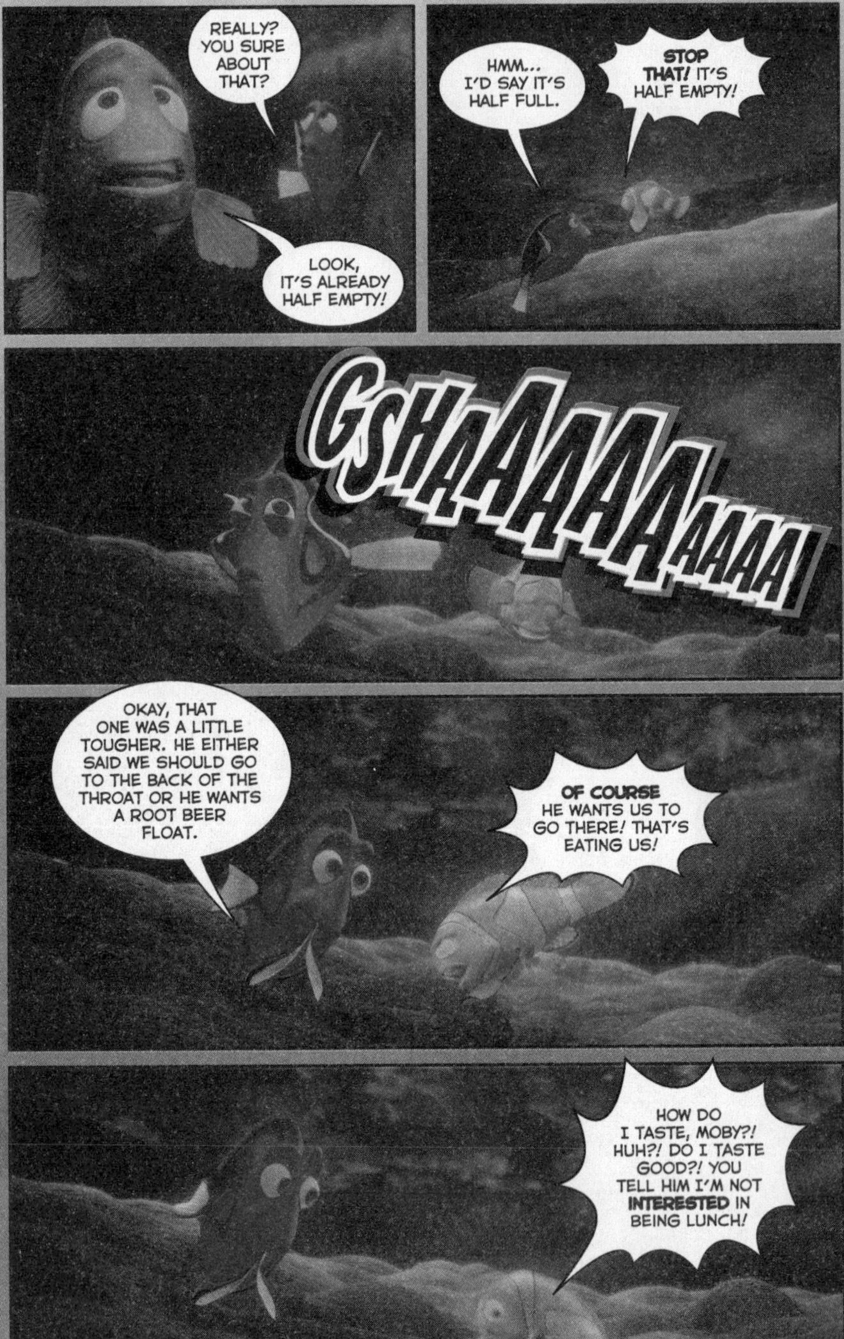
REALLY? YOU SURE ABOUT THAT?
LOOK, IT'S ALREADY HALF EMPTY!
HMM... I'D SAY IT'S HALF FULL.
STOP THAT! IT'S HALF EMPTY!
GSHAAAAAAAAAA!
OKAY, THAT ONE WAS A LITTLE TOUGHER. HE EITHER SAID WE SHOULD GO TO THE BACK OF THE THROAT OR HE WANTS A ROOT BEER FLOAT.
OF COURSE HE WANTS US TO GO THERE! THAT'S EATING US!
HOW DO I TASTE, MOBY?! HUH?! DO I TASTE GOOD?! YOU TELL HIM I'M NOT INTERESTED IN BEING LUNCH!

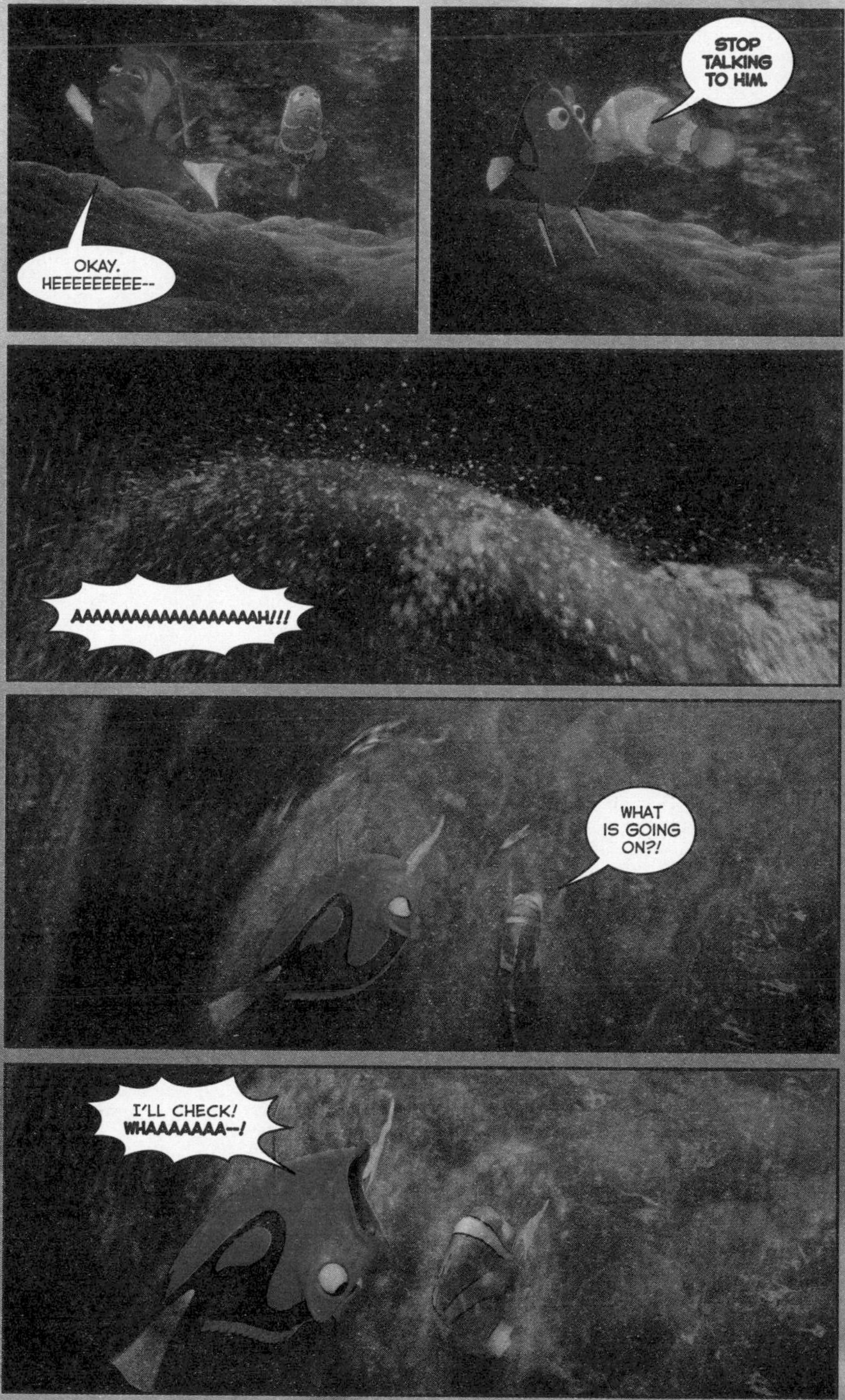
OKAY. HEEEEEEEEE--
STOP TALKING TO HIM.
AAAAAAAAAAAAAAAAAAAAH!!!
WHAT IS GOING ON?!
I'LL CHECK! WHAAAAAAA--!

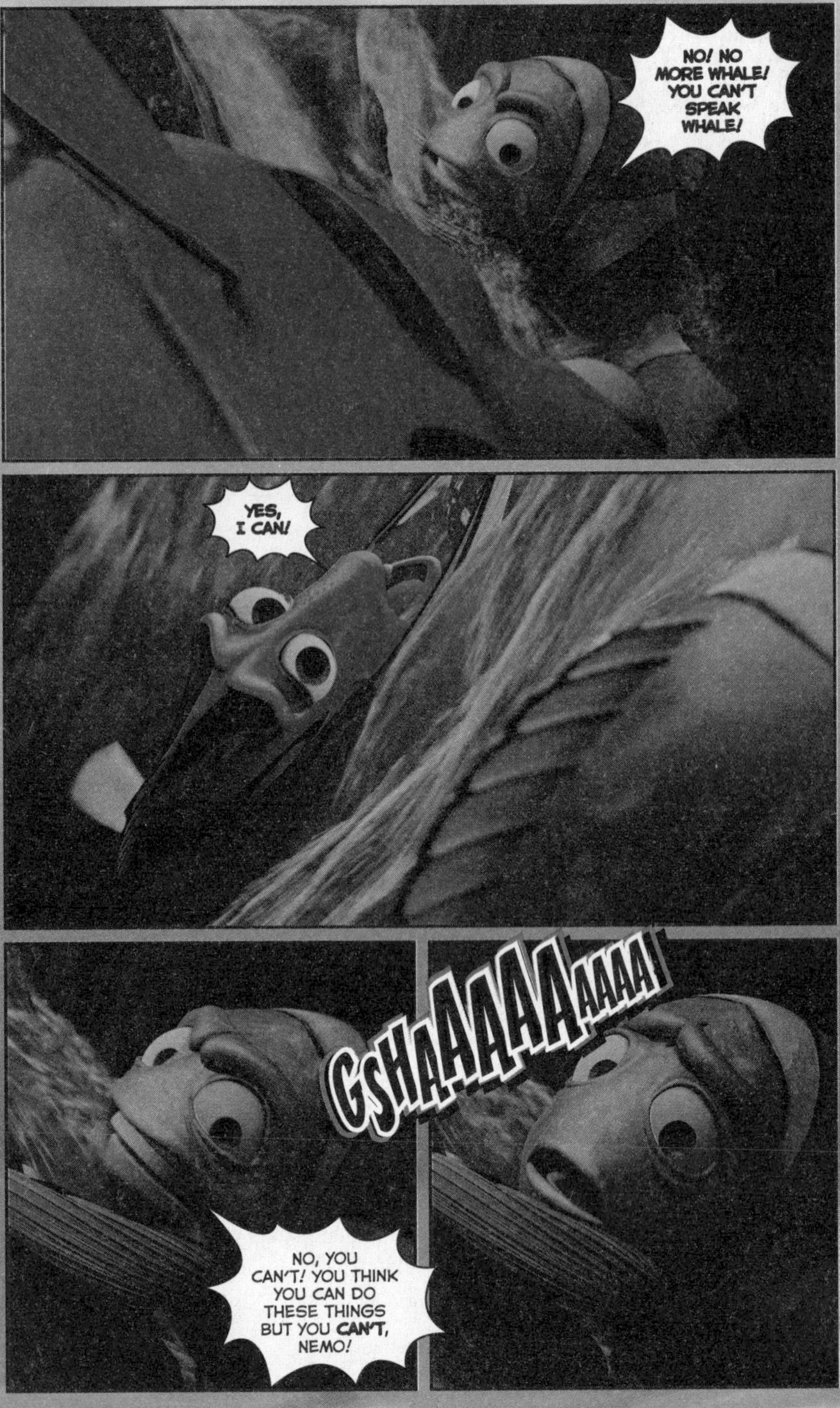
NO! NO MORE WHALE! YOU CAN'T SPEAK WHALE!
YES, I CAN!
GSHAAAAAAAAA!
NO, YOU CAN'T! YOU THINK YOU CAN DO THESE THINGS BUT YOU **CAN'T**, NEMO!

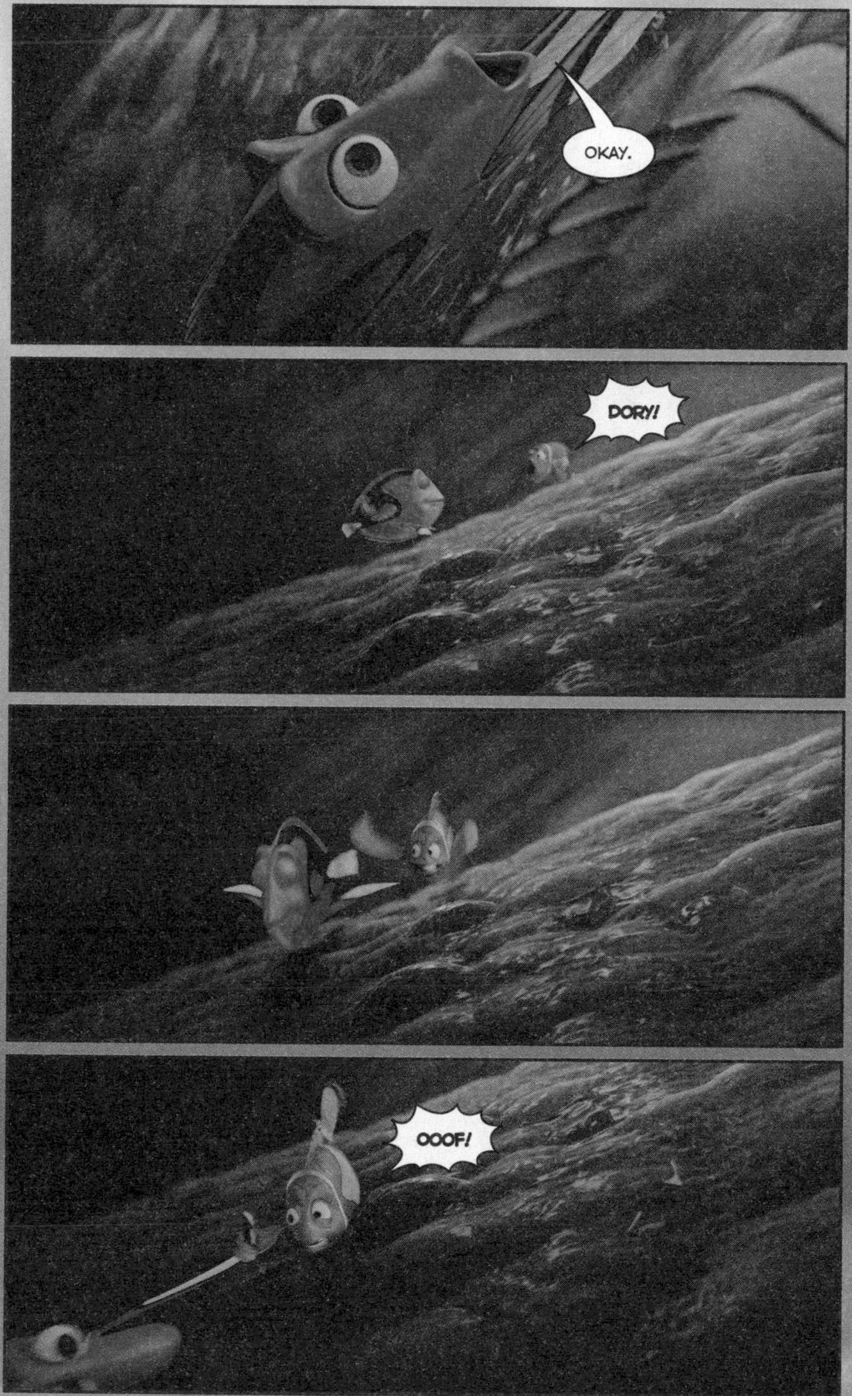
OKAY.
DORY!
OOOF!

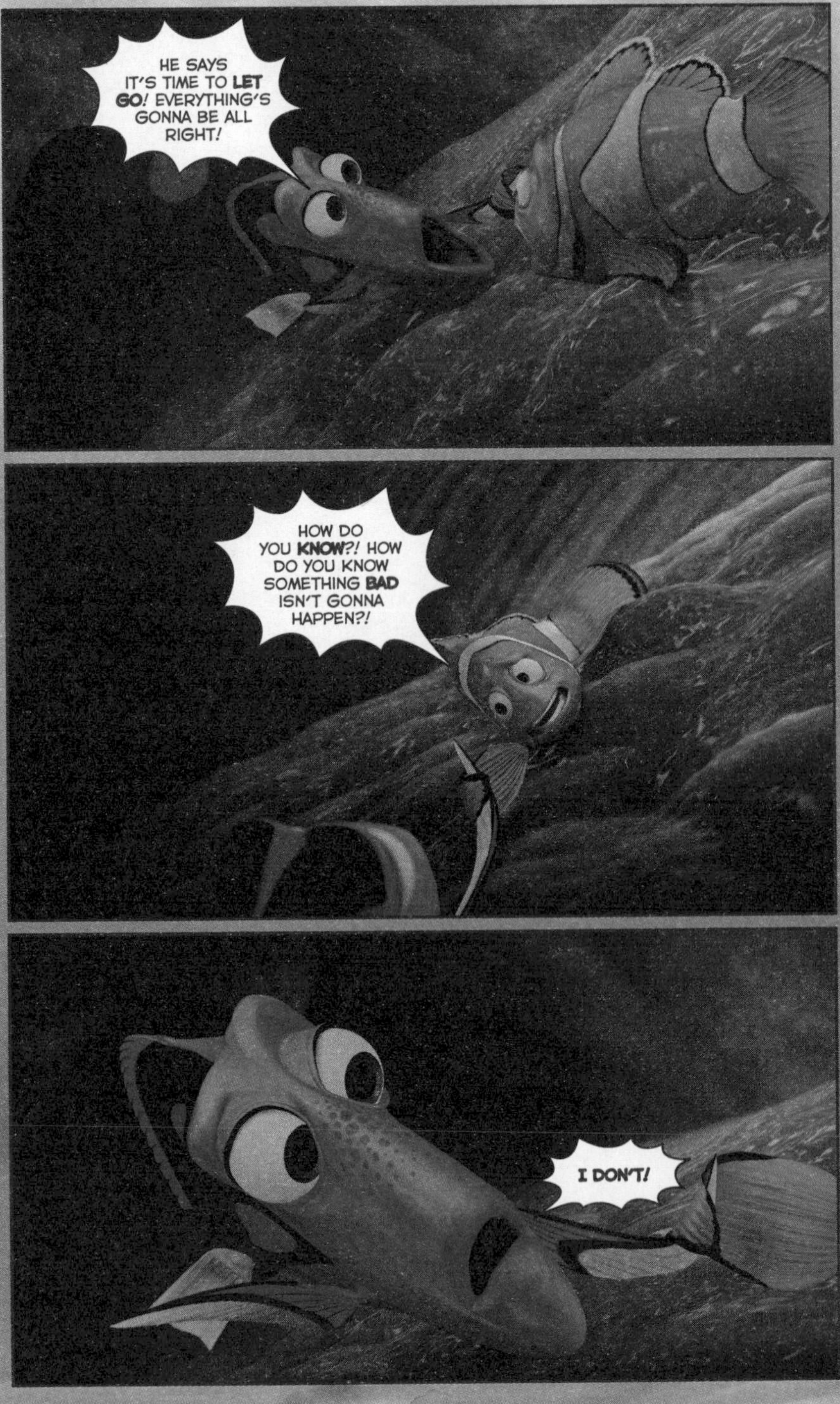
HE SAYS IT'S TIME TO **LET GO!** EVERYTHING'S GONNA BE ALL RIGHT!
HOW DO YOU **KNOW?!** HOW DO YOU KNOW SOMETHING **BAD** ISN'T GONNA HAPPEN?!
I DON'T!

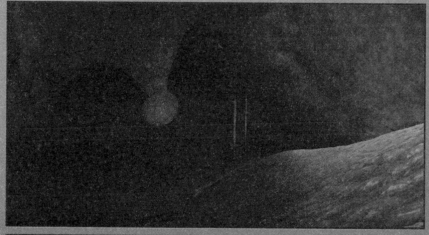

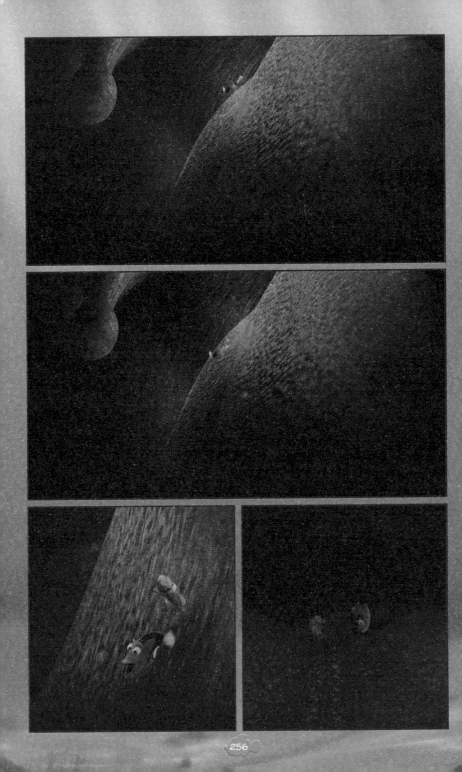

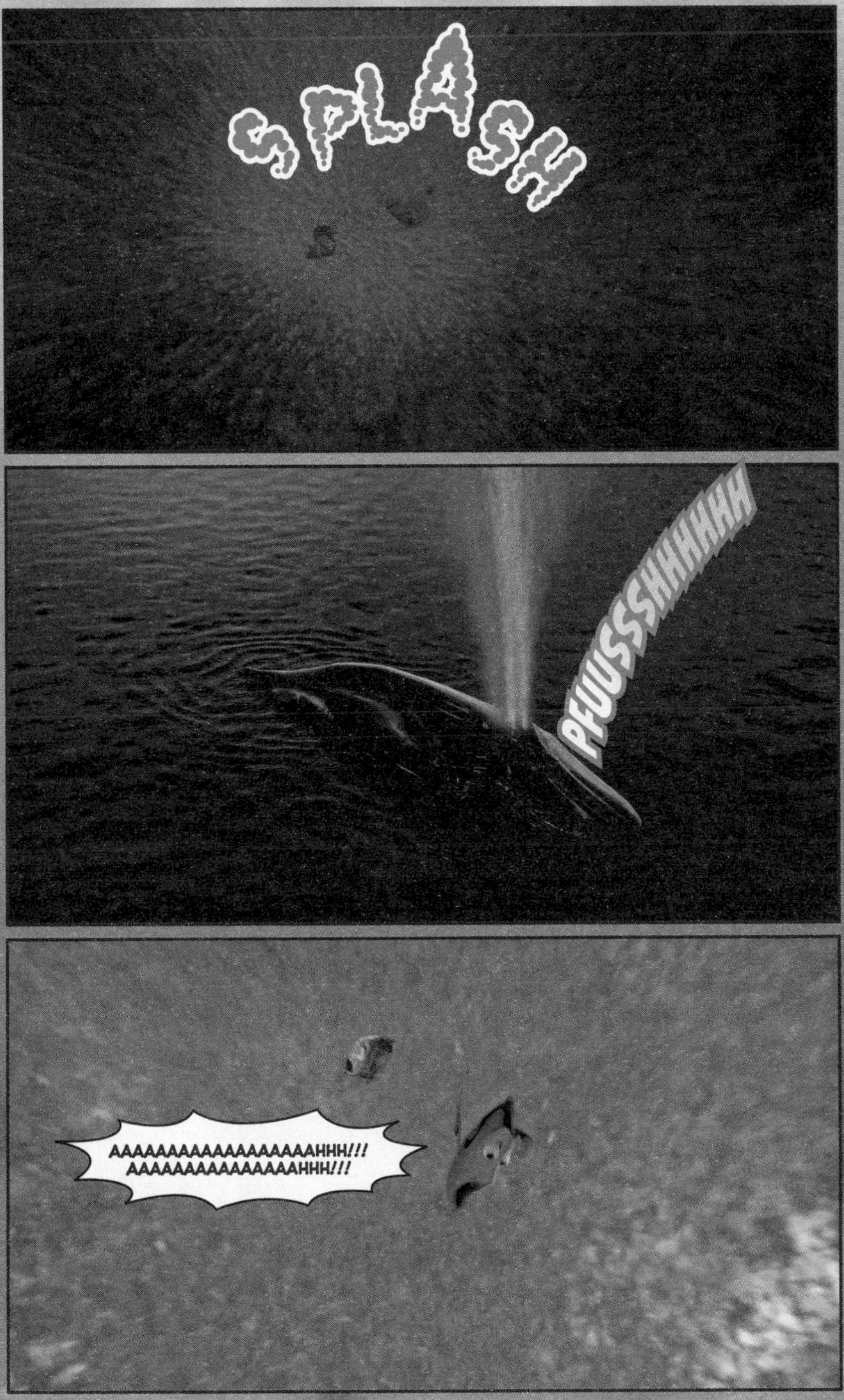
SPLASH
PFUUSSSHHHHHH
AAAAAAAAAAAAAAAAAAAAHHH!!!
AAAAAAAAAAAAAAAAAHHH!!!

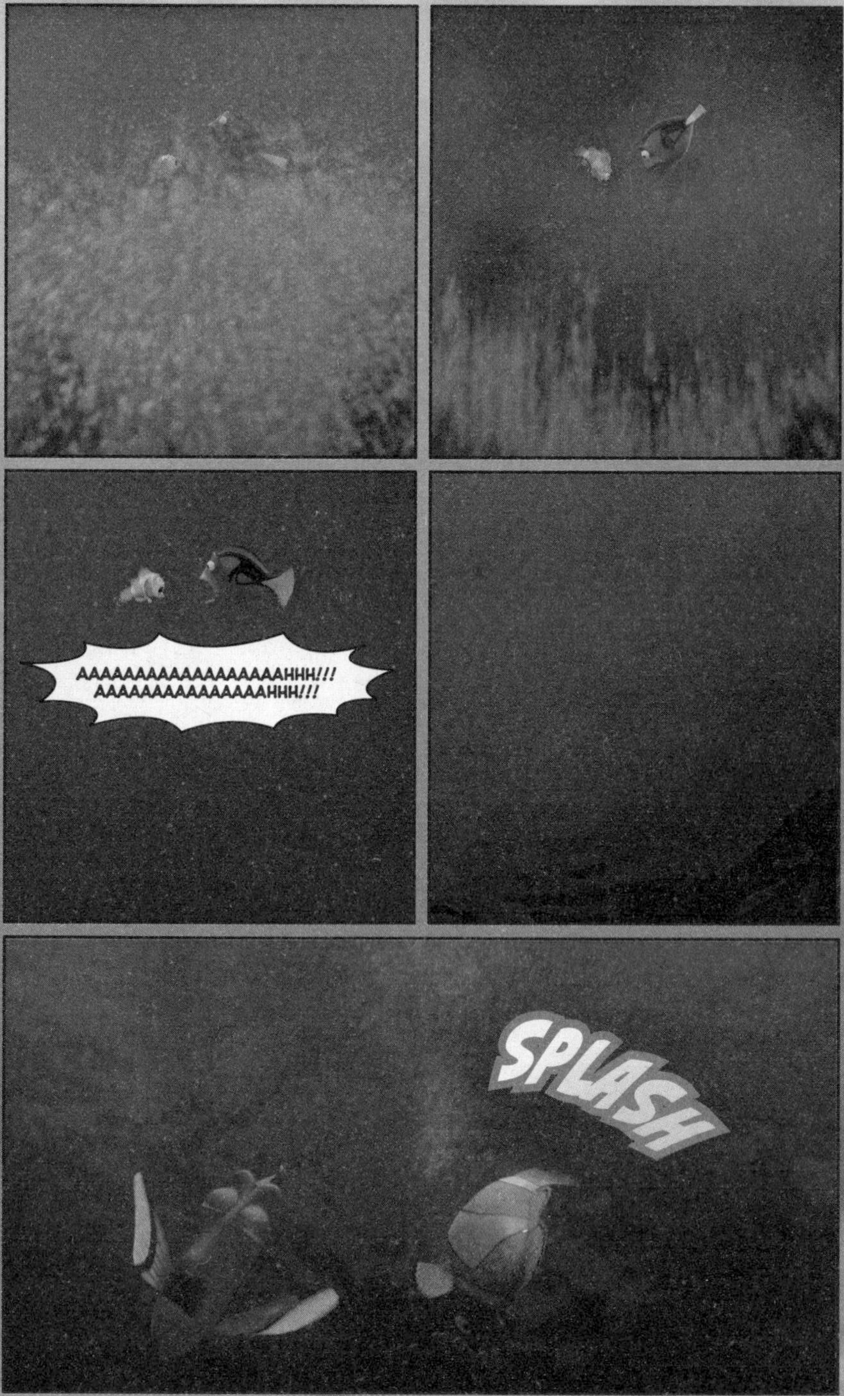
AAAAAAAAAAAAAAAAAAAAAHHH!!!
AAAAAAAAAAAAAAAAAAAHHH!!!
SPLASH

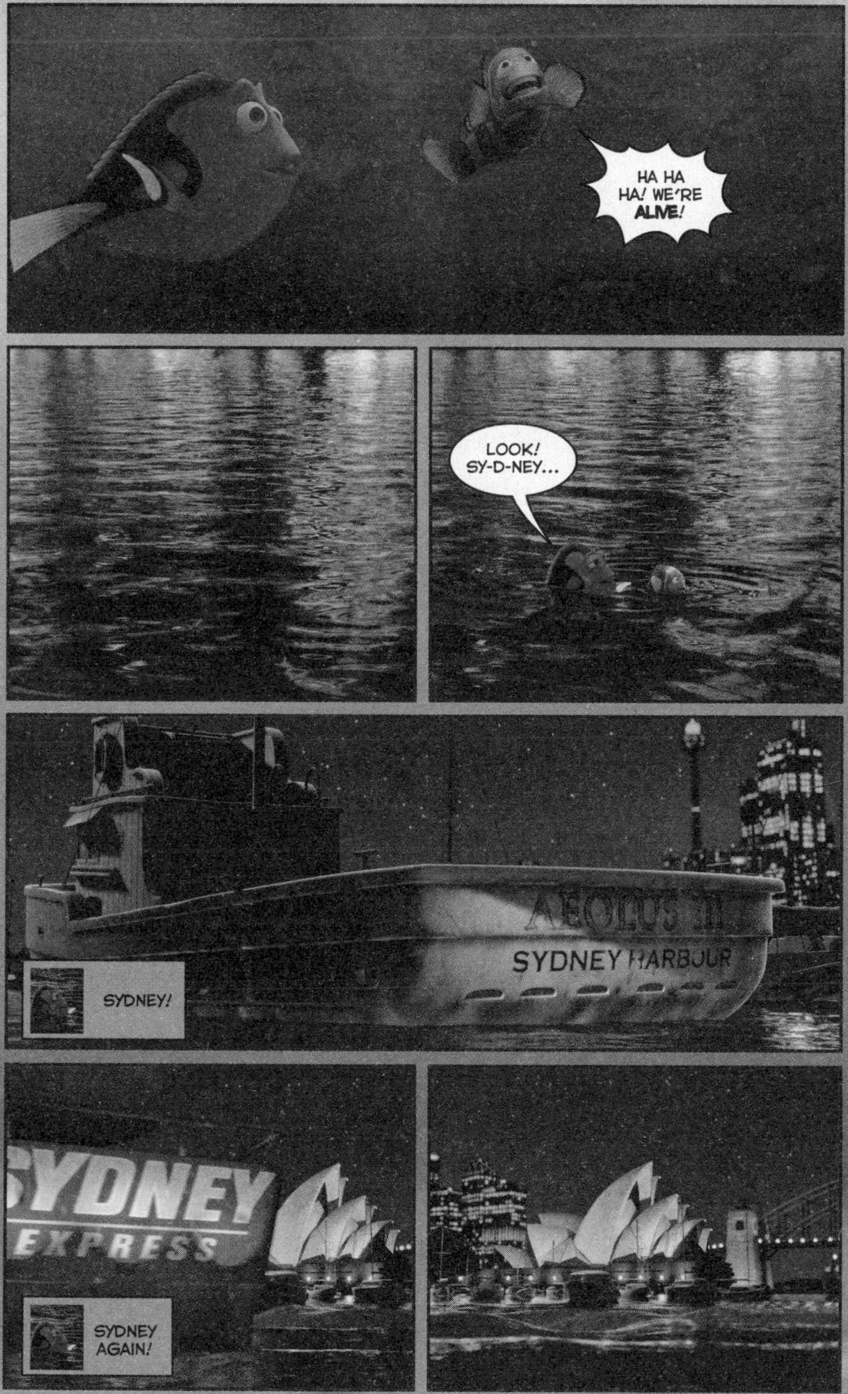
HA HA HA! WE'RE ALIVE!
LOOK! SY-D-NEY...
AEOLUS III
SYDNEY HARBOUR
SYDNEY!
SYDNEY EXPRESS
SYDNEY AGAIN!

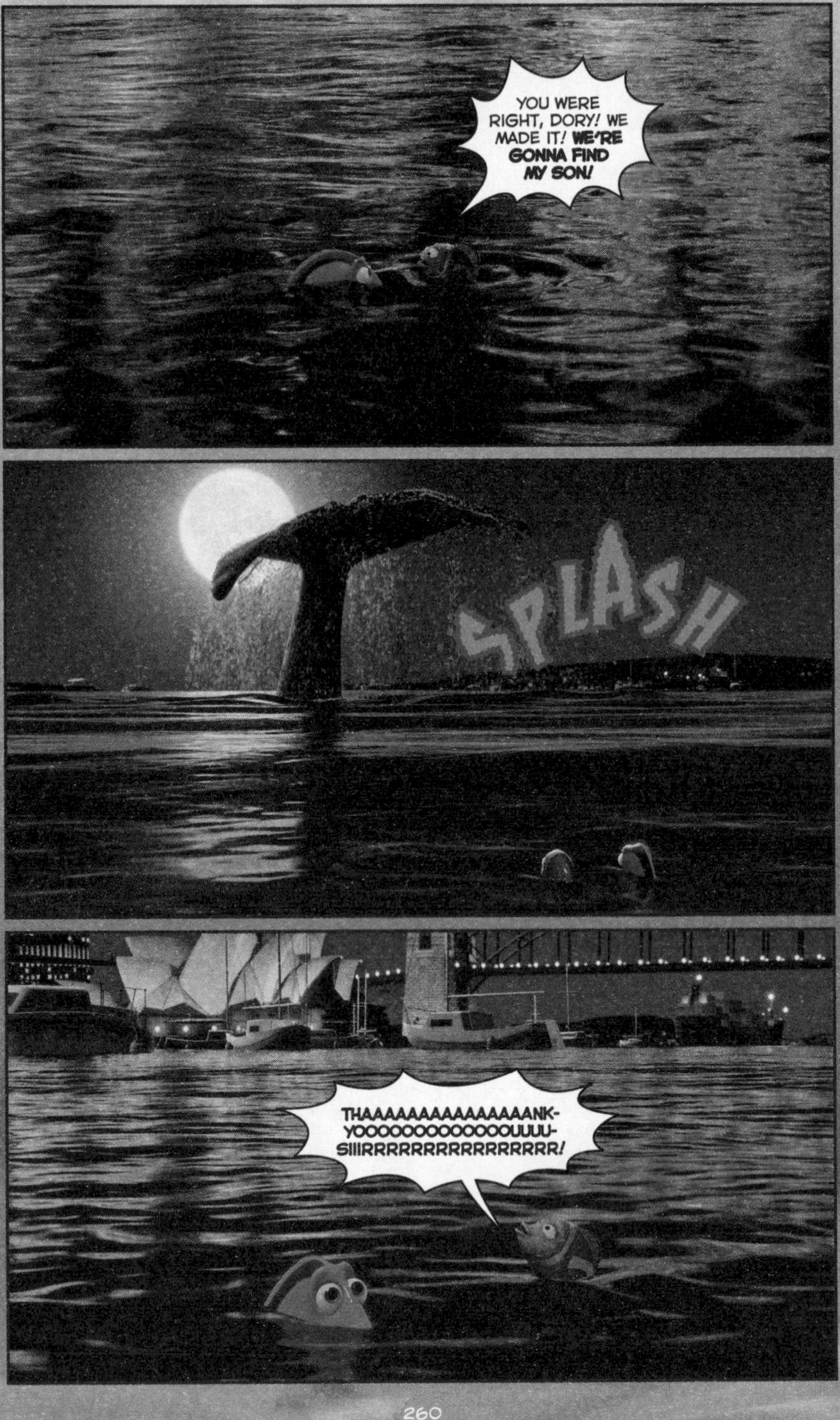
YOU WERE RIGHT, DORY! WE MADE IT! WE'RE GONNA FIND MY SON!
SPLASH
THAAAAAAAAAAAAAAAANK-YOOOOOOOOOOOOOUUUU-SIIIRRRRRRRRRRRRRRRR!

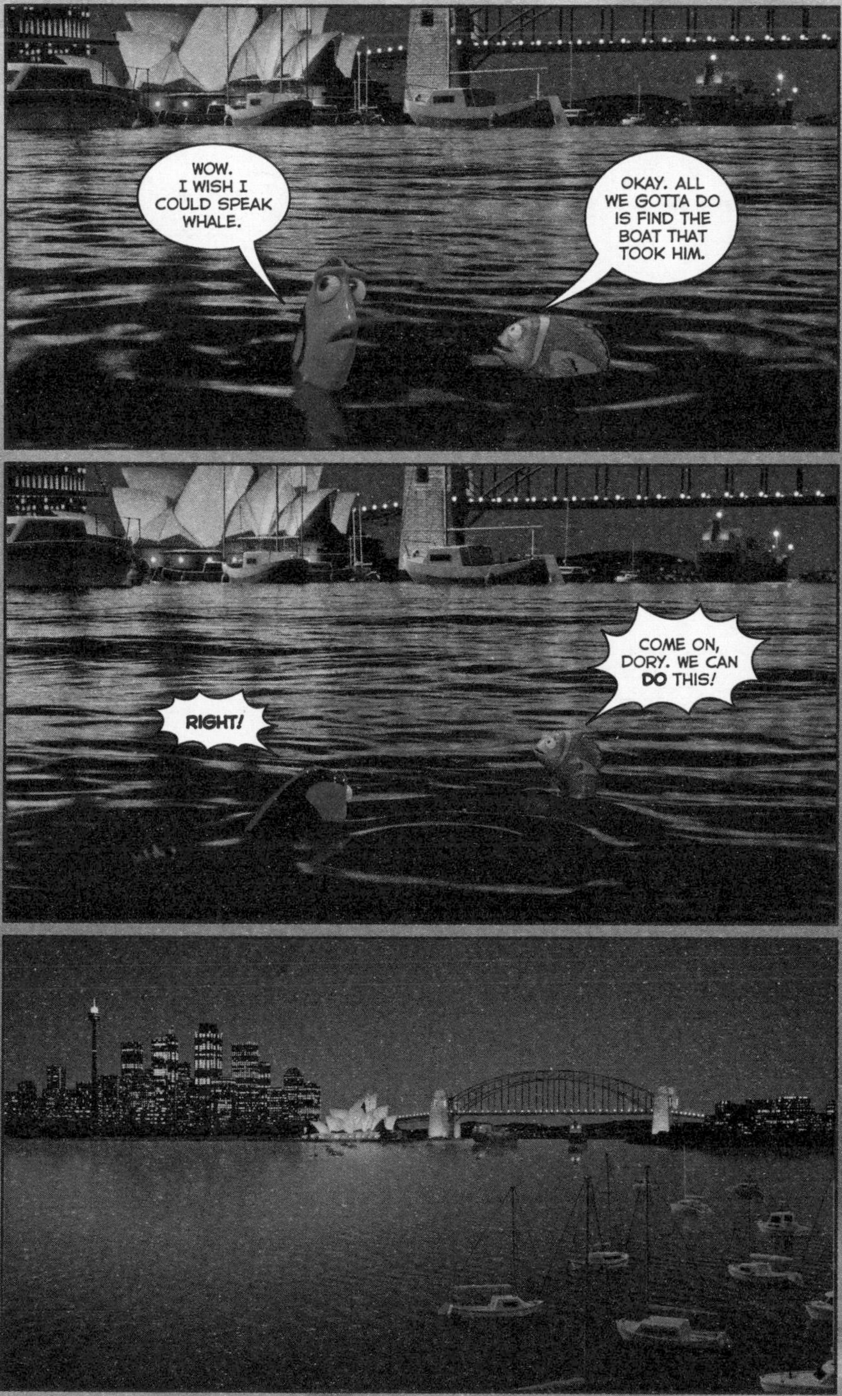
WOW. I WISH I COULD SPEAK WHALE.
OKAY. ALL WE GOTTA DO IS FIND THE BOAT THAT TOOK HIM.
COME ON, DORY. WE CAN DO THIS!
RIGHT!

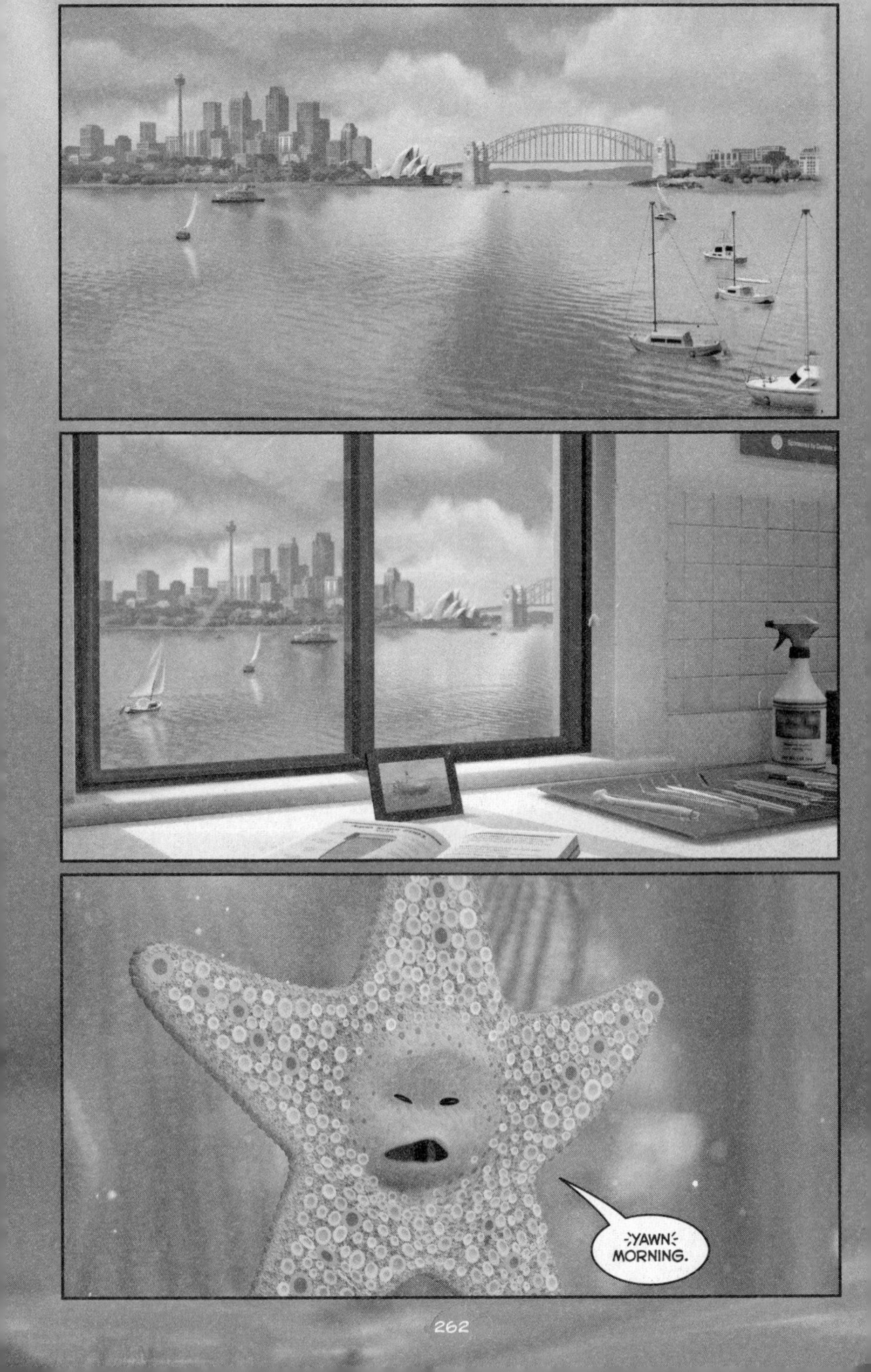
YAWN MORNING.

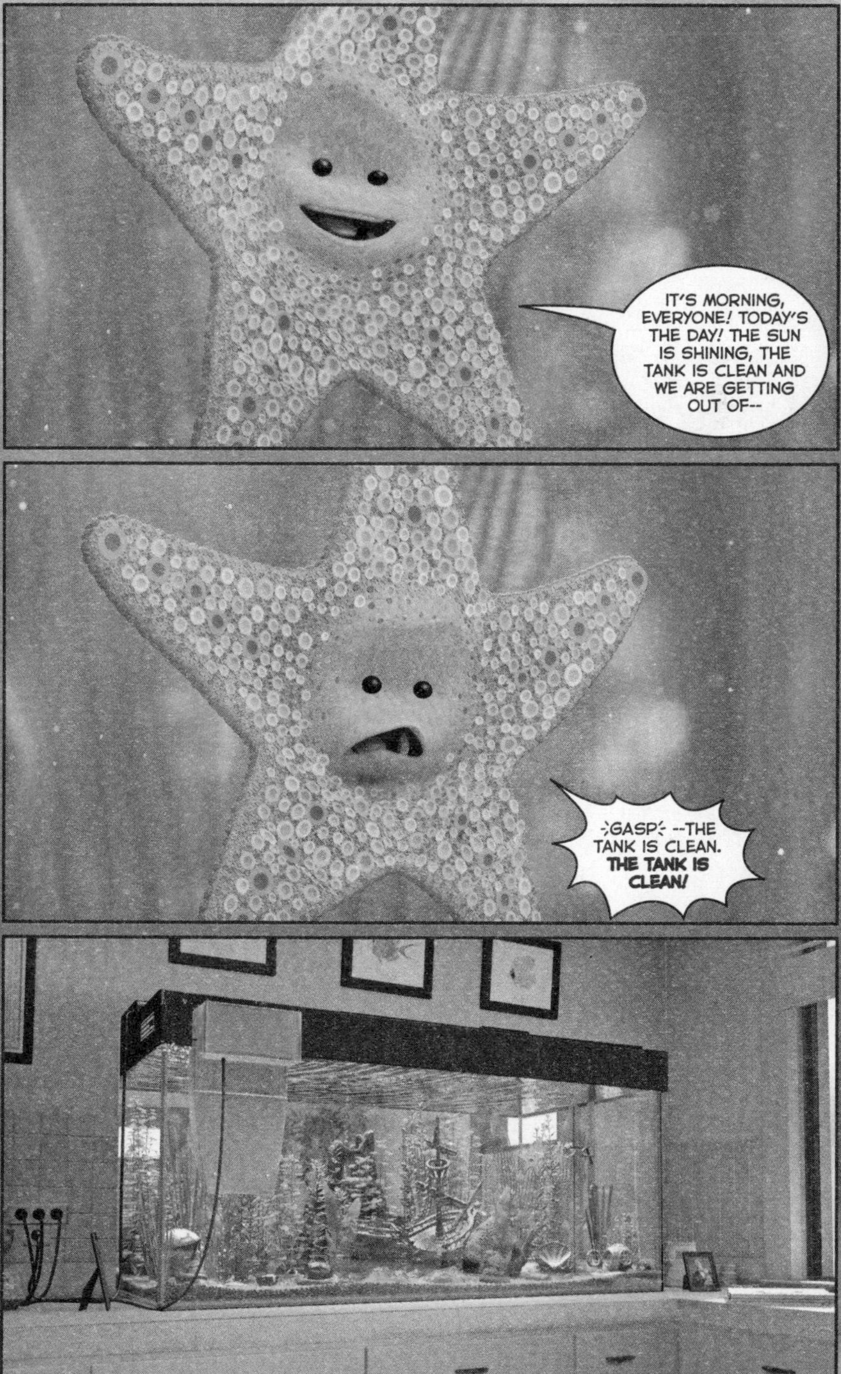
IT'S MORNING, EVERYONE! TODAY'S THE DAY! THE SUN IS SHINING, THE TANK IS CLEAN AND WE ARE GETTING OUT OF--
-GASP- --THE TANK IS CLEAN. THE TANK IS CLEAN!

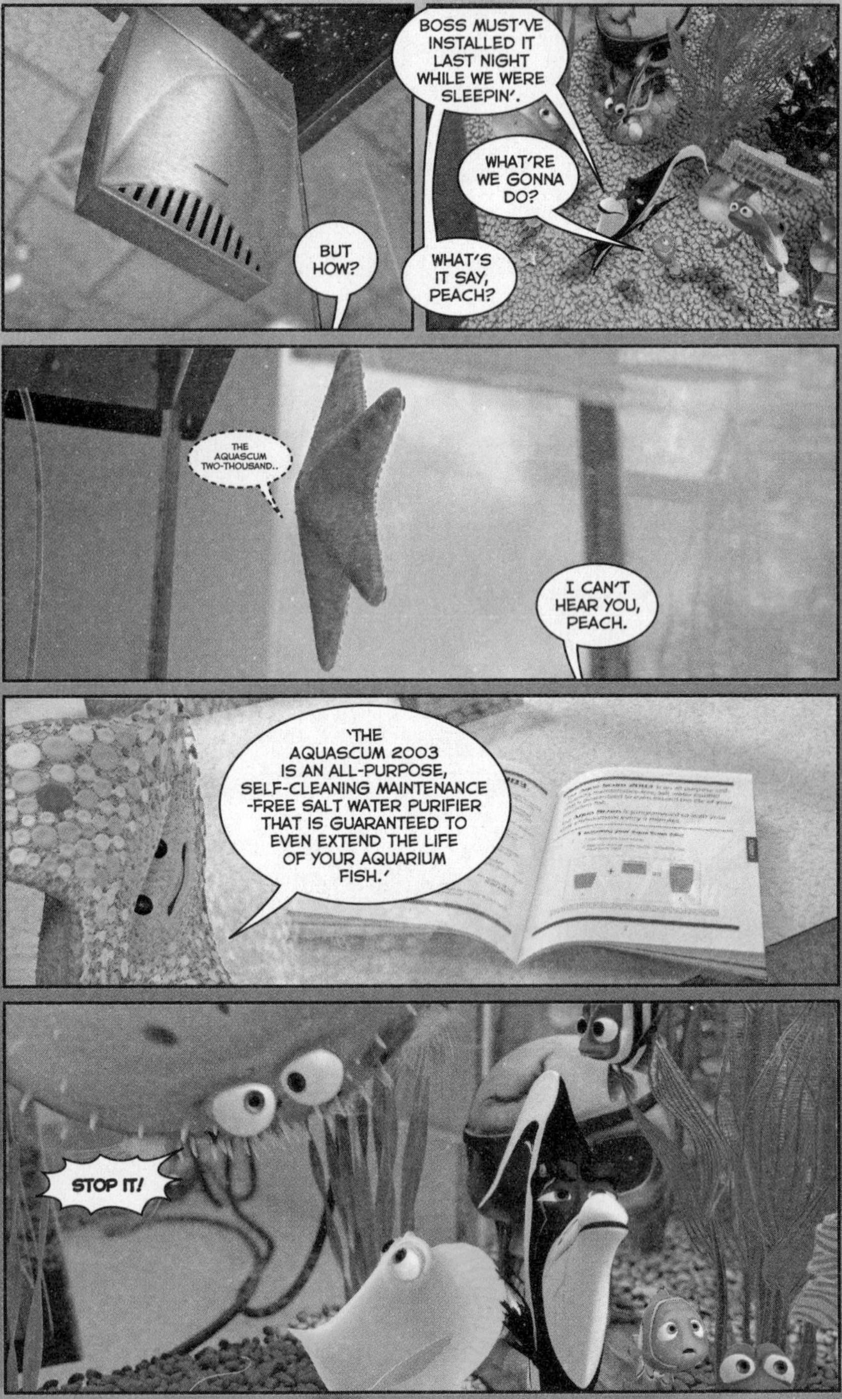
BUT HOW?
BOSS MUST'VE INSTALLED IT LAST NIGHT WHILE WE WERE SLEEPIN'.
WHAT'RE WE GONNA DO?
WHAT'S IT SAY, PEACH?
THE AQUASCUM TWO-THOUSAND..
I CAN'T HEAR YOU, PEACH.
'THE AQUASCUM 2003 IS AN ALL-PURPOSE, SELF-CLEANING MAINTENANCE -FREE SALT WATER PURIFIER THAT IS GUARANTEED TO EVEN EXTEND THE LIFE OF YOUR AQUARIUM FISH.'
STOP IT!

'THE AQUASCUM IS PROGRAMMED TO SCAN YOUR TANK ENVIRONMENT EVERY FIVE MINUTES?'

SCAN? WHAT DOES THAT MEAN?

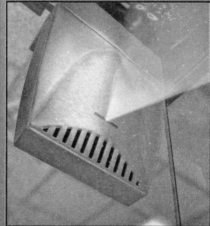

POOF

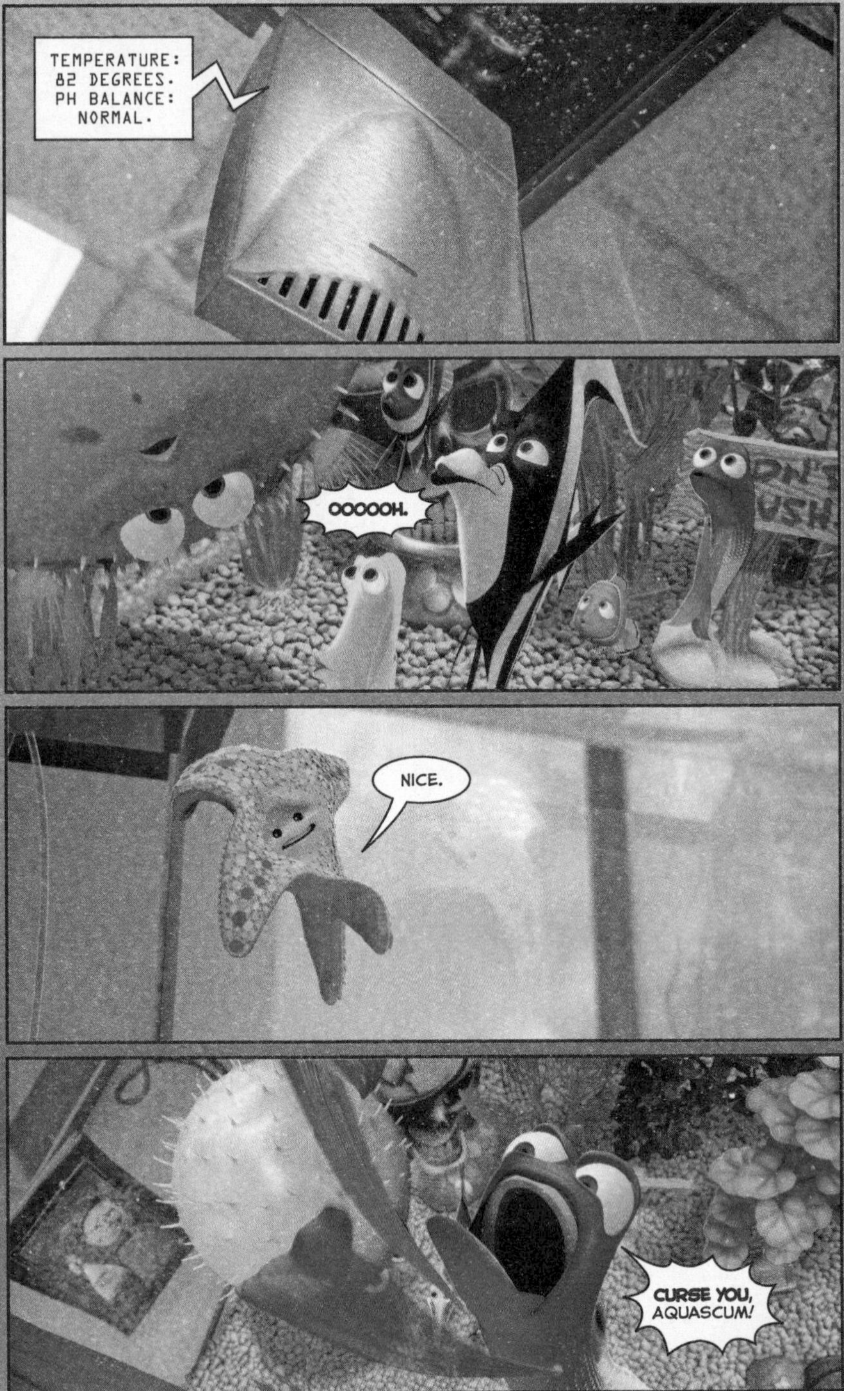
TEMPERATURE: 82 DEGREES. PH BALANCE: NORMAL.
OOOOOH.
NICE.
CURSE YOU, AQUASCUM!

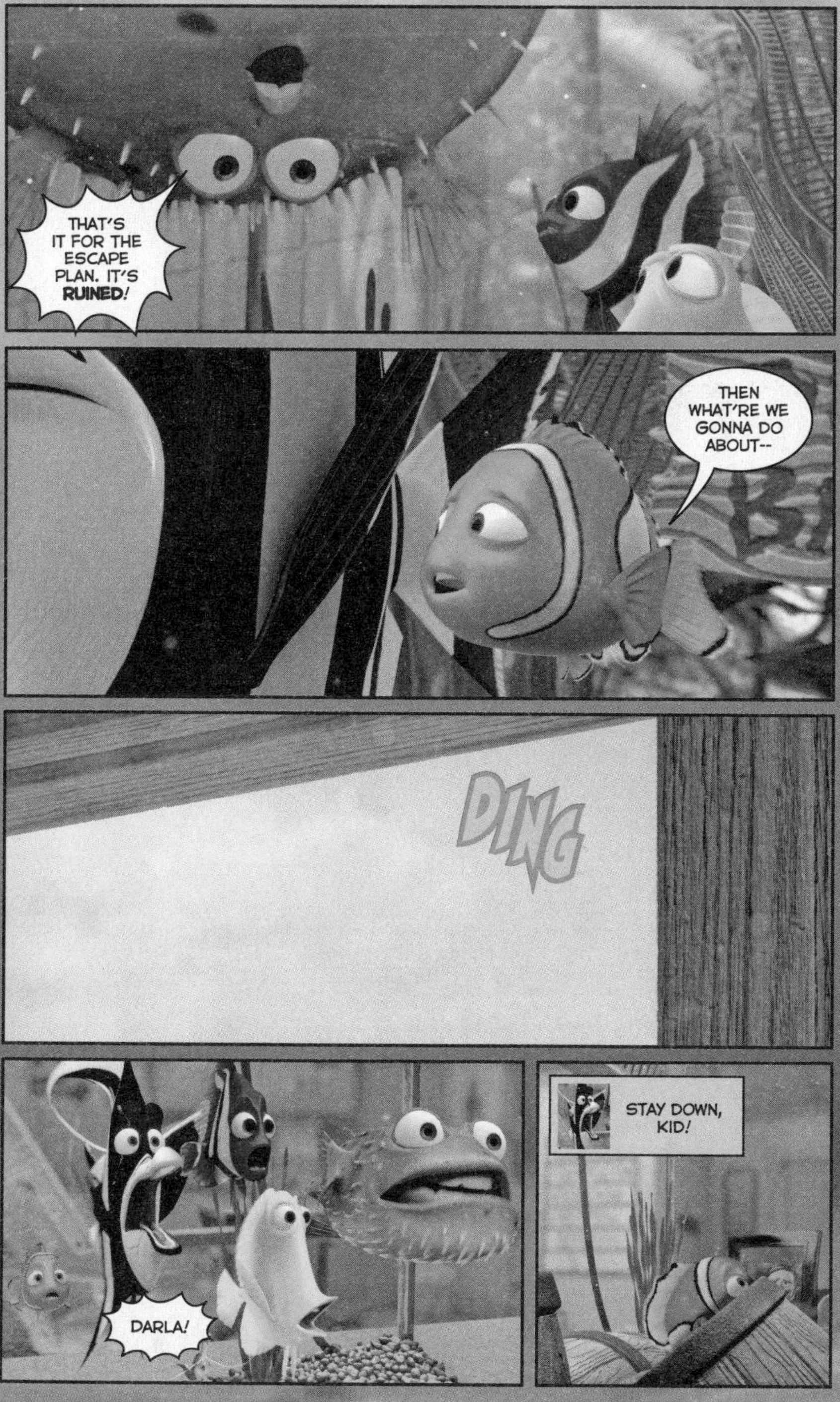
THAT'S IT FOR THE ESCAPE PLAN. IT'S RUINED!
THEN WHAT'RE WE GONNA DO ABOUT--
DING
DARLA!
STAY DOWN, KID!

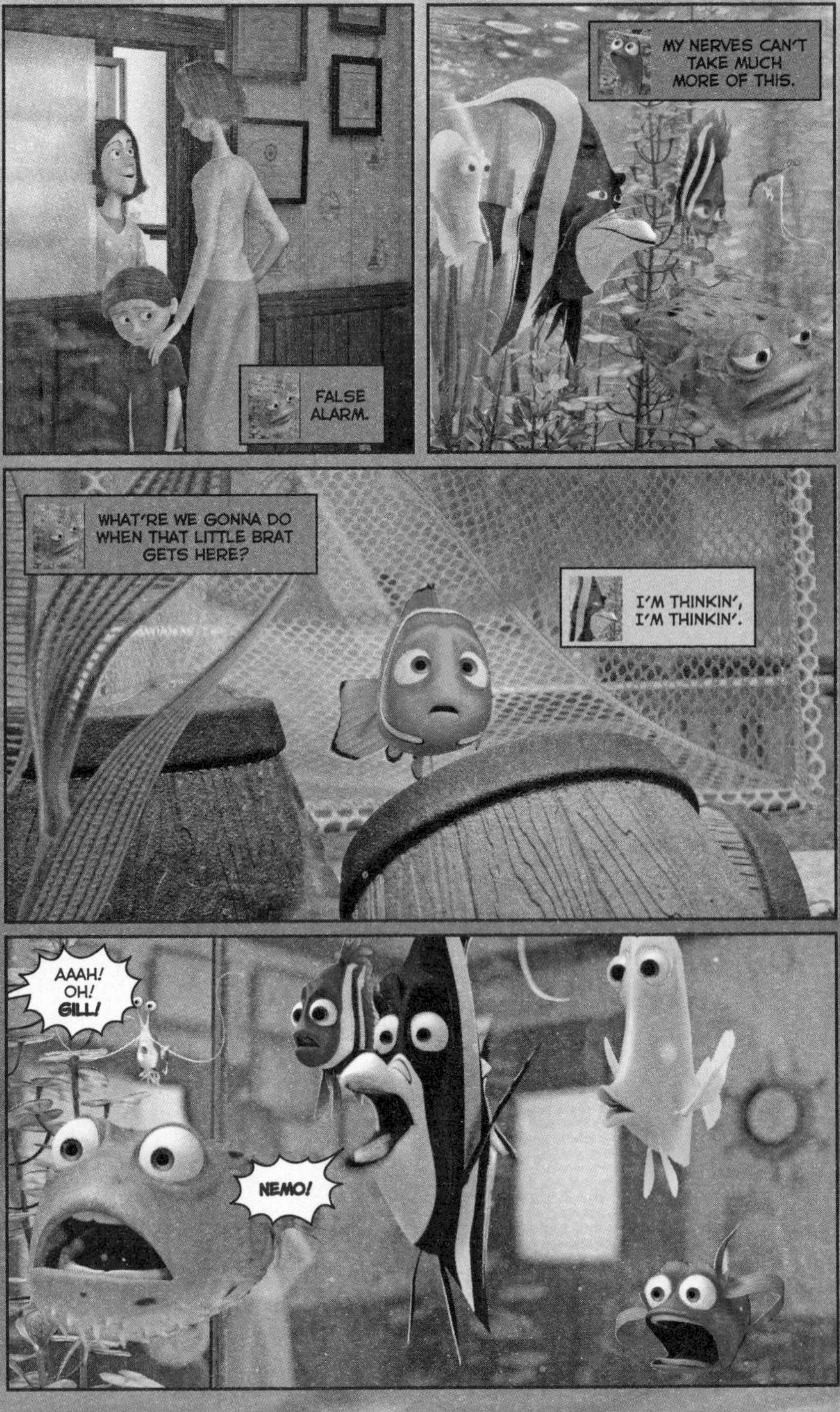
FALSE ALARM.
MY NERVES CAN'T TAKE MUCH MORE OF THIS.
WHAT'RE WE GONNA DO WHEN THAT LITTLE BRAT GETS HERE?
I'M THINKIN', I'M THINKIN'.
AAAH! OH! GILL!
NEMO!

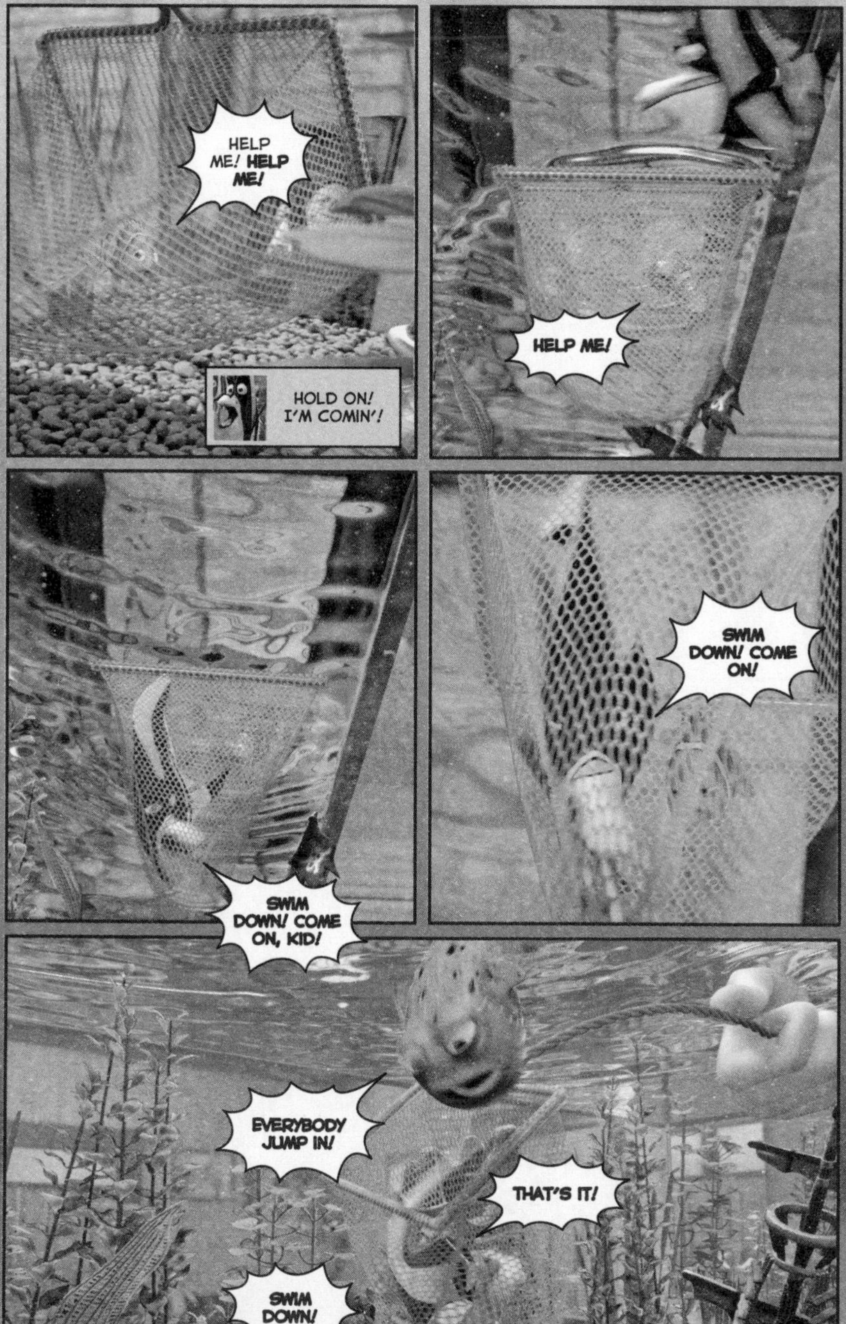
HELP ME! HELP ME!
HOLD ON! I'M COMIN'!
HELP ME!
SWIM DOWN! COME ON, KID!
SWIM DOWN! COME ON!
EVERYBODY JUMP IN!
THAT'S IT!
SWIM DOWN!

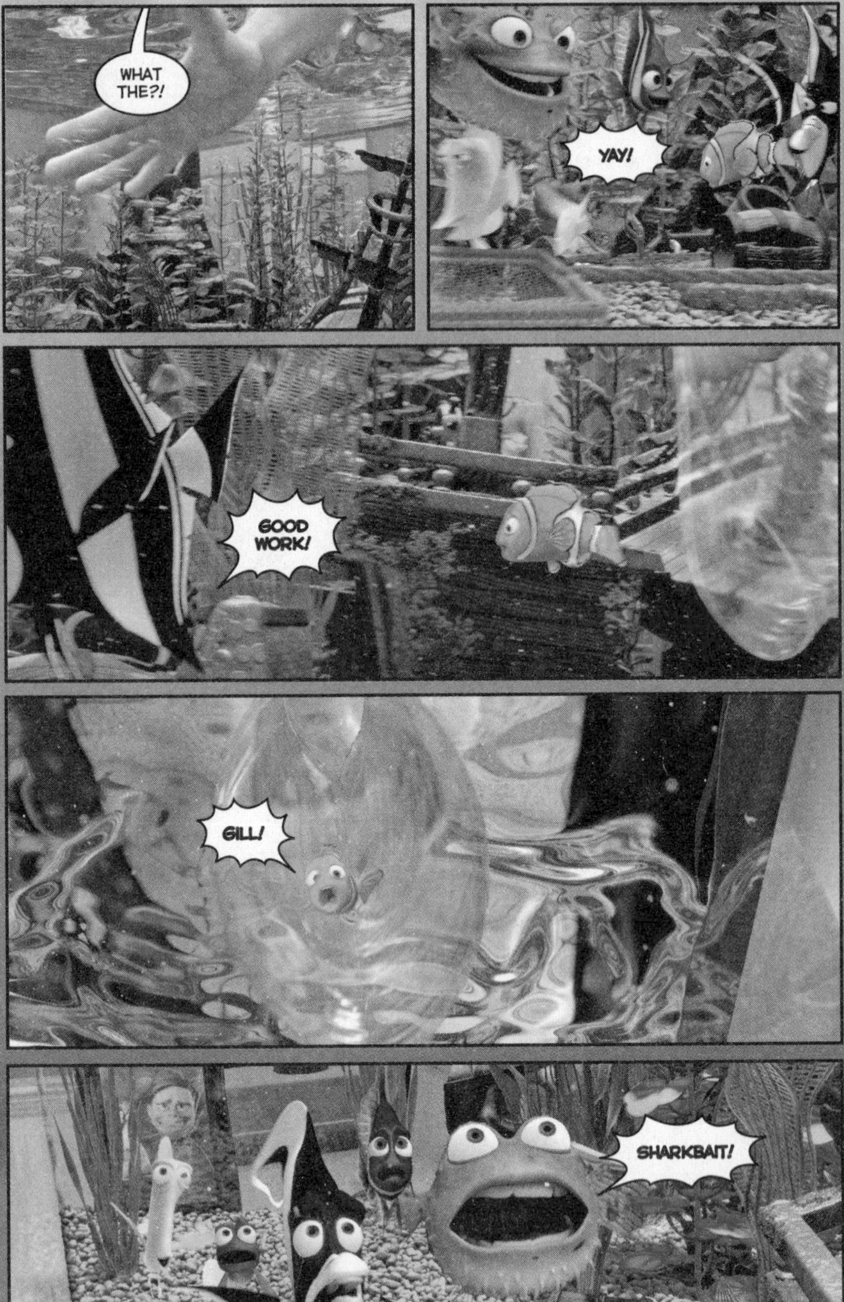
WHAT THE?!
YAY!
GOOD WORK!
GILL!
SHARKBAIT!
NEMO!

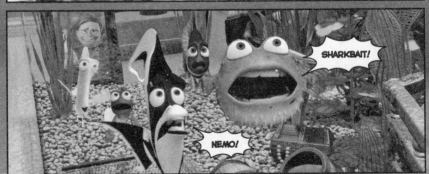

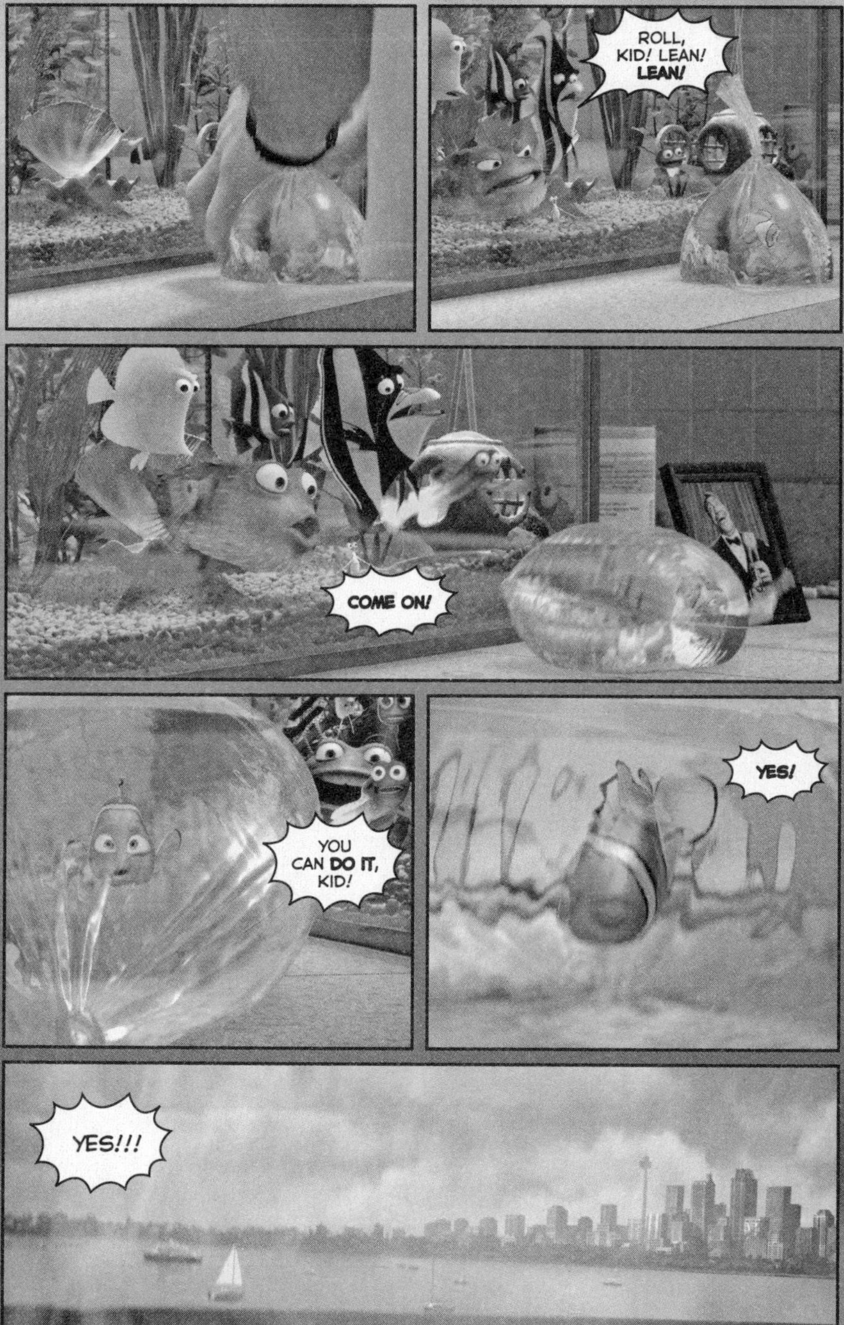

ROLL, KID! LEAN! LEAN!
COME ON!
YOU CAN DO IT, KID!
YES!
YES!!!

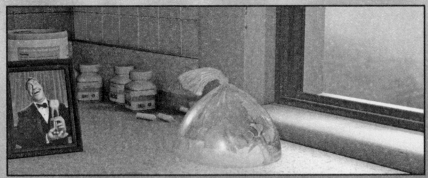

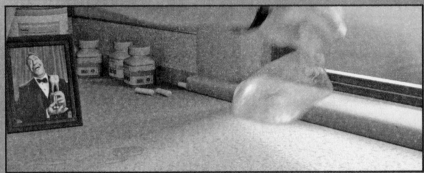

WHOOPS.
THAT WOULD
BE A NASTY
FALL.

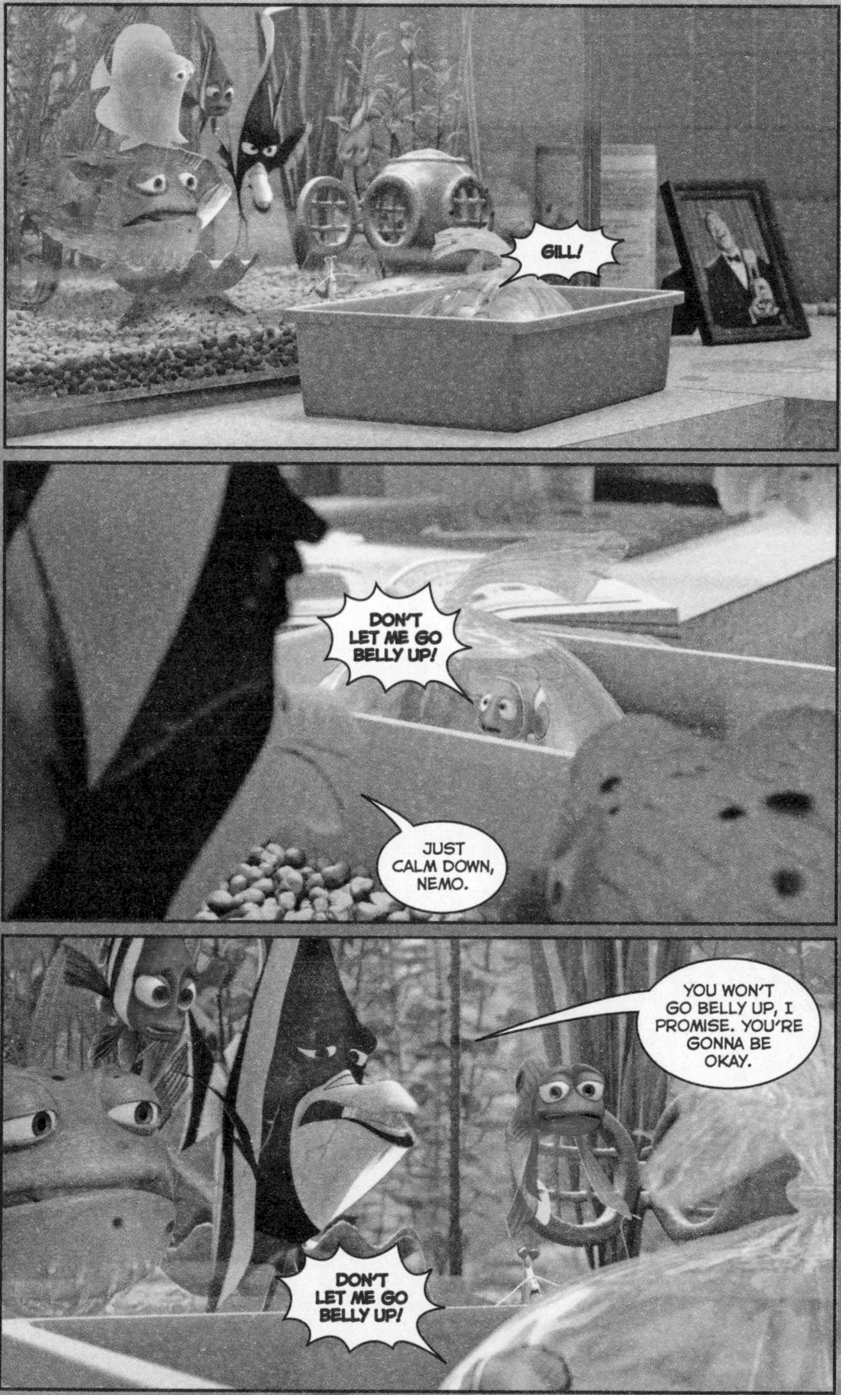
GILL!
DON'T LET ME GO BELLY UP!
JUST CALM DOWN, NEMO.
YOU WON'T GO BELLY UP, I PROMISE. YOU'RE GONNA BE OKAY.
DON'T LET ME GO BELLY UP!

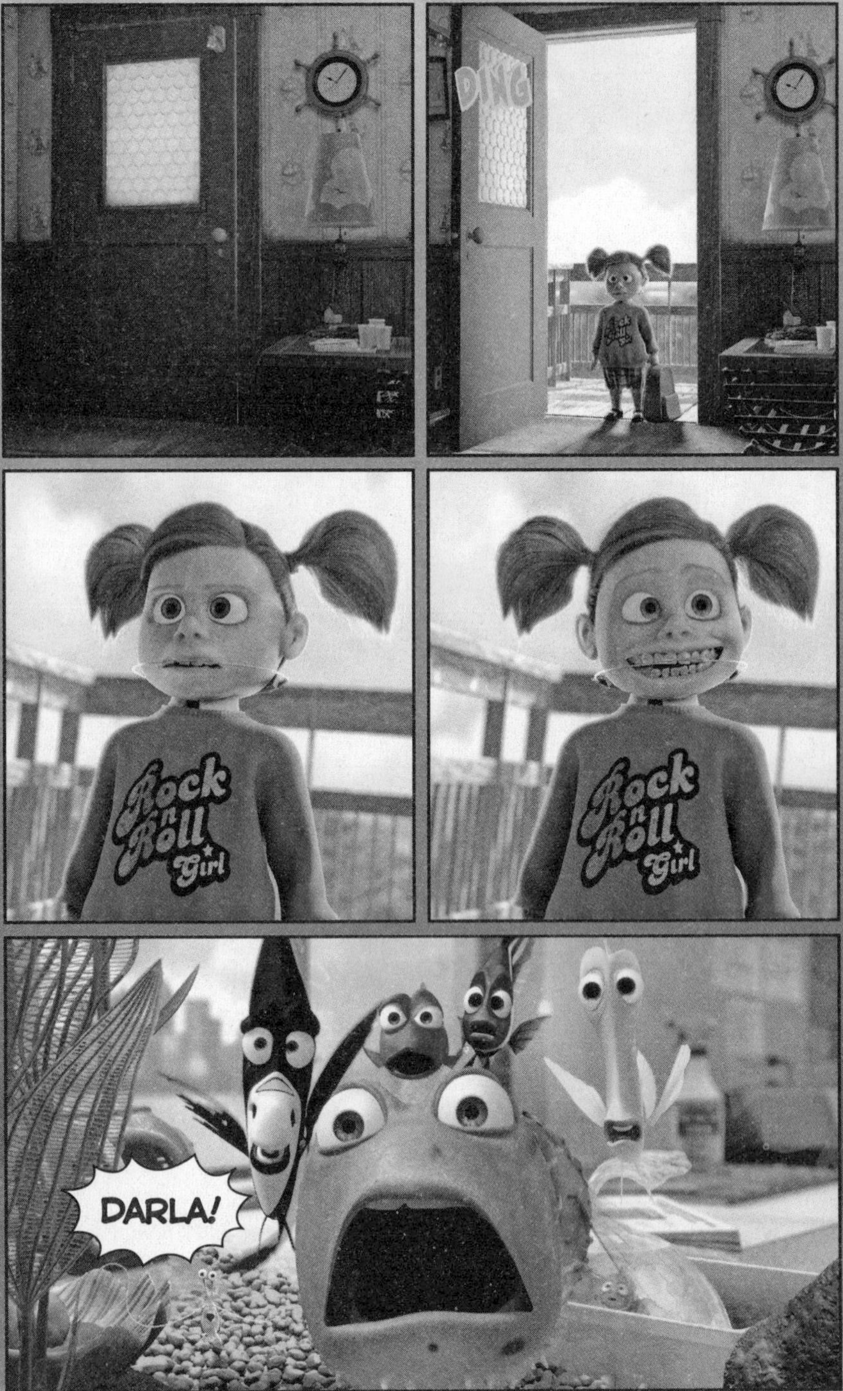
DING
Rock n Roll Girl
Rock n Roll Girl
DARLA!

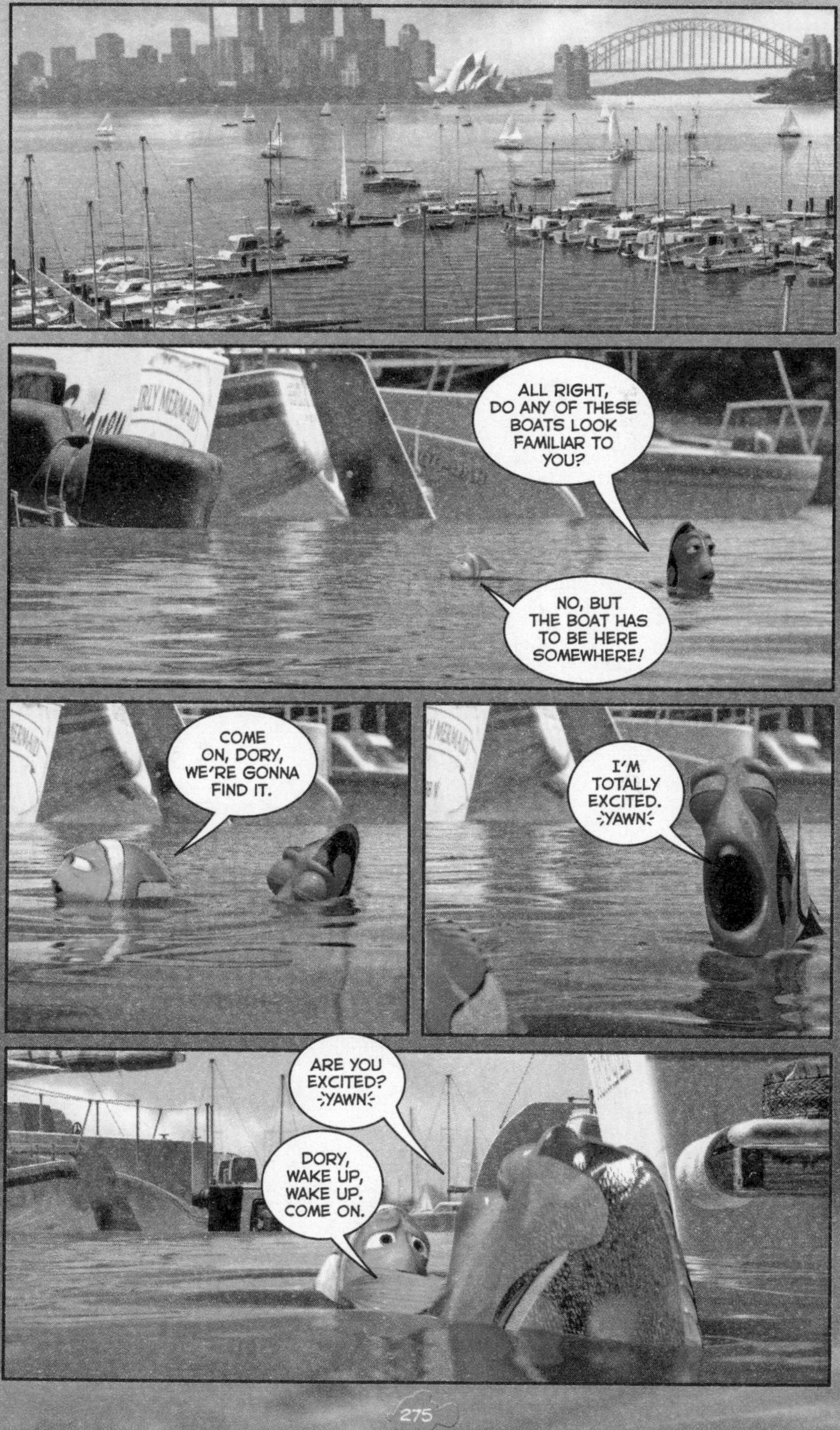
ALL RIGHT, DO ANY OF THESE BOATS LOOK FAMILIAR TO YOU?
NO, BUT THE BOAT HAS TO BE HERE SOMEWHERE!
COME ON, DORY, WE'RE GONNA FIND IT.
I'M TOTALLY EXCITED. YAWN
ARE YOU EXCITED? YAWN
DORY, WAKE UP, WAKE UP. COME ON.

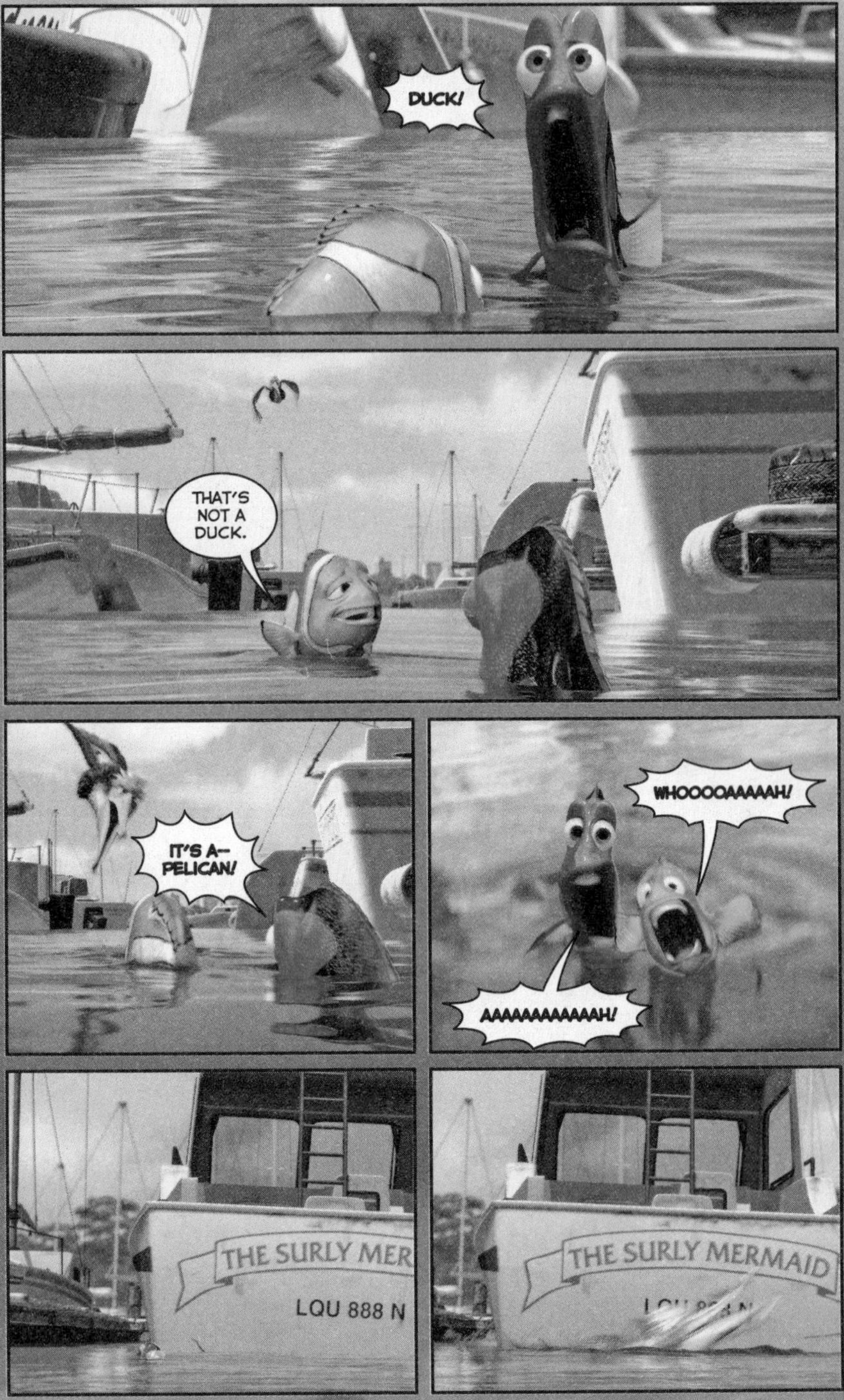
DUCK!
THAT'S NOT A DUCK.
IT'S A— PELICAN!
WHOOOOAAAAAH!
AAAAAAAAAAAAH!
THE SURLY MER
LQU 888 N
THE SURLY MERMAID

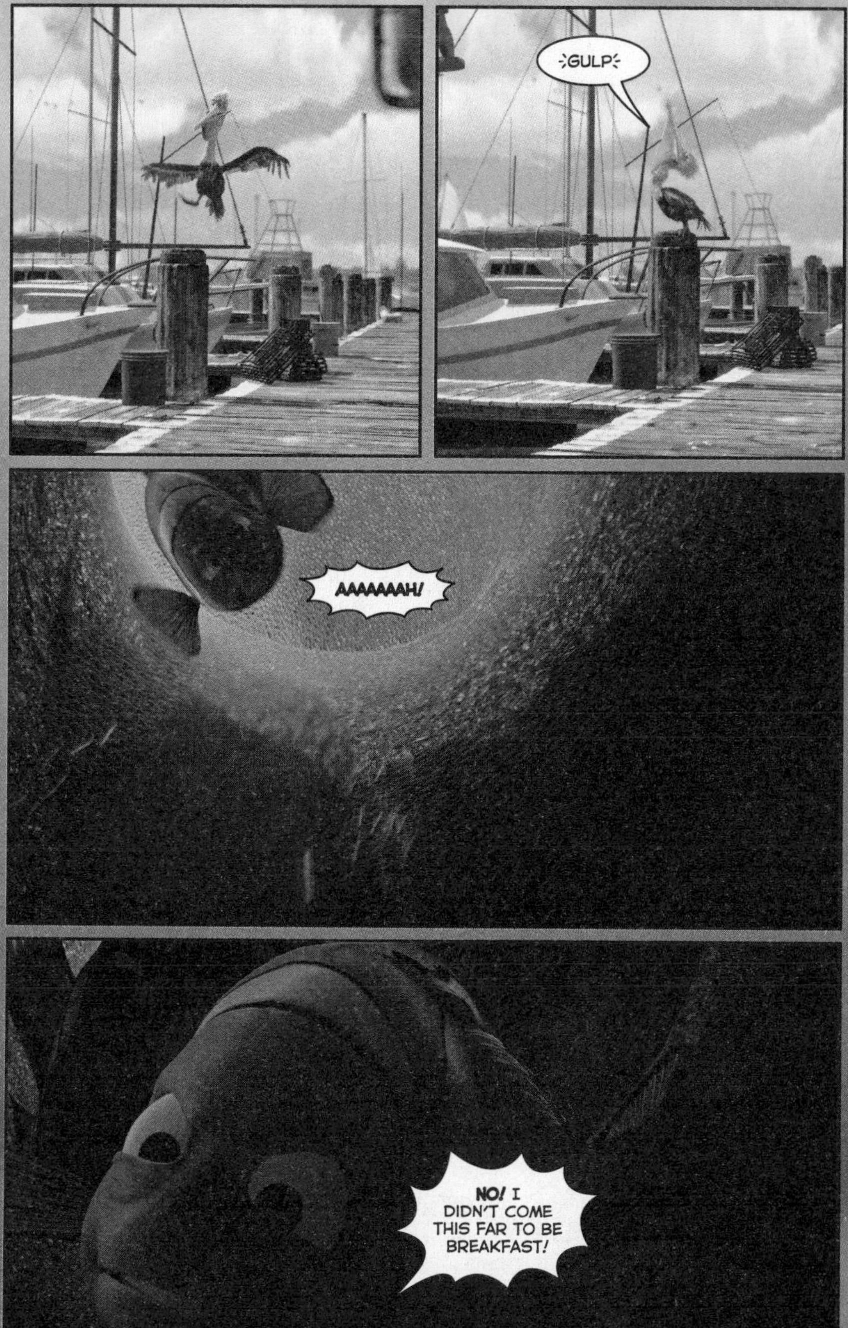
GULP
AAAAAAAH!
NO! I DIDN'T COME THIS FAR TO BE BREAKFAST!

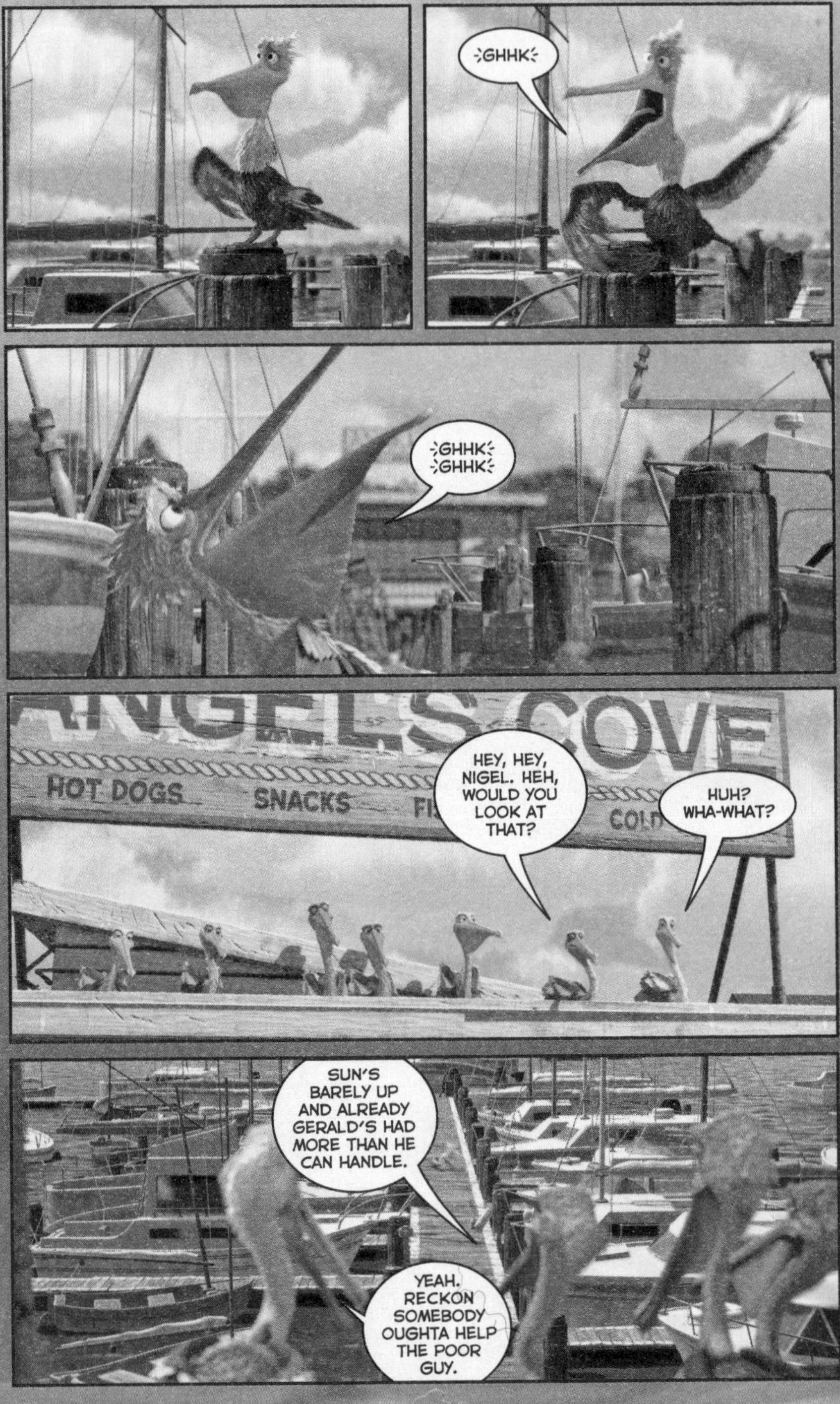
GHHK
GHHK GHHK
ANGELS COVE
HOT DOGS SNACKS
HEY, HEY, NIGEL. HEH, WOULD YOU LOOK AT THAT?
HUH? WHA-WHAT?
SUN'S BARELY UP AND ALREADY GERALD'S HAD MORE THAN HE CAN HANDLE.
YEAH. RECKON SOMEBODY OUGHTA HELP THE POOR GUY.

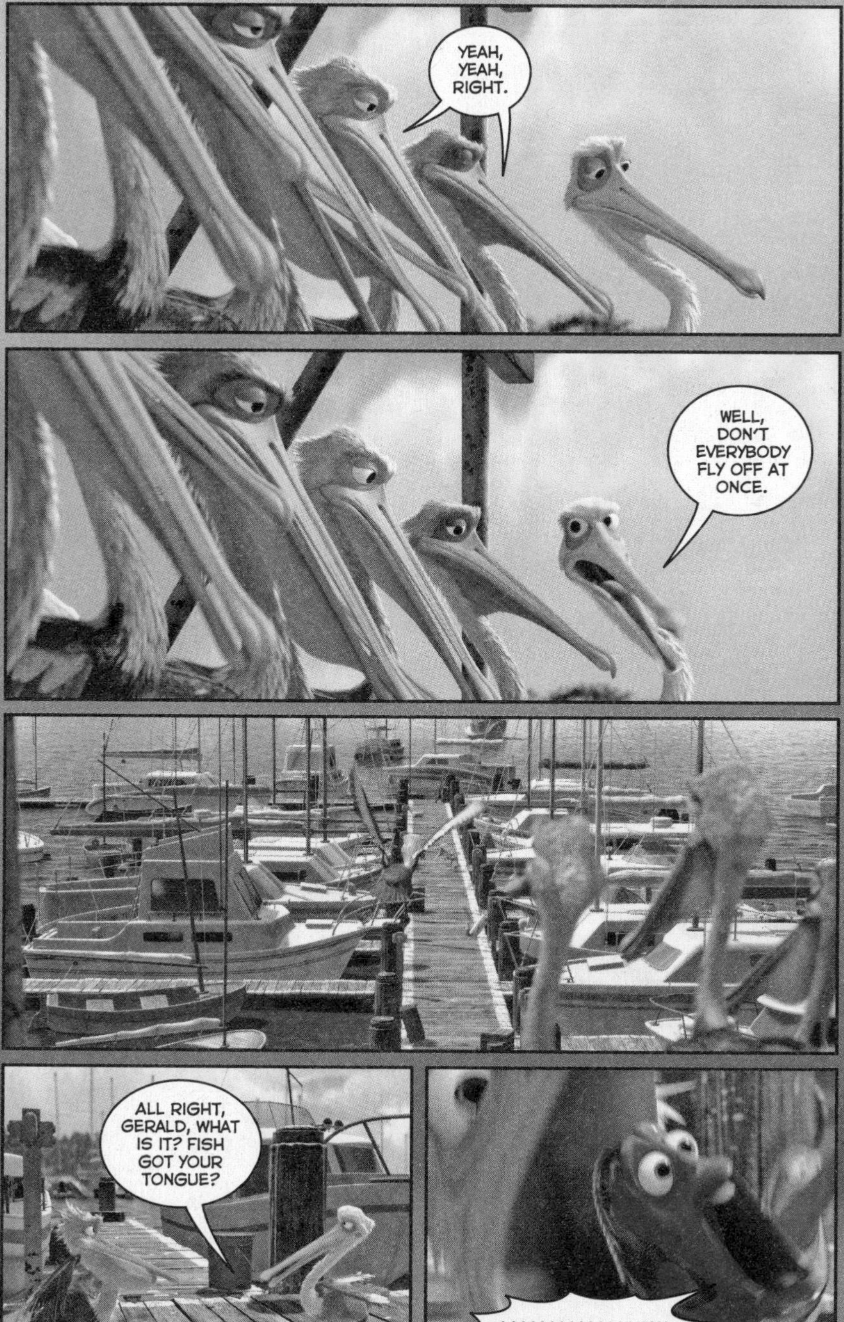
YEAH, YEAH, RIGHT.
WELL, DON'T EVERYBODY FLY OFF AT ONCE.
ALL RIGHT, GERALD, WHAT IS IT? FISH GOT YOUR TONGUE?
AAAAAAAAAAAAAAAH!!!

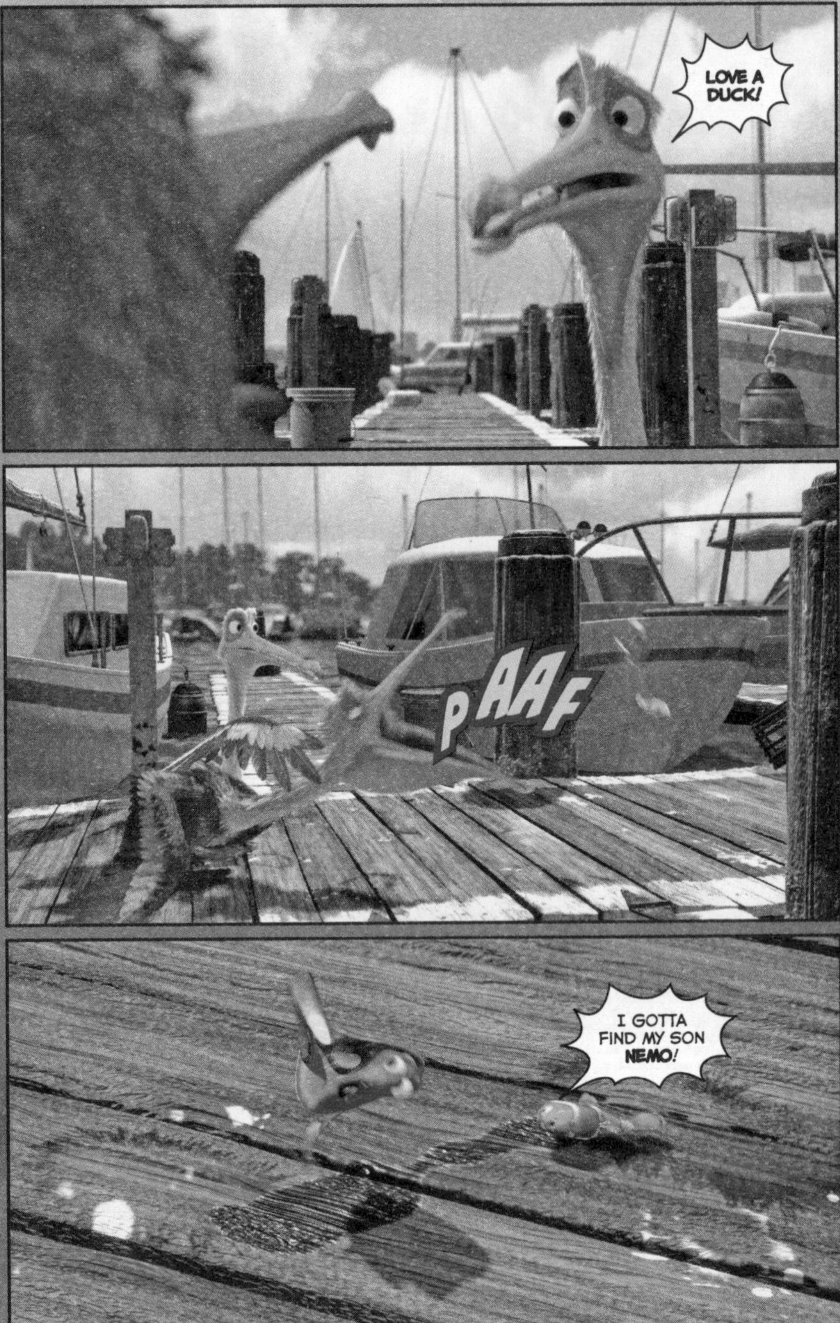
LOVE A DUCK!
PAAF
I GOTTA FIND MY SON NEMO!

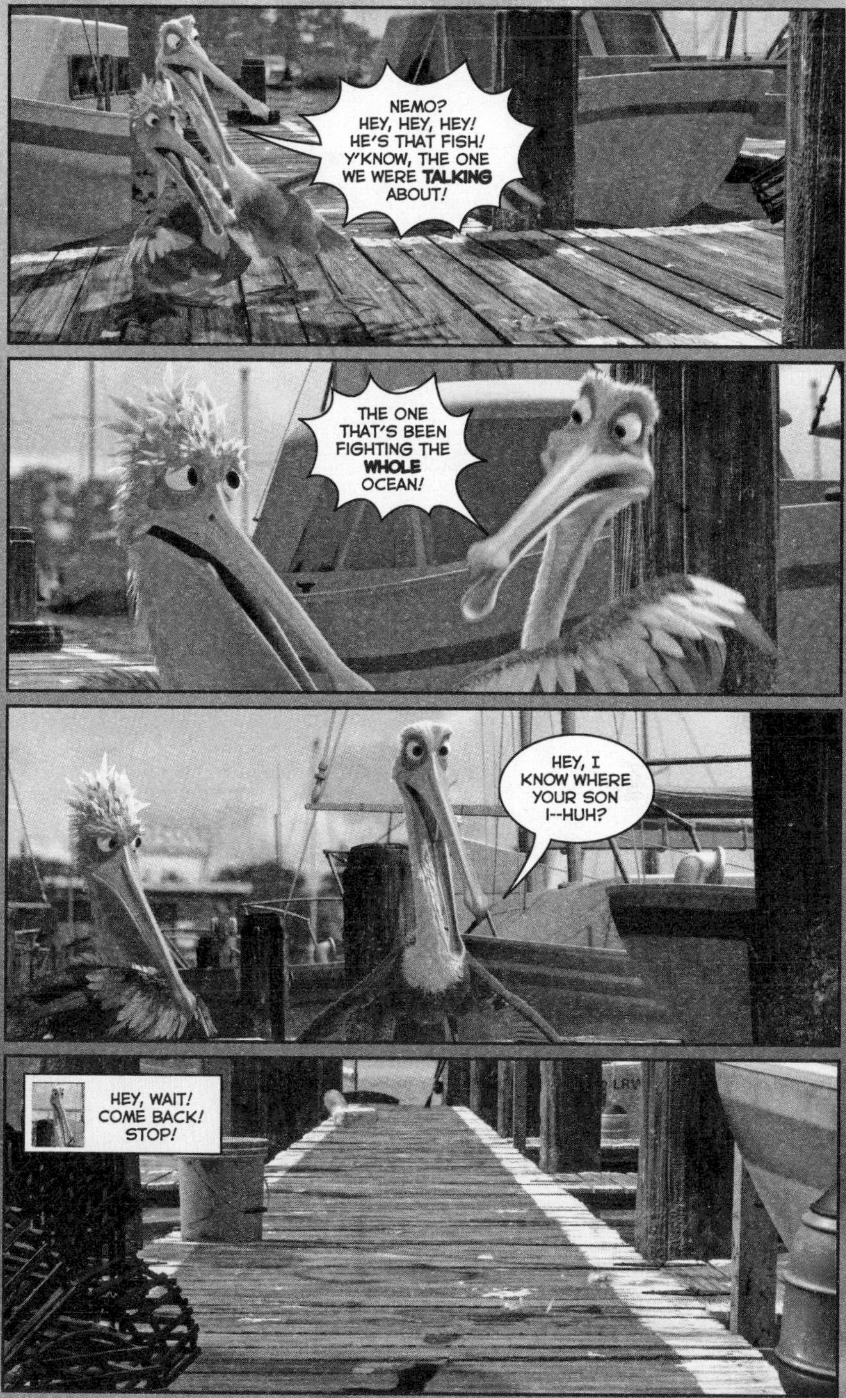
NEMO? HEY, HEY, HEY! HE'S THAT FISH! Y'KNOW, THE ONE WE WERE TALKING ABOUT!
THE ONE THAT'S BEEN FIGHTING THE WHOLE OCEAN!
HEY, I KNOW WHERE YOUR SON I--HUH?
HEY, WAIT! COME BACK! STOP!

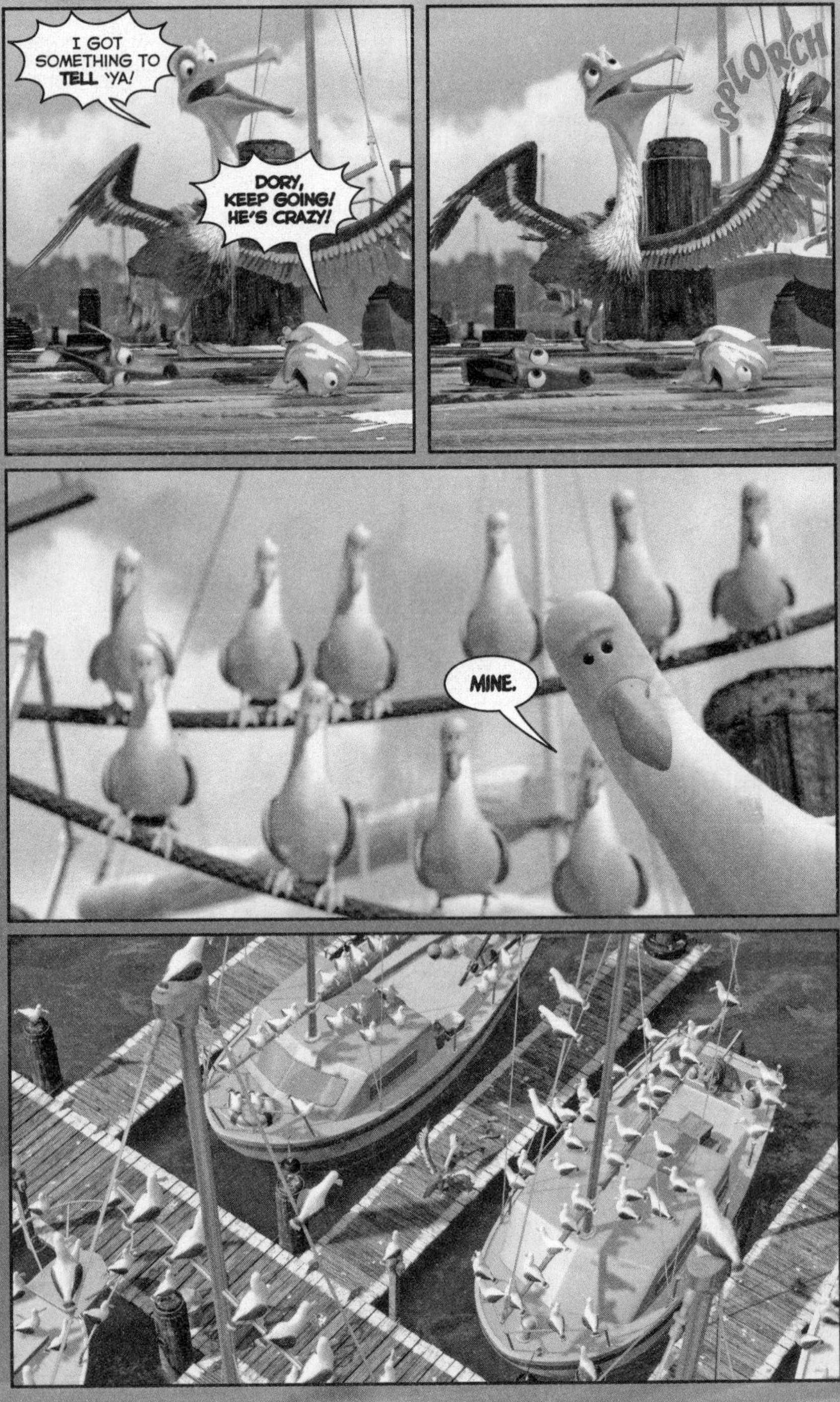
I GOT SOMETHING TO TELL 'YA!
DORY, KEEP GOING! HE'S CRAZY!
SPLORCH
MINE.

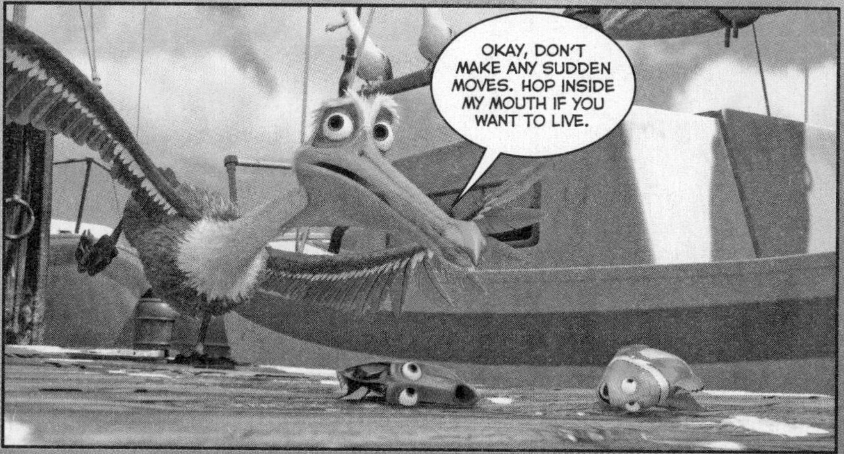
OKAY, DON'T MAKE ANY SUDDEN MOVES. HOP INSIDE MY MOUTH IF YOU WANT TO LIVE.

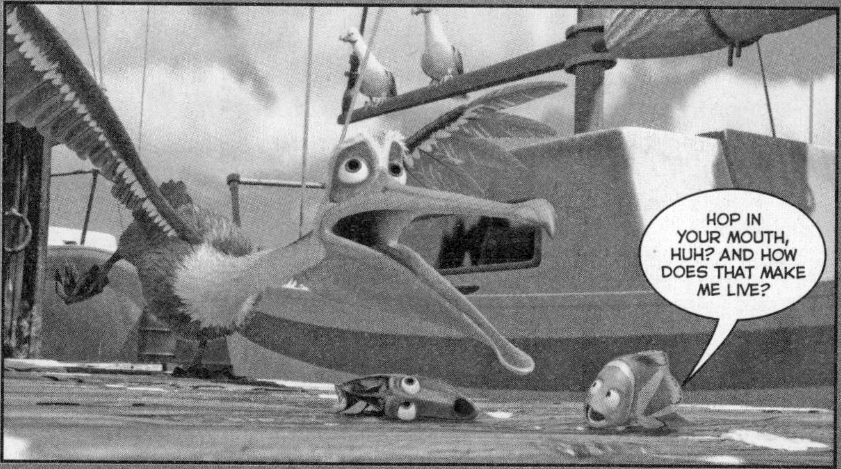
HOP IN YOUR MOUTH, HUH? AND HOW DOES THAT MAKE ME LIVE?

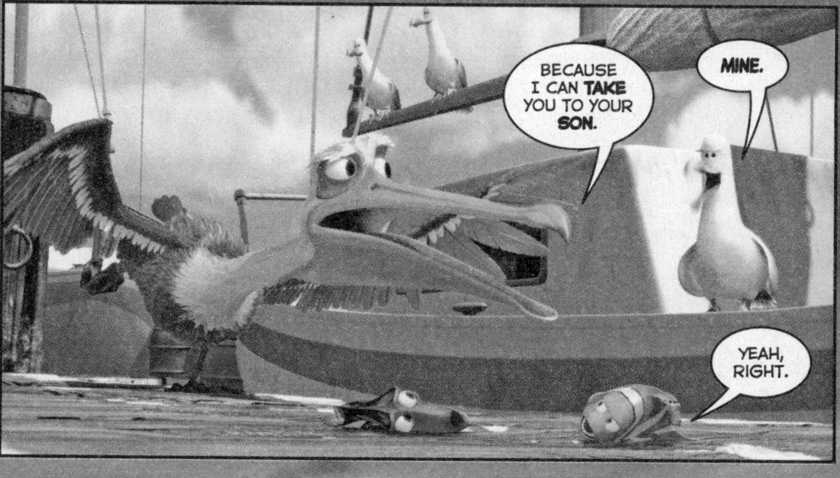
BECAUSE I CAN **TAKE** YOU TO YOUR **SON**.
MINE.
YEAH, RIGHT.

NO. I KNOW YOUR SON. HE'S ORANGE, HE'S GOT A GIMPY FIN ON ONE SIDE...

THAT'S NEMO!

MINE! MINE! MINE! MINE! MINE! MINE!

AAAAH!!!

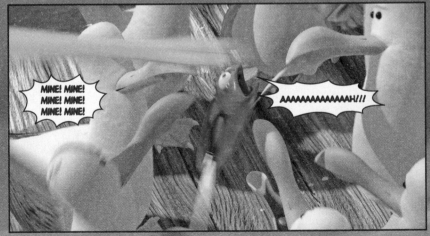

MINE! MINE! MINE! MINE! MINE! MINE!

AAAAAAAAAAAAAH!!!

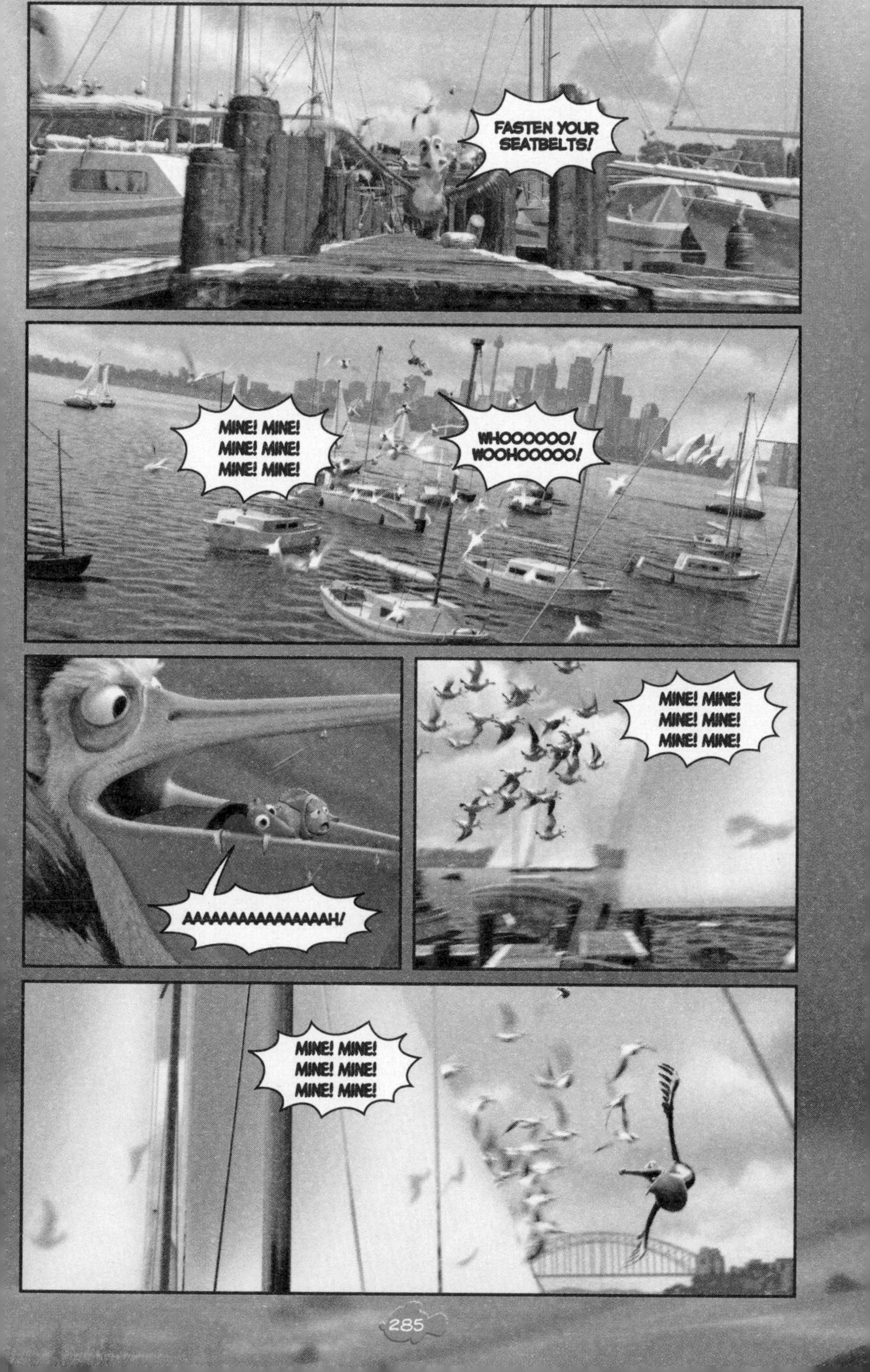
FASTEN YOUR SEATBELTS!
MINE! MINE! MINE! MINE! MINE! MINE!
WHOOOOOOO! WOOHOOOOOO!
AAAAAAAAAAAAAAAAH!
MINE! MINE! MINE! MINE! MINE! MINE!
MINE! MINE! MINE! MINE! MINE! MINE!

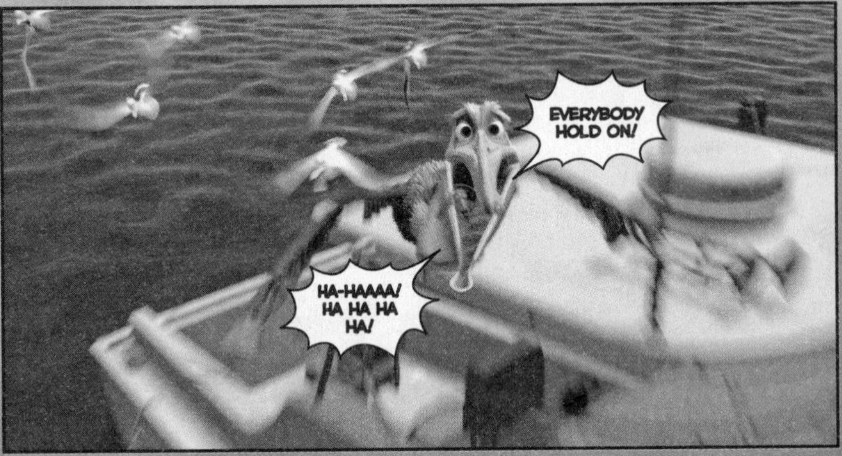
EVERYBODY HOLD ON!
HA-HAAAA! HA HA HA HA!

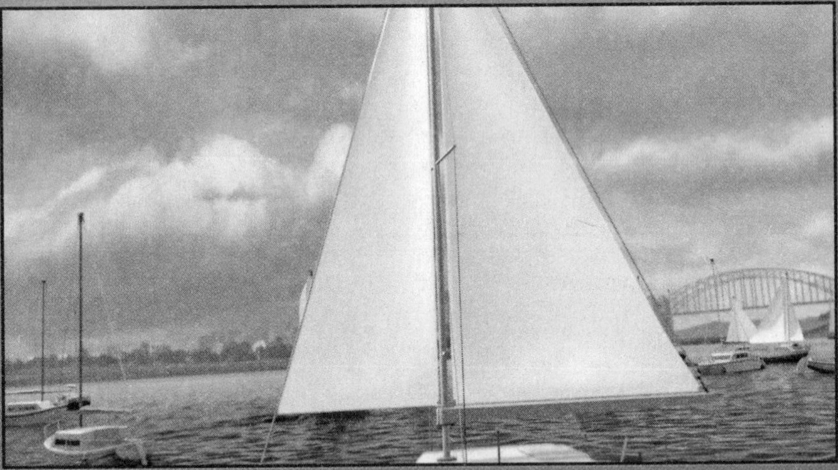

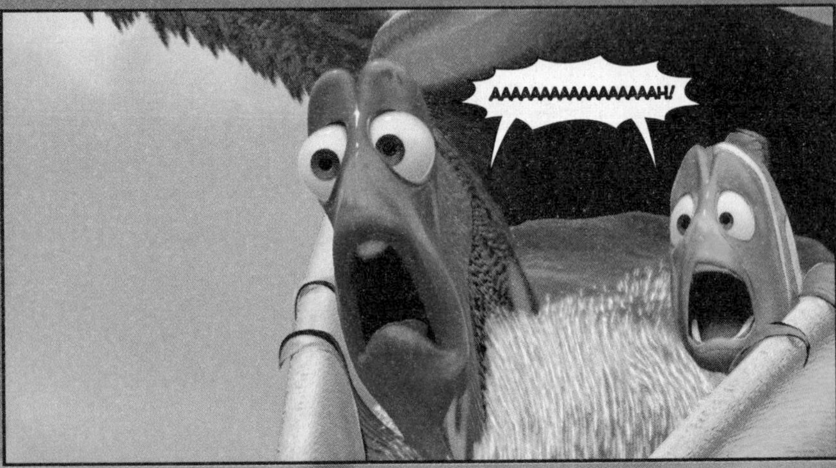
AAAAAAAAAAAAAAAAAAH!

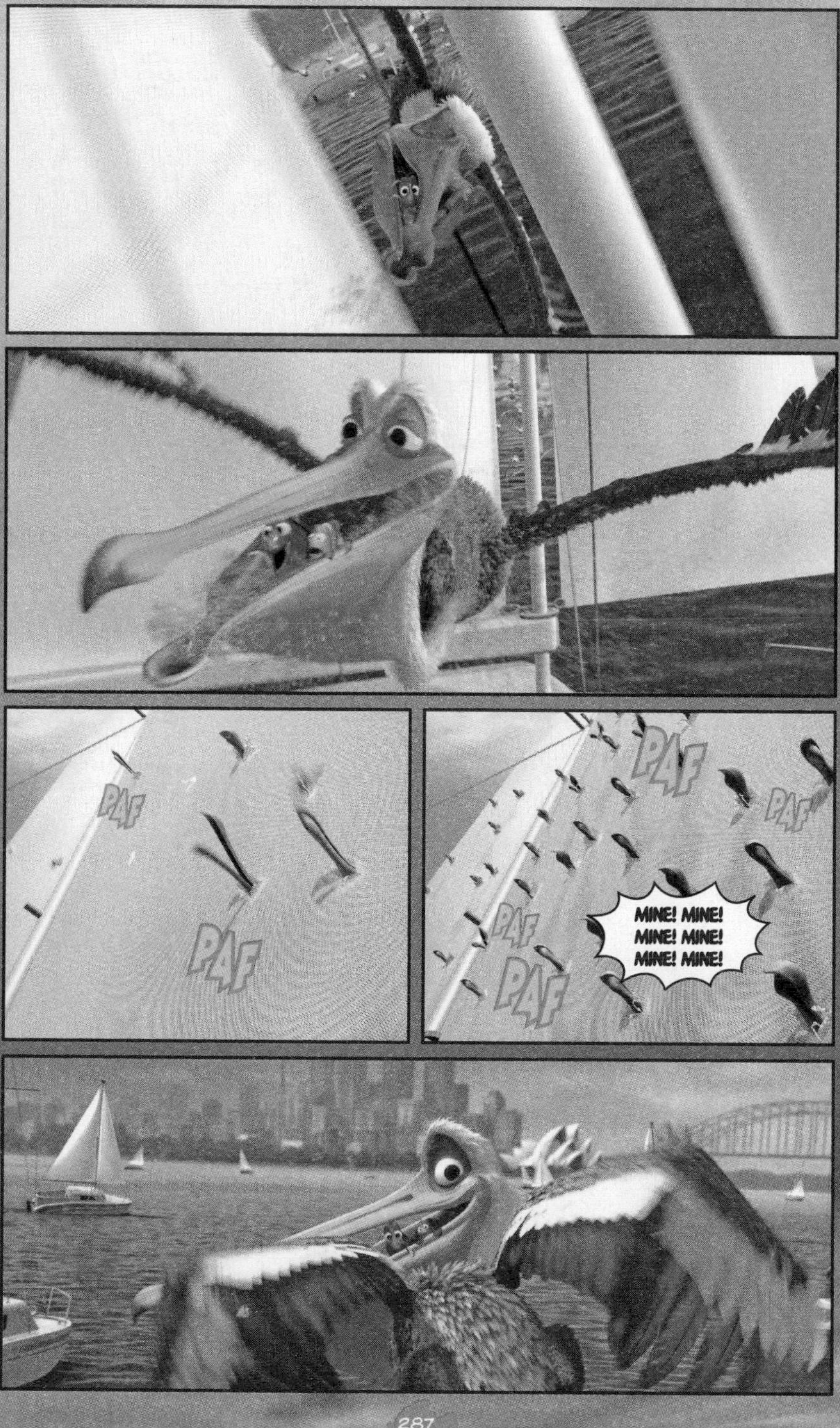
PAF
PAF
PAF
PAF
PAF
PAF
MINE! MINE!
MINE! MINE!
MINE! MINE!

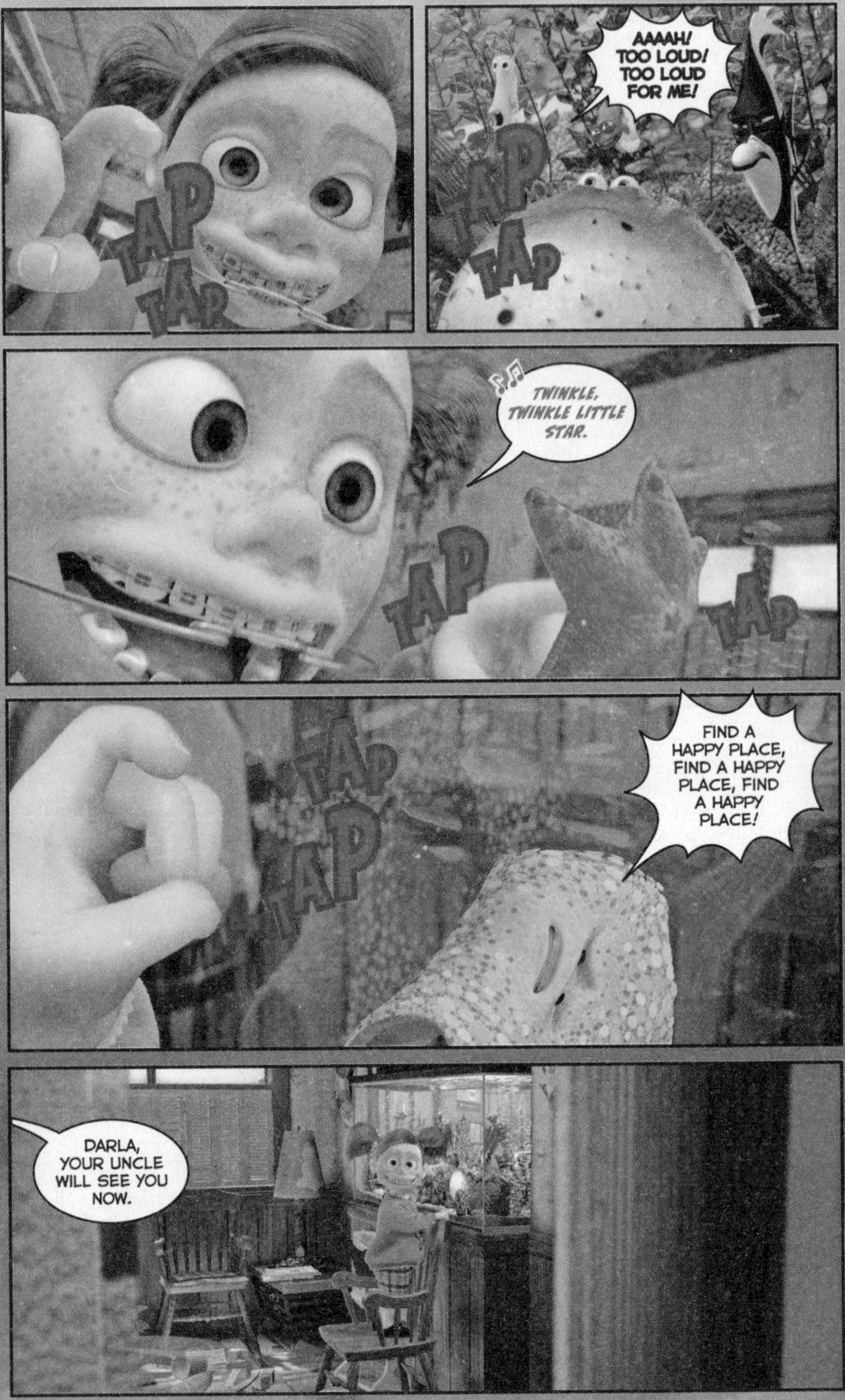
TAP
TAP
AAAAH! TOO LOUD! TOO LOUD FOR ME!
TAP
TAP
TWINKLE, TWINKLE LITTLE STAR.
TAP
TAP
TAP
TAP
FIND A HAPPY PLACE, FIND A HAPPY PLACE, FIND A HAPPY PLACE!
DARLA, YOUR UNCLE WILL SEE YOU NOW.

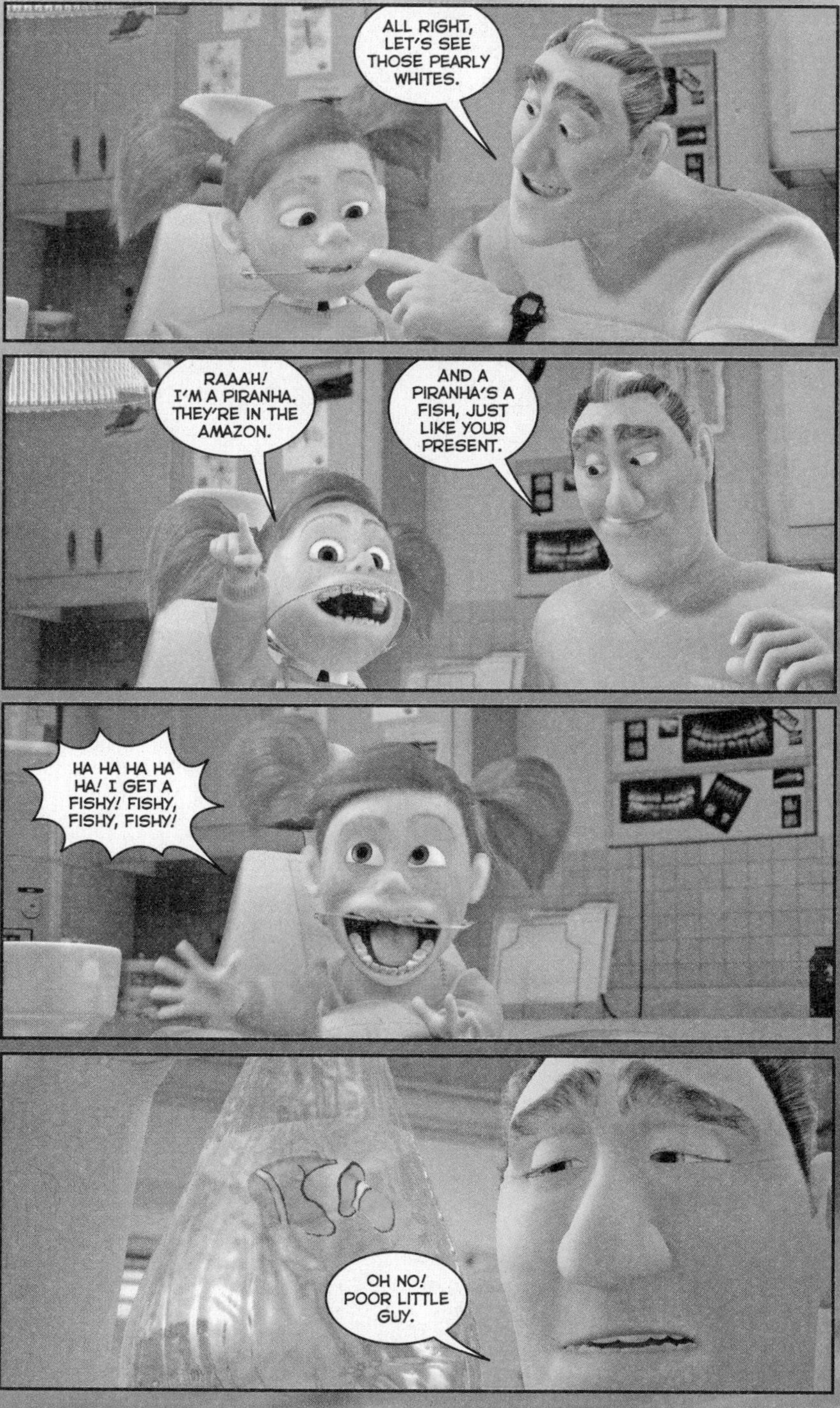
ALL RIGHT, LET'S SEE THOSE PEARLY WHITES.
RAAAH! I'M A PIRANHA. THEY'RE IN THE AMAZON.
AND A PIRANHA'S A FISH, JUST LIKE YOUR PRESENT.
HA HA HA HA HA! I GET A FISHY! FISHY, FISHY, FISHY!
OH NO! POOR LITTLE GUY.

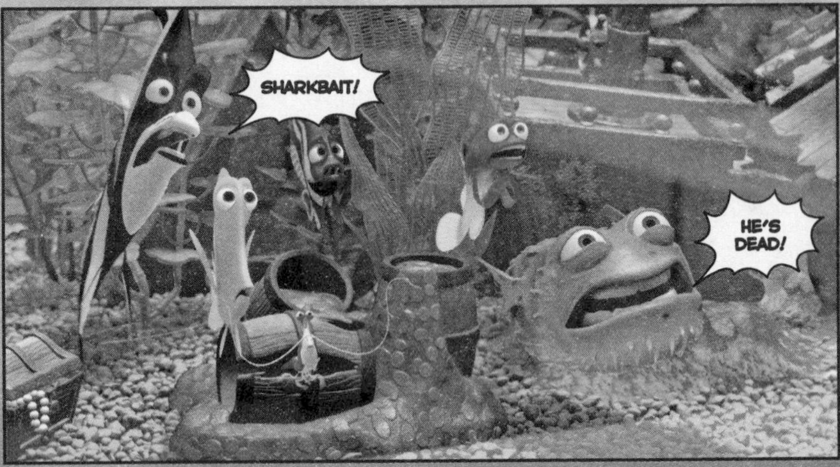
SHARKBAIT!
HE'S DEAD!

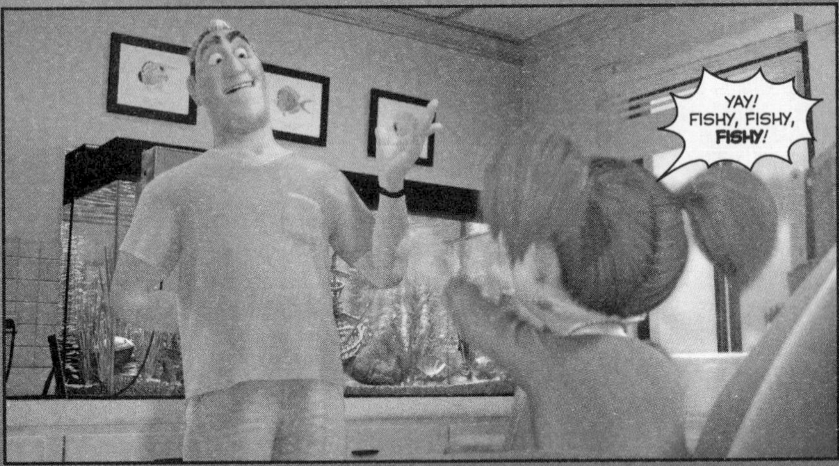
YAY! FISHY, FISHY, FISHY!

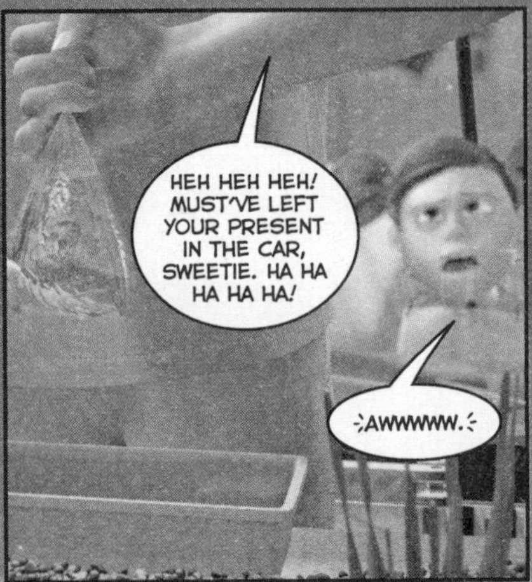
HEH HEH HEH! MUST'VE LEFT YOUR PRESENT IN THE CAR, SWEETIE. HA HA HA HA HA!
AWWWWW.

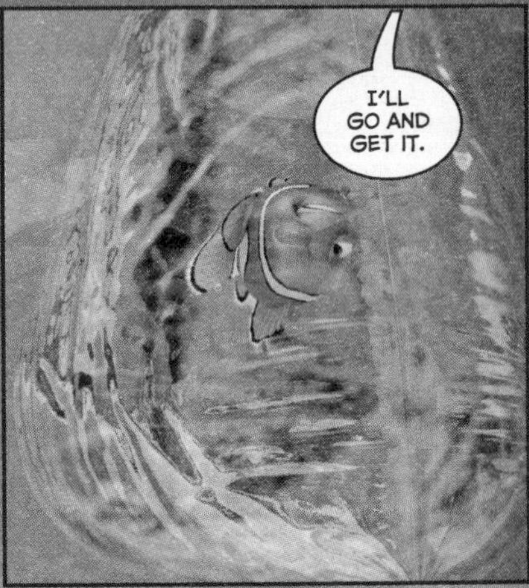
I'LL GO AND GET IT.

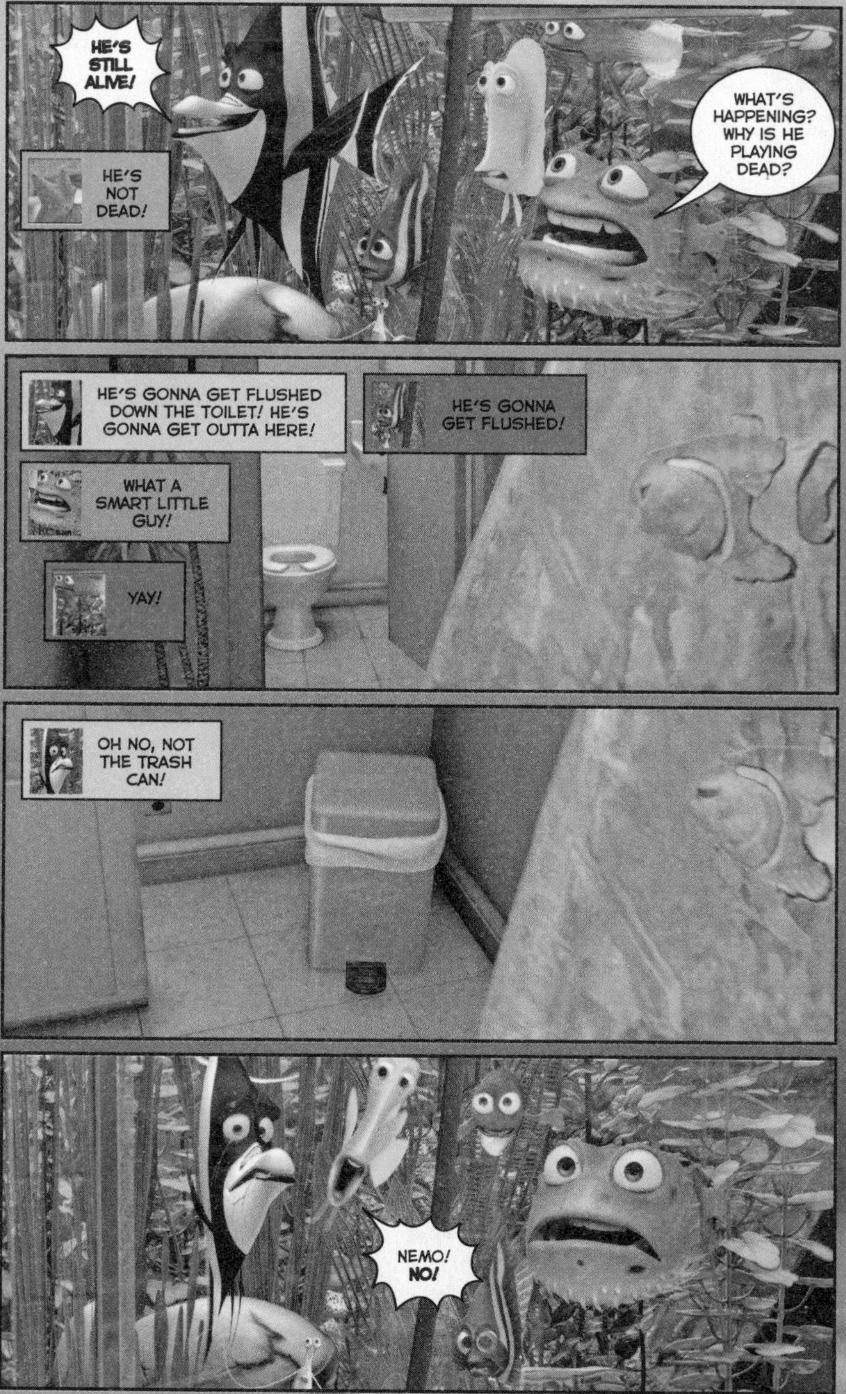
HE'S STILL ALIVE!
HE'S NOT DEAD!
WHAT'S HAPPENING? WHY IS HE PLAYING DEAD?
HE'S GONNA GET FLUSHED DOWN THE TOILET! HE'S GONNA GET OUTTA HERE!
HE'S GONNA GET FLUSHED!
WHAT A SMART LITTLE GUY!
YAY!
OH NO, NOT THE TRASH CAN!
NEMO! NO!

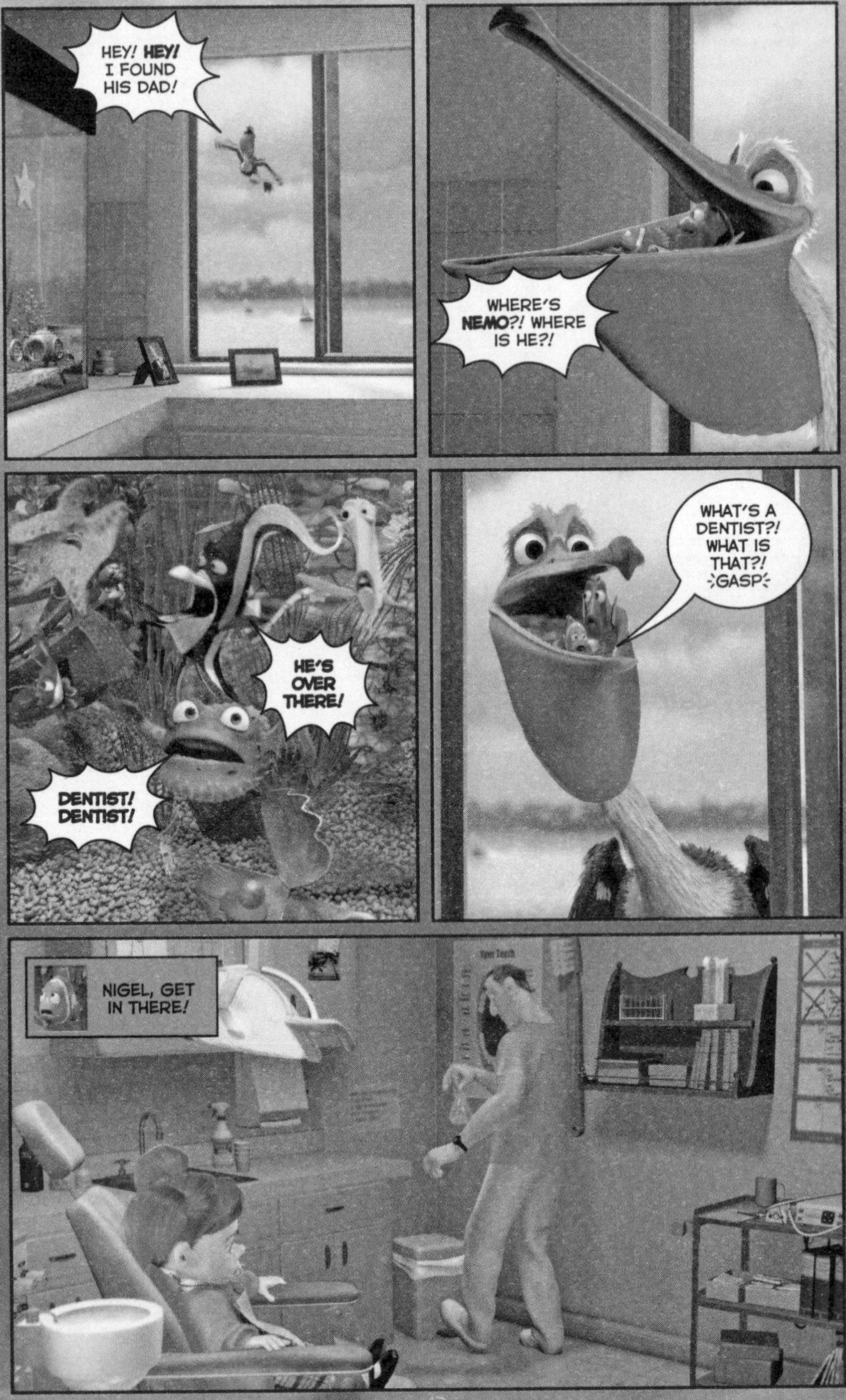
HEY! **HEY!** I FOUND HIS DAD!
WHERE'S **NEMO**?! WHERE IS HE?!
HE'S OVER THERE!
DENTIST! DENTIST!
WHAT'S A DENTIST?! WHAT IS THAT?! GASP
NIGEL, GET IN THERE!

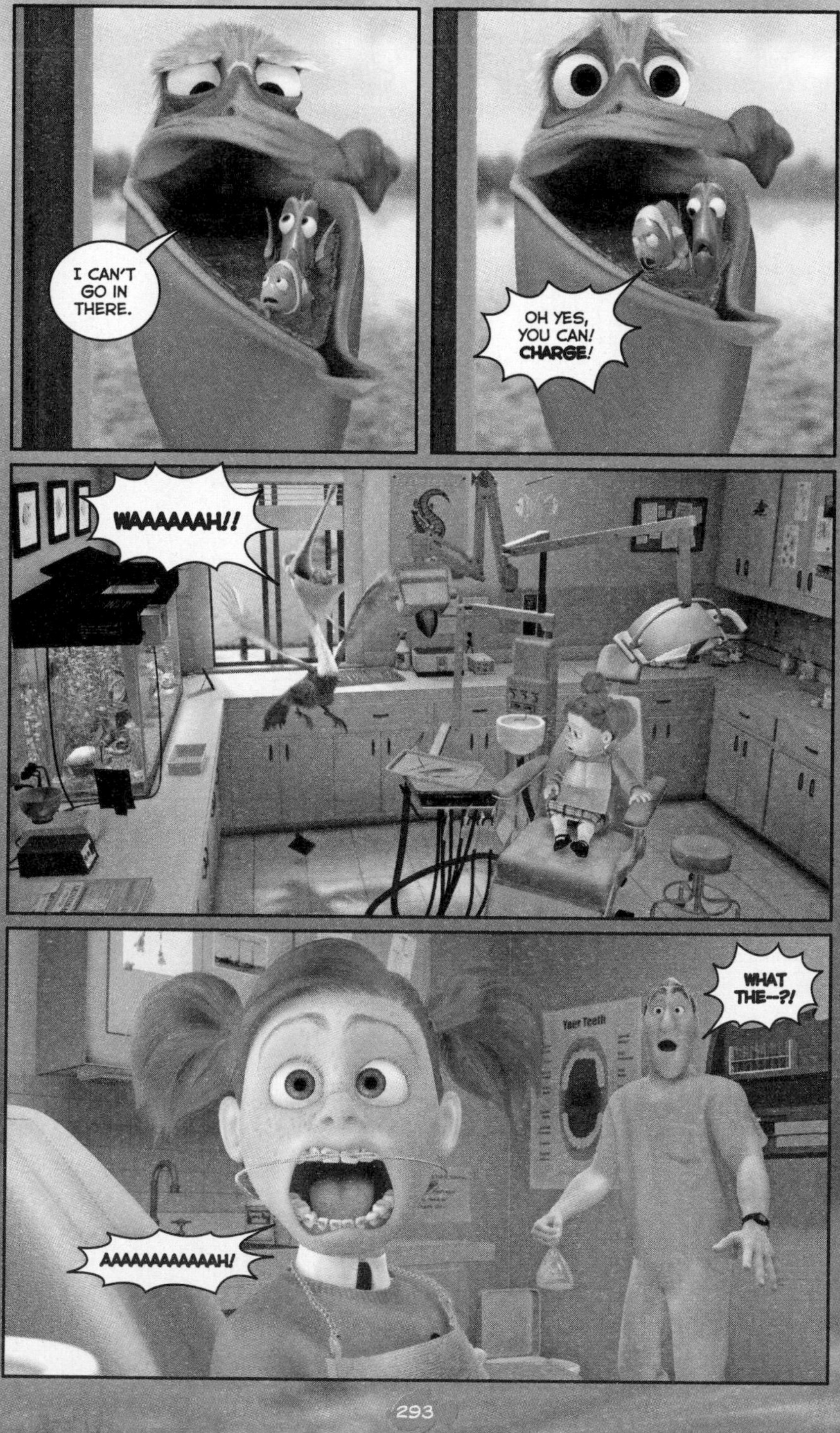
I CAN'T GO IN THERE.
OH YES, YOU CAN! CHARGE!
WAAAAAAH!!
WHAT THE--?!
AAAAAAAAAAAAH!

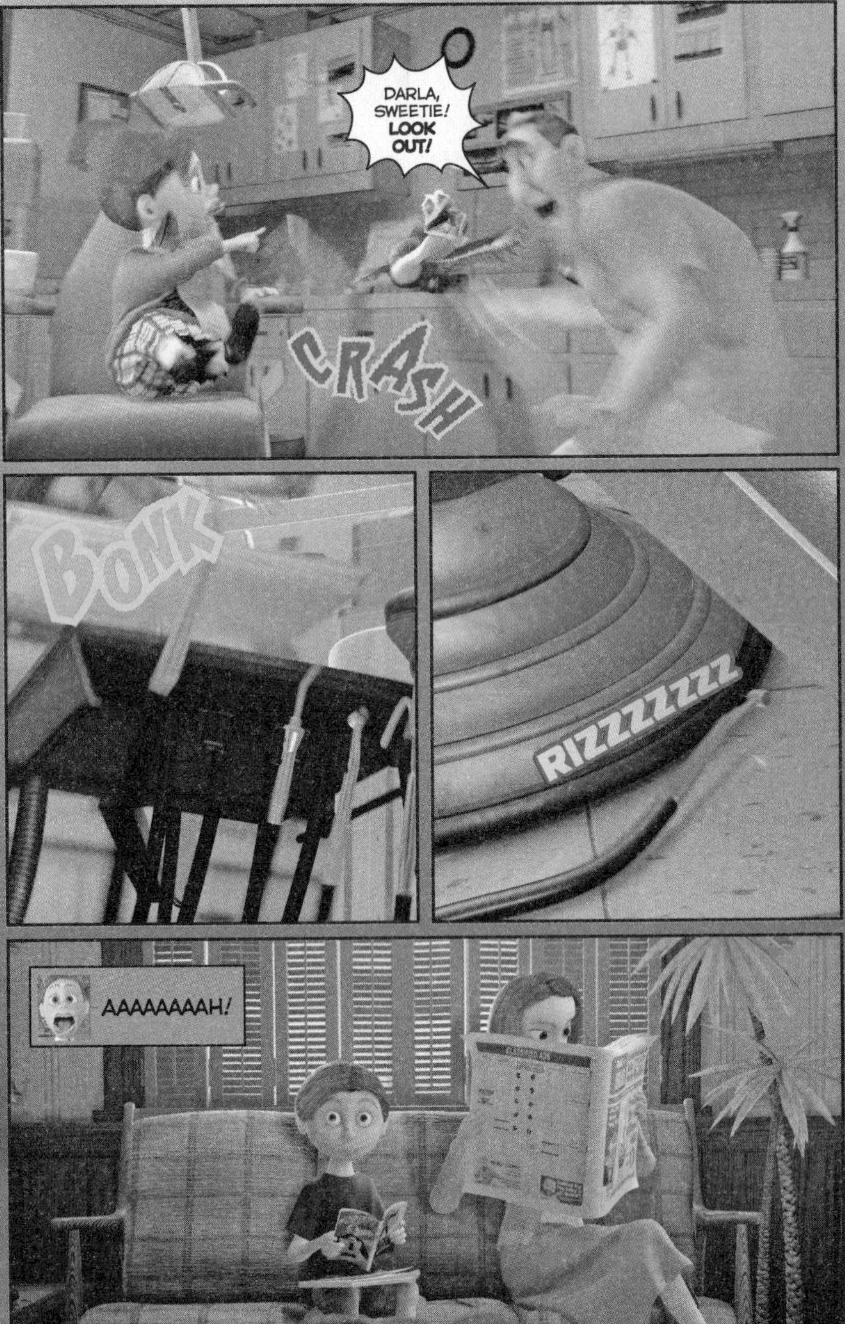
DARLA, SWEETIE! LOOK OUT!
CRASH
BONK
RIZZZZZZZ
AAAAAAAAH!

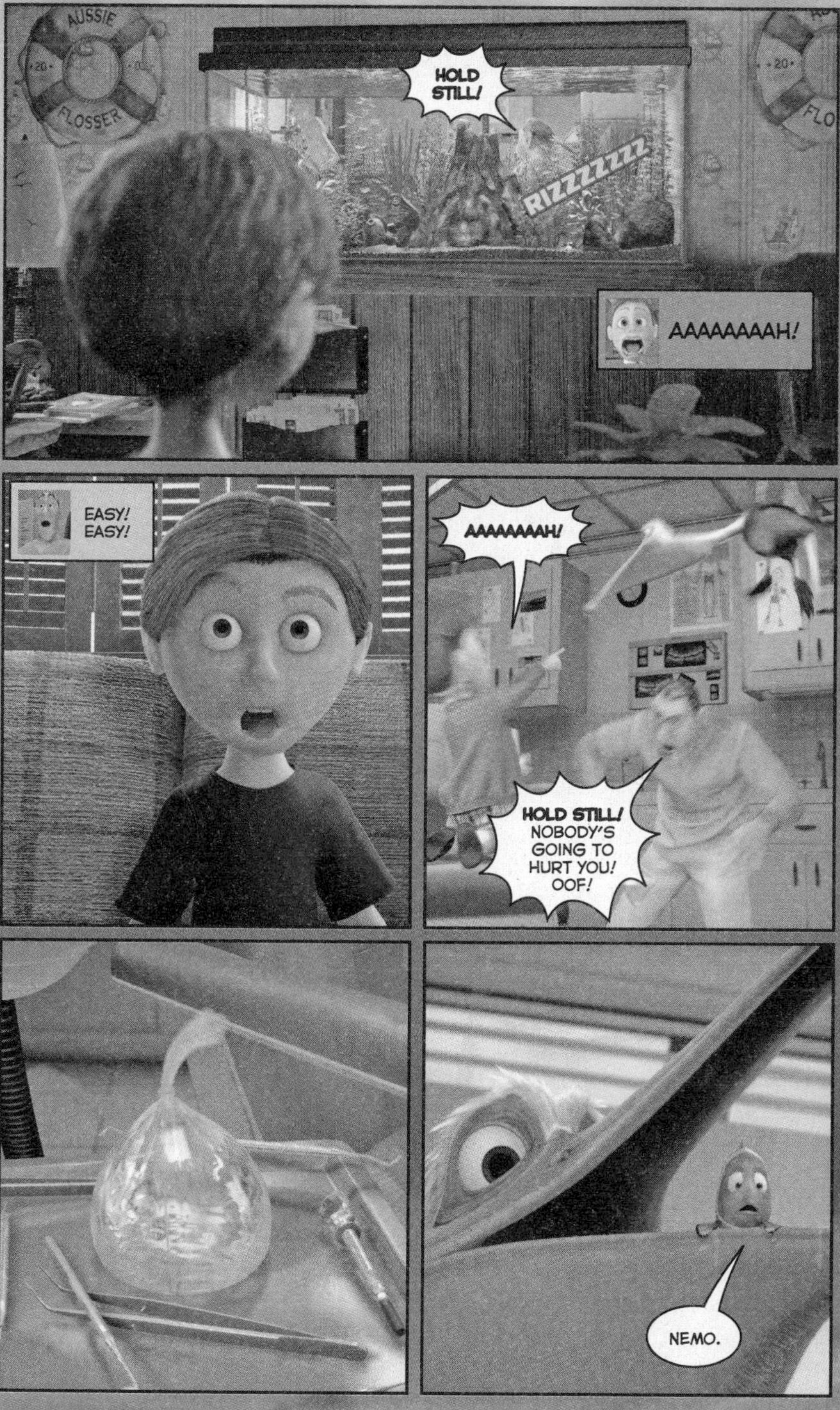
AUSSIE
FLOSSER
HOLD STILL!
RIZZZZZZZ
AAAAAAAAH!
EASY! EASY!
AAAAAAAAH!
HOLD STILL! NOBODY'S GOING TO HURT YOU! OOF!
NEMO.

OH MY GOODNESS.

GOTCHA! KEEP DOWN!

NEMO!

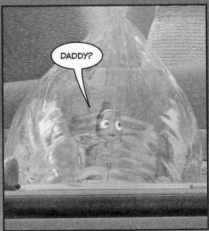

DADDY?

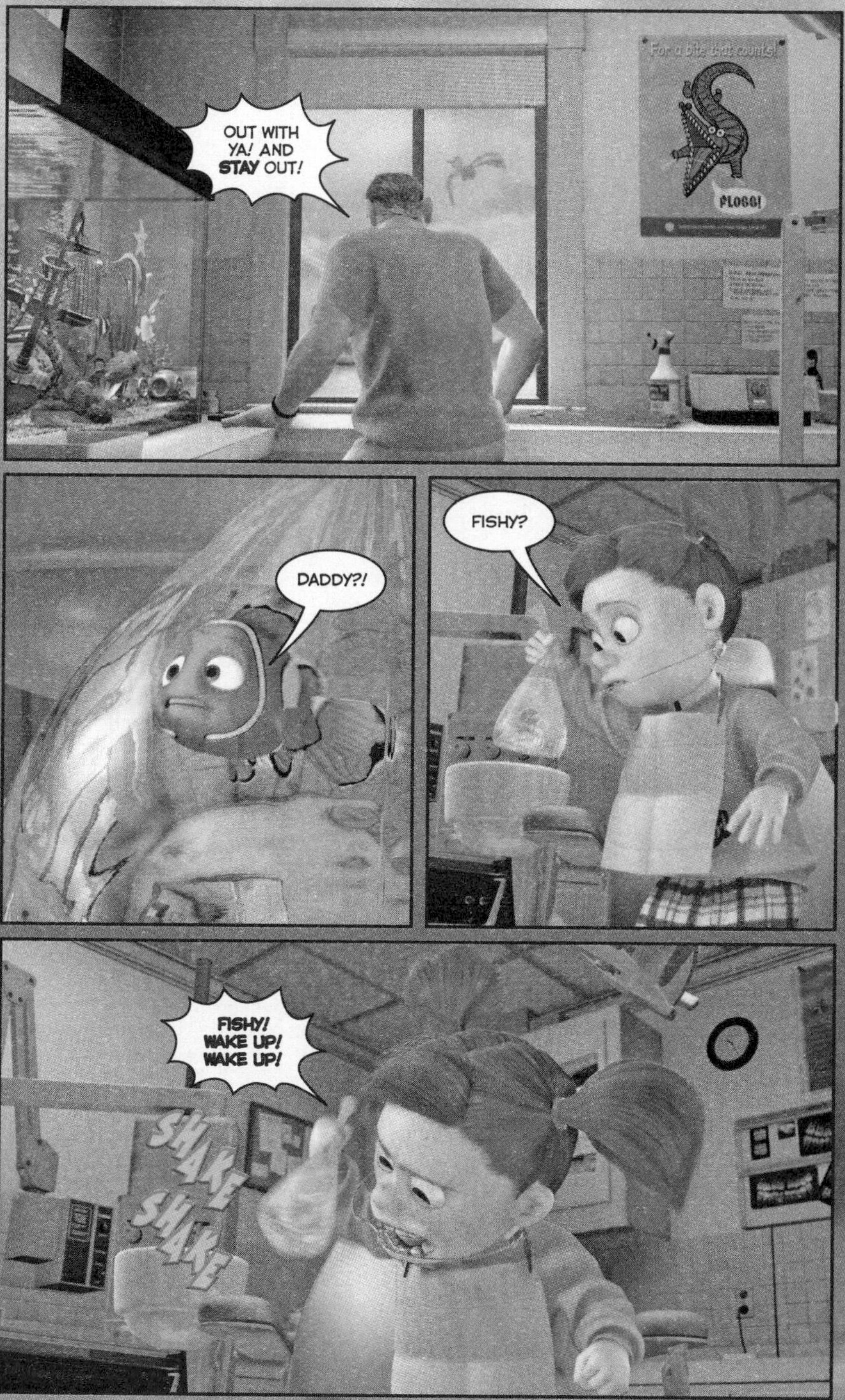
For a bite that counts!
FLOSS!
OUT WITH YA! AND **STAY** OUT!
DADDY?!
FISHY?
FISHY! WAKE UP! WAKE UP!
SHAKE
SHAKE

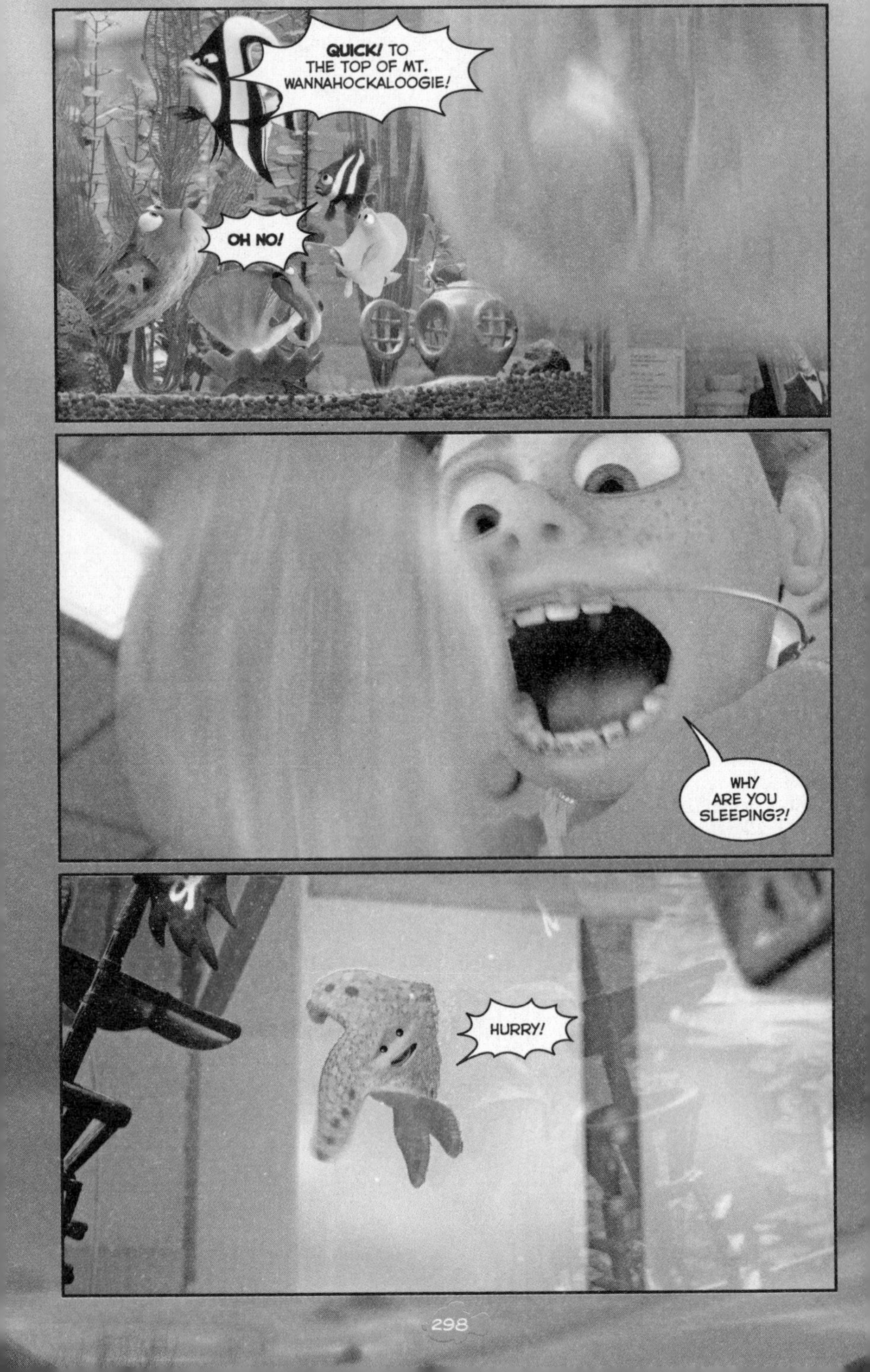
QUICK! TO THE TOP OF MT. WANNAHOCKALOOGIE!
OH NO!
WHY ARE YOU SLEEPING?!
HURRY!

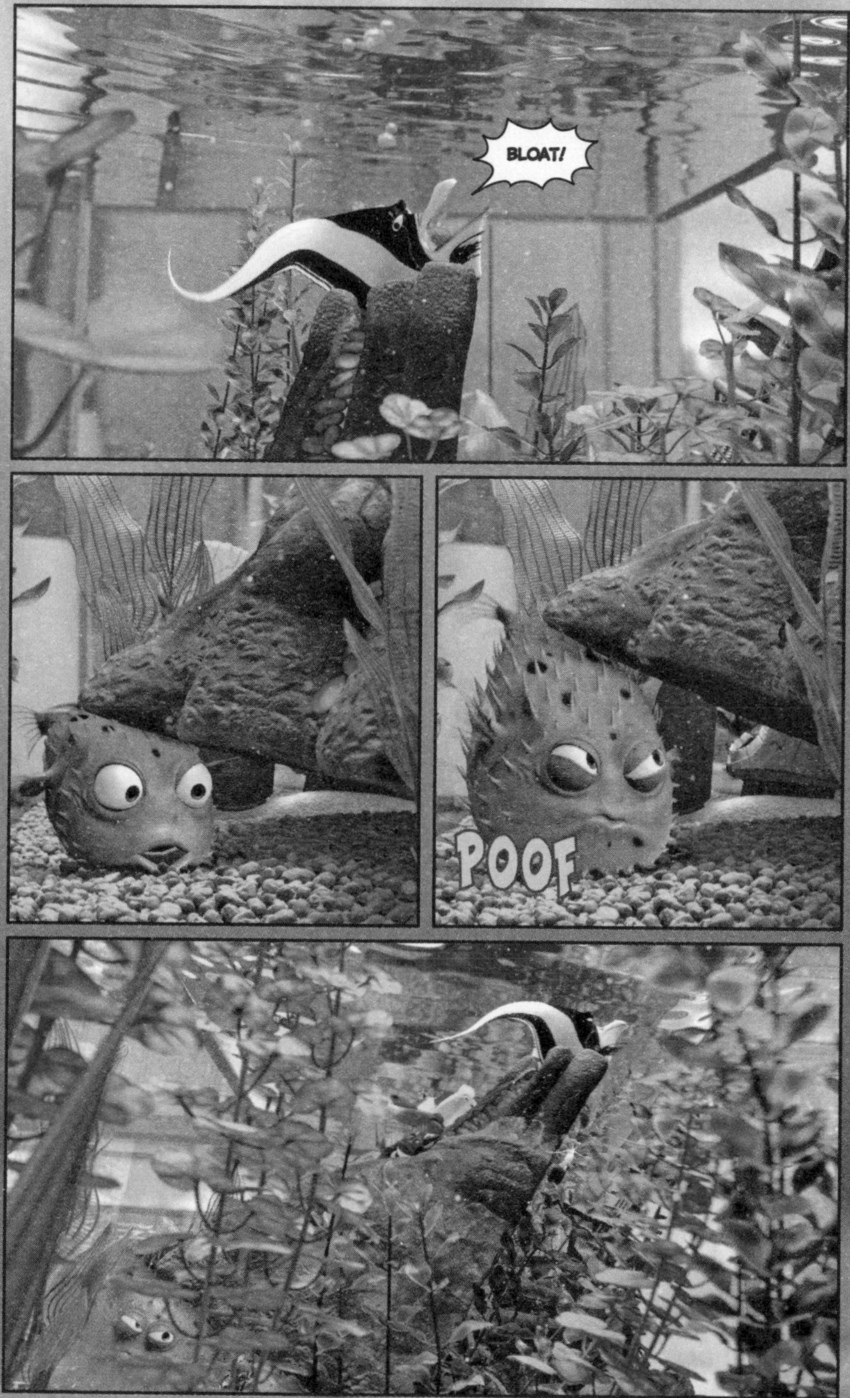
BLOAT!
POOF

RING OF FIRE!

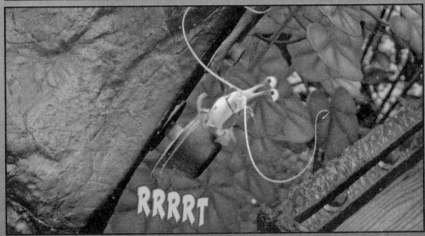

RRRRt

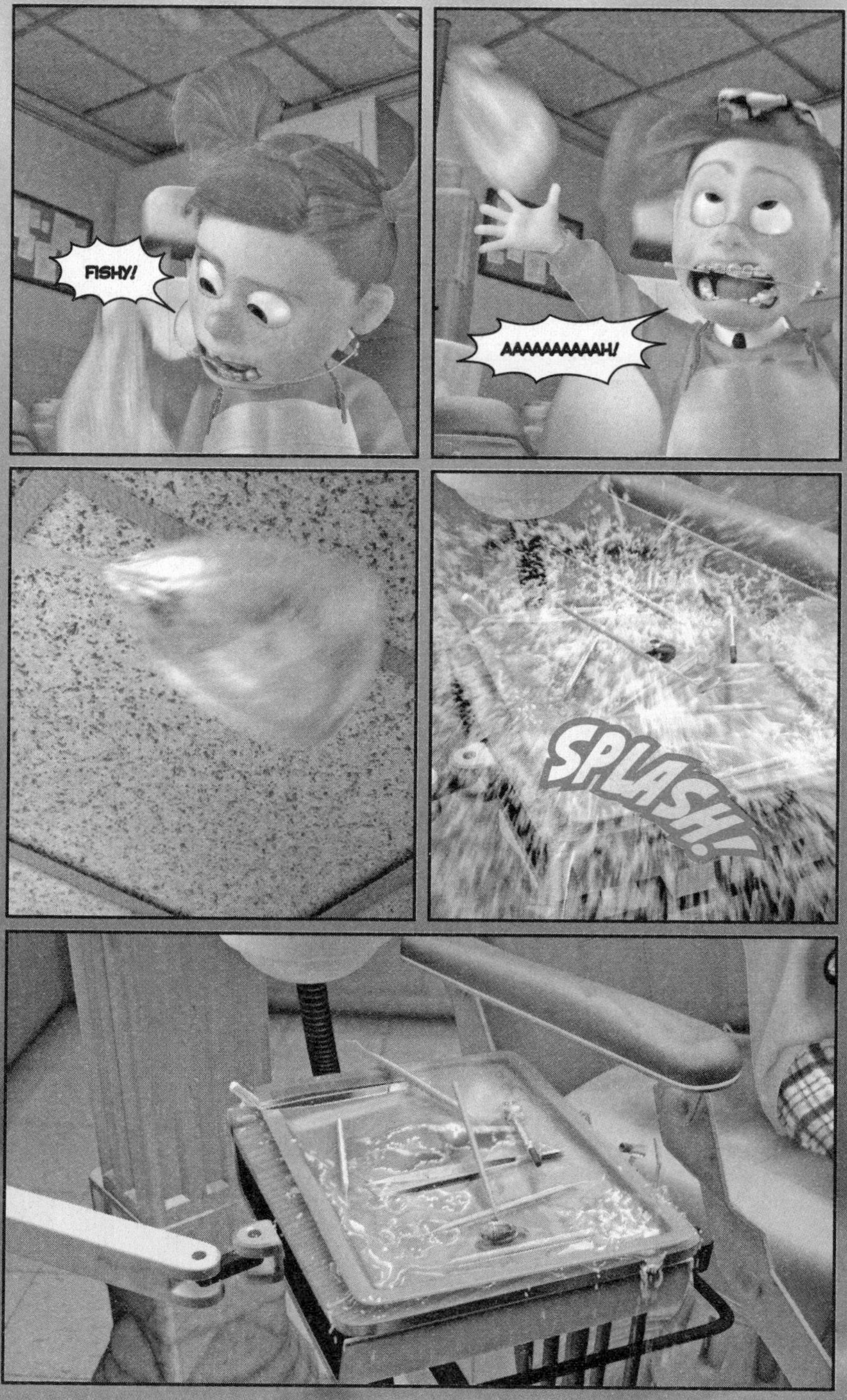
FISHY!
AAAAAAAAAAAH!
SPLASH!

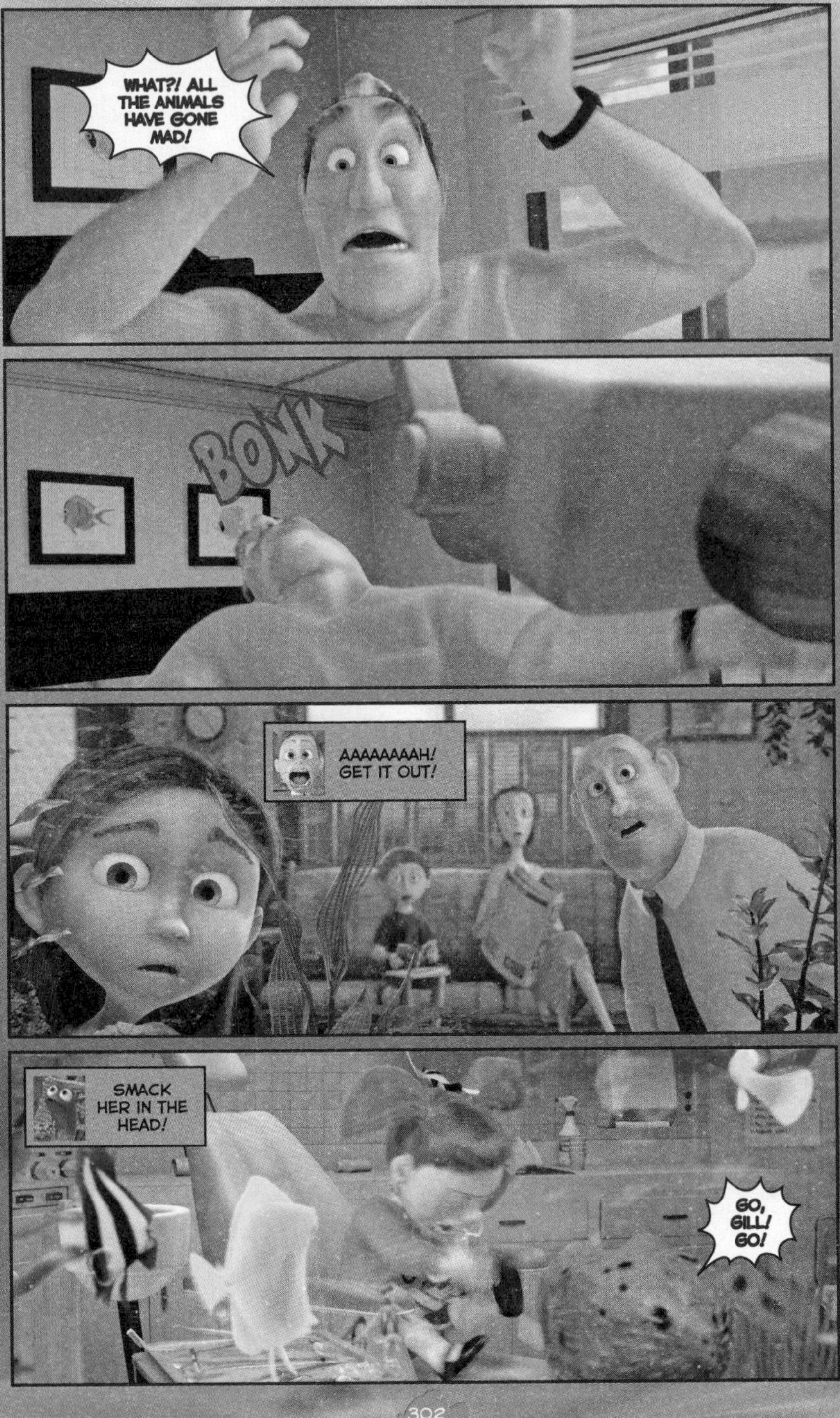
WHAT?! ALL THE ANIMALS HAVE GONE MAD!
BONK
AAAAAAAAH! GET IT OUT!
SMACK HER IN THE HEAD!
GO, GILL! GO!

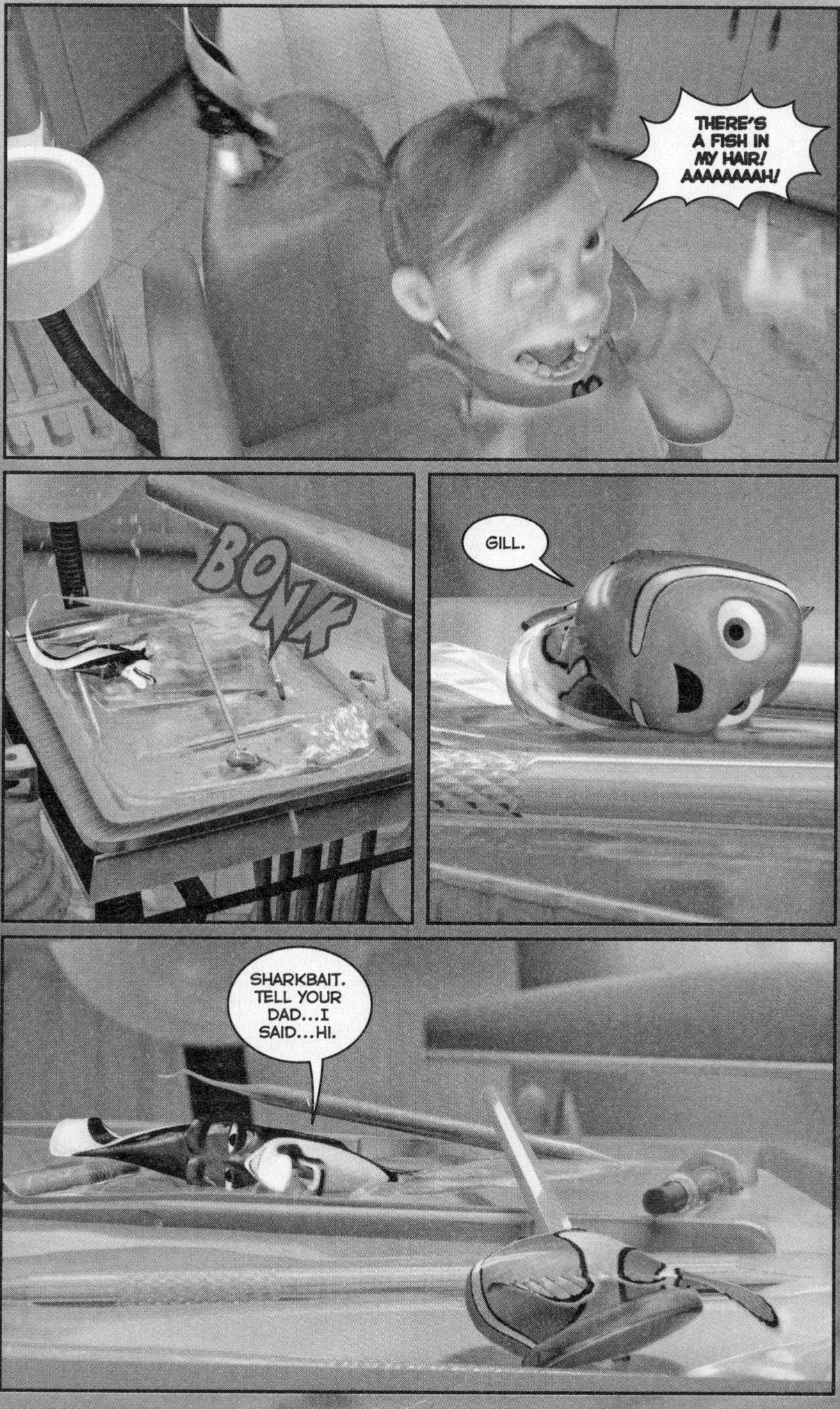

THERE'S A FISH IN MY HAIR! AAAAAAAAH!
BONK
GILL.
SHARKBAIT. TELL YOUR DAD...I SAID...HI.

WITH THAT, GILL LEAPS...

...AND COMES BACK DOWN, LAUNCHING NEMO INTO THE AIR...

...SENDING HIM FLYING INTO THE SINK!

FSSH

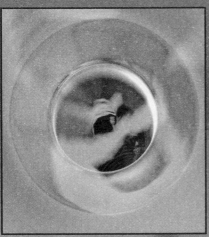

GO GET 'EM.

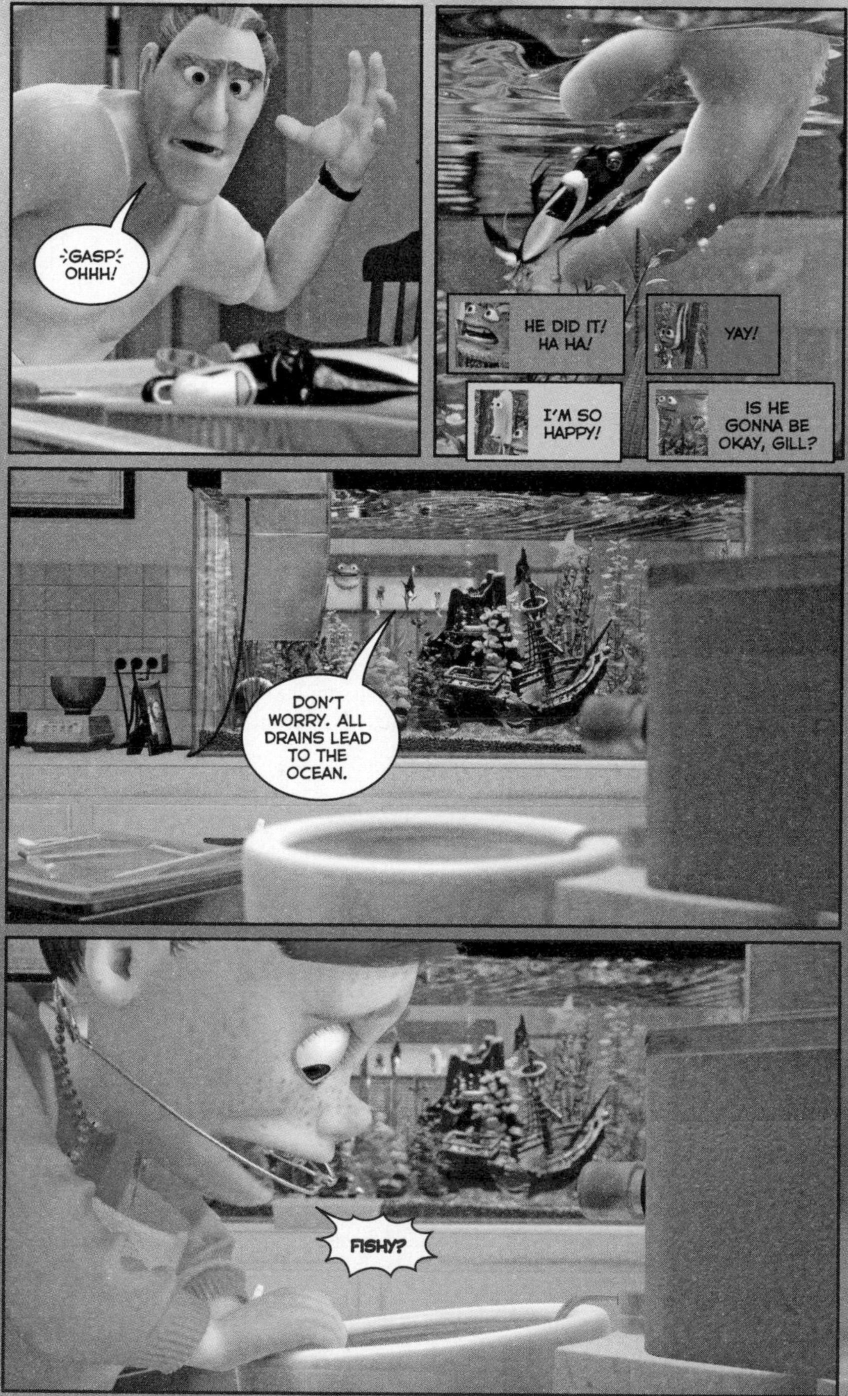

GASP
OHHH!
HE DID IT! HA HA!
YAY!
I'M SO HAPPY!
IS HE GONNA BE OKAY, GILL?
DON'T WORRY. ALL DRAINS LEAD TO THE OCEAN.
FISHY?

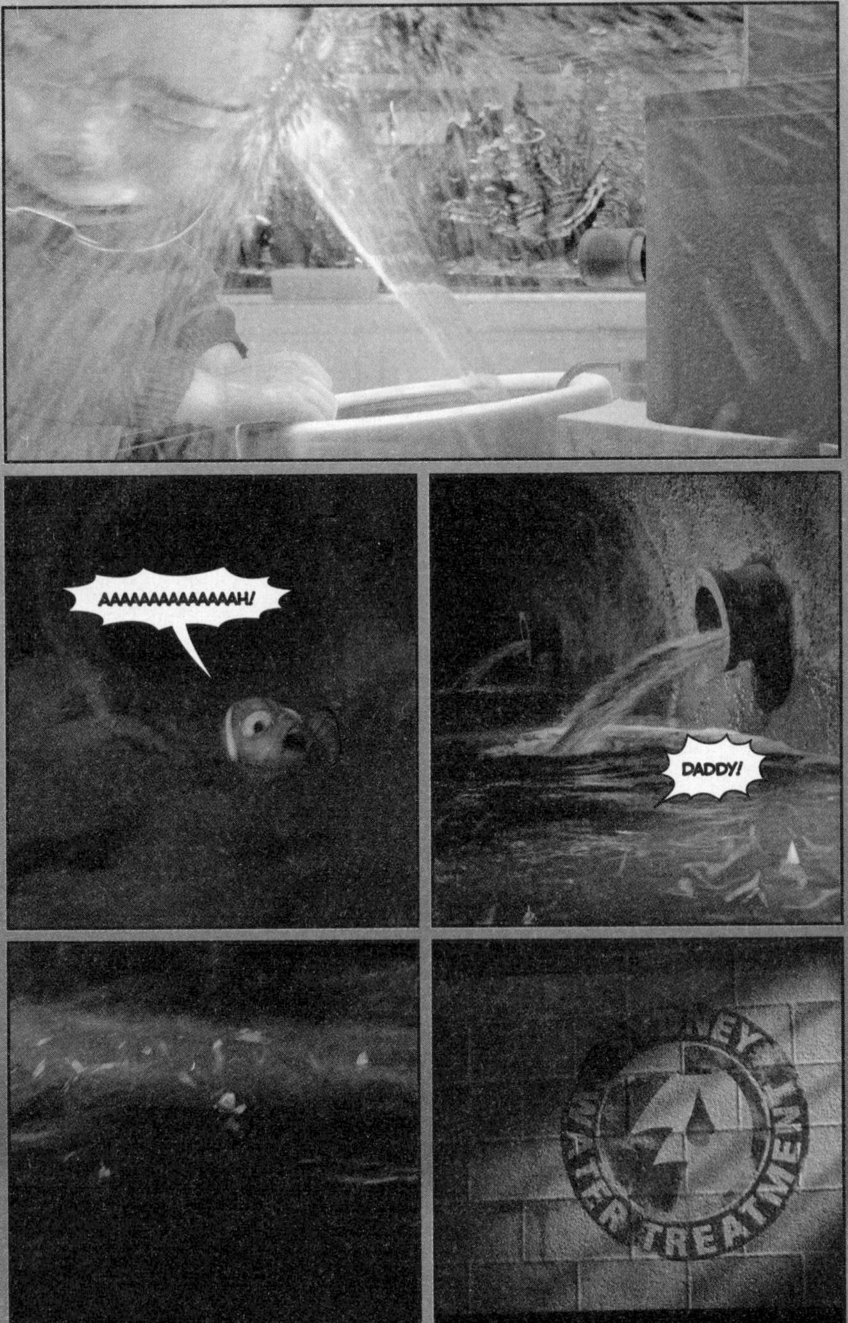
AAAAAAAAAAAAAAH!
DADDY!
WATER TREATMENT

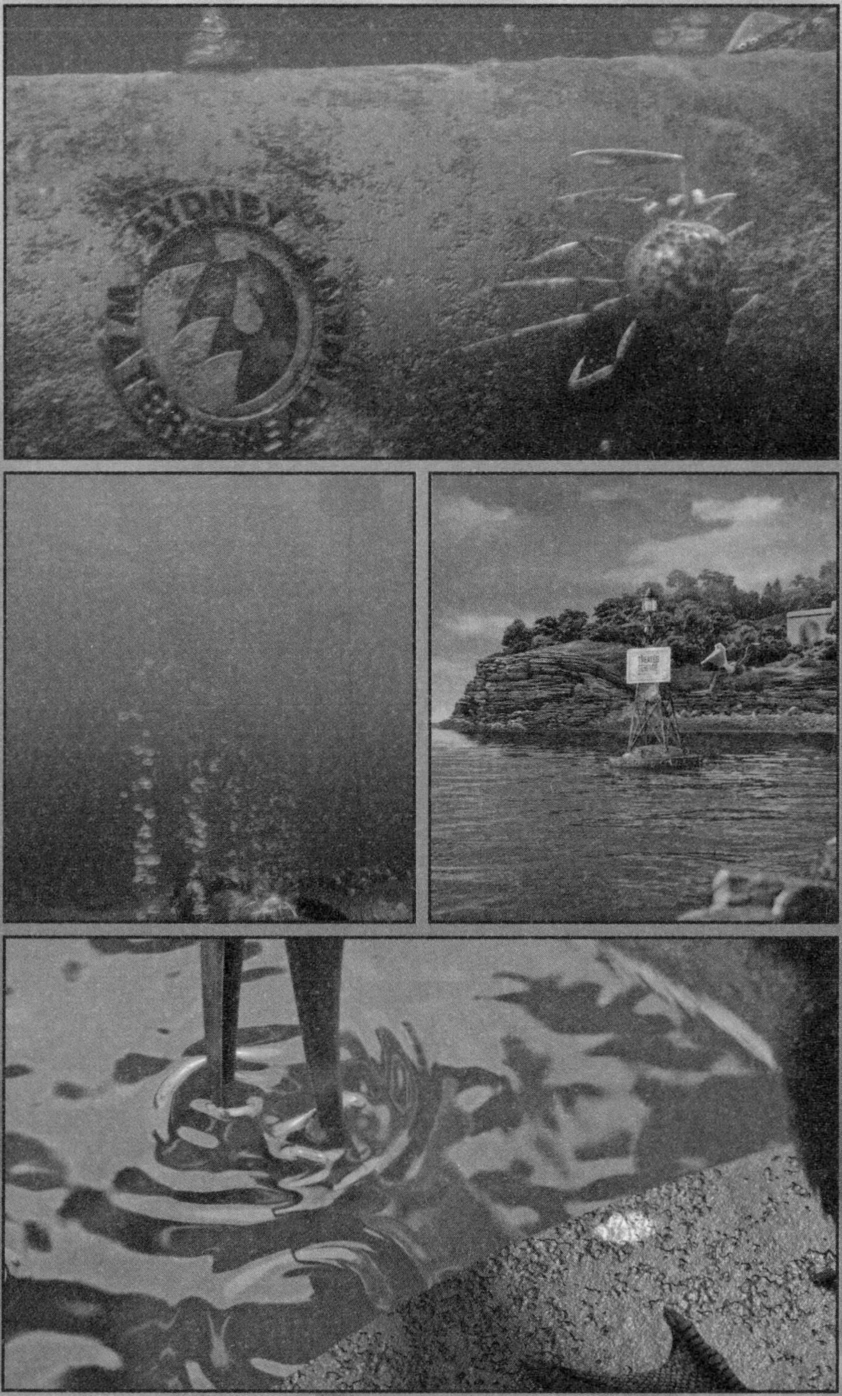
SYDNEY

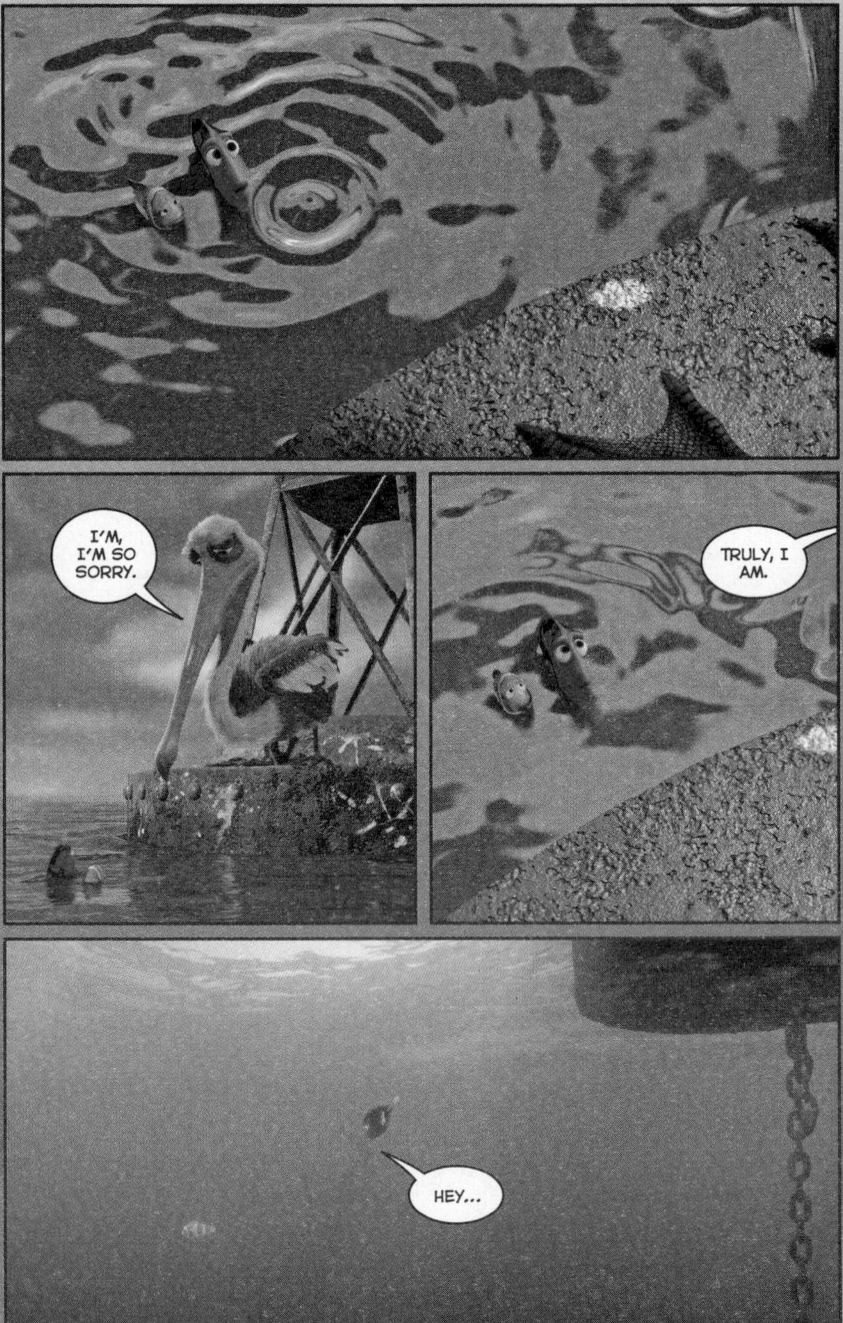
I'M, I'M SO SORRY.
TRULY, I AM.
HEY...

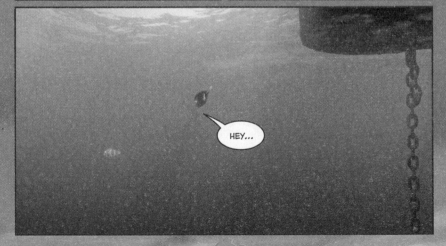

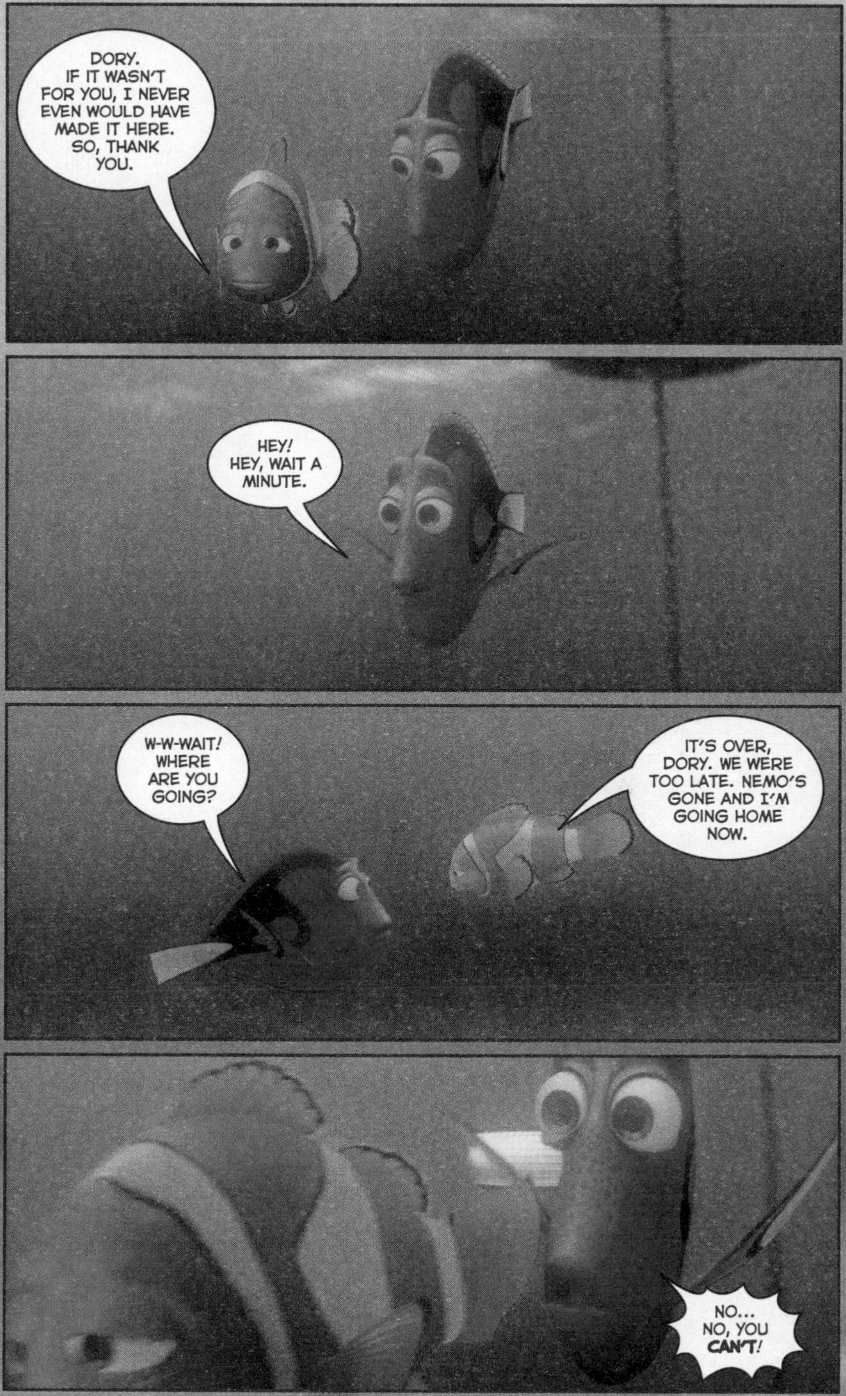
DORY. IF IT WASN'T FOR YOU, I NEVER EVEN WOULD HAVE MADE IT HERE. SO, THANK YOU.
HEY! HEY, WAIT A MINUTE.
W-W-WAIT! WHERE ARE YOU GOING?
IT'S OVER, DORY. WE WERE TOO LATE. NEMO'S GONE AND I'M GOING HOME NOW.
NO... NO, YOU **CAN'T**!

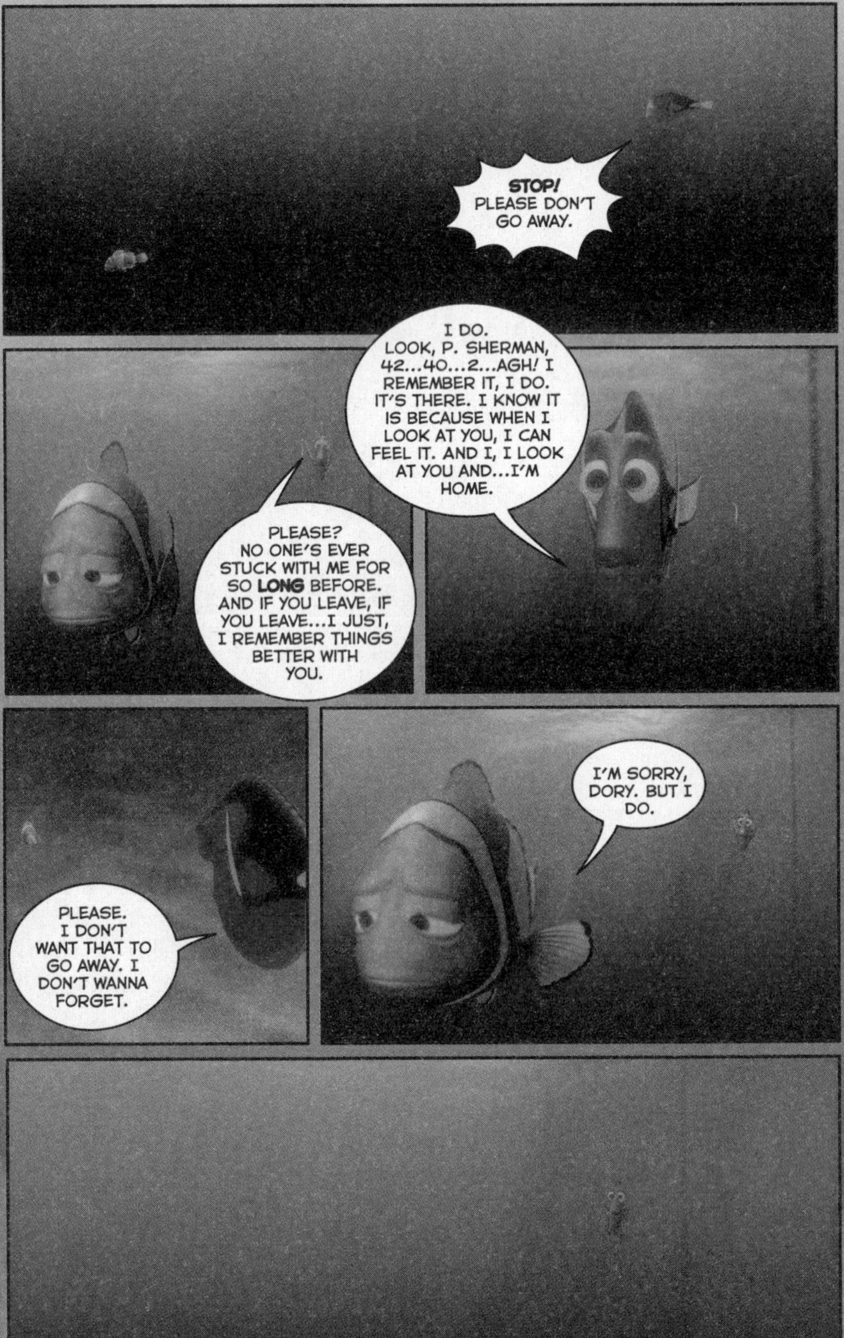
STOP! PLEASE DON'T GO AWAY.
PLEASE? NO ONE'S EVER STUCK WITH ME FOR SO LONG BEFORE. AND IF YOU LEAVE, IF YOU LEAVE...I JUST, I REMEMBER THINGS BETTER WITH YOU.
I DO. LOOK, P. SHERMAN, 42...40...2...AGH! I REMEMBER IT, I DO. IT'S THERE. I KNOW IT IS BECAUSE WHEN I LOOK AT YOU, I CAN FEEL IT. AND I, I LOOK AT YOU AND...I'M HOME.
PLEASE. I DON'T WANT THAT TO GO AWAY. I DON'T WANNA FORGET.
I'M SORRY, DORY. BUT I DO.

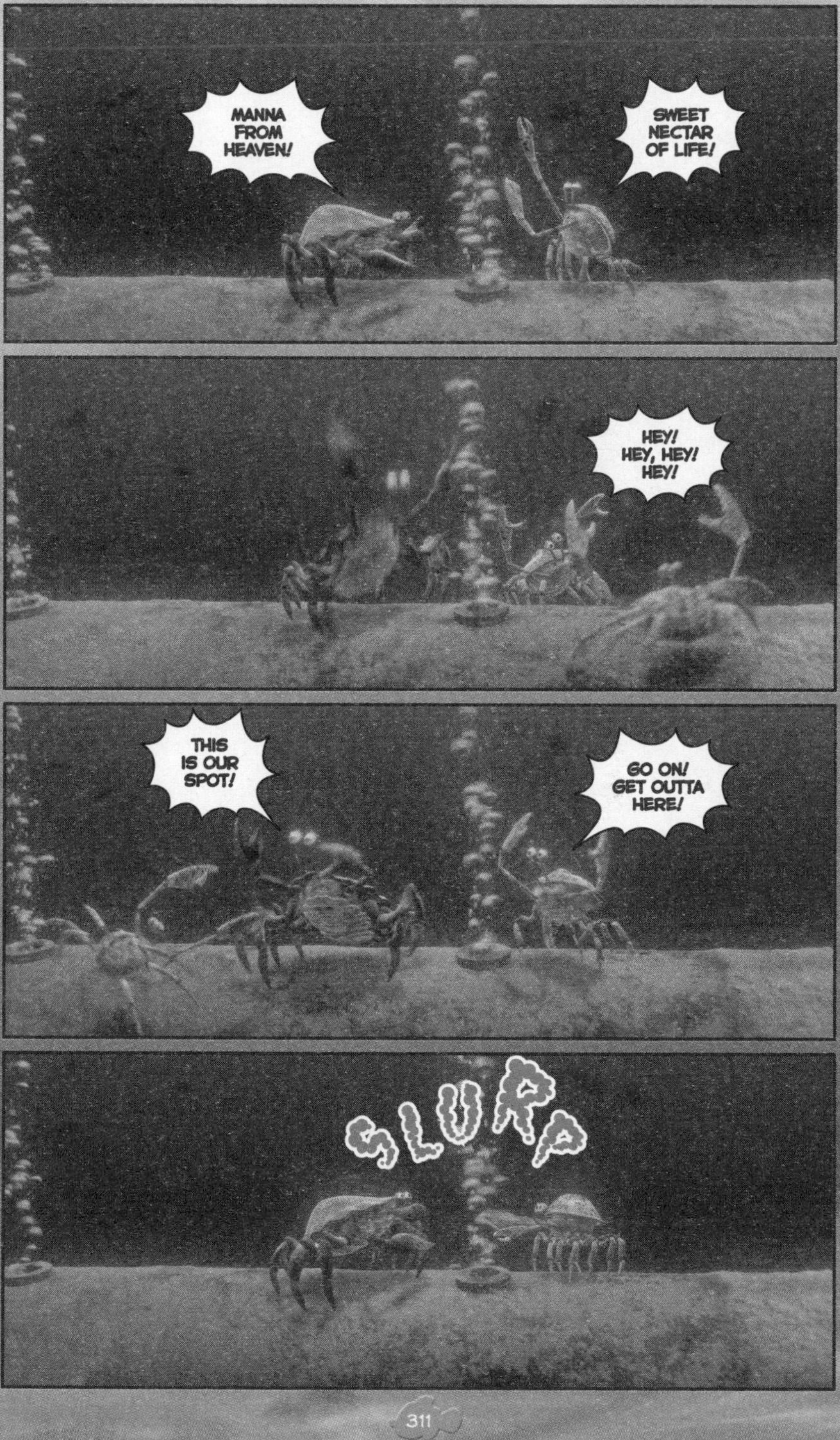
MANNA FROM HEAVEN!
SWEET NECTAR OF LIFE!
HEY! HEY, HEY! HEY!
THIS IS OUR SPOT!
GO ON! GET OUTTA HERE!
SLURP

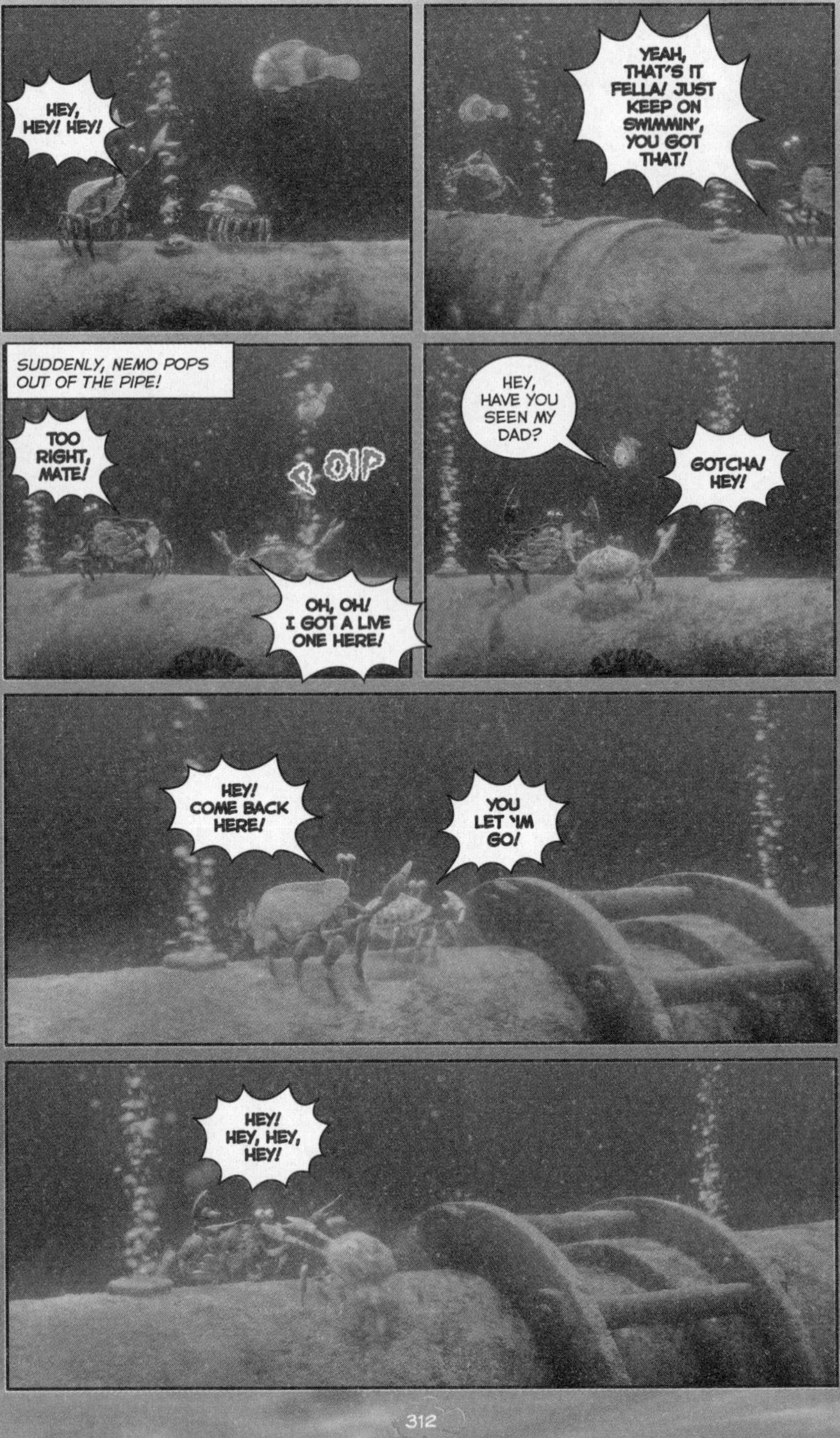
HEY, HEY! HEY!
YEAH, THAT'S IT FELLA! JUST KEEP ON SWIMMIN', YOU GOT THAT!
SUDDENLY, NEMO POPS OUT OF THE PIPE!
TOO RIGHT, MATE!
POIP
OH, OH! I GOT A LIVE ONE HERE!
HEY, HAVE YOU SEEN MY DAD?
GOTCHA! HEY!
HEY! COME BACK HERE!
YOU LET 'IM GO!
HEY! HEY, HEY, HEY!

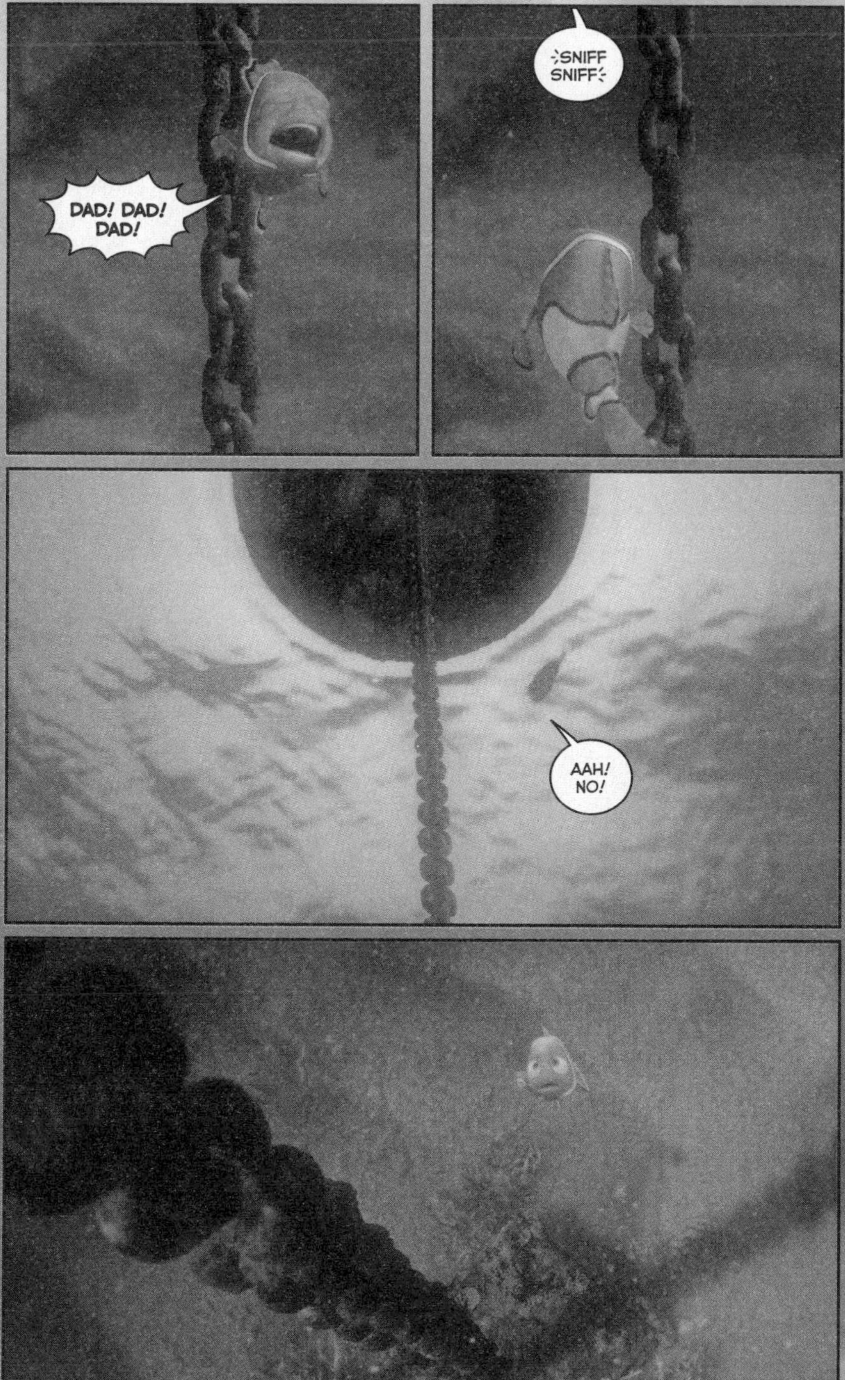
DAD! DAD! DAD!
SNIFF SNIFF
AAH! NO!

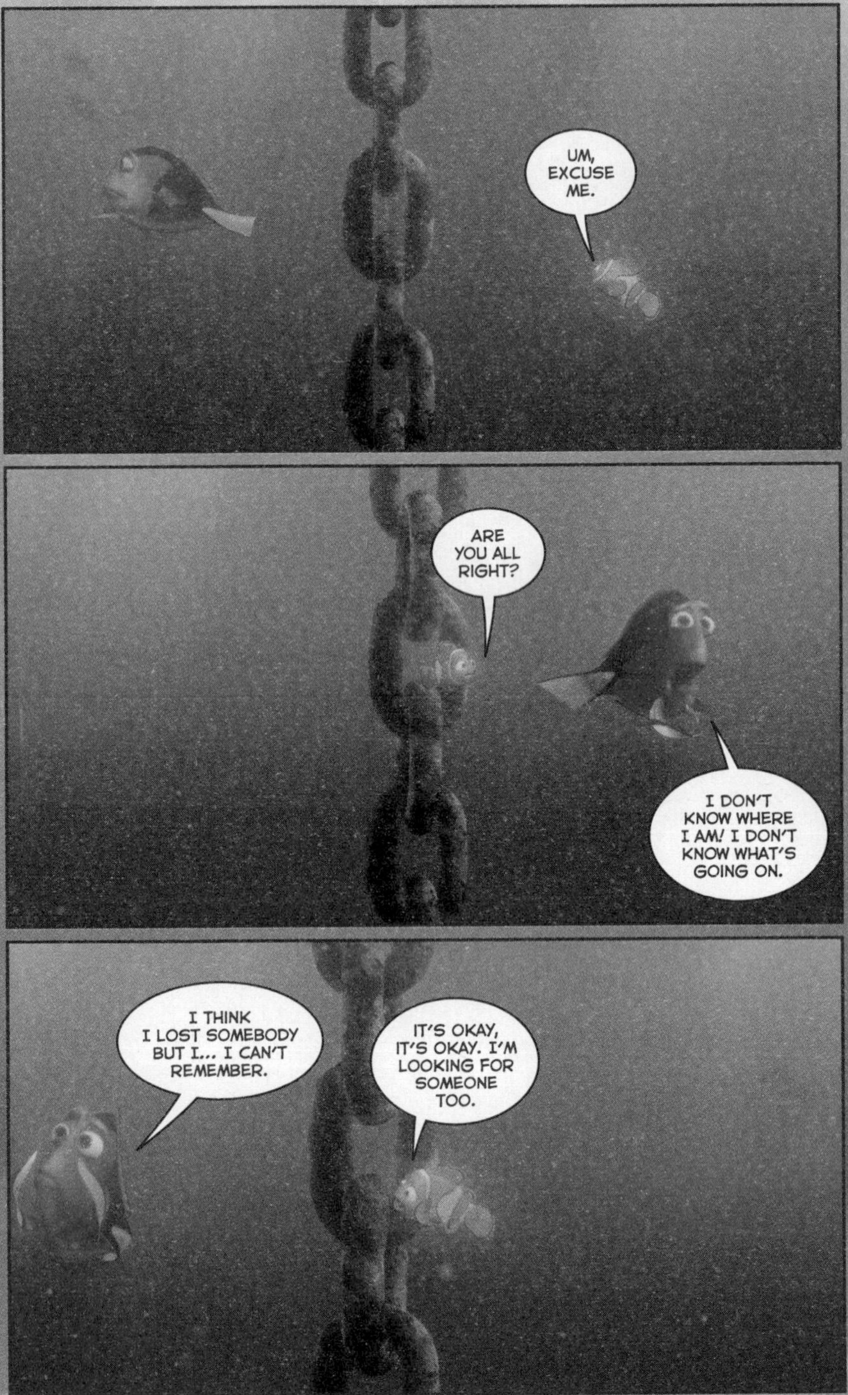
UM, EXCUSE ME.
ARE YOU ALL RIGHT?
I DON'T KNOW WHERE I AM! I DON'T KNOW WHAT'S GOING ON.
I THINK I LOST SOMEBODY BUT I... I CAN'T REMEMBER.
IT'S OKAY, IT'S OKAY. I'M LOOKING FOR SOMEONE TOO.

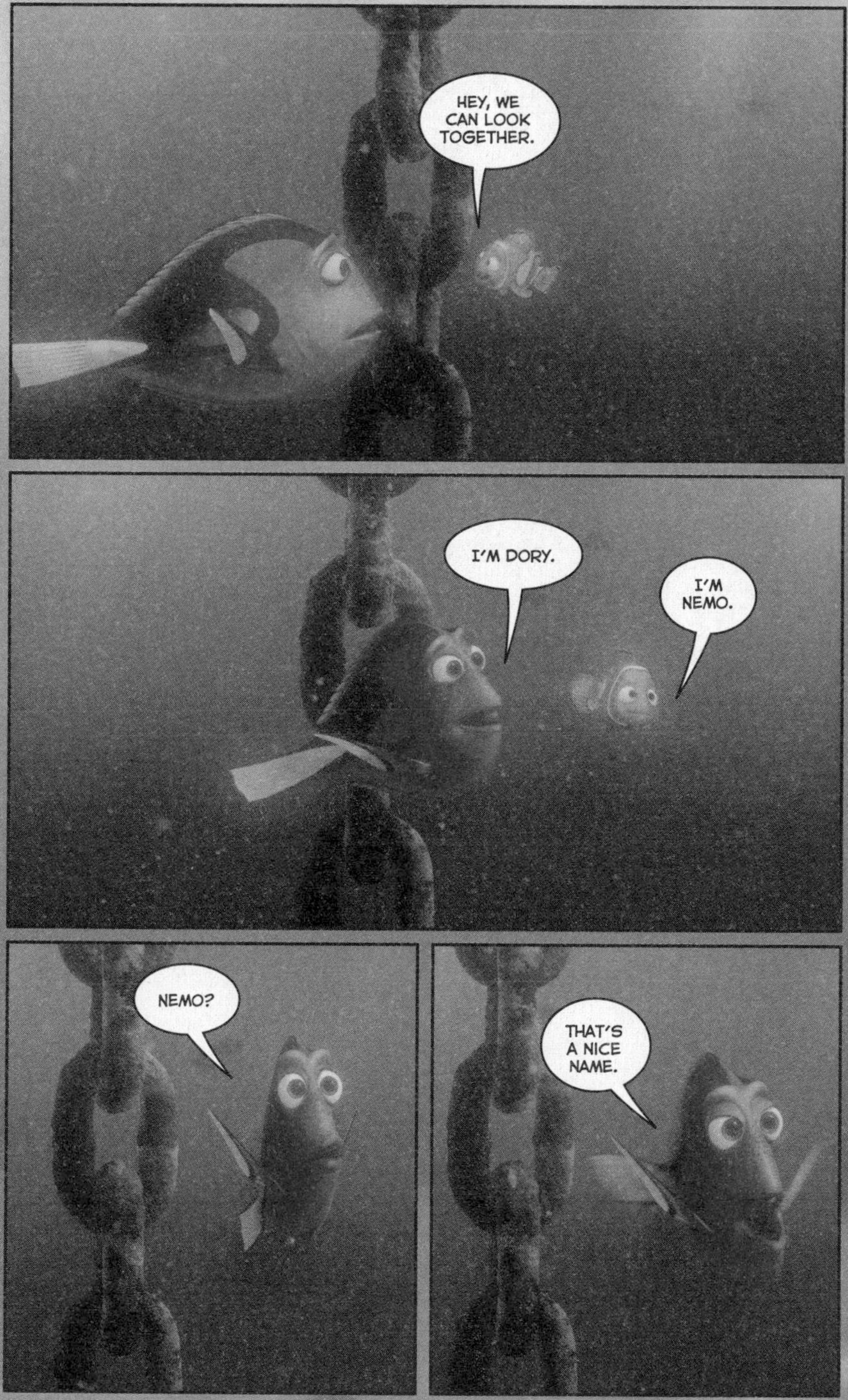
HEY, WE CAN LOOK TOGETHER.
I'M DORY.
I'M NEMO.
NEMO?
THAT'S A NICE NAME.

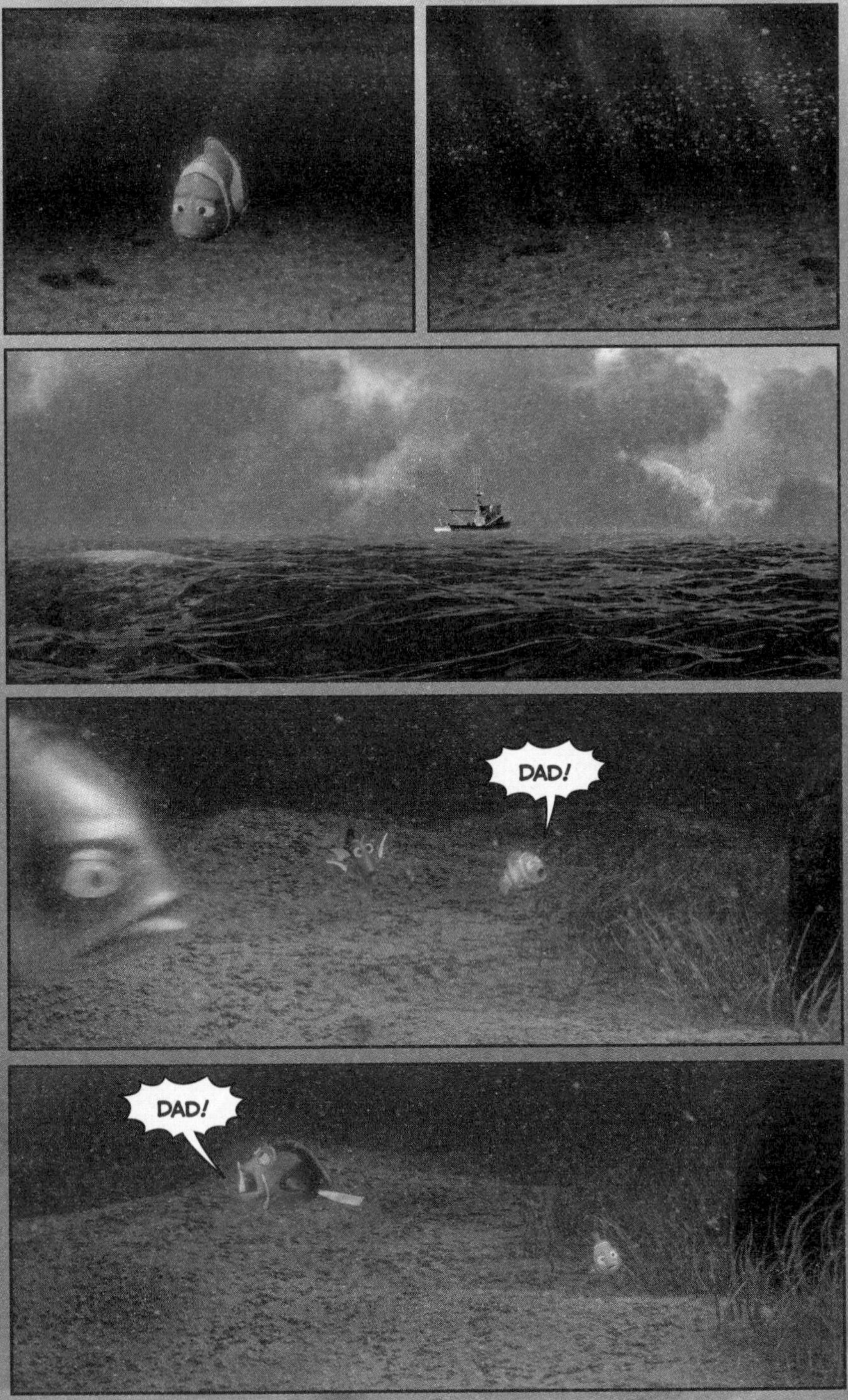
DAD!
DAD!

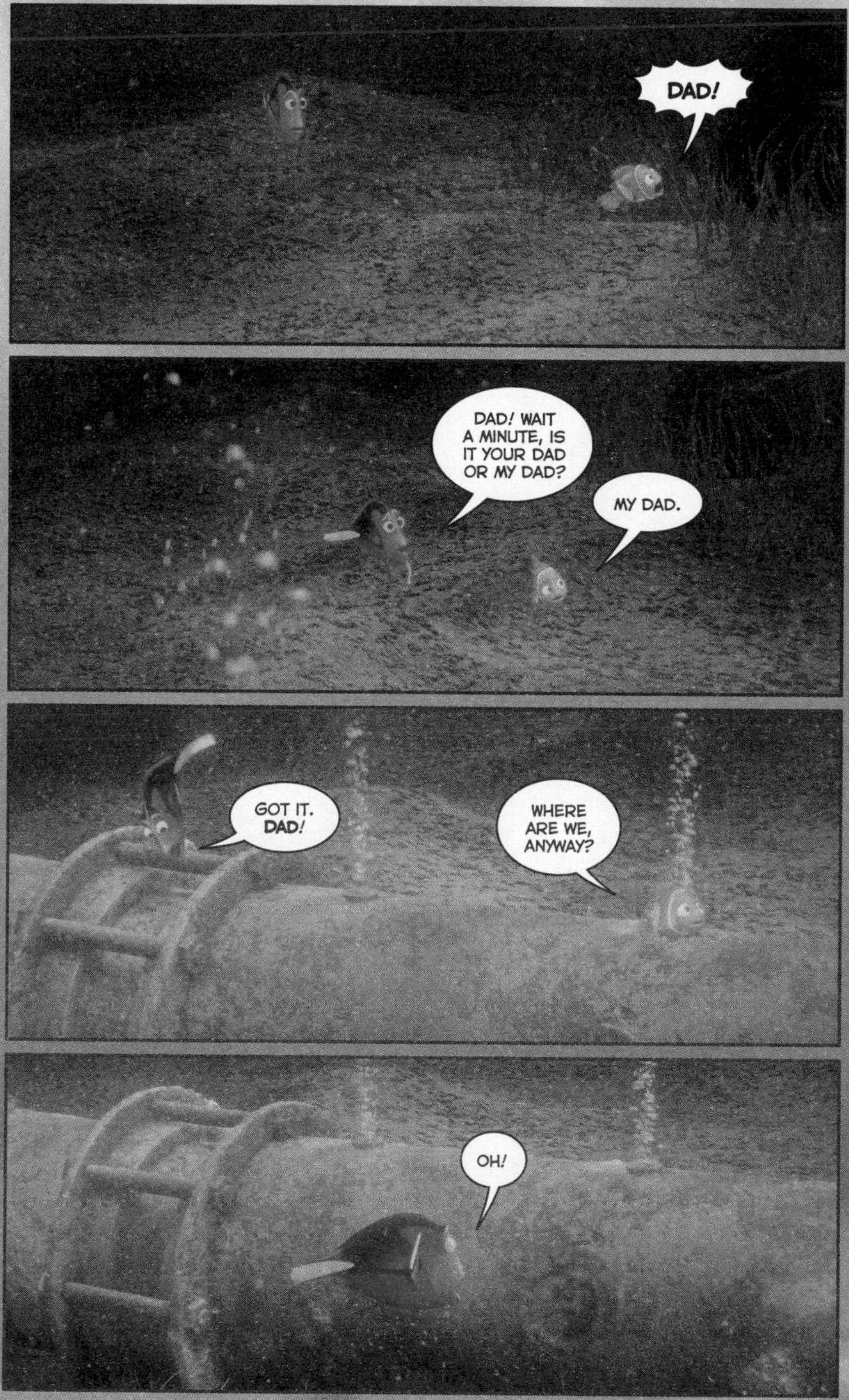
DAD!
DAD! WAIT A MINUTE, IS IT YOUR DAD OR MY DAD?
MY DAD.
GOT IT. **DAD!**
WHERE ARE WE, ANYWAY?
OH!

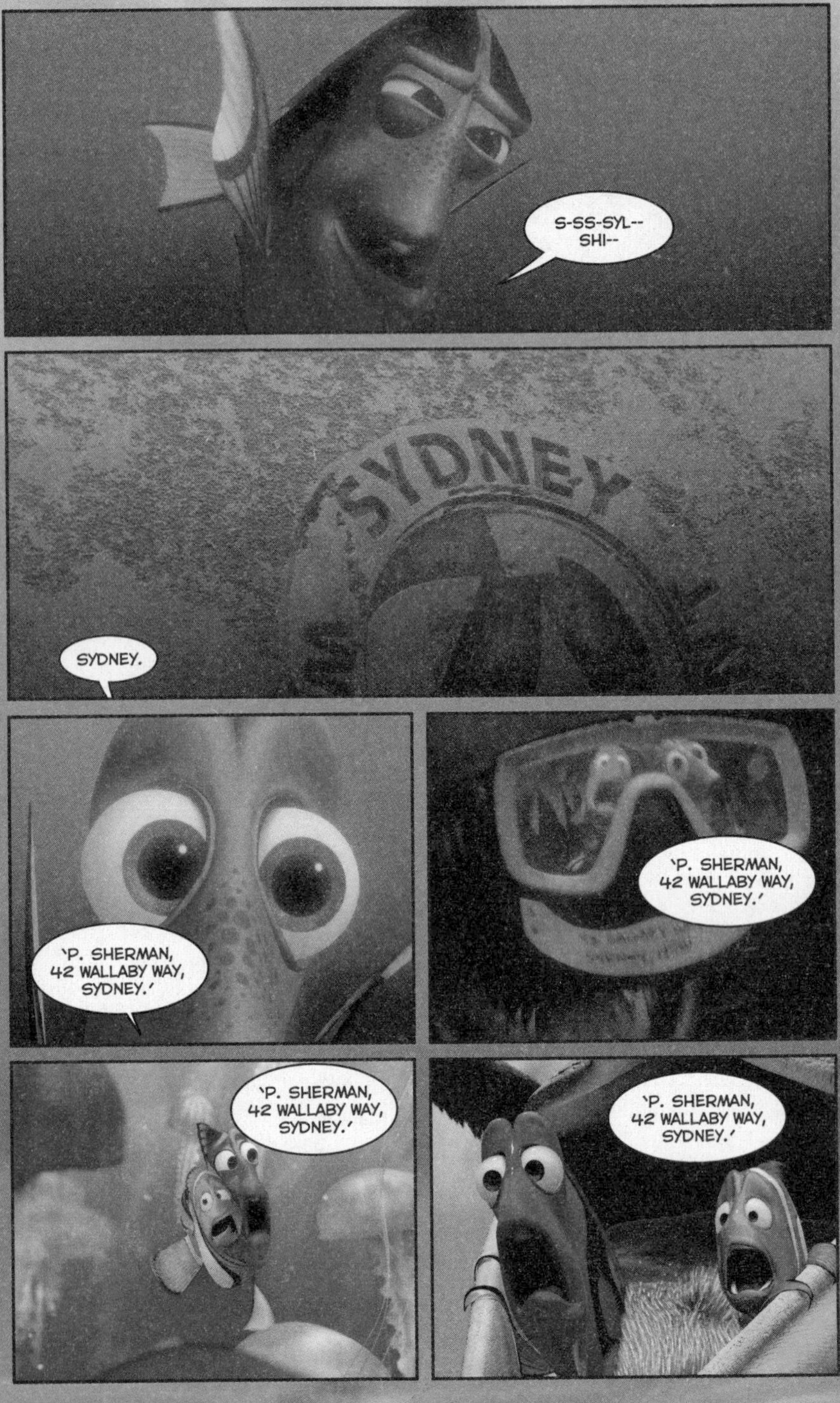
S-SS-SYL--
SHI--
SYDNEY
SYDNEY.
'P. SHERMAN,
42 WALLABY WAY,
SYDNEY.'
'P. SHERMAN,
42 WALLABY WAY,
SYDNEY.'
'P. SHERMAN,
42 WALLABY WAY,
SYDNEY.'
'P. SHERMAN,
42 WALLABY WAY,
SYDNEY.'

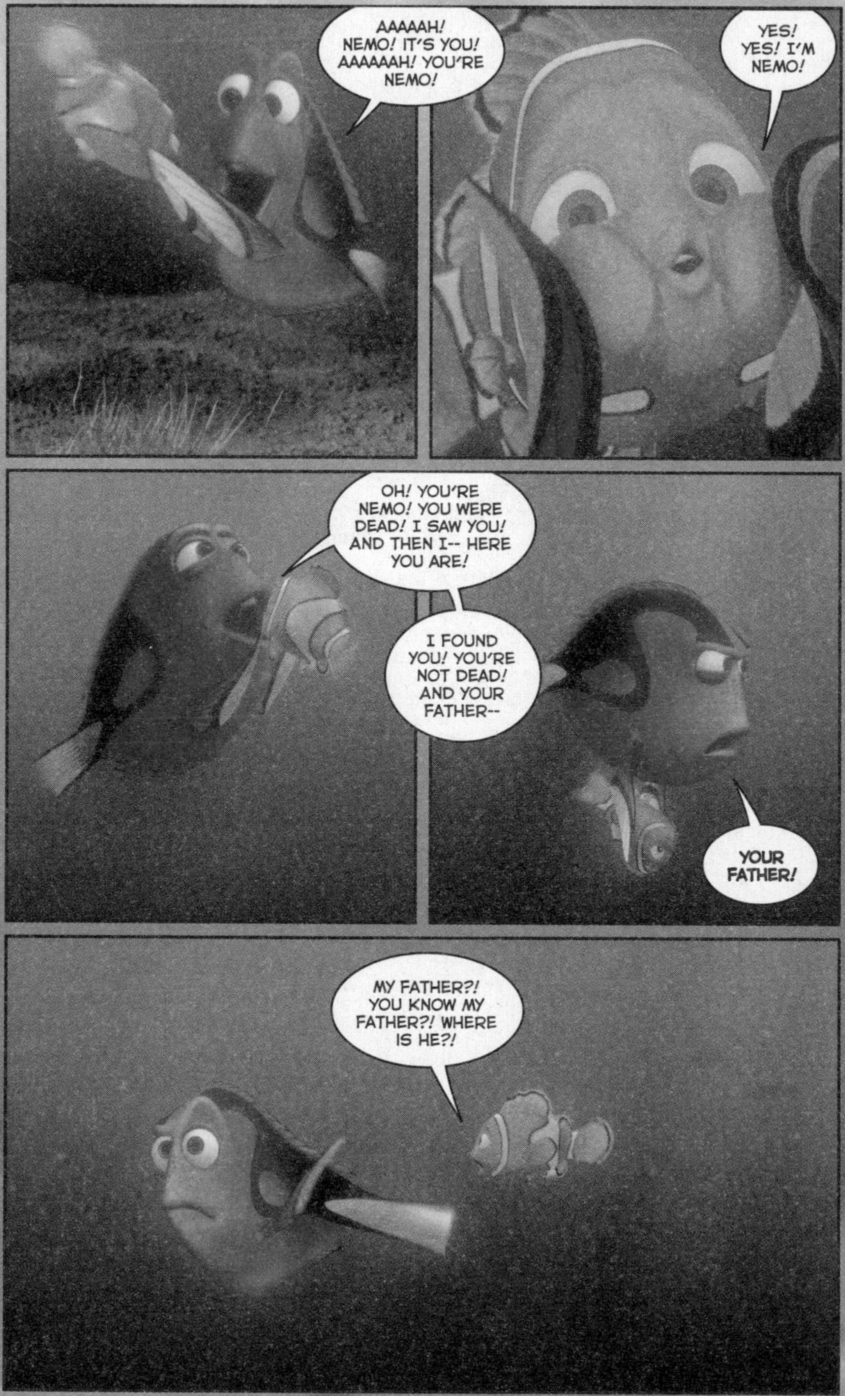
AAAAAH! NEMO! IT'S YOU! AAAAAAH! YOU'RE NEMO!
YES! YES! I'M NEMO!
OH! YOU'RE NEMO! YOU WERE DEAD! I SAW YOU! AND THEN I-- HERE YOU ARE!
I FOUND YOU! YOU'RE NOT DEAD! AND YOUR FATHER--
YOUR FATHER!
MY FATHER?! YOU KNOW MY FATHER?! WHERE IS HE?!

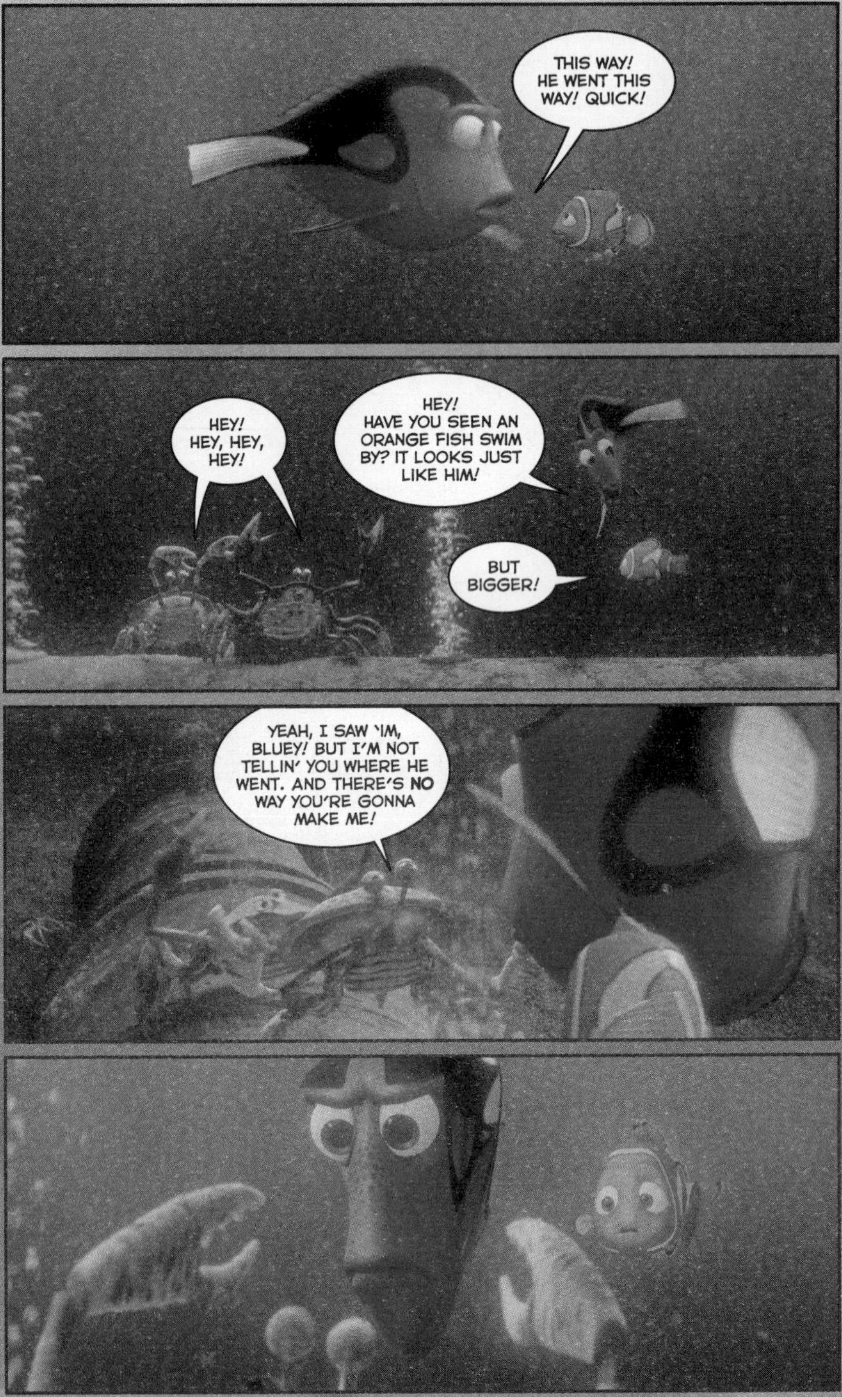
THIS WAY! HE WENT THIS WAY! QUICK!
HEY! HEY, HEY, HEY!
HEY! HAVE YOU SEEN AN ORANGE FISH SWIM BY? IT LOOKS JUST LIKE HIM!
BUT BIGGER!
YEAH, I SAW 'IM, BLUEY! BUT I'M NOT TELLIN' YOU WHERE HE WENT. AND THERE'S **NO** WAY YOU'RE GONNA MAKE ME!

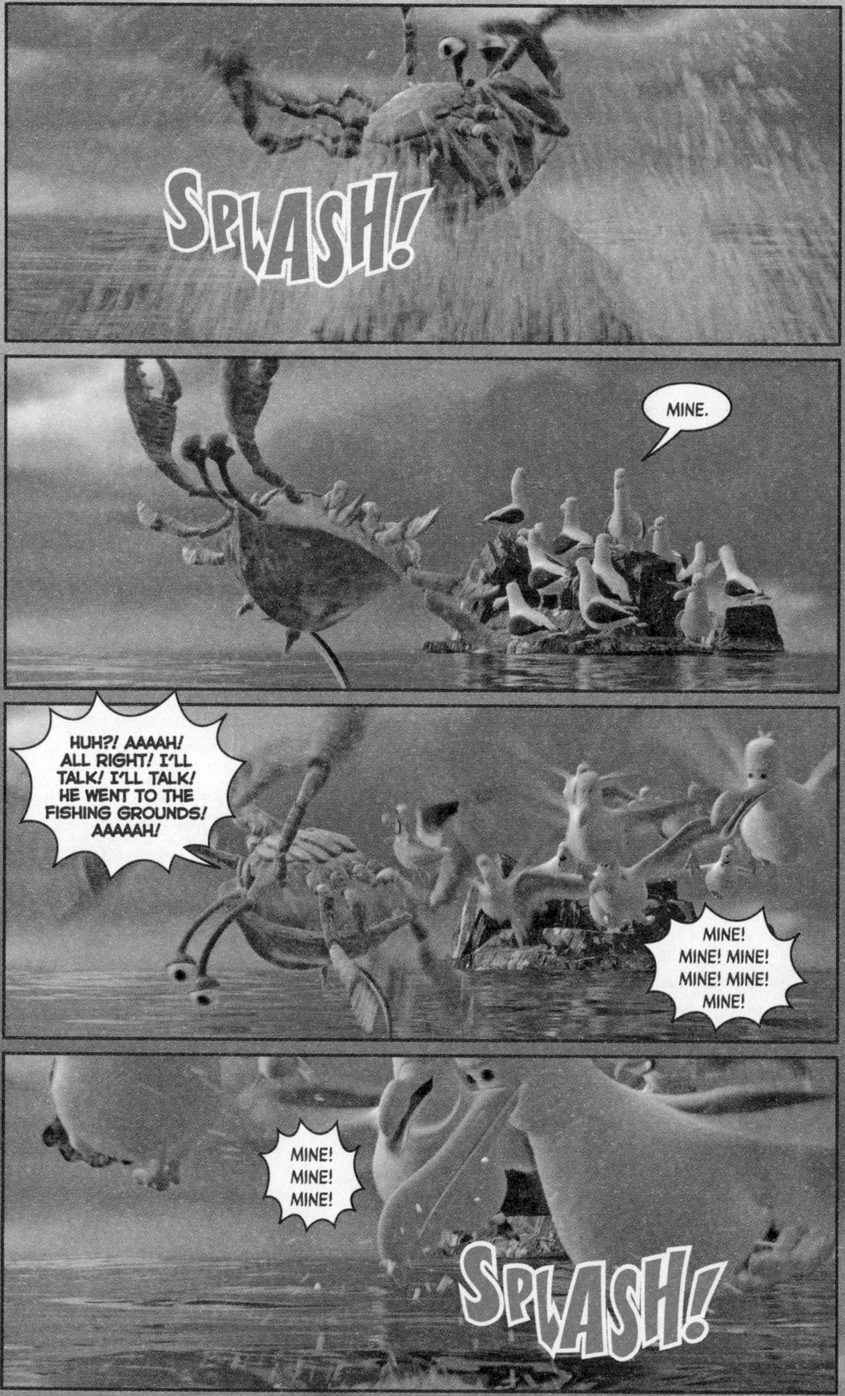
SPLASH!
MINE.
HUH?! AAAAH! ALL RIGHT! I'LL TALK! I'LL TALK! HE WENT TO THE FISHING GROUNDS! AAAAAH!
MINE! MINE! MINE! MINE! MINE! MINE!
MINE! MINE! MINE!
SPLASH!

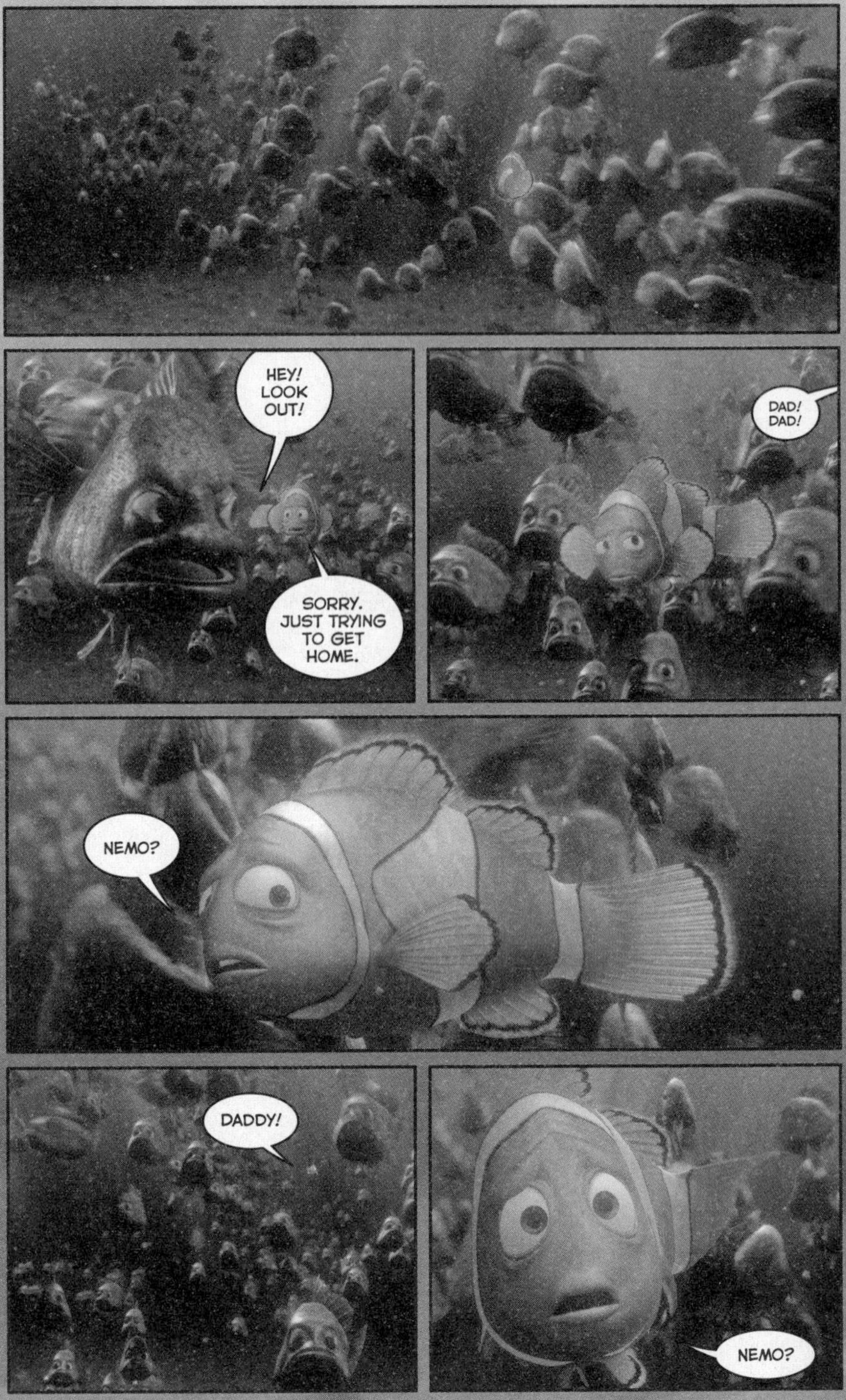
HEY! LOOK OUT!
SORRY. JUST TRYING TO GET HOME.
DAD! DAD!
NEMO?
DADDY!
NEMO?

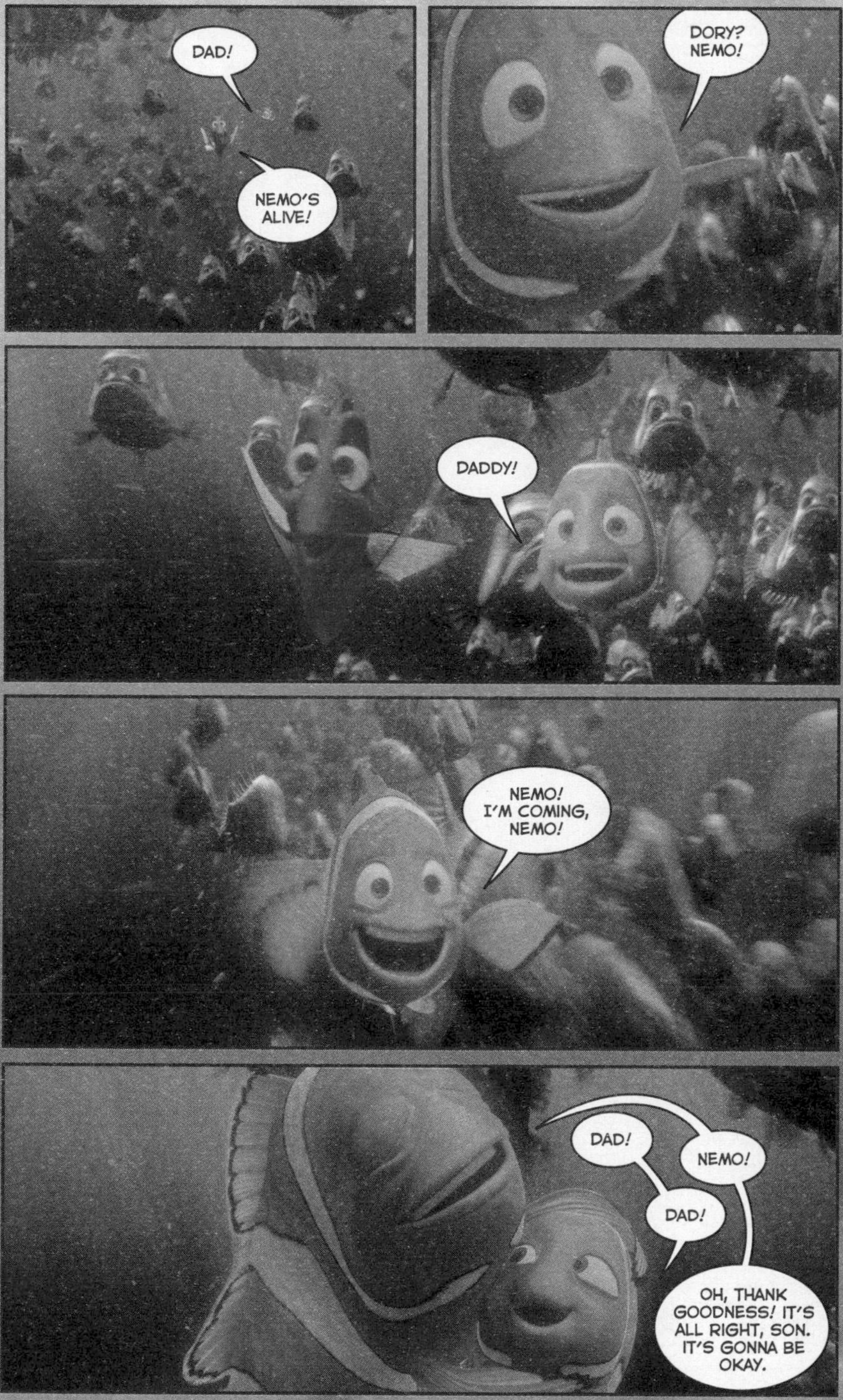
DAD!
NEMO'S ALIVE!
DORY? NEMO!
DADDY!
NEMO! I'M COMING, NEMO!
DAD!
NEMO!
DAD!
OH, THANK GOODNESS! IT'S ALL RIGHT, SON. IT'S GONNA BE OKAY.

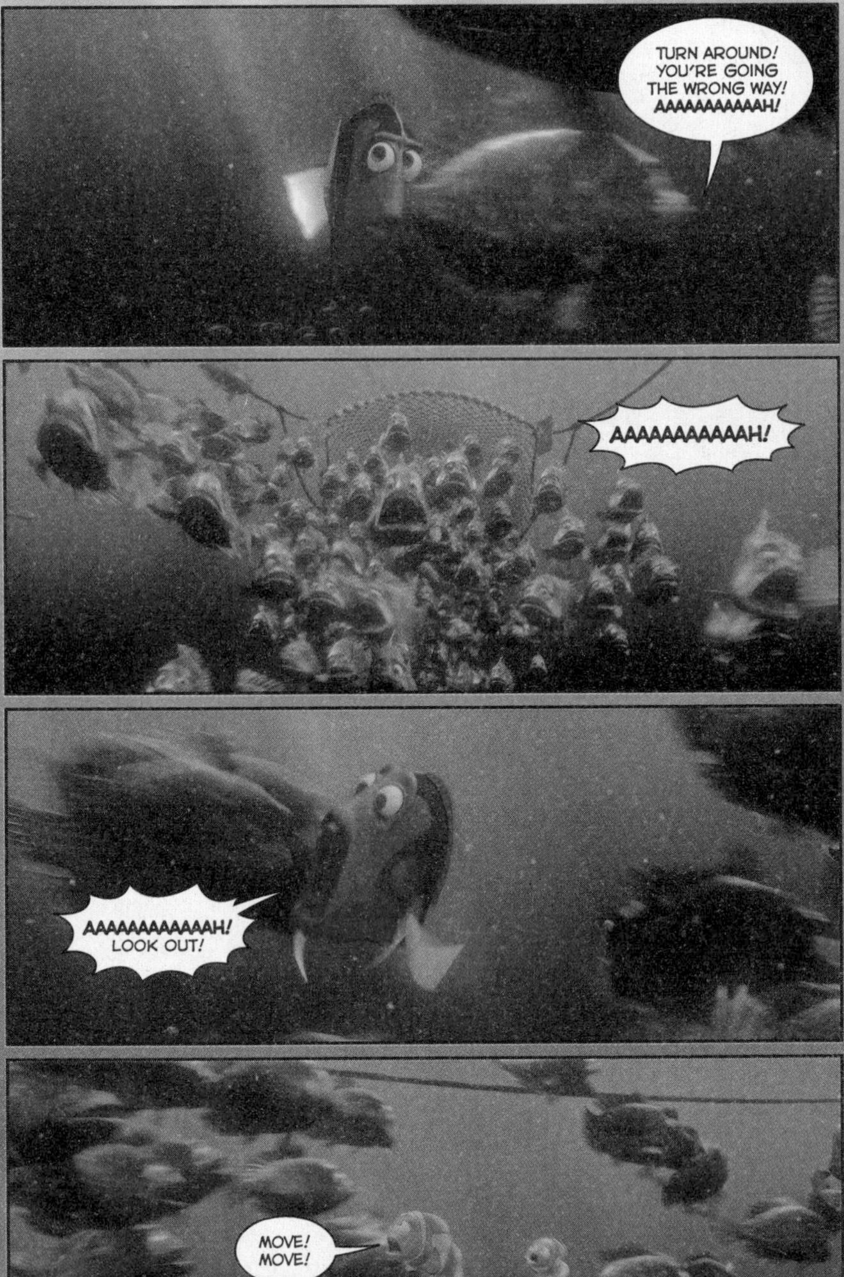
TURN AROUND!
YOU'RE GOING
THE WRONG WAY!
AAAAAAAAAAAH!
AAAAAAAAAAAAH!
AAAAAAAAAAAAH!
LOOK OUT!
MOVE!
MOVE!

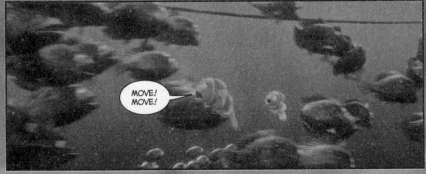

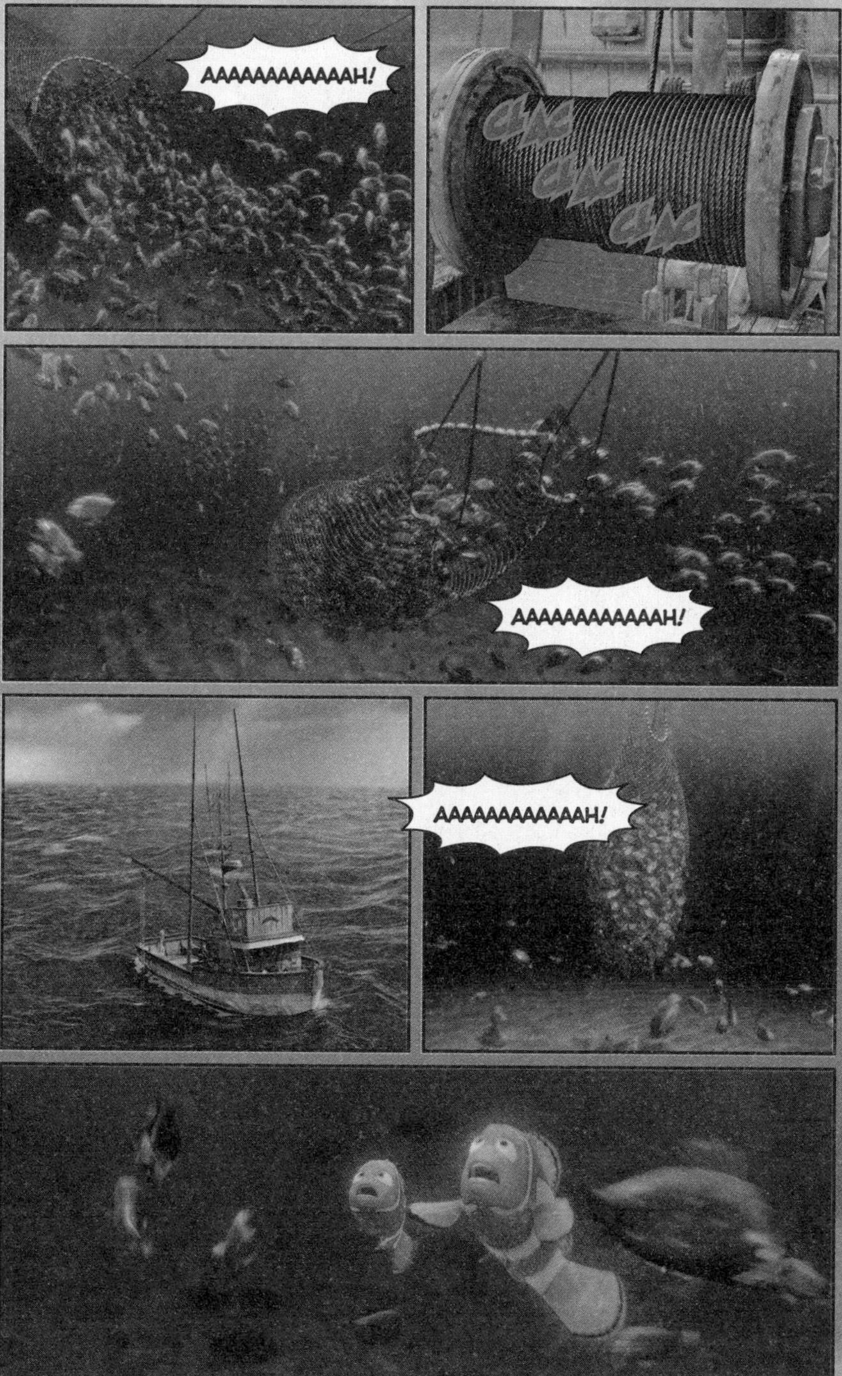
AAAAAAAAAAAAAH!
AAAAAAAAAAAAAH!
AAAAAAAAAAAAAH!

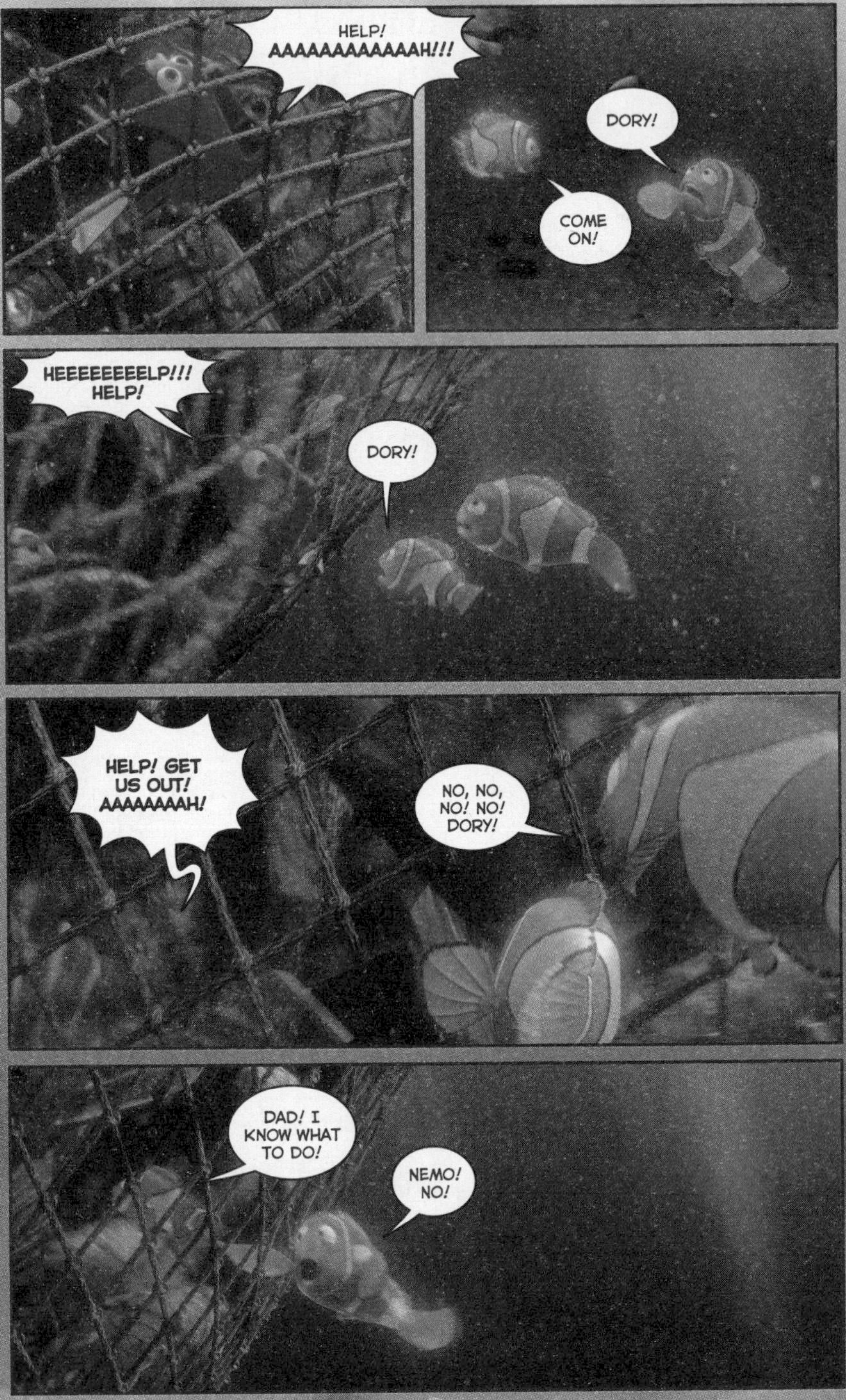
HELP! AAAAAAAAAAAAAH!!!
DORY!
COME ON!
HEEEEEEEELP!!! HELP!
DORY!
HELP! GET US OUT! AAAAAAAAH!
NO, NO, NO! NO! DORY!
DAD! I KNOW WHAT TO DO!
NEMO! NO!

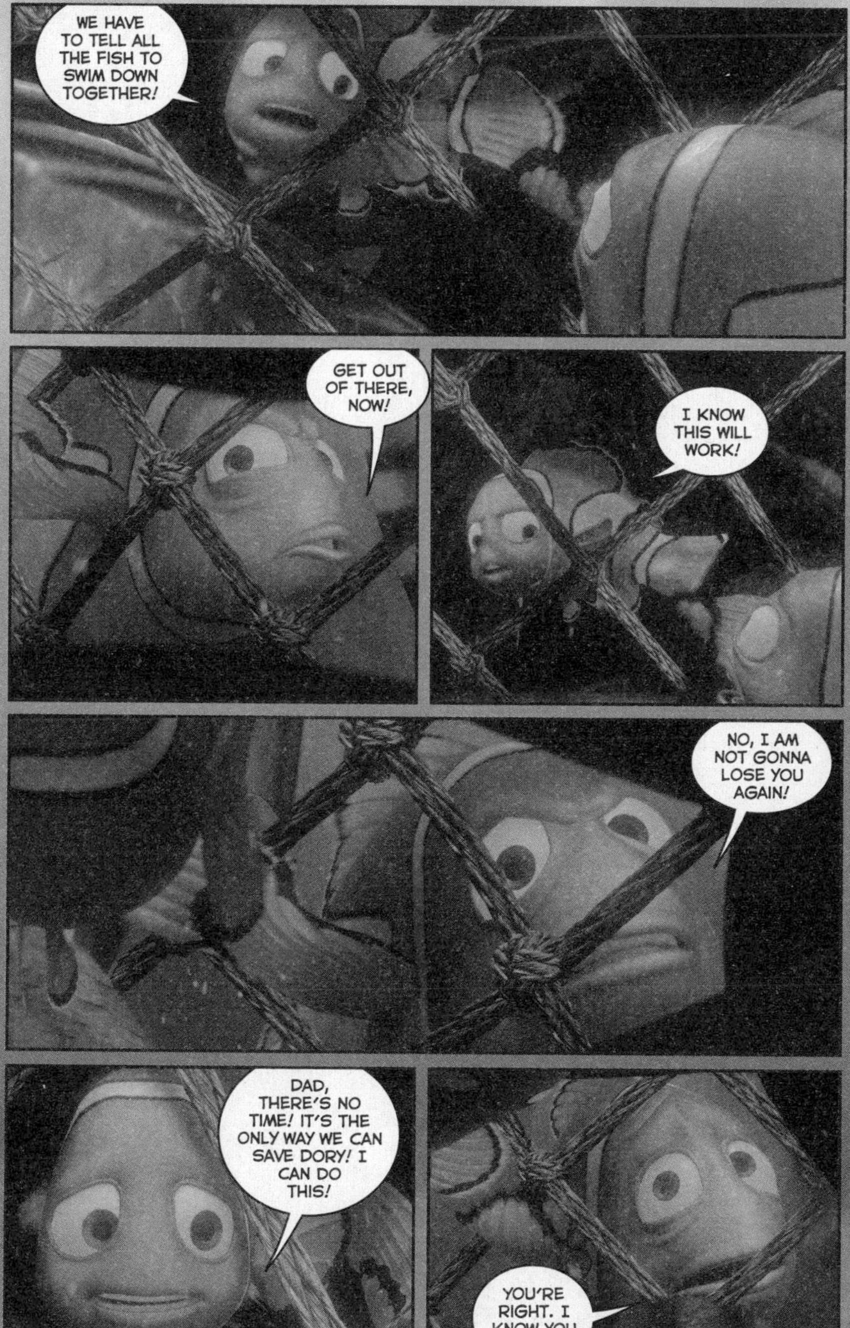
WE HAVE TO TELL ALL THE FISH TO SWIM DOWN TOGETHER!
GET OUT OF THERE, NOW!
I KNOW THIS WILL WORK!
NO, I AM NOT GONNA LOSE YOU AGAIN!
DAD, THERE'S NO TIME! IT'S THE ONLY WAY WE CAN SAVE DORY! I CAN DO THIS!
YOU'RE RIGHT. I KNOW YOU CAN.

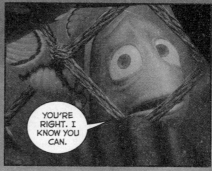

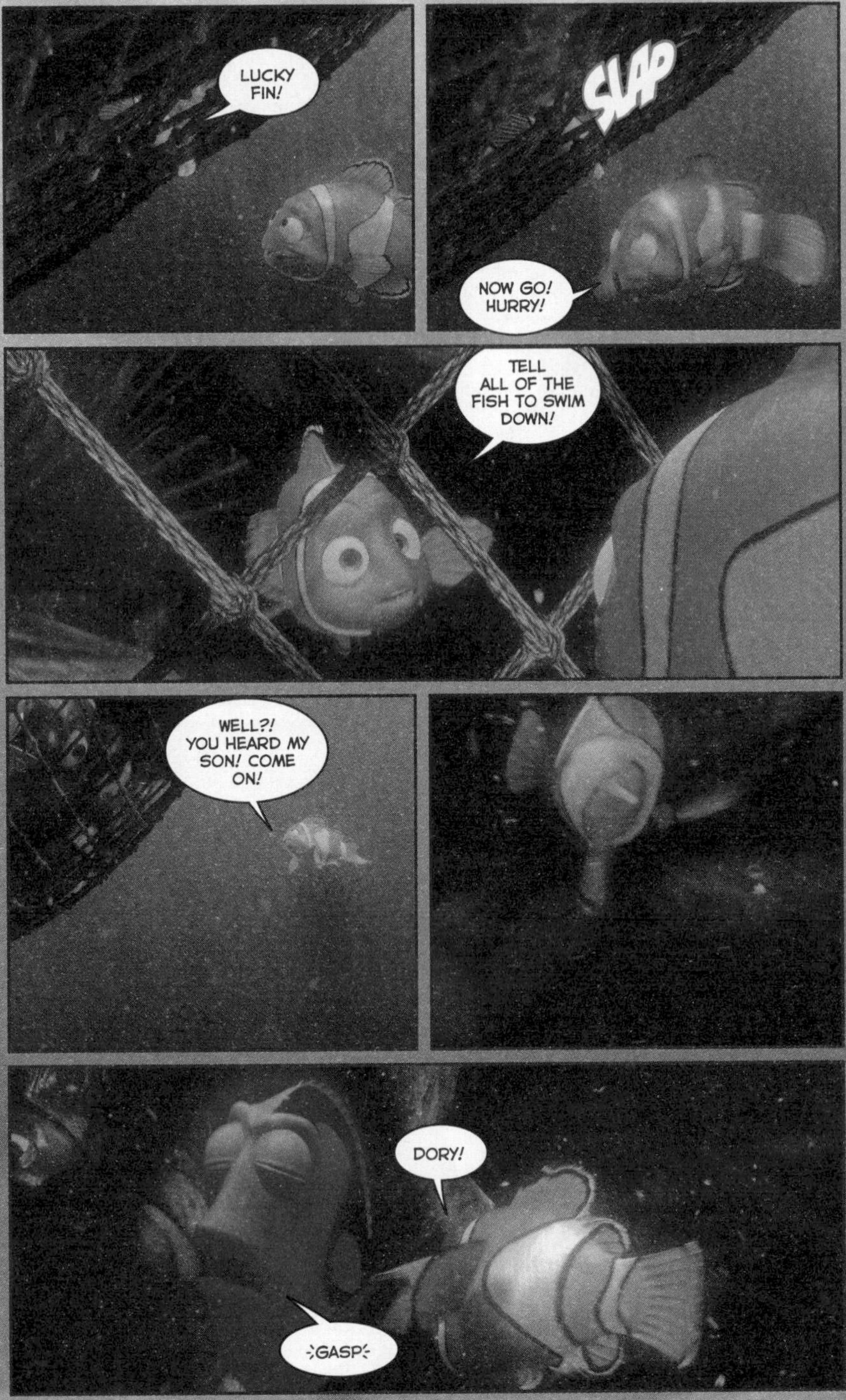
LUCKY FIN!
SLAP
NOW GO! HURRY!
TELL ALL OF THE FISH TO SWIM DOWN!
WELL?! YOU HEARD MY SON! COME ON!
DORY!
GASP

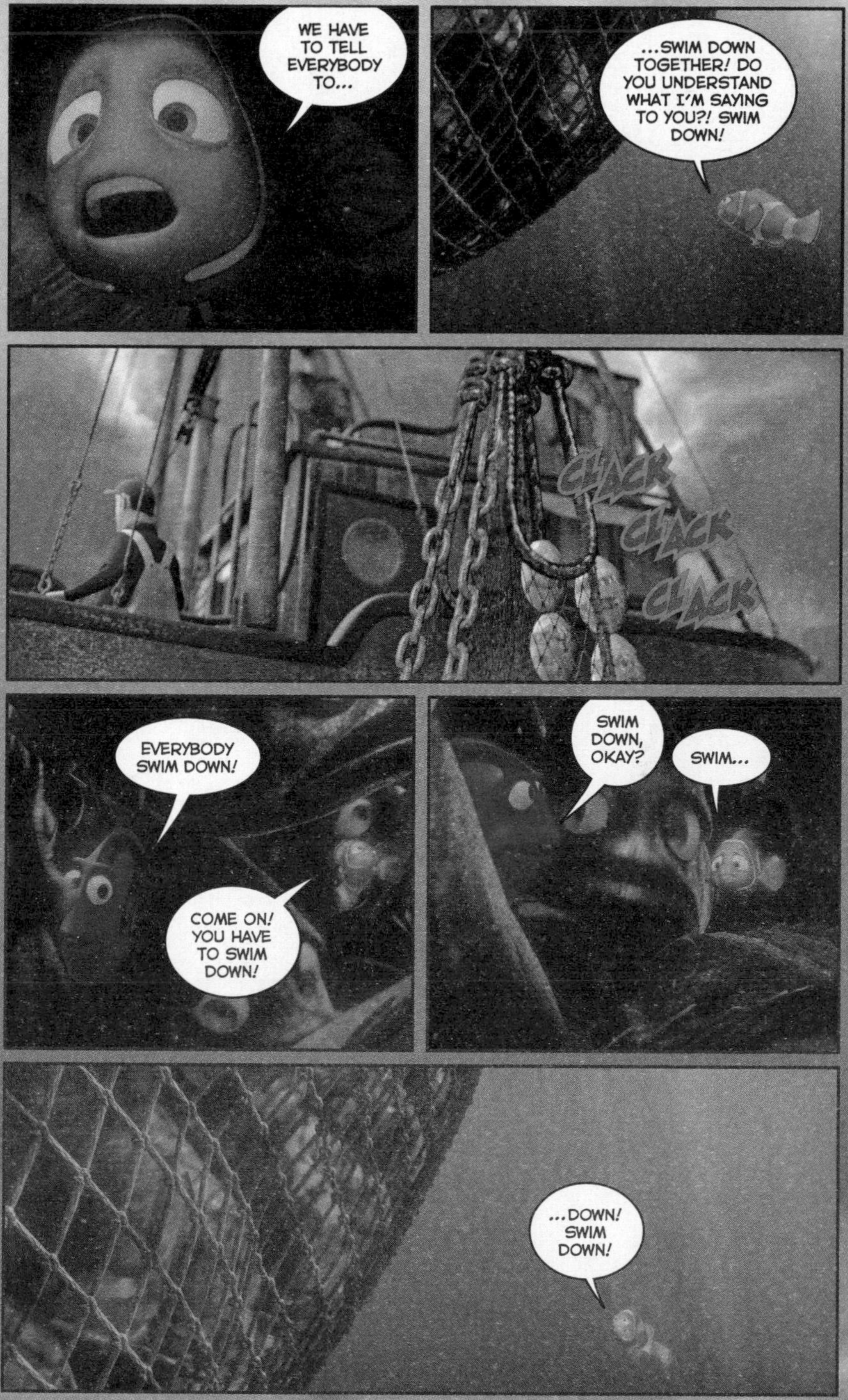
WE HAVE TO TELL EVERYBODY TO...
...SWIM DOWN TOGETHER! DO YOU UNDERSTAND WHAT I'M SAYING TO YOU?! SWIM DOWN!
CLACK
CLACK
CLACK
EVERYBODY SWIM DOWN!
COME ON! YOU HAVE TO SWIM DOWN!
SWIM DOWN, OKAY?
SWIM...
...DOWN! SWIM DOWN!

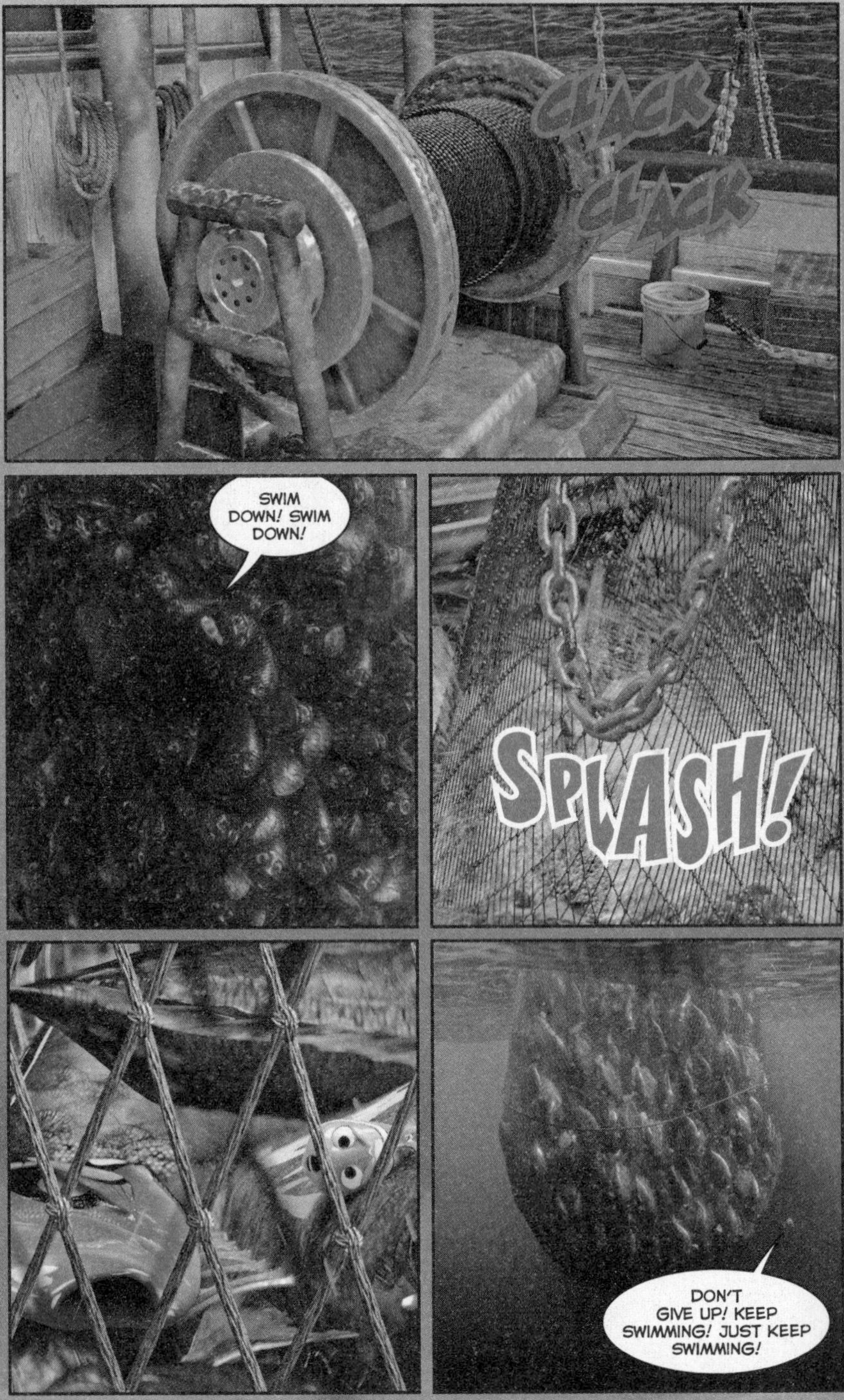
CLACK
CLACK
SWIM DOWN! SWIM DOWN!
SPLASH!
DON'T GIVE UP! KEEP SWIMMING! JUST KEEP SWIMMING!

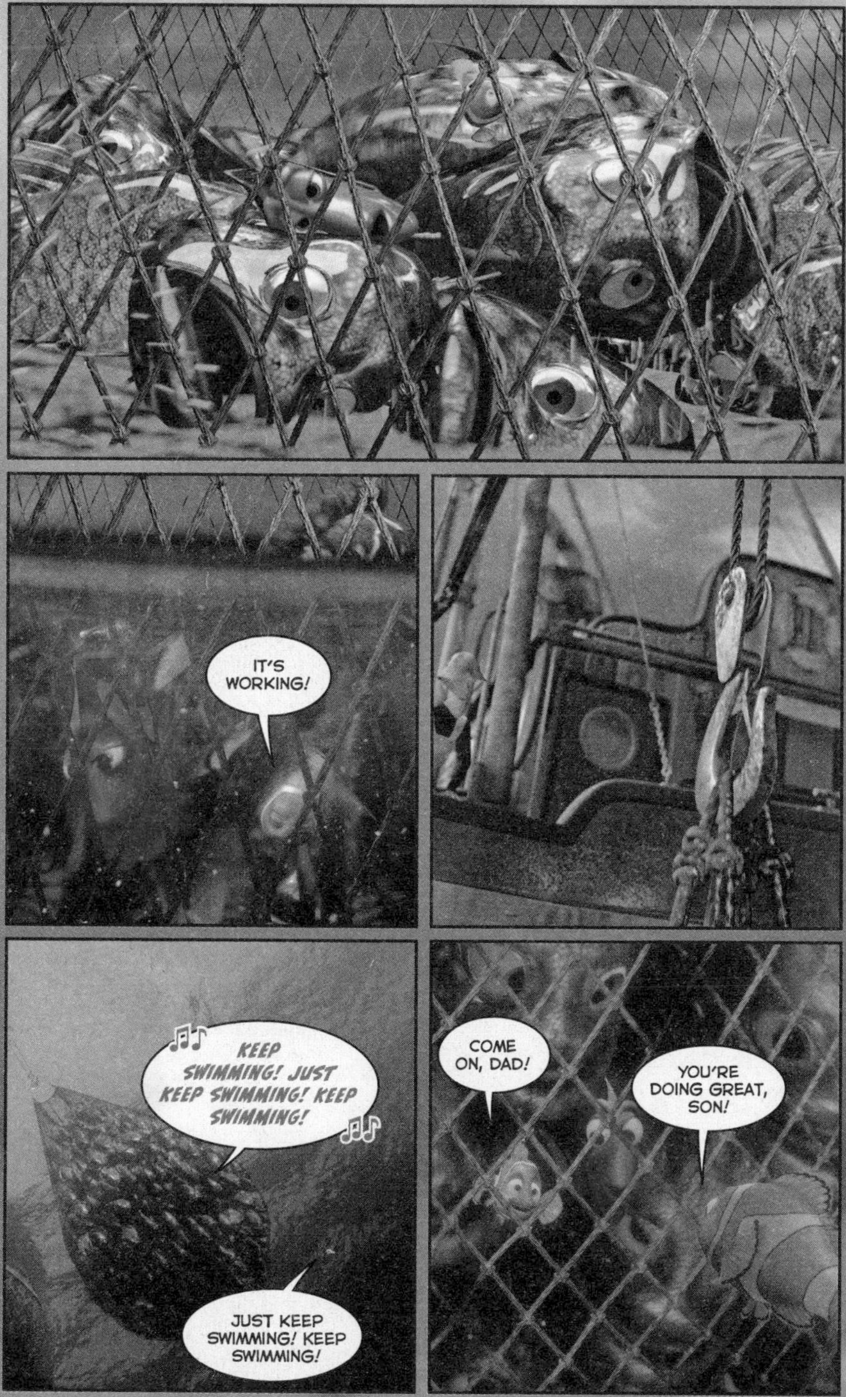
IT'S WORKING!
KEEP SWIMMING! JUST KEEP SWIMMING! KEEP SWIMMING!
JUST KEEP SWIMMING! KEEP SWIMMING!
COME ON, DAD!
YOU'RE DOING GREAT, SON!

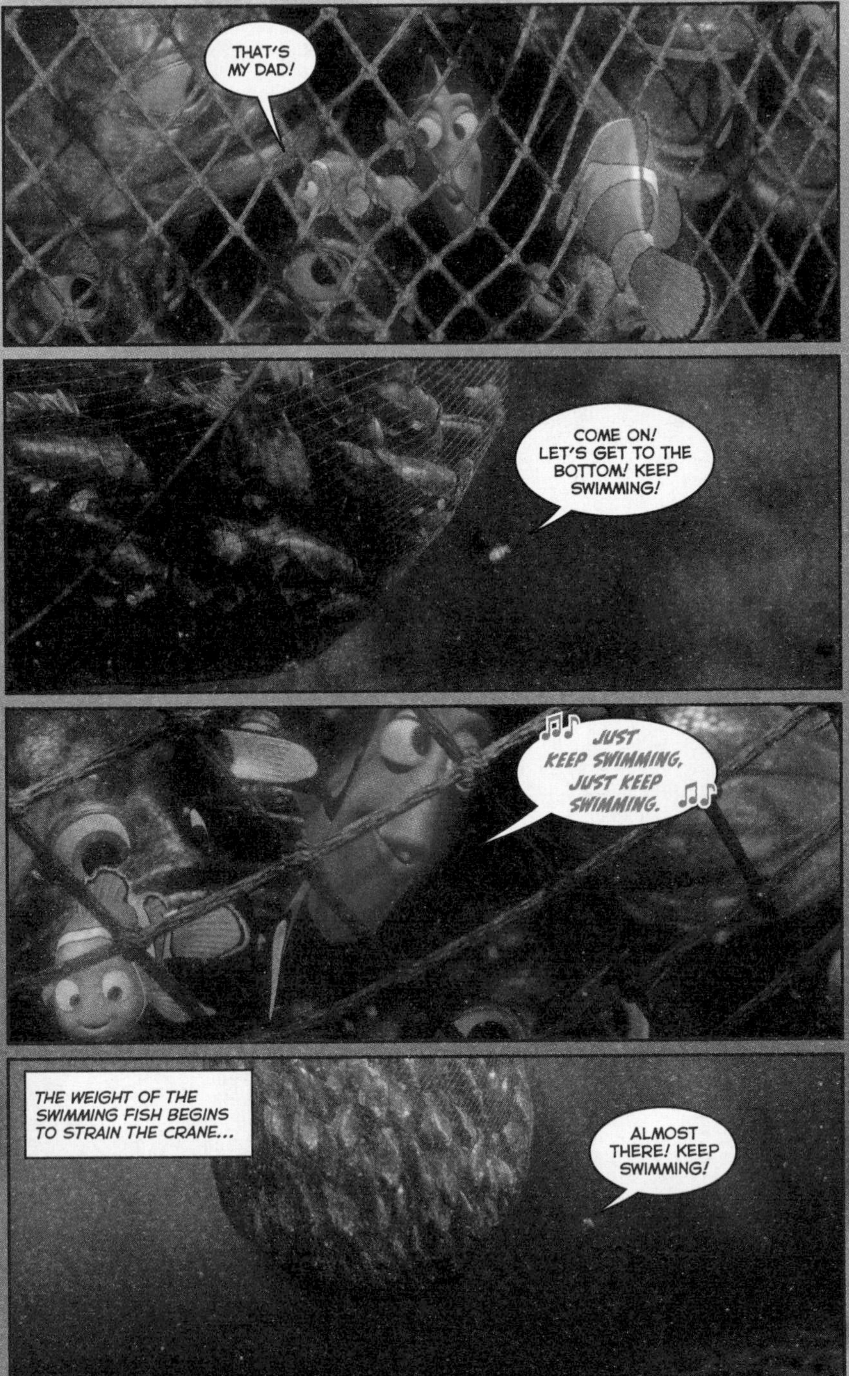
THAT'S MY DAD!
COME ON! LET'S GET TO THE BOTTOM! KEEP SWIMMING!
JUST KEEP SWIMMING, JUST KEEP SWIMMING.
THE WEIGHT OF THE SWIMMING FISH BEGINS TO STRAIN THE CRANE...
ALMOST THERE! KEEP SWIMMING!

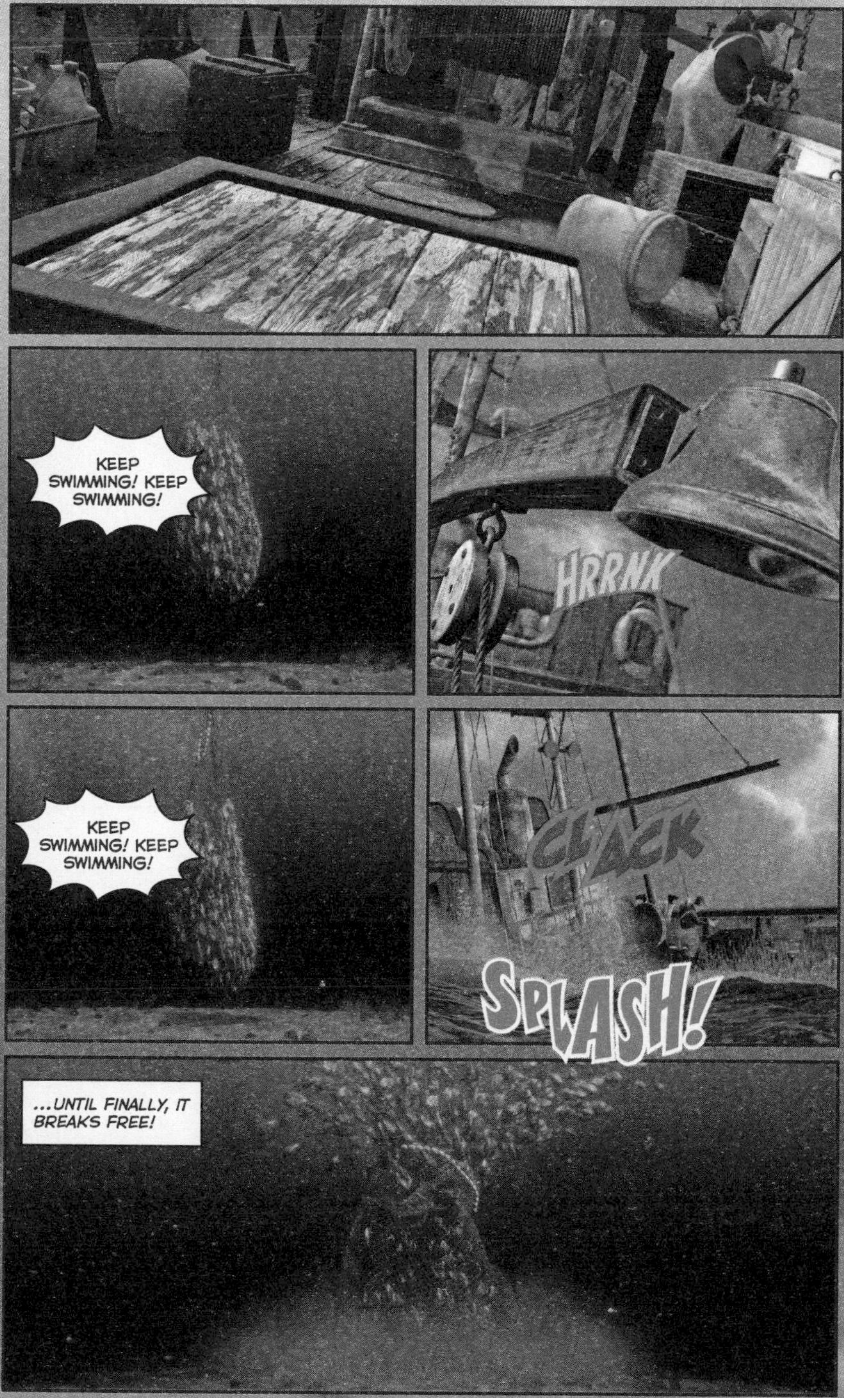
KEEP SWIMMING! KEEP SWIMMING!
HRRNK
KEEP SWIMMING! KEEP SWIMMING!
CLACK
SPLASH!
...UNTIL FINALLY, IT BREAKS FREE!

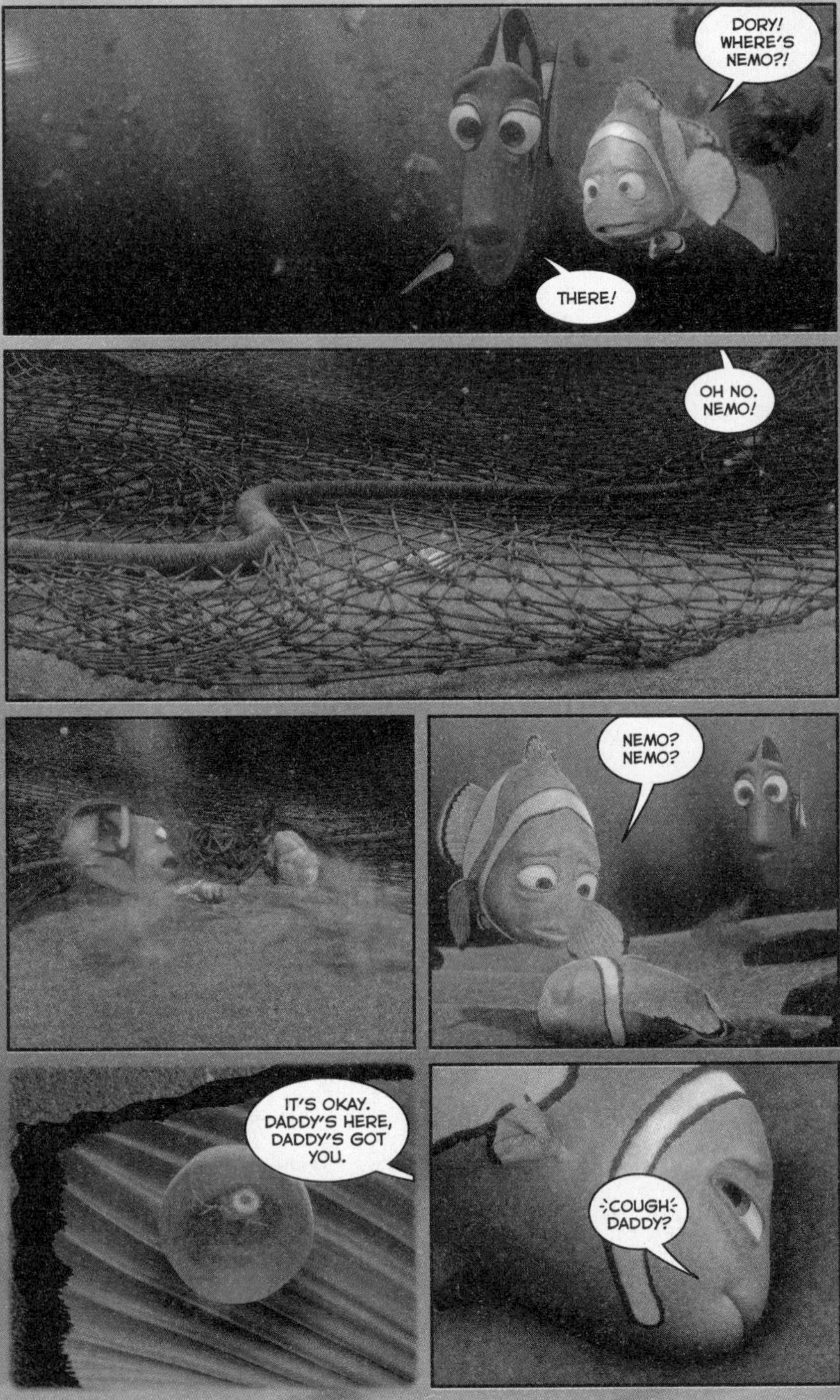
DORY! WHERE'S NEMO?!
THERE!
OH NO. NEMO!
NEMO? NEMO?
IT'S OKAY. DADDY'S HERE, DADDY'S GOT YOU.
-COUGH- DADDY?

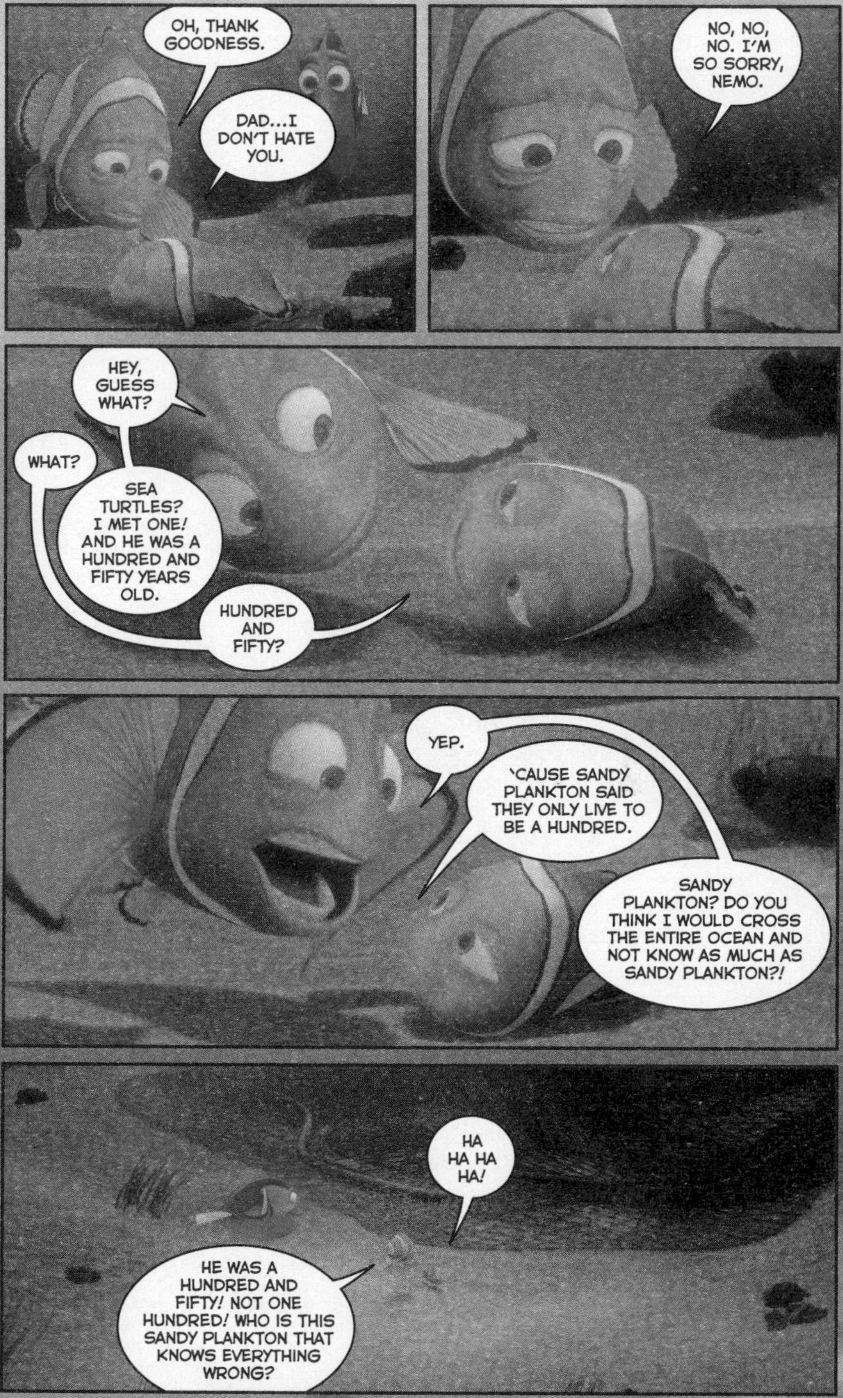
OH, THANK GOODNESS.
DAD...I DON'T HATE YOU.
NO, NO, NO. I'M SO SORRY, NEMO.
HEY, GUESS WHAT?
WHAT?
SEA TURTLES? I MET ONE! AND HE WAS A HUNDRED AND FIFTY YEARS OLD.
HUNDRED AND FIFTY?
YEP.
'CAUSE SANDY PLANKTON SAID THEY ONLY LIVE TO BE A HUNDRED.
SANDY PLANKTON? DO YOU THINK I WOULD CROSS THE ENTIRE OCEAN AND NOT KNOW AS MUCH AS SANDY PLANKTON?!
HA HA HA HA!
HE WAS A HUNDRED AND FIFTY! NOT ONE HUNDRED! WHO IS THIS SANDY PLANKTON THAT KNOWS EVERYTHING WRONG?

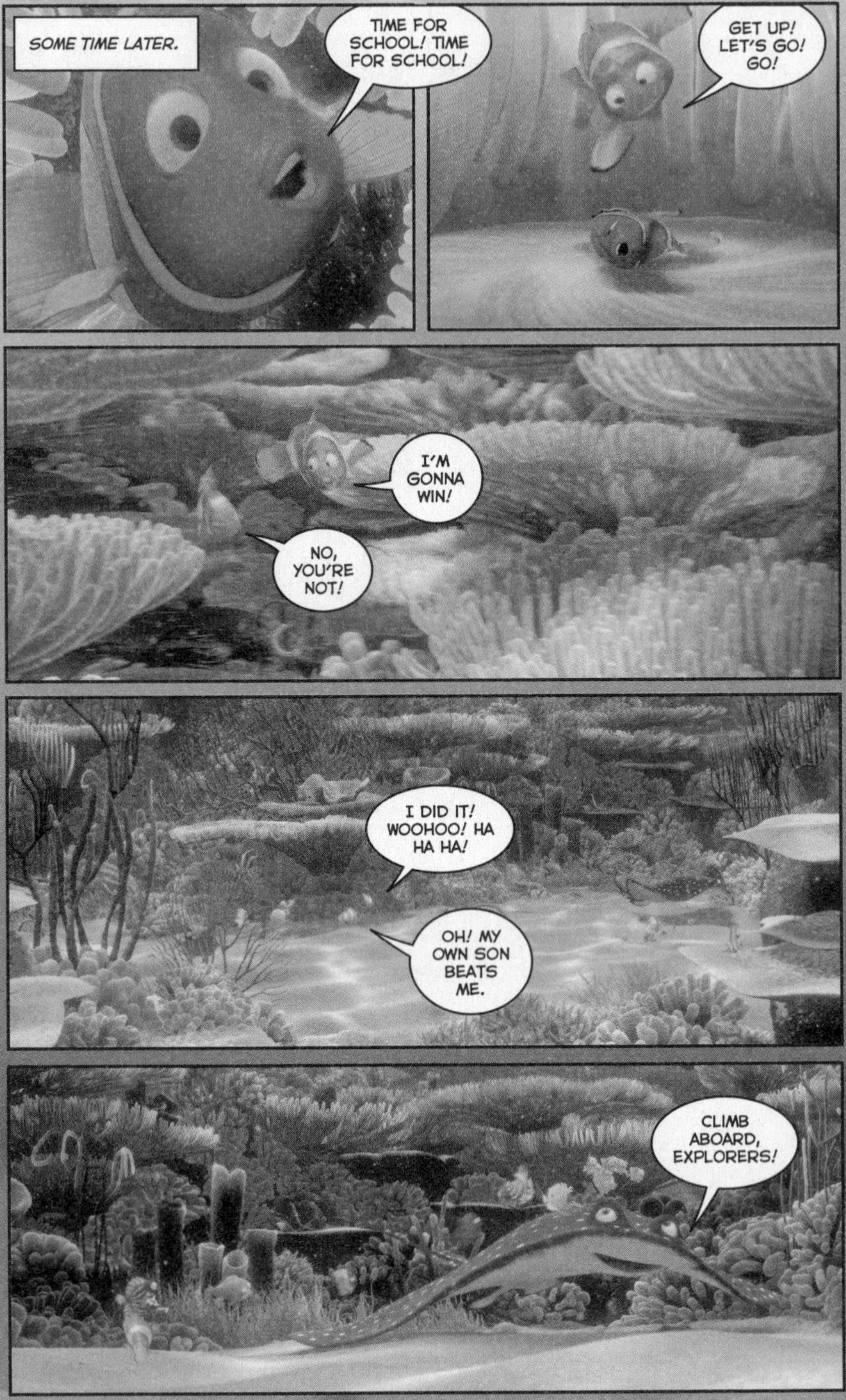
SOME TIME LATER.
TIME FOR SCHOOL! TIME FOR SCHOOL!
GET UP! LET'S GO! GO!
I'M GONNA WIN!
NO, YOU'RE NOT!
I DID IT! WOOHOO! HA HA HA!
OH! MY OWN SON BEATS ME.
CLIMB ABOARD, EXPLORERS!

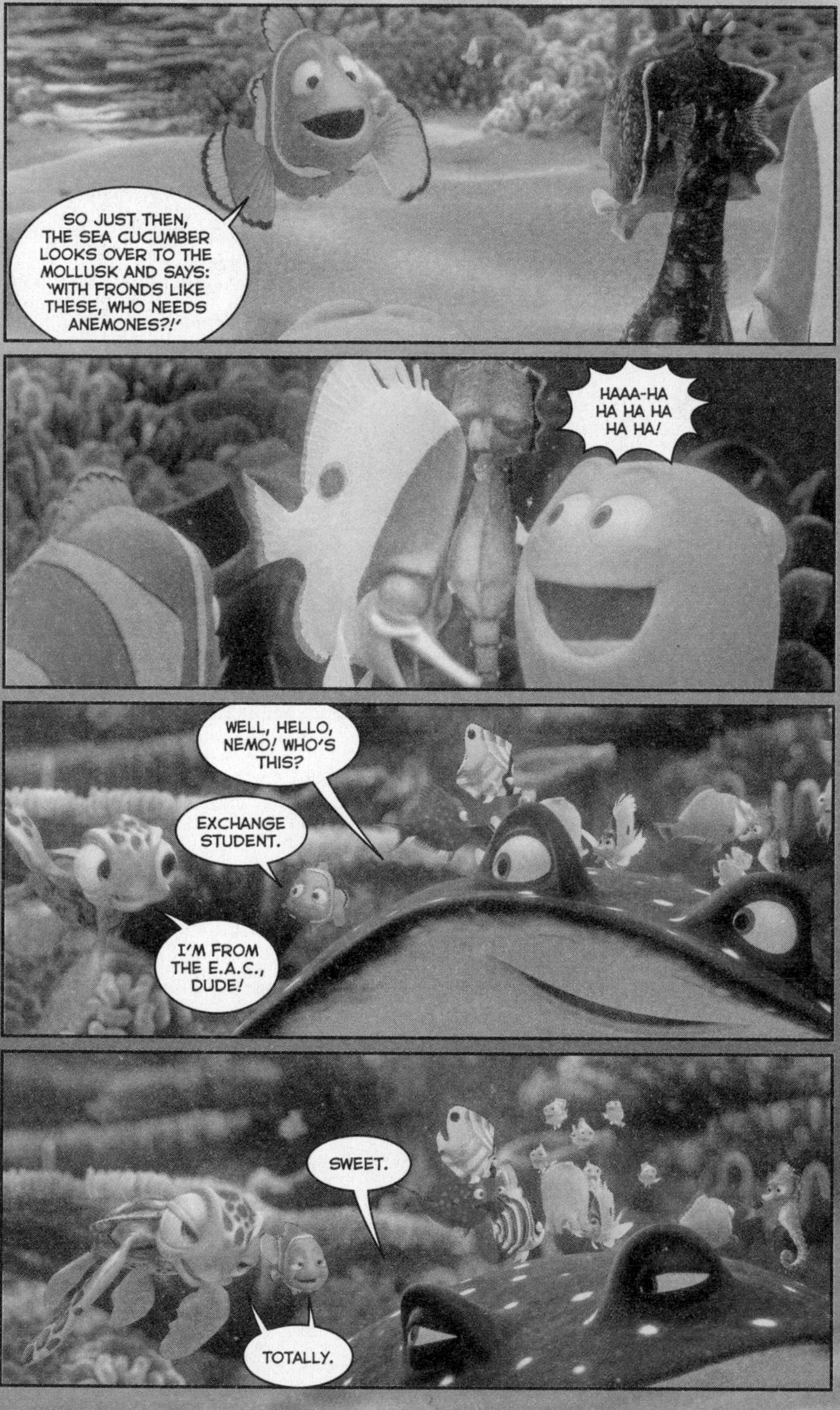
SO JUST THEN, THE SEA CUCUMBER LOOKS OVER TO THE MOLLUSK AND SAYS: 'WITH FRONDS LIKE THESE, WHO NEEDS ANEMONES?!'
HAAA-HA HA HA HA HA HA!
WELL, HELLO, NEMO! WHO'S THIS?
EXCHANGE STUDENT.
I'M FROM THE E.A.C., DUDE!
SWEET.
TOTALLY.

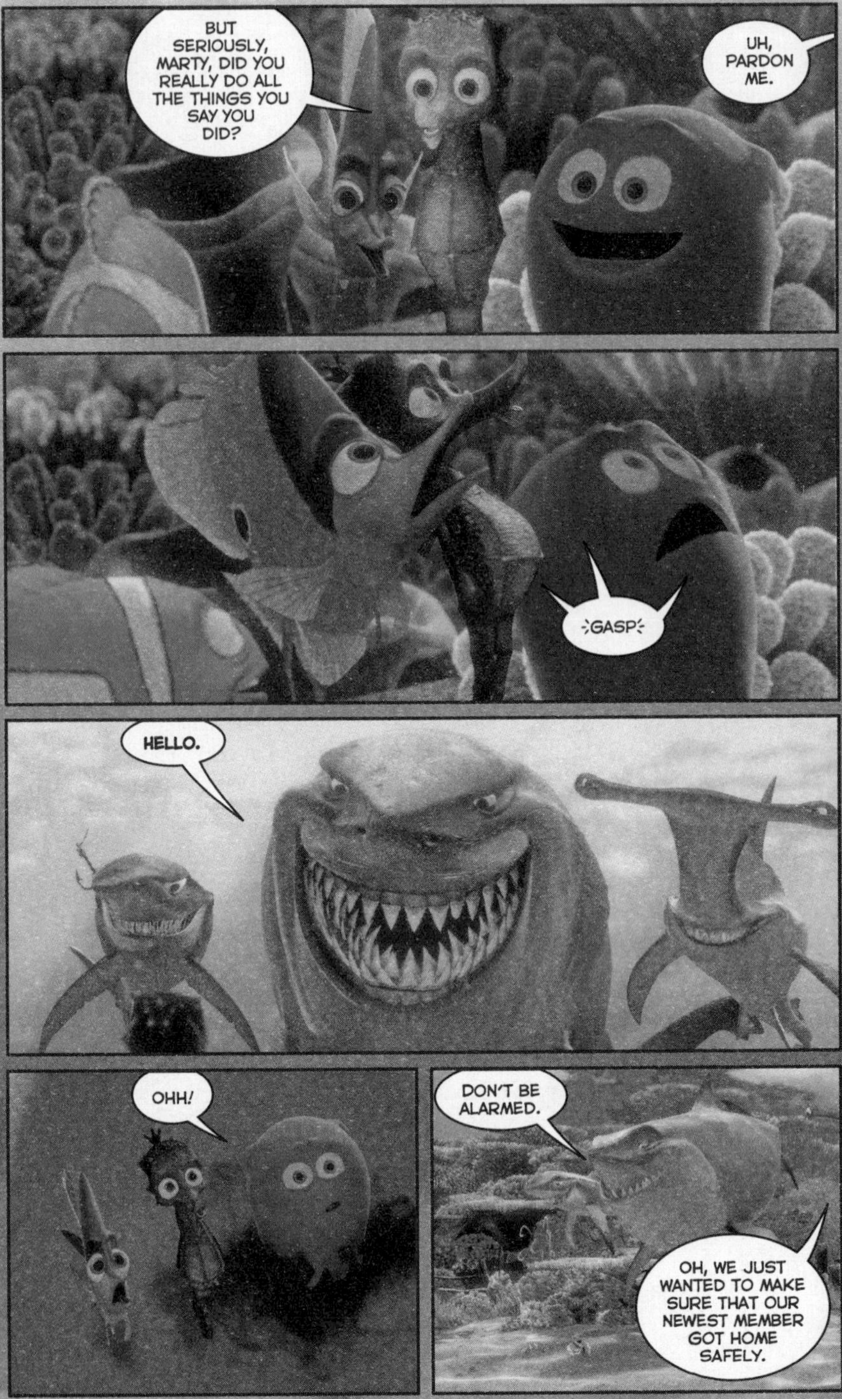
BUT SERIOUSLY, MARTY, DID YOU REALLY DO ALL THE THINGS YOU SAY YOU DID?
UH, PARDON ME.
GASP
HELLO.
OHH!
DON'T BE ALARMED.
OH, WE JUST WANTED TO MAKE SURE THAT OUR NEWEST MEMBER GOT HOME SAFELY.

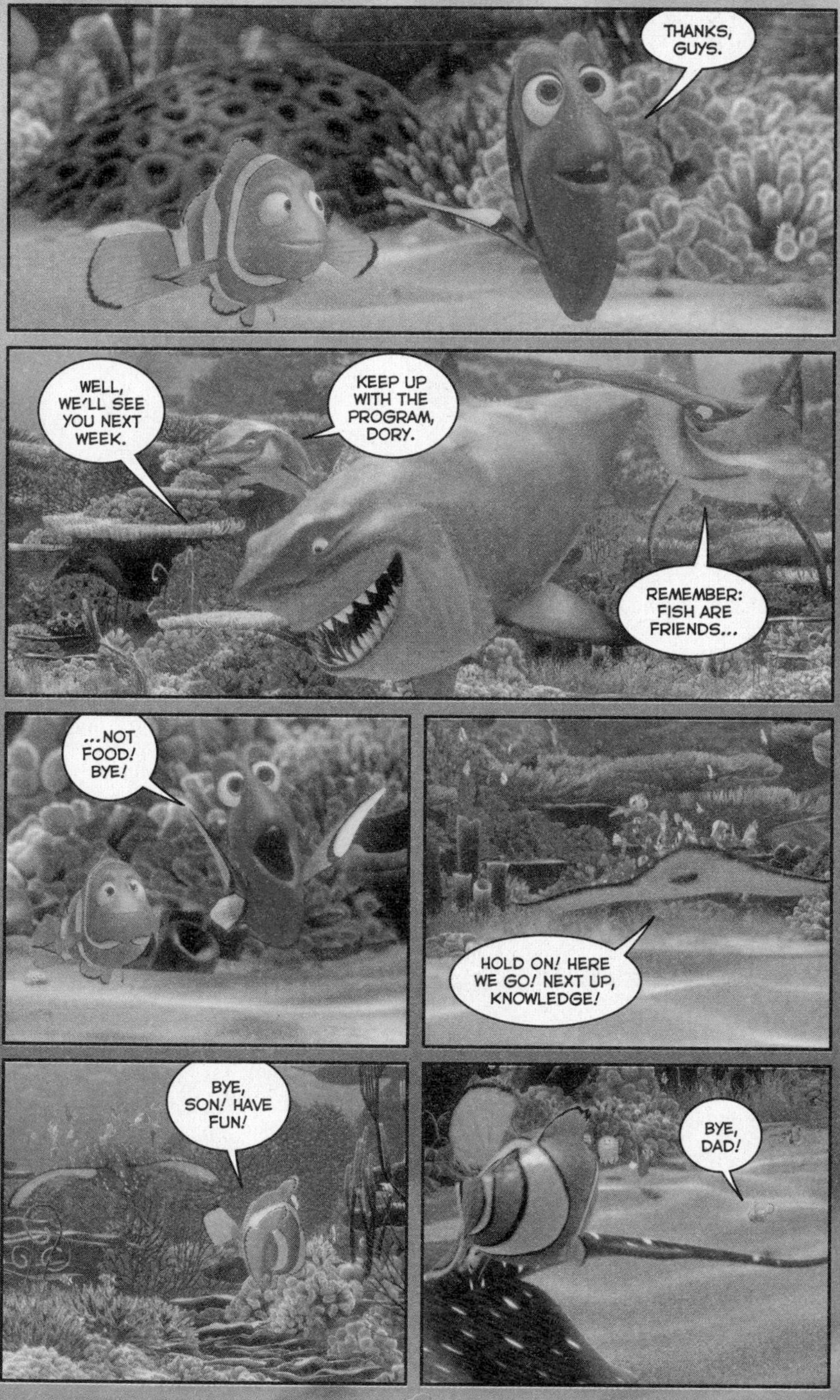
THANKS, GUYS.
WELL, WE'LL SEE YOU NEXT WEEK.
KEEP UP WITH THE PROGRAM, DORY.
REMEMBER: FISH ARE FRIENDS...
...NOT FOOD! BYE!
HOLD ON! HERE WE GO! NEXT UP, KNOWLEDGE!
BYE, SON! HAVE FUN!
BYE, DAD!

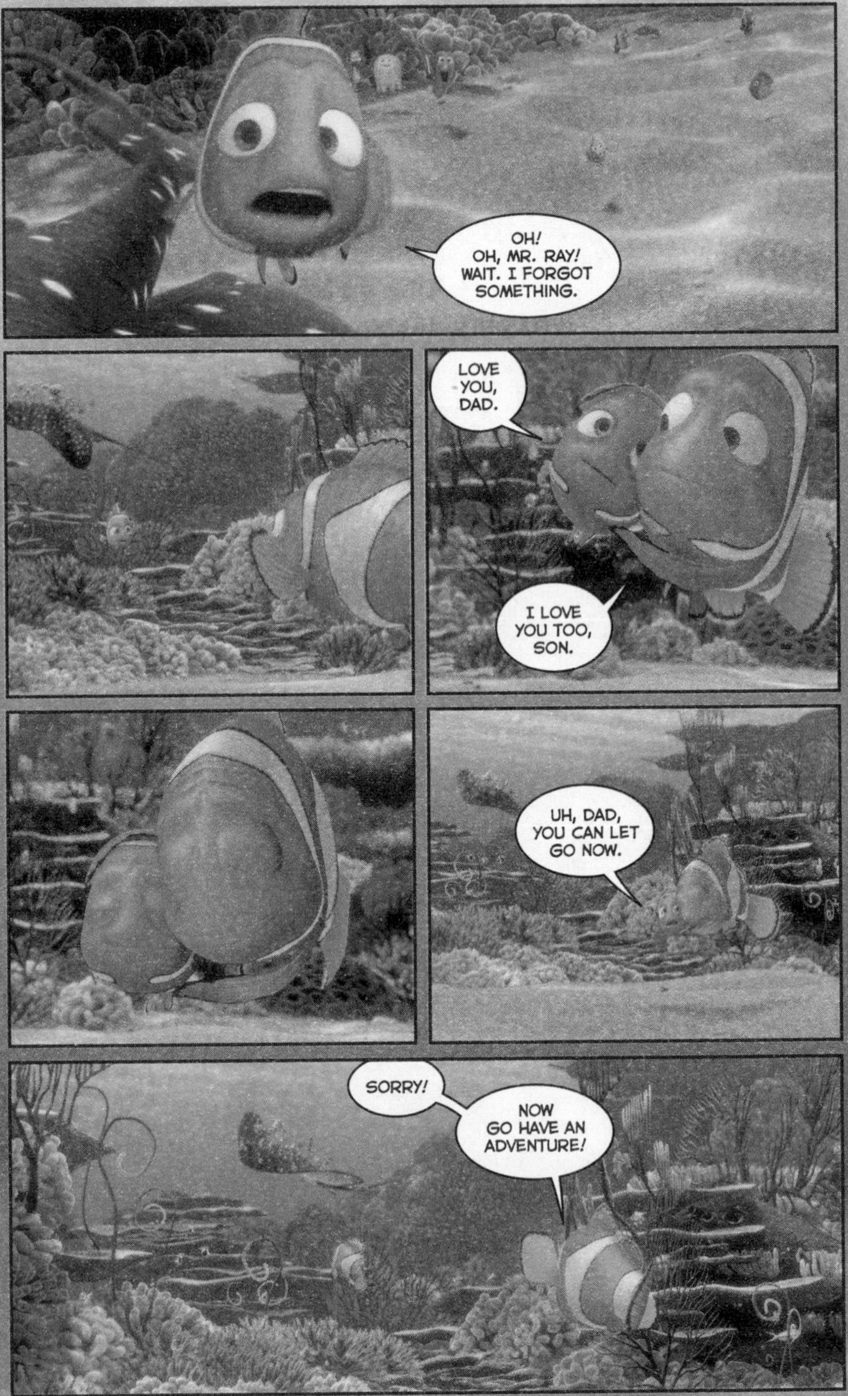
OH!
OH, MR. RAY!
WAIT. I FORGOT
SOMETHING.
LOVE
YOU,
DAD.
I LOVE
YOU TOO,
SON.
UH, DAD,
YOU CAN LET
GO NOW.
SORRY!
NOW
GO HAVE AN
ADVENTURE!

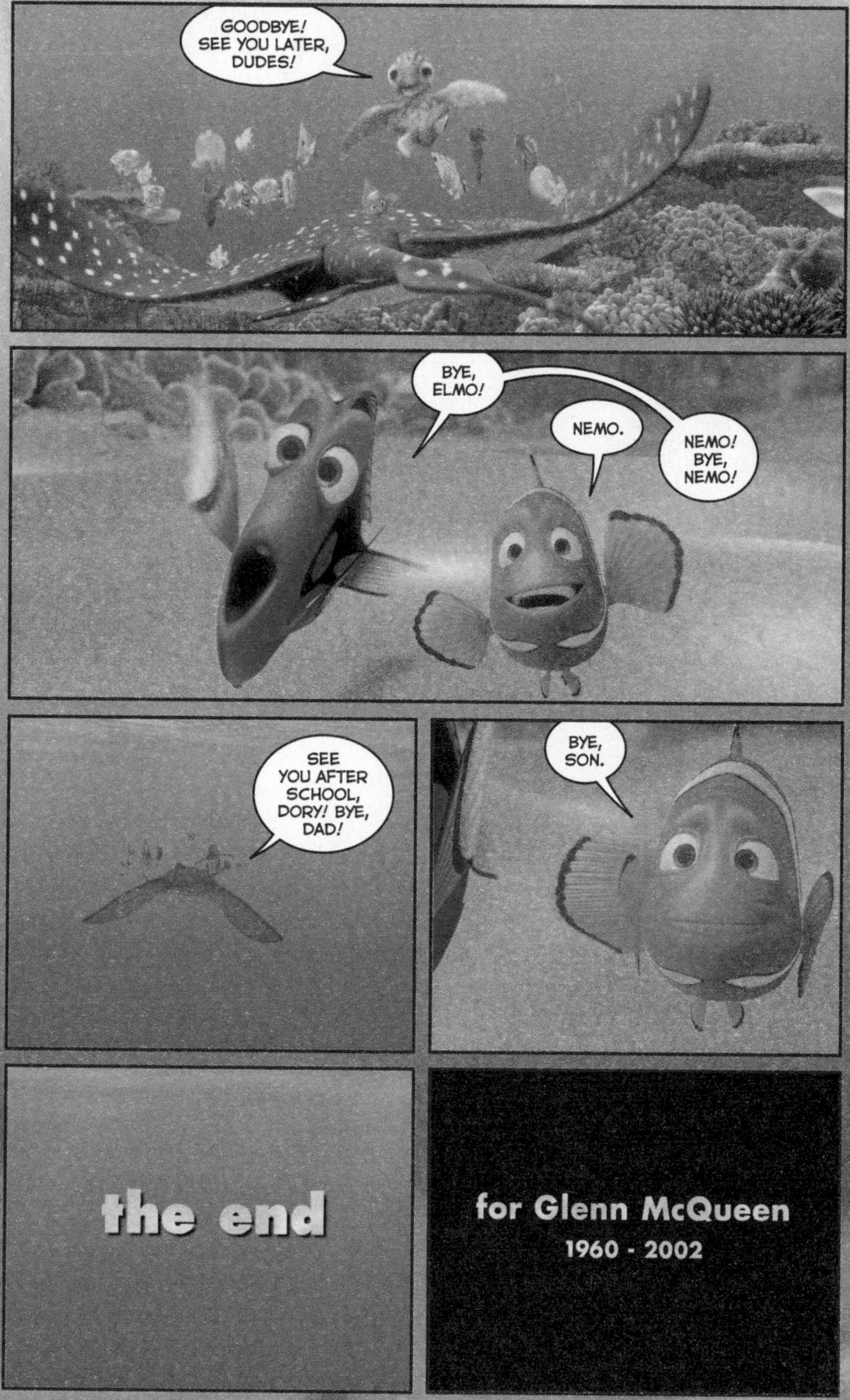
GOODBYE! SEE YOU LATER, DUDES!
BYE, ELMO!
NEMO.
NEMO! BYE, NEMO!
SEE YOU AFTER SCHOOL, DORY! BYE, DAD!
BYE, SON.
the end
for Glenn McQueen
1960 - 2002

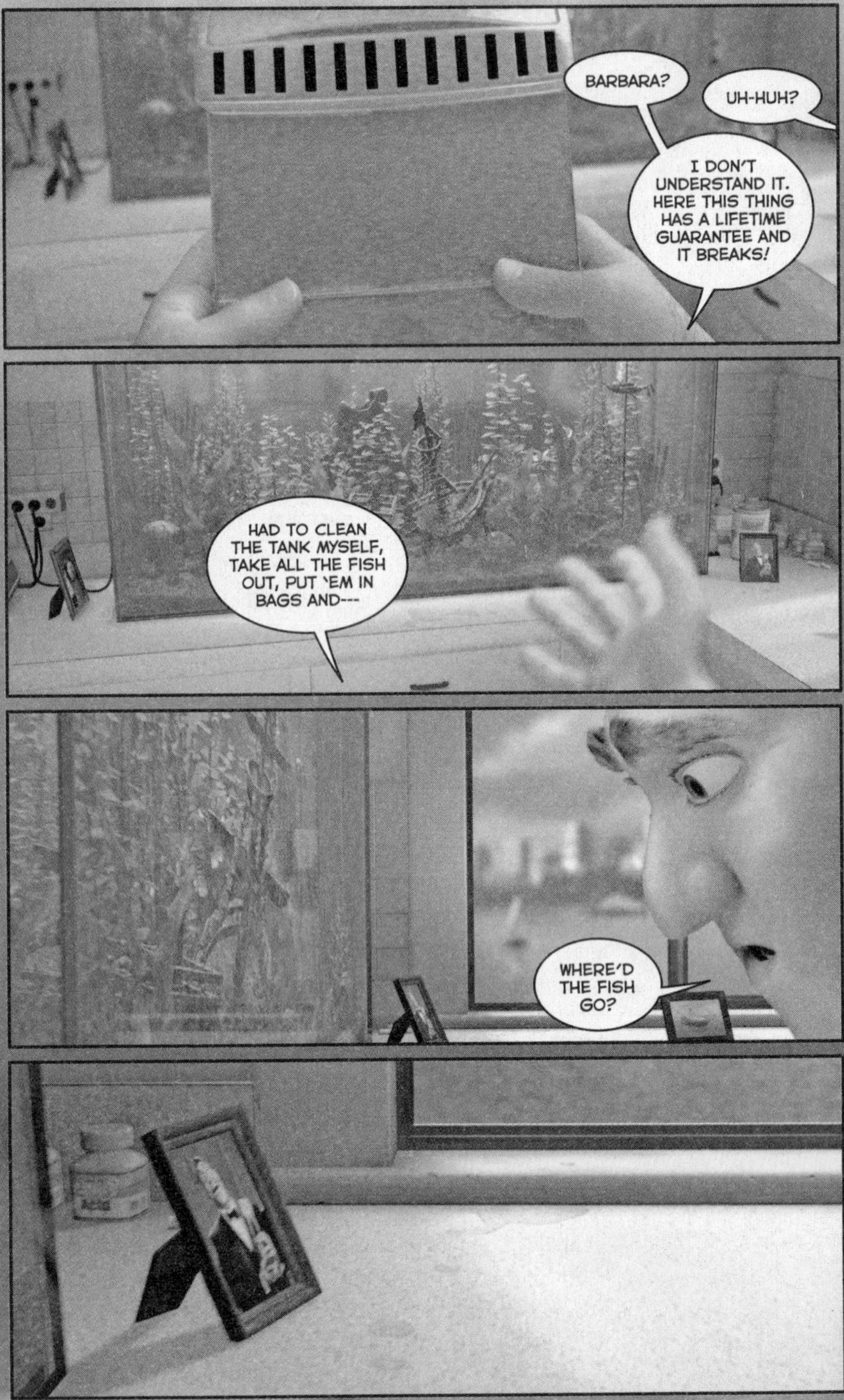
BARBARA?
UH-HUH?
I DON'T UNDERSTAND IT. HERE THIS THING HAS A LIFETIME GUARANTEE AND IT BREAKS!
HAD TO CLEAN THE TANK MYSELF, TAKE ALL THE FISH OUT, PUT 'EM IN BAGS AND---
WHERE'D THE FISH GO?

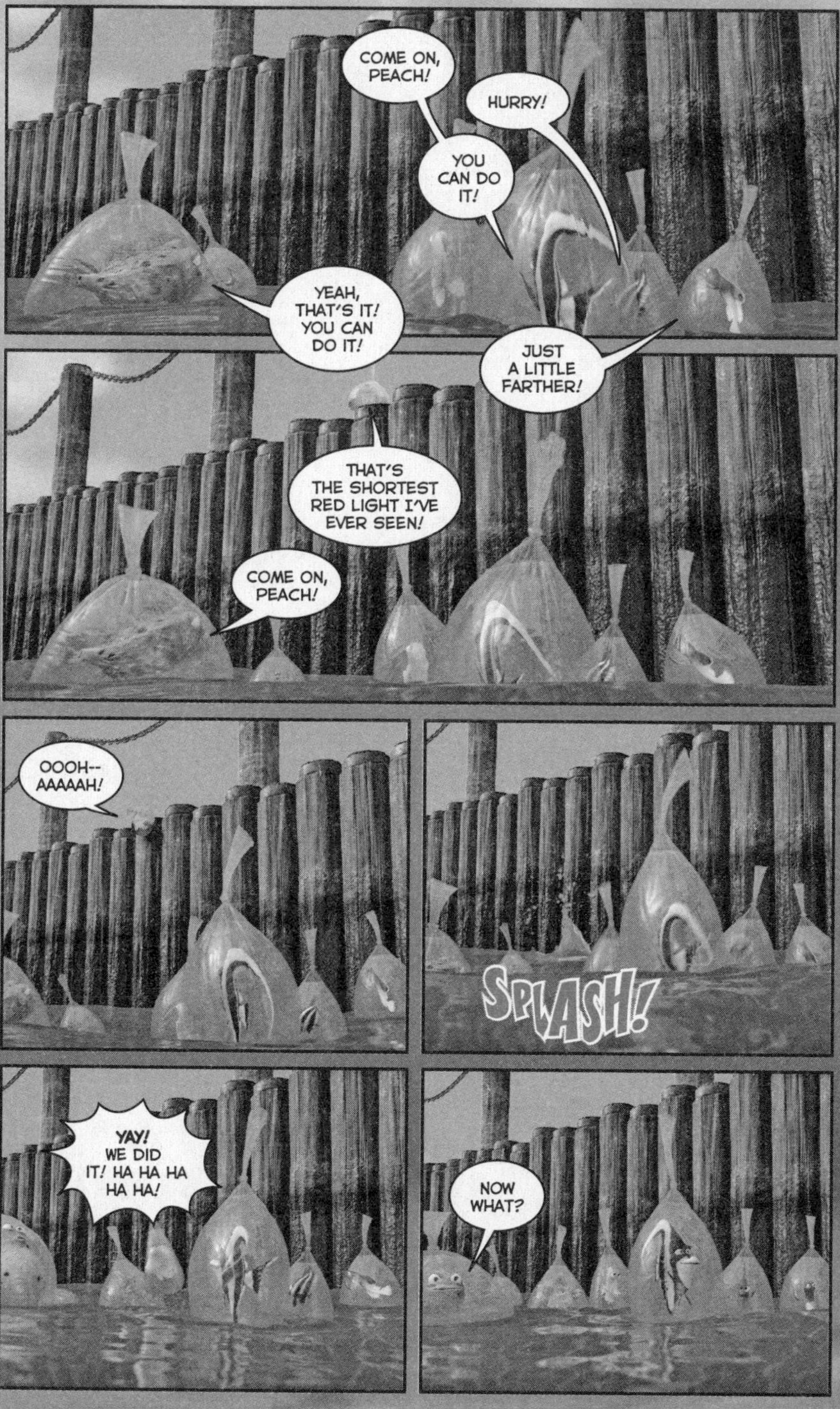
COME ON, PEACH!
HURRY!
YOU CAN DO IT!
YEAH, THAT'S IT! YOU CAN DO IT!
JUST A LITTLE FARTHER!
THAT'S THE SHORTEST RED LIGHT I'VE EVER SEEN!
COME ON, PEACH!
OOOH-- AAAAAH!
SPLASH!
YAY! WE DID IT! HA HA HA HA HA!
NOW WHAT?

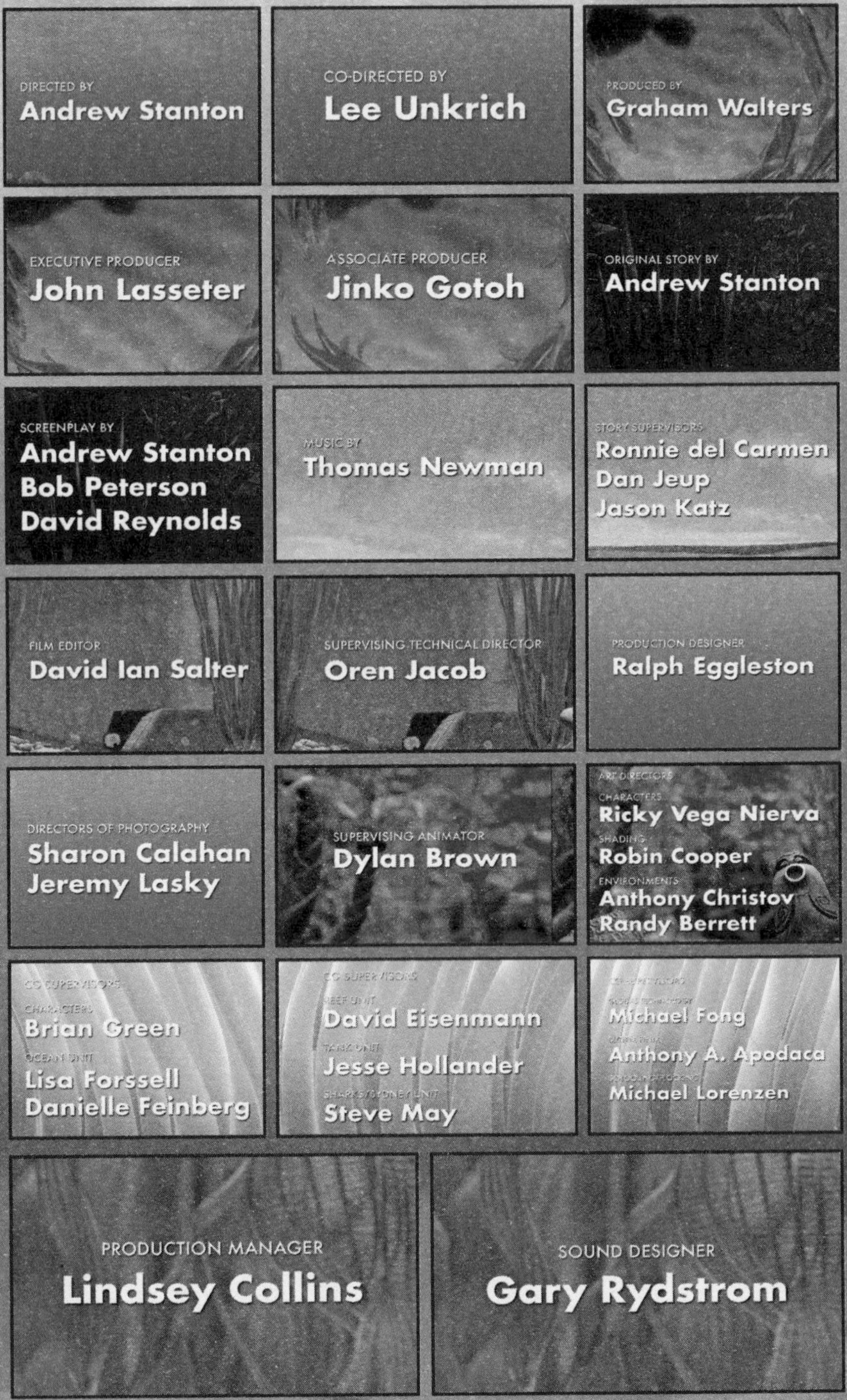

DIRECTED BY
Andrew Stanton

CO-DIRECTED BY
Lee Unkrich

PRODUCED BY
Graham Walters

EXECUTIVE PRODUCER
John Lasseter

ASSOCIATE PRODUCER
Jinko Gotoh

ORIGINAL STORY BY
Andrew Stanton

SCREENPLAY BY
Andrew Stanton
Bob Peterson
David Reynolds

MUSIC BY
Thomas Newman

STORY SUPERVISORS
Ronnie del Carmen
Dan Jeup
Jason Katz

FILM EDITOR
David Ian Salter

SUPERVISING TECHNICAL DIRECTOR
Oren Jacob

PRODUCTION DESIGNER
Ralph Eggleston

DIRECTORS OF PHOTOGRAPHY
Sharon Calahan
Jeremy Lasky

SUPERVISING ANIMATOR
Dylan Brown

ART DIRECTORS
CHARACTERS
Ricky Vega Nierva
SHADING
Robin Cooper
ENVIRONMENTS
Anthony Christov
Randy Berrett

CG SUPERVISORS
CHARACTERS
Brian Green
OCEAN UNIT
Lisa Forssell
Danielle Feinberg

CG SUPERVISORS
REEF UNIT
David Eisenmann
TANK UNIT
Jesse Hollander
SHARK & SYDNEY UNIT
Steve May

CG SUPERVISORS
PRODUCTION MANAGER
Michael Fong
OPTIMIZATION
Anthony A. Apodaca
GLOBAL TECHNOLOGY
Michael Lorenzen

PRODUCTION MANAGER
Lindsey Collins

SOUND DESIGNER
Gary Rydstrom

CASTING

Mary Hidalgo
Kevin Reher
Matthew Jon Beck

CAST

Marlin	. . . . . .	**Albert Brooks**
Dory	. . . . . .	**Ellen DeGeneres**
Nemo	. . . . . .	**Alexander Gould**
Gill	. . . .	**Willem Dafoe**
Bloat	. . . . . .	**Brad Garrett**
Peach	. . . . . .	**Allison Janney**
Gurgle	. . . . .	**Austin Pendleton**
Bubbles	. . . . .	**Stephen Root**
Deb (& Flo)	. . .	**Vicki Lewis**
Jacques	. . . . .	**Joe Ranft**

Nigel	. . . . . .	**Geoffrey Rush**
Crush	. . . . . .	**Andrew Stanton**
Coral	. . . . . .	**Elizabeth Perkins**
Squirt	. . . . . .	**Nicholas Bird**
Mr. Ray	. . . .	**Bob Peterson**
Bruce	. . . . . .	**Barry Humphries**
Anchor	. . . . .	**Eric Bana**
Chum	. . . . .	**Bruce Spence**
Dentist	. . . . .	**Bill Hunter**
Darla	. . . . . .	**LuLu Ebeling**
Tad	. . . .	**Jordy Ranft**
Pearl	. . . . . .	**Erica Beck**
Sheldon	. . . . .	**Erik Per Sullivan**
Fish School	. . .	**John Ratzenberger**

PRODUCTION SUPERVISOR
Marcia Gwendolyn Jones

STORY

STORY MANAGER
Blake Tucker

STORY ARTISTS
Jim Capobianco   Joseph "Rocket" Ekers
Bruce M. Morris   Peter Sohn
Nathan Stanton

ADDITIONAL STORYBOARDING
James S. Baker   Max Brace
Rob Gibbs   Matthew Luhn

DIGITAL STORYBOARDING
Courtney Booker

STORY CONSULTANT
Will Csaklos

STORY COORDINATOR
Rachel Raffael-Gates
Adam Bronstein

STORY PRODUCTION ASSISTANT
Romney T. Marino

ART

ART MANAGER
Doug Nichols

CHARACTER DESIGN
Dan Lee

ADDITIONAL CHARACTER DESIGN
Jason Deamer

PRODUCTION ARTISTS
Nelson "Rey" Bohol   David Fulp
Ellen Moon Lee   Albert Lozano
Nathaniel McLaughlin   James Pearson
Peter Sohn   Bud Thon

SCULPTORS
Jerome Ranft
Greg Dykstra

LEAD CG PAINTER
Belinda Van Valkenburg

CG PAINTERS
Bert Berry   Jamie Frye
Yvonne Herbst   Glenn Kim
Laura Phillips   Andrea Warren

VISUAL DEVELOPMENT
Geefwee Boedoe   Peter Deseve
Tony Fucile   Carter Goodrich
D. J. Cleland-Hura   George Hull
Dominique Louis   Simon Varela
Mark Whiting   Bruce Zick

ADDITIONAL VISUAL DEVELOPMENT
Rikki Cleland-Hura

ART COORDINATOR
Bert Berry

EDITORIAL

SUPERVISING FILM EDITOR
Lee Unkrich

SECOND FILM EDITORS
Katherine Ringgold
Stan Webb
Kevin Nolting

FIRST ASSISTANT EDITOR
Axel Geddes

SECOND ASSISTANT EDITORS
Luis Alvarez y Alvarez   Jason Hudak
David Suther   Elizabeth Thomas

TEMP MUSIC EDITOR
David Slusser

OMF COORDINATOR
Kathleen Relyea

EDITORIAL PRODUCTION ASSISTANTS
Gregory Amundson
Gabrielle Siegel
Jacob Parsons

ANIMATION

ANIMATION MANAGER
Jenni Tsoi

DIRECTING ANIMATORS
Alan Barillaro
Mark Walsh

ANIMATORS

Carlos Baena	Bobby "Boom" Beck
Misha Berenstein	Ben Catmull
Scott Clark	Brett Coderre
Tim Crawfurd	David DeVan
Doug Dooley	Ike Feldman
Andrew Gordon	Stephen Gregory
Travis Hathaway	Jimmy Hayward
Steven Clay Hunter	Rob Jensen
Nancy Kato	Karen Kiser
Shawn P. Krause	Wendell Lee
Angus MacLane	Matt Majers
Daniel Mason	Dale McBeath
Amy McNamara	Jon Mead
Billy Merritt	Cameron Miyasaki
Dave Mullins	James Ford Murphy
Rodrigo Blaas Nacle	Peter Nash
Victor Navone	Bret Parker
Michael Parks	Bobby Podesta
Brett Pulliam	Rich Quade
Roger Rose	Gini Cruz Santos
Andy Schmidt	Doug Sheppeck
Ross Stevenson	Patty Kihm Stevenson
Doug Sweetland	David Tart
J. Warren Trezevant	Michael Venturini
Tasha Wedeen	Adam Wood
Kureha Yokoo	Ron Zorman

SENIOR LAYOUT ARTIST
Craig Good

FIX ANIMATORS
Paul Mendoza
Christopher DiGiovanni

ANIMATION COORDINATOR
Graham Moloy

ANIMATION WRANGLER
Christopher DiGiovanni

ANIMATION FIX COORDINATOR
Kearsley Higgins

CHARACTERS

UNIT MANAGERS
Kelly T. Peters
Joshua Hollander

LEADS
Paul Aichele
Keith Olenick

CG ARTISTS

Byron Bashforth	David Batte
Chad Belteau	Jason Bickerstaff
Brian Boyd	Martin Costello
Ziah Sarah Fogel	Lucas R. A. Ives
Steven James	Rob Jensen
Kristifir Klein	Sonoko Konishi
Krummhoefener	Daniel McCoy
Casey McTaggart	Brandon Onstott
Adrienne Othon	John Singh Pottebaum
Jeff Pratt	David Ryu
Tom Sanocki	Andrew H. Schmidt
Bill Sheffler	Eliot Smyrl
Keith Stichweh	Danny (Dani) Sukiennik
Colin Hayes Thompson	Brian Tindall
Erin Tomson	Dirk Van Gelder

Christine Waggoner

UNIT COORDINATOR
Pamela Darrow

OCEAN UNIT

UNIT MANAGER
Michael Warch

LEADS
Liz Kupinski Carter	Jun Han Cho
Scott G. Clifford	Derek Williams

CG ARTISTS
Cortney Armitage	Airton Dittz, Jr.
Louis Gonzales	Stefan Gronsky
Jae H. Kim	Keith Daniel Klohn
Mike Krummhoefener	Tom Miller
Amy Moran	David Munier
Jack Paulus	Justin Ritter
Apurva Shah	Erik Smitt
Michael L. Stein	Maria Yershova

UNIT COORDINATOR
Marcia Savarese

REEF UNIT

UNIT MANAGER
Kim Collins

LEADS
Robert Anderson
Don Schreiter
Kim White

CG ARTISTS
Jessica Abroms	Chris Bernardi
Simon Dunsdon	Steven James
Sungyeon Joh	Michael Kilgore
David MacCarthy	Michael K. O'Brien
Eileen O'Neill	Lisa Kim
Burt Peng	Andrew Pienaar
Timothy Swec	Sophie Vincelette
Brad Winemiller	

UNIT COORDINATORS
Suzanne Hightower-Purcell
Seth Murray

SHARKS/SYDNEY UNIT

UNIT MANAGER
Siouxsie Stewart

LEADS
Michael Fu
Ken Lao
Derek Williams

CG ARTISTS
Brian Boyd	Chris Chapman
Jun Han Cho	Kevin Edwards
Christina Garcia	Christina Haaser
Jean-Claude J. Kalache	Steven Kani
Keith Daniel Klohn	Ivo Kos
Holly Lloyd	Martin Nguyen
Kelly O'Connell	Phat Phuong
Gabriel Schlumberger	Suzanne Slatcher
Peter Sumanaseni	Erdem Taylan

UNIT COORDINATOR
Sheri Patterson

TANK UNIT

UNIT MANAGER
Michael Warch

LEADS
Brad Andalman
Scott G. Clifford
Sylvia Wong

CG ARTISTS

Frank Aalbers, Mark Adams, Fareed Behmaram-Mosavat, Chad Belteau, Shawn Brennan, Gary Bruins, Liz Kupinski Carter, Airton Dittz, Jr., Ziah Sarah Fogel, John Halstead, Nigel Hardwidge, Patrick James, Ewan Johnson, Thomas Jordan, Jae H. Kim, David MacCarthy, Amy Moran, Dan Schoedel, Sajan Skaria, Suzanne Slatcher, Erik Smitt, Keith Stichweh, Maria Yershova, Brian Cordan Young

SCHOOLING & FLOCKING

UNIT MANAGER
A. J. Riebli

LEAD
Justin Ritter

CG ARTISTS
Dale McBeath
George Nguyen
Michael L. Stein

DIGITAL FINAL

UNIT MANAGER
Ethan Owen

CG ARTISTS
Claudia Chung, Richard Thompson, Michael Kilgore, Matthew Webb

UNIT COORDINATOR
Dana Leigh Murray

TECHNICAL DEVELOPMENT

TECHNICAL DEVELOPMENT LEAD
William Reeves

TECHNICAL DEVELOPMENT TEAM
Jessica Abroms, John Alex, John R. Anderson, Anthony A. Apodaca

Larry Aupperle, David Baraff, Ronen Barzel, David Batte, Fareed Behmaram-Mosavat, Chris Bernardi, Daniel Campbell, Cynthia Dueltgen, Tom Duff, Stefan Gronsky, John Halstead, Lauren Alpert Hoffman, Thomas Jordan, Michael Kass

Shirley Konkle, Ben Koo, Ken Lao, Casey McTaggart, Tim Milliron, David Munier, George Nguyen, Martin Nguyen, John Singh Pottebaum, Brian M. Rosen, Apurva Shah, Tom Sanocki, Bill Sheffler, Erdem Taylan, Richard Thompson, Mark VandeWettering, John Warren, Brad West, Brad Winemiller, Andy Witkin, Adam Woodbury, Wayne Wooten

ADDITIONAL CG ARTISTS

Michael Chann   Brian Clark   Andrew Jimenez
Frances Kumashiro   Michelle Lin   Paul Seidman

STUDIO TOOLS R&D

LEADS

Dana Batali	Tony DeRose
Kurt Fleischer	Mary Ann Gallagher
Thomas Hahn	Michael B. Johnson
Josh Minor	Guido Quaroni
Brian Smits	Galyn Susman
Karon Weber	Andy Witkin

DEVELOPMENT TEAM

Brad Andalman	John R. Anderson
Katrina Archer	Jim Atkinson
Sanjay Bakshi	David Baraff
Sam "Penguin" Black	Malcolm Blanchard
Ian Buono	Gordon Cameron
Loren C. Carpenter	Per Christensen
Christopher Colby	Bena Currin
Peter Demoreuille	Brendan Donohoe
Max Drukman	Tom Duff
Susan Fisher	Julian Fong
F. Sebastian Grassia	Eric Gregory
Susan Boylan Griffin	Mark Harrison
Jamie Hecker	Jeff Hollar
Jisup Hong	Mitchell Im
Michael Kass	Chris King
Shawna King	Cybele Knowles
David Laur	Eric Lebel

Mark Leone	Tom Lokovic
Antoine McNamara	Gary Monheit
Nghi (Tin) Nguyen	Peter Nye
Shaun Oborn	Michael K. O'Brien
Hans Pederson	Fabio Pellacini
Katrin Petersen	Sudeep Rangaswamy
Arun Rao	Martin Reddy
David Ryu	Rudrajit Samanta
Chris Schoeneman	Kay Seirup
Michael Shantzis	Sarah Shen
Marco da Silva	María Milagros Soto
Heidi Stettner	Paul S. Strauss
Dirk Van Gelder	Kiril Vidimče
Brad West	Audrey Wong
Adam Woodbury	Wayne Wooten
Jane Yen	David G. Yu

Hans Pederson	Fabio Pellacini
Katrin Petersen	Sudeep Rangaswamy
Arun Rao	Martin Reddy
David Ryu	Rudrajit Samanta
Chris Schoeneman	Kay Seirup
Michael Shantzis	Sarah Shen
Marco da Silva	María Milagros Soto
Heidi Stettner	Paul S. Strauss
Dirk Van Gelder	Kiril Vidimče
Brad West	Audrey Wong
Adam Woodbury	Wayne Wooten
Jane Yen	David G. Yu

CAMERA

CAMERA MANAGER
Joshua Hollander

CAMERA SUPERVISOR
Louis Rivera

CAMERA SOFTWARE & ENGINEERING
John Hee Soo Lee   Matthew Martin
Drew TTV Rogge   Babak Sanii

CAMERA TECHNICIANS
Cosmic Don
Jeff Wan

PHOTOSCIENCE MANAGERS
David DiFrancesco
James Burgess

DEPARTMENT ADMINISTRATOR
Beth Sullivan

PRODUCTION

PRODUCTION ACCOUNTANT	**Nephi Sanchez**
SCHEDULING COORDINATOR	**Heidi Cruz**
DIRECTOR OF PRODUCTION FINANCE	**Robert Taylor**
SUPERVISOR OF PRODUCTION RESOURCES	**Susan T. Tatsuno**
ASSISTANT PRODUCTION ACCOUNTANT	**Kesten Migdal**
ASSISTANT TO THE PRODUCER	**Marguerite K. Enright**
ASSISTANT TO THE DIRECTORS	**Lisa Marie Schwartz**
PRODUCTION OFFICE ASSISTANTS	**Jon Darrell Handy**
	Peter T. Schreiber
DISNEY PRODUCTION REPRESENTATIVE	**Jenny Aleman-Holman**

ADDITIONAL PRODUCTION SUPPORT

Cindy Cosenzo	**Xanthe Hohalek**	**Jennifer Kinavey**
Susan E. Levin	**David Lortsher**	**Julie McDonald**
Wendi McNeese	**Roger Noyes**	**Adrian Ochoa**
Karen Paik	**Marc Prager**	**Dan Sokolosky**

INFORMATION SYSTEMS

MANAGERS & LEADS

Peter Kaldis	**Erik Forman**
Alisa Gilden	**May Pon**
Alex Stahl	**Christopher C. Walker**
Warren Hays	

SYSTEMS ADMINISTRATORS & SUPPORT

Domenic Allen	**Neftali "El Magnifico" Alvarez**
James Bartel	**Jennifer Becker**
Gabriel Benveniste	**Bryan Bird**
Sean Brennan	**Lars R. Damerow**
james g. dashe	**Ross Dickinson**
Miles Egan	**Edward Escueta**
Sandy Falby	**Grant Gatzke**
Joshua Grant	**Bethany Jane Hanson**
Jason B. Hendrix	**Ling Hsu**
Kenneth "Yo" Huey	**Jason "Jayfish" Hull**
Jose "Gayle" Ignacio	**Humera Yasmin Kahn**
Elise Knowles	**Cory Andrew Knox**
Matthew Lindahl	**Jessica Giampietro McMackin**
Bob Morgan	**Terry Lee Moseley**
Michael A. O'Brien	**Jeanie T. Oh**

Mark Pananganan	**Kathleen H. Parmelee**
Wil Phan	**Edgar Quiñones**
A.U.B.I.E.	**M.T. Silvia**
Nelson Siu	**Elle Yoko Suzuki**
Andy Thomas	**Jason "JTOP" Topolski**
Chuck Waite	**Jay Weiland**
Ian Westcott	**Adam Wood-Gaines**

POST PRODUCTION

POST PRODUCTION SUPERVISOR	**Paul Cichocki**
SENIOR MANAGER EDITORIAL AND POST PRODUCTION	**Bill Kinder**
PROJECTION	**John Hazelton**
EDITORIAL SERVICES	**Phred Lender**
	Andra Smith
	Jeff Whittle
POST PRODUCTION COORDINATOR	**Courtney Bergin**
ORIGINAL DIALOGUE MIXER	**Doc Kane**
DIALOGUE RECORDIST	**Jeanette Browning**
ADDITIONAL DIALOGUE RECORDING	**Vince Caro**
	Charlene Richards
	E.J. Holowicki

ADDITIONAL ADR VOICE CASTING	**Mickie McGowan**
ADDITIONAL AUSTRALIAN VOICE CASTING	**Ceri Davies**
END CREDIT DESIGN	**Ellen Moon Lee**

POST PRODUCTION SOUND SERVICES BY
SKYWALKER SOUND
A Division of Lucas Digital Ltd., Marin County, California

RE-RECORDING MIXERS	**Gary Rydstrom**
	Gary Summers
SUPERVISING SOUND EDITORS	**Michael Silvers**
	Gary Rydstrom
SOUND EFFECTS EDITORS	**Shannon Mills**
	Teresa Eckton
	E. J. Holowicki
FOLEY EDITOR	**Al Nelson**

ADR EDITOR	**Steve Slanec**
ASSISTANT SOUND DESIGNER	**Dee Selby**
ASSISTANT SUPERVISING SOUND EDITOR	**Stuart McCowen**
FOLEY ARTISTS	**Dennie Thorpe**
	Jana Vance
FOLEY MIXER	**Frank "Pepe" Merel**
FOLEY RECORDIST	**Travis Crenshaw**
MIX TECHNICIANS	**Jurgen Scharpf**
	Juan Peralta
RE-RECORDIST	**Brian Magerkurth**

FACILITIES

Tom Carlisle	Craig Payne
Cherise Miller	Joe Garcia
Aaron Burt	Edgar A. Ochoa
Keith Johnson	Paul Gillis
William de Ridder	Kenny Condit

HUMAN RESOURCES

Sangeeta Prashar	Dawn Haagstad
Lisa Ellis	Shelby Madeleine Cass
Kimberly Adair Clark	Monica VanDis

PIXAR SHORTS

Roger Gould	Osnat Shurer
Bill Polson	Gale Gortney
Steve Bloom	Daniel A. Goodman
Alice Rosen	Alex Orrelle
Chris Vallance	Erin Cass
Omid Amjadi	

PIXAR UNIVERSITY & ARCHIVES

Randy Nelson	Elyse Klaidman
Christine W. Freeman	Elizabeth Greenberg
David R. Haumann	Brandon T. Loose
Andrew Lyndon	

PURCHASING & RELOCATION

Dennis "DJ" Jennings
Jody Giacomini

RENDERMAN PRODUCTS

Ray Davis	Renee Lamri
Jonathan Flack	Dylan Sisson
Lola Gill	Wendy Wirthlin

SAFETY & SECURITY

Keith Kops	Chris Balog
Jonathan Rodriguez	Joni Superticioso
Marlon Castro	Michael Jones
Valerie Villas	Sequoia Blankenship

CRAFT SERVICES

Osvaldo Tomatis	Luis Alarcon-Cisneros
Francisco Figueroa	Loretta Framsted
Candelaria Lozano	Jose Ramirez
Guillermo Segovia	Fernando Contreras
Olga Velaszquez	Maricela Navarro
Meagan Miller	

PRODUCTION BABIES

A.J. IV	Aislinn	Amaey	Ayana
Benjamin	Bergen	Colin	Cynthia
Daniel	Dorri	Ella	Emma
Fiona	Haiden	Hanako	India
Isaac	Jack	Jacob	Jake
Jeremiah	Joshua	Louis	Lucas
Margaret	Matthew	Maximilian	Miles
Nico	Nina	Noah	Oona
Owen	Parker	Rachel	Reese
Riley	Sophia	Sophie	Tallulah
Thomas	Tobias	Yonatan	

SPECIAL THANKS

Adam P. Summers, Fabulous Fish Guy
University of California - Irvine

Aquarium of the Pacific	Steinhart Aquarium
Hal Beral	Maria Elena Magana Cervantes
Roni Douglas, DDS	Dive Makai Charters
Craig Gillespie	Mike Severens Diving

City and County of San Francisco, Public Utilities Commision,
Oceanside Water Pollution Control Facility
Marcia Peck, RDH

"The Girl from Ipanema"

WRITTEN BY
Antonio Carlos Jobim,
Vinicius De Moraes
and Norman Gimbel

"Psycho (The Murder)"

WRITTEN BY
Bernard Herrmann

"Fandango"

WRITTEN BY
Bob Bain

"Beyond the Sea"

WRITTEN BY
Charles Louis Trenet
Albert Lasry
and Jack Lawrence

PERFORMED BY
Robbie Williams

COURTESY OF EMI RECORDS UNDER
LICENSE FROM EMI FILM & TV MUSIC

FINAL RENDERING SYSTEMS **Sun Microsystems, Inc.**
ANIMATED ON **Marionette™**
RENDERED BY **RenderMan®**
FILMED IN **PixarVision™**

Prints by Technicolor®

Kodak
MOTION PICTURE FILM

DOLBY
DIGITAL
IN SELECTED THEATRES

SDDS Sony Dynamic Digital Sound.
IN SELECTED THEATRES

DIGITAL
dts
SOUND
IN SELECTED THEATERS

No. 39772

MOTION PICTURE ASSOCIATION OF AMERICA

THIS PICTURE MADE UNDER
THE JURISDICTION OF

AFFILIATED WITH
A.F.L.-C.I.O.-C.L.C.

FINDING NEMO BOOKS
AVAILABLE WHEREVER
BOOKS ARE SOLD

LOOK FOR THE FINDING NEMO
VIDEO GAMES
WHERE GAMES ARE SOLD

EXCLUSIVE FINDING NEMO MERCHANDISE
AVAILABLE AT THE DISNEY STORE
WWW.DISNEYSTORE.COM

THIS MOTION PICTURE WAS CREATED BY PIXAR TALKING PICTURES
FOR PURPOSES OF COPYRIGHT LAW IN THE UNITED KINGDOM

ORIGINAL SOUND TRACK AVAILABLE FROM

Walt Disney
RECORDS

DISTRIBUTED BY
Buena Vista Pictures Distribution

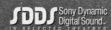

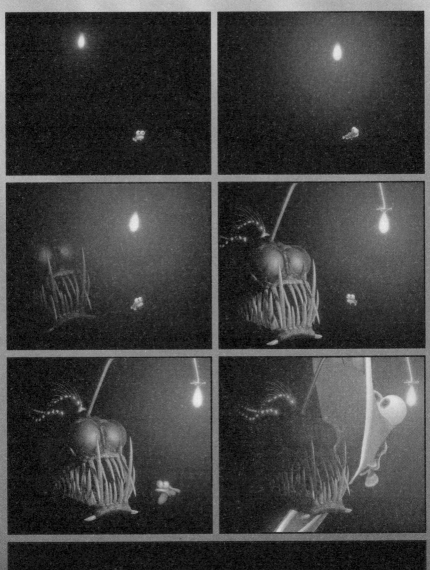

CREATED AND PRODUCED AT

Pixar Animation Studios

EMERYVILLE, CALIFORNIA

STEREOSCOPIC 3D

STEREOSCOPIC SUPERVISOR
Bob Whitehill

3D TECHNICAL SUPERVISOR
Daniel McCoy

DIRECTOR OF 3D PRODUCTION
Joshua Hollander

RENDERING LEAD	**Reid Sandros**
MANAGERS	**Paul McAfee**
	Tamsen Mitchell

TECHNICAL & RENDERING

Sean Feeley	Philip Graham	Patrick Guenette	Chris Horne
Jay-Vincent Jones	Joshua Mills	Roxanne Paredes	Jonathan Penney
Nadim Sinno	Eliot Smyrl	Yaa-Lirng Tu	Brett Warne

POST PRODUCTION

SUPERVISOR	**Erick Ziegler**
COLORIST	**Mark Dinicola**
RE-RECORDING MIXER	**Tom Myers**

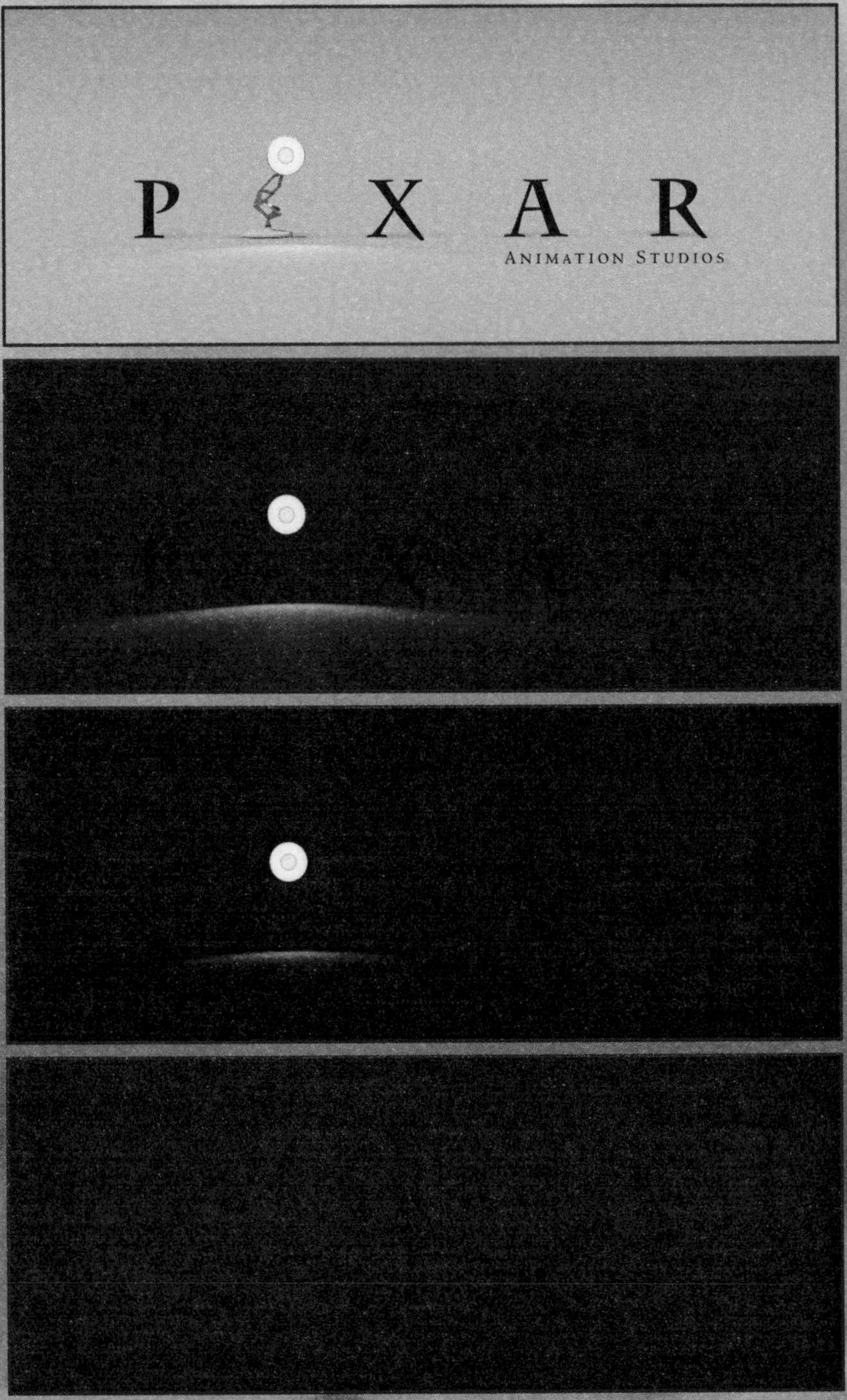
PIXAR
ANIMATION STUDIOS

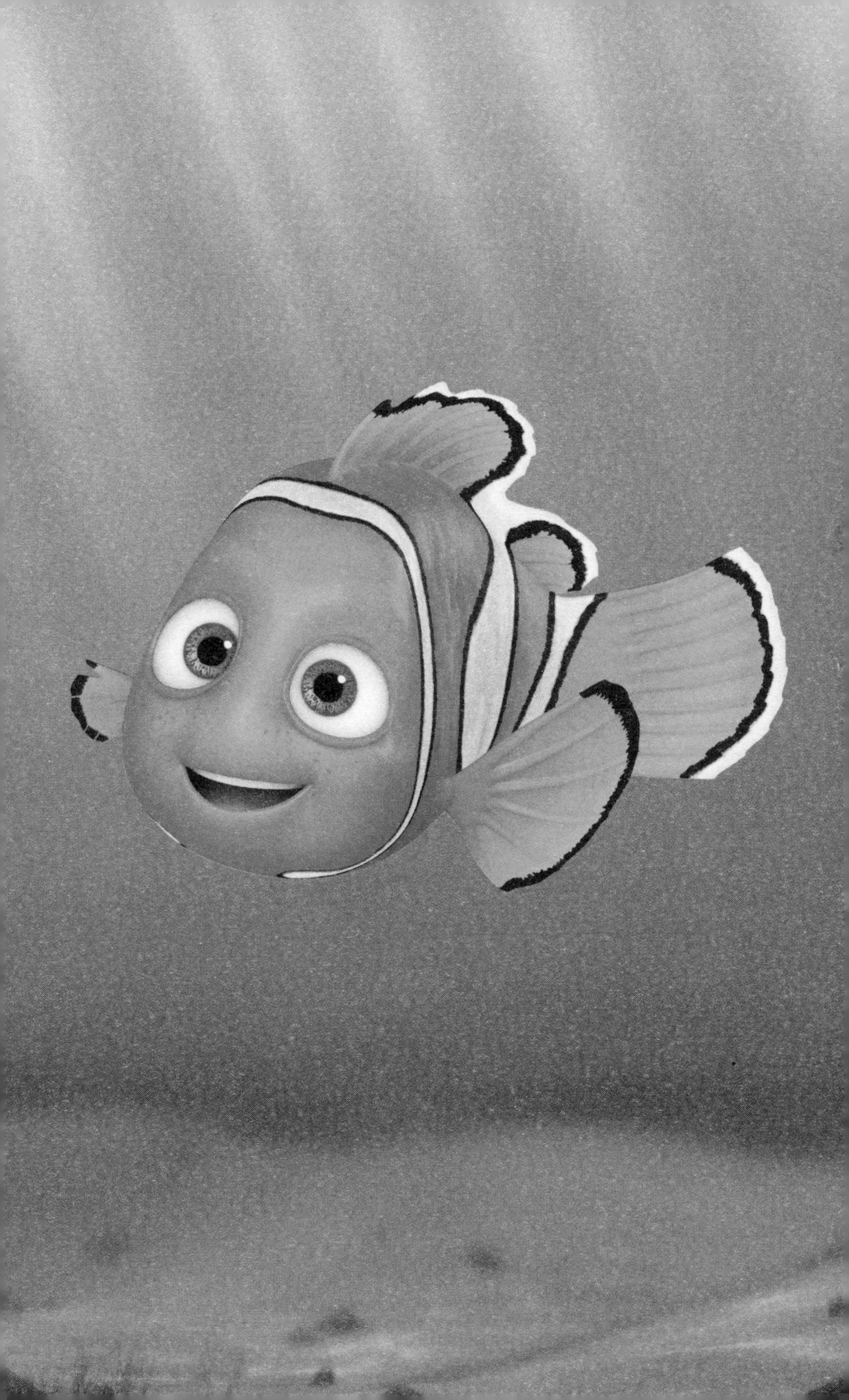

Who's Who in the

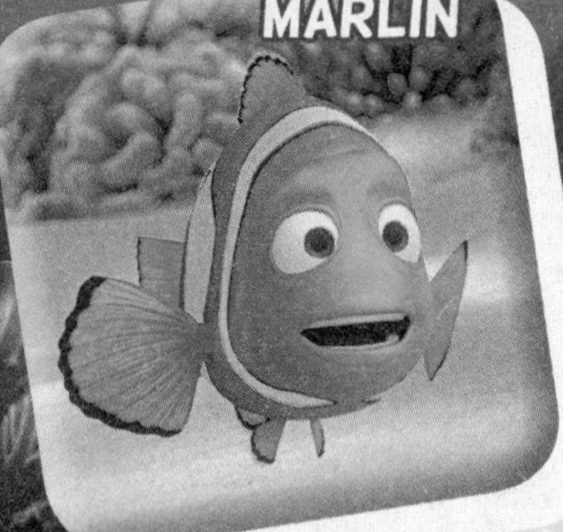
MARLIN

FIN FACT: Clownfish

FUN FACT: Nemo's dad, Marlin, fears the world beyond his safe little reef. Marlin is so nervous he thinks that school-age Nemo should wait five or six years before going to school.

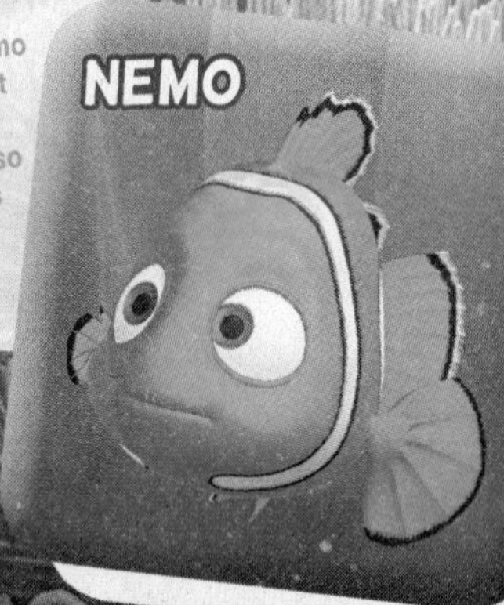
NEMO

FIN FACT: Clownfish

FUN FACT: Nemo has a "lucky" fin that doesn't look like the other one. Nemo is so excited to get to his first day of school, if he can only get Dad to hurry up!

FIN FACTS: Flapjack octopus (Pearl), sea horse (Sheldon) and butterfly fish (Tad) are all in Mr. Ray's class at school. They'll make great friends for Nemo once they meet him!

FUN FACTS: Prankster Tad likes to startle Pearl, which makes her let out her ink. So embarassing! And Sheldon the sea horse has a very inconvenient allergy to, yes, water — but he doesn't let that slow him down!

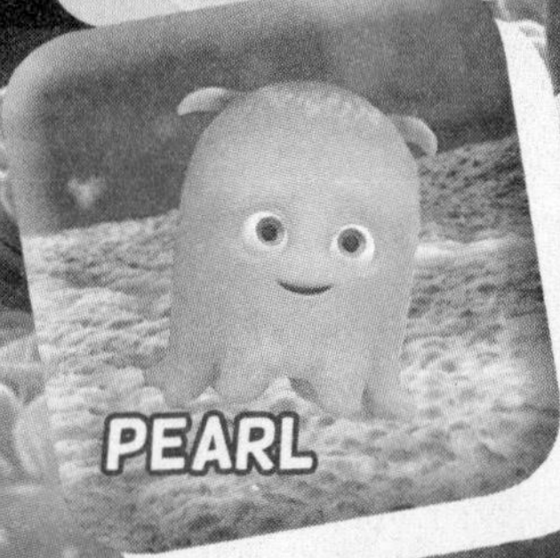
PEARL

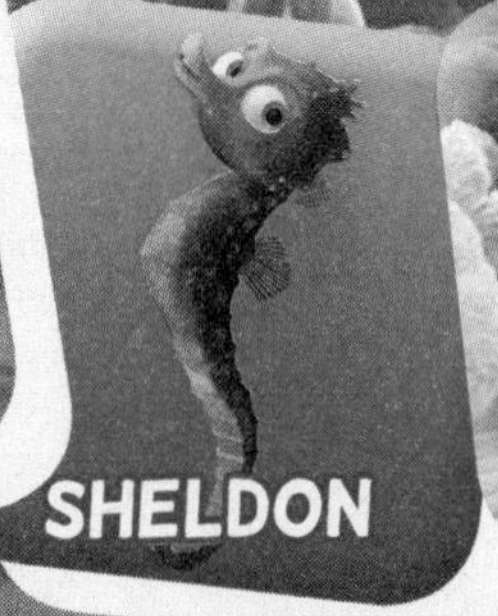
SHELDON

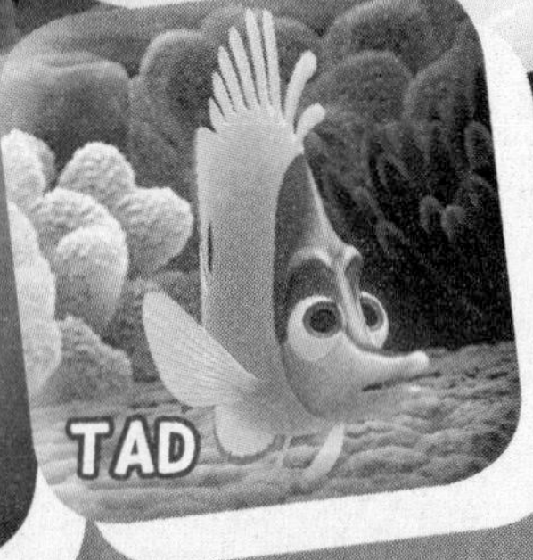
TAD

Ocean Blue!

Learn about the funky fish in Nemo's world!

FIN FACT: Regal blue tang fish

FUN FACT: Dory is just minding her own business until she meets Marlin, who needs her help! There's just one problem: Dory has no short-term memory, so she can't remember who they're searching for...Elmo? Fabio?

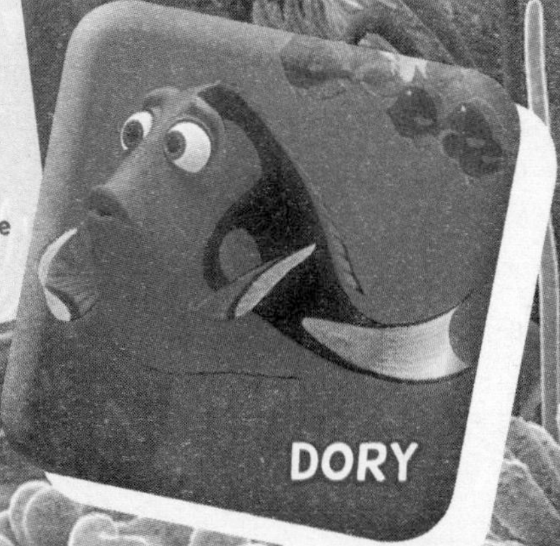

DORY

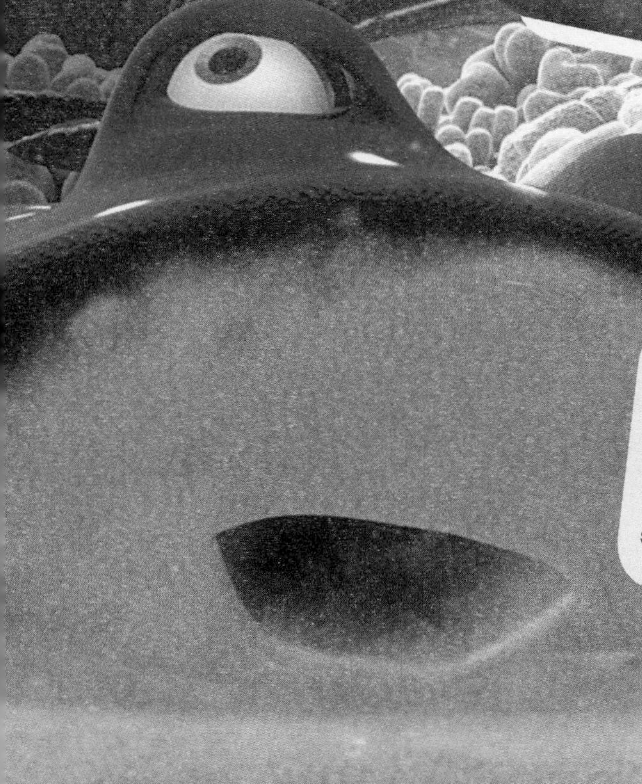

MR. RAY

FIN FACT: Eagle Ray

FUN FACT: Mr. Ray is the science teacher for the youngest fish in school. There's nothing he likes better than taking a field trip to teach his students something new about the seabed they all live in!

the following is excerpted from the *FISHIPEDIA PACIFICA*

WHO'S WHO *in the* OCEAN BLUE

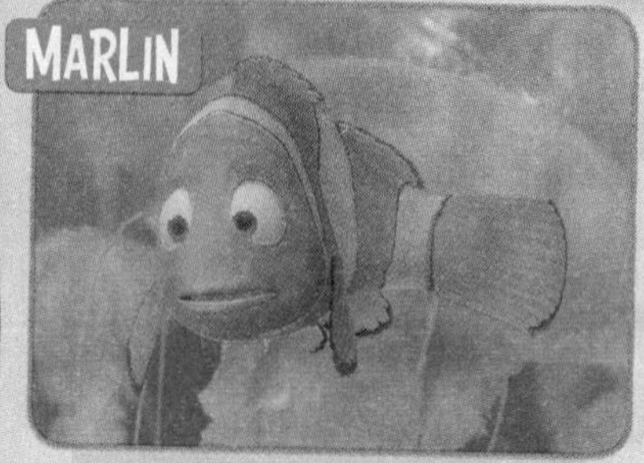
MARLIN

CLOWN FISH
(Humorii Jellymanicus)

Forced to leave the safety of the reef, Marlin searches for his son. He sees danger everywhere, but keeps on swimming to save Nemo.

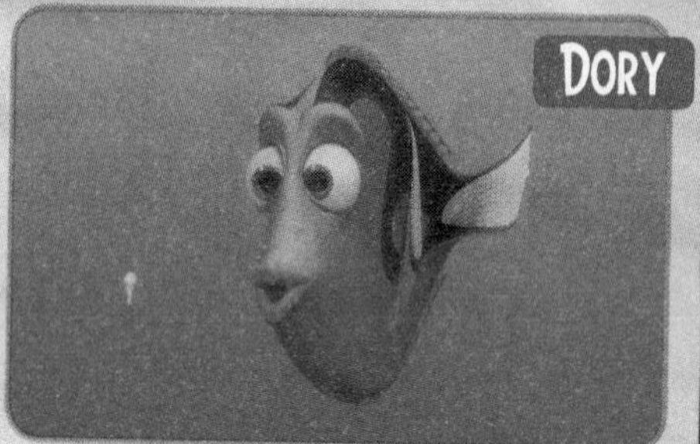
DORY

REGAL BLUE TANG FISH
(Memorus Forgeticci)

Dory is Marlin's partner in his search for Nemo. Dory almost never remembers anything, but she can read human and is fearless!

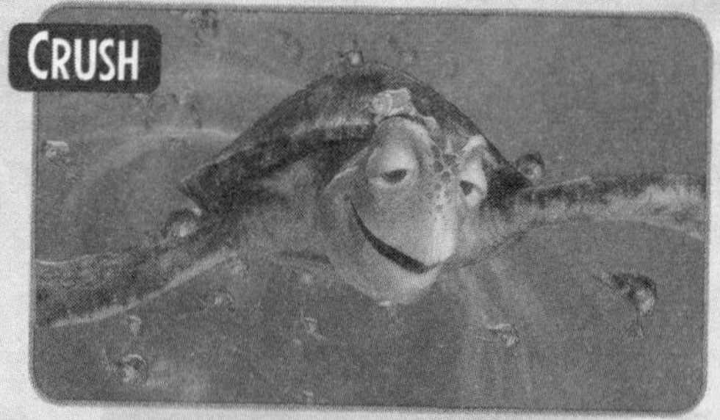
CRUSH

SEA TURTLE *(Dudius Turtlicus)*

150 year old sea turtle that surfs along the EAC (East Australian Current) with his turtle tribe, and his son Squirt.

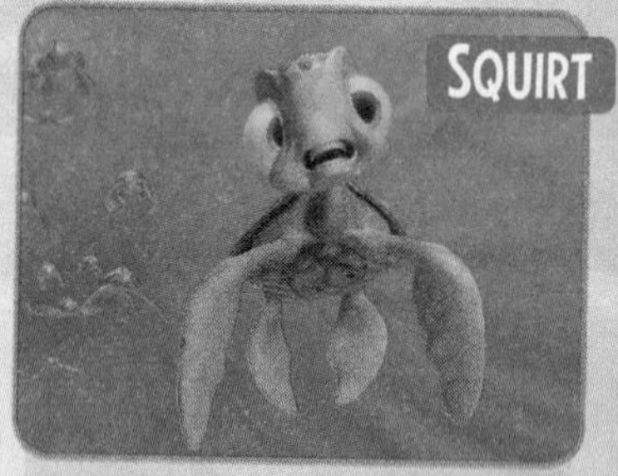
SQUIRT

SEA TURTLE *(Sweeticci Turtlicus)*

A tiny surfing sea turtle, Squirt rides the current with his dad and the turtle tribe. He's a strong swimmer for his age, and a bit of a show off!

NEMO

CLOWN FISH
(Lostimus Clownfisherus)

A young, energetic clownfish captured by a diver, Nemo now finds himself in a dentist's aquarium! Nemo is scared and just wants to see his dad again.

GILL

MOORISH IDOL FISH
(Leadirus Escapai)

The leader of the Tank Gang, Gill has a deep scar on his face and a damaged fin. He seems scary, but he befriends Nemo and plots to help him escape.

GURGLE

ROYAL GAMMA
(Germaphobus Negatii)

Gurgle is a nervous fish that is a part of the Tank Gang. He is scared by any germs and needs everything to be clean.

JACQUES

CLEANER SHRIMP
(Germus Purgicus)

Jacques is the cleaner of the Tank Gang. He loves to eat the scum and bacteria in the tank. Yum!

DEB

BLACK & WHITE HUMBUG
(Twinicus Reflectus)

Deb likes to talk with her twin sister, and by her twin sister we mean her reflection. She also likes to watch the dentist drill teeth...yikes!

BLOAT

PORCUPINE PUFFERFISH
(Ballooniffi Scaredius)

He may not be as nervous as his friend Gurgle, but it doesn't take much for Bloat to blow up to twice his size!

PEACH

STARFISH *(Clingius Starfisherus)*

Peach is a starfish that clings to the side of the fish tank. She likes watching the dentist work and giving the rest of the fish updates.

BUBBLES

YELLOW TANG *(Crazii Bubblicus)*

The energetic Bubbles likes to babble about his bubbles! He's weirdly obsessed with the bubbles that come out of the treasure chest in the fish tank.

Who's Who IN THE OCEAN

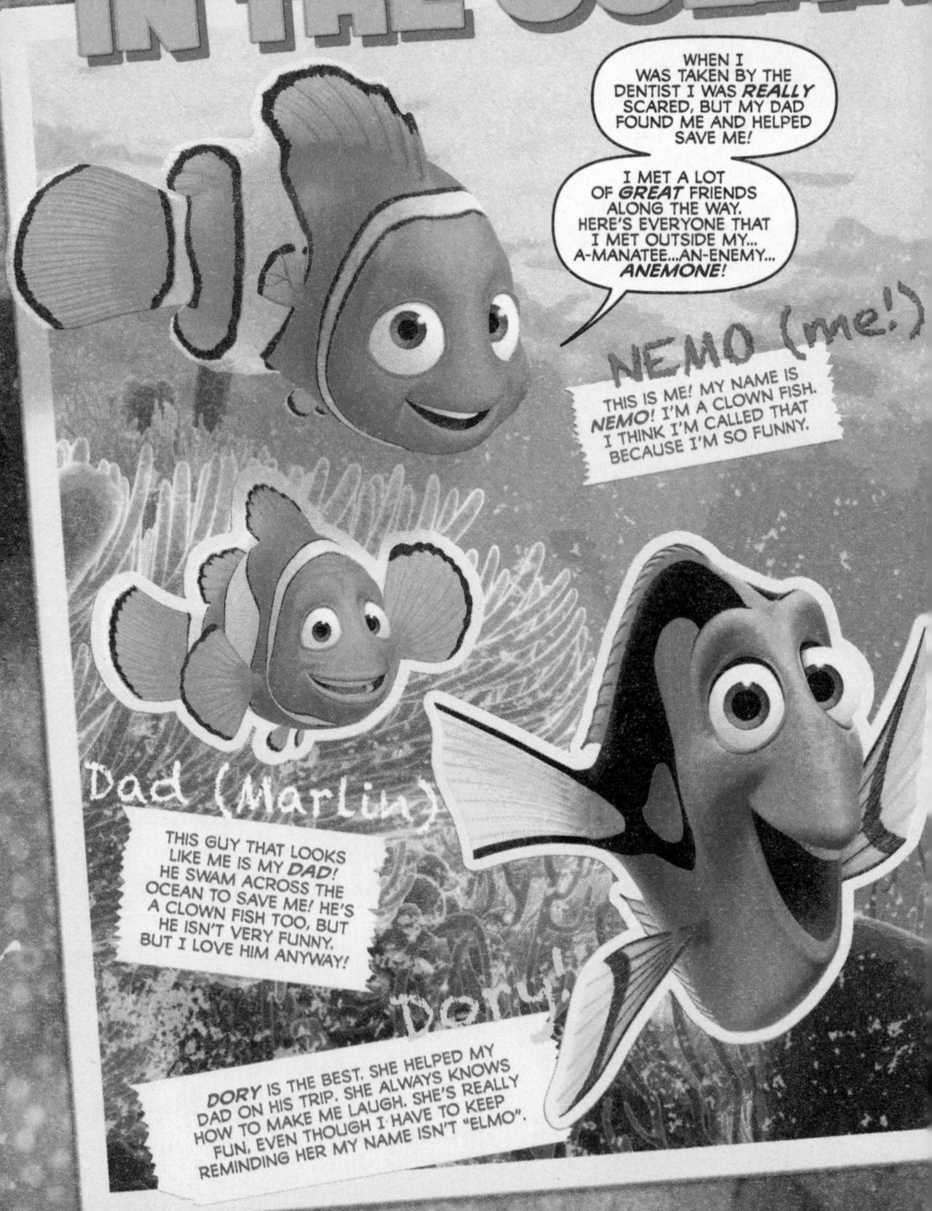

BLUE

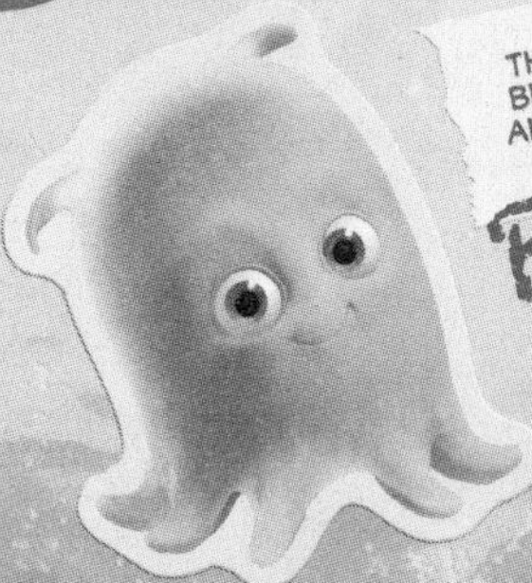

THE EIGHT TENTACLES IN THIS PICTURE BELONG TO MY FRIEND ***PEARL***. SHE IS AN OCTOPUS! WHEN SHE GETS SCARED SHE SHOOTS OUT INK. ***GROSS!***

Pearl

Sheldon

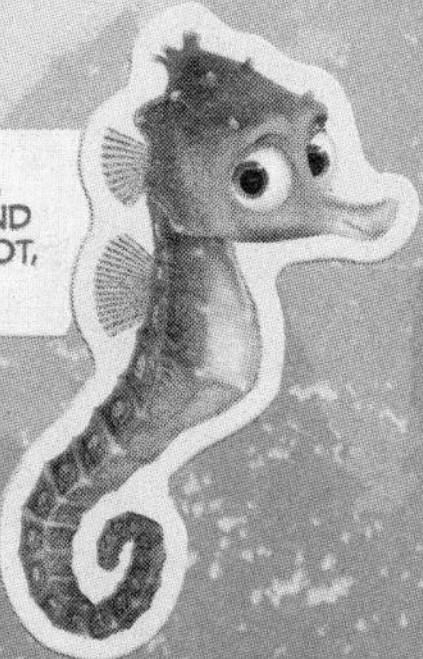

SHELDON IS A SEAHORSE. HE IS ALLERGIC TO WATER, AND THAT MAKES HIM SNEEZE A LOT, WHICH IS PRETTY FUNNY!

Tad

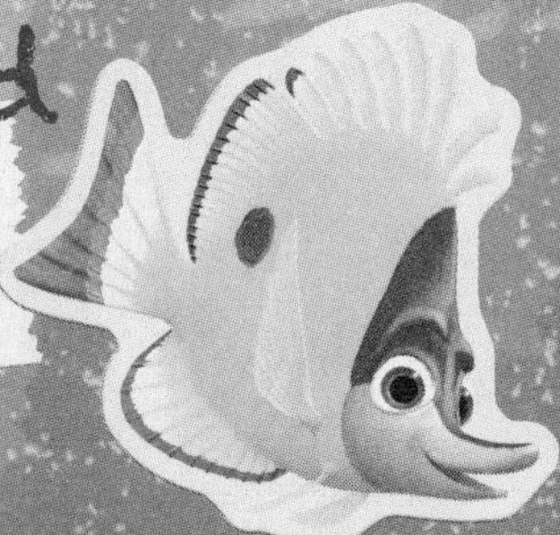

TAD IS MY OTHER FRIEND. HE'S REALLY DARING, BUT NOT AS DARING AS ME! HE DIDN'T TOUCH THE BOAT! HE ALSO REALLY LIKES BEING OBNOXIOUS, BUT HE'S STILL MY FRIEND.

Crush

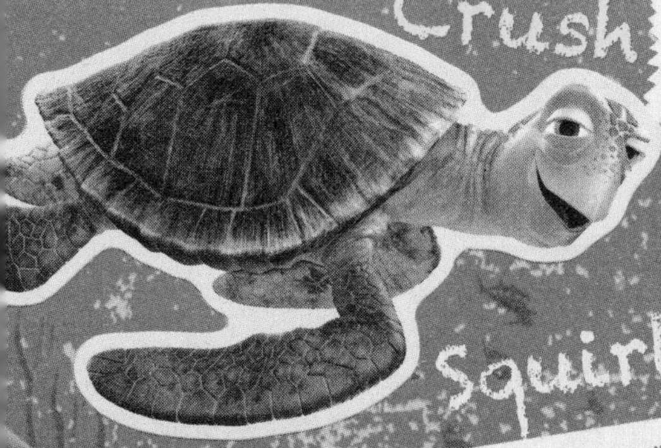

THIS IS THE COOLEST TURTLE EVER, ***CRUSH!*** HE HELPED MY DAD SWIM ON THE EAST AUSTRALIAN CURRENT (***EAC***). HE'S 150 YEARS OLD AND STILL YOUNG!

Squirt

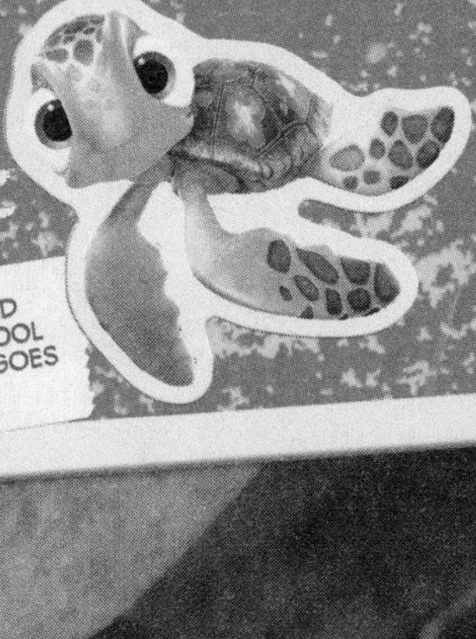

CRUSH HAS A SON NAMED ***SQUIRT***. HE'S JUST AS COOL AS HIS DAD, AND NOW HE GOES TO SCHOOL WITH ME!

Who's Who IN THE OCEAN BLUE

Gil

THIS SCARY LOOKING FISH, ***GIL***, IS THE LEADER OF MY FRIENDS FROM THE TANK. HE NAMED ME ***"SHARKBAIT"*** AFTER I SWAM THROUGH THE RING OF FIRE. I WASN'T SCARED.

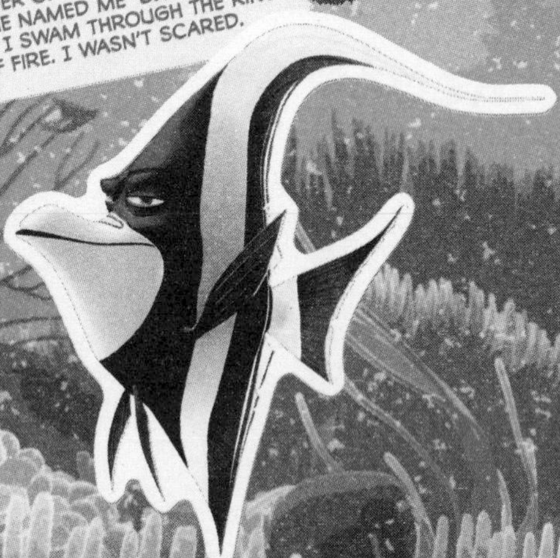

DEB LOVES WATCHING THE DENTIST DRILL TEETH, AND TALKING TO HER TWIN SISTER ***FLO***. I DON'T WANT TO BE MEAN AND TELL HER THAT HER TWIN SISTER IS REALLY JUST HER REFLECTION.

Deb

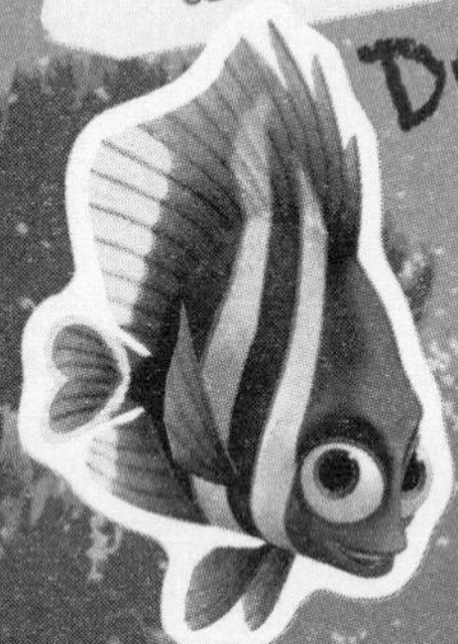

Peach

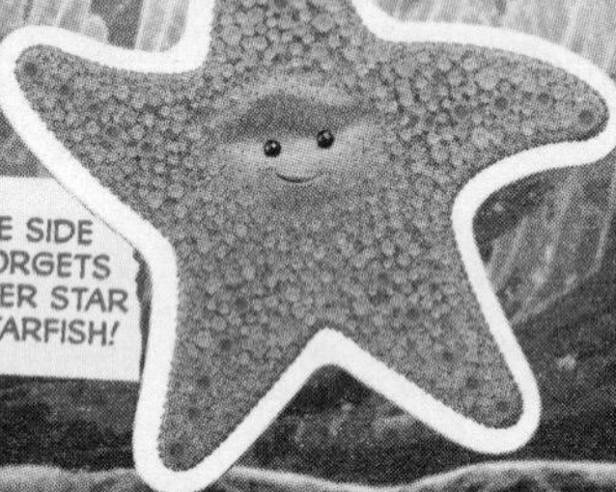

PEACH LOVES CLINGING TO THE SIDE OF THE TANK BUT SHE ALWAYS FORGETS TO GET OFF THE GLASS TO TALK! HER STAR SHAPE IS WHY SHE IS CALLED A STARFISH!

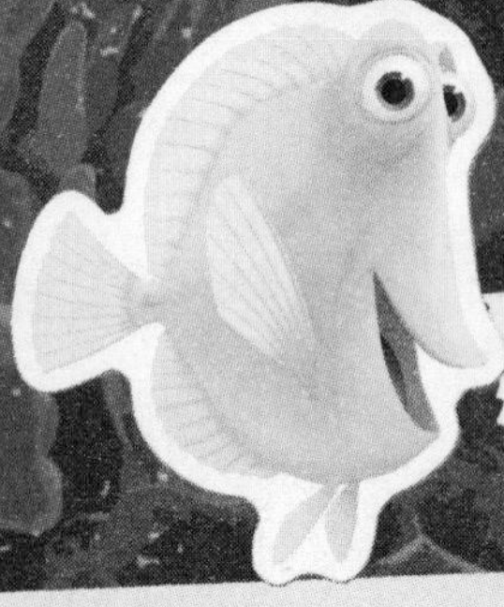

Bubbles

THIS IS ***BUBBLES***. I DON'T REALLY KNOW ANYTHING ABOUT HIM, BESIDES THAT HE ***REALLY*** LIKES BUBBLES.

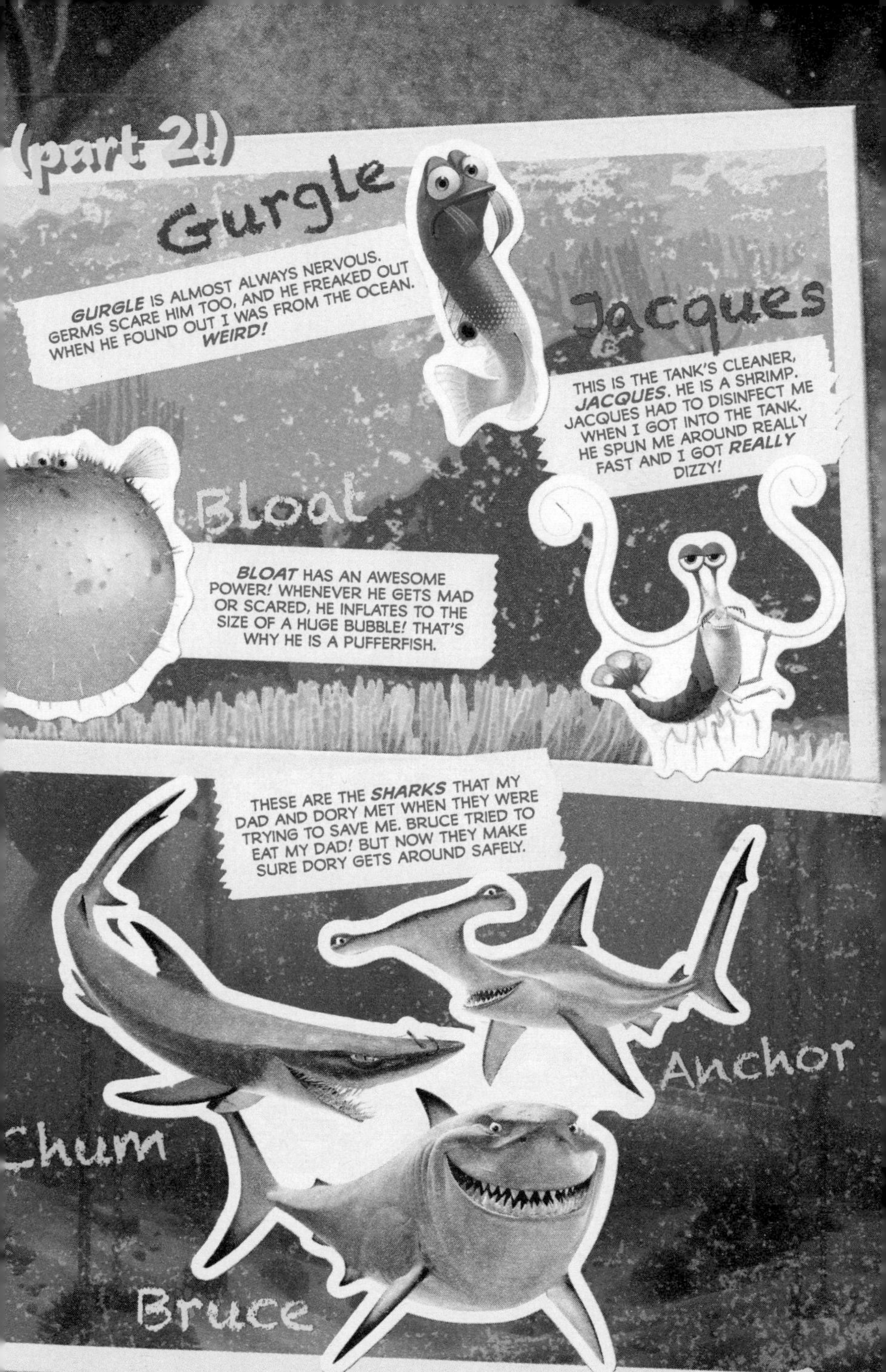
(part 2!)
Gurgle
GURGLE IS ALMOST ALWAYS NERVOUS. GERMS SCARE HIM TOO, AND HE FREAKED OUT WHEN HE FOUND OUT I WAS FROM THE OCEAN. WEIRD!
Jacques
THIS IS THE TANK'S CLEANER, JACQUES. HE IS A SHRIMP. JACQUES HAD TO DISINFECT ME WHEN I GOT INTO THE TANK. HE SPUN ME AROUND REALLY FAST AND I GOT REALLY DIZZY!
Bloat
BLOAT HAS AN AWESOME POWER! WHENEVER HE GETS MAD OR SCARED, HE INFLATES TO THE SIZE OF A HUGE BUBBLE! THAT'S WHY HE IS A PUFFERFISH.
THESE ARE THE SHARKS THAT MY DAD AND DORY MET WHEN THEY WERE TRYING TO SAVE ME. BRUCE TRIED TO EAT MY DAD! BUT NOW THEY MAKE SURE DORY GETS AROUND SAFELY.
Anchor
Chum
Bruce

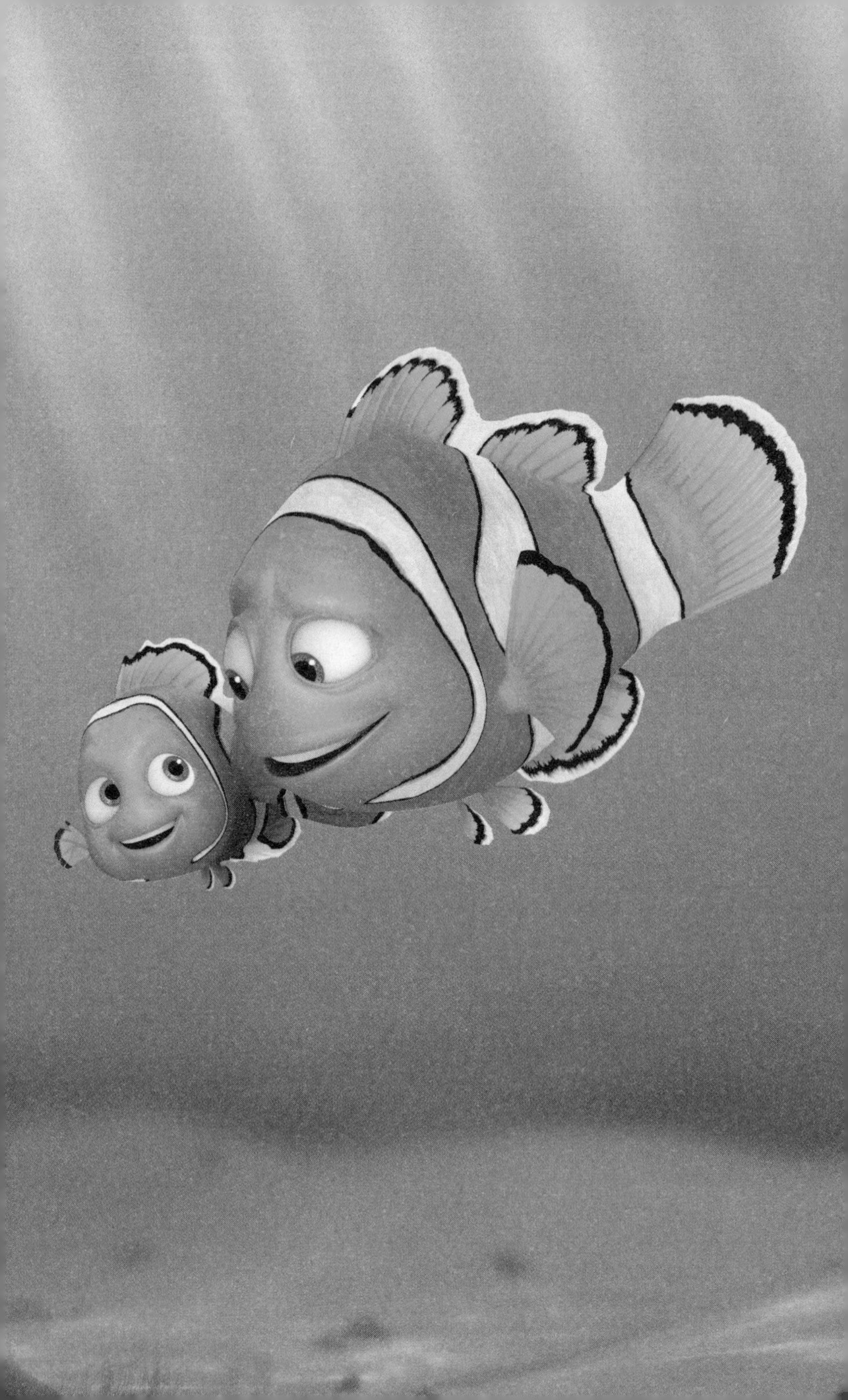

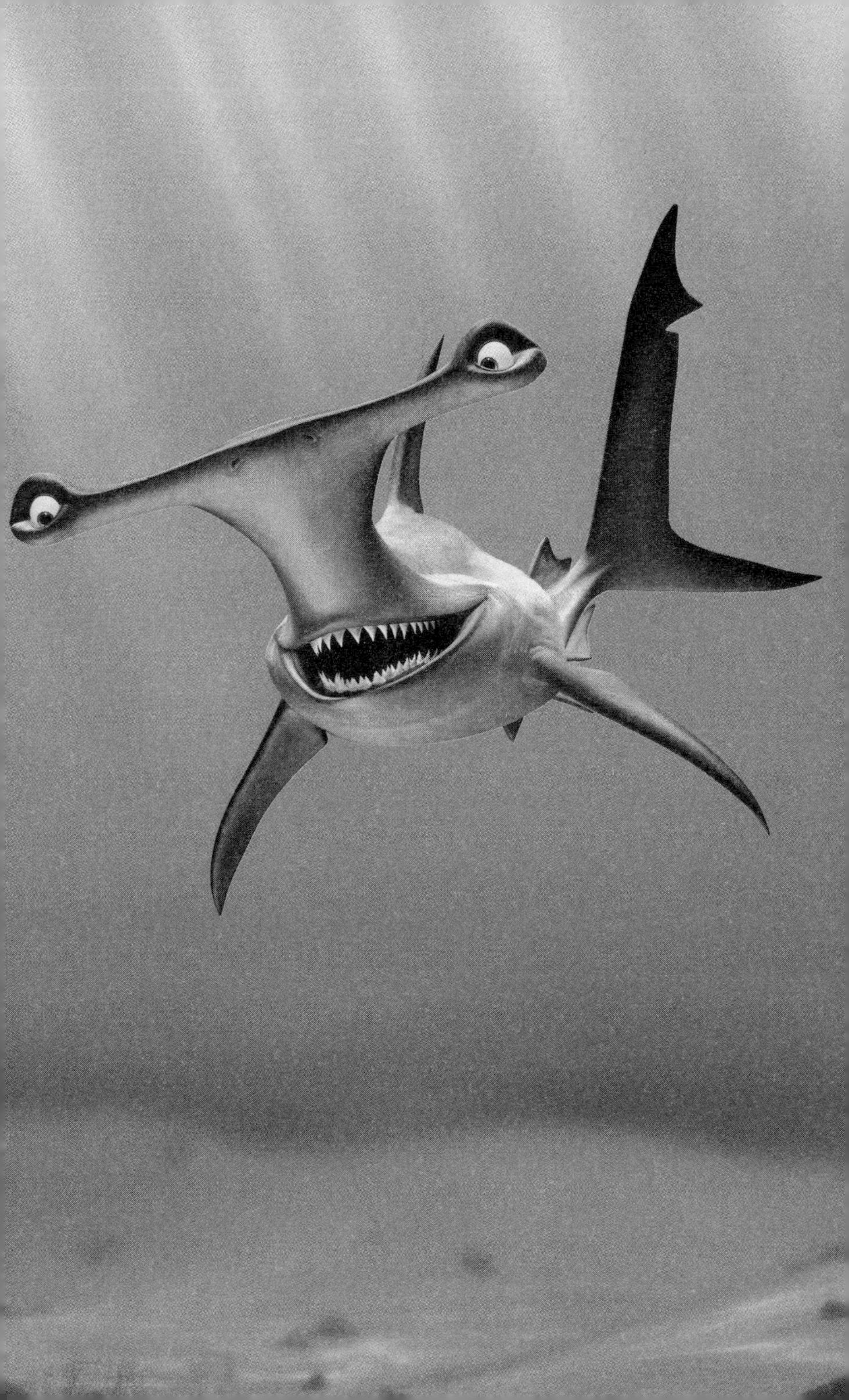

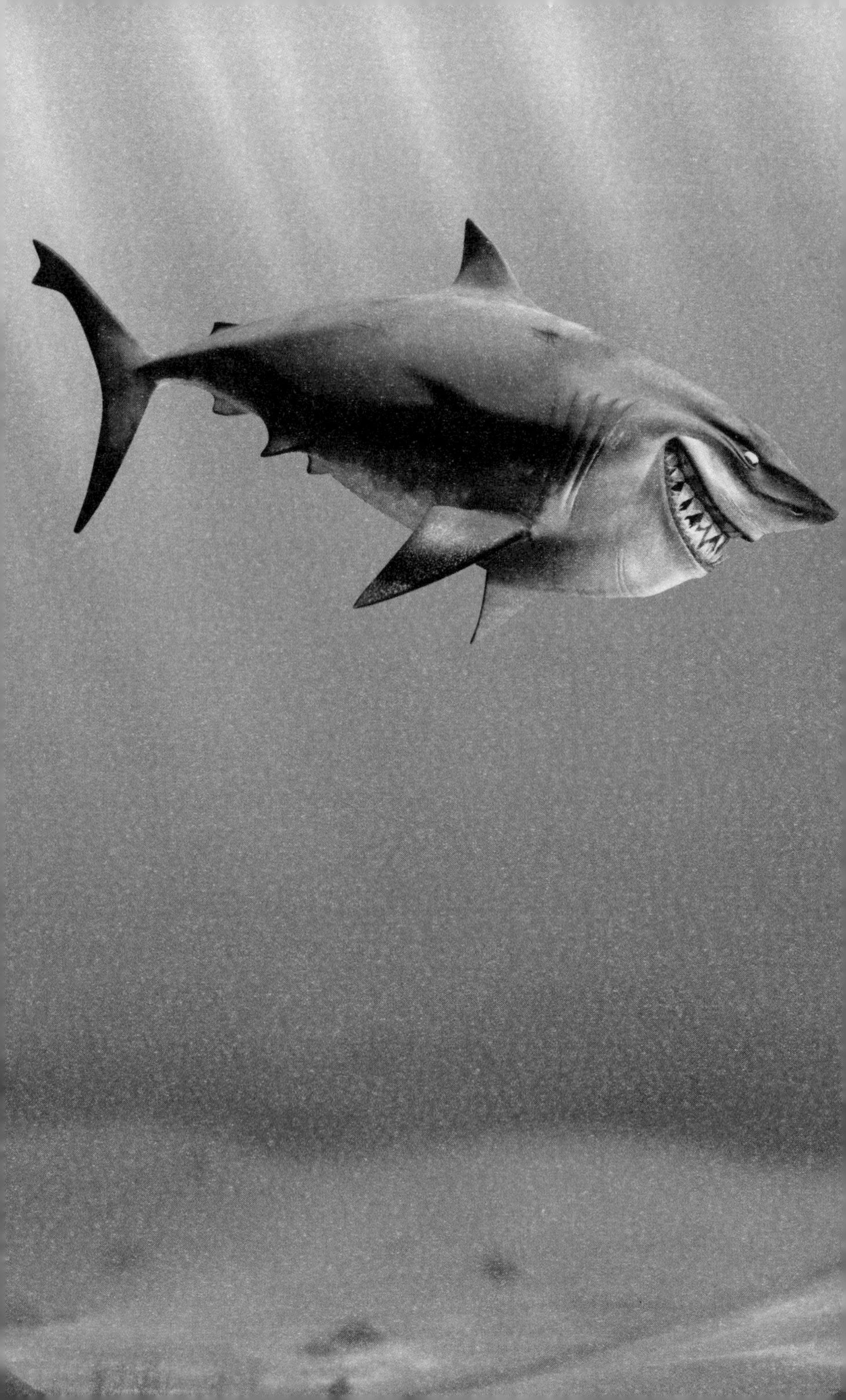

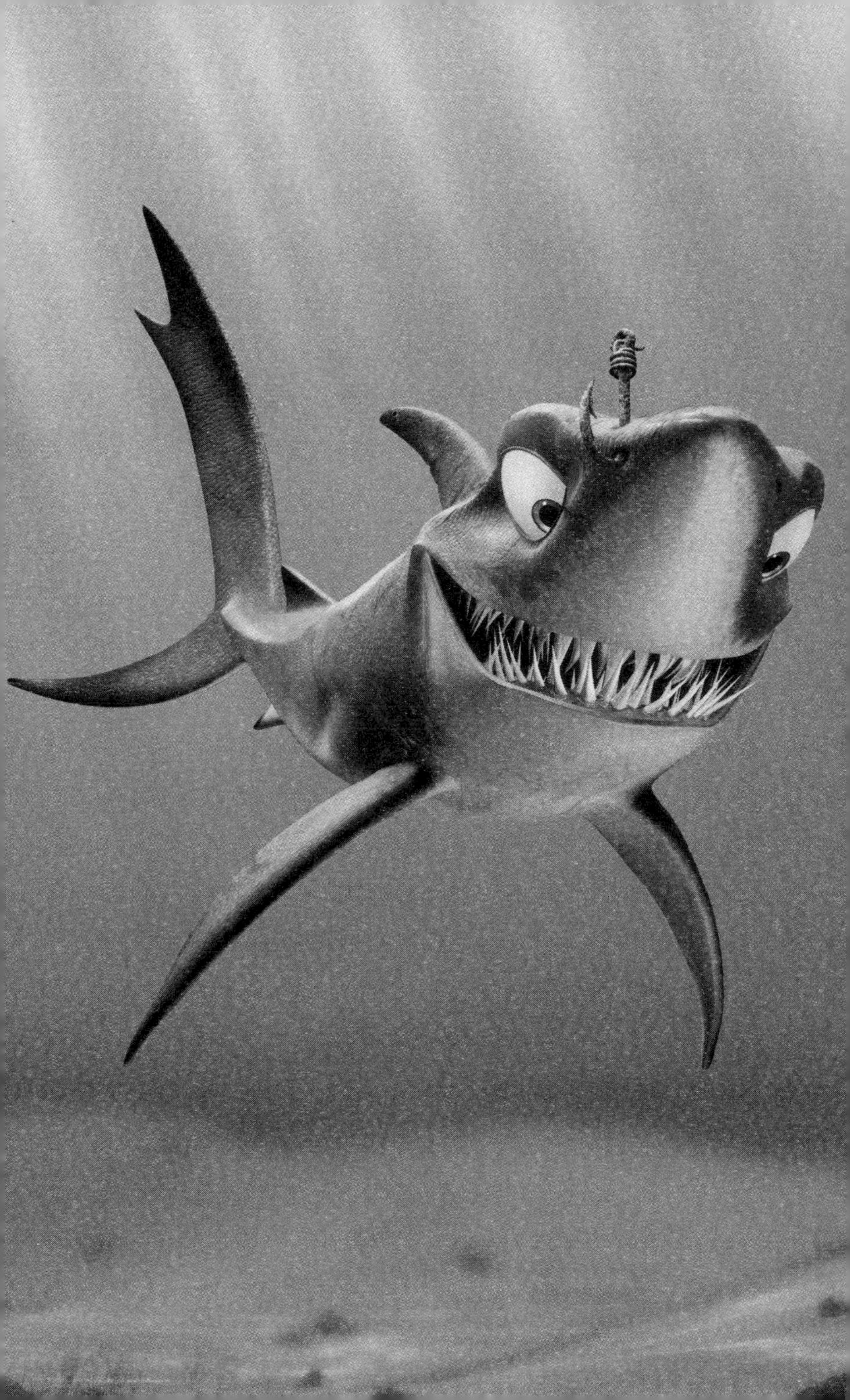

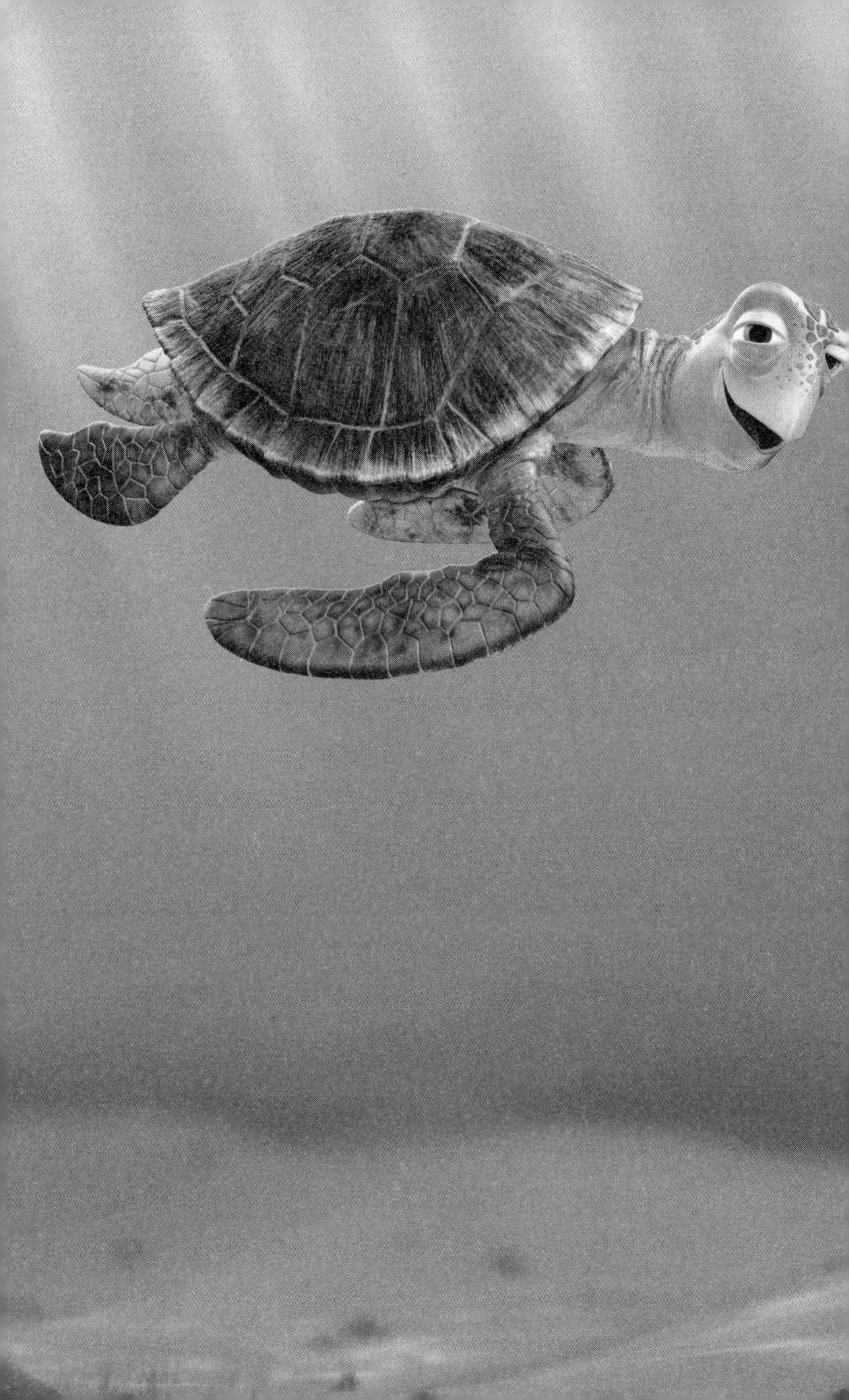

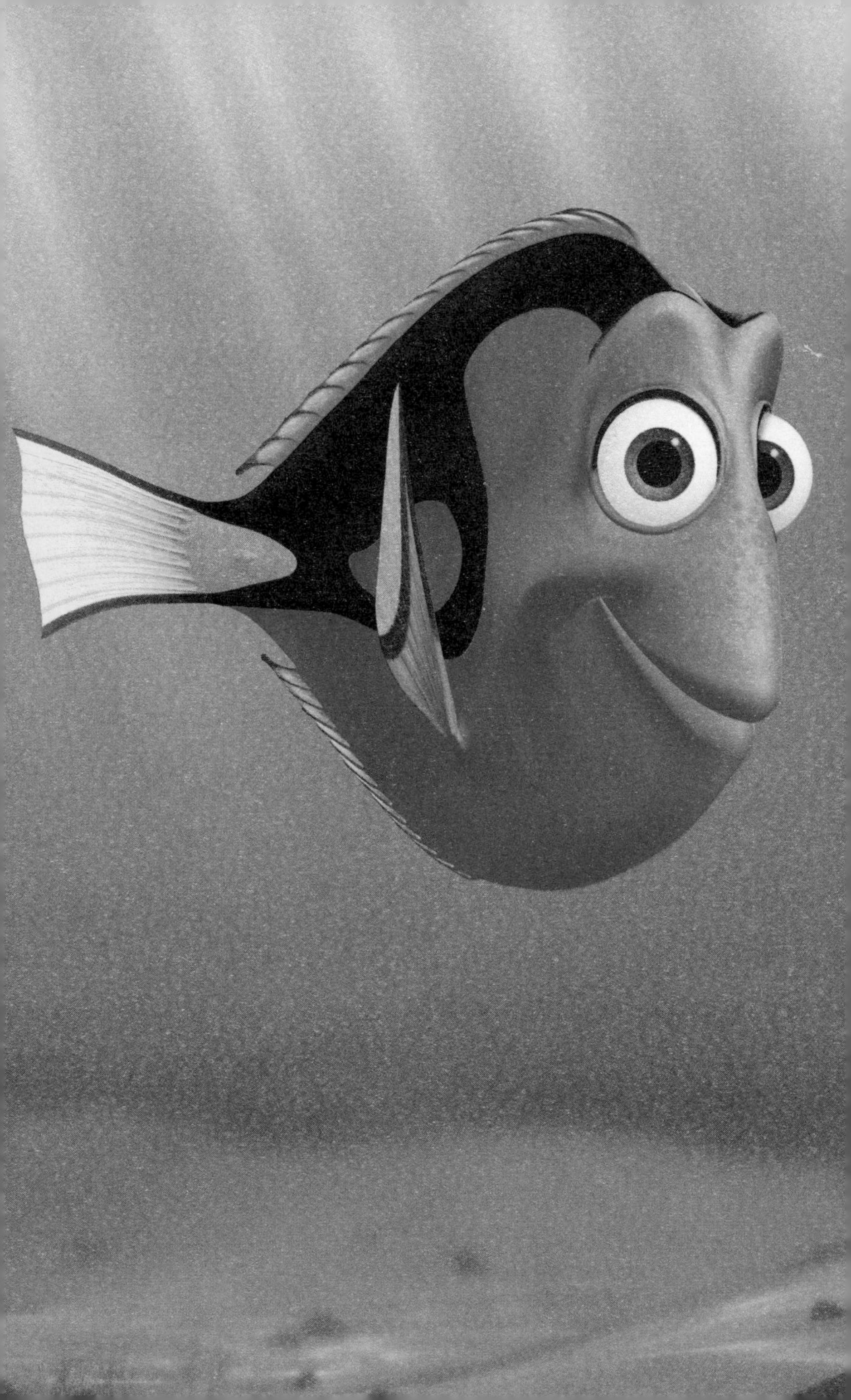

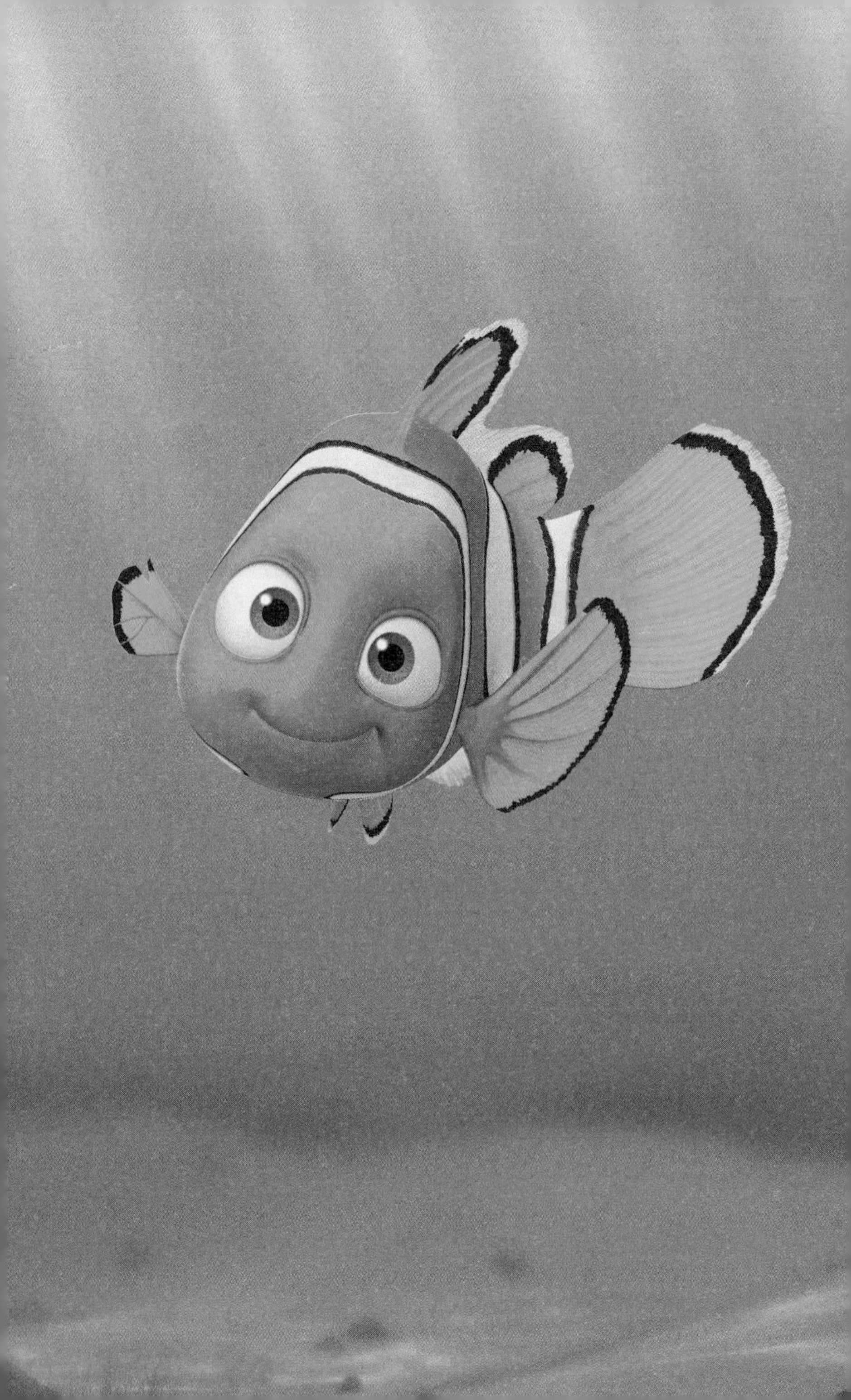

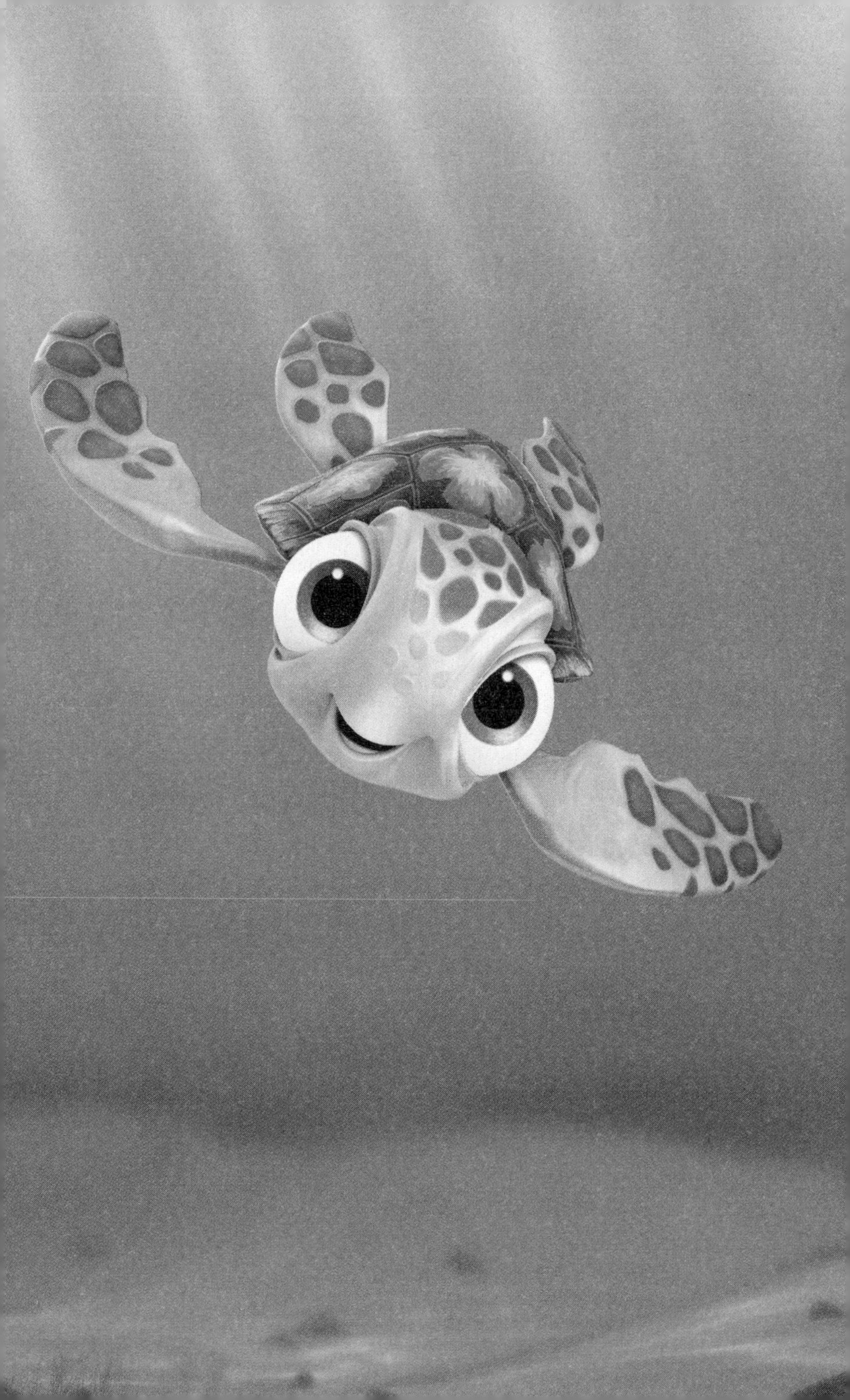

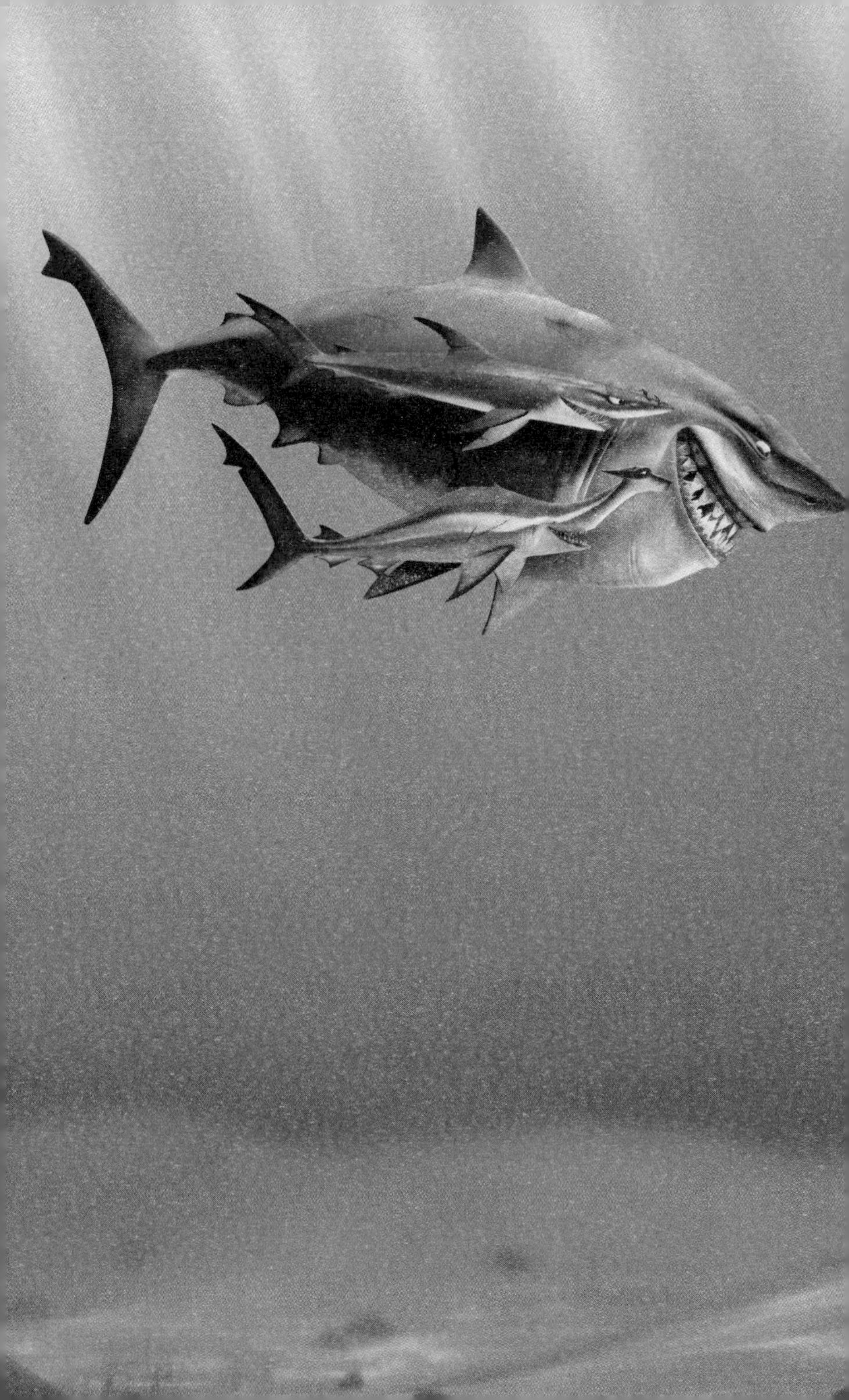

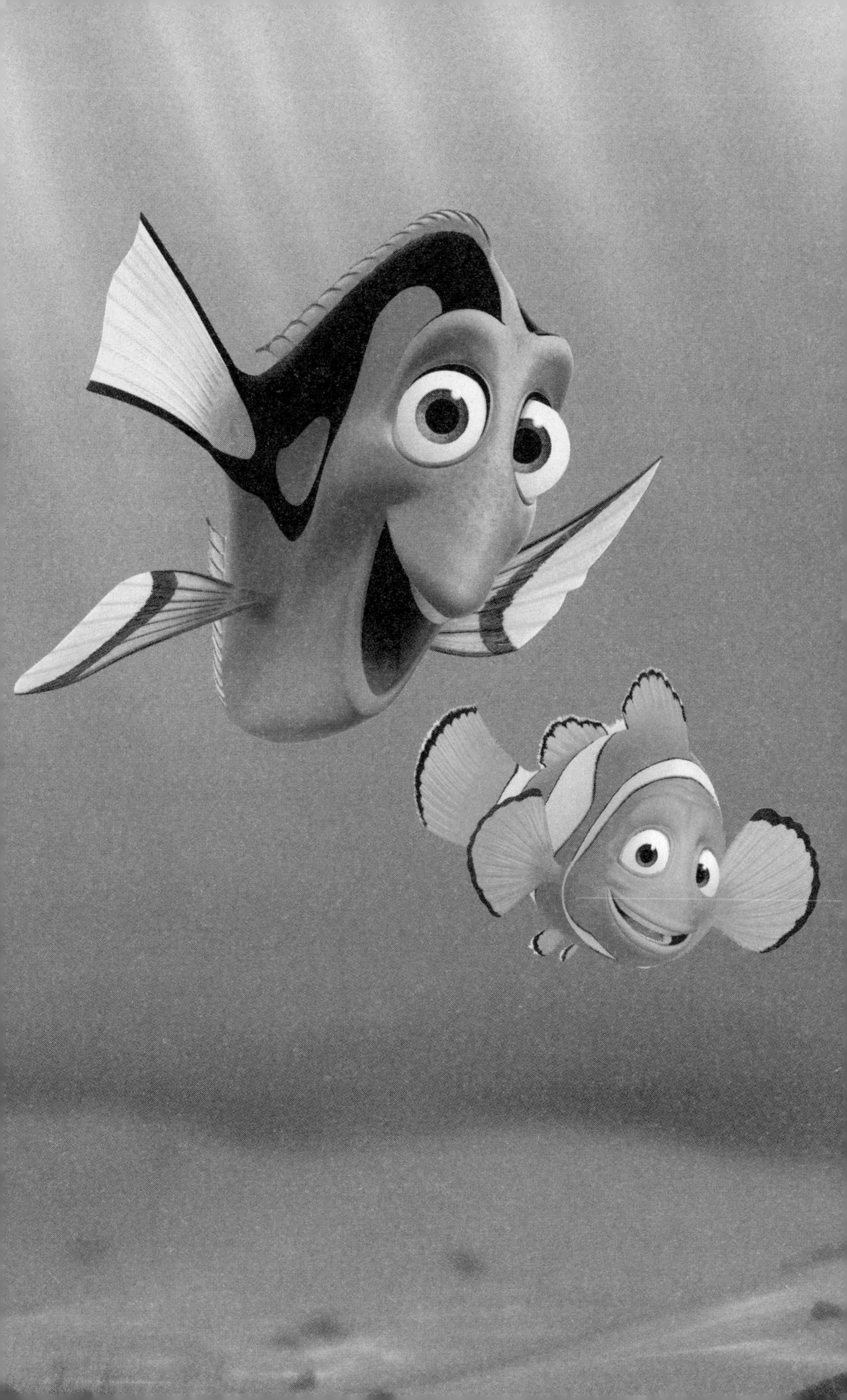

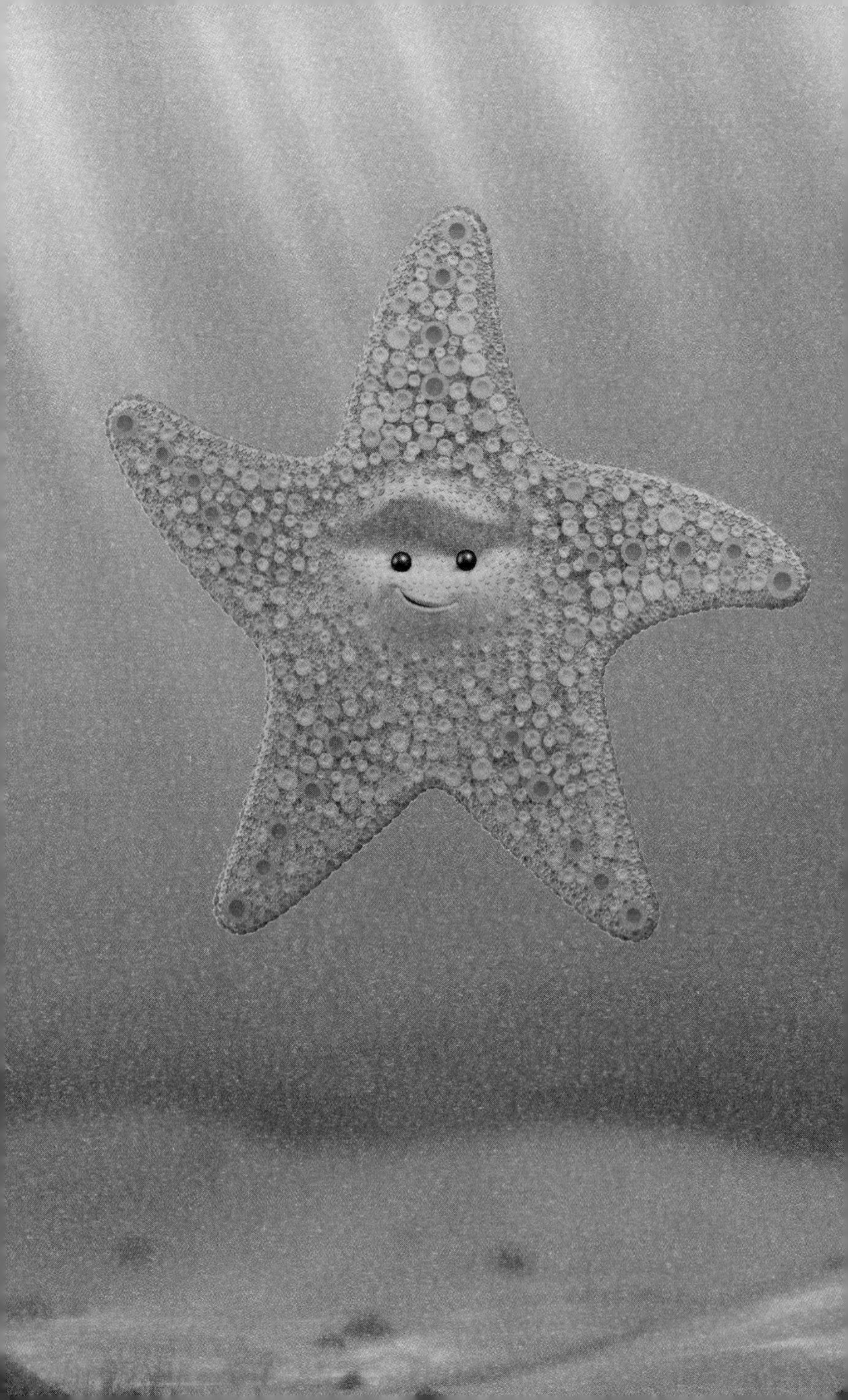